Legends of Ogre Gate

by Jeremy "Deathblade" Bai

LEGENDS OF OGRE GATE

Legends of Ogre Gate is a work of fiction. Names, organizations, places and incidents portrayed in this novel are either products of the author's imagination or are used fictitiously. Any resemblance to actual, events, locales, or persons is purely coincidental.

Edited by Crystal Watanabe
Cover art by Mario Saggia
Map art by Michael Prescott and Josephe Vandel

ISBN: 978-0-578-49477-7

Dedicated to my wife, who makes everything possible.

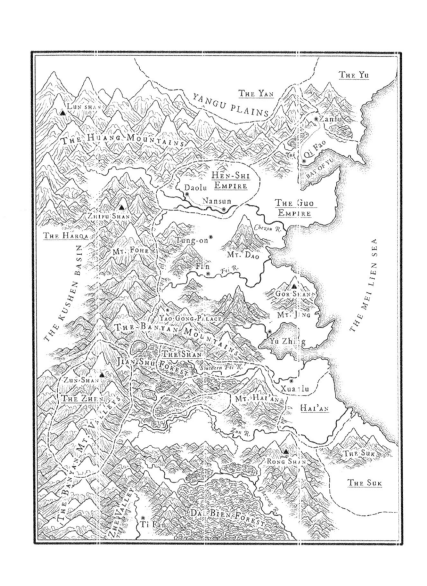

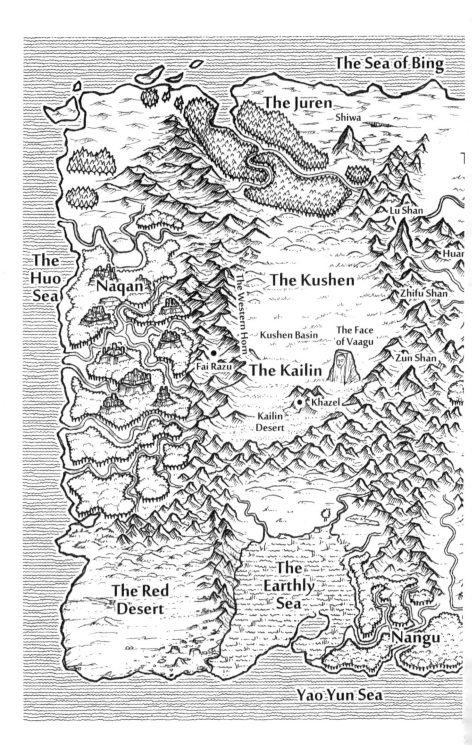

The Sea of Bing

The Juren

Shiwa

Lu Shan

Huar

The Huo Sea

Naqan

The Western Horn

The Kushen

Zhifu Shan

Kushen Basin

The Face of Vaagu

Fai Razu

The Kailin

Zun Shan

Khazel

Kailin Desert

The Red Desert

The Earthly Sea

Nangu

Yao Yun Sea

Qi Xien
The Human Realm

The Yangu Plains

Yangu

g Mts

The Chai Yun

Daolu

Mt. Dao

Zhan Dao

Empire

Li Fan

Gor Shan

Banyan Mts.

Hu Qin

Banyan Region

Hai'an

Rong Shan

Dhamma

Desert Island of the Hechi

The Eastern Archipelagos

The Mei Lien Sea

Cosmology of Qi Xien

Heaven

Moon · Stars · Sun

Upper Realms

Infinite Sky Realm

Skypoles

Earth/Qi Xien

Ocean · Emo Cheng

Ogre Realm

Mt. Zhizhu

Lower Realms

PROLOGUE: TIME

Year 1075
Reign of the Demon Emperor

An arrow smacked into the mud in front of Hui's nose, and she blinked. The entire left side of her face was pressed down into the muddy street, her head spinning like a top.

The sounds of fighting met her ears. Clashing metal. Screaming. Dying.

Pain stabbed through her right eye all the way to her left temple, jolting her into lucidity.

She blinked again, then swiveled over and pushed herself up onto her knees. She saw chaos.

People were fighting everywhere. A bolt of lightning illuminated the night sky, followed by a clap of thunder that reverberated in her ears.

A drop of rain hit her nose.

She slowly shook her head, trying to clear it, and that was when another arrow stabbed into the ground, this time next to her foot. Then another and another, eventually becoming a volley aimed directly at her.

Just as she was about to be turned into a pincushion, a blur emerged in front of her, and someone grabbed her by the shoulder. A sword spun through the air to deflect the oncoming arrows.

"Get her out of here!" someone shouted, and whoever had grabbed her arm pulled her off her feet.

Her vision blurred again, and she felt herself being thrown over a shoulder. Her head smacked against someone's back, and whoever it was then began to run at top speed.

The sword, she thought. *Where is it?*

"I have it," the person responded. Only then did she realize that she had actually spoken those words aloud. The voice belonged to a man, a man she recognized.

"Just hold on," he said. "I've got you."

More running. Turns left and right and left until she lost count, but as the man ran, her thoughts grew even clearer.

We were betrayed. By who? And… Bao Yang has the sword. Bao Yang? BAO YANG?

She tried to turn her head to confirm the identity of the man who was carrying her. She was almost sure it was Bao Yang, but then again, it was hard to say.

Bao Yang has the sword.

Hui's teeth started to chatter. Everything was falling apart. All their plans. All their training. Had it been all for nothing?

All of a sudden, she felt herself swinging off of Bao Yang's shoulder, and then she was plopped down onto a hard surface. A box, a crate of some sort. She looked around.

They were in an underground chamber or warehouse. She heard running water and saw the glow of torches. Somewhere in the background, she was sure she could detect the chatter of rats and mice.

Bao Yang crouched down in front of her. He was tall, powerfully built, with perpetually suspicious eyes. In his younger days, he had been considered one of the top rising figures in the martial world and had even managed to build a powerful criminal organization that controlled much of the southern reaches of the continent.

In the end, he ran afoul of the Demon Emperor. Rumor had it that he had been forced to watch while his wife and daughters were raped and beheaded, his lieutenants skinned alive, and his apprentices boiled to death.

After escaping somehow, he sold his services to the highest bidder as a mercenary. Although he was not a villain, he was no hero, and Hui happened to dislike him. What made it worse was that the character Bao that made up his surname was the same character as the name of the most famous woman in history: Heroine Bao.

Hui idolized Heroine Bao for many, many reasons, and she dreamed of accomplishing heroic deeds just like her. The only thing that made the connection tolerable was that while Bao was Bao Yang's surname, Hui happened to know that Heroine Bao's actual surname was something completely different.

Bao Yang looked her in the eye. "Are you clearheaded?" he asked. "You took a hard knock to the head."

She put her fingers to her temples and rubbed them gingerly. "I'm fine," she replied. "What are you going to do with me?"

His face was virtually expressionless as he stared back at her. "What do you think? Get this sword to your master."

Her brow furrowed. "But you… you're…"

This time he frowned. "I'm what? Not one of you idealistic idiots? No, I'm not. But I'll take any chance I can get to stick a thorn in the side of the Demon Emperor, and helping you people is exactly that. Plus, I have lots of money on the line here. Can you walk? Can you run?"

She rose to her feet and slowly shook out her hands and feet. "I can run."

"Then let's go."

Bao Yang started running, and she followed. It was then that she noticed the cloth bundle strapped to his back, the bundle that, until recently, she had been entrusted with. The sword.

That sword was the key to everything. It was hope. Their only hope.

Bao Yang had obviously taken it when she was knocked unconscious.

As she ran, her head cleared, and the pain from before faded into a dull throb. Her training took over, and she began to circulate her qi. It took a while, but she got her bearings.

She knew these alleys. They were in Yu Zhing, an ancient city that went back thousands of years. Back to the time before the Demon Emperor came. Back before the world began its descent into darkness.

Some legends said that Heroine Bao was born in Yu Zhing, and Hui couldn't help but wonder if she might have run down this very alley at one point in her life.

As she followed Bao Yang through the alleys, she quickly realized what he was doing. He was taking a circuitous route to their original destination, to the place where her master waited.

As she settled into running, she focused her breathing and her thoughts. Perhaps the plan could still be carried out. If Bao Yang could really bring the sword to the underground temple, to her master, if the ritual really could be carried out, then perhaps things would change.

Time passed.

Twenty minutes later, they were in a wide underground corridor, in the middle of which was a channel filled with flowing water. The rain had clearly picked up outside.

"Everything look normal to you?" Bao Yang asked.

She nodded.

"Well," he said, "you know what to do. Hurry it up."

She took the lead and led him through the corridor, carefully avoiding the stones she knew to be traps. In one place, she motioned for him to duck down, and he did. When they reached the thick wooden door at the end of the corridor, she checked the secret symbols carved off to the side to make sure that it was safe, then knocked in the prescribed fashion.

The door was unbarred and opened, and light spilled out to reveal a hall filled with candles.

Her master sat cross-legged at the far end of the hall, flanked on either side by various robed figures. Some were monks or nuns, devotees of Hen-Shi, who most people said had been killed along with the wind god, Gushan, countless years in the past. The others were disciples of her master, the remnants of one of the most ancient sects in the world, whose robes were embroidered with a symbol resembling an intertwined dragon and phoenix, the mark of Sunan and Bao.

Whenever Hui saw that symbol, her heart filled with awe and hope. She had grown up hearing stories about Sunan and Bao and could recite every one of them by heart. She knew the Betrayal of the Emerald Monk, the Fall of Daolu, the Ballad of the Timeless Master, the Defeat at Heart's Ridge, Sunan and Bao Steal the Zhizhu Coral, the Battle of the Cat Demons, and so many more.

Bao Yang brushed past the disciple who had opened the door, who smiled oddly at him as he passed, although neither Bao Yang nor Hui noticed that. As Bao Yang stalked across the temple toward Hui's master, he reached up and untied the bundle strapped to his back. The sword.

Hui quickly trotted to catch up.

"Greetings, Iron Crab," her master said. He was a middle-aged man with long salt-and-pepper hair and piercing eyes.

"Dispense with the formalities," Bao Yang replied. "Here's the sword. Now where's my money?"

Hui hurried around to sit down cross-legged next to her master.

"As direct as ever, I see," her master said. "Give me the sword. Once the ritual begins and the sword is proven to be legitimate, I'll give you your money." He reached into his robe and pulled out a plump bag, which he placed on his knee with a muffled clink.

Bao Yang glared for a moment, then frowned. Finally, he threw the bundle over.

Hui's master grabbed it and quickly unwrapped the cloth. Inside was what appeared to be nothing more than an ordinary sword.

When Bao Yang saw it, he snorted. "That's it?"

Hui's master breathed out slowly. "This is most definitely it."

He held the sword aloft with both hands, whereupon one of the monks who had been kneeling off to the side rose to his feet and took it into his hands.

"Begin the ritual," Hui's master said. "Our friend here is anxious to leave, as am I."

The monk nodded. Two nuns appeared from the nearby shadows, carrying a small iron cauldron filled with white sand between them. They placed it on the floor in front of Hui's master, and the monk carefully stabbed the sword down into the white sand. A handful of incense sticks appeared in the monk's hand, which he then placed into the sand around the sword, arranging them in a complex formation. The nuns produced a brazier, which they used to light the incense sticks.

Nothing happened.

Bao Yang snorted again. "You people are crazy," he said. "I told you from the beginning your little trick wouldn't work. Did you really think you could force that sword to fail in its function? Now give me my money."

"There is more to it than that," Hui's master said.

As if on cue, green smoke began to rise up from the incense. At first it simply swirled around the cauldron like ordinary smoke, but then it began to form the shape of an hourglass. Complex green and yellow symbols began to appear on the blade of the sword. Light began to shine.

Hui's master smiled. "It is authentic," he said. "Very well, take your money and go."

With that, he tossed the bag over to Bao Yang.

Bao Yang snatched it out of the air, and without another word, turned to leave.

It was at this point that a cold voice split the air.

"You won't be going anywhere, Bao Yang!" The voice came from the disciple who had opened the door for them moments ago.

Bao Yang stopped in place, and his hand went to the handle of the sturdy mace he kept tied to his belt.

The disciple stepped forward, and as he did, his facial features began to ripple like water. He grew taller, his clothes changed, and a moment later, he was a different person.

He looked like a scholar, with long green robes and a fan tucked into his belt.

"Hidden Arrow!" growled Bao Yang. "I should have killed you when I had the chance!"

The man he had referred to as Hidden Arrow smiled. "You always knew how to pick the wrong side, Bao Yang. Are you sure you don't want to come work for me? I could always use some brute force to crack skulls here and there."

Bao Yang spat on the ground. "I'd rather bash my own skull in than be a whore for the Demon Emperor!"

Hidden Arrow's eyes flashed. "If it's death you seek, I can accommodate you!"

Bao Yang hefted his mace. Farther back, Hui's master rose to his feet, as did all the monks and nuns. Weapons were drawn with the sound of steel on leather.

"Hidden Arrow," Hui's master said, "why do you tread this path? Surely you see that our world is a dismal one. A world of pain and suffering, of choking clouds and fire. If you schemed against the Demon Emperor instead of people like us, we might be able to live in a very different world."

Hui looked between Hidden Arrow and her master. He was trying to buy time.

Hidden Arrow chuckled. "I have my own plans, and they're none of your concern. This little revival of the Dragon-Phoenix Sect that you have worked out is ridiculous. Sunan and Bao died a millennium ago, and their sect went with them. What is done cannot be undone."

"Yet again you prove your ignorance, Hidden Arrow. The Dragon-Phoenix Sect did not fall a thousand years ago. It has been hiding in the shadows, planning and preparing for this very day. What was done *can* be undone, and it will!"

Hidden Arrow snorted. "Hand over that sword immediately, and you might leave this place alive!"

It was at this point that Hui noticed the rustling sounds coming from the shadows in the corners of the room.

The House of Paper Shadows? she thought, and her heart began to pound even harder.

A voice rang out in Hui's mind. Her master's voice. *Hui, Hidden Arrow is a profound master and utilizes deadly poisons. Prepare yourself!*

Yes, Master.

Hui needed no prompting from her master. She was young, only about fifteen or sixteen, but she was more experienced than many fighters in the world.

"Screw you, bastard," shouted Bao Yang, lunging forward with his mace. "Bone Blasting Mace!"

His mace smashed through the air toward Hidden Arrow but ended up blasting nothing but air. Hidden Arrow shot backward at incredible speed, then snapped his fan open.

A metallic droning filled the air, and Hui twirled her fingers, causing her twin daggers to whirl as she spun into the move Deflecting Canopy.

Her master's sword flashed through the air in front of her as he utilized a profound master's version of the art.

The world seemed to slow down in Hui's eyes.

A storm of needles spread out through the room, a tempest,

more needles than she had ever seen in her life. Bao Yang, the closest to Hidden Arrow, deflected some of the needles but was hit by at least two and dropped down to his knees.

At some point, shadows had stretched out from the walls and attached themselves to the monks, nuns, and other disciples, making their arms and legs leaden and immobile. One of the monks took a needle to the eye and started to flip backward into the air. Another was hit in the shoulder, and it spun him to the left.

Hui watched in horror as one ally after another was hit with needles. Only her master, with his brightly spinning sword, seemed capable of deflecting all the needles. Hui was positioned directly behind him and was thus able to benefit from his shield. That, coupled with her own Deflecting Canopy, ensured that she was not hit by a single needle.

The entire fight was over in a matter of seconds. Bao Yang was on his hands and knees, vomiting blood. Most of the monks and nuns had been killed in the initial volley, and those who had not were vomiting blood or twitching in seizures.

Her master stood in front of the cauldron, only an arm's length from the sword, which was now thrumming with magical power.

"You're too late, Hidden Arrow," he said. "The ritual is complete. The time has come."

Hidden Arrow sauntered forward, chuckling. "I think not. You're getting slow in your old age."

To her shock, Hui's master staggered slightly. He reached his hand up to his neck, and when he pulled it away, a needle could be seen held between his thumb and index finger. A tiny drop of blood rolled off the end.

Hui's heart lurched.

Her master's voice spoke in her mind again.

Hui, prepare yourself. I will throw you the sword in the moment before it is activated. You must take my place to accomplish this mission.

Hui's mind spun, her heart pounding. *Master, I can't! I was supposed to stay here!*

Hidden Arrow walked up to Bao Yang and grabbed him by the hair. "Your martial arts fell behind mine decades ago. When we first met, you might have been able to defeat me with a bull rush, but now? Don't make me laugh." He lifted his foot up to Bao Yang's shoulder, then kicked, sending him toppling to the ground in a pool of vomit and blood. "Cutting your head off would be too quick. I think watching you die this way will be much more enjoyable." He turned toward Hui's master.

You must accomplish the mission, Hui. I've been hit with Hidden Arrow's enhanced hellebore poison. Even if I use the sword, I'll still die after reaching the destination. When I throw it your way, all you have to do is grab on and hold tight.

Hui resisted the urge to cry.

Master, I've memorized the Song of Bao, but I haven't mastered the Trance Touch incantation!

"I don't think that sword does what you want it to," Hidden Arrow said, folding his hands behind his back. "But I don't really care. Even if you somehow manage to *force* it to fail, you'll still die within minutes, no matter where you end up."

"Fine, then," her master said.

Hui, you have the foundation, you just need practice and more power. Once you reach your destination, you will have plenty of time. Now, prepare yourself.

Her master's hand snaked out, grabbed the sword, and sent it shooting toward Hui with a burst of qi. Hui leapt forward, hand outstretched toward the hilt.

Her heart trembled as Hidden Arrow's hand also shot out from behind his back. He made a flicking motion, and a needle began to speed toward her.

It moved faster than the sword, much faster. Backed by Hidden Arrow's profound master qi, the impact itself would likely kill her, and if it didn't, the poison surely would. She watched the needle get closer and closer, but before it arrived, her hand clamped down on the hilt of the sword.

Time seemed to slow, and then it stopped altogether. Brilliant colors burst out from the blade, surrounding her. They filled her eyes until all she could see was painful whiteness.

Then she vanished.

The needle smacked into the stone wall. Cracks spread out for at least a meter in all directions from the point of impact.

Hui's master chuckled. "It's done."

Hidden Arrow gritted his teeth. "I still don't believe that you can manipulate the Sword of Time in that way."

"It doesn't really matter what you believe, does it? One thing is for certain, Hidden Arrow: I might be about to die, but I'll be taking you with me!"

CHAPTER 1
A BRUSH

Year 50
Reign of the Demon Emperor

Somewhere in the distant northeast of Qi Xien lay a quaint village. It was the kind of village that at one time could have been found almost anywhere, and according to the stories passed down by the village elders, it had existed in the legendary Era of the Thundering March, which was before Qi Xien even truly existed.

The village was neither large nor small. Few famous people had been born there. For the most part, the villagers were happy to live their lives, as they had for the past thousand years. Dynasties had risen and fallen, but this village remained the same.

The adults of the village were mostly fishermen, farmers, and craftsmen. Although stories had been passed down about men from the village being recruited as soldiers, it had mostly been to fight against marauding tribesmen of the Yangu Plains or the Chai Yun, not to participate in grand military campaigns.

Stories of epic warfare were viewed by the village folk as something of legend, and they often questioned whether they were real. None of the men from the village had ever risen to prominence as heroes or generals.

Couple that with the hundreds of years of peace and prosperity that the village had experienced, and one could say that the villagers were complacent. Happy and complacent.

Except for one.

There was one person in the village who was anything but complacent, and his name was Fan Sunan, though he hated being called by his full name and insisted on being called Sunan. He was ten years old, and he bristled with energy and curiosity. Of course, energy and curiosity are things most young boys possess, but they seemed to thrive without limit in young Sunan.

He was interested in anything and everything. He asked questions of everyone and wanted to learn all there was to learn. He liked to fight and wrestle, loved to climb trees, and adored horseback riding. Or perhaps it would be best to say donkeyback riding, as horses weren't exactly common in the village.

He got bored easily when talking to people. However, that was not because he was easily distracted, though it seemed that way to some. Rather, his brain was in a constant state of motion. It never stopped. He never stopped. He thought and pondered and considered and mulled over everything constantly. He read the village records, something that few other people his age would ever think to do.

He did this because he wanted to know about the ancient legends. He wanted to hear the old stories.

Some young people yawned when the village elders spoke of how humans came from the tears shed by the Enlightened Goddess Xian Nu Shen, but when Sunan heard such things, his eyes glittered. He also devoured the scraps of stories about Hen-Shi and Gushan and legends such as that of Mount Zhizhu, the enormous mountain that held up the entire world.

Sunan was born into unique and momentous times. Roughly

fifty years before his birth, the world had changed. A spectral palace had appeared in the depths of the Banyan Mountains. No one knew when exactly it appeared, because it was originally in a location few people ever traveled to. Eventually, armies poured out of that palace and began to conquer whatever cities lay in their path. The dynasty of that time, the Hen-Shi Dynasty, fought back, but years of complacency had made them weak.

That dynasty fell, and a new government took its place. The leader of this new government was called the Demon Emperor, although few people had ever seen him. According to the stories which began to spread throughout Qi Xien, he was a twisted monster who had risen from the depths of Emo-Cheng, the underworld, and that all he wanted was to enslave the lands.

Sure enough, after wiping out the Hen-Shi Dynasty, the Demon Emperor's armies began to spread out and inflict terror upon the populace.

Something else happened around the same time as the appearance of the Demon Emperor, although few people connected the two events. A new energy rose up in the land, which gave new power to plants, animals, and other living things. It even seemed to interfere with the previous barriers that existed with the spirit world.

Little of that chaos affected Sunan. In fact, the energy spread through the lands so slowly that it hadn't even reached his village. It was a place of little consequence, nestled in a cove off of the Bay of Yu, a day's travel from the great city of Qi Fao.

For years and years, the effects of the violence and terror did not affect the villagers. For decades, the armies of the Demon Emperor were mostly focused on the resistance in the south and west, and they had little time to pay attention to the insignificant northeastern frontier regions.

Because of that, Sunan was born into peaceful conditions and grew up only hearing about the horrific things that were happening farther south. Passing travelers told bloodcurdling tales that parents used to threaten their children into doing chores. Despite these stories, the villagers' lives were not affected in any meaningful way.

However, when Sunan was a teenager, things began to change.

The Demon Emperor had subjugated the majority of the realm, and now he was turning his attention to those small places which he had ignored for so long. As his forces marched farther and farther north, more and more refugees began to seek shelter in the village.

Life changed.

The villagers finally began to feel their hearts thumping with fear.

The Demon Emperor had already defeated all the major forces that existed, and now he was headed their way.

There were rebels, of course, some of whom passed through the village and attempted to drum up support for their causes. Few villagers were impressed. Despite the lingering fear they felt, the Demon Emperor was still just a vague concept, a story, something frightening but amorphous.

The villagers were complacent.

Except for Sunan.

Whereas the village elders tended to look to the past and think about how stable things had been, Sunan was filled with a sensation of imminent change. All the stories of the fighting and wars filled his mind with thoughts of adventure. Although he never considered running away from home, he thirsted for action.

As chance would have it, one of the refugees who stayed in the village for a few months happened to be a retired soldier. It took some urging, but the soldier agreed to teach Sunan a few things about fighting.

When his parents found out, it caused a bit of a scene. It was dinnertime when one of Sunan's young sisters piped up and said, "Sunan, did you learn anything from your master today?"

"Master?" his mother asked.

"Sunan is learning to fight people!" another sister declared.

"Is that so?" his father said, taking a sip of yellow wine.

Sunan's jaw jutted out. "Shut up, sis, I don't want to fight people. I just want to be able to defend myself."

His mother smiled. "Sunan, you remember how your grandmother always quoted that saying of Kong Zhi? 'Boys fight with fists, men fight with words.'"

Sunan rolled his eyes. "Mom, you just made that up, didn't you? I was just reading a history scroll the other day that said Kong Zhi was a noble who knew how to fight. He could even ride a chariot! Why would he say something like that?"

"He became a philosopher long after that," his mother replied primly, and then went on to change the subject.

Later that night, he and his father were outside looking at the stars.

"Son, I agree with your mother and your grandmother. But if you want to learn to fight, to be a soldier or a warrior, then… I support you."

Sunan smiled. "Thanks, Dad."

"Figure out what it is that you want to do in life, and do it. I'll always be here to help you, no matter what."

The next day, Sunan decided that his sister was right: He should call his teacher Master. They trained mornings and evenings, and Sunan absorbed his lessons like a dried-out sponge.

"Put your foot there, and there," his master would say. "Remember, you're young and small, but that can be an advantage. Use your opponent's weight against him."

They sparred and practiced to the point where Sunan could defeat him three times out of ten.

One summer night when Sunan was seventeen years of age, he woke up because of the heat. It was a strange thing, because he was used to the intense summer temperature, having lived with it his entire life.

His eyes were blurred by sweat, and it took a moment for him to realize that the heat was not from summer, but from fire. His bedroom was aflame!

He tumbled out of bed, bleary eyed, to face a wall of fire. Covering his face with his arm, he leapt out of the paper window into the night outside.

What met him was a scene from a nightmare.

The Demon Emperor's armies had finally arrived. Soldiers were everywhere, laughing and slashing about with swords. Villagers who Sunan had known since birth were cut down in front of his very eyes.

He saw Third Uncle Fan kneeling on the ground, his intestines spilling out of his belly.

He saw Granny Chu's head lopped off, causing blood to spray out like a fountain.

He saw the village chief's throat being cut with a wickedly curved serrated blade.

He stood there in shock as a burly man began to stride toward him. He wore odd-looking leather armor emblazoned with a mark that looked like the face of a monster.

Sunan immediately cleared his mind. His master's words echoed in his mind, and he quickly struggled up and placed his feet and hips in the correct position.

He's bigger than me, thought Sunan, *but if I'm careful, I can toss him to the ground like a sack of flour.*

As the burly man neared, Sunan prepared. However, instead of lurching forward to attack, the man stopped about a meter away.

"What do you think you're doing, kid?" he growled. "You're gonna try to fight me?"

Sunan didn't respond. Instead he extended his left hand in front of him and placed his right hand near his waist.

The burly soldier laughed and strode forward.

At the last moment, Sunan's hand shot out toward the soldier's hip. Then he twisted his waist and knee, only to find that it did nothing.

The soldier sneered, then reached out toward Sunan's shoulder. He brushed his hand in a dismissive motion, and Sunan felt as if a tree had hit him. He flew backward through the air, flipping head over heels numerous times until he slammed into a wall, which collapsed over him.

Hours passed.

When Sunan awoke, what he first took to be the smell of roasted pork turned out to be the reek of burning flesh. Nothing remained of the village but ashes and blood. He found his parents decapitated. His master had been ripped limb from limb. He found one sister, and the realization of what had happened to her caused him to immediately vomit. As for his other two sisters, they were nowhere to be seen.

Eventually his mind went blank. He collapsed, weeping until there were no more tears left within him.

Finally, he fled, heading north toward the Huang Mountains, his heart filled with sorrow and terror. Time blurred, and eventually he took up residence in a cave.

The horrific memories that played over and over in his mind haunted him for weeks and months. In order to escape them, he began to travel, carefully making his way west through the mountains. Time had no meaning to him.

One day, he happened to be crossing a ravine via a fallen log when the log snapped, and he fell, landing in a small pool of water below.

As soon as he splashed down into the water, he noticed that the water was different. It seemed to glow and sparkle in a way that was different from the water he was used to seeing in the well back in the village.

Sunan didn't know it at the time, but because of the natural landscape of the area, this pool had become infused with the special energy that the Demon Emperor brought with him. When he took a sip of the water, the energy began to flow through his body, causing him to gasp.

The sensation was strange at first but also pleasant. Sunan quickly took another drink of water and felt more of the energy seep into him. Gradually, the weariness and aching in his bones and muscles began to fade away.

Sunan took up residence near the pond. Every day he would drink from the pond water and gather food from the surrounding forest.

One day, while sitting cross-legged on a stone outcropping, looking up at the stars in the sky, Sunan closed his eyes and focused inwardly. The pain and horror from the slaughter of his friends and family in the village was something that still haunted him, and he remembered reading about a way to deal with such feelings.

Back in the village, he had learned a bit about something called meditation. It was something the village elders usually practiced, something laughed at by the children, of course, who said it was just sleeping while sitting up.

According to what Sunan had been told, it was a way to calm the mind and heart, which was something he desperately needed to do.

Therefore, he closed his eyes and began to breathe in a set, rhythmic fashion. Slowly his mind emptied, and his heart grew calm. In that state of peace and quiet, Sunan became aware of something that seemed almost like a spark, burning deep inside his body. Curious, he focused his attention on the spark, prodding it with his mind. The spark responded, twitching, moving, almost as if it were alive, and yet not.

Fascinated, Sunan spent the rest of the night experimenting with the spark. He pushed it, pulled it, stretched it, and finally began to send it circulating into other parts of his body.

That was how Sunan began to learn about that special energy.

It was on that same night that he had a strange dream, a dream of golden statues and shining light. Normally Sunan did not remember his dreams, but this one was different. The following morning, he could remember it in detail. And that wasn't all. It felt… real. However, he had more pressing concerns than a dream about golden statues, so he dismissed it and concerned himself with more practical matters.

Strangely, the following morning, he noticed a strip of gray cloth hanging from a branch near where he had been sleeping. Looking down at his clothing, he realized that his garments were slowly deteriorating into rags. And yet that strip of cloth didn't seem to have come from his own garb. It was a mystery to be sure, but it only occupied his mind for a short time before he pushed the matter aside.

In the following weeks, he continued to drink from the pond water, to live as part of nature, and to learn more about that energy. Soon he realized that the energy had come to be part of him because he had been drinking the pond water. However, as more energy built up in him, and he became more skilled in manipulating it while meditating, he realized that it could be absorbed in other ways.

Furthermore, by controlling his breathing in certain ways, he could improve the rate at which the energy flowed into and through his body. Soon he reached the point where it wasn't even necessary to drink the pond water, except as a source of refreshment when his tongue was dry.

As time passed, he became more proficient in manipulating the energy. However, other than the invigorating effects it had on him, Sunan wasn't sure how it could truly benefit him.

Eventually the weather started to turn cold. Autumn was about to turn into winter. If he stayed by the pond, he would very likely end up stranded by a winter storm, and then he would surely die.

Now was not the time to be complacent.

Without a backward glance at the pond, he headed down out of the mountains and made his way toward the nearest city.

Daolu.

CHAPTER 2
FIVE SPADES

Sunan was not used to cities, but considering his circumstances, he didn't pay much attention to his surroundings. After the long trek down from the mountains, he was famished.

After months of living off the land, as soon as the fragrant smell of sweet buns and fried food reached his nose, his stomach began to scream at him. He spied one dish that appeared to be made from long strips of very thin bread, all piled together, and it looked delicious.

Unfortunately, he didn't have even a single spade of money to his name, which meant that if he wanted to eat immediately, he would have to steal or worse, beg.

His eyes flickered as he took in the sights and sounds while strolling along the busy streets. From his observations, he soon realized that the beggars in the city were organized. He learned that the hard way, of course. At one point, he decided to rest by squatting down on a street corner, only to be accosted by an angry beggar who told him, "Get lost, this is my street corner!"

At first he was confused as to why he would be taken for a beggar, until he remembered that he'd worn the same set of clothes his entire time in the wilderness.

The longer Sunan walked to and fro, the more his stomach grumbled. He began to glance at the food stalls out of the corner of his eye, and he even started to eye the bulging purses tied to the belts of passing merchants and aristocrats.

In the end, he was the type of person who couldn't bear to lower himself to the criminal element.

He would rather be a dog than a thief.

And that was how he ended up squatting in an alley, picking through a heap of trash. He found some half-eaten buns, a bottle gourd with a bit of yellow wine sloshing around in the bottom, and a few other miscellaneous items.

After sating his hunger, he crossed his legs and meditated for a bit to calm himself. Then he left the alley and began to explore the city.

The city had a long history that Sunan remembered reading about once upon a time. In the ancient dialect of Classical Fei, the name of the city meant "Road of Blades," and there were numerous legends and stories about why that was the case.

It was part of one of the last sovereign nations in the land, the Hen-Shi Empire, which was the shrunken remnant of the Hen-Shi Dynasty that had ruled Qi Xien decades before. And yet Demon Emperor soldiers, who Sunan learned were called the Lions of Peace, could still be seen occasionally in the streets.

Like most old cities, it was well organized and laid out, sturdy and built to withstand the ravages of war. Sunan found a few locations such as restaurants or inns that were hiring staff. However, after only two inquiries, he learned that such establishments required that all new staff members provide paperwork to establish legal residency in the city, stamped with an official seal.

His heart sank. Honest employment seemed impossible to

acquire, leaving him with few choices. He could resort to crime, or he could try to join whatever guild or sect the beggars ran.

He had just decided to seek a way to join the beggars when he noticed that across the crowded square from where he stood was a small booth with a banner hanging next to it that read: "Scholar Sun Mai's Sundry Services."

Sitting behind a rough wooden table was a young man dressed like a scholar, frowning as he read a bamboo scroll. His robe was disheveled, his hair unkempt, and his face was smudged with ink. Spread out on the table in front of him were various scholar's instruments, including sheets of paper, brushes, ink, and the like. Furthermore, leaned up against the table next to him was a guqin, a type of seven-stringed zither that was the signature instrument of a true scholar.

After seeing the young man sitting there, an idea bloomed in Sunan's mind. Eyes glinting shrewdly, he strode across the square until he stood directly in front of the table.

"Greetings, scholar," he said, clasping his hands respectfully.

"Mm-hmm," was the reply from the young scholar, who stared intently at the bamboo scroll for a moment before inserting his thumb into his mouth and beginning to chew it slowly.

Sunan cleared his throat. "I'm in need of certain services. Sundry services, perhaps?"

"Sun Mai's Sundry Services," the young scholar replied.

Sunan frowned. "Are you Sun Mai?"

"I am Sun Mai. Sun Mai I am." The young scholar looked up from the bamboo scroll. "Perfect."

"Excuse me?"

"Do you know what perfect means? Perfect."

Sunan was a bit taken aback. "Umm… I believe so."

"You believe so…"

Sunan began to back up slowly. Perhaps this hadn't been the

best idea after all. "Sorry, I mistook you for someone else," he said. "I'll be taking my leave and—"

Sun Mai slapped his hand down onto the table. "Perfect and imperfect. They're just states of mind, opinions, impressions. Beliefs! You believe so, and therefore you know." A profound gleam appeared in his eyes, and he looked Sunan square in the eyes. "You, sir, are potentially a genius. Did you know that? Genius! How could I have overlooked this?"

He pulled out a sheet of paper and a small brush and began to furiously write down a steady stream of characters, muttering incoherently as he did. "Perfect... imperfect... beliefs are just systems... the sky... moon and sun... Dehua... interesting, interesting, interesting... YES!" He leapt to his feet and held the paper aloft with a triumphant smile.

"This is it! The beginning of my classic scripture!" He looked back at Sunan. "Of course, it won't be classic until much later, so it will start out as an ordinary scripture. But one day, my friend, one day, it will be a classic. A classic, I tell you!" He blinked as if just noticing Sunan. "Who are you?"

Sunan stared in shock for a moment before regaining his senses. "Fan Sunan, but... just call me Sunan."

"Sunan? I'm Sun Mai." The young scholar clasped his hands and bowed. "I'm in your debt for this bit of enlightenment. How can I repay you? Do you need a poem written for a lover? Music for a feast? A painting, perhaps?"

Sunan felt a bit put on the spot. He wanted to simply turn on his heel and walk off into the crowd, but he couldn't quite bring himself to be so impolite.

"I need some writing done," he said finally. "Something similar to... proof of residency in the city. Do you happen to have official sealing stamps on hand?"

Sun Mai cocked his head to the side for a moment, after which he chuckled and lifted his left eyebrow. "Ahh, a recommendation letter. So, you need *that* type of writing." He chuckled. "Of course I can accommodate you."

He sat back down and began to shuffle through his brushes. "You know, back when the Hen-Shi Empire was really on top of things, I would never have done something like this. It is most… inappropriate. But Emperor Tian really ran things into the ground, and times are tough. So, in this *one* case, I will bend my moral compass to help a soul as equally destitute as myself. Oh, by the way, the cost will be a total of five spades."

Sunan cleared his throat again and was just about to launch into a counter proposal when he noticed that he was not alone at Sun Mai's booth.

A tall, muscular man was now standing next to him on his left, and to the right were two shorter men. Although Sunan had grown up in a village, it was obvious to him that these men were ruffians. From the way they held themselves to the expressions on their faces, he knew that they were people he couldn't afford to offend.

"Sun Mai, Sun Mai," the tall man said, "please tell me you have good news for me."

Sun Mai looked up, and when he saw the tall man standing next to Sunan, his face went a bit pale.

"G-g-green Tiger Zheng," he stammered. "Long time no see! How can I help you?"

"Long time no see?" Green Tiger Zheng replied. "I was here yesterday afternoon. And my patience is running thin. Where is my money?"

"Money?" Sun Mai said. "Er, money, oh… right… money! Money." His face brightened. "Well, as a matter of fact, I do have some money. What do you say to a ten percent payment, right here and now!"

Green Tiger Zheng's eyes narrowed. "Ten percent? That's only five spades."

Sun Mai tilted his head up, and a solemn expression appeared on his face. "Sir, I assume that you are not very familiar with Dehua, but allow me to point out that Kong Zhi said, 'Strive to be poor but joyful, wealthy but civilized.'"

Green Tiger Zheng stared at Sun Mai for a moment. "As far as I'm concerned, you can take that brush and stick it up Kong Zhi's—"

"Hey, *hey!*" interrupted Sun Mai, throwing his hands up in air. "Please, sir, show at least *some* respect for the ancient sages. I have five spades to give you today. Isn't that better than nothing? And I promise that… I promise that I'll provide the same amount every other day until the whole amount is paid off!"

"Why should I believe you? You haven't paid a single spade back for the past two months!"

Sun Mai cleared his throat. "I have a wealthy new patron," he explained. "I am very much looking forward to paying back your fifty spades."

Green Tiger Zheng's hand closed around the handle of the wooden cudgel he had strapped to his belt. "Very well. Five spades now. Five more in two days, and the same until your debt is clean." He held out his hand. "Now give me those spades."

Sun Mai nodded solemnly and then pointed to Sunan. "He has them."

Sunan's eyes went wide. "Me?" he blurted.

"Of course," Sun Mai said. "Didn't you just hire me for my writing services?"

"I don't have any money! I was just about to tell you when—"

Before he could finish his sentence, Sunan saw a blur of motion out of the corner of his eye.

The tall burly man was reaching for him, clearly intent on grabbing him by the shoulder. For some reason, Sunan found his hands, feet, and waist falling into that same move that his master, the soldier, had taught him. He twisted to the side, leaning just the right way, and then pushed.

Before he even knew what was happening, the tall burly man was flying through the air. He crashed into Sun Mai's table, crushing the entire thing and sending paper, ink, brushes, and all his scholarly tools flying up into the air.

"My table!" Sun Mai exclaimed with a choked cry.

The burly man groaned, and his two companions stared in shock for a moment. However, it didn't take but a moment for the two of them to pull cudgels from their belts. No words were spoken, but it was clear what was happening.

Sun Mai's eyes went wide, and Sunan stood there gaping. Despite Sunan's intelligence, he was not a streetwise person. Sun Mai was.

"Run!" he cried, scooping up his zither, some scattered papers, and a few brushes. He leapt over the groaning man buried in the rubble of the table.

Sunan was simply too stunned to react. Before he could start running, one of the other ruffians took a swing at him with a wooden cudgel. Acting on mere instinct, Sunan leaned his head back to avoid the blow, then managed to reach out and grab ahold of the man's wrist. Then he leaned backward quickly, simultaneously kicking at the man's knee, another move he remembered learning from the soldier.

The ruffian collapsed face-first onto the dusty street.

Sunan had recovered his senses. Not waiting for the third man to make a move, he turned and began running as fast as he could in the other direction.

Off in the distance, Sun Mai was scrambling around a corner into an alley, juggling his zither and writing utensils the entire time. Sunan followed, speeding into the same alley moments later, whereupon he just managed to catch sight of Sun Mai ducking into a dark door.

For the subsequent quarter hour, Sunan followed Sun Mai as he fled in and out of buildings, alleys, streets, squares, stables, a library, a cricket shop, and even a brothel, before finally coming to stop behind a temple dedicated to Supreme Judge Yu. There, he plopped down beneath a cypress tree, dumped his zither and other items onto the ground next to him, and pulled a rag out of his sleeve, which he used to wipe the sweat from his face.

"That... was... a... close... one..." he said, breathing heavily the entire time.

Sunan rested his hands on his knees and gulped in huge lungfuls of fresh air. All of a sudden, he realized that he was starving again. He was of half a mind to curse Sun Mai, but for some reason, he felt that it wouldn't do any good. After catching his breath, he dropped down cross-legged and said, "This was not how I envisioned my first day in the city."

Sun Mai sighed deeply. "My apologies. Although if I were you, I would refrain from swindling others in the future."

Sunan's eyes went wide. "What did you just say?"

Sun Mai stretched out his hands placatingly. "Sunan, listen to me. The past is the past. It can be changed no more than the pigeon can restore the egg from which it just hatched." He stopped talking and cocked his head to the side. "Say, that makes a lot of sense! Maybe I should write that one down to include in my classic scripture."

He looked back at Sunan. "Anyway, the point is, we can't change the past, right? So why worry about it? The most important thing is that I figured out something very important. I know how to make some money, Sunan. Big money. You and I are going to be rich!"

CHAPTER 3
BENCHES

In the northwest corner of Daolu was the warehouse district, a place where the buildings were large, utilitarian, and filled with things like grain and cloth, even jade. Of course, there were street vendors, beggars, and the like, but generally speaking, it was a quieter area than the other parts of the city.

One of the buildings in that area was different from the others. It looked like a warehouse, but it wasn't. Most buildings in the warehouse district were well guarded, but this one had double the amount of guards. There were lookouts posted on nearby buildings who had special whistles fastened to their wrists that they would use if the wrong people approached.

Inside the main door of that building were more even more guards. Furthermore, the building had four secret entrances and at least seven secret exits.

Upon first entering the main door, you would think that you were in a packed warehouse, but that was just a facade. Beyond the facade was a stone wall with a tightly locked door. After the door was a staircase that led down below ground level.

When Sunan and Sun Mai knocked on the main door of the building itself, their hearts were pounding in their chests.

The sound of the knock echoed out into the streets and slowly faded away until everything was silent.

"Are you sure this is the place?" whispered Sunan.

"Of course I'm sure!" hissed Sun Mai. "I've lived in this city for years, and you just arrived. I'm a scholar, for heaven's sake. You're what, a vagabond at best? I'm street smart, do you hear me? Worldly wise! Did you know that once—"

Before he could finish speaking, the door opened a crack. Faint light spilled out, making it impossible to clearly make out the features of the face that appeared.

"The word?" growled a gruff voice.

Sun Mai tilted his chin up. "Green elephant eating rice!"

Sunan's eyes went wide, and he stomped his foot down onto Sun Mai's toe. "It's sesame, you moron!"

Sun Mai grunted, cleared his throat, and then said, "Green sesame eating rice!"

Sunan's eyes nearly bulged out of his head. "You fool! Not the elephant. The rice!"

Sun Mai slowly turned to look at Sunan, his eyes flashing. "Please! There's no need to be so insulting!" He turned back to the shadowy face in the door. "Green sesame eating sesame!"

Sunan quickly grabbed Sun Mai by the shoulders and nudged him to the side. "Hey, friend," he said to the shadowy face. "My friend has just... had a bit too much to drink. The word is 'green elephant eating sesame.'" He chuckled. "Sorry about that."

The shadowy face snorted and closed the door. Shuffling and clanking sounds could be heard, and then the door opened.

Sunan strode in, pulling Sun Mai along with him. They were led past the facade to a staircase lit by oil lamps, which they began to descend.

"Fan Sunan!" Sun Mai growled as they proceeded down. "Enough with the lies!"

"Lies?"

"I had too much to drink? I never drink until the day is over and I'm finished with all scholarly pursuits. Drinking clouds the mind. It confuses the soul. If I drank, how could I ever keep my thoughts straight?"

Sunan clenched his teeth and declined to respond. He and Sun Mai followed the staircase downward until they reached a short corridor. After another locked door that required the same password, they reached their destination.

It was a large room filled with people, a crowd that included merchants and farmers, soldiers and beggars. The din of conversation filled the air, as well as a melange of sawdust, sweat, alcohol, and dried blood. In the center of the room was a raised circular stone platform roughly five meters wide and a meter tall. Most of the people in the room milled around the platform itself, although there were others clustered in the balconies that ringed the room, plus some small private booths interspersed along the balconies.

Before Sunan and Sun Mai could even take in the whole scene, a skinny, shifty-eyed man limped over. "You're Fan Sunan?"

Sunan gulped and nodded. "That's me."

"Don't you have something flashier to go by? Fan Sunan sounds like the name of a farmer."

"Just call me Sunan. Leave out the Fan part."

The man examined him suspiciously for a moment before nodding. Looking at Sun Mai, he said, "Who are you?"

"I'm Scholar Sun Mai, student of the erudite, ponderer of truth, friend to the—"

"He's my agent," interrupted Sunan.

The man frowned. "Very well. Fan Sunan, you come with me. 'Agent,' you can stand in the managers' section over there. Tell them you're with a fighter and that I sent you. I'm Rat-Hearted Li."

Without waiting for a response, the man began to limp off toward the raised platform.

"This is it, Sunan," Sun Mai said. "May Xian Nu Shen guide you."

Sunan glanced over. "You believe in the Enlightened Goddess?"

"Not really, but you'll surely need some divine help up there tonight."

"*What?* You were the one who said I should do this! Fast reflexes, you said. Instincts!"

Sun Mai cleared his throat. "I see someone over in the managers' section waving to me. Good luck!"

Shaking his head, Sunan followed Rat-Hearted Li over to the platform. They came to a stop on the north side, where a set of benches were lined up. The benches were about half full; eight men were seated there, all of them rough-looking characters.

Rat-Hearted Li spat onto the sawdust floor. "Since you're new, you'll be the first fight of the night. Do you know the rules?"

"No killing?" Sunan said with a shrug.

Rat-Hearted Li rolled his eyes and then proceeded to recite a long explanation of various rules, including which types of strikes were allowed or not, how points were awarded, grounds for disqualification, and other complicated topics.

During the several minutes it took him to explain everything, the crowd slowly grew larger, and more tough-looking men showed up and sat down on the nearby benches.

Sunan's heart was starting to pound. The previous day, Sun Mai had somehow convinced him that they could both make a lot of money by fighting in underground martial arts matches. Sunan was now unsure of why he possibly believed Sun Mai's rambling explanation of why it would be safe and how there was nothing to worry about.

This is foolish, he thought to himself. *I learned a few silly fighting moves from a soldier, and almost got killed using them. What happened with those street thugs was just blind luck. This is ridiculous. I'm going to get myself killed here. Look at these guys. That one has only one eye. That other one has more scars than I have fingers and toes. I have to get out of here!*

He took a deep breath and was just about to turn and leave when he realized that at some point Rat-Hearted Li had left his side and was now standing on the fighting platform.

"Ladies and gentlemen, welcome!" he cried out. "This week's fighting platform tournament will begin now!" His words were met with a few cheers and a spattering of applause. "The first fight will feature a returning champion from last week, Chen Zhisheng, the, er… Bloodstained Murderous Bear!"

More applause could be heard as a man shouldered his way past Sunan and then leapt up onto the platform. He was stocky, with a patchy beard and glaring eyes. He beat his chest a few times and roared as he stalked back and forth on the platform.

Sunan's heart sank down into his chest. *What am I doing?*

"His adversary will be… the, er… new guy… Sunan." Rat-Hearted Li's somewhat anticlimactic conclusion was met with the sound of one person applauding. Sunan looked over to see Sun Mai clapping his hands and nodding enthusiastically.

Swallowing again, Sunan shook his head, walked over, and vaulted up onto the platform.

Rat-Hearted Li climbed off of the platform, walking over to stand behind a wide desk located off to the side. Perched on the desk was an incense burner and a candle, and stacked next to that was a large pile of incense, each stick carefully cut in half. He took out one of the incense sticks and placed it carefully into the incense burner.

"Begin!" he shouted, and at the same time, he lit the incense stick with the candle.

Before Sunan even knew what was happening, Chen Zhisheng let out a bellowing roar and rushed toward him. The fighting platform was only five meters wide, so in the blink of an eye, the man's fist was flying through the air directly toward Sunan's face.

He instinctively ducked back and could almost feel the hairs on the man's knuckles brushing against his chin.

As he stepped back, Chen Zhisheng staggered a few steps to the left, thrown off balance by his wild swing.

Sunan clenched his jaw and thought back to the very few things he had learned about fighting. Chen Zhisheng settled back into a fighting stance, clenching his fists and roaring again.

I need to focus, thought Sunan. *Clear my mind. Observe his movements.*

For some reason, he thought to utilize the mind-clearing techniques that he had practiced so often while meditating. Chen Zhisheng began to charge him again, and he flushed his mind of all extraneous thought.

Everything became clearer. He saw Chen Zhisheng's right shoulder twisting back and knew that the man was going to swing just as wildly as before, and with his right hand.

At first, Sunan's hands began to curl into fists, but then he remembered something his master had taught him. Oftentimes, the best way to end a fight wasn't to use your own power to defeat the opponent, it was to use the opponent's power against them. Although that advice had proved useless against the soldiers of the Demon Emperor, for some reason, Sunan couldn't help but feel that there was some truth to it. His hands opened, exposing his palms.

As Chen Zhisheng closed in, something else happened.

Sunan was so used to manipulating that spark of energy inside of him that it happened again, without him even intending to do so. The energy flared to life deep within him, and then, because his thoughts were focused on his left palm, it surged through the passageways in his body in that direction.

As Chen Zhisheng's fist approached, Sunan leaned slightly to the side and then reached out with his left palm. Bolstered by the energy, his palm moved faster than he expected, and with even more force than he had intended.

He originally meant to simply use Chen Zhisheng's momentum to knock him to the ground. Instead, what happened was that as the wild fist swung through the air past Sunan, an explosive slap landed on the man's shoulder. A miserable shriek could be heard as he was knocked violently off his feet. He flew off the platform, spinning through the air to land in the benches next to the platform.

A crash could be heard, as well as several bellows of rage as a handful of the rough-looking characters were all sent into a heap of arms and legs by the spinning Chen Zhisheng.

The entire underground warehouse chamber filled with silence for the span of about four seconds. Then it erupted into a huge commotion.

Rat-Hearted Li leapt up onto the platform, which Sunan would have found surprising considering the man's previous limp. However, he was so stunned that he could do nothing more than look down at his own open palm.

"A stunning knockout by Sunan!" yelled Rat-Hearted Li. "He's a powerhouse! A warrior! A... a dragon among men! Sunan the Dragon! SUNAN THE DRAGON!"

The following minutes were a blur.

Sunan was hustled off the platform and led through a series of formalities that he forgot. He barely noticed what was happening around them. Instead, he was reviewing what had happened during the fight. He thought about the mental state he had been in and how he had directed the energy to his hand. He remembered the movement, the weight of his feet, the angle of his arms and legs.

Before he realized it, he and Sun Mai were back out on the street, and Sun Mai was pulling him along by the arm at a virtual run.

"What's going on?" Sunan asked. "Where are we going?"

Sun Mai looked over his shoulder and smiled. "We're going to a feast!"

CHAPTER 4
A SISSY TO FIGHT

They truly did attend a feast, though it was not a feast of rich, delicious fare. An enterprising establishment near the docks offered never-ending food for a cheap price. Called the Heavenly Meat Palace, it was not very clean, and it was filled with sweaty sailors and drunken soldiers.

The food was simply prepared but plentiful. There were skewers of suspicious-looking meat served by the handful, boiled yellow beans, spicy prawns from the nearby river, and loads of flatbread. Most of the food was unseasoned, but Sun Mai was aware of that ahead of time and purchased a pack of peppers and spices from a nearby vendor.

The restaurant also provided endless pots of cheap yellow wine, which Sun Mai began to down with a vengeance.

At one point, Sunan thought of something and asked, "How are we paying for this?"

Sun Mai stared at him for a moment. "Seriously? Did you forget? We're rich! You won! Do you hear me? You *won!*" He reached into his robe and then threw a purse down onto the table. It landed with a clunk. "That's an entire string of cash!"

Sunan nearly choked on a mouthful of grilled meat. "A string of cash? You mean a thousand *spades*?"

Sun Mai grinned and drank another mouthful of yellow wine. "Like I said, we're rich!"

"But I thought you said we would earn 250 spades?"

Sun Mai chuckled. "That was if you lost."

Sunan's mouth dropped open. "You expected me to lose?"

Sun Mai stuck his chin up. "Of course not. I was just prepared for the worst." His eyes flickered, and he looked around. "Now tell me, how did you do it? Was it… magic? Black magic? Most men of learning don't believe in such things, but I'm no ordinary man. So… was it?"

Sunan guffawed. "Magic? Magic's not even real! No, it was… I don't know how to explain it."

"Don't know how to explain it?" Sun Mai asked incredulously. "What does that mean? You knocked that buffoon a full ten meters through the air! The physician said his arm was broken, plus three or four ribs, although that could have been from the fall. If it wasn't magic, then what was it?"

Sunan frowned and picked up a pot of yellow wine. After taking a long swig, he said, "Something happened to me out in the mountains…"

Sun Mai chuckled. "I guessed as much from your clothing, if you could even go so far as to call it clothing. More like rags, really. Dirty rags, or even—"

"Anyway," said Sunan, "when I was out in the mountains alone, I… I felt something. Something that's part of nature, I think, but then… it became a part of me. It felt like an energy or a wind of some sort, like air. It began to flow through my body, and then it started to grow. Somehow I pushed that wind-air energy into my hand, and… well, you saw what happened."

"Wind energy, huh?" Sun Mai cracked open a spicy prawn and devoured it. A distracted look appeared in his eyes. "Wind. Energy. Wind and energy. Windy energy. Energetic wind? Energetic windiness? Windy energeticness? No, that's not right. Hmmm. Qi. Classical Fei. Qi. Yes, that's right." His gaze turned sharp. "You know, not many people can read Classical Fei nowadays, let alone speak it. Were you aware that in ancient times, people believed that the whole world was made of only five elements?

"Sounds funny, of course, because later that was proven wrong. However, in Classical Fei, the character for 'air' was the same one they claimed was one of the five elements, a type of energy that kept the world in motion. In Classical Fei, the pronunciation of that character is 'qi.' Wind-air energy is a pretty cumbersome term, so why not just call it qi?"

"Chee?"

"Qi," Sun Mai said, correcting his pronunciation slightly.

"Qi," echoed Sunan. He nodded. "I like it."

The conversation veered off in other directions after that, and the more yellow wine they consumed, the stranger the conversation got. Eventually the night transformed into one long blur, much of which Sunan was later convinced was a hallucination.

The following morning, his pounding head was filled with images of himself and Sun Mai singing songs with a group of pretty girls with too much makeup, an argument with a beggar over a melon, and something about a tiger.

It took hours to recover. When his head was finally clear and his stomach settled, he had a more serious discussion with Sun Mai about what had happened and what they would do going forward.

With the seemingly vast fortune they had won, they rented a small room in an inn near the docks, not too far from the Heavenly Meat Palace, which was surely destined to become one of their favorite destinations.

Sun Mai explained more to him about the underground

platform duels. Everyone got paid, even the losers. However, the winners could earn exorbitant sums. According to Sun Mai, if he could win the next fight, they would get 1,500 spades, not just 1,000. And the numbers increased from there. Rumor had it that the top fighter, who went by the flashy nickname Golden Immortal, earned fifty strings of cash per fight and never lost.

At Sun Mai's urging, he began to spend most mornings meditating and practicing with his qi. He also began to teach Sun Mai the meditation techniques from his village.

Five days passed. On the morning of the sixth day, one day before the next underground platform tournament, Sun Mai finally made a breakthrough.

He let out a whoop of excitement and leapt to his feet.

"I did it! I felt it! The qi! This is incredible! What do I do now?"

Sunan sat down cross-legged next to him and began to instruct him in the most basic ways of manipulating the qi inside of the body.

That night, Sunan had a strange dream. He heard laughter, maniacal laughter. And then there was a black hurricane whipping across the lands, flaying trees, sending men and soldiers flying about. He woke up in a cold sweat and couldn't go back to sleep for nearly an hour.

The following day, after a morning spent meditating and circulating qi, Sunan and Sun Mai went to the market to buy some new clothing. Sun Mai upgraded his scholar's robes to silk, and Sunan purchased a tunic and trousers of sturdy hemp, something he felt was more befitting of a rough-and-tumble duel.

Sun Mai tried to convince him to buy a jacket with a dragon embroidered on the back, but Sunan refused.

"But you're Sunan the Dragon!" exclaimed Sun Mai.

Sunan merely snorted and continued on through the market.

Later, as they ate an afternoon meal, Sun Mai asked, "So, who was that girl?" He raised his eyebrow suggestively.

"Girl?" Sunan replied, confused.

"Come, come, no need to be so shy. When I got up last night to talk to the moon, I saw a girl in your room last night. Gray robe? Pretty? Had a sword strapped to her back?"

Sunan stared for a moment. "Hold on, what did you just say? Talk to the moon?"

"Yeah, don't you talk to the moon?"

Sunan shook his head. "Uh, no. Were you drinking again? There was no girl."

Sun Mai gave a cold snort. "If you don't want to admit it, fine. She was pretty, though. You have my approval."

Sunan shook his head and continued eating.

Later that night, they found themselves once again in the underground warehouse. Last time they had come, people had paid no more attention to them than they would a pair of flies. This time, eyes turned in their direction, and the buzz of conversation rose up in the room.

Rat-Hearted Li appeared at their side. "Greetings, Young Masters. Young Dragon, are you ready for your fight?"

"Just Sunan. There's no need for the 'dragon' part."

"Er, very well, Young Master Sunan, please come with me to the fighter's corner. Young Master Sun, a table is waiting for you in the managers' corner."

There were other fighters sitting on the benches, who eyed Sunan coldly as he approached.

"Your performance last week was spectacular," Rat-Hearted Li said, the words pouring out of his mouth. "Chen Zhisheng is still bedridden! And from a single blow, at that. Because of the stunning fashion with which you achieved victory, you moved much higher in the rankings. You will fight fourth, against Wang Li, the Killer of Daolu."

"Killer?" Sunan said. "I thought it was forbidden to kill your opponent?"

"Of course it is, but you know... accidents can happen."

After leading Sunan to the benches, Rat-Hearted Li limped off into the crowd. Sunan looked over at the champions' corner and saw a man wearing a golden robe. Presumably, he was the famed Golden Immortal, the reigning champion.

Before long, the fights proceeded. This was Sunan's first time to truly watch people in organized combat. The first match was between a burly man who looked like a sailor and a shorter but even stockier man who was obviously a soldier. Seeing them exchange blows, Sunan felt lucky that his opponent last time had been Chen Zhisheng. The sailor and the soldier were clearly no strangers to a fight.

They're definitely good, probably not good enough to be considered experts, though, he thought.

As Sunan watched, he picked up on some of the things that the men were doing, such as where they placed their feet, how they delivered their blows. In many of the situations, he saw how a failed blow could have connected or how twisting in a slightly different way could have resulted in avoiding a strike.

The two men battered each other back and forth for three rounds before the sailor was finally knocked unconscious by a fist to the side of his jaw.

As the man slammed face-first onto the fighting platform, a glob of blood flew out of his mouth and narrowly missed Sunan.

Sunan swallowed hard.

The following fight was less dramatic but longer. The two fighters were clearly experienced, and they spent a lot of time dancing around each other. Neither of them landed a single blow during the entire first round. About halfway through the second round, someone sat down next to Sunan.

Sunan looked over to see a skinny fellow with a long scar down the side of his cheek and a mustache with long, curled ends.

"Hey, kid, you're the one they call the Dragon, right?" he asked, keeping his eyes fixed on the fight.

Sunan nodded. "Yeah, that's me, but you can just call me Sunan."

"My boss is Iron Awl Hu. Have you heard of him?"

"No, I don't think so."

"He's an important man in Daolu. We're aware that you're new in town, so you probably don't know the lay of the land here. Let me just spell it out for you: Iron Awl Hu runs things here. The constables, the soldiers, everyone answers to him. Got it?"

Sunan nodded.

"Good. You seem like a smart kid. Listen, the man you're fighting tonight, Wang Li, he's a friend of Iron Awl Hu's nephew. I think it would in your best interest to just let him win the fight. Don't make it seem obvious. Throw in a few good punches and kicks. But in the end, you go down and you stay down, understood?

"Since you're in the fourth match, you would normally make 625 spades for losing. We'll kick it up to 1,000. Not a bad deal, right?" He finally turned to look at Sunan. "You hear me, kid?"

Sunan clenched his jaw. "I hear you."

"Good. Don't let it go past two rounds."

With that, the man stood up and wandered off into the crowd.

The current fight ended about then, and the third match started. However, Sunan couldn't concentrate on what was happening on the platform. His mind was working furiously regarding the words spoken to him by the mustachioed man.

Finally, the moment arrived in which his name was called, but he still hadn't formulated a plan. For some reason, he wished he could consult Sun Mai about it. Although Sun Mai tended to ramble, and sometimes incoherently at that, he often ended up making interesting points and profound statements.

As he hopped up onto the platform, he heard a few people cheering for the Dragon, but most were obviously rooting for Wang Li, the so-called Killer of Daolu.

As Rat-Hearted Li made the introductions, Sunan looked over

at his opponent. He was young and well-built, with cold eyes and a mouth twisted into a perpetual scowl. He actually did look like the type of person you would expect to be a killer.

The round began, and Wang Li immediately went on the offensive, albeit cautiously. Before he could get close, Sunan began to circulate his qi, raising his hands defensively at the same time. He could tell how vastly different this match was going to be compared to his first fight.

Wang Li was obviously a trained fighter, with experience to boot. However, with qi flowing through him, Sunan didn't find it very difficult to avoid the man's blows. The few that connected didn't cause him very much pain.

But then one particular jab caught him across the chin, sending him staggering to the left, stars dancing in his eyes.

How did I let that through? he thought. *I won't let that happen again.*

He shook his head to clear it, then sidestepped to avoid a follow-up blow.

After some more back and forth, the round ended. Sunan didn't strike a single time.

When the second round started, Sunan still wasn't sure what to do. He didn't like the idea of throwing the fight, but in the end, he would still make a lot of money. Sun Mai probably wouldn't object. And it wouldn't be a good idea to offend a powerful crime lord, which was what Iron Awl Hu seemed to be.

Wang Li edged forward and began to look for an opening.

Fine, I'll just throw the match. It doesn't matter.

However, it was in the exact moment that Sunan was about to throw the fight that Wang Li spoke for the first time.

"Hey, little bitch, where did you learn to fight, some village somewhere? Who taught you, your mother? Or was it your sister? Tell me where you come from so that I can go thank them for giving me such a sissy to fight. Afterward, I'll make sure to give them a real good time!"

CHAPTER 5
CRUNCH

Blood rushed into Sunan's head, and he could almost feel the veins popping in his eyes, causing them to become murderously bloodshot. He had read about something called "killing intent" before but had never experienced it. Village life had always been idyllic and enjoyable. Even the times he had gotten in "fights" with other young boys, it had really been little more than spirited wrestling.

However, the moment Wang Li mentioned his mother, Sunan understood what killing intent was. His heart began to pound so hard it felt like it would burst out of his chest. His ears pounded with soundless thunder. His cheeks were hot, his eyes burned, and his hands clenched so hard into fists that blood welled up around his fingernails.

Images of his mother and his sisters flashed through his mind, and they were not the happy images of his childhood. He had not been the type of boy to argue with his sisters, nor the type of son to harass his mother. Tragically, the images which welled up in his mind were that of their bloodstained and ravaged forms lying bent, broken, and burning among the wreckage of his village.

He had never experienced rage like this before, and the way it burned within him seemed to give him access to a power he had been unaware of before. This was not the power of qi, nor was it some other magical ability. It was something that existed in all people, a fuel of rage that could burn beyond control.

Sunan could think of nothing else but killing the person in front of him. He forgot who Wang Li was. He forgot about Iron Awl Hu. He even forgot who he was himself.

Without thinking about it, he circulated his qi, and then, he did more. He summoned the qi that had built up in his body during his time in the Huang Mountains, not just to his fists, but to his eyes and to his feet.

Somehow the killing intent raging inside of him also burned his mind into a state of clarity. In some ways, he had lost control, but in other ways, he was more in control than ever. His observations of the fights earlier coalesced subconsciously, and he moved his left foot slightly forward. He shifted his weight and twisted his shoulders.

Based on the back and forth from earlier, he was highly confident that he could predict the speed, direction, and angle that Wang Li would attack from.

And that he did.

The qi in his feet allowed him to move faster than he normally could have had he been running, and he took three steps to the left. The qi in his eyes made everything seem to slow down. He could see Wang Li's angles and momentum, and it was as easy to see where he was moving as it would be to watch a stream of honey flow off of a spoon.

This time, he timed his movement carefully. Even before Wang Li's blow sailed past his face, Sunan's clenched fist began to move. He poured every scrap of qi he could into that fist, into the fingers, and especially the knuckles. He braced his arm, his muscles, his bones, and his flesh, imbuing them all in a way that would both protect them and endow them with ironlike power.

And speed.

A crunching sound could be heard as his knuckles made contact with the side of Wang Li's face. One knuckle hit a cheekbone, another hit the temple. In the end, it didn't matter. Sunan's fist was like an iron cudgel, and Wang Li's face was like a pumpkin.

Bone shattered. Flesh tore. Blood sprayed.

Teeth flew through the air.

But that wasn't all.

Sunan's single blow shattered half of Wang Li's head and sent his body spinning several times through the air before it landed on the edge of the platform. Wang Li still wasn't dead yet, and his lone remaining eye stared in shock at Sunan. He reached out shakily as if to steady himself, made a gurgling sound, then died. His body toppled backward off of the platform, leaving behind a streak of blood and gore.

The rage and fire in Sunan's heart slowly began to subside. For some reason, he looked out into the crowd and found himself staring into the eyes of the mustachioed man. Sunan held his gaze for a moment while he wiped the spatters of blood off of his face, then looked down at the crumpled body lying down below.

This time, the crowd did not erupt into wild cheering. Everyone was deathly silent. No applause burst forth from Sun Mai.

The only sound to be heard were the drops of blood plopping down from Sunan's fist onto the stone platform beneath his feet.

***

Sunan and Sun Mai sat across from each other, separated by a huge pile of grilled meats and vegetables, none of it touched yet, steaming in the night air.

Sun Mai raised a bowl of yellow wine up into the air, as did

Sunan. Then he looked up at the moon, his expression somber.

"A bowl of wine, a table of meat," he said poetically.

"And a friend like a brother with which to dine,

"I raise my bowl to the moon up high—" He looked down at the grilled meat.

"And this poor sheep, which makes us three.

"But the moon won't drink

"And our shadows—"

Before he could continue with his poetry, Sunan interrupted. "All right, all right! Enough already. To you!"

"No!" Sun Mai said. "To you."

"To us," Sunan conceded.

"To us!"

They downed the bowl of yellow wine and then began to eat and drink voraciously. After a few minutes passed, Sun Mai belched loudly and said, "Sunan?"

"Yes?"

"That. Was. INCREDIBLE!" He slammed his palm down onto the table, causing all of the meat to hop up into the air and then plop back down loudly. "I've never seen anything like it! What happened?"

Sunan shrugged. "He said something insulting, and I hit him as hard as I could. That's all."

"But didn't you hit that other guy as hard as you could? You didn't... you know..." He held his balled fist up in front of his face and then opened his fingers wide. "Poosh!"

Sunan grimaced and shrugged again. "I'm stronger than before. I'm not sure how it happened, but... it's almost like I broke through to a higher level than before."

"A breakthrough, huh?" Sun Mai held another bowl of yellow wine up into the air. "Come on, let's drink," he said. They downed another bowl together. "You know, even after they fined you for killing 'the killer,' we're still completely rich. And you rose even higher in the ranks! Now you're only two ranks below the Golden Immortal. Did you see those golden robes he was wearing? I'm telling you, we need to get you some clothes with dragons on them.

"Do you know where the legends of dragons come from? You might be surprised. I was reading one of the classics the other day, and…"

Sunan tuned Sun Mai out as he ate and drank. Time passed.

At some point, Sunan realized that everything had become very quiet. He looked up from a spicy prawn to find Sun Mai staring at him with eyes as wide as the moon. Sunan frowned, and Sun Mai mouthed a word which he couldn't quite make out.

"What did you just say?" he asked.

"S-s-s…"

"What?"

"Sp-sp-sp…"

Sunan cocked his ear. "Huh?"

"Sp-sp-spear!" Sun Mai choked out.

It was at this point that Sunan felt something cold pressing lightly in the side of his neck. The tip of a spear. His heart began to thud, and a cold rage welled up in his heart.

A voice spoke out, oily and vicious. "What. Were. You. *Thinking?*"

Even before the owner of the voice strolled into view, Sunan knew exactly who it was. It was the mustachioed man from the tournament earlier. He walked into Sunan's field of vision but remained a distance of at least three or four meters away from the table.

"I told you to throw the fight, and you said you understood. Did you? Did you really understand? Apparently not. Not only did you not throw the fight, you defeated your opponent. And not only did you defeat him, you *killed* him! Splattered his brains all over the platform. Impressive. Very impressive."

Sunan looked over at Sun Mai, who was staring directly into his eyes. Ever so slightly, Sun Mai's lips moved, forming a single word: *Fight.*

Sunan nodded almost imperceptibly and began to circulate the qi in his body, sending it into his arms.

"Iron Awl Hu isn't happy," the mustachioed man continued. "In fact, 'not happy' doesn't even begin to describe how he feels. I think that he—"

In the middle of the man's sentence, Sunan jerked to the side, twisted, and batted the spear away from him. The man holding the spear was a thuggish fellow, burly, with hands the size of small cats.

Without the slightest pause, Sunan clenched his hand into a fist and poured all of his qi into it. He bent his knees and cocked his fist, then lunged forward, aiming what he knew was a deadly blow directly toward the man's face. It wouldn't matter if his fist hit the man's jaw, temple, nose, or any other place—the resulting damage would be mortal, beyond the shadow of a doubt.

Die, you bastard!

Sunan's anger, fury, and humiliation burned like fire, fueling his lunge. He let out a shout as he flew through the air.

And then he found himself airborne, his fist having connected with nothing. His punch had completely missed the target.

The thug was burly but quick. He easily dodged Sunan's wild blow and swung his spear in a full circle, slamming the haft into Sunan's torso.

Sunan flopped down face-first onto the hard-packed dirt floor. The wind was knocked out of his lungs, and the qi inside of him was sent into chaos.

Before he could force air back into his lungs, before he could struggle to his feet, before he could do anything, he felt six or seven spearheads pressing into his back and legs and arms. The razor-sharp tips pierced his skin, pinning him down. Moments later, hands gripped him, vicelike and hard as iron.

He heard a shriek, and his eyes swiveled to the right. Sun Mai was being held tightly by thugs, a knife pressed up against his throat.

Someone grabbed Sunan's hair, and his head was jerked up. He found himself looking into the eyes of the mustachioed man.

The man chuckled. "I've seen people like you before, you know. People always come along with some special move, some special weapon, some special poison. It's nothing new. *You're* nothing new.

"And now, you're going to do what they all do. You're going to listen to me. From now on, you work for Iron Awl Hu. When he says fight, you fight. When he says lose, you lose. Got it?

"You think you're special? You think you've... *got what it takes* to be your own man?" He laughed and slowly pulled a thin, razor-sharp knife out of his sleeve, which he slowly ran down the side of Sunan's jaw. "Think again, boy. And don't forget, you might be able to take a punch or a cut or a stab... but not everyone can."

Sunan's head was jerked to face Sun Mai. One of the men holding Sun Mai looked Sunan in the eye, grinned, and then twisted Sun Mai's arm. Sunan winced at the cracking sound as Sun Mai's arm was broken.

Sun Mai screamed in anguish and began to sob.

"If hurting your friends won't work, there's more we can do," the mustachioed man continued. "So, let me say this one more time. You do what *we* say. You think you're fast? You think you're strong? We will always have people who are faster. And stronger. And better. Fall in line, you pitiful bastard. Otherwise..."

The mustachioed man held Sunan's hair tightly, forcing him to look in Sun Mai's direction as the other man holding him slowly drew his own wicked-looking knife out from his belt and then slowly pressed the blade against Sun Mai's throat.

Then he pulled Sun Mai's head back hard, holding it there until the veins and arteries in his neck began to bulge. Sun Mai gurgled and whimpered.

Then the man slowly began to draw the knife across Sun Mai's throat.

CHAPTER 6
FINGERNAILS

It would be hard to find someone more different from Sunan than Bao. Sunan was born and raised in a remote village in the northeast. Bao was born and raised as nobility in the metropolitan city of Yu Zhing, at the base of the Banyan Mountains. Sunan lived his young life having heard of the Demon Emperor as nothing more than a vague bogeyman who existed far, far away, if at all. Bao virtually grew up in his shadow.

In fact, she had even laid eyes on him on more than one occasion. He was ugly. Very ugly.

Bao was born years after the Demon Emperor had secured tyrannical control over the majority of central Qi Xien. Yu Zhing had been one of the first cities to fall to his initial military onslaught, and the noble clans there had almost universally capitulated. Some, such as the Dongmen and Zhongli clans, chafed under the new rulership. Others, such as the Sima and Gongye clans, thrived. Bao was born into one of those noble clans.

Eventually, hatred for the Demon Emperor began to come to

a head within the city, and after decades of clandestine planning, a full-fledged rebellion was nigh. But then, with no warning whatsoever, the conspiracy was betrayed, and the Demon Emperor sent the Bone General to settle matters.

Yu Zhing and its noble clans were purged mercilessly. Numerous prominent members of many of the clans were called out as traitors, then tortured and executed publicly. Some were burned or skinned alive. Others suffered worse fates.

Whether or not the victims were innocent or guilty didn't matter. The heart of the rebellion was ripped out, and the smell of the burning flesh would linger in the noses of the survivors for years to come.

Bao occasionally had nightmares about the things that had happened. Her mother had been one of the accused, and although Bao never found out whether or not she was actually part of the rebellion, it didn't matter. She was tortured and then burned alive in a public square. Other relatives had their own bones extracted and sharpened into instruments of torture, which were then used to kill them. Bao's father committed suicide shortly thereafter.

From then on, she was a ward of the clan, her basic needs cared for, but she was ignored for the most part.

Bao had always been pretty, and as she reached her teens, she began to blossom into beauty. However, there were many beauties in the noble houses of Yu Zhing, even in her own clan. A rose growing up in a cabbage patch will attract much attention, but a single rose in a bed of roses will not. Bao was the latter.

Perhaps because of the horrors she had witnessed and the oppressive nature of noble life in a city controlled by the Demon Emperor, Bao developed a love of reading. She read anything she could get her hands on, but she especially favored the tales of legends and myths that most nobles frowned upon. She didn't care that people looked down on such stories, and truth be told, few people cared about her obsession or even noticed.

Of course, it wasn't easy to keep up a hobby of reading, since books came almost exclusively in the form of bamboo or wood scrolls. Most stories were told by storytellers on the streets, but Bao wasn't allowed to go wandering around the streets, so she really had no other choice but to read.

She would read any chance she could get, and that reading fueled her imagination with thoughts of adventure and reckless abandon. Everything that was the opposite of the drudgery of her actual life.

Eventually she began to itch for more, and it was at about this time that she realized that her greatest asset was the very thing she hated most: her boring anonymity. Since few people in the clan cared about her or even noticed her, she began to take advantage of that to go places a young noble lady shouldn't go or do things that were technically forbidden.

It started in the clan estates, after she managed to get her hands on a servant girl's dress. On one particularly dull evening, she found a discreet place to change her clothes and rub some dirt on her face, after which she snuck into the kitchens. Her heart pounded the whole time, but shockingly, nobody even looked at her. She pilfered some dried fruits and a small pot of wine, which she enjoyed later in the privacy of her room.

From the servant girl's dress, things escalated. She used that very dress to sneak into the laundry room, where she stole a male servant's uniform. As long as she kept her long hair tied up beneath a hat and made sure her chest was bound, nobody noticed that she didn't look like an ordinary servant.

Eventually, sneaking around the clan estates got boring, and soon she identified one section of the clan gardens where a tree made it easy to shinny over the wall, after which she began going out at night into the city.

That day, her life got very exciting. And that was how she met Geng Long.

On her third excursion outside of the clan estates, she was prowling the streets dressed as a waif. Although homelessness and begging were officially outlawed by the Demon Emperor, in the sketchier areas of the city, such practices were alive and well. Those were the places Bao found most exciting to visit.

She was prowling through an alley when she happened to notice a tattered bamboo scroll lying in a pile of trash next to a door. She squatted down next to the trash and gingerly pulled the bamboo scroll out. It was so old and worn out that it was on the verge of falling apart, and many of the characters were faded into near illegibility. The title read: *Romance of the Hen-Shi Knights.*

Bao's eyes lit up. Wiping the scroll off with her sleeve, she was just about to tuck it under her arm and hasten back to the clan estates when someone spoke behind her.

"Hey, Little Sis, are you really so desperate for reading material that you pick books up out of the garbage?"

She spun around to find a lanky young man leaning up against the wall across from her. She stood up and shrugged casually. "I just haven't seen this one before."

The boy chuckled. "If you say so. I haven't seen you before. What's your name?"

"I'm, er, Bao," she replied.

"Bao? Is that your surname or your given name?"

"Just call me Bao," she said. Bao was in fact her given name. She didn't dare to tell him her surname, as it would reveal that she was from a noble clan.

"Bao it is, then," the boy said. "I'm Geng. Geng Long. Long like dragon, you know?"

Bao nodded.

"Look," Geng Long said, "I'm into books too. I know a place where you can get as many as you want."

And that settled it. After a bit more chatting, Geng Long led her from this corner to that corner, until they were in another dark alley, in front of the door of a shop. The shop was closed, and the door clearly barred. Above the door was a sign that read "books."

"A bookshop?" Bao asked. "But it's closed…"

"Exactly," Geng Long replied, grinning. He then proceeded to break into the shop, albeit carefully, in such a way that, after leaving, no one would be able to tell that they had come.

After slipping into the darkness of the shop, Geng Long said, "All right, take a look around and pick one or two. Old Man Guo is virtually blind. As long as we bring the books back in a few days, he'll never be the wiser. Hurry up, I'll stand watch."

Thus, Bao made her first real friend.

In the following weeks and months, she spent most days reading in the gardens of the clan estate and most nights gallivanting with Geng Long. It was an exciting life, albeit slightly dangerous.

On one particular night, Bao met Geng Long in their usual meeting place, and she had a small sack slung over her shoulder.

"What's that?" he asked.

She grinned. "I managed to get my hands on some nice food and wine." Although Bao was used to the fine delicacies available at her clan's estates, Geng Long was not. When she showed him the contents of the sack, his eyes gleamed with anticipation.

"I know the perfect spot," he said. "Come on."

He led her to the Yu Zhing docks, where they sat down beneath the eaves of a warehouse and began their late-night picnic.

They had been eating and chatting for only a few minutes when a shadow fell across Bao's legs. She looked up to see a swarthy teenage boy looming over her, flanked by two other teenagers.

"Well, look who we have here," the boy said, grinning maliciously. "Geng Long and his mistress." He cracked his knuckles.

Geng Long and Bao both scrambled to their feet.

"Screw off, Peng Lin," Geng Long said.

Peng Lin snorted coldly. "This is our territory. If you wanna have a tryst with this slut, do it somewhere else."

Geng Long's hands clenched into fists, and he took a step forward. "I dare you to say that again!"

Geng Long was about a head taller than Peng Lin, but Peng Lin had much broader shoulders and far thicker arms; if Geng Long looked like a race horse, Peng Lin looked like an ox.

Peng Lin spat onto the ground at Geng Long's feet. "I said, if you wanna have a tryst with this slut—"

Geng Long roared and leapt forward, swinging wildly at Peng Lin. The blow just managed to graze him, causing him to stagger backward a few paces. He spat out a mouthful of blood, wiped his mouth clean, and then growled, "You're *dead*, Geng Long. Boys, you get the slut and hold her down. I'm coming for her next!"

As Geng Long and Peng Lin began to batter each other with fists and feet, Peng Lin's two companions advanced on Bao.

Her heart pounded, and she backed up until she ran into the wall of the warehouse. The two boys chuckled as they closed in.

Bao was a young woman who had never been in a fight in her life. However, she had seen many an exhibition match between soldiers in the clan, and in her boredom had even spent some time watching them train. Even though she didn't have a lick of experience, she knew how to fight, at least on a theoretical level.

As the boys reached out to grab her, something strange happened. Her pounding heart suddenly went completely calm. Everything seemed to slow down. Her eyes flickered down for a brief moment as she confirmed that lying on the ground near her left foot was a knife, which she had brought along to cut a slab of cured donkey meat.

Her eyes flickered back up, and she sprang into motion. Before either of the two boys could react, she lunged forward and grabbed one of them by the forearm, then kneed him in the groin with all the strength she could muster. The boy let out a muffled squawk, then dropped to the ground and rolled into the fetal position.

The other boy was so taken aback that he froze in place.

Bao whirled, ducking down to grab the knife, and then jumped toward the second boy. By this point, he had overcome his initial shock and just managed to dodge to the side and avoid the wild slash of the knife.

Then he swung out with his right fist, landing a blow directly on the side of Bao's face. Pain lanced through her head, and colors flashed in her eyes as she was knocked off balance and toppled to the ground. The knife clattered off to the side.

Then the boy kicked her in the stomach, or at least he tried to. The kick actually connected with her hip bone, which hurt the boy's foot more than it hurt Bao. Ignoring the pain, Bao tried to struggle to her feet, but her head was still spinning.

"You're dead, bitch!" the boy growled, lifting his leg back to kick her again. Before he could, Bao forced her head to clear and then pushed herself into a lurching near-somersault, crashing into the boy's legs, one of which was planted firmly on the ground, the other of which was just beginning to kick.

Caught off guard yet again, the boy tumbled to the ground, and as he did, Bao grabbed his shirt with her hands, pulling herself across his body toward his head.

"I'll show you who's the bitch," she whispered. Grabbing his hair with her left hand, she jabbed her sharp fingernails into his right eye.

The boy screamed as blood spurted out of his damaged eye. He then tried to push Bao off of him. In response, she wrapped her legs around his waist in the same way the clan soldiers would do when wrestling, then slashed at his face with her fingernails.

Someone grabbed her by the arm. Geng Long. He pulled her off of the boy, who immediately crawled away from her, moaning and clutching his bleeding eye.

"Bao, let's get out of here," he said. "Constable Guo Minghan runs this part of the city, and he never lets anybody off the hook if he catches them fighting! Come on!"

Holding her hand tightly in his, he pulled her away, and they scrambled into a nearby alleyway.

They ran through the city as fast as they could, eventually finding themselves on a rooftop overlooking a river. As they sat there catching their breath, Geng Long said, "I can't believe you ripped Xie Song's eyes out! That was crazy!" He looked over at her. "Are you okay?"

She nodded. Somewhere along the way, her heart had begun pounding again.

"You're bleeding," Geng Long said. He reached over and touched her jaw, tilting her head so that he could see the side of her face. Where the boy had struck her, a little tear had opened up near her ear.

"It's nothing," she said, reaching up and brushing the blood away. "I'm fine."

Then Bao realized that Geng Long's face was only a few inches away from her own, and he was looking into her eyes.

For some reason, she found herself leaning forward, and a warm explosion of heat bloomed from her lips as he kissed her.

CHAPTER 7
A FINGER

Bao had read that a girl's first kiss can change everything. In her case, though, things didn't change in the way she had expected.

That night, when she finally found herself back in her bed at the clan estates, she lay there, staring up at the ceiling, head aching a bit but filled with wild thoughts of romance and adventure.

She imagined running away from Yu Zhing with Geng Long. They would travel far to the south, away from the Demon Emperor. They would get married, have children, and live near the ocean, where they would eat fresh seafood every day and spend their time reading on the beach.

The following day, when the bruise on the side of her head was noticed, she made an excuse about falling during the night. She could hardly wait until the following evening, when she snuck out of the clan estates to the place where she and Geng Long usually met.

Except Geng Long wasn't there. She waited for three hours before finally giving up and returning to the clan. This wasn't the first time such a thing had happened. Occasionally Geng Long had other matters to attend to, although he never told her exactly what he did. In fact, sometimes she was the one who missed one of their meetings for some reason or another.

However, the following day, the same thing happened. And again the third day.

Where are you?

By the fourth day, Bao had slipped into a deep sadness. It wasn't until the seventh day that Geng Long finally appeared.

When she saw him leap over the nearby wall and then hurry up to the spot beneath the peach tree, she wasn't sure whether to laugh or cry. Or maybe smack him across the face.

Before she could say anything, though, and before he even reached her, he spoke.

"I'm sorry," he said.

Instantly her heart softened.

"I wanted to send a message, but I couldn't." Then he was in front of her, slipping his hands around her waist. He kissed her again, and that wild heat once again raced through her body.

Finally, she pushed him away. "What happened?" she whispered somewhat breathlessly.

He shrugged. "Business. And I have some more bad news. I need to go away again. A few weeks. Maybe a month or two."

She nodded, declining to press him with any questions. "Okay," she whispered. "I understand."

He nodded back. "All right, this is our last night together for a while. Come with me. I found a new place where we can watch the moon reflecting on the water."

He clasped her hand, and the two of them dashed off into the night.

Over the following year, time progressed in this same fashion as Geng Long came and went. They devised a method to leave messages, and whenever he was available, they would spend time together, although it was usually no more than a day or two every few weeks or months.

Every time they met, he would kiss her, and it felt like lava scorching her mind and heart.

When Geng Long was away, she prowled the streets on her own. After the fight with the three boys at the docks, Bao realized that she needed to be prepared for the unexpected. One night she visited the clan's woodworking shop, where she appropriated a few carving knives from a drawer. Then, with a bit of clever manipulation of some leather strips she found, she fashioned some sheaths to keep them in her sleeves.

She also spent more time observing the clan soldiers training and even began to memorize the fighting forms they practiced, which she would then imitate in her room when she was alone. Sometimes they didn't feel right, maybe because they were designed to be used by burly, sweaty men wearing armor, so she made adjustments here and there.

Throughout the months, she only got into three dangerous situations. One of them was resolved by simply drawing her knives threateningly. In another situation, she didn't have time to draw the knives, as someone tried to jump her from behind. Thanks to her time practicing the clan fighting techniques, she managed to throw her attacker to the ground. It was another young girl, clearly a homeless beggar, who immediately scurried off into the night before Bao could even say a word to her.

The third dangerous situation was when she ran into the same three boys she and Geng Long had fought months before. One of them wore an eye patch now, and he had three pale scars running down the opposing cheek. As soon as the boys saw her, they began to give chase.

It was a situation in which neither her knives nor her slight increase in knowledge about fighting would do her any good. They chased her for the better part of twenty minutes before she finally managed to lose them.

She began to grow familiar with some of the others who roamed the streets at night. Generally speaking, they were beggars, pickpockets, and the like. At most, she knew their names and knew which ones were territorial or aggressive.

She even began to venture outside of the city, although that was more difficult because of the sheer distance involved.

Time passed.

One night, she found a message waiting for her from Geng Long.

Meet tomorrow night. Alley behind the pork butcher.

Bao's heart lifted, and she smiled. It had been nearly two months since she'd seen him last.

The rest of the night and the following day passed in a slog that seemed to last forever. When it was finally safe to sneak out into the night, she hurried through the city to the appointed spot, her heart pounding harder and harder by the moment.

However, the person waiting for her wasn't Geng Long.

It was an older man, wearing the clothes of a working man, along with a broad smile. As soon as she realized it wasn't Geng Long, her hands moved toward the knives in her sleeves.

The man held his hands up in front of him placatingly. "Don't worry," he said. "I'm a friend of Geng Long. He got tied up at the last minute and won't be free for another hour. He sent me to bring you to him."

Her brow furrowed. "Where is he?"

The man smiled. "On a job near the south market. He told me to give you this." The man pulled out a bamboo scroll that had been tucked into his belt and held it out to her.

It was a brand-new copy of *Romance of the Hen-Shi Knights.* Inwardly, she was shocked. A scroll like this would be very expensive, even if it weren't new.

She took the scroll and smiled, then nodded to the man.

He turned and began to lead her to the south part of the city. Eventually they reached an alley just across the street from the main market. The man knocked in what was clearly a prescribed fashion, and the door slowly opened.

"In here," he said, ducking quickly into the doorway.

Bao followed close behind.

As soon as the door shut behind her, she felt something hit her in the back of the head, and everything went black.

***

She awoke to find herself in almost complete darkness. She was lying on a wooden cot in an iron cage. She blinked groggily, then sat up and gingerly touched the back of her head. It was painful, but there was no blood. Despite that, she felt nauseous and completely out of sorts.

Where am I?

As she looked around, she realized she was in a room filled with cages, at least ten of them. They were all empty except for one on the opposite side of the room from her, where a huddled figure lay sleeping on the cot.

There were no windows, at least none that she could see.

Groaning, she swung her feet over and sat up on the cot. That immediately led to a wave of dizziness, but after a moment it passed. She thought of her knives, but a quick check confirmed that they were gone.

About that time, she heard indistinct voices, and a very faint light revealed a doorway in the side of the room. The light was spilling from underneath the door, which was closed.

As the light grew stronger in the doorway, the voices grew clearer. When she realized that one of them belonged to Geng Long, her heart surged.

He's here to rescue me! she thought.

Soon the voices were distinct enough to make out a few words.

"Always busy," Geng Long said. "Just... time for this stupid... my own plans."

The other voice was gravely and deep. "We have to watch out... Make some big money and we can get... if you know what I mean." The voice chuckled.

The crack of light beneath the door went dark. Apparently Geng Long and the other man were walking right by it.

"What's this girl to you?" asked the gravelly voice.

"Oh, nothing, one of my many projects." Geng Long chuckled. "I set her up for a whole year, believe it or not."

The gravelly voice laughed. "So you knew all along she was nobility?"

The voices began to fade away.

"Of course. Otherwise it wouldn't have been worth it. So much money for... have enough money to get out of here... join the..."

"Join them? Why not join us? We're the ones... going to be..."

And then they became too indistinct to hear clearly.

Bao sat there on the cot, her hands gripping her trousers tightly. Her heart felt cold, empty, and sinking. Tears began to well up in her eyes. She clenched her jaw and closed her eyes, causing the tears to seep out and roll down her cheeks.

The tears streamed down, but she refused to cry out loud.

***

She couldn't sleep that night. The next morning, she realized that there was a window in the room, a very tiny one up in the far corner. Around dawn, the room began to light up, and soon thereafter a fat man with a beard opened the door and slipped a tiny bowl of millet congee into her cage, as well as the other cage in the room.

Bao's mind was filled with questions, but she didn't give voice to any of them. When the fat man left, she tried to start a conversation with figure in the far cage, but whoever it was refused to speak.

That afternoon, she finally slept, all the way until the fat man returned with dinner, a bowl of plain noodles with sesame sauce.

That night, it took a while, but she managed to fall asleep.

The next day, before breakfast was served, the door burst open and the fat man stalked in, joined by a tall, muscular young man with a square jaw. They walked over to the other cage, which the fat man opened. He stepped in and physically dragged out the prisoner, a young teenage boy who looked vaguely familiar to Bao.

The fat man shoved him up against the iron bars. "This is your last chance. Tell us something that will help!"

"I don't know anything!"

The fat man spat on the ground. "Wrong answer." He turned toward the burly young man. "All right, Mao Yun. Do it."

The burly young man named Mao Yun grimaced. "I don't feel—"

"Shut it!" the fat man said. "You know your place here. Be a coward on your own time. *Do it.*"

With that, the fat man grabbed the prisoner's forearm and slammed his hand up against the bars.

Mao Yun's jaw clenched, and he stepped forward. A long, sharp knife appeared in his hand.

"What are you doing?" the prisoner shrieked. Then he began to babble. "I'm telling you, I don't know anything. My uncle! My uncle has gold hidden… in his bed! Hidden in the bed or in the—No! STOP!"

Mao Yun's meaty hand grabbed the prisoner's pinky finger and cut it off. Then he dropped it in disgust.

Blood spurted, and the prisoner screamed in pain. The fat man threw him back into the cage, tossed a rag in his direction, then picked up the finger and walked out of the room.

Mao Yun followed, and as he passed the cage, he looked over at Bao. Their eyes made contact for a brief moment before he was gone.

Later, Bao realized why her fellow prisoner looked familiar. He was from another of the noble clans, someone she had seen earlier that year on some formal occasion.

The following day, three men came to take him away, and he never returned.

More days went by in a blur.

One day, the fat man opened the door, yet again joined by Mao Yun.

After unlocking Bao's cage, the fat man said, "Come with us."

Clenching her jaw, she stood up from the cot and followed as he led her out of the room. Mao Yun followed a few paces behind her.

She was led down a few corridors to a meeting hall filled with numerous unsavory characters. As soon as Bao laid eyes on these people, she knew who they were. Ruffians. Thieves. Criminals.

There were at least twenty of them, one of them the man who had led her to this place that night. Geng Long was nowhere to be seen. The man in the seat of honor was obviously their leader. He wore fine silks and furs and sat on a raised platform that put him above everyone else in the room. At his right sat a swarthy man with a perpetual sneer, and to the left was a beautiful woman.

Other than the beautiful woman, everyone else in the room was male. There were tall ones, short ones, young and old, all sorts. But Bao could tell that they were rough, violent people.

The fat man led her to a position a few meters in front of the leader, then said, "This is her, Chief."

The chief looked her over for a moment, then spoke, his voice smooth like oil. "Why won't your clan pay the ransom for you?"

As soon as she heard the words, Bao's suspicions were confirmed. She had been kidnapped for ransom. She couldn't help but laugh out loud. "Ransom? I'm nothing to my clan. You might as well have kidnapped a tree from the garden."

The chief frowned and tapped his fingers on his knees. "You'd better come up with something to get them to pay. Otherwise we'll start cutting off fingers. Why do you say you aren't worth anything?"

Anger sparked in Bao's heart, and she looked away.

The chief snorted. "What do you think, Underchief Wang?"

The swarthy man standing next to him chuckled. "Maybe she got taken to the Demon Emperor's bed one too many times."

That provoked laughter from the others in the room.

Bao's face flushed with anger, but she refused to reply.

A moment passed, and the chief said, "Take her back. We'll try one more time before sending a finger."

The fat man and Mao Yun led her back to the iron cages. After the cage door clicked shut, the fat man walked out. Mao Yun also turned to leave, then paused for a moment and looked over his shoulder at her.

"Try to think of something," he said. "Otherwise… you know." His jaw clenched, and he shook his head. Then he closed the door and was gone.

CHAPTER 8
HALL OF ARROWS

The following day, nothing happened. Sometimes Bao lay down on the cot, sometimes she sat, sometimes she stood, sometimes she paced. She thought about many things, and she thought about nothing. She tried to make plans of how to escape, but everything she thought of seemed silly after only a few minutes.

Despite her show of fearlessness in front of all the criminals, icy terror was beginning to worm its way into her heart.

I'm just a girl. I can't fight. I have no magic. What can I do?

What she had said about her clan's attitude was true, although now she wished she hadn't spoken the words out loud.

She mattered little to her clan. Her only value would be as a wife to marry off to some other clan to strengthen ties or form an alliance. However, there were many other young w~~ do the same thing. Although the clan lea~ abandon her to be killed, she worried that tl the type of ransom these criminals were after.

She stewed in her thoughts the whole day before finally managing to fall asleep.

Late in the night, she awoke with a start.

Candlelight poured down onto her face, causing her to squint slightly. The candle was being held by none other than the swarthy man who had stood next to the leader of the criminal gang. Bao remembered him being called Underchief Wang.

He was staring at her, a slight grin on his face as he leaned up against the iron bars.

She quickly scrambled into a sitting position, folding her arms around her knees. Apparently he was waiting for her to speak first, so she resolved to deny him of that and said nothing.

After a long moment passed, his lips twisted into a sneer, and he said, "Things aren't looking good for you, girl."

Again, she said nothing in response, even looking away from him into the darkness that was the far corner of the room.

He snorted. "Play tough all you want. If your clan won't pay up, bad things are going to happen to you." He chuckled. "Maybe more than just a missing finger."

When it became clear that she was not going to speak, he began to slowly tap the metal bars of the cage with an iron cudgel that he had been holding behind his back with his free hand.

"So tell me, what's the Demon Emperor like?" he asked. "How is he with, you know… the ladies?"

Bao slowly turned to look Underchief Wang in the eyes, then spat on the floor of the cage.

He laughed. "Oh, come on. Everyone knows the nobility is in bed with the Demon Emperor. Both figuratively and literally. Girls like you jump at the chance to spread your legs for him at night. How many times have you let His Majesty stick his—"

"Shut the hell up!" Bao spat. "I'd kill myself before I let the on Emperor touch me."

"h, really? I heard he has a different noble girl every night, except the ones he likes, who he calls back for second helpings."

"That's a lie, and you know it."

Underchief Wang chuckled again, then pointed the iron cudgel at her through the bars. "I say you're the Demon Emperor's whore, which is a good thing for me." He chuckled. "You'll be all loosened up and ready when I—"

Bao jumped off the cot and lunged for the iron cudgel, but she was too slow. Laughing, Underchief Wang jumped back.

Bao gripped the cage bars so tight her knuckles creaked. "I hate the Demon Emperor!" she said, her voice quavering. "You hear me? I *hate* him! I wish I could rip his arms and legs off and beat him to death with them!"

"Feisty!" Underchief Wang said, licking his lips. "I might just have to tie you down when the time comes."

"If you lay a hand on me, you're *dead*!" Bao said, her voice rising to a shout.

"You know, I used to work in Xuanlu, and I ran into a girl a lot like you. At first she fought back, but eventually she was asking for it. I bet you'll be just the same."

"I take it back," Bao said, her voice now cold. "If you lay a hand on me, I'll cut it off! I'll rip your intestines out and strangle you with them, you bastard! I'll dig your eyes out with your own fingernails! You're just as bad as the Demon Emperor. Fuck you! Fuck you and the Demon Emperor. *Fuck you!*"

Almost the exact moment that Bao shrieked the curse words at the top of her lungs, the ground vibrated, and a muffled boom followed. It sounded almost as if something had exploded nearby.

Underchief Wang immediately strode over to the door and walked out, not even bothering to shut it behind him.

Bao stood with her hands clenching the iron bars, breath coming in ragged pants. Finally, she gritted her teeth, turned, and kicked the cot as hard as she could, although nothing much happened to the sturdy cot.

She had never lost control in that way, nor had she ever uttered such filthy words. However, no one had ever spoken so vilely to her in her life, either. She sat down on the cot and put her head in her hands.

She didn't have much time to think about the matter, however, as the sounds of a commotion drifted into her ears. Based on what she remembered of the layout of the facility she was being held in, the commotion seemed to be coming from the direction of the reception hall where she had briefly met the gang's chief, which would also likely be near the main entrance.

Soon Bao realized what the commotion sounded like: battle. She could hear the clanging and clashing of metal hitting metal. People were shouting and screaming, and soon the aroma of smoke hit her nose. Bao stood back up and walked forward, trying to get a better view of the corridor outside.

The sounds of fighting grew more intense, but then they suddenly stopped. Next she could hear people running. First one figure, then two, then three, scrambled past the door. She recognized at least one of them from when she'd gone out into the main hall. They appeared to be fleeing, running for their lives.

Has the clan come to rescue me? she thought. It seemed unlikely.

Another figure ran past, a burly young man who she recognized as Mao Yun. Almost as soon as he ran past the door, she heard him stop and turn back. A moment later, his face appeared in the doorway, and he was looking right at her.

He glanced back the way he had come and finally hurried over to her cage. Wasting no time, he unhooked the bronze axe he kept at his waist and began to batter at the cage lock.

It took him several blows, but the lock finally broke, and he swung the cage door open.

"I suggest you follow me," he said.

"Why should I?"

"The people out there… it's not your clan, and they're not here to rescue you. It's the Bone General himself, and his Bone Slicers."

The blood drained from Bao's face. "The Bone General?"

"They're torturing the chief right now, and when they're done, they'll torch this place. The chief dabbled in matters he shouldn't have. Come on, there's no time to talk now. Let's go." Not waiting for her to respond, Mao Yun turned and headed toward the door.

Bao didn't even need to consider the matter; she immediately followed.

The Bone General was one of several ogre generals, devoted servants of the Demon Emperor. Everyone in cities occupied by the Demon Emperor knew that they weren't even human but rather monsters that people said were summoned from the underworld of Emo-Cheng. Considering that there were five of them, some people even claimed that they were incarnations of the Five Ghosts who ruled the underworld.

Each of the ogre generals served the Demon Emperor in a different way. As for the Bone General, he was used like a hammer to crush threats, which he always did in an efficient and barbaric fashion. The Bone Slicers were his most elite fighters. According to some stories, they got their name from the way they would cut slices of bone out of living victims, then use those slices to torture them further.

Bao knew that to be true. She had seen such horrors during the purge of Yu Zhing, an event in which the Bone General played an important role.

As a bloodcurdling scream echoed down the hall from the main audience chamber, Bao hurried out the door and followed Mao Yun.

The first thing she noticed was a table next to the door, upon which rested her knives and leather sheaths. She quickly grabbed them and hurried after Mao Yun, strapping the sheaths to her wrists as she went.

After hurrying through several corridors, she and Mao Yun ended up in relatively large chamber with a large barred door at the end. A group of about twenty or thirty rough-looking individuals were congregated there. Standing between the larger group and the door was the man named Underchief Wang, as well as another young man. The two of them appeared to be arguing.

"What's going on, Third Zhou?" Mao Yun said in a booming voice.

The young man turned. "Big Bro Mao, Underchief Wang won't open the door!"

Mao Yun strode up to face off with Underchief Wang. "What's the meaning of this? You're going to get us all killed!"

"Either that or save our lives!" Underchief Wang replied. "They've surely blocked off the exits. We'll likely open this door to find a hail of arrows punching holes in our hides!"

"The Bone General is right behind us, Underchief. If we don't get out of here, we'll be pierced by more than arrows!"

As the two men argued back and forth, Bao looked nervously over her shoulder at the corridor they had just walked out of, her mind filled with horrific scenes of brutality from years past involving the Bone General and his Bone Slicers.

Time ticked by, and the argument between Underchief Wang and Mao Yun grew more heated. Neither party seemed willing to back down.

Bao began to chew her lip, tapping her foot on the ground. Finally, she had had enough.

Clenching her hands into fists, she walked directly between Underchief Wang and Mao Yun, straight up to the door. Before anyone could react, she placed her shoulder under the door bar and then heaved up and tossed it to the side.

"Hey, what are you—" Before Underchief Wang could finish his sentence, she was pushing the door open.

The door slammed against the outside wall, and Bao leapt out into a wide corridor with a channel of water running down the center. It was raining.

She looked around vigilantly, but no hail of arrows shot through the air toward her. Actually, the corridor almost seemed deserted. Back when the purge of Yu Zhing had just begun, she clearly remembered what everyone said about the Bone General. She remembered him being described as a hammer used to crush resistance. He wasn't a thinker or a strategist like the Skin General or the Hate General.

He wasn't known for secrecy or plots; he tended to barge in, kill or torture everyone he could, and then burn the place to the ground.

Because of that, Bao had been fairly confident that there wouldn't be an ambush waiting outside. Not waiting to see who else came out of the door behind her, she sprinted down the corridor. When she reached the end, she knew which part of the city she was in and was about to turn in the direction of the clan estates when she paused.

There's nothing for me there, she thought.

Gritting her teeth, she instead turned in the opposite direction, toward the north wall of the city. Relying on everything she had learned about the city during the last year of stalking it during the night, she began to run as fast as her legs would carry her.

CHAPTER 9
UNDER THE PILLOW

At first, the ruffians followed Bao as she ran through the city, but eventually Mao Yun and Underchief Wang took the lead. Bao considered ducking into a side alley to lose them but decided against it. Although it seemed crazy to join with the people who had kidnapped her and threatened her physically, for some reason, Mao Yun made her feel safe. That, coupled with her desire to escape from Yu Zhing and all the horrible memories there, was a powerful driving force.

Mao Yun and Underchief Wang wasted no time leading the group out of the city, utilizing a remote crumbling section of the north city wall to sneak out into the night.

Once outside of the city, they headed north, walking about an hour under the moonlight until they reached a cave network, an oft-used way station and supply depot that the group had used for various criminal purposes.

The group was exhausted and quickly spread out into the various caves to find places to sleep. Mao Yun led Bao to a small side chamber where a cot was propped up in the corner.

"You sleep on this," he said, laying the cot out. "I'll guard the door. I don't trust Underchief Wang." With that, he lay with his back against the door, which would make it impossible for anyone to enter the room without knocking him aside.

Bao nodded. If someone had told her a few days ago that she would be sleeping alone in a room in a cave with a strange man, she would scarcely have believed it, and yet here she was.

The following day, as the group ate some rice millet, Underchief Wang stood up, cleared his throat, and said, "Listen up, everyone.

"Our old chief is dead, and his group is a thing of the past. From here on out, I'm Chief Wang, and I'm in charge. Anybody got a problem with that?" His gaze flickered toward Mao Yun, who didn't look very happy but didn't say anything.

Chief Wang nodded. "I say we make our way north. Things are going to be too hot in the city for us. The farther north you get, the less presence the Demon Emperor has. We head to Fan City, or maybe Mt. Dao. We should be able to do some business there. Agreed?"

Nobody offered any objections, so the matter was settled. After eating, the group ransacked the cave hideout for provisions, then set out to the north. They stayed off the public roads, heading through the countryside, camping at night and eating mostly off the land. To Bao, it was a life vastly different than the one she had lived before, and for some reason, it was invigorating.

She began to train with Mao Yun. He was far larger and stronger than she was, but in her mind that was a good thing. She needed to be able to deal with opponents just like him, and as the days went by, she became more adept at defending herself.

After about a week of travel, a mountain peak appeared in the distance. According to Mao Yun, it was Mount Jing, the location of Gor Shan, one of the five most famous mountain peaks in Qi Xien.

Ironically, although Bao had never traveled outside of Yu Zhing, she knew much of Gor Shan, whereas Mao Yun, who had actually been there before, was unfamiliar with the legends behind the place.

"Gor Shan is associated with the dragon Shui Long as well as the phoenix Li Huang," Bao explained to Mao Yun as they sat on a sun-soaked boulder, eating a lunch of rice and wild vegetables. "According to most of the stories, Shui Long encountered Li Huang when she was looking down at a long, empty valley. When she said the emptiness of the valley made her sad, the dragon roared, and the entire valley became a river. And that's where the Chezou River came from."

Mao Yun shrugged. "Nice story."

"There's more…"

Soon they were passing Mount Jing and heading in the direction of Fan.

One morning, Bao woke to find the group abuzz with conversation. Chief Wang had taken to sending some of the men out as scouts, and one of them had just returned with news that they had spotted a traveling merchant.

Chief Wang immediately declared that it was gift from the heavens. He quickly selected ten men, including Mao Yun, who he took with him to "relieve" the merchant of some of his goods.

They returned an hour later bearing chests and sacks full of dried meat, silk, and other goods.

Later, when she and Mao Yun were eating dinner together, Mao Yun grumbled, "We're turning into bandits."

Bao swallowed a mouthful of cured pork. "So?"

He sniffed. "I just never thought I would be a common bandit."

"What were you before, then?"

He shrugged. "Not a bandit."

She decided not to push him any further.

Eventually they reached the Fei River, and their progress slowed as Chief Wang began to focus more on finding merchants and less on traveling. Soon they were robbing people almost every other day, and Bao realized that Mao Yun was absolutely right. They were bandits, and she was one of them.

Bao's duties were relatively domestic. She cleaned, packed bags, tended to equipment, even cooked. Although she had never done such things before, the actions seemed to come naturally.

Some of the men, especially Chief Wang, tended to cast inappropriate glances in her direction, but thanks to Mao Yun, nothing ever happened.

One day they reached a riverside trade outpost, where Chief Wang finally agreed to spend a few days of rest and relaxation at a sprawling inn. They had accumulated quite a bit of wealth in their weeks of banditry, and this would be the first time they'd truly enjoy themselves in a civilized manner.

On the first night, Mao Yun and Bao decided to buy some food and wine and enjoy it together, away from the other bandits. Chief Wang had extravagantly agreed to arrange for private quarters for everyone, so Mao Yun joined Bao in her room to drink and eat.

Before long, the wine was flowing through Bao's veins, and she was laughing and singing. Mao Yun joined in, and eventually the evening turned into a blur.

When the stabbing sunlight woke Bao up the next day, Mao Yun was slumped over the table, and she lay fully clothed in the bed, her head pounding and her tongue dry.

After stumbling downstairs to get some food and water, she returned to find Mao Yun awake and rubbing his temples.

"Well, that was fun," he said, chuckling.

Bao sat down across from him and handed him some of the food. She looked up and noticed a scroll hanging on the wall next to the window, and on it were a few lines of poetry. She didn't recall having seen it the day before. "What's that?" she asked.

Mao Yun looked over and laughed. "You don't remember? Just before you passed out, you leapt up and wrote that poem. You almost seemed like you were in a trance or something."

Bao squinted her eyes and looked at the poetry. "What's that third character? I don't recognize it."

Mao Yun laughed again. "I've never seen it either. Last night you said that it read 'wyrm,' whatever that means."

Bao recited the poem out loud.

The shining Wyrm strides ever north
The graceful Bird due south takes wing

Bao shook her head and thought little more of it. After all, this was her first time getting truly drunk.

When Mao Yun and Bao finally emerged into the light of day, they found that the entire trading outpost was abuzz with news of a fight that had occurred the night before, which had resulted in the death of one of the hired guards. According to the rumors, the man's head had literally exploded during the fight, a shocking scene which was described by another guard, who claimed to have witnessed the entire fight.

"It was a gray ghost. A woman. With a sword!" he said. Few people believed him.

The days passed at the inn, and Bao started to get bored. However, it soon became apparent why Chief Wang had agreed to stop at this place. It wasn't just because he sought rest and relaxation; rather, this was the type of place where local ruffians tended to gather. And Chief Wang was recruiting.

By the time the final day came, their group numbered thirty in total, quite an increase from before. Chief Wang also purchased some supplies and arms, ensuring that their bandit group was now much better equipped than before.

To Bao's surprise, he even bought her a pair of long, thin knives, not crude carving knives like the ones she had used before, but fine steel, sharp and deadly.

She wanted to refuse, but she accepted them in the end.

The group never reached Fan. Chief Wang found some caves near a tributary of the Fan River, where he began to build a fortress to serve as the group's headquarters. From there, the bandit group began to exert its authority in the region.

Chief Wang issued orders that all members were required to participate in raids, which Bao wasn't happy about but couldn't avoid. The first raid she participated in was more of a con than a raid, and there wasn't even any fighting. The second raid did devolve into fighting, though Bao managed to avoid having to participate.

Months passed.

Eventually, Bao's friendship with Mao Yun deepened. They often drank together late into the night, though never to the point of passing out like they had that first time. Bao soon learned that Mao Yun's father had been an important man. And although Mao Yun never explained the specifics, she got the feeling he was a highly ranked official, perhaps even a general, one who had defied the Demon Emperor and paid the price. She also learned that Mao Yun had a sister, Mao Mei, although they had been separated for years, and he had no idea where she was in the vast world of Qi Xien.

One night after Bao had been drinking in Mao Yun's quarters, she headed across the hall to her own room. After barring the door, she walked toward the bed and had just begun to unbutton her collar when she realized she wasn't alone.

Chief Wang was slumped against the wall by the door, staring up at her with drooping eyes. He was clearly drunk.

"Hello, Bao," he said, chuckling.

She tried to jump back and unbar the door, but he lurched to his feet and blocked her way.

"What do you want, Chief?" she said warily, trying to clear her spinning head. Her eyes flickered to a nearby shelf, where the two knives Chief Wang had given her as a gift sat. She hadn't strapped them to her arms when she went to drink with Mao Yun, a decision she instantly regretted.

Chief Wang licked his lips, his eyes wandering up and down her body. "Oh, I think you know what I want. Weren't you just about to take your clothes off? Why did you stop?"

She backed up toward the bed, even as he walked toward her unsteadily.

"Chief, you're drunk. Let me take you back to your room."

"My room? Oh, your room will do just fine." His lips twisted into a sneer. "Now get out of your clothes! Or do you want me to cut them off of you?"

He lunged forward, somehow managing to grab both of her wrists, and then pushed her down onto the bed. She grunted as his knee jabbed into her side. She could smell the alcohol on his breath, along with the aroma of garlic and mutton.

"I've been wanting this for a long time," he said, releasing her wrist to grab at the collar of her shirt.

That was all the chance she needed.

He began to rip her shirt off, and her left hand slipped under her pillow and closed around the hilt of a knife. This was one of her original weapons, a carving knife she had pilfered from the workshop back in the clan.

Before Chief Wang knew what was happening, her hand shot out from under the pillow and stabbed the knife into the side of his neck. Blood spurted out, and his eyes went wide. Not waiting for a reaction, Bao pulled the knife out of the wound and then ran it viciously across his throat, sending a waterfall of blood down onto her face. He made a gurgling whimper, and as his grip on her right hand loosened, she shoved him off of her. He toppled over onto the bed, and she straddled him, then stabbed him in the chest, once, twice, three times. Five. Ten times. And she didn't stop.

Blood was everywhere, soaking the sheets, causing her hair to stick to her face. It smelled both sweet and pungent at the same time. Bao was breathing in ragged pants as she plunged the knife into Chief Wang over and over again. It was almost as if she wasn't in control of her own body, as if some powerful force were raging inside of her, causing her to become consumed by fury.

Finally, she stopped for a moment to catch her breath. Looking down at Chief Wang's mangled, bleeding corpse, she gritted her teeth and then slowly stabbed the knife into his right eye, all the way to the hilt. Then she twisted it.

"Fuck you," she snarled. "And fuck the Demon Emperor."

CHAPTER 10
THAT SPOT

B ao lurched off the bed and staggered to the corner of the room, where she emptied the contents of her stomach. She looked at her hands, which were drenched with blood, and then took a shaky breath. Her mind began to race.

What have I done? she thought. *What will I do? I need to run! Get out of here!*

For a moment, panic welled up, but she quickly quashed it. It was not the time for panicking.

It's actually not that bad. It's not like any of these people are his friends.

That was true. Over the months that she had been a part of the bandit troupe, she had come to realize that Chief Wang ruled by force and power. The bandits respected him, but they didn't love him.

No one would mourn his loss, that was for sure.

However, there would now be a power vacuum, a position that

needed filling. A wild thought popped up in her mind, a thought so insane that it seemed impossible.

What if I took over? she thought. After a moment passed, she dismissed the notion. *Ridiculous. I'm just a girl.*

She looked down at her bloody hands, and she knew what to do.

Not bothering to even wipe the blood off her face, she walked to the door, unbarred it, and strode down the hall to Mao Yun's room. She knocked lightly, leaving bloody knuckle prints on the rough wooden surface of the door.

After knocking three times, she heard a muffled response from inside, then shuffling. Finally, the door opened to reveal an irritated Mao Yun. As soon as he laid eyes on her, though, his expression changed to that of shock.

"Bao! What happened, are you okay?"

He reached out as if to prop her up, but she stepped back and waved her hand dismissively.

"I'm fine. Come with me." Not waiting for a response, she turned walked back to her room.

Mao Yun hurried along behind her, and when he saw carnage on her bed, his eyes went wide. He opened his mouth as if to speak, then held back.

"You can probably imagine what happened," Bao said, "and there's no need to get into the details. The question is… what do I do now?"

Mao Yun's mouth opened and closed a few times, but apparently he couldn't compose his thoughts. Bao's heart began to sink with the realization that perhaps her idea wasn't going to work. Despite that fear, she pressed on.

"Pull yourself together, Big Bro Mao. I'm the one who just killed someone, not you."

"R-r-right," he said, shaking his head. "What will you do now? Run?"

Bao rolled her eyes. "Run? To where? Back to Yu Zhing? I don't think so. Besides, there's no need to run. Nobody here cares about Chief Wang. They only care about the money he earns them."

"So… what do you mean?"

Bao was getting impatient. "Listen, as long as there's a strong leader who's willing to take charge and make sure these guys keep getting money, they'll follow anybody who claims the title of chief."

"You? But aren't women called chieftainesses?"

Bao was about ready to smack Mao Yun across the face. "Not me, you fool. YOU!"

"Me?"

"Yes. People here look up to you. They respect you. Plus, you're one of the manliest men here. Look at your shoulders. And your arms. As long as you exert the authority, they'll follow you."

Mao Yun appeared to be completely taken aback.

"Me…?" he repeated.

Closing her eyes for a moment, Bao began to explain her plan in detail.

***

An hour later, in the main audience hall, the bandits were assembled. Lounging in the seat of honor, where Chief Wang usually sat, was Mao Yun. He even wore the same fur-lined cape that Chief Wang often wore in formal settings.

Standing at his right hand was Bao. She had straightened her hair and clothing but hadn't cleaned away any of the blood. Her face was caked with it, as were her arms, and in her left hand, she held Chief Wang's head by the hair.

The only sound that could be heard at the moment was the occasional plopping sound as thick drops of blood oozed off of Chief Wang's head. They would then land in the increasingly large pool of blood at Bao's feet.

Time ticked by, and inwardly, Bao began to smile.

It seemed her idea was working. She and Mao Yun had woven the perfect tale to try to convince the bandits of why they had slain Chief Wang and why Mao Yun was now the perfect person to lead them. They had even made it seem as if Bao had intentionally lured Chief Wang into a trap and then defeated him after a brutal fight.

However, it was in that moment when the very person Bao had feared would speak up did just that.

His name was Chun Chuixi, and he had the reputation of being the best fighter among the bandits. He was ruthless, popular, and the exact person Bao had hoped to cow with the bloody spectacle of Chief Wang's severed head.

Chun Chuixi was even taller than Mao Yun, although he was sinewy and lithe as opposed to Mao Yun, who was built like a bear.

"Hold on a moment," Chun Chuixi said. "Maybe things with Chief Wang happened the way you said, and maybe not. I don't really care. But are we sure Mao Yun really qualifies to be the new chief?"

"What makes you think he doesn't qualify?" Bao growled immediately.

Chun Chuixi frowned slightly. "I mean no disrespect, Little Sis Bao, but Big Bro Mao doesn't seem to be fond of... our line of business. He spends more time coming up with excuses why we shouldn't go on raids than actually raiding. Why would someone like that want to lead people like us?"

Okay, Mao Yun, thought Bao. *You have to say something. Say the right thing and put this guy in his place.*

Mao Yun slammed his palm down onto the arm of the seat. "How dare you!" he shouted. "I lead because... because I want to lead! I don't need a reason!"

Inwardly, Bao groaned.

Chun Chuixi chuckled, sauntering forward a few steps and then turning to face the other bandits. "Brothers, this isn't a decision that can be made lightly. Perhaps we should consider more than one option. After all, it wasn't Mao Yun who killed Chief Wang. Look! That stingy old bastard's blood is caked on Little Sis Bao's face and arms. Maybe we should make *her* the chief!"

One of the other bandits called out, "Don't you mean chieftainess?"

Everyone laughed.

Things were rapidly spinning out of control, and Bao wasn't sure what to do. Before she could say anything, though, Mao Yun rose to his feet and took a step forward.

"Big Bro Chun, there's no need to beat around the bush," he said. "If you want to challenge me to a fight, then we can do it here and now!"

Chun Chuixi chuckled. "Oh no, I don't want to fight you. The person who has the most right to take over for Chief Wang is none other than Little Sis Bao!"

Bao's heart began to pound. Things were not playing out how she had imagined. She had been able to kill Chief Wang because he had been blind drunk, and she had surprised him. There was no way she could beat a full-grown man in a fight. It didn't matter that she and Mao Yun had been spending so much time training. Bao was under no illusion that sparring and practice was anything akin to real fighting.

Mao Yun snorted coldly. "You're challenging a girl to a duel? Are you a man or not?"

"There's no need for a duel," Chun Chuixi said. "Clearly Bao doesn't want to lead us; she just wants to… *support* the leader. So let her decide. Me, the best fighter among us, the most famous bandit in the region, Chun Chuixi the Spring Thunderbolt! Or the soft, lazy, obscure son of a loser, Mao Yun, who doesn't even have enough of a reputation to have a martial name!"

Bao took a deep breath. Chun Chuixi had played his hand well, and in truth, what he said made sense. At this point, if Bao said she chose Mao Yun, both of them would be laughingstocks. Even if Mao Yun somehow defeated him in a duel, he would still be in a very tenuous position at best.

Her mind raced as she tried to formulate some argument to defeat him with words.

Chun Chuixi glanced at the people behind him and smirked triumphantly as he saw their nodding expressions. He prepared the final nail to settle the matter. "That is why I—"

Suddenly, an arrow sprouted out of Chun Chuixi's right eye. A wickedly sharp, bloody arrow.

The horrified bandits turned toward the entryway of the main hall to see a man standing there with a crossbow, a man dressed in the armor of the Demon Emperor. He tossed the crossbow aside and stepped into the room, drawing a saber.

A strangely accented voice behind the man growled, "Attack!"

More men poured into the room, all of them wearing the same armor.

The bandit force had grown in recent months, and they now numbered nearly fifty in total, and it soon became apparent that there weren't nearly as many Demon Emperor soldiers. However, these soldiers were trained fighters, and some of them even used the seemingly magical fighting abilities of the Demon Emperor and his ogre soldiers, making them vastly superior in terms of speed and strength.

Fierce fighting broke out all over the main hall.

It was at this point that another figure entered the room. He was tall and powerfully built, with features that didn't even look human. He looked vaguely feline, with dark skin and sharp teeth almost like tusks that protruded from his lower lip. He wore strange clothing and armor but held no weapon in hand.

He was definitely an ogre, one of the inhuman creatures who came with the Demon Emperor from the hellish Emo-Cheng, or whatever other place they came from.

As soon as he entered the room, he looked around with cold

eyes, and in that strangely accented voice barked, "Kill them all!"

Bao and Mao Yun were at the opposite end of the hall, so the fighting didn't reach them immediately. They simply stood there in shock, unsure at first of what was happening.

However, as soon as Bao saw the ogre, she knew. *The Demon Emperor*, she thought. *He tracked us down.*

In the blink of an eye, Bao knew what she had to do. Leaning her head over, she said, "Mao Yun, you have to lure that ogre into… that spot! Hurry!"

Mao Yun blinked a few times, then nodded in understanding. Unhooking the axe from his belt, he took a few steps forward and then pointed straight at the ogre. "Hey, you, dog! Come over and fight me like a man! Or are you scared?"

The ogre grinned and then flew forward with inhuman speed, coming to a stop just a yard or two in front of Mao Yun, standing atop a stone tile that was slightly darker than the surrounding tiles. "You want to die, human? I can oblige!"

Bao dropped Chief Wang's head and lunged toward the seat of honor, where Mao Yun had been sitting moments ago. Her hand shot out toward the left side of the seat, searching for a hidden wooden switch. Fortuitously, her finger landed directly on the switch, and she pushed down hard.

Rumbling sounds filled the entire main hall, causing the fighting to pause momentarily. Even the ogre looked around cautiously.

What happened next was something that not even the ogre's superhuman speed and strength could protect him against.

A chute in the ceiling opened up, and a massive pile of stones and boulders fell directly onto the ogre. He tried to leap out of the way but was too slow. All he could do was let out a muffled grunt as he was first knocked to the ground and then crushed into a bloody pulp as the rubble piled up.

Within the space of only a few breaths of time, the spot where the ogre had been standing was now a pile of rocks and stone a full meter and a half tall.

The eyes of the bandits went wide, and the Demon Emperor soldiers' jaws dropped.

In the shortest of moments, the tide of the battle had turned. Now the playing field was even.

It was a critical moment, a moment in which hesitation could lead to death. But Bao didn't hesitate.

"KILL THEM!" she shouted.

CHAPTER 11
CATS AND RATS

Sunan would never forget what it was like to awaken in a haze, his body aching and twinging with pain, to see his friend lying face down in a pool of blood.

Fortunately, the mustachioed man's cohort hadn't actually slit Sun Mai's throat. He'd run the knife slowly over the surface of the skin, drawing some blood but doing no fatal damage. Laughing, the mustachioed man had then ordered Sunan and Sun Mai to be beaten unconscious.

Sunan was the first to wake up. He wasn't sure how much time had passed. It seemed like weeks or days but was most likely hours. It may even have been minutes.

The first thing he did was crawl over to Sun Mai and pull him up off the ground.

"Sun Mai!" he cried, choking back a sob. *Be alive. Please be alive!*

He felt Sun Mai's wrist, and after detecting a pulse, sighed in relief. Holding Sun Mai in his arms, Sunan struggled to his feet. He staggered out into the street, his first inclination to find a physician, but then he realized that this late in the evening, such places would surely be closed for business, front gates barred and shut tight. It was still before the local ward curfew time, though, so Sunan was able to get them back to the inn with no incident.

A shocked staff member let them in and then helped him carry Sun Mai up the stairs to their room. After settling him in his bed, Sunan collected some water and rags and began to clean up his friend up and examine him.

Other than the nasty cut on his throat and some other bruises and scrapes, Sun Mai seemed to be in good condition.

At this point, it occurred to Sunan that he should examine himself, which he did, finding no evidence of any serious injury.

Finally, he leaned up against the side of Sun Mai's bed and fell asleep.

That night he had more dreams. He saw a strange symbol that looked like an intertwined dragon and phoenix, which then began to shine with golden light. Somehow the symbol seemed familiar, although he was sure he had never seen it before.

The next morning, he woke to find rays of sunlight piercing in through the window to land on his knees. He turned his head and saw Sun Mai sitting cross-legged on the bed, meditating.

Sunan likewise crossed his legs and began meditating, sending his qi flowing through his body. He was shocked to find that after sleeping for several hours, he felt much better, almost as if nothing had happened the night before.

When he opened his eyes and reexamined his body in the same way he had last night, he discovered that many of his bruises were completely gone, and even the cuts were mostly healed. He could tell that by the next day, he would be completely recovered.

Shocked, he rose to his feet and looked at Sun Mai, whose eyes snapped opened.

Astonishingly, the long cut on Sun Mai's neck was more than half healed!

"Are you as surprised as I am?" Sun Mai asked.

Sunan once again looked himself over. He stretched his neck and shook out his arms and legs. If he wasn't sure that the events of the previous night had occurred, he might almost take them to be a hallucination.

"This is incredible!" Sunan said.

"I know," Sun Mai replied. "I almost couldn't believe it myself when I realized the truth."

"How could it be? What happened? Magic?"

"I don't think magic has anything to do with it. It's all cats and rats!"

"It must be the qi. In addition to making us stronger and faster, it probably heals u— Wait. What did you just say? Cats?"

"Yes, it's the cats and rats. Or maybe both. Haven't you ever noticed that there seems to be an alarming abundance of cats in the city, whereas there are few rats? I think we all know the reason now."

"Sun Mai, what are you talking about?"

"Sunan, I just asked you if you were as surprised as me that the Heavenly Meat Palace serves fake meat. You agreed. It's little wonder that we can get so much meat for such a cheap price. I just realized why. Because it's not real lamb and pork meat, of course. The city has plenty of cats, and no rats. It's something I always wondered about throughout the years. Daolu would often fluctuate between the two. Some years, the cat population booms. Then the cats vanish and the rats come. Then vice versa. It all makes sense. The main question now is what that yellow wine actually is…"

Sunan shook his head. "Sun Mai, we nearly got killed last night! Now, only a few hours later, we've almost completely recovered from our injuries. Don't you find that… astonishing?"

"Oh, that. Well, it's because of the qi, obviously. Our bodies heal faster than normal, it's not really very surprising if you ask me. In fact, based on my calculations, my broken arm should be mended within the week. At most two."

Sunan rubbed his temples and sat back down on the floor. "Well, what do we do now?"

Sun Mai rubbed his chin. "Obviously they were giving us a warning. They'll probably expect us to take a few weeks to recover, then go back to the fighting arena and follow their rules to make them some money."

"Right. So we can't go out the next day as if nothing happened. What do we do, hole up in here?"

"Just what I was thinking. We can take the time to do a bit of training away from prying eyes. As luck would have it, I was preparing to suggest just such an arrangement leading up to your next match. I even made some inquiries and purchases. Look in that cabinet over there."

Sunan opened the cabinet Sun Mai was pointing to and found a stack of bamboo scrolls and even a few paper books. He pulled one out and read the title.

"*Nine Chapters of Hand Fighting*." He picked up another. "*Wrestling Techniques from the Kushen Basin*." Another, this time one of the paper books. "*Suk Assassins*."

"As you probably can guess, that last one is quite rare," Sun Mai said, "considering it's made from paper."

"Fighting manuals," Sunan murmured. He sat down cross-legged and unrolled the scroll labeled *Nine Chapters of Hand Fighting* and began to study the contents.

Sun Mai hopped off the bed, walked over, and sat down next to him, picking up *Wrestling Techniques from the Kushen Basin*. "Exactly. As was made painfully obvious last night, we know nothing about fighting. We have an advantage because of our qi, but sometimes power and speed mean nothing when compared to skill and experience. Or lots of weapons." Sun Mai's eyes went wide. "Wait, that's great material for my classic scripture!"

He immediately dropped the bamboo scroll and scrambled to another cupboard to look for writing materials.

Time passed.

Sunan and Sun Mai spent most of the following two weeks locked in their room, studying, meditating, and practicing.

Sunan had reached a point in his meditation where he was on the verge of another breakthrough. Things were now much clearer to him than before. From the time he started building up qi in his body back in the Huang Mountains all the way until his first fight in the arena, it was as if there was an empty pool inside of him that had been slowly filling with water.

Something happened after his first fight, some sort of breakthrough in which he reached a higher level. To him, there was a clear distinction in his speed, power, and other capabilities. After that, the qi had continued to build up.

After discussing the matter with Sun Mai, he realized that Sun Mai was reaching the point of making his second breakthrough.

"Breakthroughs," Sun Mai said one day.

Sunan opened his eyes from meditation. "Excuse me?"

"We'll just refer to it as having breakthroughs. After your fights and all the sparring we've done during practice, it seems fairly obvious. I've had one breakthrough, you've had two. By building up qi in the body and then using it, it's possible to reach higher levels, which make you faster, stronger, more resilient. Right now, you need to figure out how to achieve a third breakthrough."

Sunan nodded. "I wonder if a fourth breakthrough is possible?"

After two weeks had passed, both Sunan and Sun Mai were firmly in the position to make breakthroughs. Both of them had absorbed various aspects of the different martial arts manuals, taking things that made sense to them and adapting them in various ways.

Sunan, being mostly concerned with remaining safe in arena matches, and yet also being able to win, focused more on molding his body into a weapon. He put much thought into the movements of his hands and legs, how to use his weight to his advantage, and how to inflict damage as quickly and efficiently as possible.

Sun Mai was more interested in exploring the mysteries of qi and how it interacted with the human body. In fact, he was quickly becoming more adept at manipulating qi than Sunan. He was at a lower level than Sunan and had less experience than him, but given his scholarly leanings, such a use of qi was more suited to his personality and interests.

One afternoon after a long session of meditation, Sunan found Sun Mai shaking him by the shoulders excitedly.

"Sunan, look, look! Watch that lamp!"

On the table in the corner of the room was a simple oil lamp, lit.

Sun Mai took a deep breath, then placed his hand out in front of him with his index finger and middle finger extended. Then he waved his hand in a complicated gesture, during which time Sunan could sense the qi flowing within him. Sun Mai ended with a chopping motion, whereupon a blurry light shot out from his fingers toward the lamp, extinguishing it.

Sunan's jaw dropped.

Sun Mai looked over at him with a triumphant grin.

"That was amazing!" Sunan exclaimed. "How did you do it?"

For the rest of the evening, Sun Mai went on to instruct and guide Sunan regarding the technique he had begun to develop.

A few more days passed. It had been well over two weeks since the incident at the Heavenly Meat Palace, and Sunan was started to get frustrated and antsy. Being cooped up in one room with Sun Mai was a test unto itself. Thankfully they had plenty to occupy their time, but even still, it was getting to the point where Sunan needed to be outside, to walk the streets.

"Sun Mai, I've had it. No more hiding."

"Hiding?" Sun Mai replied indignantly. "We're not hiding!"

"Well, then what do you call it? We're here behind closed doors, refusing to see or speak to anyone. All we do is meditate and practice while our enemies roam the streets, plotting how to either use us or kill us."

Sun Mai rubbed his chin. "Hm, good point. Well, I still think that hiding is the wrong term. We're just removing ourselves from the outside world, secluding ourselves, so to speak. We're spending most of our time in meditation, improving ourselves, refining ourselves. The right state of mind is essential to self-improvement, you know. So we're secluded, in meditation. Secluded meditation! That's what we're doing!"

Sunan frowned. "Fine. Secluded meditation. Well, I've had it with this secluded meditation. I want to go out. I'm ready to fight again. In fact, I'm itching to. All of these stances and moves I've been working on are great, but I won't know how effective they will be until I actually use them in a real fight."

Sun Mai sighed. "But Sunan, you yourself said that you're on the verge of major progress. Don't you think it would be better to achieve that third breakthrough before you compete in the arena again?"

Sunan shrugged. "Maybe, but I don't know how to break through. I'm stuck. Stuck in the second level."

"Why don't you—"

Sun Mai was interrupted by a knock at the door. A message had arrived for them. A burlap envelope sealed shut with a crude iron awl.

When Sun Mai and Sunan saw that iron awl, their gazes met, and they could see the anxiety in each other's eyes.

Sunan let Sun Mai open the envelope. Inside was a sheet of coarse paper with a simple message written on it, which Sun Mai read out loud.

"Your wounds should be healed. Come fight tonight. This time, win." Sun Mai looked at Sunan. "Well, that settles it, apparently."

Sunan nodded.

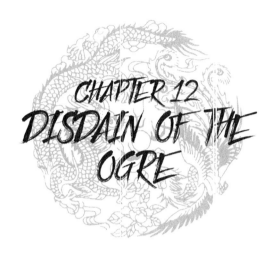

CHAPTER 12
DISDAIN OF THE OGRE

Sunan was nervous stepping back onto the platform to fight. Rat-Hearted Li gave them a long, telling look but didn't say anything. The other fighters looked at him out of the corners of their eyes.

They looked more nervous than he did.

When the time came for the actual fight, Sunan was shocked. His opponent moved incredibly slowly, telegraphed his each and every move, and left holes in his defense wide enough to ride elephants through.

All that training paid off, he thought. *Or is it just that this guy is a terrible fighter?*

The difficulty in the fight was making it look realistic. Because of Sunan's recent increase in speed, power, and fighting ability, the platform seemed small, even restrictive. He had to hold back from countering the man's strikes, and eventually he allowed the man to land some blows. They felt like the blows of a sleeping baby.

He somehow managed to make it through two full rounds before finishing the fight off by knocking the man clean out. Although he tried to make it look like a wild punch, Sunan knew that he could have killed the man without the slightest effort, and he actually had to work hard to make the blow look realistic without seriously injuring him. He was even confident that he could have knocked the man out with the brush of a hand, which made him think back to when his village had been invaded, and he had been struck by that Demon Emperor soldier.

This must be why the Demon Emperor and his army are so invincible. They're all qi fighters!

Time passed. Sunan followed the orders of Iron Awl Hu, winning and losing fights when instructed to do so. While he focused on fighting, Sun Mai ingratiated himself with the other managers. Whether that was intentional or not, Sunan wasn't sure, but in the end, Sun Mai managed to fit in and even made some friends.

Eventually they learned that only about a quarter of the matches were fixed ahead of time. Most of the fighters who participated had no idea about the arrangement—only the select elite were part of the system.

After they identified who these select elite were, Sunan spent more time observing their matches. He quickly realized that although they were skilled, that was only in terms of fighters with no qi.

The Golden Immortal was the exception.

The first time Sunan watched the Golden Immortal fight, he saw the man use a move in which he jumped up into the air to an impossible height—to quite a few oohs and ahhs from the crowd—and then dropped down with a spinning back kick that leveled his opponent.

He can use qi, Sunan realized almost immediately. *I wonder how many breakthroughs he's achieved.*

Sunan watched him more and more closely over the coming weeks and months, and soon he realized that the Golden Immortal was also studying him.

He was now only one rank behind, so it was inevitable that a showdown would occur eventually.

Sun Mai and Sunan were now regulars at the Heavenly Meat Palace. After some discussion, they decided that they didn't care what kind of meat it was they were eating, as long as it was well cooked and they added enough spice. After some clandestine investigation, they came to the conclusion that the "yellow wine" was genuine, although of low quality and quite watered down.

One night after another profitable fight, they were wolfing down "lamb" skewers and guzzling yellow wine, when Sun Mai suddenly slapped his hand down onto the table.

"Twenty-one!" he declared.

By now Sunan was quite used to Sun Mai's odd way of beginning conversations, so he took the sudden statement in stride. "Twenty-one what?"

"Twenty-one moves. The Golden Immortal. Haven't you noticed?"

Sunan was also learning to follow Sun Mai's seemingly random trains of thought. "You're talking about how he relies on a fairly limited set of moves?"

"Yes! Excellent. Great minds think alike."

"I noticed it but haven't really been paying attention. You're saying that he only uses twenty-one moves?"

"After much thought and analysis, I believe so. In fact... Waiter!"

A waiter scurried over. When Sun Mai demanded some paper and writing utensils, the boy looked at him oddly for a moment but eventually hurried off and returned a few minutes later with the requested materials.

Sun Mai prepared some ink and then cleared a space in front of him. Placing down a sheet of coarse paper, he began to draw a man in a pose that Sunan recognized as the Golden Immortal's opening fighting stance. Then Sun Mai made some notations below it and went on to draw another figure.

Over the course of the next hour or so, Sunan continued to eat and drink while Sun Mai worked. In the end, he had a sheet of paper with twenty-one illustrations and accompanying notes.

"Those are his moves," he said, handing the paper over to Sunan. After packing the writing materials away, Sun Mai then descended upon another pile of meat.

Sure enough, the illustrations Sun Mai had just laid out on the paper were all of the moves Sunan remembered seeing during the handful of matches he had observed. Of course, in actual combat, there would be plenty of variations involved, but the foundation was relatively simple.

Combined with the observations Sunan had already made, this information caused his mind to spin into overdrive. Of course, his mind had already been spinning a bit from the yellow wine, but in this instance, it actually helped.

He began to analyze the moves he often used, including their strengths and weaknesses. Then he fell into a trance. Brilliant light began to flow through him, light that only he could see. He could feel energy coursing through his blood vessels and qi passageways. All the meridians in his body felt as if they were being cleaned. Popping sounds rang out, sounds that no one else could hear, and then he felt completely calm.

His eyes opened to find a dark noxious mist surrounding him, which quickly faded away. He felt clean. And strong. The spinning sensation caused by the alcohol was no longer present.

Shockingly, the table had been cleared at some point, and it was no longer nighttime, but rather, dawn. Sun Mai still sat across from him, although his chin was resting on his hand, and his eyes were closed.

Sunan took a deep breath then cleared his throat.

Sun Mai opened his eyes. "Ah, you're back. If I'm not mistaken you..."

"Yes, I had that breakthrough."

"The third?"

"Yes."

Sun Mai nodded. "Excellent. Now, let's go get some breakfast. I stood watch over you the whole night, and I'm famished."

Sunan chose not to point out that Sun Mai had just been sleeping, casting a bit of doubt into the words "stood watch the whole night."

He and Sun Mai left the Heavenly Meat Palace and headed south to where vendors sold breakfast food from stalls.

They were only halfway there when something caught Sunan's ear. He stopped in place, cocked his head, and turned toward a nearby alley. As he approached, he heard a gruff voice speaking.

"Tell me where the money is, bitch, otherwise I'll slit your throat!"

Sunan's eyes turned cold, and he hurried into the alley, Sun Mai following close behind. What he saw caused the coldness in his eyes to turn into fire.

A tall, lanky man was holding a woman up against the stone wall of the building. His hand was gripped around her throat while her hands clutched at his forearm. She was pregnant.

When she spoke, she could barely force the words out of her throat. "I don't… have any money… I promise…"

"Hmph," the man said. "Then you're no use to me." He then began to draw a long, curved dagger from his belt.

"HEY!" Sunan shouted, breaking into a dead run.

The man turned his head to look at Sunan and almost immediately dropped the woman. His shoulders swiveled as he continued to draw the knife and charged toward Sunan.

As soon as Sunan saw the man's chest, his heart began to thump in nervousness. Clearly visible on the man's garment was the insignia of the Demon Emperor.

He's one of the Lions of Peace! Dammit, a Demon Emperor soldier!

Wishing he'd had more time to think and plan, Sunan's hands

twisted into claws like that of a dragon. As the Demon Emperor soldier neared, Sunan planted his left foot and slashed out with both hands. The soldier was still two meters away, but the power of Sunan's qi caused two translucent illusory dragons to appear and surge toward the soldier.

It was hard to say whose eyes widened first, Sunan's or the soldiers. However, the soldier was clearly a trained fighter. He crossed his arms in front of his chest and splayed them wide, shouting, "Disdain of the Ogre!"

A shimmering, circular ripple appeared, which the two dragons slammed into and then dissipated.

Sunan's attack had been completely countered.

Grinning, the soldier stopped in place. "So you know a bit about the divinity brought to this world by the King of the Pure Ones. A Misos attack? Did you invent it, or did someone teach you? Either way, the Lions of Peace could always use more hands. Why don't you come with me? Become one of the greatest soldiers in the world."

The two illusory dragons had surprised Sunan. He had simply used one of the moves he had been practicing for the past few weeks with Sun Mai, except in the heat of the moment, he had sent the qi flowing a bit differently, slightly adjusting the angles of his arms. Based on the feeling of how the qi had flown through him and the way it stuck slightly in some of the meridians in his arms, he could already guess how to improve the move.

So they name their moves, huh? Fine!

Not deigning to respond to the soldier, he unleashed the same attack as before, except tweaked slightly, and shouted, "Rebuke of the Dragon!"

This time the dragons shimmered like flowing water as they shot toward the soldier.

The soldier immediately crossed his arms. "Disdain of the— URG!"

He was too slow. The dragons slashed into his chest, ripping his leather armor, sending blood splashing in all directions. The soldier shouted in pain as he staggered backward a few paces, but just as quickly, he snarled and slashed out with his dagger. This time he didn't yell out the name of the move, and yet the blade sent a blast of light in Sunan's direction.

Sunan instinctively spun to the left, but he wasn't fast enough to avoid the blast. It hit his shoulder, sending piercing pain down through his torso, knocking him off his feet. He flew through the air, and he saw a trail of blood flying out from a gaping wound. Then he slammed hard into the ground.

As the soldier closed in, Sunan struggled to his feet. The soldier raised his dagger. "How appropriate to kill you with a move called the Peasant-Beheading Slash!" He laughed loudly.

Dammit. What do I do? Sunan thought.

That was when Sun Mai made his move. He extended his index and middle finger, and while the soldier was completely focused on Sunan, he slashed his hand down.

An invisible force flew through the air, hitting the soldier in the side of the neck. He shouted in rage as blood spurted out onto his shoulder.

Sunan took advantage of the man's distraction to lurch to his feet and blast him with another Rebuke of the Dragon.

The force of the blow landed directly in the man's face. His jaw was broken as his head snapped back violently. He was knocked off of his feet and then slammed down flat on his back on the ground.

Sunan's hands clenched into fists, and Sun Mai once again extended his index and middle fingers.

However, the soldier didn't get up, nor did he move. After a long moment passed, Sun Mai carefully approached the man. After nudging him with his toe, he carefully reached out and felt the man's pulse.

When Sun Mai turned to look back at Sunan, his upper lip was twisted in the slightest of smiles. "As dead as a rat in the Heavenly Meat Palace. Although not as tasty, I imagine…"

CHAPTER 13
LESSONS NOT LEARNED

Sunan turned at the sound of muffled weeping. He turned his head and saw the pregnant woman who the soldier had been accosting, huddled against the wall a few meters away.

Her right arm was cradled protectively around her swelling belly, and her left hand was covering her mouth. Although her eyes were closed, tears streamed down her cheeks, and she couldn't stifle her sobs.

Sunan walked over to the woman and squatted down onto his heels about a meter away from her.

Now that he was close up, he could see that she was young, probably not much older than he was.

"Big Sis," he said softly, "it's over now. You're safe."

The woman struggled to calm herself, then brushed the tears off of her face and opened her eyes.

She looked over at the blood-soaked body of the dead soldier, shuddered, and then looked back at Sunan.

"Who are you?" she asked.

Sunan heard soft footsteps from behind him as Sun Mai joined them. "We're friends," Sun Mai said.

The woman nodded.

"Why did that man want to hurt you?" Sunan asked.

The woman sniffed. "He wanted money that my husband owed him. But... I don't have any money."

"Is your husband not in the city?" Sun Mai asked.

She looked down. "I don't know where he is. He told me that he had a business opportunity in Nansun. That's why he borrowed the money from Iron Awl Hu. But he left three months ago, and he's sent no word back. Eventually Iron Awl Hu sent people for the money."

Without even thinking, Sunan pulled a money purse out of his tunic and offered it to her.

"This isn't much, but it should help. It's just a few spades."

The woman eyed the purse but didn't reach out to take it.

"Take it, please," Sunan said.

She hesitated for a long moment, but in the end she reached out and took the purse.

"Wait a moment," Sun Mai said, his eyes flickering. "You said your husband borrowed money from Iron Awl Hu?"

She nodded.

Sun Mai's brow furrowed, and he turned to look at the nearby corpse. "But that man was a Demon Emperor soldier."

She nodded again. "I was surprised too."

Sun Mai turned his head and looked at Sunan, who looked back at him for a long moment. They both nodded.

"Big Sis," Sunan said, "do you have a safe place you can stay?"

The woman made to rise to her feet, and Sunan and Sun Mai both stepped forward to help her up.

"My brother has a farm outside of the city. I can go there."

"You should hurry," Sun Mai said. "Once word starts to spread about this soldier, things could get dangerous."

She nodded, then clasped hands and bowed to both of them. "Many thanks, heroes. I hope that one day I can repay your kindness." With that, the woman hurried out of the alley, cradling her belly.

After she was gone, Sunan and Sun Mai walked back over to the corpse of the soldier. Sunan looked at it for a long moment, then crouched down and began to search the man. He quickly relieved him of a money purse, a Lions of Peace identification medallion, and a narrow wooden box sealed with wax.

"Sunan, we should leave," Sun Mai said, looking nervously up and down the alley. "If we get implicated in this man's death, it could lead to serious consequences."

Sunan nodded and rose back to his feet. Glancing once more around the alley, he hurried back toward the street.

***

As expected, news that one of the Demon Emperor's soldiers had been killed soon spread like wildfire through the city. That night at the Heavenly Meat Palace, Sunan and Sun Mai didn't talk to each other at all as they ate. Instead they eavesdropped on the surrounding conversations.

"Did you hear that one of the Lions of Peace was killed?"

"Good riddance! Nobody wants that damn Demon Emperor up here!"

"Supposedly, he was killed by some wandering hero! Stabbed through the eyes is what I heard."

"You're wrong there, friend. His head was chopped clean off. I saw it myself!"

"Do you think it will draw the attention of the Demon Emperor?"

"Probably not. He was just an ordinary soldier."

"I heard he wasn't just a soldier, he was actually a spymaster.

They say that the Demon Emperor is turning his attention to the north!"

"That's right. I heard some villages on the Bay of Yu were raided and sacked recently. We're probably next!"

Throughout the course of the night, Sunan and Sun Mai learned little helpful information.

Later, as they prepared to sleep, Sun Mai said, "You know what I was thinking?"

Bracing himself for another bizarre conversation, Sunan replied, "What's that?"

"What was a Demon Emperor soldier doing debt collecting for Iron Awl Hu?"

The sheer normality of the conversation topic surprised Sunan. After blinking a few times, he took a deep breath and said, "It seems pretty obvious to me. Iron Awl Hu must be working for the Demon Emperor."

"That's what I was thinking. Hmm…" Sun Mai fell into silence.

A few minutes passed, during which Sunan's eyes slowly began to close. Just when he was about to drift into sleep, Sun Mai sat up loudly. "Righteousness and social order."

Sunan's eyes fluttered open. "What?"

"Righteousness and social order are among the key tenets of Dehua. Kong Zhi told us that 'The righteous man who sees wrongdoing but does nothing to stop it is no righteous man.'"

"Are you sure that was Kong Zhi?" Sunan asked sleepily. "I think I heard that in a street opera before."

It was dark, so Sunan couldn't see the dark look that flashed across Sun Mai's face.

"Of course it was Kong Zhi. And of course it's true. Sunan, getting rich in the platform tournaments is not inherently wrong, but we have been blessed with a great power. What Iron Awl Hu is doing is wrong. If he's selling out the city to the Demon Emperor, we, as righteous men, have a duty to stop him!"

Sunan was rapidly being dragged back from the brink of sleep into being fully awake. Slowly sitting up in bed, he rubbed his eyes and said, "Sun Mai, what are you talking about? Selling out the city to the Demon Emperor? You have no proof of that! For all you know, that soldier was making extra money on the side by working for Iron Awl Hu."

"Well, that's… I mean…" Sun Mai spluttered a bit but couldn't come up with anything to say in response at first. After a bit of incoherent muttering, he finally said, "Well, they're both bad guys!"

Sunan shook his head. "Bad guys? Perhaps so, but that still doesn't mean Iron Awl Hu is involved in some conspiracy to sell the city to the Demon Emperor."

Sun Mai sighed, placing his elbow on his knee and resting his chin on his hand. "I guess you're right. My judgment wasn't really clear, I suppose. Wait. Judgment. Clarity. Perfection. Dehua." He leapt out of the bed. "Sunan, you're a genius! This is just what I need for my classic scripture!"

With that, he began banging around in the dark to prepare writing utensils and paper, then started muttering and taking notes.

Sunan rolled his eyes and tried to sleep.

The following day after eating breakfast, Sun Mai resumed the conversation from the night before. "Sunan, after that bit of enlightenment last night, I wrote down many ideas. Unfortunately, it was so dark that not much of my notes make sense. However, one thing I wrote down was completely eye-opening. Zhui zhen qiu shi!"

Sunan stared blankly. "What?"

"Oh, right, that's Classical Fei, which you don't understand. You should really start studying it, you know. Hm, how to translate it? I guess the best translation would be 'Seek the truth, pursue the actual.'"

Sunan shrugged. "Sounds… profound?"

"Yes, you were right last night. We can't accuse Iron Awl Hu of working for the Demon Emperor unless we have proof. And that's why starting today, we're going to get that proof. We will investigate this matter and get to the bottom of it! As righteous men, we will seek the truth and pursue the actual! We will determine what is really going on in Daolu!"

Sunan's face twisted into a grimace. "Sun Mai, isn't that the job of the sheriff and the city constables?"

Sun Mai guffawed. "Constables? Everybody knows that they all report back to Iron Awl Hu himself. No, my friend, we have been blessed by Xian Nu Shen herself with the power of qi, and we will use it to carry out justice!"

"I thought you didn't believe in the Enlightened Goddess…"

"Ahem. Well, I was speaking figuratively, of course. Anyway, what do you think? Don't you agree? We need to start investigating right away!"

Sunan rubbed his chin. What Sun Mai said made sense, but Sunan wasn't sure that was the path for him. He had seen what the Demon Emperor's soldiers could do, both in his hometown and in that alley the day before. They were clearly trained in how to use qi to fight, and with that in the picture, it changed everything.

I don't want to be a hero, he thought. *I just want to… Well. Hmm. What do I want?*

It was a question he had never considered. In the Huang Mountains, he had been focused on survival and healing. After coming to Daolu, events had proceeded along so quickly he had allowed himself to be swept up and had never stopped to think about a purpose or goal in life.

He looked up to find Sun Mai waiting expectantly, clearly expecting an answer, eyes burning with passion.

This seems stupid. Dangerous! We could get ourselves killed! But Sun Mai was right. They couldn't just let the Demon Emperor take over every corner of the entire world and not do anything about it.

One day, I'm going to make him pay for what he did to my family and my friends.

He nodded decisively. "Yes, I agree. We will seek the truth and pursue the actual. Where do we start?"

***

Meanwhile, somewhere near the north gate of the city was one of the most luxurious mansions in all of Daolu. Within that mansion was a courtyard with a fish pond and willow trees. Two men occupied the courtyard. One of them wore golden-colored robes and sat in a pavilion sipping tea.

The other man was a few meters away in a portion of the courtyard paved with wide stone slabs. He was tall and broad-shouldered and was currently shirtless, revealing a powerfully muscled upper torso. In his left hand he held a metal spike with a knob at the end, roughly a third of a meter long in total.

The bare-chested man was none other than one of the most powerful men in Daolu, if not *the* most powerful: Iron Awl Hu.

The man in the golden robes was, of course, the Golden Immortal, the most famous fighter in the underground platform tournaments.

Lined up in front of Iron Awl Hu were several dummies crafted from bamboo and straw that bore the rough semblance of men.

Iron Awl Hu hefted his awl for a moment, then he let out a powerful shout, spinning through the air and then hurling the awl at one of the dummies.

The awl screamed through the air and plunged into the chest of the first dummy.

A hail of wood chips and straw flew into the air as the awl crashed through the dummy's chest and then continued on to the next dummy. The awl smashed through the second dummy's chest and flew toward the third.

Finally, the awl embedded itself in the third dummy, all the way to the knob.

Iron Awl Hu grunted and walked over to the pavilion, where he sat down next to the Golden Immortal and accepted a cup of tea.

"Still not perfect," he said.

"When it is," the Golden Immortal said, "it will be formidable."

Iron Awl Hu nodded. "The final version should be able to pierce through at least three men in one blow. I just need to think of a good name for it."

"Have you completed negotiations for the work on the tempest stone?"

"Yes. We can begin work with it as soon as Geomancer Po arrives from the Banyan Region."

"He'll bring feathers from the windhawks that live near the Falls of Sura?"

"Of course."

A servant appeared, who wound his way through the courtyard and then prostrated himself in front of Iron Awl Hu, holding aloft a sealed message. Iron Awl Hu took it and dismissed the servant, then opened the message and read it.

"Trouble?" the Golden Immortal asked.

"Perhaps. One of the Lions of Peace was killed in an alley yesterday. Blood everywhere."

The Golden Immortal frowned. "An officer?"

"No, one of the weaker ones. Even still, only someone with... abilities like ours could do something like this. Perhaps..."

The Golden Immortal nodded. "The boy from the platform tournaments? Didn't you send some men to teach him a lesson?"

"I did, but perhaps the lesson didn't sink in."

"Shall I handle it?"

"Yes, but wait for a bit, until the commotion of the soldier's death dies down. No more lessons this time. If it was him, put an end to him. I would do it myself, but I'm very close to a breakthrough."

The Golden Immortal smiled. "Very well. Shall I make it painful or quick?"

Iron Awl Hu's lips twisted into a grim smile. "Painful."

CHAPTER 14
ROOFTOPS

Weeks went by. Their discreet inquiries around the city earned them a bit more information about Iron Awl Hu, but regarding his connection to the Demon Emperor, virtually everyone seemed to have their own version of an explanation.

Some people said the Demon Emperor had promised him official lordship of the city. Others said the Demon Emperor was paying him to kidnap children to be used in human sacrifices.

There were even some people who believed that Iron Awl Hu actually was the Demon Emperor, in hiding because of a coup.

Sunan and Sun Mai were starting to get discouraged.

They even stopped fighting in the platform tournaments for a while in an attempt to keep a low profile.

One day during the second week, Sun Mai had his own breakthrough. Furthermore, the technique he had been working on grew more refined. Instead of a simple blast of air, he was able to form something that almost resembled a shadowy sword.

As for Sunan, he continued to refine his Rebuke of the Dragon technique. He began to develop other techniques, especially ones designed for defense and deflection of attacks. Now that he had achieved his third breakthrough, he found his progress with his qi to have slowed considerably. He could sense that a fourth breakthrough was indeed possible, but reaching it would be much more difficult than before.

Staying out of the platform tournaments meant that they weren't making any money, but they still had quite a bit saved up from their previous victories.

Nothing eventful happened until one particular morning during which Sun Mai was practicing with his zither. They were told someone had requested an audience with them.

"An audience?" Sun Mai said incredulously. "With us?"

"Yes, Young Master," the boy replied, one of the numerous servants who worked in the inn and called it home. "He said he's a friend of yours. Green Tiger Zheng?"

Sunan and Sun Mai exchanged a glance. Green Tiger Zheng was none other than the man who Sun Mai had owed money to and had chased them through the city the day they met.

They had seen him a few times since then in the city, but he always avoided them, even when Sun Mai called out his name and said he wanted to settle the debt.

"Send him up," Sunan said.

The servant boy nodded and disappeared.

Sun Mai snorted coldly. "Presumably he's heard about your victories in the platform fighting tournaments and is worried we're holding a grudge."

Sunan and Sun Mai quickly straightened the room up and prepared to receive Green Tiger Zheng. They both felt a little silly, especially considering how small their room was, but there was little option.

A few minutes later, Green Tiger Zheng appeared in the doorway. Despite his height and muscular frame, he didn't seem threatening at all, and in fact, he even looked nervous. As soon as he entered the room, he clasped his hands and bowed deeply.

"Greetings, Young Masters," he said.

Sunan and Sun Mai clasped their hands and bowed in return.

"Greetings, Green Tiger Zheng," Sun Mai said. "What is the purpose of your visit? I can pay back your twenty-five spades right now, with interest."

Sunan's brow furrowed. Didn't he owe fifty spades?

Green Tiger Zheng's expression flickered, but he quickly bowed his head and said, "No, no, of course not. I don't need those fift— er, uh, twenty-five spades. Consider it a gift. I've come bearing an invitation. The Golden Immortal would like to entertain you for dinner tomorrow night at his residence."

Sunan looked over and could see Sun Mai frowning.

"The Golden Immortal?" Sun Mai asked. "Hmm. Is there a special occasion?"

"He said that he wishes to become better acquainted with one of the most promising fighters he's seen in years." When he said that, Green Tiger Zheng's eyes flickered in Sunan's direction.

Sun Mai looked over at Sunan, and they exchanged the slightest of nods.

"Very well," Sun Mai said. "We accept."

"Excellent, Young Masters!" Green Tiger Zheng said. Clasping his hands once again, he said, "In that case, I'll take my leave."

After Green Tiger Zheng left, Sunan began tapping the table. "What do you think he really wants?"

Sun Mai plucked a string on his zither. "Excellent question. Let me think." He plucked another random string, then another. "Green Tiger Zheng. Small-time loan shark. Southern Market. Yams. Carrots. Star anise." He looked up from the zither. "Sunan, do you like the flavor of star anise?"

Sunan thought for a moment. "Yes, I suppose so."

"Perfect. My mother used to make a wonderful dish with yams, carrots, and star anise! Perhaps the inn would let me use their kitchen."

Sunan's eyes narrowed. "Sun Mai, what does that have to do with Green Tiger Zheng and the Golden Immortal?"

"Hrnm? What? Oh. Right, that. Green Tiger Zheng operates mostly around Southern Market. We went there a few days ago when we were asking questions about Iron Awl Hu and the Demon Emperor, remember?"

"Sure, I remember."

"When we were there, I saw him lounging next to a fruit cart operated by Old Granny Wang. Now, that might seem like it's nothing out of the ordinary, but Old Granny Wang's nephew is Wang the Leek. They call him that because his hair sticks straight up like a leek. In any case, Wang the Leek happens to operate the Silk Peony brothel!" Sun Mai triumphantly plucked another string on his zither.

Sunan squinted. "Okay...?"

Sun Mai sighed. "Come on, Sunan. Even you know that Iron Awl Hu runs all the brothels in the city. If Green Tiger Zheng is close with Wang the Leek, then obviously he's connected to Iron Awl Hu's gang. Now, the Golden Immortal is supposedly just a fighter. I've never heard any talk that he works for Iron Awl Hu. But now, one of Iron Awl Hu's flunkies comes to invite us to have dinner with the Golden Immortal? And this just weeks after we killed that Demon Emperor soldier, who was also working for Iron Awl Hu?" He shook his head. "Too many coincidences."

"You're saying that the Golden Immortal works for Iron Awl Hu?"

"I'd definitely make that bet. And it makes sense too. Why wouldn't the top fighter in the city be in cahoots with the top gang boss? The *only* gang boss, really. It's probably not even a secret. We never thought to care about it, so we never asked anybody, and it's not like people just randomly chat about that kind of thing."

"So you think this dinner with the Golden Immortal is a trap or something?"

"Definitely."

"Then what do you suggest we do about it?"

Sun Mai grinned. "We need some black clothes."

***

The city walls of Daolu were enormous, towering things, but most of the residences within the city itself were one story tall. Some two-story structures existed, mostly in the commercial districts. The only larger structures were the various temples, guard towers, or other government buildings that rose up high above everything else.

Thankfully, that night was moonless and overcast. Sun Mai and Sunan were dressed in all black, with black cloths tied over the lower halves of their faces. They crouched in the shadow of one of the guard towers, which rested atop one of the smaller walls that divided the city into its various sections. From this vantagepoint, they could overlook the sizeable courtyard residence occupied by the Golden Immortal.

Getting into this position had not been difficult. Sunan and Sun Mai had long since discovered that it was possible to use qi to make their footsteps lighter and faster. Sun Mai actually seemed more adept at it than Sunan, but both of them could use this skill to run and jump from rooftop to rooftop, making it much easier to get around the city.

"Nothing's happening," Sunan whispered. "We've been here for an hour already."

Sun Mai sighed. "He's probably asleep already."

"I have an idea. You must know where Iron Awl Hu lives, right?"

"Of course."

They exchanged a glance.

"Good idea," Sun Mai said.

They proceeded to leap from rooftop to rooftop as they headed toward the north part of the city.

It didn't take long before they were perched on the eaves of the two-story Drunk Ox Wine Shop, looking down at a residence that was easily three times as large as the Golden Immortal's. It had been built in the shadow of the city's largest temple, which was dedicated to the Enlightened Goddess.

"That's it," Sun Mai said. "Iron Awl Hu's mansion."

"Seems pretty quiet too."

They observed the residence for roughly an hour before finally deciding that they had wasted their time. Then, at that exact moment, a bright light flared in the main courtyard.

A well-built man could be seen standing in the courtyard, wearing a long robe of brocaded silk. He was flanked by two men with sabers strapped to their waists, one of whom held an oil lamp in his left hand.

Two additional men could be seen, thuggish-looking brutes. They stood a few meters in front of the man in the silk robe, and between them knelt a woman. The thugs were holding her wrists and shoulders at a painful-looking angle, and her hair was draped down, concealing her face.

Staring at the man in silk, Sunan whispered, "Is that...?"

"Yes," Sun Mai replied. "That's Iron Awl Hu."

Even from this distance, Sunan could tell that Iron Awl Hu was a fighter, and almost immediately, he began to speculate as to whether or not he could use qi.

After a moment passed, Iron Awl Hu began to speak. Despite how far away they were, Sunan and Sun Mai could still make out the words being spoken, thanks to their qi-enhanced hearing.

"Where did you find her?" he asked.

One of the men holding the woman responded, and his words caused Sunan's heart to go cold. "A farm outside the city."

"I see," Iron Awl Hu said. "Well, girl, tell me what you know."

He reached forward and lifted the girl's face up by the chin.

It was none other than the pregnant young woman they had saved from the Demon Emperor soldier.

"I don't know anything!" the young woman said with a growl. Despite the tears staining her cheeks, her eyes flashed with anger.

"That's what people always say. I can make you talk one way or another. Why not just do it the easy way?"

"Just kill me!" the woman said. "I know you killed my husband, you murderer!"

Iron Awl Hu chuckled. "I've killed a lot of people. Tell me about the two boys. The ones who slew the soldier. Who are they? Who are they working for? Who have they told about me?"

When the young woman didn't respond, one of the brutes twisted her arm a bit, provoking a whimper of pain. "I really don't know, I promise!"

"I see." Iron Awl Hu stood there quietly for a moment. "Very well. I guess it doesn't matter. The boys will be dead by tomorrow night anyway." He turned to the two men with the sabers. "Get rid of her. Feed her remains to the dogs." With that, he began to walk away.

The thugs with the sabers stepped forward and began to draw their weapons.

The killing intent burning within Sunan's heart could no longer be contained. Without even consulting Sun Mai, he dashed across the rooftop, vaulted over a wall, and leapt into the courtyard. It only took the span of a few breaths to accomplish this, and before the two thugs had even finished drawing their weapons, Sunan was only a few meters away from them.

In the blink of an eye, Sunan's hands had twisted into dragonlike claws. Just as the two thugs turned to look his way, eyes flashing in surprise, Sunan planted his left foot and slashed with both hands.

"Rebuke of the Dragon!"

CHAPTER 15
IT HAS TO WORK THIS TIME!

Two shimmering dragons shot out at lightning speed toward the two thugs. The first thug was completely caught off guard. The dragon slammed into his throat, causing blood to spray out like a fountain as the man was sent spinning off to the side, where he fell to the ground, dead. The oil lamp he had been holding clattered away and went out, plunging the entire courtyard into almost total darkness.

The other thug was faster. As soon as he saw Sunan, he ceased drawing his weapon and stepped back. As the shimmering dragon bore down on him, he crossed his arms in front of him and waved them to the side.

That's Disdain of the Ogre! He is *a qi fighter.*

A shimmering ripple appeared, and yet the dragon blasted through it, slamming into the man's chest and shoving him backward.

Sunan saw a flash of motion in his peripheral vision. Glancing to the side, he saw Sun Mai flying through the air toward the two brutes who were holding down the young woman.

Before Sunan could do anything to help, the man he had just attacked drew his saber and lunged forward.

Don't get distracted, Sunan told himself.

As the saber slashed down toward him, he dodged to the side, grabbed the man's wrist, and punched his throat. This was a new move he had been working on, devised to counter attacks from bladed weapons like this, which he knew were the preferred weapon for most soldiers, bodyguards, and thugs like this.

He's a qi fighter, but he's not as fast or as strong as I am. Probably has only had a single breakthrough.

The thug's eyes went wide as Sunan's hand slammed into his throat. A gurgling sound came from his throat, and he staggered backward, his sword clanging to the ground a few meters away. Coupled with the blow from before, the man didn't appear to be in very good shape.

Need to end this fast. Where's Iron Awl Hu? Sunan's eyes flickered to the right, but he saw no trace of Iron Awl Hu. For the briefest of moments, one of the new techniques he had been working on flashed through Sunan's mind, and he considered trying it out.

I need this man down for the count now!

With that, he again unleashed Rebuke of the Dragon. This time, two shimmering dragons bore down on the thug, who once again tried to use Disdain of the Ogre, only to fail miserably. One dragon slammed into his shoulder, the other into his knee. Blood spattered, and a crunching sound rang out as bones were broken. The man spiraled through the air for a full two seconds before slamming into the ground near his fellow.

Sunan spun toward Sun Mai only to find that the other two brutes were lying face-first on the ground, either unconscious or dead. Sun Mai was helping the young woman to her feet.

The sound of soft clapping rang out from within the shadows of a nearby willow tree.

"Not bad, you two," Iron Awl Hu said. "And I have to say, I'm quite surprised to find you here."

Sunan backed up toward Sun Mai, peering into the shadows of the willow tree, trying to catch a glimpse of Iron Awl Hu.

"Just let us go," Sunan said. "We don't have any beef with you."

"Oh, I'd say you do. You killed one of the Lions of Peace, who was under my care. Do you think the King of the Pure Ones takes kindly to such things? Not only might you ruin my plans, you might cause his wrath to be unleashed on Daolu. Is that what you want?"

"What plans?" Sunan asked.

Iron Awl Hu chuckled. "I won't be telling my plans to a nobody like you. Now, you listen to me. I'll tell you what's going to happen now. It's obvious you've taught yourself a bit about the divinity of the King of the Pure Ones. However, I can also see that you are weak, weaker than me, and also less experienced. Besides that, I have a whistle here in my hand. If I blow that whistle, twenty of my soldiers will be in this courtyard within two minutes.

"You might be able to fight with divinity but not against twenty men at the same time. You're nowhere close to such a level yet.

"Therefore, you will lie down on the ground and place your hands behind your neck.

"I will not kill you. Instead, I will teach you more of the divinity and how to use it in combat.

"That is what you will do. Or you will die. I will give you to the count of five to comply. One."

What is this divinity? wondered Sunan. *It must be qi.* And was the King of the Pure Ones the Demon Emperor?

"Two."

Sunan glanced over at Sun Mai, who was glaring into the shadows of the willow tree, one hand held out protectively in front of the pregnant young woman.

"Three."

Sunan took a deep breath. *He must be bluffing. He would have called his soldiers already if he really had some.*

"Four."

Sunan's hands twisted into the shapes of dragon's claws, and he leaned back on his right leg.

"Five."

Then there was silence. Sunan frowned slightly, craning his neck, still unable to pierce the darkness of the shadows beneath the willow tree.

Then the piercing sound of a whistle broke the stillness of the night. Sunan sensed an explosive burst of qi coming from the willow tree. Something flew out, radiating power, moving with such incredible speed that Sunan didn't even have a chance to blink before it was two meters from his chest.

It was an iron awl, razor sharp, a third of a meter long.

Based on the raging qi power he could sense within that awl, Sunan knew that if it struck his chest, he would be very seriously injured, if not killed.

Flying out behind the iron awl itself was none other than Iron Awl Hu, his brocaded silk robe fluttering in the wind.

In recent days, Sunan had been working on a few special techniques, one of them being the counter he had just used on the thug with the saber. Another was a move he hoped would be effective against arrows, darts, or other such weapons. He had not used it in a real fight, not even against Sun Mai when sparring. At the moment, though, he had no time to think, nor any time to devise a plan.

As the iron awl pierced through the air toward his chest, he began to tilt back at the waist, pouring qi into his leg, which shot up, aiming toward the spot he hoped the iron awl would occupy in the following second.

His foot made contact with the awl at just the right moment. His leg continued to fly through the air, and he flipped backward, the iron awl spinning away into the darkness of the courtyard.

Sunan landed on his feet two meters back from his original position, where he immediately crouched into a ready position to meet Iron Awl Hu.

However, he was shocked to find that in the time he had spent flipping backward, Iron Awl Hu had changed directions and was now heading toward Sun Mai and the pregnant woman.

As Sun Mai prepared to make a move, Sunan unleashed Rebuke of the Dragon, sending two shimmering dragons toward Iron Awl Hu.

Iron Awl Hu was clearly no stranger to a fight. He waved his hand to the left, sending a gust of wind out that sent the two dragons spinning away, not stopping for even a moment as he closed in on Sun Mai.

It was at this point that Sunan noticed for the first time that Iron Awl Hu's left hand was clutching at something behind his back. It was another iron awl, but this one was ridiculously oversized. It was two-thirds of a meter long, and Sunan might have mistaken it for a club were it not for the razor tip.

As Iron Awl Hu closed in on Sun Mai, he pulled the huge iron awl out from behind his back and raised it high into the air.

"Awl Tribulation!" he growled, and the awl crackled with electricity.

Sunan had already begun to dash toward Iron Awl Hu and Sun Mai, but there was nothing he could do. His heart sank from the intense feeling of destructive power he could sense from the massive, descending awl.

But then Sun Mai's lips twisted into a grin. Grasping the young pregnant woman by the robe, he said, "Dance of Kong Zhi!"

The iron awl descended, and he pushed down with his left foot, shooting backward and into the air with jaw-dropping speed.

The awl slammed into the ground, causing the entire courtyard to tremble, and a booming thud echoed out. The paving stones two meters around the point of impact cracked and shattered.

Dance of Kong Zhi? thought Sunan. Somehow he couldn't imagine the austere and proud philosopher Kong Zhi dancing through the air. *He needs to come up with a new name for that one.*

When Sun Mai landed several meters away from his original position, he turned to the young woman and said, "Get into the shadows!"

Iron Awl Hu grasped the huge iron awl and wrenched it up from the ground.

Only a few seconds had passed, but already shouting sounds were coming from the buildings surrounding the courtyard, and lights were beginning to shine.

Sunan knew that it wouldn't be long before soldiers arrived.

Iron Awl Hu hefted his massive weapon as he turned toward Sunan, his lips twisted into a snarl.

Now is the time to go all out and take him down.

As Iron Awl continued to turn in his direction, Sunan dashed forward, building up his qi in a meridian near his right thigh. Then he planted his left foot and leapt into the air, kicking his right foot out, powered by all the qi he could muster.

Slash of the Dragon's Tail! He didn't shout the words, but in his mind that was the perfect way to describe the way his right leg slashed with blinding speed toward Iron Awl Hu's neck.

Iron Awl Hu lifted his awl up in an attempt to block the move but was too slow. Sunan's foot landed square on the side of his neck, accompanied by a blast of wind that sounded like a roar coming from ancient times.

A cracking sound rang out as Iron Awl Hu staggered to the side, accompanied by a roar of rage.

A hit! But he's not down.

An illusory sword slashed down from the other direction, accompanied by a shout from Sun Mai. "Sword of the Scholar!"

Iron Awl Hu could do nothing to block this attack, and the illusory sword slashed across his chest, sending blood spurting out into the darkness of the courtyard.

More shouts came from the surrounding buildings, along with the clank of weapons.

It was in this moment that Iron Awl unleashed yet another sweeping attack with his awl, this one directed at Sunan.

Sunan tried to evade but was unsuccessful, and when the awl hit him, it felt like being kicked by ten horses at the same time. He was knocked backward several meters, fiery pain stabbing through his chest.

Sunan was sure that the soldiers were only moments away.

This is it. It has to work this time! He gathered his qi into his right hip, then dashed forward and leapt into the air.

"Slash of the Dragon's Tail!"

CHAPTER 16
THE ONLY QUESTION

Bao took a moment to catch her breath. The sudden death of the ogre cast such terror into the hearts of the Demon Emperor soldiers that the tide of battle shifted instantly. A moment ago, they had been ready to slaughter everyone they saw. But now, they were fighting for their lives.

Bao wasn't sure how long the fighting lasted. It seemed like hours, and at the same time, seconds. Screams and howls of rage rang out in the hall. Blood flowed.

Bao helped Mao Yun to fell one of the Demon Emperor soldiers who Bao knew to be a ranking officer, based on his uniform. He fought with seemingly supernatural power and abilities, and they won only because of a lucky stab by Bao that punctured a major blood vessel in the man's leg.

Soon silence filled the hall.

Bao looked around. There were bodies everywhere, and the stone floor tiles were smeared with blood and gore.

Only around twenty bandits remained standing. Clearly, if she and Mao Yun hadn't managed to bring the ogre down so quickly, the bandits would have been slaughtered.

Bao glanced at the pile of rubble that was the ogre's burial mound, and her heart began to pound.

In the heat of the moment, she hadn't hesitated at all to cut the creature down. And really, there had been no other choice. However, Bao knew that the Demon Emperor viewed each and every one of his ogres as precious.

There was a fairly common story that Bao had heard recounted on more than one occasion about the city of Yun Hu. There were different versions of the story, but most involved an ogre that died of a broken neck after being bucked off of a local horse. In his rage, the Demon Emperor ordered Yun Hu burned to the ground and all of its inhabitants slaughtered. The city was later rebuilt, but it was a chilling tale, and Bao was fairly certain it was true.

She wasn't sure why an ogre had been sent here to handle some petty bandits, but the fact that the creature had been killed would not be overlooked. People even said that the Demon Emperor cast spells on his ogres so that if one of them died, he would be instantly informed.

The surviving bandits looked around blankly at the carnage. All of them were injured in some way, some worse than others. A few even lay on the ground moaning softly.

Everyone seemed confused, unsure of what to do.

As time trickled by, Bao began to grow more and more nervous. *We need to get out of here, and fast.* She glanced over at Mao Yun, but he seemed as much in a daze as everyone else. Finally, she gritted her teeth.

"All right, listen up, people," she said. "You, you, and you." She pointed to three of the bandits with her knife. "Bandage up the severely injured. You five over there, go prepare the horses. You three, gather together all of the weapons and armor you can find and get them to the stables and packed onto the horses. You three, pack some food, as much as you can. Get everything ready. We need to leave as soon as possible. The rest of you, prepare travel supplies. Tents, cookery, lamps. You have thirty minutes! Now go!"

Whether it was her terrifying, blood-soaked appearance or the fact that she had been the one to kill the ogre, the bandits all looked at her in a different light than before.

No one questioned her orders, and in fact, as soon as she said "go," everyone sprang into action.

"Mao Yun, you come with me!" With that, she spun on the balls of her feet and headed toward Chief Wang's quarters.

Mao Yun hurried to join her, walking by her side. "What's the plan now?"

"Leave," she replied. "There will be repercussions because of this, and we need to be far away from this place as soon as possible."

It only took a minute to wind through the stone corridors until they reached Chief Wang's room. Reaching into her sleeve, Bao pulled out a set of keys, which she had taken from Chief Wang after decapitating him. It only took a moment to find the correct key to unlock the sturdy bronze padlock, whereupon the door swung open.

The room was luxuriously decorated and very messy.

"Find the strongbox," Bao said and immediately began to rifle through the room. Mao Yun quickly joined her.

A minute or two later, they uncovered a sturdy wooden chest, which contained the main accumulation of the bandits' wealth. There were numerous strings of cash and silver taels, and even some gold taels. It was quite a sum.

After opening the chest, Mao Yun and Bao exchanged a glance.

"We can't just carry this chest out there," Mao Yun said.

"I know." She stood up and looked around the room, quickly spotting some leather satchels piled in the corner. "Split it up into those. One bag of you, one for me, one for everyone else."

He nodded, and they set to work.

***

Thirty minutes later, the surviving bandits were gathered in the stables.

"All right, listen up," Bao said. "I'm sure most of you have heard the story of Yun Hu. The Demon Emperor will not ignore the fact that one of his ogres was killed. If the rumors are true about the magic he uses, then he might already know. There could be soldiers on the way here right now. I plan to go to the north, where the Demon Emperor is weak. Supposedly, the Hen-Shi Empire still rules there, and I've heard of cities like Daolu and Nansun, where not even a single Demon Emperor soldier can be found.

"The rest of you have two options. The first is to come with me. Travel north to where there is still freedom from the Demon Emperor. The second option is to go your separate way. Head south, east, west... wherever you want. The choice is yours, but you need to make it quickly."

Not even a second passed before Mao Yun said, "I'm with you, Big Sis Bao. Let's ride to the Hen-Shi Empire."

Bao looked back at him and nodded, then turned to the rest of the bandits.

A moment passed, and one of them spoke up. "I have no friends or family anywhere else in Qi Xien. I'll ride with you, Big Sis Bao."

"As will I," another said.

"Me too!"

In the end, only one bandit chose not to join them, a jovial fellow known as Fatty Bo. "I wish you all the luck in the world, Big Sis Bao," he said. "But I have a sweetheart back in Yu Zhing, I can't just travel to the other end of the world and leave her behind."

Bao nodded. "I understand."

There were only fifteen horses. They gave one to Fatty Bo and then split the others between the remaining bandits, with Bao getting the finest of them, a Harqan steed from the Kushen Basin that was likely worth ten thousand spades or more.

And then, they rode off into the night.

***

Once again, they were traveling through the countryside. This time, though, they didn't live off the land. They had plenty of supplies and were well equipped with tents and other traveling equipment.

They stayed away from the roads, which wasn't too difficult in the lands north of the Fei River, which were mostly wide grassy plains. Before long, they were in the foothills of Mount Dao, about a day's ride east of the city of Tung-On, where they set up camp.

As they were eating dinner, the bandit known as Third Zhou cleared his throat and said, "Big Sis... Er... Chieftainess Bao... the road leading from Fan to Tung-On is sure to have plenty of merchant caravans. Should we maybe... get back to work?"

Bao didn't respond at first. She had been pondering this issue as they fled north, even discussing the matter with Mao Yun. Considering the wealth that Chief Wang had built up, their little group could definitely be considered rich. However, that wouldn't last forever. They needed some source of income, some way to survive, especially once they reached the Hen-Shi Empire.

Banditry was an option, but to both Bao and Mao Yun, it was a distasteful one at best.

A long moment passed, after which Bao said, "Third Zhou, let me ask you a question. What did you do for work... before?"

Third Zhou frowned for a moment before replying. "I used to be a pig merchant in Xuanlu."

"So how did you end up like this?"

"The Demon Emperor accused the pig merchants' guild of conspiring against him. Most of the other pig merchants were killed, but I fled north to Yu Zhing."

Bao nodded, then turned to another of the bandits. "How about you, Second Zhou?"

The bandit called Second Zhou replied, "I was a soldier in Qi Fao. After the Demon Emperor conquered the city, I managed to escape south."

"And you, First Zhou?"

"My family was killed in the purges in Yu Zhing."

Raising her voice, Bao said, "How about the rest of you? How many of you reached this point because of the Demon Emperor?"

Of the twenty bandits present, nineteen raised their hands.

"Think back to your life before the Demon Emperor ruined it. Did you ever imagine that you would be a bandit? Did you ever want to be? No. None of you.

"Things happened, your life changed, and in order to survive, you had to break the law. Well, I say the time has come to rise above being bandits." As she spoke, the words rang true for Bao as well.

"The common people are suffering because of the Demon Emperor, so there's no need for us to cause them more suffering. We have money now. We have horses. We have weapons. Why not use them for good? Or at least refuse to use them for evil!

"We are only a few days' ride from the Chezou River, beyond which is the Hen-Shi Empire, and Nansun. I say that tomorrow we go into Tung-On to resupply. If we can, we sell our services as escorts. Instead of robbing the merchants, we make money off of them, open and aboveboard. If no such work is to be found, we make haste for Nansun.

"We have plenty of spades in our coffers, plenty of money to last for many, many days without having to resort to banditry.

"When we get to Nansun, I'll find a way for us to earn money. The righteous way.

"What do you say?"

This time, Mao Yun held his tongue, for which Bao was grateful. The other bandits exchanged glances, and a long moment passed.

Finally, Third Zhou broke the silence. "Very well, Chieftainess Bao. I'm willing to try."

One by one, the others voiced their consent.

Later that night, Bao and Mao Yun were sitting on a boulder, drinking together under the moon.

"Nice speech," Mao Yun said. He held his drinking glass up. "To you. Bottoms up!"

Bao nodded, and together they drank. Wiping her lips dry, she sighed. "The only question is, is it really possible to make money the righteous way?"

***

About that same time, much farther to the south, at the base of Mount Jing, a camp had been set up. Numerous tents of varying sizes stood at the center, with the horses neatly hobbled on the western side of the camp, and guard posts had been erected.

In the central tent, the largest of them all, a long table had been set up. Tied down to the table with thick hemp ropes was an overweight man whose eyes bulged with fear.

A hulking figure loomed over him, a figure who was clearly not human. He had broad shoulders and wicked, protruding teeth. He wore a helmet that appeared to be fashioned from the skull of some bizarre creature, and his armor was apparently constructed from the rest of that creature's skeleton.

"Do you know who I am?" the figure asked in a growling voice. His accent was strange. Clearly this was no human, but an ogre.

The overweight man nodded, and sweat dripped down the sides of his face.

"That's good," the ogre replied, slowly drawing a long knife out from his belt. "Then you've no doubt heard why they call me the Bone General." He rested the knife on the man's forearm. "Now, tell me who it was that killed the ogre five days ago. And where is that person now? The sooner you tell me, the less pain there will be."

A moment later, a bloodcurdling scream ripped through the night.

CHAPTER 17
CRAZY!

Tung-On was a typical city, situated almost exactly halfway between Fan on the Fei River and Nansun on the Chezou River. It had a longer and more complicated name that came from a foreign tongue, but to most people it was simply referred to as Tung-On. To the west was the Little Demon Forest of Zhang Chang, and to the east was Mount Dao. There were rumors that the Demon Emperor planned to build a canal connecting the two great rivers, a canal which would run directly through Tung-On. However, those were just rumors.

It was a bustling travel hub, and in some ways a frontier town as far as the forces of the Demon Emperor were concerned, being the northernmost city under his control. Everything north of the Chezou River was considered free, although some regions to the far northeast of Qi Xien had been invaded or sacked in recent years.

Trade still went on between the Hen-Shi Empire and the southern cities. After all, the rich gold deposits in Jinxu were controlled by the Hen-Shi, and even the Demon Emperor needed gold to run an empire and fund his campaigns into southern regions such as the Dai Bien and Jin Suk Forest.

In the end, Bao decided to take only a small group into Tung-On—herself, Mao Yun, Third Zhou, and Li Runfa, who had previously handled supplies for Chief Wang and had even been to Tung-On in the past. They split into two groups, with Bao and Mao Yun entering through the north gate and Third Zhou and Li Runfa through the south gate.

Despite the fact that Tung-On was a frontier town with more strange-looking characters than you would expect to see in the central regions of the empire, Bao still didn't feel comfortable riding into the city gates as a woman. Therefore, she disguised herself as a man, something she had become quite adept at doing in her days wandering the streets of Yu Zhing at night.

As planned, Bao and Mao Yun wandered the city for a few hours to become familiar with the place before meeting up with Third Zhou and Li Runfa at a teahouse in the middle of the city. After the scouting, the group confirmed that nothing much had changed in the city since Li Runfa's previous visits. Thus, they quickly split up to handle their assigned tasks.

Third Zhou went to purchase dried meat. Li Runfa acquired staple food, which this far north in Qi Xien meant wheat-based foodstuffs like buns and a newly invented food called "noodles." Mao Yun found wine and tea, and Bao hunted down some basic spices like star anise and cumin.

Fortuitously, Bao found what she was looking for almost immediately, leaving her with plenty of extra time to search for what she really wanted to find in the city: a bookstore. After a bit of asking around, she found a wonderful shop that even had paper books, which she found surprising considering how far Tung-On was away from the center of the empire.

Two hours later, she was back in the teahouse, reading a copy of *The Tears of Emperor Chanku*, a colorful account of how the last emperor of the Hao Dynasty had been assassinated. According to the official histories, when Emperor Chanku attempted to purge his government of perceived corruption with a string of executions, his enemies united against him.

However, in this more romantic version of the story, a jilted concubine allied with the Empress to slay the Emperor out of revenge for the excessive attention he lavished upon his newest and youngest concubine.

Nearly an hour before the appointed meeting time, Li Runfa hurried into the teahouse and sat down across from Bao. He looked out of breath and a bit flustered.

Shoving the bamboo scroll he held in his hand into his sleeve, he said, "Chieftainess, Mao Yun has been arrested!"

Bao's eyes went wide. "What? How?"

"One of the local constables recognized him and accused him of being a rebel just like his father!"

Bao clenched her jaw. She had never pressed Mao Yun for more information about his past, including his father, but from various comments she had overheard during her time with the bandits, she knew that he came from a famous family.

"Dammit, where did they take him?"

"The constabulary next to the west gate."

"Were you with him at the time?"

"No, but I was just across the street."

"What about Third Zhou?"

"Last I saw him, he was negotiating with a vendor to buy some Harqa drinking vessels."

Bao ground her teeth. "All right. You wait here for Third Zhou. I'm going to go check out the situation."

"Be careful, Chieftainess."

***

You can do this, Bao, she said to herself. It was a seemingly ridiculous situation. She, a young woman who had lived virtually her whole life within the walls of her clan's estates, was now leading a group of newly reformed bandits. One of them had been arrested by constables loyal to the Demon Emperor and needed rescuing. By her.

She shook her head as she first looked up at the moon overhead, then down at the ornately decorated cask of yellow wine she held in her hand. Then she straightened her long silk dress and took a deep breath. The dress was a type she had never worn in her entire life, nor would ever have imagined herself capable of wearing.

It was not a dress a lady would wear but rather the type of dress that "professional" women would be seen in. Bao could not be considered voluptuous, but she was clearly a woman, and this dress made that embarrassingly clear. Just thinking about how revealing it was made her blush.

Finally, she took a deep breath and strode forward. When she entered the door of the constabulary, she quickly looked around. There were two constables on duty, and in the far corner, Mao Yun was locked up in a cage with iron bars. As soon as she entered, he looked up, whereupon his eyes went wide and his jaw dropped.

Tilting her chin up, she turned to look at the two constables and smiled in the most seductive manner she could.

The constables' eyes narrowed, but before they could say anything, she said, "I've come bearing gifts!"

She held the wine flagon out and cocked an eyebrow.

The two constables exchanged a glance, then one of them said, "Gift? Or gifts?"

Bao's smile deepened, and she said, "That depends."

Inwardly, her heart was pounding and her mind was racing.

What am I going to do? I can't just murder them! Her original plan had been to somehow kill the constables, probably by slitting their throats. But now that she was standing in front of them, real, living people, men who had actually done her no wrong, she realized that she was not so cold-blooded. They might be employed by the Demon Emperor and were surely corrupt, but she couldn't simply end their lives.

"Who is this gift from?" the other constable asked.

Think of something, she thought inwardly, swaying forward and coming gracefully to her knees across the table from the constables. She produced three drinking vessels from within her sleeve.

"Oh, I think you know who it's from," she said with a wink, placing the drinking vessels on the table and filling them, making sure that her own cup was much less full than the other two.

The first constable thought for a moment and then said, "You mean it's Lord—"

Before he could finish, the other constable elbowed him and said, "Don't say it out loud!"

Bao chuckled. "That's right, no need to say it out loud." With that she raised her cup. "Big Bro constables, please, let's drink! I wish you health and prosperity!"

The constables chuckled, raising their cups and drinking.

Meaningless banter and drinking following. Bao's alcohol tolerance had grown thanks to spending so much time drinking with Mao Yun. Furthermore, she was careful to pour herself the bare minimum and the constables the absolute maximum. Soon they had had enough to drink that they didn't notice she wasn't even pouring anything into her cup.

She occasionally glanced over at Mao Yun, who seemed both nervous and angry.

After about an hour, the constables were clearly intoxicated, whereas Bao only felt slightly tipsy. By this time, she had her plan fixed firmly in mind.

Her eyes flickered to the side of the room where an oil lamp burned, one of the three sources of illumination in the room. It rested on the wall next to a rack that contained numerous bamboo scrolls and paper books, which were clearly the records of this constabulary.

She had also identified the location of what appeared to be the key to the cage, which was within the sleeve of one of the constables.

She bit her lip as she tried to decide when to make her move. The alcohol flagon was almost empty. She didn't have much more time left.

It's almost time, she thought.

However, that was when one of the constables said, "Hey, darling, didn't you mention gifts?" He chuckled and leaned forward, grabbing her by the wrist.

Before she could do anything, he pulled hard, causing her to slide across the table and land halfway into his lap. His arm slipped around her waist, and he leaned forward as if to kiss her.

Time seemed to slow down as Bao's hand shot toward her sleeve. As the constable's face neared hers, her hand closed around the hilt of her knife. This constable was lucky, because his hand happened to be placed on the table next to him, making it the perfect target. Were it not for that, Bao might have aimed for his throat or heart.

A thud could be heard as Bao violently stabbed the knife down, pinning the man's hand to the table.

His head swiveled in shock, and his eyes went wide, and Bao shoved herself out of his grasp, reaching into his sleeve and grabbing at the key ring tucked therein.

The other constable's jaw dropped at the sight of his partner's hand pinned to the table, blood already oozing out.

A miserable shriek spilled out of the first constable's lips.

While the two constables were focused on the knife, Bao leapt up and dashed across the room, tucking the key into her sleeve. She grabbed the oil lamp and was just about to toss it onto the rack with the bamboo scrolls and paper books when something caught her eye.

It was a small paper book with the words "True Fighting Manual" on it. Not hesitating, she grabbed the book and then smashed the oil lamp on the rack. Flames leapt up.

The constable had pulled the knife out of his hand and was on his feet, as was his fellow.

"You're dead, bitch!" roared the first constable, cradling his hand as he took a step toward her.

The other constable drew a dagger from his belt and also began to approach. Instead of facing them, Bao danced to the side. Only a meter away to her left was another oil lamp, the second in the room, which she immediately smashed onto the ground, causing flames to leap up.

"Dammit, this whore is crazy!" barked the second constable, backing away from the flames.

Bao continued to hug the wall as she dashed toward the third oil lamp. The entire east wall of the constabulary was in flames, and the constables were hesitating.

Then her hands wrapped around the third oil lamp.

"Let's get out of here!" the first constable said. "Let her die in the fire!"

As the two constables ran out, Bao, keeping the third oil lamp held in one hand, hurried over to the cage and used the key in her other hand to open it up.

"Bao, you're crazy!" Mao Yun blurted.

"I know. Come on. Let's get out of here!"

CHAPTER 18
THE WHOLE BOWL!

The subsequent events in Tung-On were something that Bao preferred not to think about. She and Mao Yun had expected to find a ring of constables waiting for them outside. However, once they burst out of the main door of the constabulary, smoke curling up from the edges of their singed garments, what they saw was a scene of chaos. The flames from the fire Bao had started were rapidly spreading from the constabulary to adjacent buildings.

The constable Bao had stabbed was nowhere to be seen, but the other constable was shouting orders to nearby citizens. Buckets of water were being hauled over to try to stave the spread of flames.

Mao Yun and Bao exchanged a glance and quickly snuck off into a nearby alley.

The fire continued to spread through the night. By dawn, nearly a third of the city was in flames, and the city gates to the north, east, and south were opened hours ahead of schedule to allow the populace to escape the city.

That made it every easy for Bao and the others to leave. Most of the city guard was focused on containing the fire, leaving the gates almost completely unguarded.

It was with pounding hearts that Bao, Mao Yun, Third Zhou, and Li Runfa galloped away from burning, smoking Tung-On.

After reuniting with the rest of the group, they decided that the best course of action was to lay low. They headed higher up into the foothills of Mount Dao, to a relatively isolated valley, where they set up temporary camp.

After more discussion, Li Runfa agreed to head back down into the plains the following day to check on the situation in Tung-On. The final decision about how to proceed would be made after that.

The next morning, Bao was sitting in her burlap tent, studying the fighting manual she had taken from the constabulary. She wasn't sure what had inspired her to take it, but as soon as she opened it up, her heart began to pound.

The characters were small and precisely written. The introduction read as such:

The True Fighting Manual shall be bestowed only with the express permission of the King of the Pure Ones or his direct subordinates. Any who unlawfully comes to possess or study the manual will be killed, along with their entire family and clan.

She shivered and almost dropped the book. She knew exactly who the King of the Pure Ones was.

The Demon Emperor, she thought.

But then a determined gleam flickered in her eyes, and she continued to read.

It didn't take long for her to determine exactly what this True Fighting Manual was. It was a detailed explanation regarding the basic techniques used by the loyal fighters of the Demon Emperor. It was common knowledge that many Demon Emperor soldiers could fight in ways that were virtually magical in nature. Bao had seen such things with her own eyes.

There were various rumors about how these feats were possible.

Some people said it had to do with human sacrifices or pacts with vile beings from the underworld of Emo-Cheng.

But as Bao studied the True Fighting Manual, it was as if she had received sudden enlightenment. The fighting abilities of the Demon Emperor had nothing to do with any agreement with ghosts or goblins.

According to the first pages, the key to power lay within nature itself. Some of the characters and words in the book were strange to her, but the overall message and ideas described therein were relatively simple. The first third of the manual or so was dedicated to the method for absorbing and cultivating the energy that apparently existed everywhere in the world, and the rest of the book went into detail about how to use that in combat.

For the time being, Bao ignored the portions of the book which talked about combat and focused on the section regarding how to absorb the energy of nature. She spent a full two hours reading and rereading those pages of the manual until she was sure she understood the general meaning. With the exception of the characters she didn't recognize, all of it seemed relatively simple, and even the meaning of those odd characters could mostly be deciphered from the context.

It's all about breathing and posture. Anybody can do this.

According to the book, the location where one absorbed the energy of nature was important. Certain terrain features could concentrate that energy and would make the process much easier. She rose to her feet and emerged from her tent into the afternoon sun.

When she told Mao Yun that she would be going for a walk into the surrounding hills, he demanded to accompany her. She protested, but he staunchly refused to back down, so in the end she agreed. They headed out of the encampment and farther up Mount Dao. After hiking for about fifteen minutes, they found a place that seemed to match the description in the manual, a boulder situated in a clearing surrounded by trees.

"I need to be alone for a little bit," Bao said.

Mao Yun raised an eyebrow. "Are you okay?"

"I'm fine. Look, see that boulder? I'm going to go sit there for a bit. You wait here for me, okay?"

Mao Yun shrugged his shoulders. "Suit yourself."

"Thanks. And I'd like a bit of privacy, okay?"

He nodded.

Bao headed into the clearing and climbed up onto the boulder, where she sat down cross-legged and pulled out the manual again.

This is basically just like meditation, she thought. Meditation was not an uncommon practice in Yu Zhing, especially among the elderly. In fact, in her clan, it was common for the old-timers to meditate every morning at sunrise.

In some ways, the illustrations in the manual looked similar to the meditation postures Bao had seen before, and yet in other ways, they were different. The meditation she had seen always involved sitting cross-legged with the hands folded in the lap.

There were differences in the illustrations in the manual. Instead of the legs being crossed casually, the feet were tucked up uncomfortably next to the opposite thigh. Strangely, the index and middle finger of the right hand were to touch the spot between one's eyebrows, whereas the middle and ring fingers of the left hand were to touch the thumb and be held at the level of the navel.

It all felt very strange to Bao, but she assumed the posture. It took a few tries before she could get it right while also managing to sit still.

Next was the breathing technique, which required her to breathe in for a certain length of time, hold the breath, then breathe out. After remaining perfectly still for a set time, the cycle repeated.

Shockingly, when Bao began the second cycle of breathing, she felt something hot entering her nose, causing her to jerk in shock. The movement disrupted the posture and the breathing, and she almost fell off the boulder.

However, that brief moment of success caused her eyes to light up.

Taking a deep breath, she continued to practice.

By the time the sun set, Bao had mastered the basics of the meditation and breathing exercises. To her shock, she found that there really was some strange energy that could be breathed in. It could even be stored inside her body.

At the moment, only a small amount existed within her, but she could sense that if she continued to breathe and meditate in this way for a long period of time, she could build up even more of that energy. Right now, it was like a spoonful of water placed into a bowl.

She wanted the whole bowl!

She and Mao Yun headed back to camp. After dinner, before the sun set, she was back in her tent, where she began to study the fighting techniques described later in the book.

What she found was that most of the section on fighting was actually a list of prescribed movements and poses that could then be used when fighting. Furthermore, it was possible to draw upon that reserve internal energy to make those moves faster and stronger, or even unleash fantastic abilities. However, the more she studied the poses and movements, the more she felt that they weren't appropriate for her.

Back in Yu Zhing, when she had studied the clan soldiers during their training, and in the subsequent months practicing and training with Mao Yun, she had already developed ways of attacking and defending that seemed to work better for her.

Closing the manual, she looked up, and her eyes flickered with understanding.

Screw the Demon Emperor's stupid fighting techniques. I'll make my own!

***

Although no smoke could be seen in the air above Tung-On, the entire city smelled like a fire pit.

More than half of the city had burned before the fire was brought under control. Only two soldiers and one constable died, and no civilians. Although that might seem miraculous, it had more to do with the fact that Tung-On had nearly burned to the ground twice in the past several decades, first during the Demon Emperor's initial siege and once again later in a rebellion.

Apparently the citizens were used to such things.

The Tung-On yamen had been spared from the fire, and a very important meeting was underway there. Early-morning sunlight streamed into the main hall. The city magistrate was not sitting in the seat of honor, where he normally would. That position was occupied by a hulking figure wearing bone armor, who was, of course, none other than the Bone General.

The city magistrate was sitting to his right, opposite of whom was the local inspector, who led the city's military force. Next to the inspector was the sheriff, who led the constables.

"The son of Minister Mao?" the Bone General said in his deep, accented voice.

The sheriff quickly nodded. "Yes, Your Excellency. One of my constables was the son of one of Minister Mao's bodyguards, and as such, recognized Minister Mao's son, Mao Yun."

The Bone General's eyes flickered. "And there was a girl?"

"Yes. A young girl came to the constabulary and…" He cleared his throat. "Well, she poisoned the constables and then managed to free Minister Mao's son. In the process, they instigated local rebels into setting the city aflame."

"I see. Poisoned… Where are those constables now?"

"Your Excellency, that vile young woman used hellebore poison.

Neither lived, and in fact, their corpses were lost in the fire. That is one reason I would like to request special compensation to give to their families. They were brave men, after all, cut down in the line of duty by murderous rebels."

"Were there any others helping the son of Minister Mao and the girl?"

"No, Your Excellency. They appear to have been acting alone."

"Their current location?"

"Unknown, Your Excellency. According to reports, they were last seen heading south to Fan."

"I see. So, a young girl, a prostitute for all you know, outwitted and killed two of your constables, set fire to the city, and escaped both law enforcement and military forces, to vanish into the wind?"

The sheriff and the inspector shared a glance. The sheriff cleared his throat and said, "Well, er… yes, but to be fair, sir, what actually happened was—"

"Silence." The Bone General closed his eyes and sat there completely motionless.

The sheriff, inspector, and city magistrate looked at each other nervously but didn't dare to speak any further. Minutes passed, although to the city officials it seemed like hours.

All of a sudden, the Bone General's eyes snapped open.

"Nightfall," he said, turning to stare at the sheriff.

The sheriff gulped. "Your Excellency?"

"Sheriff Wu, how much of a fool do you take me for?"

"Your Excellency, I would never—"

"You have until nightfall to give me a full report. I'm not interested in the pack of lies you just spewed. Conduct an investigation like a man of your office should. I want to know how many individuals were in the group of supposed rebels who rescued the son of Minister Mao. Find out why they were here in Tung-On, what they did, and where they are headed. If I don't have satisfactory answers by nightfall, I'll help you to become more familiar with how I came to be called the Bone General."

CHAPTER 19
YOUNGER AND SKINNIER

Five days passed. Bao took to meditating every morning and every night. When Mao Yun asked what she was doing, she brushed it off and told him that she would explain later.

Soon, the spoonful of energy grew into two spoonfuls, and then three. She was still a far cry from a whole bowlful.

She began experimenting with how to incorporate that energy into her fighting, but it was difficult. For the first four days, the energy was completely static and didn't respond to any prodding on her part.

On the fifth day, the energy stirred, and she managed to move some of it toward her right arm. However, the effort left her sweating and even gasping for breath. Reaching a level where she could use the energy in fighting would clearly be a difficult task.

An hour after the sun set on the sixth day, Li Runfa returned to the camp, riding his horse at a full gallop. He hardly waited for the horse to come to a halt before leaping off its back to find Bao, whereupon he breathlessly explained the situation in Tung-On.

Just that morning, the Bone General had arrived in Tung-On, and a major investigation began regarding Bao and Mao Yun.

The camp was about a day's journey from Tung-On, but Li Runfa had ridden his horse hard the entire way to make the trip in a shorter time. After explaining the state of the city in general, he got to the most important bit of information.

"They know who you are, Mao Yun," Li Runfa explained. "The whole city is abuzz. When I first arrived, nobody was talking about you, but after the Bone General arrived, questions started being asked, and soon everyone was talking about what happened. The constables went crazy, asking for information about who was with you. Thankfully I disguised myself and skirted around to enter the city through the west. The west gate was entirely burned down, by the way."

Li Runfa shook his head and frowned. "The biggest question was the direction we left in."

Bao's eyes narrowed. "We left to the south, then waited until we were on an abandoned stretch of road before veering off to the east. But this is the Bone General we're talking about. I wouldn't be surprised if he tracks us down in a day or two."

After a moment of silence, Mao Yun said, "We can't stay here."

"I agree," Third Zhou chimed in. "Let's just go to Nansun."

Others in the group began voicing their assent.

After a long moment passed, Bao shook her head. "No. The Bone General is no fool. He's obviously after us because of the ogre we killed, and we've made a beeline for the north. He'll know that we're heading for the Hen-Shi Empire, and Nansun is the closest and most obvious choice.

He's probably already sent word ahead to have soldiers watching for us at the Chezou River."

No one said anything in response. Another minute or so passed in silence before Bao finally spoke again. "We go south. He definitely won't be expecting that. Ride two days south, then head west to the Little Demon Forest. From there we can make our way north toward Daolu."

The other members of the group exchanged glances, but no one seemed opposed.

Finally, Third Zhou asked, "When do we leave, Chieftainess Bao?"

Bao looked up into the sky, where the moon shone brightly. Normally night travel wouldn't be safe, especially in mountainous country like this, but she couldn't stop the anxiety which was worming away at her heart. She imagined the sight of the Bone General striding into their camp, and that thought caused her scalp to tingle.

"We leave now. Pack and be ready to go in ten minutes."

***

For the following week, Bao felt like her heart had changed position within her body to rest directly behind her throat. They rode long and hard every single day, following her plan of first going south, then west.

They were as careful as possible, scouting ahead when they could, setting sentries at night, and yet none of them ever felt safe.

That didn't stop Bao from continuing with her regimen of meditation, though, and soon she could successfully manipulate the energy within her body. She had even begun to experiment with methods of integrating it into her fighting techniques.

After a lot of thought, she even began to teach Mao Yun how to meditate and breathe, although it took him a lot longer to master the techniques than it had for her.

It wasn't until more and more trees began to appear, indicating that they had reached the Little Demon Forest, that Bao finally breathed a sigh of relief.

With one last look out over the plains that led to Tung-On, she led her group of ragged ex-bandits into the trees.

Once in the forest, their speed slowed significantly. Soon the sky began to grow dark as evening approached.

"Look," said Mao Yun, motioning ahead with his chin.

Bao looked. A man was standing up ahead of them in the forest. He had his hands clasped behind his back and was unarmed. He merely stood there smiling, looking completely at ease as their group approached.

When they were about ten meters away, the man brought his hands to the front and clasped them. "Greetings, travelers."

Mao Yun, who was in the lead position, clasped his hands in response and said, "Greetings. I am Mao Yun. You are…?"

"I am a messenger from Lord Shu, who controls this part of the Little Demon Forest. Since evening is falling, he would like to invite you to dine with him and stay the night in his estate."

Mao Yun looked over his shoulder at Bao and Third Zhou. Bao cocked her head to the side, and Mao Yun nodded.

"What if we would prefer to camp on our own?" he asked.

A wry smile appeared on the messenger's face. "This is a dangerous forest. Lord Shu would prefer for guests in his territory to remain safe in his estate, not vulnerably exposed out in the open. There are bears and brown leopards in these parts, you know."

"I see. Please wait a moment." Mao Yun turned his horse and headed back toward Bao and Third Zhou. Lowering his voice, he said, "The message seems clear. We won't be allowed to set camp in this man's territory, and it's late. Who is this Lord Shu?"

Bao glanced at Third Zhou.

"I've heard the name," Third Zhou said. "But that's about it. However, this far north, and this far into the forest, I doubt he's anything more than a, uh"—he cleared his throat—"than a bandit."

Bao smiled. "I see."

If they're bandits and they want to attack us in the night, what would stop them? she thought.

"Fine, we play along. But make sure everyone has weapons in hand or ready to draw at a moment's notice." Third Zhou nodded and began to spread word while Mao Yun led his horse back toward the front of the group.

And that was how, roughly an hour later, they found themselves attending a feast in the middle of a bandit fortress.

Lord Shu's "estate" was exactly that, a stronghold with wooden walls that housed what appeared to be no less than thirty bandits, plus family members and some servants and workers.

Bao and her group were treated cordially and were not threatened, but considering how heavily armed Lord Shu's people were, she immediately tensed with worry.

However, they weren't asked to remove their own weapons, so she, Mao Yun, Third Zhou, and everyone else allowed their horses to be stabled. They entered a large hall where a feast had been laid out.

Lord Shu was younger than she would have imagined, with a flashy smile and green robes.

Formal introductions were made, in which Mao Yun claimed that they were armed escorts traveling north to Daolu to look for work. When it was announced that Bao's title was chieftainess, looks of shock flashed across the faces of Lord Shu's men, whereas wry, embarrassed smiles could be seen among Bao's followers.

As the formalities proceeded, Bao continued to wonder what exactly was going on. There had to be a trick or a con being played, although she wasn't sure what.

And then it began.

"Chieftainess Bao," Lord Shu said, raising his drinking vessel, a traditional northern-style cup, bronze, and essentially large enough to contain one mouthful of alcohol. "Allow me to toast you!"

She raised her own glass and nodded, and together they drank, downing the mouthful of clear alcohol. Ordinarily she might have worried about poison, but all of the alcohol was being served from the same casks. As soon as the liquid entered Bao's throat, it burned like fire, and she had a hard time not coughing.

What is this? It was much stronger than what she and Mao Yun usually drank together. Bao could immediately tell that the alcohol was at least twice as strong as their preferred yellow wine, perhaps even three or four times as strong. As was the custom, she immediately refilled her glass.

"So... Chieftainess Bao," Lord Shu continued, "how did a... young woman like yourself come to lead this... mighty group of armed escorts?"

"Oh, you know," she replied with a cool smile. "Coincidence."

"Ah, coincidence." He raised his glass. "Let us drink. To coincidence."

Her expression the same as ever, she raised her glass and drank again.

After some more idle conversation, Lord Shu said, "Chieftainess Bao, I'm not sure about where you're from, but up here in the north, it's customary to return the honor of a toast with a toast of your own."

Is he trying to get me drunk? she thought. At that, she almost laughed. One thing she had noticed after she began to build up the strange energy within her was that alcohol affected her differently. Whereas before Mao Yun could usually drink three glasses to her one, over the course of the past week or so, her alcohol tolerance seemed to have doubled.

"My apologies, Lord Shu," she said. Refilling her glass, she raised it high and said, "To you, Lord Shu. Many thanks for your hospitality."

They drank. And then again. And again.

All of a sudden, a loud banging sound rang out as Mao Yun slammed his hand down onto the table.

"Enough!" he shouted. "This is preposterous! Chieftainess Bao is, is..."

"Is what?" Lord Shu prompted.

Mao Yun bit his tongue.

Smiling, Lord Shu raised his voice and said, "A little woman! That's what!"

His men chuckled.

"A frail little woman!" Lord Shu declared.

This ignited a spark within Bao, an anger that she barely managed to prevent from appearing on her face. The energy within her stirred. Perhaps it was because of the alcohol, or the anger, or a combination of both, but in that moment the energy began to flow through her in a way it never had before.

Bao could feel it coursing through her blood vessels, and as it did, she was astonished to find that she could identify the difference between the blood and the alcohol in her body.

Grim expressions had appeared on the faces of Bao's people, but Bao just smiled coldly.

"Now, now, men," she said, raising her own voice. "Lord Shu is right. I'm just a woman. Unlike him, a would-be farmer living in a log cabin in the woods, leader of pack of lice-ridden dogs who lick their own master's ass in the hopes of finding a bit of food leaking out the back that tastes better than the trash he serves them for dinner."

Gasps rang out among Lord Shu's men, whose faces quickly turned stony. Many a hand came to rest on the hilts of daggers and knives, causing a similar reaction from Bao's people.

Lord Shu's eyes flickered with flames of anger. However, before he could respond, Bao continued, "Lord Shu, please forgive my men. They are used to the civilized behavior of city folk and are unfamiliar with the manners of pig farmers like yourself."

Lord Shu's eyes went wide, and he opened his mouth, but Bao cut him off. "I come from Yu Zhing, where true men can drink far more than the few swallows you've taken. In fact, I know many girls younger and skinnier than myself who could likely outdrink you even if your drink were more watered down than I suspect it is already. Therefore, if it's a drinking contest you want, then a drinking contest you shall have. Unless you're afraid?"

CHAPTER 20
LIKE A GRAPE

Lord Shu's teeth were clenched so hard it seemed they might shatter. His followers were equally infuriated. Eyes twitched, lips quivered, veins bulged on foreheads.

Lord Shu's hand had come to rest on the hilt of the long dagger at his waist.

Unfortunately for him, Bao had worded things perfectly, leaving him no choice but to agree to her suggestion. If he refused, the resulting loss of face would be virtually fatal. If he tried to do something to physically harm her, the result would be the same.

Plus, she had implied that it was normal in Yu Zhing for women to engage in drinking contests, making it impossible for him to cite her being a woman as a reason to not compete.

Several long seconds passed in which Lord Shu was clearly trying to think of what to do.

Finally, Bao took a deep breath and was about to say something when Lord Shu slammed his drinking vessel down on the table.

"Very well!" he said. "Since you want to drink, we'll drink.

There is no more famous drinker in these parts than Lord Shu, so what have I to fear? Right, men?"

A cheer rose up from Lord Shu's men, although it seemed less enthusiastic than it should have been.

"Bring four pots of Wuxing sorghum wine!" he said loudly.

Sorghum wine, thought Bao. *So that's what this stuff is. Tastes like fire!*

Sorghum wine was a relatively new innovation that had appeared in Qi Xien, with an alcohol content that supposedly vastly exceeded the more common yellow wine, alcohol made from various other fruits or berries. It was mostly popular in border regions and among rough-living men.

Bao surmised that, based on her current alcohol tolerance, she could finish four pots of yellow wine and still not pass out. But she had just experienced a moment of inspiration regarding how to use the strange energy to help her drink even more than that. All of these thoughts ran through Bao's mind in a split second.

So Lord Shu thinks he can put me under with two pots of sorghum wine? Bao chuckled.

"Four pots?" Bao said, an incredulous look flashing onto her face. "Just for you? Wait. Don't tell me you're planning to drink four pots yourself and only give me three? Because I'm a woman?" She threw her head back and laughed heartily. "Will your insults never end, Lord Shu? If you wish to drink four pots, then bring me five!"

Lord Shu's face paled, and his eyes went wide. However, he quickly regained his composure. "That... that wouldn't be fair." Raising his voice, he called out, "Bring five pots of sorghum wine for me, and five for Chieftainess Bao."

"How manly of you, Lord Shu," Bao said. "By the way, I would like to appoint Mao Yun as my official wine vanguard."

Lord Shu's brow furrowed. "Wine vanguard?"

Bao gave an exaggerated sigh. "How difficult to be so far away from the more... courtly parts of the world. Lord Shu, in official drinking contests, participants appoint a wine vanguard to sample each pot of wine that the opponent drinks from. This is to prevent both poisoning as well as cheating by using watered-down wine. As my wine vanguard, Mao Yun will sample your pot of wine before the round starts, and your wine vanguard will sample mine."

This was something Bao had just made up on the spot. However, considering that neither Lord Shu nor any of his men had challenged her previous, wildly inaccurate statements on Yu Zhing drinking culture, it was clear that they knew little or even nothing about it, leaving her much more confident in being able to pass off complete fabrications as truth.

Lord Shu continued to frown, but then he nodded. "Er, of course. I'm obviously aware of the wine vanguard arrangement. We just call it something else where I come from. Very well, my wine vanguard will be my most trusted attendant, Shi Fanzhuo!" Then he raised his voice again and called out, "Furthermore, make it ten pots of Zun Shan sorghum wine, not Wuxing sorghum wine."

Hmph! Switching wines after I bring up the wine vanguard arrangement? I'd wager ten to one that he was planning to cheat with that Wuxing sorghum wine.

Lord Shu looked at Bao, his eyes flickering coldly. "Chieftainess Bao, are there any other random requirements you'd like to bring up before we begin?"

"Oh, just one," she said, holding up her cup. "I'm afraid these dainty bronze drinking vessels aren't really appropriate for a true drinking contest. Drinking so many pots of alcohol only one mouthful at a time can get tedious. I suggest we use something else." Turning to Third Zhou, she said, "Third Zhou, do you remember those three Harqa drinking vessels we happened to come across before we headed north? Do you still have those?"

Third Zhou smiled immediately. He clearly had no idea what Bao was planning, but he knew that there must be some trick up her sleeve. "Of course, Chieftainess."

"Please bring them out."

Third Zhou rummaged through a pack off to the side before producing the very three vessels to which she had referred. They were ceremonial drinking vessels of the Harqa people, who were nomads and warriors of incredible renown. Although they were also made of bronze, that was where the similarities ended. The drinking vessels provided by Lord Shu, which were typical in this part of the north, were so small that they could barely hold a quail egg. Harqa drinking vessels were larger. Much larger. In fact, each vessel seemed large enough to hold half the liquor of one of Lord Shu's pots. Of course, Harqa nomads didn't drink sorghum wine—the type of alcohol they used such cups for were much less potent.

When Lord Shu saw the Harqa drinking vessels, his eyes widened.

"Ah, that's much better," Bao said, smiling. Accepting the vessels from Third Zhou, she took a moment to examine them. "Yes, just as I remember, this one has a phoenix engraved on the side. I've always liked phoenixes." She placed it on the table in front of her. "Lord Shu, of the other two, one is engraved with an ox, the other, a flying crocodile. Which would you prefer?"

"The ox, I suppose."

Bao nodded and then threw the ox-engraved vessel toward Lord Shu, who caught it. The remaining vessel she placed next to her knee, behind her table and out of sight to anyone except for perhaps Third Zhou.

Lord Shu cleared his throat as he looked the drinking vessel up and down. "This…"

"Remarkable, isn't it?" Bao said. "We can get this contest done a lot faster with the drinking vessel of a true drinker."

About this time, a few servants returned bearing ten pots of alcohol, which were split between Lord Shu and Bao. Without waiting for Lord Shu to even say anything, Bao unsealed the first pot of wine and began to pour the alcohol into the Harqa drinking vessel. "Mao Yun," she said as she poured, "please take your place at Lord Shu's side to act as wine vanguard."

As Mao Yun rose to his feet and walked over toward Lord Shu, Lord Shu sent his attendant Shi Fanzhuo over to sit next to Bao.

Over the course of the next few minutes, Bao made up a set of formalities off the top of her head that she claimed was the proper form for a formal drinking contest. The first pot of alcohol was sampled by Mao Yun and Shi Fanzhuo, who both gave their approval. Then the contest began.

Bao didn't waste any time. She immediately raised her Harqa drinking vessel to Lord Shu and said, "To your health and prosperity, Lord Shu!"

He nodded at her, and they began to drink, maintaining eye contact the whole time. Since Bao initiated the toast, she would determine how deeply to drink, and she did not hold back. She let the burning alcohol pour down her throat slowly but surely. As the seconds ticked by, Lord Shu's eyes began to grow wide. Even Bao felt some tears welling up in the corners of her own eyes.

Finally, she leveled her glass and set it down, doing her best not to cough or allow the tears to spill out of her eyes.

Wow! This sorghum wine is not for babies!

The alcohol she had already consumed was reaching her head. Combined with the long drink she had just taken, things were starting to spin a bit. According to the customs she had cited, she and Lord Shu would now have a short period of time to munch on some of the cold dishes that had been provided and drink fresh water, if they wished, before beginning again.

As she took a sip of water, Bao closed her eyes and circulated the energy inside of her. Just like before, she sent it through her body, specifically into her bloodstream. It didn't take long to identify the alcohol therein, which she then began to push through her blood toward a specific direction: her right hand.

Her right hand happened to be grasping the extra Harqa

drinking vessel, which was behind the table, out of the view of Lord Shu or anyone else for that matter. As the alcohol in her bloodstream flowed toward her hand, she pushed the tip of her index finger down hard on the engraving of the flying crocodile, specifically, one of its teeth. It was really a tiny bronze spike, and when she poked her finger with it, it pierced her skin, and a drop of blood oozed out. She then quickly moved her index finger into the glass. Moments later, a mix of blood and alcohol began to ooze out of her finger into the cup.

Over the course of the next minute or two, she continued with this process until the cup was about a third full. By that time, it was Lord Shu's turn to drink.

Not surprisingly, when he toasted her, he also drank half of a Harqa drinking vessel's worth of alcohol, with Bao following suit. In a short few minutes, the two of them had imbibed an entire pot of extremely potent alcohol.

While they rested, Bao once again used the strange energy to force the alcohol out of her blood and into the extra drinking vessel. Of course, she couldn't get it all, so her head continued to spin. However, if her calculations were correct, she was likely drinking only about one third of the amount of alcohol Lord Shu was drinking.

Time passed, and eventually it was Bao's turn again. She looked over at Lord Shu and could see that his eyes were a bit blank, and his head was swaying back and forth slightly.

"Lord Shu, would you like to concede?" she asked, smiling.

"Of course not!" he blurted. "I'm waiting for you, frail little woman!"

Her eyes glinted with a flicker of anger. *Fool, I was about to go easy on you!*

Maintaining her smile, she raised the Harqa drinking vessel. This time, she drank only a third of the entire vessel before stopping. During the respite, she drained as much alcohol as she could. The hidden drinking vessel was about three-quarters full.

Bao's head was spinning but not too badly. From the way she felt, she could tell that she wasn't even halfway to her limit.

It was Lord Shu's turn next. "That last drink was a bit on the safe side, girl," he said, his voice slightly slurred. "It's time to narrow the gap! The time has come to show you what real drinkers can do. No Yu Zhing slut can outdo Lord Shu!"

With that, he began to guzzle alcohol down with a vengeance.

Bao took a deep breath and began to follow up. It soon became apparent that Lord Shu was going to down the entire glass. Bao's throat was burning, and her stomach was beginning to clench up. Her arms twitched, and sweat had broken out on her scalp and down her back. However, she continued to drink, draining her drinking vessel only moments after Lord Shu did.

Lord Shu devolved into a fit of coughing, and when that was over, he sagged, panting. But then he straightened up and looked at Bao with cloudy eyes.

Bao took a moment to compose herself, suppressed the urge to vomit, and then quickly began forcing more alcohol out of her system.

Lord Shu was now swaying back and forth visibly, whereas she was sitting there calmly. A quick glance around the room confirmed that nervous expressions could be seen on the faces of all his men.

"Lord Shu, it seems your men are losing confidence. Are you sure you can handle the pressure?"

Lord Shu's expression darkened. "Pressure? There's no pressure! I feel more pressure taking a piss than I do in this supposed contest. I've half a mind to just have my men kill your men and then take you to my chambers to give you a spanking!" He roared with laughter.

A nervous chuckle rose up from Lord Shu's men, whereas Bao's people muttered angrily.

"Lord Shu," Bao said, "the teat of a cow feels great pressure when the milk comes out. Do you know why? Because the teat is so small! I wonder… if you feel great pressure when taking a piss, could it be because…"

Lord Shu leapt to his feet, eyes blazing with fury. "Bitch!" he yelled. Fumbling at his waist, he managed to draw his dagger, which he pointed directly at Bao. "I *dare* you to say another word!"

Bao looked him directly in the eye. She tucked a hand into her sleeve and felt the knife there, sending the strange energy swirling in the same direction. Then, her voice cold, a slight smile on her face, she said, "You have a tiny dick, you bastard."

With an enraged roar, Lord Shu leapt over the table in her direction. However, as he jumped, his robe caught on the table leg, twisting him to the side. His foot landed on the ground at a strange angle, and with a squawk, he tumbled toward the ground.

As he fell, his hands instinctively flew out in front of him to break his fall. And that was when a sound rang out like a grape being squashed beneath a boot, as Lord Shu's dagger stabbed him in the eye. He lay there, the dagger poking out of the back of his skull.

***

The Bone General reined his horse to a halt and looked at the trees off in the distance. "So she's in that forest?"

Off to the side was his most trusted lieutenant, who wore armor similar to the Bone General. "Yes, General Gu. The scouts say she's holed up in a primitive fort roughly a day's journey into the forest."

"I see." The Bone General frowned. "Unfortunately, the orders that came in were very clear. Insurrection in Hai'an requires my immediate attention."

"Your orders, sir?"

After a moment of thought, the Bone General sighed. "We ride south immediately. We'll return for this girl once things are settled in Hai'an."

CHAPTER 21
I REFUSE!

Iron Awl Hu's eyes went wide as his head was violently ripped off of his shoulder's by Sunan's Slash of the Dragon's Tail.

As soldiers poured into the courtyard, his head spiraled through the air, trailing droplets of blood like tiny red flower petals. It almost seemed to move in slow motion as it arced up, then slowly descended, smacking onto the paving stones with a splurching sound, after which it rolled across the ground briefly before plopping into a small fishpond.

Iron Awl Hu's body teetered for a moment and then toppled over.

Sunan landed on his feet in a defensive stance, immediately glancing around to determine what he was up against.

There were roughly twenty soldiers in the courtyard, wearing leather armor and carrying long spears.

I hate spears, he thought.

Almost to a man, the soldiers' mouths were wide open in shock. One poor fellow even stumbled off to the side and started retching.

A long moment passed that seemed to stretch on for hours and hours, but in reality, it lasted for only a few breaths of time.

Then the soldiers seemed to recover, and one by one they began to point their spears at Sunan and Sun Mai. However, their eyes flickered with fear, and some of them were even trembling visibly.

Sunan was just about to say something when Sun Mai strode forward, hands clasped behind his back.

"Who's in charge here?" he asked in a commanding voice.

The soldiers looked around nervously, their eyes soon coming to rest on one of their number in particular, a stocky man with a wide nose and a coarse beard.

"Er, I'm... I'm the leader here." The man's eyes flickered down to the decapitated corpse of Iron Awl Hu and then over at the nearby pond where the severed head was.

"Very well," Sun Mai said. "Who is the most powerful person in this compound?" He took a menacing step forward. "You?"

The bearded man subconsciously stepped back. "*No!* No, of course not!" His eyes once again flickered down to Iron Awl Hu's corpse.

Sun Mai chuckled. "I see. And what is your honored surname and respectable name?"

"Tie Gangwen."

"A very manly name. Tie Gangwen, let me rephrase my question. Who is in charge now that Mr. Hu has met a most unfortunate and untimely demise?"

"Ritual Master Zhen."

"Take us to him. Now. You lead the way."

Tie Gangwen gulped and nodded, issuing orders to the other soldiers to fall into formation.

Sunan glanced around to look for the pregnant woman, but she was nowhere to be seen. Presumably she had slipped away during the commotion.

The soldiers quickly led Sunan and Sun Mai out of the courtyard and into the corridors of the compound.

As they walked along, Sunan leaned over and whispered, "What are you planning to do?"

"First, save our hides. Second, take over."

Take over?"

"That is the natural state of affairs. When the leader of the pack is eliminated, a new leader emerges. It is the way of nature, and only by following the way of nature can we achieve true harmony." He gasped. "Dammit, where are writing materials when you need them? Remember that thought! I need to put it in my classic scripture."

"Fine, we take over. But what about this Ritual Master Zhen? And what about the Golden Immortal?"

"I don't know about the Golden Immortal. My bet is that he was not any greater a fighter than Iron Awl Hu. If we can truly seize control of Hu's power structure, we can deal with him when the time comes. Right now, this Ritual Master Zhen is the rightful successor. Considering his title, he must be a Yen-Li priest."

"What's that?"

Sun Mai gave Sunan a sidelong glance. "You don't know about the Yen-Li priests? Where did you grow up, a—" Sun Mai bit his tongue. He had learned long ago that Sunan tended to be sensitive when it came to his home and family. Sun Mai quickly began a new sentence. "They're sorcerers. Although, the more I think about it, the more I suspect that what they are doing is not magic at all. It's most likely manipulation of qi. Just in a different way than we have come to use it."

"So what, we recruit him?"

"No." Sun Mai lowered his voice even beyond what it had been, to a nearly inaudible whisper. "We kill him."

What?"

"Listen to me, Sunan. We have to kill him immediately. Any person who worked directly for Iron Awl Hu is clearly a vile person, allied with the Demon Emperor, a person who kills the husbands of pregnant mothers, who forces young girls into brothels, a monster, someone who has plotted and murdered and slandered and—"

"All right! Even still, I won't just murder someone. We talk first!"

Sun Mai grimaced. "Fine. He'll have one very limited chance to submit. If not…"

Sunan took a deep breath, then nodded grimly.

Before long, they were below ground level in the complex. As they walked along, both Sunan and Sun Mai remained vigilant. Soon they reached a wide corridor that ended at a red wooden door. The soldiers quickly fell into place along the walls of the corridor.

Tie Gangwen nervously cleared his throat. "This is Ritual Master Zhen's workshop. He… spends most of his time in here."

Sunan studied the door briefly but didn't notice anything out of the ordinary. "Well, open it up!" he said after a moment.

"Open it up?" Tie Gangwen asked, making a slight choking sound. "Sir, no one just opens up the door of Ritual Master Zhen's workshop. Not even His Excellency Lord Hu. To do such a thing would be… dangerous."

Sunan looked over at Sun Mai.

"Fine, then," Sun Mai said. "Knock or do whatever it is you would normally do."

Tie Gangwen swallowed hard. "No one knocks either…"

Sun Mai started, and Sunan frowned.

"Then how does one go about seeing him?"

Tie Gangwen shrugged. "Wait?"

There was little more discussion. Sunan and Sun Mai stood in front of the red door, arms crossed, waiting. The soldiers appeared to be completely terrified, and virtually all of them were sweating profusely despite the fact that the corridor was relatively drafty and cold.

After a few minutes passed, Sunan realized that there was indeed a draft, and strangely, it was a wind that was blowing against his back. However, he was only standing a meter or two in front of the door. He turned to look behind him and saw nothing unusual, but he was able to confirm that there was indeed wind blowing down the corridor toward the door. Even the flames of the torches lighting the corridor seemed to be bending in the same direction—toward the door.

Sunan leaned toward Sun Mai. "Do you feel that?"

Sun Mai nodded. "What do you say we just let ourselves in?"

Sunan grinned.

"Rebuke of the Dragon!"

"Sword of the Scholar!"

As Sunan and Sun Mai unleashed their most powerful techniques, the soldiers began to run in the opposite direction, clearly terrified. As for the red door, it didn't stand up long. A few moments later, red splinters of wood showered about as the door virtually exploded.

As the dust and wood chips settled, the chamber beyond the door slowly became visible.

It was large, but thanks to the vast accumulation of books, artifacts, and other objects, it seemed much smaller than it actually was. At the far end was a raised platform and a table, and there sat an extremely skinny, short man wearing what appeared to be a roughly sewn cloth robe, tied around his waist with a thick rope.

He lounged there lazily, a slight smile on his face. His eyes were sunken into his face, making him look almost skeletal, and his fingernails were long and jagged.

"Well, it took you long enough," the man said, chuckling. "I've been watching you." He held up a simple copper mirror and tapped it with the long fingernail of his left index finger. "Magic mirror. You certainly dispatched Iron Awl Hu with gusto. I also saw you whispering in the halls. I suppose you're here to... recruit me? Kill me?"

If Sun Mai was taken aback by the man's words, he didn't show it. Clasping his hands behind his back, he said, "Recruit isn't quite the right word, good sir. We would like to extend an invitation for you to join us."

"I see," Ritual Master Zhen said, stroking his chin with his long fingernails. "And who exactly is 'us,' if I might ask?"

"Oh," Sun Mai said. "Well, I will allow our esteemed sect leader to tell you." He looked over at Sunan.

Sunan blinked as he scrambled to think of a name. The first adjective that popped to mind was Golden, probably because he and Sun Mai had just discussed the Golden Immortal. Clearing his throat, Sunan said, "We are the Golden... Dragon Sect!"

Ritual Master Zhen nodded slightly. "The Golden Dragon Sect. Interesting. Well, I think your offer is worth discussing. Please, come have a seat and we can talk."

Sunan took a step forward, already formulating the questions he wished to ask the man.

Sun Mai followed close behind. However, before either of them had taken more than five steps, they experienced a strange sensation in their arms and legs. It was almost as if they were wading through water. The feeling grew more intense, until it was like they were trying to walk through thick mud. After only a few breaths of time had passed, they couldn't even move.

Sunan's eyes went wide, and Sun Mai gritted his teeth.

Chuckling could be heard as Ritual Master Zhen set the copper mirror down. "As expected, you two are complete and utter fools. Do you think someone like me, Ritual Master Zhen, master of the arcane, summoner of demons, would even consider 'joining' two buffoons like you?"

Sunan couldn't see what Sun Mai was doing, but he could feel the blood pounding in his own veins, and he could sense the killing intent rising up in his heart. He realized that he really had been a fool. How could someone who worked so closely with someone like Iron Awl Hu possibly be an honorable and righteous person? How could a person like that possibly be trusted to discuss things in a rational manner?

How could I even have thought that this man would sit down and talk?

Ritual Master Zhen continued to speak, unleashing a variety of scathing insults upon Sunan and Sun Mai. He picked up a wooden box from off to the side, which was filled with knives and daggers. Some were long and straight, others wickedly curved. Some shone brightly, others were rusty and old.

While Ritual Master Zhen began to rifle through the daggers, Sunan closed his eyes.

Sun Mai said that this guy's magic is probably just qi. If that's the case, then there's nothing supernatural at all about what he's done to us. I must *be able to break free.*

Tuning out the droning of Ritual Master Zhen, Sunan entered a state of complete and utter focus.

Qi is just energy. Energy is force. Force pushes and pulls and can also be resisted. Whatever force it is that is pushing against me... I can push back! I refuse to give in to this. I REFUSE!

It took so much effort that Sunan began to tremble, but by sheer force of willpower, he managed to clench his hand into a fist.

I REFUSE!

Focusing his mind and his will, he filled himself with the desire to reject whatever force it was that Ritual Master Zhen was using to lock him down. He lifted his leg in the air and took a step forward. Opening his eyes, he realized that Ritual Master Zhen was still completely focused on the daggers. But then the man suddenly stopped talking and pulled a bronze dagger out of the box.

"Ah, this is the one!" he exclaimed.

By that point, Sunan was walking toward him, slowly but surely. As Ritual Master Zhen began to look up at him, Sunan formed dragon's claws with his hands and circulated his qi in preparation for an attack. He was now roughly three meters away from Ritual Master Zhen.

When Ritual Master Zhen caught sight of Sunan walking toward him, his eyes went wide. But then he smiled.

And the unimaginable happened.

CHAPTER 22
WU – SUNAN

Ritual Master Zhen calmly placed the blade of the bronze dagger across his left palm, then closed his hand around it and pulled the dagger out. Blood immediately oozed out, which he poured onto the ground in front of him. Then he began to speak in what Sunan now recognized to be Classical Fei.

"Ren xue wei di, shu shi wei yu, shu yu zhan di, shu li tao tian!"

Then, he slammed his hand down on the table next to him.

Sunan was picking up speed, and considering he had no idea what the words meant, they didn't distract him at all. However, before he could get even a meter closer to Ritual Master Zhen, he heard a clicking sound, and something fell from the ceiling.

More clicking sounds followed, and more objects fell from the ceiling to land on the ground with muffled thuds.

Before Sunan could take another step, a clicking sound could be heard from directly above his head, and then something dropped down onto him. It tumbled down across his face and fell to the ground at his feet.

LEGENDS OF OGRE GATE

He looked down and was surprised to see the corpse of a rat!

Then there were more clicking and thumping sounds. Panels in the ceiling opened up, and rat corpses fell like rain. Some of the corpses were fresh, others were little more than skeletons.

The grisly sight left Sunan completely astonished.

Ritual Master Zhen began to laugh maniacally. "And now I shall draw upon the power of the rats to cut you down!"

Slicing himself again with the bronze knife, he waved his hand violently, sending droplets of blood flying out in all directions. In response, black mist began to rise up from the corpses of the rats, forming tendrils that shot through the air toward Ritual Master Zhen.

Now was not the time for shock. Sunan steeled himself, suppressing the urge to vomit as he took another step forward.

I REFUSE! I REFUSE! I REFUSE!

The more he rejected whatever force it was that Ritual Master Zhen had used to lock him in place, the easier it became to move. As his foot touched down on the ground after taking another step, the black tendrils of mist began to pour into Ritual Master Zhen's eyes, ears, nose, and mouth.

Then Ritual Master Zhen began to transform. Hair popped out all over his skin, and his fingernails grew long and sharp. His face began to stretch out, and his ears grew larger. He seemed to be in the process of transforming into an enormous rat.

Lips twisting with disgust, Sunan planted his foot and unleashed Rebuke of the Dragon, which slammed into the ratlike Ritual Master Zhen, sending him tumbling backward.

Moments later, Sun Mai's Sword of the Scholar sliced through the air. Apparently Sun Mai had also managed to free himself from the initial trap. The illusory blade slashed Ritual Master Zhen across the throat, sending blood spraying out in a fountain.

Sunan unleashed one more Rebuke of the Dragon, ensuring

– 196 –

that Ritual Master Zhen was well and truly dead. There was no force at all trying to lock him in place.

Before the man could complete his grisly transformation, he was cut down.

Rats were still dropping down from the ceiling.

The bizarreness of the scene was such that Sunan almost wondered if it was all real.

He slowly turned to find Sun Mai approaching.

"You were right," Sunan said. "We should have just killed him. A few more seconds, and who knows what would have happened."

Sun Mai stepped past Sunan and squatted down over the corpse of Ritual Master Zhen. Taking an iron knife out of the nearby box, he prodded the corpse a few times before turning to look up at Sunan.

"This is problematic," he said.

"What do you mean? Getting rid of all the corpses?"

"No." Sun Mai rose to his feet, a grave expression on his face. "It appears my entire theory about the Heavenly Meat Palace is invalid."

*　*　*

Other than Iron Awl Hu and Ritual Master Zhen, there was no one else in the criminal organization who could use qi, which made it very easy for Sunan and Sun Mai to take control.

Originally, Sunan had no wish to be in a leadership position, but Sun Mai somehow convinced him. They renamed the organization the Golden Dragon Sect, with Sunan as the sect leader and Sun Mai as the chief minister.

They quickly found that, exactly as the rumors stated, Iron Awl Hu controlled virtually the entire city. Sunan was also relieved to find that, although many of their activities were less than legal, for the most part their income came from legitimate business. As such, few changes needed to be made to the general operations.

However, Sun Mai and Sunan both agreed to immediately end any trafficking in addictive herbal powders and liquids. Other arrangements of the less-than-moral type were also eradicated. The only disagreement they had was when it came to the brothels. Sunan wanted them banned completely, whereas Sun Mai said that to do such a thing would earn too much ill will from the people, especially from the soldiers. In the end, Sunan begrudgingly agreed to let the brothels stay.

Another area in which they disagreed was regarding the local sheriff and constables. Sunan wanted to end the "gift" payments that Iron Awl Hu had been sending them on a regular basis, which were really just bribes. Sun Mai was of the opinion that controlling the policing of the city was a good thing. Sunan wouldn't budge, though, and thus, the local constable force finally became an autonomous force after years of what had essentially been servitude.

They burned the former workshop of Ritual Master Zhen, leaving the shell of the room empty for the time being.

The Golden Immortal disappeared the same night Iron Awl Hu was killed. Sunan and Sun Mai investigated the matter but turned up few clues.

The forces of the Demon Emperor also disappeared. However, theirs was apparently less of a vanishing act and more of a calculated retreat. A message was left behind for Sunan, written in elegant calligraphy.

To Your Excellency Sunan, sect leader of the Golden Dragons:

The news of the death of Master Hu is unfortunate but not entirely unexpected. Things such as this are known to happen to men in such lines of work. Sadly, many plans have now gone awry because of the sudden change. As such, we will be leaving Daolu for the time being. When we return, I hope that

you will be as willing to work with us as the late Master Hu.
Regards,

    Huang Dayang
    Third Lieutenant to the Love General

"Love General?" Sunan asked Sun Mai.

"The Demon Emperor has five ogre generals. The Hate General, the Bone General, the Fire General, the Love General, and the Skin General. They're quite mysterious, really, some more than others. For example, the Bone General is very famous. People say that he is the hammer the Demon Emperor uses to crush any and all plots against him.

"The Fire General is the spear which slashes across the battlefield. He trains the troops in the ways of killing. Supposedly the Love General is the dove of peace which the Demon Emperor sends to allies.

"As far as the Skin General and the Hate General…" He shrugged. "I haven't heard any rumors about them at all."

Sunan looked down at the message. "The dove of peace to send to allies, huh?" He frowned. "I'd rather drink a cup of nails than be an ally of the Demon Emperor. What do you think we should do?"

Sun Mai took a deep breath but didn't say anything for a long moment. "The Demon Emperor has long since allowed this part of Qi Xien to rule itself. Perhaps an alliance would be nothing more than a formality."

"Perhaps."

"But…"

"But what?"

"It probably wouldn't hurt to prepare to defend ourselves…"

Sunan nodded.

Daolu had a sheriff and the city constables but no standing army. Neither did its sister city of Nansun, the other major city in the Hen-Shi Empire. It was commonly held that the lack of said army was one reason the Demon Emperor had mostly ignored this part of Qi Xien for so many decades.

After some debate, Sunan agreed that they needed to start training fighters, although they would do it mostly in secret to avoid attracting unwanted attention from the Demon Emperor. It was with that goal in mind that Sunan agreed to allow the underground platform fights to continue, although he did away with the practice of fixing the fights, standardizing the rules to make the fights safer. He also increased the prizes, which made the contests even more popular than they had been before.

It also enabled him and Sun Mai to begin to identify the talented fighters in Daolu.

They also spent time with the soldiers who were already part of Iron Awl Hu's organization, identifying the good men among the bad, both in terms of fighting ability as well as moral character.

Months passed.

As they had planned to do some time before, they began to identify and codify the moves and stances that they used in their fighting and practicing. The process took a full month, but in the end, they perfected twenty-seven stances, which they linked together into one form that could be practiced within a few minutes. After they were both satisfied with the results, Sun Mai created an illustrated version on a bamboo scroll, complete with detailed text descriptions.

"What about your Rebuke of the Dragon?" he asked of Sunan.

Sunan thought about the question for a moment. "That will come later. I'll wait until I find someone worthy of being able to unleash power like that."

Sun Mai nodded. After having put the final touches into the contents of Sunan's fighting methods, he rolled the bamboo scroll up and said, "So, what do we call it?"

"Come on, Sun Mai, you're the scholar."

"Right." Sun Mai thought for a moment and then wrote some

characters on the cover of the bamboo scroll, then handed it over to Sunan.

"What's this first character?" he asked.

"That's Classical Fei, of course. An archaic character that means 'martial' or 'war.' It's pronounced Wu."

With that, Sunan read the title: "*Wu-Sunan, the Ultimate Fighting System.*" He looked at Sun Mai. "Sounds a little pretentious."

"People will love it, trust me."

They eventually picked a group of ten men—five from Iron Awl Hu's organization and five from the platform competition, and they began to train them in the ways of the newly dubbed Wu-Sunan fighting system.

***

Deep in the Banyan Mountains was a legendary location that most people had only heard of in whispered stories.

Yao Gong Palace.

The headquarters of the Demon Emperor.

In a tall tower in Yao Gong Palace, overlooking a sprawling ceremonial square, was a room filled with books and scrolls. Seated behind a desk in that room was an ogre dressed in red and pink robes. Even someone who had never seen an ogre before would likely be able to discern that this ogre was a female.

She sat there, leafing through a stack of reports.

Her eyes went wide as she read the contents of one particular report from the north.

"Iron Awl Hu is dead? The Golden Dragon Sect? Hmm…"

With that, she rang a bell. A moment later, a servant appeared in the doorway.

"I need to speak with His Excellency the emperor," she said, a slight frown on her face.

CHAPTER 23
WE'VE GOT COMPANY

Over the months, Sunan's students made excellent progress in Wu-Sunan. Three of them experienced at least one breakthrough.

Despite their sudden access to a level of wealth that would formerly have been incomprehensible, Sunan and Sun Mai continued to live much the same as they had before, except that they now resided in the former mansion of Iron Awl Hu.

They even continued to frequent the Heavenly Meat Palace.

Of course, Sunan was quite famous in Daolu now, therefore his patronage of the Heavenly Meat Palace made its popularity grow tenfold. Mysteriously, the quality of the meat seemed to increase, and the wine became more potent. They even began to season the meat before serving it. The entire establishment even closed for an entire month for renovations.

When it reopened, it was twice as large and ten times as luxurious.

However, the premise remained the same: unending piles of meat for a cheap price.

The restaurant created a private room for use by the Golden Dragon Sect, although most of the time, Sunan and Sun Mai preferred to eat in the common room.

On one particular evening, they were there in their usual spot, consuming massive quantities of meat with their disciples, when Sun Mai began to expound on his philosophies. The discussion quickly turned lively. Although the disciples respected Sun Mai, none of them took him very seriously when it came to philosophy. Truth be told, neither did Sunan.

On this particular night, Sun Mai was ranting about the Perfect Realm, which was supposedly a higher level of existence, a heaven to which many people hoped to reach by means of enlightenment over the course of many lives. Belief in the Perfect Realm had existed in the culture of Qi Xien for countless years, even before the arrival of the Demon Emperor. However, after his invasion, it became the subject of much discussion among philosophers and religious figures.

At one point, when Sun Mai took a short break to wolf down some "lamb" skewers, a young man appeared next to their table. Clasping his hands, he bowed to Sun Mai and said, "Greetings, Senior. I am a humble student of Dehua, and I have a few questions I wish to ask. You are the Heavenly Scholar everyone is talking about, correct?"

Sunan rolled his eyes. People had indeed taken to calling Sun Mai the "Heavenly Scholar" in recent days. Although he hadn't completed his "classic scripture," people had begun to repeat some of the things he said most commonly. For example, "Seek the truth and pursue the actual" was already a common saying in Daolu.

"Why, yes, there are some who have called me the Heavenly Scholar. However, to a true scholar, humility is the greatest virtue. Please, just call me Sun Mai. You are…?"

The young man bowed again. "Just call me Little Mao."

"Little Mao. Very well. So, you are a student of Dehua?"

"Yes, Master Sun."

"I see. And what are these questions of which you speak?"

Little Mao hesitated for a moment, giving Sunan a moment to study him more closely. He wore simple robes and had his hair bound at the top of his head in the common fashion. He was slender, with a face that was less handsome and more… beautiful. He had delicate, pursed lips and piercing eyes that seemed to radiate thoughtfulness.

Finally, Little Mao spoke. "I'm wondering about the Perfect Realm. You were just speaking about it, and you said… it's not real. But… how could you claim to be a follower of Dehua if you don't believe in the Perfect Realm?"

"My young friend, before answering your question, I must first ask you a question. How closely were you listening to my speech just now?"

Little Mao's brow furrowed slightly. "Quite closely, actually."

"I see. Then please explain which part of my speech indicated that I don't believe in the Perfect Realm."

Little Mao shrugged. "The entire speech, really. At one point you said, and I quote, 'Kong Zhi's belief that the Perfect Realm is real couldn't be further from the truth.' If you believe Kong Zhi is wrong, that means you believe the Perfect Realm is not real. Therefore, you don't believe in it."

Sun Mai chuckled. "My young friend, are you familiar with the Harqa people?"

"Of course. Nomads who live in the Kushen Basin. They're the greatest horsemen in the world, and their horses are the finest to gallop under the skies of Qi Xien."

"Do you know what is the most important celebration among the Harqa?"

"Of course. In their language, it's called Chul'kashar, which means 'Birth of the Great Horse.' They believe that the world was created not by Xian Nu Shen but by the Great Horse, who was born on the winter solstice. They commemorate his birth by racing horses all day, drinking all night, and exchanging hats woven from grass."

"Let me ask you, Little Mao, do you think the world was created by the Great Horse or by the Enlightened Goddess, Xian Nu Shen?"

"By Xian Nu Shen, of course."

"Suppose you were traveling in the Kushen Basin during the winter solstice and happened to be there during Chul'kashar. Would you participate in the festival? Would you watch the horse races? Would you drink with the Harqa people? Would you wear a grass hat?"

Little Mao shrugged. "I suppose so. Why wouldn't I?"

"Of course. Why wouldn't you? And yet, do you believe that participating in that festival would please the Great Horse?"

"Of course not!"

"So you don't believe in their festival, correct?"

"I suppose I don't."

"And yet their festival exists, does it not? It is real, is it not?"

Little Mao frowned but didn't respond.

Sun Mai chuckled again. "Do you see my point?"

"I don't believe in their festival, and yet it exists. It is real. The festival is real, but I don't believe in it."

"Exactly. You do not believe in something that is, in fact, real. The Harqa people, on the other hand, do believe in the festival, and the festival is just as real. Belief in something has nothing to do with whether or not it is real."

Little Mao's expression flickered. "Therefore, a statement about something being real or not real cannot be used to extrapolate whether or not you believe in it."

Sun Mai slapped the table. "Exactly!" He turned to Sunan and said, "Isn't that right, Brother Sunan?"

Sunan's eyes had glazed over a bit, as he had virtually no idea what was being discussed. "Of course," he said, quickly laying into a slab of meat to avoid having to say anything further.

"Following this line of reasoning," Little Mao went on, "it would be possible to say that you think the Perfect Realm is not real, and yet you believe in it. But why would you believe in something that isn't real?"

"Because," Sun Mai replied, tapping his temple, "it's here."

"In your mind?"

"Yes, according to Kong Zhi, the Perfect Realm is another world beyond our own, a perfect world that we imperfect humans should emulate. But does that really sound plausible to you? Do you really think that there could be some other magical world that has always existed, and yet throughout the thousands of years of recorded history of Qi Xien, we don't have a single scrap of evidence of anyone visiting that world or anyone from that world visiting ours?"

At this point, Sunan couldn't help but interrupt. "Little Mao, please join us. Sit here next to Sun Mai and discuss your ideas… somewhat more privately. What do you say?"

Little Mao clasped his hands respectfully, and soon he and Sun Mai were engaged in an animated discussion, leaving Sunan free to interact with his disciples.

From that day on, Sun Mai took Little Mao under his wing. Although Little Mao didn't agree with everything Sun Mai said, the fact that there was now someone who seemed to understand Sun Mai's way of thinking completely changed him. With Little Mao's encouragement and help, Sun Mai even began compiling and organizing his notes, and he declared that he would soon begin work on his classic scripture. He also began to personally instruct Little Mao regarding qi manipulation and Wu-Sunan.

More months passed, during which time Sunan grew increasingly bored, until finally a momentous event occurred. During the eighth lunar month, the Phoenix month, on the first day of the first cycle, a star fell from the sky.

Sunan didn't witness the matter. He was in the courtyard sparring with one of his most talented disciples, Yuwen Huo, when Sun Mai rushed in.

"Sunan, I was just talking with the moon, and you wouldn't believe what I saw. A falling star!"

Sunan continued to exchange fluid punches and kicks with Yuwen Huo. "So? Shooting stars aren't that rare."

"Not a shooting star. A falling star, pure silver! I actually saw it fall from the sky down to the earth. It landed somewhere to the south."

Sunan's ears perked up, and he stopped sparring to look over at Sun Mai. Yuwen Huo also looked over.

"What do you think it means?" Sunan asked.

"I don't know. I think we should go consult our astrologer."

And that is how they found themselves leaving Daolu the following day on horseback.

According to their astrologer, a silver star falling to the earth on the first day of the first cycle of the eighth lunar month, which was the Phoenix Moon, was a rare sign. He told them that if they could find where exactly that star fell, it would surely lead them to incredible good fortune.

Frankly, Sunan was somewhat skeptical of matters pertaining to astrology, but Sun Mai was enthusiastic about the matter, and Sunan had been getting bored anyway. A jaunt out of the city to search for a fallen star seemed like just the break from monotony that he had been hoping for.

They left the Golden Dragon Sect in the hands of Tie Gangwen and Yuwen Huo and took a group consisting of three disciples and seven soldiers on what would surely be a journey of less than a week total.

They rode south out of Daolu's Zhen Gate, then crossed the bridge over the Chezou River before heading in the general direction of the fallen star's supposed final resting place, as calculated by the astrologer, based on information from Sun Mai and several other eyewitnesses.

The terrain was mostly flat plains, but the farther west they got, the more hills and trees appeared, until they were clearly in mountainous foothills. As for the trees, one of the disciples, a new recruit named Sima Zikang, who had been born and raised in the area, mentioned that they were in the northern part of the Little Demon Forest.

On morning of the fourth day, they found themselves at the top of a hill that sloped downward so steeply that it might almost count as a cliff. Only someone in the most desperate of circumstances would even consider riding a horse down such a hill.

Down below was a ravine-like valley that stretched roughly east and west. Not too long ago, the valley had clearly been filled with lush vegetation, but this was no longer true. Almost the entire valley was nothing more than ash, including a long furrowed ditch that ran down the very center of the valley, ending in front of a crater, which they were perched almost directly above.

"That must be it!" Sun Mai said excitedly.

Sunan nodded, and he was just about to start riding to the east, toward an area a few kilometers away where the steep angle of the hill turned into more of a slope, making it possible to enter the valley, when a flicker of motion caught his attention. He looked up to see a group of people emerging from the trees on the other side of the valley. After spotting the crater, they began pointing excitedly, and in fact, their loud exclamations were just barely audible from across the valley.

"We've got company," Sunan said.

As he studied the group, one of their number looked up, and

their eyes met. It was a young woman, quite beautiful, with eyes that, even at this distance, seemed sharp enough to pierce into the soul and stab at the heart.

As soon as she spotted Sunan, her eyes narrowed, and she turned to speak to a tall, muscular man who rode at her side. He looked over at Sunan and Sun Mai's group, and then a moment later, shouted out a command. The entire group turned their horses and sent them galloping to the east.

"Dammit!" growled Sunan. "Come on, men. Don't let this trip be a waste. Let's get to that crater!"

CHAPTER 24
DON'T DO THAT

The geography on Sunan's side of the valley favored his group by just a bit. There were fewer trees, and the land was more stable, making it much easier for them to gallop at top speed toward the area where the cliff turned into more of a slope.

They flew like the wind.

For a brief moment, Sunan thought back to his life in the village, before everything changed. Although horses were rare in the village and he had never actually ridden one, donkeys were common, and as a child he had always fancied himself somewhat of an expert. He had even raced donkeys with his friends in the village and had won more often than not.

After he and Sun Mai took over Iron Awl Hu's organization, he had had access to real horses, and as a result he had quickly become familiar with how to ride them. In fact, the horse he was currently riding was one of the finest in the stables.

The wind buffeted his face, and his unbound hair was whipping around his head as he galloped along. The pounding of his horse's hooves into the turf vibrated through his body, and when he glanced to the right and saw the valley so far down below, he almost felt like he was an eagle.

He couldn't hold back from letting out a long whoop.

After about a minute of riding, the distance to the sloping downward hill had been halved. He looked across at the other side of the valley and could just barely make out a flicker of motion—it was the other group riding their horses through the dense forest opposite. They had not made much progress. Obviously Sunan and his people would reach the valley floor first.

Sure enough, after another minute or two of riding, they were able to descend into the valley itself.

It only took a few seconds of riding before Sunan reached the area completely devoid of trees and vegetation. He tapped his heels against his horse's side, sending it into the fastest run possible. The valley whizzed by as he drew closer and closer to the crater.

He was only about halfway there when something flickered in his peripheral vision. He turned his head in shock to find that the young woman he had seen before was rapidly catching up to him.

She was riding on the other side of the furrow that cut the valley in half. It was a strange sight to see a young woman riding a horse, but what was more surprising to Sunan was the type of horse she was riding. Even he recognized the distinctive shape of the ears that identified it.

That's a Harqa steed from the Kushen Basin! The fastest horses in the world! Who is this girl?

Sunan tried to push his horse faster, to little effect. He caught sight of the crater up ahead, and then the young woman passed him as her Harqa steed exploded with a burst of greater speed.

"Dammit!" *Beaten by a girl in a race!*

The young woman reached the crater at least fifteen seconds before Sunan. Most shocking of all was that instead of waiting until her horse came to a stop, she actually leapt out of the saddle, somersaulting through the air to land nimbly at the edge of the crater.

What was that? Can she use qi?

Despite his level of ability and power with qi and his experience fighting, Sunan was by no means confident enough to leap off of a galloping horse. He quickly reined his horse in, then jumped out of the saddle and hurried over to the cater.

As he reached the lip of the crater, the young woman was cautiously approaching its very center. There, Sunan could see something buried in the ash and soil, something that glittered with faint silver light.

Damnation! If she lays hands on that, this whole trip will have been for nothing!

Hurrying down into the crater, he yelled, "Hey! That's dangerous. Don't touch it!"

The young woman looked back at him with a raised eyebrow. "Dangerous? And how do you know that?" Looking away, she took another step forward until she was virtually on top of the object.

"My astrologer said so!" Sunan replied. "That fallen star belongs to me!"

The young woman snorted, edging closer to the object. After a moment, she pulled a knife out of her sleeve and prodded it.

Knives in her sleeves? Sunan hurried over, angling a bit to the right so that he could get closer, while still keeping a safe distance from the young woman.

Now that he was up close, he could see that the object itself, which was mostly buried in the ash, was a chunk of metal. Or rock. Or maybe a mixture of both. It was mostly black and rough, although there were flecks of silver that glowed with odd light.

This is what stars look like? He wondered if it was hot.

The young woman looked up at him, her eyes flashing. "I'm afraid you don't know what you're talking about. Not only is this thing not dangerous, it actually belongs to me."

Sunan clenched his jaw.

The sound of galloping horses could be heard as everyone else arrived. Sun Mai hurried down into the crater, followed close behind by the tall, muscular young man Sunan had noticed earlier.

"Back away from Chieftainess Bao!" the burly man said, fingering a bronze axe strapped to his waist.

"Tell your Chieftainess Bao to back away from Sect Leader Sunan!" Sun Mai retorted, taking a threatening step forward.

Bao rose to her feet. "Calm yourself, Mao Yun."

"That's right, Mao Yun!" Sun Mai continued. "Haven't you read *The Sayings of Kong Zhi*? 'The wise man knows when to back down.' This is Sect Leader Sunan, champion of Daolu, slayer of Iron Awl Hu! He slaughtered the Killer of Daolu with a single punch, so he could take someone like you down as easy as butchering a sleeping pig!"

Mao Yun glared at Sun Mai. "I've never heard of any Iron Awl Hu, but let me tell you this, Chieftainess Bao single-handedly crushed one of the Demon Emperor's ogres. So what do you have to say to that?"

Sun Mai seemed strangely at a loss for words. Before he could recover, Sunan quickly jumped back into the conversation. "Chieftainess Bao, please forgive Sun Mai's impulsiveness." He clasped his hands and bowed. "I am Sunan of Daolu. Might I ask why you claim right to this fallen star?"

Bao's eyes narrowed for a moment, but she also clasped her hands respectfully. "Greetings, Sect Leader Sunan, I am Bao of the Pure Phoenix Sect. This pure-silver star fell on the first day of the first cycle of the eighth lunar month, which is the Phoenix month. How could such an object not belong to the Pure Phoenix Sect? Sect Leader Sunan, I have heard of your illustrious name, and although my lieutenant Mao Yun has not heard of Iron Awl Hu, I have.

"I also know that you are the sect leader of the Golden Dragon Sect. Consider this, Sect Leader: If a golden star fell to the ground on the first day of the first cycle of the first lunar month, the Dragon month, I would never claim that such an object belonged to my Pure Phoenix Sect. Therefore, how can you claim that this pure-silver star belongs to your Golden Dragon Sect? It even fell into our territory."

Sunan glanced over at Sun Mai and was dismayed to find that his jaw had dropped and his eyes were as wide as saucers.

Sunan cleared his throat, mind racing as he tried to come up with some sort of response.

"As I thought," Bao continued. "Even you realize that this pure-silver star must be a gift sent to me by the Enlightened Goddess. If you attempted to steal it from me, you would in fact be interfering with the will of Xian Nu Shen. Is that something you would dare to do?"

At long last, Sun Mai seemed to recover his composure. "Hold on a moment, Chieftainess Bao. I'll have you know that the Golden Dragon Sect doesn't even believe in the Enlightened Goddess!"

Mao Yun snorted. "Hmph! A bunch of blasphemers! As to be expected from weaklings like yourselves."

Sun Mai slowly turned to look at Mao Yun. "I'll have you know that neither Sect Leader Sunan nor myself are weaklings. You might not be aware, but your Chieftainess Bao has no doubt heard that we personally killed one of the Lions of Peace. Yes, you heard me well. Killed him. With our bare hands. Don't think I didn't notice your clever phrasing earlier. You didn't say that Chieftainess Bao 'killed' an ogre. You said she 'crushed' an ogre. A clever attempt on your part to play with words. How did she crush him? In a beauty contest? Unlike you prevaricators, we seek the truth and pursue the actual!"

"Are you calling me a liar?" bellowed Mao Yun, clenching his hands into fists.

Sun Mai tilted his chin up. "I'm merely pointing out the flaws in the fanciful story you have woven to make your chieftainess sound more intimidating than she really is."

"Say one more word, you puny little bookworm, and I'll make you regret it!"

"Mao Yun—" Bao said, reaching out toward Mao Yun.

"Sun Mai—" Sunan said, reaching out toward Sun Mai.

Sun Mai interrupted them both. "Listen up, you buffoon! I'll say anything I want, any time I want. And there's nothing a lying goon like yourself can do to stop me!"

Mao Yun's eyes blazed with fire, and he sent his palm flying out toward Sun Mai.

What was most shocking of all was that Mao Yun was a full three meters away from Sun Mai when he struck. As he extended his palm with lightning speed, the illusory image of a hand sprang out and shot through the air toward Sun Mai.

Dammit, they can *use qi!* thought Sunan.

Sun Mai's eyes widened, and yet he didn't hesitate for even a moment.

"Dance of the Bixie!" Grinning, he flew off to the side at incredible speed, completely avoiding the flying hand, which faded away without hitting anything. Dance of the Bixie was the new name Sunan had convinced him to use for the same move he had once called Dance of Kong Zhi. Since bixies were mythological winged lions, they seemed much more appropriate inspiration for the name of a technique than Kong Zhi.

Mao Yun's jaw dropped when he saw Sun Mai flit away from his attack. Before he could make another move, Sun Mai's index and middle finger slashed through the air.

"Sword of the Scholar!"

The shining image of a sword appeared, which blurred through the air toward the shocked Mao Yun. Mao Yun instinctively threw his hands up to defend himself, but it did little good. Sun Mai's Sword of the Scholar slashed into Mao Yun, opening up gashes on his forearms and right shoulder, and sending him staggering back.

Mao Yun ground to a halt a few paces back, panting, blood dripping down his arms.

It was at this point that Bao took a step forward. At some point, another knife had appeared in her other hand.

Jaw clenched, eyes blazing, she said, "You really shouldn't have done that."

CHAPTER 25
PROTECT DAOLU

The fire burning in Bao's eyes seemed to contain a rage that immediately left Sunan unsettled. It was at this same moment that it also dawned on him that he wasn't armed. He had a saber strapped to his horse several meters away, but Bao was much closer than that.

Normally a strong young man wouldn't have anything to fear from a young woman much shorter and lighter than him. But Sunan was no fool.

He knew how much of a difference qi could make when it came to fighting. Some of the disciples of the Golden Dragon Sect were women, and over the months of training, it had become apparent to everyone that qi was like a great equalizer. Generally speaking, size and weight didn't matter once you mastered the flow and manipulation of that internal energy.

Furthermore, over the past months, Sunan had developed a fondness for the saber and other saber-type weapons. It was true that he and Sun Mai had taken down Iron Awl Hu without a single weapon in hand. However, that didn't make him feel any less nervous going up against an opponent with two knives.

Besides, he had no idea what her level might be. Considering the ease with which she had flipped off the horse earlier, she might have achieved four breakthroughs, the same as him. Or even more.

Clenching his teeth, Sunan took a step back and barked, "Sun Mai, back down!"

Sun Mai landed nimbly on the balls of his feet, a frown on his face as he held his two fingers out in front of him.

Sunan looked at Bao. "Chieftainess Bao, I'm afraid things are escalating too quickly. Let's all just calm down for a moment."

Bao spit on the ground off to the side, then snorted coldly. "I'll back down when you people get on your horses and ride back to Daolu. This is my territory, and it's my fallen star."

Sunan frowned. "Now hold on a moment, I think—"

"No discussions," Bao interrupted. "I'll give you to the count of five to get back on your horses and leave. One."

Sunan's face darkened. "Listen, girl, I'm not just going to leave after coming all the way here. At least we can—"

"Two."

Anger flared in Sunan's eyes as he recalled the events leading up to the fight with Iron Awl Hu. "You know, I really don't like it when people count to five on me."

"Three."

"Fine." His hands twisted into the claws of dragons. "If you really want to do it the hard way, then so be it. Just don't—"

"Four."

"Don't say I didn't warn you."

"FIVE!" As the words left her mouth, Bao's left hand flashed through the air, and one of her knives shot toward Sunan.

To a spectator, the knife might have looked to be moving with blinding speed, but to Sunan, that wasn't the case. The first time he had faced a sharp metal object flying toward him was when he fought Iron Awl Hu, and even then he had managed to counter the attack. Since then, he had perfected and practiced that very same technique.

Based on the trajectory of the knife Bao had thrown at him, he could tell that she most likely hadn't intended it to be a deadly attack. Either she had intentionally aimed the knife too far to the left to really hit him, or she was a horrifically bad shot. Regardless, countering the move was a simple thing.

"Dragon Cleaves the Clouds!" he roared, kicking out with his foot and flipping backward. A blast of air slammed into Bao's knife, sending it flying off into the distance. Sunan landed on his feet and clenched his hands back into dragon claws.

Already, fighting had broken out around them. Sun Mai was fighting Mao Yun, who was in a berserker rage after having been slashed by Sun Mai's Sword of the Scholar. The way he swung his axe made him seem like a god descended from the skies, and yet Sun Mai danced away from his blows with apparent ease. However, now that Mao Yun had already been struck once by Sun Mai, he was on the lookout, and he was able to counter the move when it was used again.

Hoarse shouts, muffled curses, and the clash of weaponry came from the other members of both groups, echoing through the valley. Clearly Bao's followers also had some training when it came to qi fighting.

However, Sunan had no time to observe or analyze any of that. As soon as he landed, he looked up at Bao, preparing to unleash another technique. But just as he was about to unleash Rebuke of the Dragon, expecting to find his opponent glaring at him angrily like she had been moments before, he was surprised to find her staring at him with a quizzical expression on her face.

"What did you just say?" she asked.

"Huh?"

"You just yelled something. What was it?"

"Um… Dragon Cleaves the Clouds?"

"Yes, that was it. Dragon Cleaves the Clouds? What's that supposed to mean?"

"Uh, that's the name of the move. The technique I just used."

"You name your moves? Your man Sun Mai did the same thing, didn't he?"

"You don't name your moves? But… doesn't everybody do that?"

Bao chuckled. "You name your moves? What are you, a child?"

Sunan's lips twisted into a snarl. "We'll see who's the child! Rebuke of the Dragon!"

Two illusory dragons snaked toward Bao, moving with indescribable speed. Her eyes widened, and before she could do anything to defend herself, the dragons slammed into her, shredding her right sleeve and sending her spinning back through the air.

For some reason, Sunan's heart trembled when that happened. He hadn't actually expected her to be hit so easily by Rebuke of the Dragon. Even novice disciples in the Golden Dragon Sect were trained in how to identify and counter moves like that.

Then she slammed down on the ground in a cloud of dust, and Sunan's heart thumped even harder. He was quite sure that a single Rebuke of the Dragon could kill men much taller and stronger than this Chieftainess Bao. He didn't want to leave her with a bruise, let alone kill her. Especially not for a rock that fell out of the sky.

How did things escalate so quickly?

As Sunan took a nervous step forward toward Bao, his heart trembled again, and this time it wasn't for fear of having hurt her.

It was because he saw her lifting her head up. A smile broke out across her face as she realized that she had landed directly in front of the fallen star.

Her eyes rose up to meet his, and they glittered with a mischievous arrogance as she slowly reached out to grab the rock.

Dammit!

Cursing inwardly, Sunan lunged forward, but it was too late.

Bao's hands closed over the silver rock, and she struggled to her feet.

Bao began to chuckle, and Sunan lurched to a stop.

She quickly held the rock behind her back and tilted her chin up, pointing the knife at him. "Now what are you going to do, Sect Leader Sunan?"

He looked around and saw that in the past few seconds of fighting, neither side seemed to have gained an upper hand. In fact, other than the blow Sun Mai had landed on Mao Yun, no blood had been drawn. He looked back at Bao and took a deep breath. "Well, it seems that—"

Before he could finish speaking, his jaw dropped.

Bao's eyes had gone wide, and not from shock or fear. They were almost bulging out of her head!

Her left shoulder was trembling slightly, and most bizarre of all was that a tiny pinprick of silver light could be seen in the very center of her pupils. Her head spasmed as she began to draw her left hand out from behind her back. Her entire arm was shaking, and the hand which gripped the silver rock was pale white, and silver streaks were running up her arm.

"Wh-what…?" she muttered.

Sunan took a step forward. "Chieftainess Bao, are you all right?"

As he watched, the whiteness in Bao's pupils grew, spreading out to fill the irises of her eyes, and then the whites, removing any traces of color, until her eyes were pure silver. Slowly the trembling in her arm stopped, and the ashen color faded away.

Bao stared at Sunan for a moment with those silver eyes, and then she spoke. Her voice was different than before. It resonated with a strange timbre, as though it were a voice speaking out from the most ancient of times, perhaps even from a different world. "I'm fine."

Sunan's eyes flickered. "Of course, you're fine."

Her head cocked to the side. "You don't want this fallen star."

Sunan felt slightly dizzy for a moment. "No, I don't want it."

A slight smile appeared on Bao's face. She then looked around at the surrounding fighting. Raising her voice, she said, "Golden Dragon Sect disciples, there is no need to fight. We won't hurt you."

A moment later, all fighting ceased.

Even Sun Mai backed off and simply stood there calmly. Bao's followers looked around in confusion for a moment and then backed away from Sunan's disciples.

Bao looked back at Sunan, her white eyes shining. "Sect Leader Sunan, you and your people really need to get back to Daolu as soon as possible. A great threat is heading its way, and you need to defend it."

Sunan shook his head as another wave of dizziness passed through him. "Yes, a great threat. I understand. Must defend Daolu." He began to walk back to his force. "Come on, men, we need to get back to Daolu as soon as possible."

Sun Mai looked over at him with a frown. "Sunan, something's not—"

"All of you Golden Dragon Sect disciples must listen to me!" Bao said, raising her voice again. "Daolu is in peril! Ride back as quickly as possible!"

Sun Mai turned toward his horse. "You heard the sect leader, men. No delays, we have to get back to Daolu!"

Shuffling sounds could be heard as Sunan, Sun Mai, and all of the other disciples mounted their horses. Then they galloped away at top speed.

***

As the Golden Dragon Sect disappeared into the distant trees, Mao Yun approached Bao. He was bleeding, but the wounds were superficial and did little more than cause him to wince.

"Bao, what's going on?" he asked.

As Bao turned to look at him, she slowly lifted the silver rock up in front of her. Her hand began to tremble, and the silver of her eyes began to fade. "Th-this rock…" she muttered. "Don't… don't touch it."

The silver left her eyes, and her hand dropped to her side, although it maintained its grip on the rock.

As for Bao, her knees gave out from under her, and she collapsed. Mao Yun lurched forward and grabbed her arm, catching her just before she hit the ground.

CHAPTER 26
METALSMITH

When Bao awoke, she recalled a strange dream, a dream of meeting a young man and of fighting him. The more she contemplated the dream, the clearer the details became, until she realized it might not have been a dream.

She was lying on her back, staring up at the sky. At first, she was so lost in her thoughts that she didn't notice how strange that sky was. It was pure white, with pink clouds that streaked by in an arcing trajectory, moving so fast it was dizzying.

She slowly sat up.

She was on the peak of a mountain. Farther below, thick fog stretched out in all directions, as far as the eye could see. The fog was black and churned like boiling water.

There was no sound except for a faint hum that bordered on music.

Bao closed her eyes and shook her head, but when she opened her eyes, the scene was just as it was before.

At this point, she noticed a woman sitting on a rock several meters away.

As soon as Bao laid eyes on her, she gasped. The woman wore pure-white robes embroidered with silver thread and was without a doubt the most beautiful woman Bao had ever seen in her life. In fact, she was so beautiful that she didn't even seem real. Her hair was white, but it was not from age. It was pure, like silver, but brighter, so dazzling that it almost hurt one's eyes to look at it.

Pure-white eyebrows arched above the woman's closed eyes, and on her forehead was a strange glowing symbol.

The woman sat there silently, motionless, her hands resting on her thighs.

Who is she? What is she? An immortal? A goddess?

Bao struggled to her feet, then clasped her hands and bowed respectfully. "Greetings, Senior, I am Bao. May I ask, where am I?"

In response, the woman sighed. In the noiselessness of the world, that sigh resounded like the rumble of distant thunder. It felt as if storm winds were battering against Bao's face, and she almost took a step back.

"So weak," the woman said, and then she opened her eyes.

Yet again, Bao gasped.

The woman's eyes were silver, and even brighter than her hair, and when she stared at Bao, it was as if daggers were piercing her mind, as if a mountain were crushing down on her from above.

Gritting her teeth, Bao clasped her hands again. "Senior? I don't understand."

The woman took a deep breath, and the pressure faded away. "You're weak. Like all humans. I tried to give you a taste of my power, but you could barely handle it for ten minutes. Weak. Very weak."

Bao thought back to how she had fought with the young man. She remembered grabbing the fallen star and then being filled with a sensation of utter power. She remembered ordering the young man and his followers to leave, and she remembered how they had followed her instructions without hesitation.

"Senior, are you the fallen star?" she asked.

The woman laughed. "I am no star. But I do come from the Upper Realms. What fell into your hands is… well, it's difficult to explain to someone with a mind so limited as yours. Let's just say it's a sliver of my will. I had a little fight with that bastard, Yu. Supreme Judge? More like Supreme Bore. Such an uptight fellow, always running around enforcing some law or another. Unfortunately, he's very strong. Quite the opposite of you. I knew I was losing, so in the chaos of the fight, I managed to slice away part of my will and send it down here to this pitiful place that you people call Qi Xien. Thankfully, that bastard Yu didn't notice. I was aiming for you, you know."

"Aiming for me?" Bao replied.

"Yes. The Perfect Realm has been boring recently, and I've been paying attention to your little Pure Phoenix Sect. Such a name… suits me. Anyway, I need your help, and I'm prepared to reward you."

"You need *my* help?" Bao's eyes narrowed.

The woman chuckled. "Yes, someone like me, asking for help from a mortal like you. It's funny, I know. I need to borrow your body for a bit. You're weak, but I can mold you into something stronger."

"Borrow my body?"

"Yes. For only a few hundred years or so."

"A few hundred years!"

"Can you do anything other than repeat my words?" the woman asked with annoyance, her white brows furrowing into a frown. "Are all humans this stupid and weak? Yes, a few hundred years. Once I've finished everything I need to do in this cesspit, you can have your body back, and it will be much more powerful than it is now. By that time, you'll already be an immortal. A nice exchange, wouldn't you say?"

Bao was so taken aback that she was at a loss for words.

The woman began to tap her finger on her knee. "Girl, do you know how many people in your world pray for power? Do you know how many people light incense in the hope of gaining blessings from the Upper Realms? Do you know how many people offer sacrifices to lower realms hoping to gain even a fraction of what I'm offering you?

"I will make you more powerful than any human alive. Even that boring, so-called Demon Emperor will shake in his boots at the mention of your name, although by that time, I'll most likely have killed him myself. Just help me achieve my goals, and you can have power beyond your wildest dreams.

"If you want to, you can ascend to one of the Upper Realms, maybe even the Perfect Realm. You can live forever, be a god! All for simply giving me a bit of help."

Bao's eyes narrowed. "What exactly are these goals of yours?"

The woman's eyes flared with brilliant light. "Destroy the world. Kill everyone. Rain destruction upon the mortals."

Bao's eyes widened.

The woman cleared her throat. "Sorry, a bit of a joke. In the Upper Realms we say things like that sometimes as a form of humor. I don't want to destroy the world, just reshape it a bit. It's not like I want to wipe out all humankind or anything. Lots of people will survive."

"No," Bao said.

The woman's eyes widened. "No? Did you just say no? Do you know who I am? Do you know how powerful I am? I don't need to ask your permission. Do you know that? I can take over your body if I feel like it. It's just that I don't want to go to the trouble. Do things the easy way, do you hear me? Give me your permission! NOW!"

"Or what?"

"Or what? *Or what?*" The woman threw her head back and screamed, clenching her fists at her sides. The entire world began to tremble as she rapidly grew larger and transformed into something far from human. Her neck stretched out, and her head transformed into that of a beautiful, fierce bird. Enormous wings took the place of her arms, wings with long silver feathers tinged with a multitude of colors. A tail of feathers spread out behind her, long and draping, and her legs stretched out and were soon covered with silver scales. At their ends were enormous talons with long, curving, razor-sharp claws.

In the blink of an eye, the woman was a hundred times her original size, towering over Bao, glaring down at her. It was then that Bao realized there was one thing that was exactly the same about her, and that was her eyes. They were the same shining silver color, and they were even the exact same shape.

A silver talon shot out and wrapped around Bao, although it didn't actually touch her.

"You call yourself the Phoenix? You are no phoenix. *I am the Phoenix!* Do you hear me? Your Pure Phoenix Sect is a joke! You are a speck of dirt on the leg of an ant compared to me.

You want to know what will happen if you refuse me? I will make you *suffer!* Yes, *that* is what will happen. I will crush you and flay you and slice you and burn you a thousand times over. You *will* give me what I want!"

Bao looked into those burning silver eyes and smiled confidently.

"You're bluffing," she said. "If you could take over my body without my permission, you would have done so already. The answer is still no. Let me out of this place."

"No? *No?*" The phoenix began to laugh, and the sound grew louder and louder until even thunder and lightning would cower in fear beneath the sound of it. "How *dare* you!"

Massive pressure crushed down onto Bao, and her mind trembled. And yet, she gritted her teeth.

She's trying to scare me, that's all. This place isn't real. It's my mind. She's here in my mind, and she's trying to trick and threaten me!

"No! Back off, you oversized chicken. This is *my* mind! GET OUT!"

***

Mao Yun carried Bao in his arms for the entire ride back to the forest stronghold. They tried to pry the fallen star out of her hands, being careful not to touch it, but the task proved impossible. Her fingers were like bands of metal that refused to budge.

Her hand was bone white, with silver streaks running up her arm toward her shoulder. As they rode along, those streaks grew longer and wider. By the time they got back to the fortress, her entire arm was white, and Mao Yun could only presume that the color was spreading to the rest of her body.

A Yen-Li priest was called up, but he proved no help. A priestess of Hen-Shi came but offered no solutions, although she was able to confirm that the whiteness was not spreading any further past Bao's shoulder.

Her grip on the fallen star never loosened.

A week passed. Two weeks. A month.

They tried to feed her, but her mouth wouldn't open. At first Mao Yun was worried, but as time passed, it seemed that her body was in a strange state that didn't require sustenance.

Gradually, day-to-day affairs returned to normal.

With the cooperation of Third Zhou and Li Runfa, rumors were intentionally spread that, according to the Hen-Shi priestess, Bao was on an astral journey to the Perfect Realm. That caused a bit of a stir and actually raised morale temporarily.

The effect lasted for only a month. Then, whisperings floated that Bao was sick, or even dead.

Another month later, people were complaining openly. Morale

was beginning to plummet, and Mao Yun wasn't sure what to do. Third Zhou and Li Runfa had no ideas.

Mao Yun even considered cutting her hand off to separate her from the fallen star, but he couldn't quite bring himself to do something so drastic, not when it was clear that her body was in no danger because of the passage of time.

One night, Mao Yun was standing watch over her and was nearly frightened out of his skin when she sat straight up in bed and opened her eyes. They were glowing silver.

She turned her head to stare at him, and then the whiteness began to fade. Then the whiteness that had covered her shoulder and arm for the past months faded away. The fallen star dropped to the ground.

Bao shivered and looked down at the rock. "Oversized chicken," she muttered. Then she looked up at Mao Yun. "Find me a metalsmith."

CHAPTER 27
AN EYE

Throughout the months during which Bao had lain there still and unmoving, her body never seemed to change at all. Her hair hadn't grown. She didn't lose weight. She remained the same as ever.

After waking up, though, she felt a wave of weakness building up deep inside of her. It was as if she hadn't slept during all of those months, and all the exhaustion was on the verge of breaking out at one time. She felt like she might fall unconscious again at any moment.

Other than willpower, the only thing that kept her awake was hunger. Deep, piercing hunger that made her stomach feel as heavy as a mountain.

She swayed a bit back and forth, then placed her hand down on the bed in front of her to stop the dizziness. For a moment, all thoughts of metalworkers vanished from her head.

"Bao, you're back!" Mao Yun exclaimed, leaping to his feet.

"Hungry," she said. "Food. Now."

Mao Yun blinked, then rushed out of the room, whereupon the entire stronghold was thrown into a frenzy.

Mao Yun returned minutes later with steamed buns, pickled vegetables, and cured meat. The food vanished almost before he could put the tray down in front of Bao.

"More," she said before she even finished swallowing the final mouthful.

Mao Yun's eyes went wide. Over the course of the next three hours, dish after dish was brought in, which Bao wolfed down with ravenous hunger. Even during the time in which the event played out, exaggerated stories already began to spread.

"Did you hear that Chieftainess Bao just ate ten bowls of noodles in a row? Without even breathing!"

"I heard that Mao Yun already sent people down to Fan to buy more pickled vegetables. Chieftainess Bao ate an entire month's worth of stock!"

"I heard that at one point she was so hungry waiting for the next dish that she ate the chopsticks!"

"The chopsticks were nothing! They even had to get a new table!"

After three hours, Bao took a deep breath. "Water," she said. Mao Yun nodded.

More stories spread.

"Third Zhou said we'll probably have to start working on a new well after this. The current one is running dry!"

"Mao Yun said that for the next month, all the alcohol and wine is free because Chieftainess Bao drank all the water!"

"Hey, what are you doing?"

"I'm going to burn this incense to Eastern Sea Goddess and beg her not to turn Chieftainess Bao into a water ghost!"

Finally, Bao finished. She wiped her lips with a cloth handed to her by Mao Yun, then yawned.

"Mao Yun," she said.

"Yes, Chieftainess Bao?"

"I… need to… sleep for a—" She promptly flopped back down into the bed and began to sleep. This time it was not a coma, but she did sleep for three days straight, during which time Mao Yun, Third Zhou, and Li Runfa took turns watching over her, just like they had during the long months in which she was in a coma.

Third Zhou was on watch when she woke up again. This time, when Bao sat up, she didn't ask for food and water, instead she requested a pen and brush. Third Zhou hurried back moments later, followed by Mao Yun. When Bao was handed the brush, she immediately began to write on the paper.

From north to east the clouds surge forth
From south to west fair feathers sing

"What's that?" Third Zhou asked.

Bao sighed and shook her head. "I'm not sure." She looked at the words she had written, then slowly handed the brush back to Third Zhou. "I just felt… as if I had to write them. They were burning within my head."

Mao Yun looked over the lines of poetry. "This reminds me of that time we got drunk."

Bao looked up and grinned wryly. "Which time?"

Mao Yun chuckled. "The first time. Remember? You jumped up onto the table and wrote a poem on the wall?"

"I remember you telling me that story." Taking a deep breath, Bao experimentally scooted to the end of the bed and swung her legs over the side. When she tried to stand up, her legs felt a bit creaky, but none the worse for wear.

After a moment passed, Mao Yun cleared his throat. "Chieftainess Bao, may I humbly ask… what happened?"

Bao looked over at the table where the fallen star sat perched on a wooden platter. "I'll explain later," she said. "First, do we have a metalworker in the stronghold?"

Third Zhou answered the question. "We do, Chieftainess. But

according to him, treasures like that fallen star are far beyond his level of skill. He said that if you want something made from the star, you should talk to Ruan the Flamingo."

"Flamingo?" Mao Yun said. "What's that?"

"A type of bird," Bao answered. "From the lands on the other side of the Banyan Mountains. I saw a painting of one when I was a child. They're pink and stand on one leg."

"That's right," Third Zhou said. "Ruan the Flamingo originally came from the south. Perhaps that is why he has the nickname. I'm not sure. In any case, he's somewhat of a hermit, but is well-known for this metalworking skill. He even made some famous swords and spears when he was younger. He fought against the Demon Emperor during the invasion of Fan, and when the city was sacked, he fled into the mountains. Nowadays he lives in a cave in the foothills of Mount Fohe."

"Mount Fohe," Bao said thoughtfully. "That's far, but not too far."

"I already made some calculations," Third Zhou said. "Most of the traveling would be through forests, hills, and mountains. Depending on the exact route we take, it should take fourteen to twenty days to get there."

Bao sucked in a breath. "A month-long trip in total, maybe even two months."

"Chieftainess Bao," Third Zhou exclaimed, "you're not thinking of going yourself, are you?"

"I have no choice," she replied. "The fallen star is too dangerous. Plus, only I know how to control it." She frowned for a moment in thought. "Make preparations. We leave the day after tomorrow."

***

The following two days were a buzz of activity as various preparations were made. They didn't leave the stronghold until noon. Third

Zhou and Li Runfa were left behind to administer the daily affairs. Mao Yun went with Bao, as well as a handful of other followers, some from the old bandit group and some from group they had assimilated after the untimely death of Lord Shu.

It wasn't until they were well into the journey on the second day that Bao finally had a chance to explain to Mao Yun what had occurred to her. Although she didn't go into explicit detail, she didn't hide anything, either. After she finished with her tale, Mao Yun shook his head.

"It's almost unbelievable," he said.

"I wouldn't believe it if I hadn't experienced it myself."

"How did you do it? How did you stand up to the… the oversized chicken? How did you defeat her?"

"I didn't defeat her. I just… suppressed her. I think it had to do with confidence. The further I go along in life, Mao Yun, the more convinced I am that confidence is the key to everything. Those who lack confidence never come out on top. Those who maintain deep and unswerving self-confidence have what it takes to be victorious."

"But Bao, that phoenix demon, she's… like a god! You said she talked about Xian Nu Shen as if she knew her personally? And she fought with Supreme Judge Yu? I don't know if I could even look her in the eye, let alone have a battle of wits with her."

"Well, from the very beginning, she made a mistake. She said that she had been watching the Pure Phoenix Sect for a long time. But the Pure Phoenix Sect was nothing more than a joke. Who was it that brought it up the first time? Second Zhou?"

"First Zhou. Well, First Zhou and Second Zhou, to be most accurate. It was actually on the trip to look for the fallen star. Somehow they started talking about how you fight, and Second Zhou said your fighting style was like a dragon. Then First Zhou said that since you're a woman, it should be a phoenix. And then they both joked that you were 'pure phoenix.'" Mao Yun chuckled.

"That's right, I remember now," Bao said, also chuckling.

"When I started talking with Sect Leader Sunan, I remembered that his group was called the Golden Dragon Sect, so for some reason that 'pure phoenix' joke popped up into my head, and told him that we were the Pure Phoenix Sect. The phoenix inside the fallen star must have heard that and taken it to be the truth. That was what made me realize that she was lying."

"Pure Phoenix Sect," Mao Yun said. "It actually sounds quite impressive."

"It does," Bao replied. "Actually, I think we should keep it."

As they traveled farther south, the terrain grew more mountainous. Eventually they hired a local guide to help them make their way to Mount Fohe.

In the end, the first leg of the journey to Ruan the Flamingo's cave took a bit over two weeks. An entire day of that time, the last day, was spent simply finding the actual cave, even though they knew they were in the right general location.

A door had been built into the cave mouth itself, somewhat defying the image that Bao had built up in her mind about what the place would look like. When Ruan the Flamingo appeared, the reason for his nickname was obvious.

He only had one leg and walked with a crutch.

As was expected, he was old, with a long scraggly beard and one eye that was milky with blindness. He opened the door of his cave dwelling, stared out at the group, then said, "Well? Whaddya want?"

"Your skill," Bao replied. "And a private audience. The matter is… sensitive."

He peered at them with narrowed eyes, then said, "Fine, come in."

As Bao dismounted, she gave a meaningful look to Mao Yun. "You stay out here with the men."

He nodded.

Ruan the Flamingo led her into his cave dwelling, which was

much more luxurious inside than she would have imagined. A small audience chamber was built into the side of the main tunnel, where the two sat down at a wooden table. Ruan served her a cup of tea.

Not waiting for him to ask questions, Bao pulled out a burlap sack, which she placed on the table with a resounding thump.

"I want something made from this," she said, carefully rolling the fallen star out into the open.

Ruan's eyes went wide. "That's…"

"A fallen star," she replied.

He reached out with his index finger to touch it, but her hand shot out like lightning to grab his wrist. "You must not touch it under any circumstances."

He looked up at her. "Do you mean to tell me…"

"There's… something inside of the star. Something like a demon."

Ruan sucked in a breath, then leaned back. "Dangerous. Very dangerous. You want me to turn this thing into a weapon of some sort and keep the demon sealed inside?"

"Have you done something like that before?"

He grinned. "Oh, once or twice."

"Very well, then. The final form doesn't matter to me. It could be a dagger or a bracer, or a bowl for all that matters. The most important thing will be to use this design as the final sealing element." She produced a piece of paper with a sketch of a magical symbol, the very same symbol she had seen on the forehead of the phoenix.

Ruan looked at the paper for a moment, then back at the fallen star. He leaned his face close and inhaled deeply, then produced a pair of wooden tongs from underneath the table. "May I?" he asked.

Bao nodded in affirmation. "Just don't touch it with your flesh."

For the next few minutes, Ruan analyzed the fallen star using a variety of methods. "I can do it," he said.

"For how much?" Bao asked.

Ruan thought for a moment. "I'm missing an ingredient. Something I don't have here in my cave. Get that for me, and we have a deal."

"What ingredient?"

He looked up and smiled. "An eye."

CHAPTER 28
CONFIDENT

An eye?" Bao asked, puzzled.

"Yes, a special type of eye." Ruan's eyes glittered. "Are you familiar with fei beasts?"

She thought for a moment. "I've heard of the term, but I always thought they were something from storybooks or legends."

"Well, of course you'll find them in stories, but that doesn't mean they're fantasies. They're definitely real. When the Demon Emperor came to Qi Xien, he unleashed a special type of energy."

Bao's ears perked up. "Energy…"

Ruan nodded. "Some people say that he brought the energy, other people say that it was always here and that his arrival unlocked it." He shrugged. "Honestly, I don't think that matters. The point is that the strange energy opened up our world in a way that defies imagination.

"Creatures, beings, entities that previously existed only in stories now walk the earth. From the clothes you're wearing and that accent of yours, I would place money on the fact that you're from Li Fan, right?"

Bao smiled. "Yes. I was born and raised in Yu Zhing."

"As I thought. You don't talk like a commoner, either. Your speech is too refined. A noble lady, perhaps?"

Bao looked back at him expressionlessly.

His eyebrow twitched. "Very well. The point is that you lived in a part of Qi Xien that, with the exception of the presence of the Demon Emperor, most closely resembles the Qi Xien of old. However, outside of Li Fan, outside of the heart of the empire, things are different than they used to be. Strange things lurk in the mountains and forests and jungles, and fei beasts are one such entity.

"I've only seen one in person once. It looked like an ox, pure white, with one eye and a tail that resembled… well, you might not believe me even if I told you. Look, bring me the corpse of a fei beast, and I'll do the job for you."

"I thought you said you just wanted the eye?"

"Well, considering that fei beasts have only one eye, do you really think you'll be able to bring me the eye without killing the thing? Probably not. And considering that creatures like that are essentially walking treasures, I'd like to have the whole thing. The eye is the most important part, but the rest of the animal can be used in other ways."

"Presumably they're dangerous?"

Ruan nodded. "Could be very dangerous. But I see you brought along a few fighters. Plus that bodyguard of yours seems stronger than two men put together. You'll probably be fine. Although I wouldn't suggest that you personally attempt to tackle the beast."

Bao snorted. "I killed an ogre and tamed the demon in that fallen star. You think I'm scared of a one-eyed cow?"

Ruan chuckled. "I like your attitude. According to the reports, a fei beast has taken up residence in a cave about three days to the west of here."

"Three days west? Isn't that the Kushen Basin?"

"Not quite, but close. I'm pretty sure this fei beast wandered in from the Kushen Basin, actually. Hard to tell. So, do we have a deal?"

Bao considered the matter for a long moment, and in the end she decided that there was little other choice. "We have a deal."

"Excellent. How soon do you need the fallen star… refined?"

"The sooner the better."

"Well, then, you have another choice to make. If you trust me, then leave the fallen star here, and I'll begin preparations ahead of time. You can even leave one of your men behind to keep an eye on me. He might even be able to help out with some of the preparations. If you don't trust me, then take it with you. However, if I wait until you bring the corpse of the fei beast back, then it will take a minimum of seven days to complete my work."

Bao was not a trusting person in general, but in this situation, she didn't see the harm in leaving the star behind. The sooner she got back to the stronghold, the better. Based on Ruan the Flamingo's reputation, she doubted he would try to flee.

"Very well, I'll leave the star here, along with two of my men. Is there anything else you can tell me about this fei beast?"

Ruan looked up in thought for a moment, then said, "Not really. Though fei beasts are extraordinarily strong, so I wouldn't recommend simply walking up and trying to kill it. Oh, another thing, their mere passage causes lesser forms of life to wither up and die. Nearby plant life, insects, everything nearby will shrivel up within moments of their hooves touching the ground."

Bao's eyes went wide. "What about people?"

"The effect doesn't reach people."

She nodded. After a bit more thought, she rose to her feet. "Very well, I'll take my leave now. We'll get you your fei beast. Remember, don't touch that fallen star."

***

After conferring with Mao Yun, they picked two disciples to stay behind with Ruan the Flamingo. Then they rode west, taking a cart along with them. The terrain was mountainous, making the travel slow. Nothing of note happened for the next three days. Thankfully, the local guide was also adept at tracking and mountain travel, which was of great help. It was on the evening of the third day that they found the cave Ruan the Flamingo had referred to.

Unfortunately, no fei beast was in sight.

However, the fact that the creature killed all lower life forms around it made it very easy to track. A swath of brown vegetation littered with dead insects trailed off to the south, which they followed at a healthy speed.

A day later, they caught up to the fei beast as it drank water from a stream. It was surrounded by dead grass and plants, and as soon as they caught sight of it, almost everyone in the party gasped. Now Bao knew why Ruan had been so evasive about the creature's tail. The tail flicked back and forth almost as if it had a life of its own, and at the end it had two pits that looked like eyes. Furthermore, the tail split open at the end in what looked like a mouth filled with sharp fangs. The tail looked like a snake!

Muttered curses and murmured exclamations could be heard from the various disciples.

"It's like a demon!" Mao Yun said.

Bao studied the creature for a bit. "I don't think so. Just something not native to our lands."

"How do we take it down?"

Bao turned to look back at the disciples. "Wang Tian, come here."

One of the men trotted his horse forward. "Chieftainess?"

"You were the one who usually led hunting parties into the forest for the late Lord Shu, isn't that right?"

"That's right, Chieftainess."

"What was the biggest animal you ever took down, and how?"

"A big deer, I suppose. Most of the time we hunted with the dogs, and then we'd take the animals down with bows."

Bao glanced over and confirmed that Wang Tian had a bow strapped to his saddle. After looking back at the rest of the disciples, she counted only one other who had a bow. "The young man back there with the bow, is he one of your hunters?"

"Yes, Chieftainess. Chieftainess, are you… going to ask us to try to shoot that… thing?"

Bao took a deep breath. "I'm thinking about it. It's called a fei beast, and its hooves can kill plants and insects but not people. It looks strange, but essentially it's just a big cow. Do you think you could take it down?"

Wang Tian studied the fei beast for a bit longer. "It's hard to say, Chieftainess. In the hunt, it's not always possible to kill the deer with a single shot or two. Sometimes you have to track it down after shooting in the first time. With this thing, tracking it down won't be a problem. So I guess there's no harm in trying. Are they fast?"

Bao frowned. "I'm not sure. Looking at it, I would guess not. Are you up for the task?"

Wang Tian grinned. "Of course. Give me a moment to prepare."

Wang Tian and the other disciple consulted each other for a few minutes before they were ready. During that time, the fei beast stayed in place by the stream, occasionally drinking but making no other moves.

When Wang Tian was ready, he and the other disciple rode their horses to a position upstream from the fei beast. Bao, Mao Yun, and everyone else rode a bit off to the side, where they had a clear view of the entire area. If the fei beast ran, they would be able to keep eyes on it from quite a distance.

After everyone was in place, Wang Tian and the other disciple sent their horses galloping toward the fei beast at the greatest speed they felt was safe. As they neared, the fei beast looked up at them and let out a grunt that echoed like thunder.

When they were roughly twenty meters away, they drew their bows and loosed arrows. One arrow slammed into the fei beast's shoulder, the other landed in its chest. The creature bellowed in rage, rearing up on its hind legs.

As Wang Tian and the other disciple let loose another volley, the fei beast charged toward them. They immediately turned their horses around to flee.

However, the fei beast was much faster than any of them could have guessed. It began to close the distance rapidly, and soon it was only a few meters behind them. Just when it was almost upon them, Wang Tian turned his horse into the water, while the other disciple veered off in a different direction.

The fei beast turned toward Wang Tian, who was currently aiming for the far bank. While the second disciple galloped back toward the group, the fei beast leapt into the water. Wang Tian looked back in alarm, kicking his horse lightly to try to gain more speed. It was useless. A moment later, the fei beast was upon him. The creature swung its head, and its horns pierced Wang Tian's horse, lifting it into the air and then tossing it violently off to the side.

As the horse and Wang Tian landed in the water with a splash, the fei beast turned to look at the other disciple, who had just rejoined the group.

And then the fei beast began to run toward them.

"Dammit," growled Mao Yun.

Various other curses could be heard.

Bao gritted her teeth. Based on how fast the fei beast was

moving, she could tell that they only had a few seconds before it would be upon them. Her thoughts spun as quickly as lightning, and a moment later, she was galloping directly toward the fei beast.

I'm only going to have one shot at this. I'd better not miss. Be confident, Bao. Confident! You can do this!

As she closed in, she leapt up to stand on the back of the horse, using the energy in her body to make herself lighter, her feet steadier. She pulled out one of her trusty knives.

The fei beast's single eye was staring at her, bloodshot and filled with rage.

When it was only a few meters away, she crouched down and leapt straight into the air, using the energy in her body to propel herself with extraordinary speed and grace.

The fei beast reared its head, but she sailed over it, grabbing one of its horns as she passed, then using her momentum to swing down and lock her legs around the creature's massive neck. Its muscles were so powerful they fairly thrummed with strength.

Before the beast could react, she reached down with a knife and drew it across the fei beast's throat, slicing it as deep as she possibly could. Blood immediately began to spill out like a waterfall, and almost instantly, the creature's legs faltered. Once again channeling the energy in her body, she leapt off its back to land a few meters away.

The fei beast staggered about a bit, but the amount of blood pouring out of its neck was such that anyone could tell it only had a few moments of life left in it. Sure enough, it soon toppled over.

Bao sheathed her knife and smiled.

Confident.

CHAPTER 29
SCOUTS

Wang Tian suffered a broken arm but nothing more. They strapped the carcass of the fei beast onto the cart they had brought with them and then headed back to the cave of Ruan the Flamingo.

The return trip seemed to go by much faster than the journey to track down the fei beast.

Before long, the cave was in sight, and this time Ruan the Flamingo was waiting outside for them. He and the disciples were outside sharing a meal when Bao and the others approached on horseback. When Ruan saw the body of the fei beast, he leapt to his feet in surprisingly nimble fashion.

"Incredible!" he exclaimed, placing his crutch underneath his armpit and hobbling over to examine the creature.

"It went surprisingly smoothly," Bao said as Ruan poked and prodded the beast. "How is the work on the fallen star?"

"Oh, it's finished."

Bao was taken aback. "Finished? But I thought you needed the fei beast's eye?"

"Hmm?" Ruan looked up. "Oh, no. I just said I was missing an ingredient. I never said the ingredient was for the work with your star."

Bao gritted her teeth. "So we just risked our lives for nothing?"

"No, of course not. That was simply the price for my services. Would you like to see the result?"

Bao felt like smacking the man in his face, but instead she took a deep breath and hopped off her horse. "Yes, I would."

Ruan seemed to have become very comfortable with the disciples she had left behind, because he quickly ordered them to butcher the fei beast and store it in the "prescribed method." The young men immediately nodded, but he turned questioningly toward Bao a moment later. She nodded and followed Ruan back into his cave.

He led her to the same room they had met in before. This time, there was a wooden box on the table, simple but elegant. After they sat, Ruan reached out and put his hand on the lid.

"I have to be honest, Chieftainess Bao," he said. "Working with your fallen star was both easier than I had anticipated, and more difficult. The rituals involved were complex and draining to say the least. Whatever demon or entity is inside of it is powerful indeed. However, the method you used to tame or seal it... is profound. I won't ask the details, but suffice to say that you have my utter respect.

"As I worked with it, the material began to take shape on its own. It was almost as if the item created itself. Considering that I didn't touch it, I have no idea its properties or what it's capable of, but my instincts tell me that they will be a lesser version of whatever it could do in its raw form. For example, if before it could shine with the light of a hundred stars, now it will probably shine with the light of twenty stars, or perhaps fifty.

"But again, I can't be sure. If the item was dangerous to you before, I would suggest exercising caution in using it now."

"I understand," Bao said.

Without any further words, Ruan lifted the lid of the box.

Inside was the fallen star, but no longer was it an ugly rock. It was a crown, as blue as the sky on a summer day, decorated with intricate feather and floral patterns, accented with pearls, gemstones, and gold. Within the flowers, she could see three dragons and five phoenixes. Strangely, the dragons were gold and the phoenixes were bright red.

"This looks like… a wedding crown?" she murmured.

"Yes, I was surprised as well. It's a wedding crown, but it's blue and not red? Why? Anyway, like I said, it took shape on its own. It was almost as if I weren't even doing the work myself. See the gold and pearls, and the gemstones? They came out from within the starstone. I didn't add them. I'm not sure if there were actually such items hidden within, or whether they were somehow transformed as if by alchemy." He shrugged. "I've worked with many strange objects and powers before, but this was one of the strangest experiences. Most strange of all was… the screaming."

Bao looked up. "What do you mean?"

"Several times during the process, I heard screaming, faint but powerful. Whatever was locked inside of that star, and now the crown, was not happy."

Bao didn't respond. Instead she reached out slowly toward the crown. As her hand neared, she half expected something to happen, but nothing did. When her fingers touched the crown itself, she felt as if a burning yet freezing wind was blasting her mind.

The sensation quickly passed. She picked up the crown and put it on her head. Somehow, she could tell that the phoenix was still in the crown, restless, angry, but unable to do anything to her. Having bested it in a battle of will, it would now be forever subservient to her.

"Well?" Ruan asked.

"It fits perfectly," Bao replied.

"And the... effects?"

"You don't want to know what it does," she said.

He nodded. "That's true. I don't want to know."

She smiled. *So it does work as I expected it would...*

With that, she took off the crown and placed it back into the box. Then she clasped her hands and bowed her head toward Ruan. "Many thanks."

He grinned. "It was nothing."

***

It would have been difficult for the trip back to the stronghold to go any worse without it turning into a complete disaster. They got lost three times. They got caught in a torrential downpour twice. One of them lasted for three straight days. One of the horses broke a leg and had to be put down. Two disciples became ill.

Bao wondered more than once if it had something to do with the crown.

It got worse when they entered the forest, which was about the time the final bout of rainfall set in. Because of the dark clouds, the choking rivers of mud, the fallen trees, and other such things, their path was almost determined for them.

It was one of the most miserable things Bao had ever experienced, and that included being kidnapped and locked in a cage.

Eventually they emerged from the forest and found themselves on a hilly part of the mostly flat lands between Tung-On and Fan. For the time being, they were content to be out of the forest, and they set up camp and waited for the rain to pass.

When the rain clouds finally belched out the last raindrops, it was late in the evening. The stars came out, and the wind blew. The entire party breathed a sigh of relief, and Bao issued orders that everyone was to rest for the morning. They would set out at noon for the stronghold.

The following morning after breakfast, a scout was sent out as usual. He came galloping back into camp less than ten minutes later.

"Chieftainess," the scout said, "there's a large force on horseback, just to the east. Only a few hills that way." He pointed in the general direction. "They're definitely Demon Emperor soldiers."

"What were they doing?"

"Nothing at the moment, just sitting there. Looks like they were doing the same thing we were, camping to wait out the rain."

Bao bit her lip. *It could be nothing, just a patrol or something. But he said a large force.* "How many were in this large force?"

"About fifty, Chieftainess."

That's no patrol. That's more like a platoon.

"I want to take a closer look. Mao Yun, you stay here, get the men ready to move. I'll be back shortly." Looking at the scout, she said, "You lead the way."

It was a short ride. Eventually Bao dismounted, leaving her horse with the scout while she crawled to the top of the hill overlooking the camp. Just as the scout had said—the soldiers weren't doing anything at the moment.

However, it only took a moment before Bao's heart began to pound. In the center of the camp was one particularly large tent, outside of which stood two men wearing very distinctive armor. Armor made of bone.

The Bone General.

Moments later, someone rode into the camp from the north, a soldier who was clearly a scout. After dismounting, he hurried over to the tent in the center of the camp and was admitted by the bone-armored soldiers.

From the direction he was riding, it's not likely he came from Tung-On. Which leaves only… the Little Demon Forest. The Bone General has finally come back for us!

There was no more time for contemplation. Bao scurried back down the hill and used a bit of the energy in her body to propel her through the air, and she literally jumped up into the saddle.

She and the horse hurried back to camp. When she arrived, she was pleased to see that everyone was already prepared to move.

Not bothering to mince words, she said in loud voice, "It's the Bone General. And he's likely going to be heading to our stronghold. We need to get back and warn everyone right away!"

Eyes went wide, and faces drained of blood. Bao didn't give them any more time to think. "Let's go!"

***

Back in the very camp Bao had just been observing, in the central tent, the Bone General sat with his top lieutenants, listening to the report of the scout.

The scout described Bao's stronghold in detail, including how many people were there, the defensive capabilities, the surrounding terrain, the path leading to the stronghold, and numerous other details.

When he was finished, the Bone General said, "What about the girl? This Chieftainess Bao?"

"I didn't see her. I suspect she might not be there."

"Hmm. I see. I think the best move would be to take action immediately. If the girl is there, we take her. If not, we extract her location from the people she left behind. We'll get to her eventually. Any other opinions?"

One of his lieutenants took a deep breath and said, "Perhaps we should send squads around to the north and west. If she is in the stronghold, she'll likely flee either to the river or into the mountains."

"Agreed," the Bone General said. "Make the preparations. We leave within the hour."

CHAPTER 30
TREE PROTECTORS

R ide like your lives depend on it!" Bao said. And that was exactly what they did. The pounding of the horses' hooves was like war drums that filled their ears as they raced north.

There was no talk or conversation. Everyone was focused on one thing: escaping.

They veered northeast as the hills began to fill with more trees, allowing them to travel faster than if they entered the thickest parts of the forest itself.

The horses were soon sweating profusely, but it almost seemed as if they could sense the danger the group was in, and they focused completely on the rhythm of galloping.

When it came time, they entered the forest, using their knowledge of the area to pick the route most likely to be free from problems because of the recent rains.

They drew ever closer to the stronghold.

Meanwhile, the Bone General was not in such a hurry.

Despite his previous order to leave within the hour, a message arrived shortly after that from the south, something that required immediate attention. There had been an assassination attempt on Magistrate Zhou in the southern city of Huisheng, an incident which the Demon Emperor took extremely seriously. The council meeting which the Bone General had just adjourned was reconvened. Deliberations with his lieutenants stretched on for hours, and soon the sky was growing dark.

The soldiers waited the entire time, ready to gallop off at a moment's notice. In the end, though, the Bone General called for another night of rest.

The following day, they set out early. They had only been riding for a short time before they came across the tracks left by the frantic flight of Bao's group.

However, considering that the tracks headed to the northeast, there was little information to indicate who the group was, so the Bone General simply passed them by.

Soon they were in the forest, and the luck which had befallen Bao seemed to be transferred over to them almost immediately.

A horse broke a leg and had to be put down. They got lost. Every form of misfortune seemed to hit them at once.

As a result, their progress was excruciatingly slow, and the Bone General's fury began to mount. And yet, they drew inexorably closer to the stronghold.

***

As soon as Bao arrived back at the stronghold, she issued orders to evacuate.

Unfortunately, she quickly realized that it was no small task to uproot the lives of enough people to form a large town. Bags had to be packed. Wagons had to be loaded. Even the name of the Demon

Emperor didn't seem to speed them along any faster. Perhaps things might have moved more quickly if the stronghold had been engulfed in flames. In fact, Bao couldn't help but think back to the incident at Tung-On and seriously considered tossing oil lamps into some of the empty rooms to spur things along.

Scouts were sent out to the north and to the south. Although they were relatively familiar with the area, considering the recent storms, Bao wanted to make sure that the way north to the Chezou River was clear. Word soon came back that the path north was without obstacle.

As for the scouts who headed south, thanks to a particularly odd way that the path wound through a gorge, they ended up running right into two scouts that the Bone General had sent north. The two parties clashed, and Bao's men managed to kill one of the Bone General's scouts. The other escaped.

Based on the distances and times involved, it seemed likely that the Bone General was about one day of travel away from the stronghold at that point.

There was no time to waste. The final preparations were made, and the stronghold was emptied. They fled north at the fastest pace possible.

The entire time, Bao felt as if the Bone General was breathing down her neck. Originally she wanted to lead the group personally, but Mao Yun convinced her that it was too dangerous, and that she should ride farther back in the middle.

As she rode along, Bao kept the wooden box close at hand. If necessary, she could open it at a moment's notice and don her Phoenix Crown. An idea had taken root in her heart, a possibility that seemed preposterously dangerous. And yet, if worse came to worst, and they ended up being cornered or trapped by the Bone General, she wouldn't hesitate to use the crown.

When night fell, they lit torches and lamps and proceeded through the forest despite the darkness. Bao didn't push them through the entire night, though. A few hours after nightfall, they set up camp to rest.

The following morning, they woke with the sun and continued north. Before long, the trees began to thin out, and they could tell that they had reached the edge of the forest.

At a certain point, only about an hour after they began moving, Mao Yun fell back to ride next to Bao and said, "We're being followed."

She looked over at him and cocked an eyebrow.

"Not the Bone General," he added.

"Then who?"

He shrugged. "Three men and two women wearing plain clothing. They're spread out about ten meters apart from each other. Shadowing us about thirty meters to the east. No weapons visible. Quite odd, if you ask me."

Bao frowned. "Keep an eye on them."

He nodded and rode back toward the front of the procession.

An hour later, Mao Yun fell back again. "More people, this time to the west."

"What about the group to the east?"

"They're still there, just walking along at the same pace."

Over the course of the following hours, the number of people flanking them grew. There were men and women, young and old, all of them dressed in plain greenish clothing, without a weapon to be seen on any of them. More people were visible farther off in the distance. Eventually it reached the point that Mao Yun and Bao were convinced that they were outnumbered.

Sometime in the hours before evening, they reached a part of the forest that looked different than the others. The forest in general was filled with a wild assortment of trees and vegetation, but this area had only small maple trees, and virtually no other vegetation. It almost seemed like a grove.

Mao Yun called a halt and rode back yet again to confer with Bao.

"There's a group of people up ahead led by a woman. She demands to speak to the leader."

Bao looked down at the wooden case she held in her hands and gritted her teeth. Well aware that the Bone General could be arriving at any moment, she decided that now wasn't the time to worry about ethics. Without any further hesitation, she opened the box and put the Phoenix Crown on her head, then rode forward.

Up ahead was a group of about twenty people, led by a beautiful woman. Oddly, the group stood between two large maple trees that had carvings of faces on their trunks. The faces' eyes were closed, but their expressions seemed to be twisted in pain. It was a very disconcerting sight.

As for the beautiful woman, she wore a fine green gown and was festooned with jewelry made from blue pearls. There was something strange about the way she carried herself, almost as if she looked down upon all other living things. Although Bao was certain that she had never seen this woman before, there was something about her that seemed strangely familiar. After a moment, she realized that the way the woman carried herself reminded her of the phoenix demon in the falling star.

Is she an immortal? Bao thought. *A goddess? A demon?*

The woman smiled as Bao approached.

"Greetings, young woman," she said. "Are you the leader of this… group?"

Bao nodded. "Yes, my lady. We're traveling north. Urgently."

"I see. May I ask where you're traveling from? Do you, by any chance, come from the stronghold to the south?"

Bao's eyes narrowed. "Perhaps…"

"The stronghold to the south is built out of trees harvested from this forest, correct?" The woman's eyes glittered in a way that caused Bao's heart to tremble.

"I didn't build the stronghold," Bao said. "My lady, we just want to leave this forest and cross the river to the north. If you have no pressing business, may I request that we be allowed to pass?"

This is ridiculous. We could crush these people like dried twigs if they tried to fight us.

"So you *do* come from the stronghold," the woman said, her expression turning grim. "That's quite sad. For you, at least. The Little Demon Forest has a new ruler. Me."

Bao was slightly taken aback. "Ruler of the forest? My lady, I don't care at all about this forest. You can have it. We just want to leave."

Shockingly, the woman's face twisted into a furious scowl. "You don't care about the forest? My forest? You chop down the trees here, torture them into your foul *furniture*? Burn it to cook your disgusting meat? Murderers! Barbarians! *Animals!*" she screeched at the top of her lungs. "Disciples, kill them! I want a chair made from human flesh and bone!"

The eyes of the faces on the trees opened, and their mouths gaped wide as they let out bellows of fury. Crackling sounds could be heard as armlike branches stretched out from the trunks of the trees toward Bao.

Faces twisting with rage, the disciples surrounding the woman reached into their garments and produced blue pearls. Most shocking of all was that the countless maple trees surrounding them began to twist and distort as they transformed into people.

Despite the fact that it was like a scene from a nightmare, Bao kept her cool. The fighters among her group all began to draw their weapons, but the last thing she wanted was a fight.

Before anything else could happen, she raised her voice and said, "If any of you move a muscle, you'll die instantly!"

The bizarre trees stopped moving, as did most of the men and women in green robes. The transformed trees looked around in confusion.

As for the woman, her face twitched, and she slowly shook her head.

"Who are you? That aura... it's so familiar. It's the aura of... no, impossible! How dare you try to compel me against my will! *How dare you!*"

With an ear-piercing scream, the woman threw her hands out to her sides and began to change shape. Her skin turned dark and brown, and she began to grow taller. Her hair transformed into leaves, and her feet became roots that sank into the ground. In the space of a few breaths of time, she had transformed into a towering maple tree.

Her face was still visible, and it was distorted with rage. "I am Shu Shu, and I am the ruler of this forest. I don't care what your relationship is with Mistress Phoenix—you will die this day!"

Bao's scalp tingled with fear. *This has got to work. Come on, Bao, you can do it!*

"Lady Shu Shu, hear my words," she said. "We are not your enemies. We are lovers of the forest, protectors of the trees! We simply wish to pass through!"

Shu Shu's lips twitched, but after a moment, her face went calm. "You are lovers of the forest..."

"Yes. We are tree protectors. You want to let us pass!"

Shu Shu blinked. "Of course. Disciples, let these tree protectors pass!"

The transformed trees seemed confused, as did the other disciples, but they didn't argue. The disciples put their blue pearls back into their robes, and the transformed trees returned to their tree forms.

The gigantic trees flanking Shu Shu closed their eyes.

Heart pounding, Bao looked back at Mao Yun. "Let's go. *Now.*"

***

A few hours later, the Bone General was conferring with a scout some distance to the south.

"Sir, there is an odd maple grove up ahead. Their tracks lead right through it."

"A maple grove? Are there people present?"

"Yes, none of them armed. Perhaps a village of timbermen."

The Bone General frowned. "Very well. If they resist, we'll tie them to their own trees and burn them alive."

CHAPTER 31
DELICACIES

Many weeks earlier

Sunan led his men back to Daolu at a breakneck pace. They rested only when necessary and were completely focused on the journey.

There was no casual chatting.

When they returned to the city, they immediately convened a council of the most trusted members of the Golden Dragon Sect. In the past, Sunan and Sun Mai had casually discussed what would be involved in defending the city against invaders. This time, they delved into it in greater detail.

Troop placements were discussed, strategies for reinforcing walls. They even considered the idea of sending men to fight outside of the walls. One of the members of the council was Sima Zikang, who had proved himself exceptionally talented when it came to matters of strategy and tactics. With his input, they soon had a masterful plan in place for how to withstand a siege.

After hours of discussion, it was Yuwen Huo who finally broached a certain subject that many of the others had been wondering about from the very beginning. "Sect Leader, why are we talking about this?"

Sunan's face darkened. "Because of the threat to Daolu!"

Yuwen Huo and Tie Gangwen exchanged a glance.

Tie Gangwen cleared his throat. "Sect Leader, what is this threat of which you speak?"

"The great threat," Sunan replied. "You know… the great threat! Isn't it an army?"

Tie Gangwen grimaced. "Sect Leader, there are no reports of any armies. Nothing has happened since the burning of Tung-On all that time ago. They even say that the Bone General headed south to fight some invaders or something along those lines."

Sunan and Sun Mai looked at each other very seriously.

"Assassination!" Sun Mai exclaimed. "It must be an assassination. Magistrate Pei Bai might be a figurehead, but killing him would send the common people into chaos."

"That must be it," Sunan replied. Subsequently, they discussed how an assassination might be carried out, how they could defend against it, and how to unveil the assassin ahead of time. They also planned how to deal with the consequences of such an assassination, were it to be carried out effectively.

Somehow, the conversation eventually switched to the possibility of a natural disaster.

Then they talked about drought and famine.

It wasn't until two days later that Sunan and Sun Mai finally realized they had somehow been compelled into believing something that wasn't true.

Neither of them was the type of person who cared a lot about face; they weren't so much embarrassed as irritated. In fact, the other disciples seemed far more embarrassed than they were.

"She must be a witch," Sun Mai mused. "Some kind of Yen-Li cultist."

"I don't think so," Sunan replied. "It was that fallen star. As soon as she touched it, something happened to her. Her eyes turned silver, and her voice changed. Then everything she said…"

"We did."

Sunan nodded grimly. Further speculation about the matter was relatively useless. Sunan and Sun Mai were determined to be on the watch for Chieftainess Bao in the future, and they spread word through the Golden Dragon Sect about her powers and potential ways to defend against it.

After the ill-fated adventure south of the Chezou River, things returned to relative monotony for a period of time. Months went by, during which the primary focus was training and the administration of the Golden Dragon Sect.

However, that calmness didn't last for long.

A letter arrived for Sunan from the south, from none other than the Demon Emperor's Love General.

It was delivered by three Lions of Peace on horseback. They swaggered about arrogantly, and yet it wasn't lost on Sunan that they were careful to show him a modicum of respect.

The letter was a simple request for information regarding Sunan's intentions regarding Daolu and the territories surrounding it, and whether or not he would "consider suggestions" provided by the Demon Emperor.

Considering that the city was officially part of the Hen-Shi Empire and ruled by Magistrate Pei Bai, the letter was very telling.

After much deliberation regarding what to say, Sun Mai crafted a vaguely worded response that they hoped would come across as deferential and yet not a declaration of support or allegiance. The letter was taken away immediately by the Lions of Peace, who didn't even stay in the city overnight.

A second letter came more quickly than either Sunan or Sun Mai had imagined it would, after less than a month had passed.

This letter contained more pointed questions, requests, and

even a few "suggestions" regarding various aspects of Daolu law and administration.

The response to this letter was much more difficult to craft. It took a full two days before both Sunan and Sun Mai were happy with the contents, whereupon the Lions of Peace rode back south.

This time, a whole month passed by with no response. Then another. And another.

Sun Mai seemed to have forgotten about the matter after the first month, but Sunan was very nervous. With each day that passed in which no response came, that nervousness grew. He could imagine numerous possible scenarios playing out, and none of them were good.

According to the news that filtered across the Chezou River, a major rebellion had broken out somewhere in the south. The Bone General, the Fire General, and the majority of the Demon Emperor's armies had been sent to quell it. But Sunan couldn't shake the feeling that the Demon Emperor would eventually turn his gaze to the north.

The so-called Hen-Shi Empire was the only thing that existed south of the Huang Mountains and north of the Chezou River. There was simply no way that the Demon Emperor would just allow it to exist free of his rule forever. And when the time came that his armies marched north, what would happen? Sunan couldn't imagine himself acknowledging allegiance and actually working for the Demon Emperor. And yet he also couldn't imagine himself leading a fight against him. A fight like that would be stupid and essentially suicidal.

But what other options could there possibly be than those two? Running? Sunan didn't care much about face, but he certainly didn't want to be labeled as a coward.

Like it or not, he had somehow ended up in a position of relative authority in the city, with people who looked up to him and respected him, even relied upon him. How could he possibly bring himself to simply abandon them?

He mulled over matters like this constantly as he waited for another communication from the Love General.

The response finally came on the first day of the second cycle of the fourth lunar month, the Demon Moon. Although Sunan wasn't given to extreme belief in signs and portents, the fact that the response came on that date was unnerving.

He became even more unnerved when he saw the contents of the letter.

To the most honorable and righteous Sect Leader Sunan:

It is my distinct pleasure to send one of my most trusted lieutenants to meet with you personally and discuss the matters which, up to this point, have been only briefly touched on in our written communications. Huang Dayang is a wise and circumspect man who is very familiar with Daolu and will surely be able to offer you the soundest of counsel. He is accompanied by Lady Yan, one of my most trusted advisors.

Unfortunately, an incident occurred in Daolu some time ago that you may or may not be aware of. One of the Lions of Peace was cruelly cut down by two unnamed assailants. I was frankly shocked by such a show of barbarism and disrespect. Because of that, I have instructed Huang Dayang to camp some distance from the city and await your presence for a meeting of the minds.

Even as you read this letter, he will be waiting patiently to speak with you in person. As a show of goodwill, the bearer of this letter also brings a chest filled with various valuables and treasures—a gift for you.

Please make the arrangements necessary to meet with Lieutenant Huang as quickly as possible.

Regards,
Love General

Discussing the matter would help little, so he and Sun Mai quickly went about making the necessary preparations. The last thing to be settled was the clothing. For Sun Mai, it wasn't a difficult matter. He wore scholar robes of the finest silk with a jade abacus tucked into the belt.

When asked about the abacus, he explained that since they might be entering into a negotiation, it might come in handy.

When it came to Sunan's clothing, things didn't go as smoothly. He wasn't fond of silk brocade, so when Sun Mai suggested he wear voluminous robes embroidered with dragons, he refused. After much bickering, Sun Mai finally said, "How about some armor?"

"Armor? What am I, a soldier?"

"You're a leader. Like a general!"

Sunan closed his eyes and rubbed his temples. "I'm not a general. I don't lead an army. Come on, Sun Mai…"

"Well, you can't go naked. Quit being a child and just pick something!"

After a bit of grumbling, he finally made a decision. "Fine. Armor. I'd rather be a general than a stuffy lord."

***

Several hours later, Sunan and Sun Mai found themselves in a strange situation. They had originally assumed that Huang Dayang would come with an entire regiment of Lions of Peace, and would attempt to cow them with threats of doom and gloom. Instead, he had only three people with him. Two were Lions of Peace. One was a woman.

They had set up a small open-air pavilion on the plains to the east of the city and were waiting just a few paces outside of it.

Considering Sunan and Sun Mai had brought an escort of fifty disciples, all armed to the teeth, they couldn't help but feel a bit silly. Stationing the men a short distance away, they approached Huang

Dayang on foot, bringing Yuwen Huo and another young soldier named Shisan with them as escorts.

As they neared the pavilion, the gazes of all four young men were drawn to the woman.

Sunan was convinced that she was the most beautiful woman he had ever seen in his life. At first he took her to be a foreigner because she had long crimson hair. But her facial features were typical of the women of Qi Xien, except this particular woman was perfect in every aspect. She wore a long pink gown of modern fashion, expertly tailored to complement her curvaceous figure.

Sunan had a hard time tearing his eyes away from her to look at Huang Dayang. Clasping his hands in greeting, he said, "I am Sunan. Greetings, Lieutenant Huang."

Huang Dayang clasped hands in return. "Greetings, Sect Leader Sunan. I've heard much spoken of your illustrious name. Please, have a seat." He gestured to a table in the pavilion, upon which was spread various delicacies. Sunan didn't recognize many of the food items, but one clay pot had the words "Naqani Heavenly Honey" on it, and there was a flagon labeled "Dhammi Rice Wine." Sunan had only heard of such distant places, let alone eaten foods from there. The other delicacies on the table were presumably equally fantastic.

The two Lions of Peace didn't sit at the table, so Sunan ordered Yuwen Huo and Shisan to wait a few paces outside of the pavilion.

After they all sat down, Huang Dayang poured some of the Dhammi rice wine into some drinking vessels and passed them around. Then he raised his own vessel and said, "If you fear poison, there is no need to drink. I won't be offended. Please, allow me to offer a toast, Sect Leader Sunan. I wish you good health and increased power here in the north. To you!"

With that, he drank deeply, as did the woman.

Sunan didn't hesitate to join them.

Huang Dayang smiled and nodded. "Before discussing the

important matters at hand, why don't we eat? I've brought many delicacies from all over Qi Xien. For example, this is cured deer meat from Heiping Valley. Over here are steamed mantis shrimps from the Yao Yun Sea. And over there…"

Huang Dayang went on to explain all of the dishes, and Sunan's mind began to spin. Each and every one seemed to be completely fresh, whether they were fried, grilled, or even baked. Most were still steaming hot, and yet there was clearly no kitchen nearby or even any people other than the Lions of Peace. How was so much fresh food here in the middle of the wilderness?

After finishing his food explanations, Huang Dayang snapped his fingers. "How could I have forgotten! Please allow me to introduce Lady Yan from Xuanlu."

Lady Yan smiled. "Greetings, Sect Leader Sunan. Greetings, Chief Minister Sun."

Sunan smiled in return. "Greetings, Lady Yan."

For the following hour or so, they sampled the delicacies and chatted randomly. Both Huang Dayang and Lady Yan seemed to be expert conversationalists. Sunan was actually surprised to find that he thoroughly enjoyed interacting with them. Somehow, matters relating to the Demon Emperor were never mentioned.

At a certain point, however, Huang Dayang cleared his throat. "Very well, enough with the pleasantries. The time has come to explain why I'm here."

Underneath the table, Sunan clenched his fists nervously.

CHAPTER 32
ANYTHING!

A day later, Sunan sat in the main reception hall, chin resting on the palm of his left hand. He sighed.

On his right was Sun Mai, like usual. To the left was someone new attending their daily meetings: Lady Yan. The conversation the previous day had been long and complicated, but in the end Sunan agreed to accept her as an honorary advisor, representing the Demon Emperor in Daolu.

He had been staunchly opposed to the idea at first, but Huang Dayang had made a strong case that even Sun Mai agreed with in the end. Lady Yan, who Huang Dayang assured Sunan had extensive political experience, would provide him with advice and help in managing affairs but would refrain from interfering in anything beyond that. She was being sent as an expression of good faith by the Demon Emperor, who supposedly wasn't interested in northern expansion and only wanted to forestall lawlessness and chaos.

Sunan reluctantly agreed.

Now here they were, hearing petitions from locals, a task which

Sunan loathed to begin with, and he felt even more uncomfortable now that Lady Yan was present to witness his ineptitude.

Thankfully, things had gone well. Lady Yan had even offered a few good pieces of advice that sped the process along. They were finally on to the last petition of the day.

A dour and unpleasant-looking man strode into the audience chamber, the final petitioner. He wore an eclectic assortment of garments and had his hair bound up with twigs, making him look like some sort of priest.

After situating himself, the man bowed formally and said, "Greetings, Sect Leader Sunan. Greetings... Chief Minister Sun." His lips twisted when he greeted Sun Mai, and his eyes flickered with displeasure. Looking over at Lady Yan, he hesitated and then said, "Greetings..."

"This is Lady Yan," Sunan said.

"Greetings, Lady Yan. I am Luo Jiabao, a local geomancer of some note, and a loyal citizen of Daolu."

"Greetings, Geomancer Luo.

"You're Smiling Luo!" Sun Mai cried.

Smiling Luo frowned. "Chief... Chief Minister Sun, that is indeed the name many people call me."

"I remember you! Your shop used to be right across from my stall in the market! Smiling Luo's Geomancy Services, right?"

"That's correct."

"Well, do you remember me? Scholar Sun Mai's Sundry Services? Calligraphy, letter writing, city guide?"

Smiling Luo snorted coldly. "Counterfeit documents? Illegal forgeries? Yes, I remember."

Sun Mai cleared his throat. "Well, nobody could ever prove I did anything illegal..."

"I'm very familiar with your *services*, Chief Minister Sun. But that's not why I'm here." He turned his attention back to Sunan, his frown deepening. "Sect Leader Sunan, a grave problem has arisen in the city. Demons. I'm aware of at least two pernicious demons that are at large, plaguing the populace. One of them has been seen numerous times around a local establishment called the Heavenly Meat Palace."

Sun Mai clapped his hands together. "Heavenly Meat Palace! We love that place."

Smiling Luo glared at Sun Mai. "I'm aware." He sniffed. "The other demon haunts the Chezou River and has reportedly taken the lives of at least three or four fishermen."

"I've heard stories of both demons," Sunan said, "but this is my first time hearing any reports that they are dangerous in any way."

"Oh, they're dangerous, Sect Leader Sunan. Very dangerous. I'm here to petition that you cleanse Daolu of these demon plagues. Restore peace to the hearts of the people."

Sunan looked over at Sun Mai, who shrugged.

"Three fishermen were killed?" Sun Mai asked.

Smiling Luo cleared his throat. "Supposedly. Regardless of the actual number, these demons won't just go away. They will continue to grow stronger, and their appetites will increase. It will only be a matter of time before children are spirited away during the night! When they're strong enough to fight soldiers, what will you do then? The time to act is now, Sect Leader Sunan. Thankfully, I happen to be very skilled in geomancy, and I know a thing or two about the supernatural. I've even killed a few demons and ghosts in my time. I would be more than happy to handle this matter for you, for a modest fee, of course."

Lady Yan chuckled. "Sect Leader Sunan, might I offer an opinion here?"

Sunan nodded.

"I've traveled all over the empire, and I have seen creatures the likes of which Mr. Luo can't even dream of. I once saw a roc kill two armored soldiers with the single sweep of a claw. I once saw a raksha demon bite the head off a man and drink his blood. In the far south,

I witnessed two fifteen-meter-long nagas fighting each other. Trees were felled and boulders crushed into dust. Being new to Daolu, I can't attest to the validity of the demon stories spun by Mr. Luo. But I can tell you that if dangerous demons were here, you would know about it. I suspect Mr. Luo is more interested in earning a few spades than protecting the safety of the citizens here."

Silence prevailed in the room for a long moment. It was broken by Sun Mai.

"I also have a question. You're called Smiling Luo, right? How come you never smile? That's kind of strange, don't you think?"

Smiling Luo's eyes widened, and veins bulged out on his neck and forehead. "Why don't I smile? *Why don't I smile?* How could I smile with a charlatan like you in the room! You con artist! I actually can perform geomancy, and I have actually killed demons. Real demons. But what about you? Back in the market, you cheated your customers constantly and lied about everything. And now you're basically in charge of the city? Damn you, Sun Mai! I hope that I don't kill those demons, I hope that I capture them. Then I'll feed you to them, one bite a time! I'll start with your feet so you can't escape! Then your hands, and then—"

"All right, enough!" barked Sunan. "Men, escort Mr. Luo out, please."

As the soldiers grabbed Smiling Luo by the arms, he shouted, "You're making a mistake! The demons are real! As real as Hen-Shi's hand! They'll get bigger and cause more problems. I really have killed demons and ghosts! It's all true…"

His voice slowly faded away into the distance as the soldiers dragged him away.

After another prolonged silence, Sunan rose to his feet. "Thank you, Lady Yan. You saved me the trouble of refusing him directly."

Lady Yan and Sun Mai also rose.

"There's no need for thanks," Lady Yan replied. "Now that court is adjourned, I'll take my leave."

Sunan nodded and prepared to head back to his residence to do some training.

Lady Yan glided toward the door, then stopped and looked over her shoulder. "Oh, by the way, Sect Leader Sunan, I was hoping to get your opinion on a certain matter. If you have the time, could I trouble you to stop by my residence later this afternoon or evening? I won't take too much of your time. We can meet in the open pavilion in the outer courtyard, so there won't be any breach in decorum."

Sunan's eyes narrowed very slightly, but after a moment he nodded. "Of course."

Lady Yan smiled and left.

"What do you think?" Sunan asked, looking over at Sun Mai.

Sun Mai shrugged. "Who knows. A few demons in the city might be kind of exciting."

Sunan sighed. "I mean about Lady Yan."

"Oh. Hmm… Well, I doubt she's dangerous. I'm almost completely certain she has no qi in her."

Sunan nodded. "I've reached the same conclusion. Well, there's only one way to find out."

***

Later that afternoon, Sunan found himself sitting in the outer courtyard of Lady Yan's residence, in a small pavilion that sat at the edge of a fishpond. The courtyard was small but beautiful, complete with a peach tree and a statue of an elephant. Lady Yan was currently pouring boiled water into two porcelain teacups, within which were some whole tea leaves. Sunan struggled to keep his eyes focused on the teacups and not her jadelike skin or ample chest.

"Sect Leader Sunan, thank you very much for providing such a lovely residence," she said.

"No need for thanks," he said, looking into her eyes and nodding. Her eyes were like limpid pools of water that almost seemed to grab him and pull him toward her. With some difficulty, he tore his gaze back to the teacups. "I have to say, I've never seen tea prepared this way. Usually it's ground up, isn't it?"

She nodded. "This is a way we drink tea back home in... well, where I come from. It's already starting to become popular down south. People say that the flavor is purer. Of course, the traditional way is still popular, but I have to admit that despite all of my traveling and experience, I never trained in the proper way to hold the ceremony." With that, she lifted her teacup and used the lid to sweep back the tea leaves. After taking a sip, she nodded. "Please, have a taste."

After sampling the tea, his eyes went wide. "Amazing!"

Lady Yan smiled. "It's a green tea from the Mount Peng region, far to the south. In the local dialect, they call it swallow-tail tea. If you look at the leaves, you'll notice that they resemble the tails of swallows."

Sunan peered into the teacup to find that the leaves did look very much like swallow tails. He took another sip. "This is truly wonderful. I've never had tea like this before."

"I imagine there are many things you haven't experienced. From what I've heard, you grew up in Daolu, is that right?"

"No, but it was close to here."

"The north is wonderful, but in the south, there is so much to see and taste and smell." She sighed and took another sip of tea.

The wind blew, rustling the leaves of the peach tree.

Sunan cleared his throat. "Lady Yan, you said you wanted my opinion on something?"

"Of course. Actually, the truth is a bit more complicated." She looked down into her teacup. "Sect Leader Sunan, I'm... I'm afraid."

Sunan was a bit taken aback. "Afraid?"

"Maybe nervous is a better word. I'm a woman... alone... I'm surrounded by, perhaps not the enemy but at least... hostile forces. Your soldiers, the way they look at me... it's disconcerting. Please, don't misunderstand: I've traveled the world and am no stranger to soldiers or to dangerous situations. But usually I'm escorted by soldiers loyal to me. Right now, I have no one to rely on."

"Lady Yan, I can assure you, you're perfectly safe."

"I know, I know. But you have to understand, there are people who hate the King of the Pure Ones with a passion beyond reason. Even in places completely loyal to him, there are some zealots who would go to any lengths to harm someone who serves him. Is there any chance you could spare a man or two to stand guard outside my residence and escort me through the streets when necessary?"

As soon as the request left her lips, Sunan felt foolish. Even if she was a servant of the Demon Emperor, she was still a spectacularly beautiful woman, and to ask her to wander the streets of a strange city alone was definitely inappropriate.

"I'll arrange it immediately, Lady Yan," he said. "I apologize for not having thought to do so earlier. It's really a breach of etiquette."

She smiled. "It's fine. I could tell right away that you are not a man of the court. It's only normal for you to overlook such matters."

Sunan took another sip of tea. "Lady Yan, since we're on the subject, do you mind me asking a question?"

"Anything."

He paused for a moment, then said took a deep breath and said, "Why are you really here?"

CHAPTER 33
THREE PIECES OF PAPER

Lady Yan's eyes flickered, and the faintest of smiles appeared on her lips. "That's a fair question."

"Lady Yan, you're right. I'm just an ordinary person. I don't like intrigues and schemes. I'd prefer to just get straight to the point. If you'd rather not answer, I understand. But maybe we could both save each other some time and be direct about things."

Lady Yan tucked a stray hair behind her ear and took another sip of tea. "The truth is that I'm here to... recruit you."

"Recruit me to work for the Demon Emperor?"

"Not quite. I don't report directly to King of the Pure Ones. I represent a faction within the empire that wishes to... restore balance."

"Balance? What balance?"

"The balance that existed before the wars began."

"You mean before the Demon Emperor began to slaughter the people of Qi Xien." Sunan said it like a statement, not a question.

A look of sadness flickered across Lady Yan's face. "Sect Leader

Sunan, there are many things that you have no way of knowing. The King of the Pure Ones came to this land long before you were even born. The truth is that originally, he had no intentions other than peaceful ones. You see, he comes from another world, a place where he was a champion of peace and justice. He fell victim to a heinous plot by the dark forces there and was exiled to this world along with his wife and other loyal friends and followers. After finding that he had no way to return, he decided to once again lead his people in the fight for good here in Qi Xien.

"Sadly, tragedy struck almost immediately. His wife was killed by a local thief, sending him into the depths of grief. Some of his advisors took advantage of his weakness to manipulate him into believing that the people of Qi Xien hated his kind, what you might call a dwarf. The campaigns and the wars were led mostly by his ogre generals, while the King of the Pure Ones languished in despair.

"He eventually fell into a coma, and he has been asleep for decades. The person who has appeared in public is not the true King of the Pure Ones but rather a body double.

I belong to a group who wishes to awaken the king and bring an end to the tyranny and evil spread by his generals. If the king were to see the misery spawned by the wars his own armies fought, he would absolutely step in to administer justice.

"Sect Leader Sunan, I'm taking a huge risk by explaining these things now. If word spread, many of my people would be in extreme risk. I'd originally hoped to win your trust before offering this explanation, but... there's something about you, something that makes me feel deep in my heart... that I can trust you." She leaned forward and looked deep into Sunan's eyes. "Please, I beg of you, keep this information secret. Too many lives are at stake, and perhaps... perhaps even the future of Qi Xien."

Sunan's heart pounded in his chest. Lady Yan's gaze seemed to penetrate all the way into his soul and wrap around it like a soft, warm hand. A moment later, she looked down to pour some more water into her teacup, and the feeling faded away. He took a deep breath.

"Of course I'll keep your secret, Lady Yan." He was quite skeptical about the tale she had just told but decided that now wasn't the best time to say so. "To tell you the truth, I didn't want to be in the position I'm in. I never wanted to be a leader or be responsible for other people. Everything just... happened. In any case, I'm not sure how I could help you. Outside of Daolu, I'm nobody, and even inside of it, I'm really just a kid from a farming village who learned a bit about fighting."

Lady Yan smiled and reached out to clasp his forearm gently. When her hand touched his arm, he almost jerked it back in shock. Now that he thought about it, he'd never really been touched by a woman before other than his mother or sisters.

"Sect Leader Sunan, you are no child anymore. Trust me, you are destined for greatness. And I just hope that when you reach that greatness, you will be willing to side with those who champion what is good and just."

"Of... of course," he stammered, thinking mostly about how smooth the skin of her hand looked.

A moment later, she pulled her hand back. "Now then, why don't you wait here for just a moment while I go fetch some more boiled water. It would be a shame to let these tea leaves go to waste."

***

For the rest of the day, Sunan couldn't stop thinking about Lady Yan. Of course, the story she'd told him lurked in the back of his mind, but it was her beauty that occupied his heart. The graceful curve of her cheeks, her fiery hair, the way her chest rose and fell when she breathed. At one point, he imagined himself reaching out to touch her and shook his head to clear his thoughts.

He was utterly distracted, to the point where Yuwen Huo

actually landed a punch on his jaw in their afternoon sparring session, nearly knocking him unconscious. At first, Yuwen Huo was horrified, until Sunan started laughing and congratulated him. That punch cleared his head of thoughts of Lady Yan temporarily.

But later that night, when Sunan was trying to fall asleep, she once again appeared in his thoughts.

Eventually, sleep took him, but later on, he was dreaming, and there she was again. She threw herself into his arms, and he could feel her curves pressing up against him.

"Sunan," she said, sounding a bit breathless, "I'm afraid. Please hold me."

"You don't need to be afraid," he replied. "I'm here." His left hand came to rest on her hip, and his right hand slid along her neck as he pulled her lips closer to his.

Suddenly, everything changed. He looked up, shocked, and found that a black wind was screaming all around him. Lady Yan vanished. He flew up into the air to find himself looking down at a black vortex, something like a swirling black hurricane. As he flew farther and farther away, he realized that the black wind was spinning above a huge circular object that resembled a dragon and a phoenix interlocked. The dragon and phoenix began to emanate golden light, which shone brighter and brighter as it rose up into the sky, which was filled with towering golden clouds.

Then, strangely, everything vanished, and he found himself staring into Lady Yan's eyes again.

A clanging sound filled his ears, and Sunan opened his eyes. In that exact moment, someone started banging on his door.

"Sect Leader Sunan, are you safe?"

Shaking his head to clear his thoughts, he sat up and mumbled, "I'm fine. What happened?"

"An intruder was lurking near your window! Lieutenant Yuwen is chasing after him right now."

"Keep me posted."

With that, Sunan lay back down and stared up into the darkness of the ceiling, thinking about Lady Yan.

***

The following morning, Yuwen Huo reported that he had chased a mysterious intruder out of the compound and across the rooftops of Daolu. Yuwen Huo was convinced that it was a woman. He said that she wore a gray robe and was definitely a qi user. She moved with incredible quickness, and at one point she even flew through the air like a bird. She eventually disappeared over the walls of the temple of Supreme Judge Yu.

The entire thing was mysterious enough to begin with, but when Yuwen Huo said it was a woman in a gray robe, a strange feeling rose up in Sunan's heart. This wasn't the first time he'd been told a woman in a gray robe had been seen lurking around him at night. Sun Mai had also mentioned something similar, though that had been quite some time ago.

Taking both Sun Mai and Yuwen Huo with him, he headed over the temple to make some inquiries, only to find that it was closed to the public. According to the priest at the gate, a red star had been spotted recently, which the abbot of the temple took to be an ill omen. As such, the temple was closed while the priests performed various rituals to beseech Supreme Judge Yu for protection.

It seemed too suspicious to Sunan and Sun Mai, so after night fell, they decided to do some investigating of their own. The temple of Supreme Judge Yu was located roughly in the center of the city, with the southern half of the temple being a lush vegetated area called the Cypress and Hibiscus Garden. Considering how far away it was from the living quarters, Sunan and Sun Mai decided that it would be the best place to surreptitiously sneak into the temple. The moon hung low in the sky as they climbed up the southern wall of the temple, clad in black garments from head to toe.

Crouching on the wall, they looked out over the Cypress and Hibiscus Garden, and Sunan immediately noticed that a fire was burning in the center of the garden.

"Sun Mai, do you see that?"

Sun Mai nodded. "Let's go."

Sun Mai hopped off the wall into the garden first, and just as Sunan was about to follow him, something flickered in his peripheral vision. He turned his head and was sure that he saw someone in a gray robe leaping over the far eastern wall. Frowning, he dropped down and began to follow Sun Mai as he ran through the trees in the direction of the fire.

Moments later, they found themselves standing outside a small pagoda. A brazier had been set up outside, within which burned a small fire. When Sunan realized that what was burning were a few pieces of paper, he immediately lunged over and pulled them out, throwing them to the ground and stamping on them to put out the fire.

Meanwhile, Sun Mai stepped closer to the pagoda. "There's a bedroll in here. A bowl. A cup. Someone's been sleeping here."

Frowning, Sunan squatted and looked down at what remained of the papers he'd rescued from the fire. One of them was a crudely drawn map of the mansion he and Sun Mai lived in. Another was a list of names, many of whom he recognized as his own disciples. A third, which had been badly damaged and was mostly destroyed, seemed to contain some poetry.

> The graceful Bird due south takes wing,
> From north to east the clouds surge forth,
> From south to west fair feathers sing.
> The fiends, a tempest dark and foul,
> A shining pillar paints the sky,
> Golden droplets spin and—

He handed the scrap of paper over to Sun Mai. "You're the scholar. Does this look familiar?"

Sun Mai looked at the poetry for a moment before shaking his head. "I've memorized all the classic poetry and have never seen those lines before. They're not even composed in the traditional manner. Amateurish at best."

They looked through the items in the pagoda but didn't find anything of note. Neither did they find anything in the rest of the garden after snooping around for an hour or so. The other areas of the temple seemed too well-lit, so they eventually abandoned their search and returned to the mansion.

Tie Gangwen was waiting for them.

"Sect Leader. Chief Minister. I have grave news. Some men on patrol outside the city were killed."

"Killed?" Sun Mai exclaimed. "How?"

Tie Gangwen took a deep breath. "A demon, Chief Minister. A river demon."

CHAPTER 34
BLUE

They set out the following morning at dawn. Tie Gangwen picked five men, and Yuwen Huo picked five men. Sunan donned his armor. Sun Mai wore his normal scholar's robes.

"I don't like armor," he declared.

"Sun Mai, we're going out to fight a demon…"

Sun Mai turned his chin up. "I'm a thinker, not a fighter."

Sunan shook his head.

They headed out of the city's Zhen Gate, which led to the south. According to the accounts, the soldiers had been ambushed by the river demon near the prawn farms west of the city. Shellfish had long been one of the primary foods for the people living along the Chezou River, and considering the sizeable population of Daolu, it was little wonder that locals had established farms to fuel the demand in the city. Sunan had often wondered how the Heavenly Meat Palace managed to get their hands on so many prawns that they could serve them endlessly, and now he knew.

Eventually they reached the spot where the fight had occurred, and sure enough, there was plenty of evidence to corroborate the soldiers' story. However, there was no river demon present. After searching the immediate area, they decided to split up. Sun Mai and Tie Gangwen would head inland a bit while Sunan and Yuwen Huo would continue west along the river.

Unfortunately, after traveling west for about two hours, they didn't find even a trace of the river demon. They asked a few farmers they saw for information and got conflicting reports. Apparently, rumors of the river demon were common, but few people had ever encountered it.

Soon it was noon, and Sunan called for a break. They found a shady spot along the river to dismount and eat a noon meal.

After they'd finished eating, Sunan headed down to the water to clean up. It was at that point that he noticed a young man a bit farther up the river, sitting on a rock, a fishing pole dangling into the water.

He approached the young man and called out, "Greetings, young sir!"

When the young man turned looked over, Sunan was surprised to see that he had blue eyes.

"Hello," the young man replied.

Walking a bit closer, Sunan said, "Do you live around here?"

"I do, sir. How can I help you?"

"I'm from Daolu, here to investigate a river demon. Have you heard any stories about it?"

"Sure, everybody around here has heard of the river demon. A few people have even seen it."

"Do you know any of those people personally?"

"Well, sure. I'm one of them."

Sunan's eyebrows shot up. "Really? Could you tell me more about it?"

"I can do better than that, I can show you. At least, I think I can. I'm pretty sure I know where the river demon's lair is. I've never gone to check, because, well, I don't want to get killed. There's a little grotto upriver from here, and I'd be willing to bet my livelihood on the fact that the river demon lives there."

"What makes you so sure?"

The young man shrugged. "I used to play in that grotto when I was young, so I know what it looks like inside. Ever since the river demon showed up, though, I stayed away."

"I see. Very well. I'd like to see this grotto of yours."

The young man rose to his feet and pointed downriver. "Sure. It's about a fifteen-minute walk that way."

After securing the horses, Sunan, Yuwen Huo, and the five soldiers followed the young fisherman down the river. Eventually he led them to an area where a bend in the river created something like a small lake. At this point, the young fisherman stopped.

"See that?" he said, pointing up ahead. "Those rocks form the mouth of a little cave. I'm almost sure that's where the river demon's lair is. I don't want to go any farther than this, though. Good luck."

Settling his qi and clenching his fists, Sunan proceeded forward, followed by Yuwen Huo and the soldiers. He'd only gone a few meters when a faint clicking sound from behind caught his attention. He looked over his shoulder, and then time seemed to slow down.

Shockingly, standing in the exact position where the young fisherman had been was an enormous, human-sized crab. It was bright blue, with wickedly curved claws and cruel-looking eyes that glistened like morning dew. It had thick fur adorning its claws and legs, which was a darker shade of blue, as dark as the depths of the Chezou itself.

The crab's claws were raised high up into the air, as if it were preparing to smash them down into the ground.

Sunan shouted a warning to Yuwen Huo and the soldiers and simultaneously swiveled in place.

The crab's claws came smashing down with a boom, sending an enormous blast of sand directly toward Sunan and his group. Sunan leapt to the side, somehow managing to evade the blast. Yuwen Huo was similarly quick footed, but the other soldiers weren't as lucky. Caught completely off guard, the sand smashed into them, sending them tumbling to the ground as patches of skin were shredded completely off their bodies. Two of the soldiers' eyes were damaged, blinding them. Bloodcurdling screams rang out into the air.

Thanks to his rigorous training in recent days, Sunan was much quicker to react than he might have been in the past. Without even thinking about it, he unleashed Slash of the Dragon's Tail, sending a blast of energy toward the river demon.

Yuwen Huo did exactly the same thing, although his Slash of the Dragon's Tail wasn't quite on the same level as Sunan's.

Unfortunately, the river demon managed to evade both attacks, and then it scuttled forward at top speed toward the fallen soldiers.

The soldiers were struggling to their feet, moaning. Before they could even draw their weapons, the gigantic crab was upon them. Its claws opened and closed with vicious clacking sounds as it attacked the two blinded soldiers at the same time.

Shockingly, one of the soldiers' heads flew off his body, blood spraying through the air as it tumbled down in front of Sunan. As for the other soldier, the river demon's other claw nearly cut him in half at the waist, sending blood and entrails flopping down into the sand.

Gritting his teeth, Sunan lashed out with Rebuke of the Dragon. This time, the blow hit true, smashing directly into face of the river demon. A crisp popping sound rang out as the gigantic crab staggered backward, only to be hit moments later by a second Rebuke of the Dragon from Yuwen Huo, which ripped off one of its clawed arms.

The crab bellowed and lashed out toward a third soldier, who just barely managed to dodge. The other two soldiers were scrambling backward, fear written across their faces.

In recent days of training, Sunan had reached a certain level of enlightenment regarding how to use qi in a fight, and he knew that it was possible to surpass the limitations of one's own body. Although he had never actually resorted to such methods in training, he was certain that by cathartically drawing upon his qi, he could unleash far greater damage with his strikes than normal.

In this desperate situation, that was exactly what he did. Pushing himself past his limit, he shouted, "Rebuke of the Dragon!"

Two enormous energy blasts shot through the air like mighty dragons, a crashing wave of blades that slammed directly into the gigantic blue crab.

The river demon was almost completely smashed to pieces. Legs flew here and there, and its only remaining claw shattered. It tumbled backward along the river bank, blue blood splashing everywhere.

Eventually it rolled to a stop, where it remained, emitting painful clicking sounds.

Sunan walked over and stood above it.

"Damn you, human," the river demon said in an odd rasping voice.

"Why did you do this?" Sunan asked. "What did I ever do to you?"

The river demon chuckled. "You humans shouldn't be this powerful. It's unnatural."

"You mean the qi? How could it be unnatural? It's part of nature itself."

"If you pour oil into sand, it becomes part of the sand, but does that mean it is innately sand?"

Sunan frowned. "I don't understand."

"What you call qi is not natural. It was brought to this world by the Demon Emperor." The crab made a gurgling sound, and its voice began to weaken. "It doesn't matter. No matter how strong you humans get, you'll always be fools. You think I didn't recognize you the minute you approached me, Young Dragon Sunan? People call you Young Dragon, but you are no dragon."

"Why can't we just live in harmony?"

"Harmony? Ha! Damn you, Sunan. I wish I could have killed more humans than I did. At least I can take delight in knowing that your precious Daolu will soon be burned to the ground."

"What?"

"That's right. Even a poor little river demon like myself can tell that you've been infiltrated. The Demon Emperor is playing you like a zither!" It chuckled. "Prepare to be cursed for all generations to come, humans. Torment of the Crab Demons!"

The river demon began to tremble and twitch. A moment later, it exploded. Countless chunks of blue-colored carapace, white flesh, and blue viscous fluid burst in all directions.

Sunan just barely reacted in time, drawing on his qi to fly backward with inhuman speed.

Yuwen Huo wasn't as lucky. Although he also flew away from the exploding crab, a chunk of flying carapace slashed across his cheek, opening a vicious gash.

Most of the exploding crab landed in the river, where it spread out in clouds of blue before slowly drifting downstream.

Sunan looked over at Yuwen Huo. The blood oozing out of the gash on his cheek was mostly red but tinged with spots of bright blue. Even the flesh around it was blue.

"Brother Yuwen, are you all right?"

Yuwen Huo looked at him and began to nod in agreement. However, his nod slowed down, and a moment later he fell over flat on his face.

***

The entire way back to Daolu, Sunan's heart was pounding with fear and anger. He berated himself over and over for leading his men into an obvious trap and getting two of them killed. Then there was Yuwen Huo, his top lieutenant, who had still not regained consciousness after being slashed by the flying chunk of cursed crab carapace.

At a certain point, they ran into Sun Mai's group. After briefly explaining the situation, they hurried back to the city as quickly as possible.

By the time they were back, Yuwen Huo's entire left cheek was completely blue, and he was still unconscious. Sun Mai had few helpful ideas.

The following morning, the blue coloring had spread down to Yuwen Huo's neck and didn't seem to be stopping. Yuwen Huo would twitch and moan occasionally. Sun Mai was at a complete loss, and none of the other physicians or priests had any clue about what to do.

"What about that Smiling Luo fellow?" Sunan asked.

Sun Mai shrugged. "Call for him, I suppose."

Unfortunately, Smiling Luo was nowhere to be found.

By noon, half of Yuwen Huo's face was blue, and the twitching and moaning had grown more intense. Sunan was so frustrated that he wanted to break something. That was when Tie Gangwen approached with news that Lady Yan had arrived.

"What does she want?" Sunan asked, distracted.

"She says she can break the curse."

CHAPTER 35
A JADE BOTTLE

As soon as Lady Yan saw Yuwen Huo, she began to bark orders. "Bring me a furnace immediately. I need violet ginseng rootlets, blackberry lily, rice wine, lotus oil, underheaven lichen, numinous mushroom…" To the astonishment of everyone present, she listed ten more ingredients. Half of the list included rare ingredients that Sunan had never even heard of.

When she finished, everyone stared at her with wide eyes.

She looked around, frowning. "There's still a chance to stop the spread of the curse. Hurry!"

It took a full hour to collect all of the ingredients and another hour for Lady Yan to concoct the medicine. Upon finishing, she forced the thick liquid down Yuwen Huo's throat. He shuddered, then went still.

It was only after the process was complete that Lady Yan offered further explanation. "The river demon you described is more common in the south. I'm not sure what such a creature was doing up here. If the spread of the curse had not been stopped, Lieutenant

Yuwen would have experienced a violent transformation and ended up becoming a crab or some other crablike creature."

In the silence that followed. Sunan shook his head slowly. "How could I have let this happen?"

Lady Yan reached out and placed her hand atop his. "Blaming yourself for mistakes does little good, Sect Leader Sunan."

Sun Mai eyed her hand and then cleared his throat. "It's true. As Kong Zhi said, 'The only true mistake is the mistake you don't correct.'"

"And how do I correct this one?" Sunan asked.

Lady Yan pulled her hand back, and Sun Mai sniffed. "Well," he said, "what was it the thing said about the city being infiltrated?"

"Not much, just that the Demon Emperor was coming for us."

"Probably idle talk," Sun Mai said.

***

Yuwen Huo woke up the following day. The bright blue discoloration on his skin remained, as did a nasty wound on his cheek, which would no doubt turn into a vicious-looking scar. Other than that, he was no worse for the wear, and in fact, he said he felt even stronger than before.

In their next sparring session, Sunan confirmed that. Yuwen Huo was significantly stronger and faster than before the incident with the river demon.

"See?" Sun Mai said. "Oftentimes good fortune comes in the midst of disaster."

Time marched by. Lady Yan continued to be of help in odd ways. Although Sun Mai didn't like to admit it, even he admired the advice she gave. Some of her minor suggestions ended up significantly changing the Golden Dragon Sect. Organizational methods, uniforms, recruiting tactics, and other things were all touched by her hand.

Sunan grew fond of walking the city walls with her in the evenings. They would talk about many things, from food to geography to art to history. Occasionally the subject of the Demon Emperor would come up, and although she always maneuvered the conversation deftly, it was clear to him that she truly viewed him as a tragic hero in his own story. Sunan still didn't quite believe her tales, but as time went on, he found her devotion somewhat endearing.

Something about Lady Yan changed that Sunan never noticed. In fact, neither did Sun Mai or any of the other members of the Golden Dragon Sect. Perhaps if Bao had been present, she might have noticed. Women can often see things in the eyes of other women that men were blind to. Lady Yan began to look at Sunan differently. Her eyes glittered in a way they hadn't before, and her smiles grew slightly more bashful.

Eventually the Golden Dragon Sect reached a milestone—the total membership in the sect had reached fifty. The most powerful fighters in the sect were Sunan and Sun Mai, both of whom had achieved three breakthroughs. Yuwen Huo and Tie Gangwen had both experienced two breakthroughs, as had a few other soldiers who had been training the longest. Twenty sect disciples had reached one breakthrough, and the rest were initiates who had not yet succeeded.

To celebrate, Sunan and Sun Mai took the entire sect to the Heavenly Meat Palace for a feast. Lady Yan, despite not being a member of the Golden Dragon Sect, was also invited.

The Heavenly Meat Palace was large enough to accommodate them, as well as a handful of other guests who had been present before they arrived.

Fiery prawns and grilled meat were piled up high on the tables, and wine flowed freely. After about two hours had passed, everyone was in a wonderful mood. Suddenly a scream pierced the air, and one of the lower-ranked disciples ran back into the common room, shouting at the top of her lungs.

"Demon! I saw a demon!" She ran up to Sun Mai and Sunan's table, panting. "Sect Leader Sunan, there's a demon back there!"

"More demons?" Sun Mai said, laughing. "Are you sure you haven't had a bit too much wine, Ma Ge?"

"Chief Minister Sun," Ma Ge said, "I'm too young to drink wine. Believe me, there's demon back there! I saw it run into one of the back storage rooms after I went to find some cumin powder!"

Sunan and Sun Mai exchanged a glance.

"I'll handle it," Sun Mai said. "I'm sure it's nothing." He turned to Tie Gangwen. "Come with me, Lieutenant."

Sun Mai was about as familiar with the Heavenly Meat Palace as he was with the back of his hand, so he needed no help from the staff to lead Tie Gangwen to the exact place that Ma Ge had just referred to.

Soon they were standing outside one of the restaurant's several large storage rooms.

"Sunan and I investigated this whole area once before," he explained. "I have a really hard time believing that a—"

Before he could finish his sentence, the door crashed open, and an enormous rat burst out. It was the size of Sun Mai's forearm, with black eyes and wide red lips that hung loosely over its curled teeth. It leapt up into the air directly toward Sun Mai, who reacted by using his technique Dance of Bixie to fly backward.

The rat demon then let out a powerful squeak that pierced the ears of Tie Gangwen and Sun Mai like daggers.

Sun Mai wasn't affected, but Tie Gangwen found himself rooted in place, completely incapable of moving.

Having missed its initial target of Sun Mai, the rat demon landed on the opposite wall and then launched into the air toward Tie Gangwen.

"Sword of the Scholar!" Sun Mai shouted, waving his finger.

An invisible sword slashed through the air, severing the rat's tail but doing little other damage. The rat landed on Tie Gangwen's shoulder, where it promptly bit down on his neck.

"Dammit!" he shouted, but he was still unable to move. He began to shake violently, to the point where he teetered on the verge of falling over. The rat turned again and looked at Sun Mai with black eyes.

"Father Zhen will have his revenge!" the rat said in a squeaky voice. Then it turned and leapt off Tie Gangwen. Tie Gangwen was sent down to the ground with a loud thump.

As the rat bolted down the hallway, Sun Mai crouched down to help Tie Gangwen up, who struggled to his feet with Sun Mai's help. Now that he could move again, he reached up to feel the bloody wound on his neck.

"Are you okay?" Sun Mai asked, examining the wound.

"I think so," Tie Gangwen replied. "I feel very weak, though."

Sun Mai looked down the empty corridor. "That was one of the most bizarre things I've seen in a long time. Come on, let's go get some food in you."

Tie Gangwen nodded, and they returned to the main hall.

When Sunan saw Tie Gangwen's neck, his eyes went wide. "What happened?"

Sun Mai sat down. "Apparently there really is a rat demon here."

Sunan's eyes went wide. "Really? Another demon? What's going on in this city?"

A familiar voice rang out from a far corner of the room. "Isn't that the question we would all like to know, *Chief Minister Sun!*"

All eyes in the Heavenly Meat Palace swiveled over to look at the dour-faced man striding toward Sunan and Sun Mai's table.

"Smiling Luo!" Sun Mai said, looking a bit puzzled. "What are you doing here?"

"I'm here to do what I should have done a long time ago, *Chief Minister Sun!*" With that, Smiling Luo turned to Sunan. "Sect

Leader Sunan, I tried to tell you before about the demons, but you wouldn't listen to me. Now look what's happened. People have died. *Died!* Well, I'm here to reveal the truth of the matter. You want to know what's going on in this city? I'll tell you. *He* is what's going on!" In accompaniment with his final sentence, Smiling Luo pointed dramatically at Sun Mai.

"Him?" Sunan said.

"Me?" Sun Mai said.

"Yes!" shouted Smiling Luo. "Sect Leader Sunan, this man you have at your side is a fraud! I've known him for years, and he's nothing but a cheater and a liar. He's in charge of the demons in this place because he is none other than their leader! He is a demon! I could never figure out why my demon-hunting business never succeeded. The reason is because Sun Mai's Sundry Services was always set up near my shop. He did it to spy on me and make sure that he and his fellow demons were safe. No wonder his shop never made any money. Because he didn't need to!"

"Hey, my shop made money," Sun Mai said indignantly. "My poetry––"

"Could be written by drunken monkey demons!" barked Smiling Luo. Then he began to laugh, which was a strange sight, because he somehow managed to frown while doing so. "You can hide your treachery no longer, Chief Minister Sun. Or should I say... Demon Sun!"

Smiling Luo then produced a small jade bottle, which he held high above his head. "It took me months to acquire this through various agents and traders, *Chief Minister Sun*, and it came at great personal cost. This is none other than the fabled Celestial Illusion Dispelling Powder from Zhe Valley. This powder will reveal the true form of any demon or similar creature. And now, *Chief Minister Sun*, it will reveal to the whole world how much of a fraud you are!"

"Stay your hand!" cried Lady Yan. "That powder... can react explosively when it contacts fire."

Everyone immediately looked around at the numerous oil lamps that filled the Heavenly Meat Palace.

Smiling Luo hesitated for a moment. "Nonsense!"

Then he reached his hand back as he prepared to throw the jade bottle to the ground.

"NOOO!" Lady Yan screamed, lunging over the table toward Smiling Luo. As she flew through the air, the jade bottle descended. Her right hand stretched out, but her fingers grasped nothing but air. The jade bottle smashed onto the ground, and a banging sound rang out as powder spread out through the room.

Lady Yan landed on the ground, her red hair spread out around her like a blanket.

Some people coughed, others placed their sleeves over their noses and mouths, others pulled out fans which they began waving through the air.

As for Smiling Luo, he threw his head back and began to laugh at the top of his lungs. "And now we can see your true form, *Chief Minister*... uh—"

Sun Mai brushed some pink powder off of his nose and then sneezed. He looked exactly as he had moments before.

Glowering at Smiling Luo, Sunan hopped over the table and walked toward Lady Yan.

"Lady Yan, are you hurt?" he said.

She remained on the ground, her hair covering her. Just before Sunan reached her, she spoke. "Sect Leader Sunan, please forgive me."

When she looked up, a collective gasp filled the room.

CHAPTER 36
THE TIME HAS COME

Lady Yan slowly looked up. As she did, her crimson hair parted to reveal her face, a face that was most certainly not the face of Lady Yan. In fact, her face wasn't even human. Her eyes were larger and wider, her nose flat and almost feline. She had odd markings on her face and sharp teeth that seemed capable of ripping flesh off of bones. Most bizarre of all was that she had three short, blunt horns sticking out of her forehead, one in the middle and two off to either side.

Her body was still voluptuous, but upon closer examination, she was taller and larger than she had been before. She seemed more powerful, somehow more muscular, but at the same time, enticing. Beautiful.

Her expression was a complex one, seemingly filled with pain, regret, sorrow, and guilt.

As soon as her face was revealed, gasps filled the room, along with exclamations of shock and even muttered curses.

"A demon!"

"What kind of monster is that?"

"What happened to Lady Yan?"

"What is that thing?"

A wave of shock ran through Sunan, and he subconsciously retracted the hand he had been reaching out toward her. He took a step back, struck speechless. He felt as if his mind had been struck by lightning, as if the world had been turned upside down. He thought about Lady Yan, about the curve of her lips when she smiled, about how he felt when she put her hand on his arm. And then he looked at the *thing* sprawled on the ground in front of him and wondered if he was dreaming. Or living in a nightmare.

"She's not a demon. I've seen her before!" The words came from Tie Gangwen, who reached out to point a trembling finger at "Lady Yan."

Some in the crowd couldn't tear their gazes away from the figure lying on the ground, but quite a few turned to look at Tie Gangwen.

"I saw her once when Iron Awl Hu went to a meeting outside of the city. She's... she's the Love General. She's an ogre!"

If the gasps of shock that rang out earlier were loud, then the response to Tie Gangwen's words this time were like thunder.

Some people staggered backward, and a few even fell down. Swords were drawn and spears were leveled. Without even thinking about it, Sunan's right hand twisted into the claw of a dragon, and Sun Mai extended the two fingers of his right hand.

"Sect Leader Sunan, please," the Love General said. "Things weren't supposed to happen like this. I mean you no harm..."

Sunan backed up another step, and Sun Mai rose to his feet. After the initial round of gasps, the room went quiet, but that lasted for only a moment.

"She's an ogre?" someone said.

"The Love General? She's one of the Demon Emperor's top advisors?"

"She's one of the Demon Emperor's people?"

Sun Mai stepped forward to stand at Sunan's side. "Sunan," he said. "If what Tie Gangwen says is true…"

Sunan had recovered from his initial shock. At first, disbelief gripped his heart, but then anger sparked to life. Looking down at the Love General, he said, "Is it?"

She looked down, almost as if she didn't dare to look him in the eyes. Taking a deep breath, she replied in a very soft voice, "Yes. It's true."

Sunan clenched his jaw and shook his head slowly. The anger in his heart began to grow hotter, burning away the disbelief, spreading out into his head, into his gut, into his hands and legs.

"You lied to me?" he asked, his voice quavering.

The Love General bowed her head, causing her hair to fall down and cover her eyes and mouth. It couldn't cover the three horns, though. "Sect Leader Sunan, I… I didn't lie… I mean, I didn't *intend* to lie…"

"Don't listen to her any more, Sunan," Sun Mai said. "She's been manipulating us this entire time. You can't trust a single word she says."

"Sect Leader," Tie Gangwen said, "the chief minister is right. She's one of the Demon Emperor's top leaders. She must have been sent here to kill the two of you."

Sun Mai took a step forward and lifted his hand. "Say the word, Sunan, and I'll kill her on the spot. Do you know how many deaths she's responsible for? She helps the Demon Emperor plan his massacres! She should be executed!"

In response to his words, more weapons were drawn in the room, and some of the soldiers even stepped closer to the Love General, pointing spears and swords at her, grim expressions on their faces.

Sunan's heart and mind were trembling. He thought back to everything that "Lady Yan" had told him about the Demon Emperor and wondered if any of it was true. The sad story about him being in a coma. Was it completely fabricated? What if it was true? It didn't make sense that she had been sent to kill them. She'd had plenty of opportunities to do so, whether by means of poison or even a knife in the back. Neither did it seem as if she'd been attempting to get him to surrender to the Demon Emperor.

Nothing made sense. Why had she come? Why had she spent so much time with him, talking about seemingly innocuous and pointless inanities? Why had they laughed so much together?

He shook his head to try to clear it.

"No," he said. "We're not murderers. She's committed no crimes in this city. I'm not going to kill someone in cold blood just for being on the wrong side. Arrange a horse and escort her outside the city."

The Love General looked up, and her expression was desperate. "Sect Leader, please, give me a moment in private to talk. I need to explain——"

"No," he interrupted. "No explanations. I won't have any more of your lies."

"Please, I was telling the truth about——"

"NO!" he barked, looking away from her. "Men, take her away."

"Sunan, I'm sorry. Please forgive me. I truly have come to lo—"

"Enough with your lies! Consider yourself formally exiled from Daolu. If you ever show your face in this city again, you'll be executed on sight! Now leave!"

The Love General bowed her head again as soldiers hurried forward and dragged her to her feet. Because her long, crimson hair covered her face, no one could see the tears glistening on her cheeks.

**

About an hour west of Daolu, on the south bank of the Chezou

River, Bao's people had set up camp and were eating a noon meal. They had taken a circuitous route to get to this point, having traveled some distance east along the Chezou River before finding a suitable place to cross.

Mao Yun approached with a bowl of prawn soup and handed it to Bao.

"Why are the prawns blue?" she asked.

"Not sure," he replied, sitting down next to her. "The farmer we bought them from said that blue prawns only showed up in the area recently. The flavor is amazing, though. Try it."

Bao pulled one of the strangely colored prawns out of the soup and cracked it open.

"You're right," she said. "You know, I ate a lot of seafood growing up in Yu Zhing. These might be the most tender prawns I've ever had in my life."

"And they go perfectly with this!" Mao Yun said, handing her a small bottle. "Local yellow wine."

Grinning, she took the bottle, raised it up to clink against Mao Yun's, and drank with him.

Over the course of the next few minutes, the two of them devoured the prawns and finished the wine.

"By now, the people in Daolu must know we're coming," Mao Yun said.

"You mean the government?" Bao replied. "Or the Golden Dragon Sect? Either way, we should be prepared for someone to ask us some questions."

"What are you going to say? Our last run-in with the Golden Dragon Sect didn't go very well. Even if Sheriff Song and Magistrate Pei Bai are fine with us entering, Sect Leader Sunan might not be too happy about it."

"I know," Bao said. Her hand came to rest on the wooden box that she always kept by her side. "But I'm sure he can be convinced."

***

Sunan stood at the edge of the pond in the courtyard of the mansion, looking down at the fish swimming lazily to and fro.

Sun Mai sat off to the side, toying with a fan.

Sunan had finally recounted to Sun Mai what the Love General had told him about the Demon Emperor, as well as certain other things she had said. After much discussion, neither of them were able to make heads or tails of it all.

"I still can't believe I was fooled so easily," Sunan said.

Sun Mai sighed. "According to Kong Zhi, 'You can cheat an honest man, but you cannot make a fool out of him.'"

"I certainly feel like a fool."

"You're no fool, Sunan. Sometimes the difference between what is real and what is not real can be very difficult to see clearly. If we could see the truth of all things at a single glance, it would mean that we are perfect up here." He tapped his temple. "That is the true Perfect Realm, you know." He cocked his head to the side. "Wait a second, that was amazing! That belongs in my great scripture!" He began patting his robes. "How come I never have writing utensils when I need them? Hold on, I'll be right back." Leaving his fan behind, he hurried off to find a brush and paper.

Sunan shook his head. *I don't even know what he's talking about half the time.*

He watched the fish for a bit longer until Tie Gangwen approached.

"Sect Leader," he said, clasping his hands in front of him respectfully.

"Yes?"

"A bit of news. A large group approached Daolu from the west only a few hours ago. The sheriff sent a party out to meet them, then escorted them into the city."

"A large group? How large?"

"Apparently a hundred or more."

"Refugees?"

"It seems so. Normally I wouldn't bother you with such a thing. A hundred people is a relatively large group but not unheard of in times like these. The thing is, the group was led by… someone you know."

Sunan looked away from the fish. "Someone I know?"

"Yes, that group… it was the Pure Phoenix Sect, led by Chieftainess Bao."

Sunan's expression darkened. "What is she doing here?"

"I'm not sure, Sect Leader."

Sunan looked back down at the fish swimming in the pond. "Send a message inviting her to the Heavenly Meat Palace for a welcoming feast. Tell her to only bring a few men, and that we'll do the same. But make sure we have plenty of men in the restaurant ahead of time. Armed. And in the meantime, summon Smiling Luo. I have some questions for him about matters relating to magic."

***

Some distance south of Daolu, the Love General was riding along on horseback when she noticed a cloud of dust off in the distance. Eyes narrowing, she was just about to ride off the road to conceal herself when her sharp eyes caught sight of who it was that was riding toward her.

It was a large group on horseback, and even if they had been farther away, she would have recognized their armor. They were Bone Slicers, and leading them was the Bone General himself.

What are you doing up here? she thought. *Maybe it has something to do with that big group that entered the city as I was leaving.*

Instead of moving off to the side, she waited in the very middle of the road. It didn't take long for the Bone General and his men to arrive. They didn't appear to be in very good shape. They were clearly travel weary, and some of the men were injured. The Love General was surprised to see such a small group.

"Don't you usually bring more men with you to border regions like this?" she asked.

The Bone General reined his horse to stop next to her. "We ran into some trouble. A pesky tree demon that needed to be taken care of. What are you doing here?"

"I could ask the same of you," she replied. "I was on a mission. It ended in failure, unfortunately."

"I see. I'm chasing a fugitive. Someone very dangerous. A girl."

"She just entered the city, I believe. I wouldn't go after her if I were you. Not with this few men. This city has become a problem. There are too many powerful people inside, and they have no love for the King of the Pure Ones."

The Bone General's expression turned even grimmer than before. "Perhaps the time has come to crush this place."

The Love General looked over her shoulder at the city, and somehow, she felt as if she could see Sunan on the city walls, looking south. Her heart twinged. "Perhaps."

CHAPTER 37
SIT DOWN

Bao strode through the streets of Daolu, her head held high. *This place is like a dump compared to Yu Zhing. Even Tung-On was better.*

Despite her show of bravado, inwardly her heart was pounding. Although the invitation from the leader of the Golden Dragon Sect, Sunan, had been worded politely, it felt more like a summons than an invitation. Not only was this strange city rumored to be a place of lawless violence, it was controlled by someone she knew could manipulate the strange energy just like she could, to fight in superhuman fashion.

Her hatred for the Demon Emperor burned as hot as ever, but she had to admit that the lands south of the Chezou River were much more orderly than this place. One thing that struck her almost immediately were the beggars. Although beggars did exist in the south, they were a rare sight, and they mostly slunk about in the shadows.

In Daolu, however, they almost seemed organized, as if they

were an actual faction within the city, on par with the constables or the Golden Dragon Sect.

In compliance with the invitation from the Golden Dragons, she only brought five of her people with her. Mao Yun was there, of course, as was Li Runfa. Of the other three, two were women and one was a middle-aged man. All three were disciples who had excelled in training over the past months.

The entire group wore silver headbands embroidered with a phoenix, an embellishment suggested by Li Runfa after they noticed that the members of the Golden Dragon Sect all wore the same type of clothing, almost like uniforms.

Considering they only had a few hours to prepare for the dinner, headbands were the best they could do. However, the zeal that had burned in the eyes of her people when they first laid eyes on the silver headbands left Bao a bit taken aback.

If I'm going to stay in charge of this group, I need to act like a leader.

Thus, it was with an air of complete confidence that she led the small group toward the dinner location, a place called the Heavenly Meat Palace. Under her left arm she carried her wooden box, while her right hand was wrapped around a cloth bundle, within which was a saber, some daggers, and a club. Technically it was illegal to carry weapons within the city itself, but Bao felt that a bit of bravado would go a long way to impressing the Golden Dragons, so she'd decided to take the risk.

Leaning close to Mao Yun, Bao asked, "You sent some people there ahead of time?"

He nodded. "Yes, but not very many. We're new in town and stick out too much. Besides, according to word on the street, Sect Leader Sunan and Chief Minister Sun Mai actually own the place and have even summoned demons from the Lower Realms to protect it. Doesn't surprise me that blasphemers like them would do such a thing."

Not too long ago, Bao would have dismissed claims of summoned demons, but after the fei beast and the tree demon, the idea didn't seem too far-fetched.

As they approached the Heavenly Meat Palace, Bao saw someone in the robes of the Golden Dragon Sect waiting out front. It appeared to be a young man, with his face turned to look in the opposite direction. When he turned and saw them, his eyes went wide, and he quickly clasped his hands and bowed low. The depth of his bow was almost ridiculous, leaving him bent over so low that his face wasn't visible.

"Greetings, Chieftainess Bao," the young man said.

She bent her head to the side to try to get a look at the young man's face but failed. "Greetings. We're here at the invitation of Sect Leader Sunan."

Before she even had a chance to pull out the invitation card to give him, the young man said, "I know, I know. Please follow me."

Remaining in a bowed position, he turned and led the way into the restaurant.

Bao turned to Mao Yun. "What was that all about? Is that some Golden Dragon custom, to bow in such ridiculous fashion?"

Mao Yun was frowning. "I'm not sure. But something about that young man seemed familiar. I can't quite put my finger on it, but I feel like I know him."

There was no time to discuss the matter further. They were led into the Heavenly Meat Palace to a table in the common room, where Sunan was already seated. Bao recognized Sun Mai from their initial meeting, but the others were strangers to her. One of them was a frightening-looking man who appeared to have a blue birthmark stretching from his cheek all the way down his neck, and another had the look of a soldier. Surprisingly, the next person at the table wasn't dressed like a Golden Dragon. A deep frown covered his face, and from the way he dressed, Bao guessed that he must be a magician or sorcerer of some sort.

Maybe they do have demons…

The young man who had led them in took the place next to Sunan, although he kept his hands clasped high, and his head bowed, making it difficult to see his face.

As soon as she entered, Sunan rose and clasped his hands respectfully. "Greetings, Chieftainess Bao."

"Greetings, Sect Leader Sunan."

"Please, have a seat."

After they were seated, Sunan immediately made introductions. "Chieftainess, as I'm sure you know, this is Chief Minister Sun, who is also a scholar and philosopher of some note."

The frowning man let out a loud snort, causing Sun Mai to glare over at him. Sunan cleared his throat. "Next are my two top lieutenants, Tie Gangwen, and Yuwen Huo, who is called the Blue Devil. Last is Smiling Huo. He is not one of the Golden Dragons but a local demon hunter and master of the magical arts."

Bao hid her frown. *Demon hunter? Why would he have a demon hunter working for him if he summons demons? Perhaps it's a lie, and this is actually their demon summoner!*

Another thing Bao realized was that her so-called Pure Phoenix Sect was really just a loose band of fugitives and fighters, whereas the Golden Dragon Sect was organized and well-disciplined, almost like an army.

We haven't even assigned any official roles to anyone! Dammit, I'm going to look like a fool if I just introduce everyone by name.

After offering the appropriate platitudes, Bao introduced her people. "This is Grand Chief of Martial Studies, Mao Yun, whom you're familiar with. Next is Li Runfa, my… Viscount of Operations. Next are my top three fighters, who are also known as the… as the Claws of the Phoenix. They are the most elite fighters in the Pure Phoenix Sect, whose each and every move is as deadly as the swiping talon of a phoenix demon."

"You've seen a phoenix demon swipe its talon?" Sun Mai asked, chuckling.

Bao slowly turned to stare him in the eye. "Yes," she said. "I have."

Sun Mai's chuckle turned into somewhat of a gurgle, then faded away.

"As I was saying," Bao continued, "these are the Claws of the Phoenix. Liu Jiahui, also known as Flying Death. Lin Qingxia, who is called the Throat-Slitting Phoenix Ghost. And Yang Ziqiong, also known as the Blood Drinker. All three of them are killers the likes of which would cause even the phoenix demon I tamed to tremble in fear."

A profound silence filled the room after her introduction. Bao felt somewhat proud of herself for being able to think so quickly on her feet. Although she had literally made up everything on the spot, it all sounded very impressive as far as she was concerned.

If Sunan and his people hadn't been so focused on Bao's introduction, they might have noticed the odd looks on the faces of Mao Yun and the others. For them, it was the first time hearing such titles and descriptions.

Now that the formal introductions were out of the way, they moved on to eating and drinking. Mounds of meat and prawns were served, along with jugs of alcohol.

"These blue prawns are new," Sunan explained. "They're especially tender. But I still favor the original spicy version."

The conversation was light and didn't touch on anything such as politics or philosophy. One odd thing that Bao noticed was that the young man who had escorted them in from outside was almost always stuffing food or wine into his mouth, making it very difficult to make out his facial features.

After about an hour passed, the topic of conversation shifted to the martial arts.

"Sect Leader Sunan, I heard people on the street talking

about something called Wu-Sunan," Bao said. "I suppose that has something to do with you."

"Yes, that's right, Chieftainess Bao. Based on our initial... meeting... it seems you're aware of the energy which surrounds us in the world and how to use it?"

"That's correct."

He nodded. "I've developed a method to cultivate that energy, which we call qi."

"That's Classical Fei," Sun Mai interjected.

"I know," Bao said. Like most youngsters in her clan, her extensive education as a youth had included Classical Fei, the most ancient language in Qi Xien.

Sun Mai's eyes went wide. "Really? You know Classical Fei?"

"Dang ran," she replied. "Ni ne?"

Sun Mai slapped the table. "Tian a! Ni tai li hai le!" He turned to Sunan. "Can you believe this? She actually speaks Classical Fei!"

Bao chuckled at Sun Mai's enthusiasm. "Sect Leader Sunan, my apologies. Please continue."

"Of course. We took the specific movements and methods of how to cultivate qi, as well as how to use it for combat purposes, and compiled them into a manual of sorts. We called it Wu-Sunan."

"In Classic Fei, Wu means—" Before Sun Mai could finish, Bao interrupted him.

"Martial. I know."

Sun Mai laughed and slapped the table. "I like this Chieftainess Bao more by the second!"

"What about you, Chieftainess Bao?" Sunan asked. "Have you thought about codifying the fighting techniques of your Pure Phoenix Sect?"

"Yes, we have," she lied. "Let's just say it's a work in progress. When it's complete, it will be something to fear. After all, my techniques enabled me to kill an ogre, tame a phoenix demon, and slaughter a fei beast. What have you done with your Wu-Sunan?"

"Well…" Sunan responded, seemingly taken aback. "Well, we defeated Iron Awl Hu."

"I remember you mentioning him last time we met," Mao Yun said, chuckling a bit. "Wasn't he just a local criminal?"

"Yes," Sun Mai said. "But he was strong. A lot stronger than you, probably. And then there was Ritual Master Zhen and his rats! You wouldn't believe how that fight went! There were—"

"Wait," Mao Yun interjected. "Your Wu-Sunan has been used… to defeat thugs, priests, and rats?" He threw his head back and laughed uproariously. "Just what I would expect from a bunch of blasphemers."

"We're no blasphemers," Sun Mai shot back. "I'm working on a classic scripture that's going to revolutionize how people think of the Perfect Realm! You just wait and see what happens when people learn the truth! And by the way, we used Wu-Sunan to single-handedly take down one of the Lions of Peace."

Mao Yun nearly spurted wine out of his mouth. "This story again? The two of you single-handedly took him down? Two on one, eh?" He laughed again. "I could probably beat you with both hands tied behind my back, scholar."

Sun Mai leapt to his feet. "I don't think so, you brainless ox! I could beat *you* with both hands tied behind my back! And my eyes closed!"

Mao Yun jumped up. "Oh, really? What are you going to do, write a book of poetry and drop it on my head?"

"Mao Yun—" Bao said, reaching out toward Mao Yun.

"Sun Mai—" Sunan said, reaching out toward Sun Mai.

Sunan and Bao's gazes met, and somehow they both knew that they were thinking the same thing.

"Sit down," they both said. It was hard to tell whose voice was colder and ironlike. Somewhat startled, both Mao Yun and Sun Mai sat back down immediately.

After a moment of silence, Bao smiled. "Sect Leader Sunan, what do you say to a little exhibition match? I hereby challenge you to a friendly competition. Let's see who is stronger, the Phoenix or the Dragon."

CHAPTER 38
DIANXUE V. CATHARTIC

"Come on, Sect Leader Sunan, you show her a thing or two!"

"Yeah, that's right, Sect Leader, there's no way she can stand up to the Rebuke of the Dragon!"

Sunan rolled up his sleeves as he stepped out into the middle of the room, which had been cleared of tables. He tried to put on a brave face, but the truth was that his heart was pounding in his chest.

The last time he had fought Bao, he'd had the upper hand at first, only to fall victim to her witchcraft, or whatever it was. The last thing he wanted was to be humiliated in front of his entire sect. However, backing down wasn't an option either. She'd openly challenged him, and to refuse would have been a clear act of cowardice.

In the traditional culture of Qi Xien, it would be unheard of for a man to fight a woman. But qi was the great equalizer. During Golden Dragon training sessions, Sunan had seen some female disciples defeat male disciples who were twice their weight.

"Chieftainess Bao, you can't show this guy any mercy!"

"Cut him down like that ogre you crushed!"

As Bao stepped into the makeshift fighting arena, she looked Sunan in the eye and smiled confidently.

"Sect Leader," she said, "this is an exhibition match only. No fatal blows. Agreed?"

He nodded in return. "No weapons, either. Agreed?"

"No weapons." With a dramatic flourish, she produced two knives from within her sleeves, which she sent flying with blinding speed back to her table.

Both knives pierced deep into the wood of the table and stood there vibrating slightly.

I should take her out as quickly as possible. I can't give her a chance to use that magic of hers. And if her eyes start to turn white...

Sunan's fingers began to curl into dragons' claws. "Chieftainess Bao, please, go ahead and make the first move."

"Sect Leader, I've killed ogres and fei beasts. I don't need your permission to go first or second. Try to hit me, if you dare."

She's intentionally baiting me, isn't she? Sunan gritted his teeth.

"Fine, I won't be polite. Rebuke of the Dragon!"

Two blasts of qi that resembled fierce dragons flew through the air toward Bao. Shockingly, she dashed directly toward them and then spun between them. The two dragons completely missed Bao and smashed into a table off to the side, reducing it to splinters.

Bao's dash had brought her within arm's length of Sunan, but he wasn't about to give her the initiative.

He immediately unleashed a new technique that he had been working on in the previous weeks. His fingers straightened out as he thrust his palm directly toward the pit of her stomach. Wanting to end the fight as quickly as possible, he drew deeply upon his qi, pouring extra power into his palm. If it connected, she would be sent flying through the air with significant wounds to her torso.

However, as his palm sailed through the air, Bao shouted,

"Infinite Counter of the Phoenix!"

Before Sunan knew what was happening, Bao's hand latched on to his forearm and tapped him viciously on the wrist, forearm, and elbow. Sunan felt power sweeping into his body, immobilizing him as it went. In the time it takes a spark to fly off of a piece of flint, his entire right arm became dead weight.

Dammit, what is this?

He quickly sent his own qi flowing toward his arm to try to combat the effect of the immobilization, wrenching it out of Bao's grasp and falling back a few paces.

As he did, the numbing sensation ceased to spread, and it even began to recede. Unfortunately, his entire right arm was now completely useless, and he could tell that it would take at least a minute or so for feeling to return.

I need to buy time.

Just as Bao was bending her legs to spring into motion again, Sunan said, "Wait!"

Bao frowned. "What is it?"

"Why is that move called Infinite Counting Phoenix? That doesn't make any sense."

"Infinite *Counter* of the Phoenix. I countered your move."

"Ohhh. *Counter* not *counting*. Well, in any case, I thought the Pure Phoenix Sect didn't name their moves. Didn't you say that was childish?"

Bao snorted. "When in the country, do as the country bumpkins do. Are you just trying to buy time, Sect Leader? How devious! Fury of the Phoenix!"

She swept her arms through the air, unleashing a wide beam of blinding white light that sped directly toward Sunan.

Sunan's eyes went wide, but he reacted immediately, leaping to the side and cradling his immobilized right arm.

Despite the speed of his reaction, part of the blast of qi still hit him in the waist, sending him spinning through the air until he slammed into one of the supporting beams that held up the ceiling.

The rest of the qi hit some tables off to the side, crushing them into pieces.

As for Sunan, after hitting the beam, he dropped down to the ground with a loud thump, blood oozing out of his nose and mouth.

Dammit, that hurts! Struggling to his feet, he wiped the blood off of his face with the back of his hand.

Chuckling, Bao began to walk toward him. "Just say the words, Sect Leader, and the fight will be over. I really don't want to hurt you. I won't hold back with my next move, and your arm won't recover in time for you to use your Rebuke of the Dragon again."

Sunan's mouth twisted into a snarl. "Not all techniques in Wu-Sunan use hands, Chieftainess. For instance… Slash of the Dragon's Tail!"

Sunan jumped up and kicked out with all his might, yet again overdrawing on his qi, destabilizing himself further. Bao lifted her left arm up to defend herself, and a moment later, Sunan's foot slammed into it, accompanied by a blast of wind and a primeval roar.

Bao let out a grunt as the massive force of the blow sent her staggering backward. She managed to take three steps before she lost her balance and fell to the ground. She even tumbled head over heels a few times before lurching to a halt in a crouching position.

Can't let her take back the initiative.

Sunan could tell that his arm was on the verge of recovering. Unfortunately, he still couldn't use Rebuke of the Dragon, so he let loose another Slash of the Dragon's Tail, sending Bao crashing backward into a table. Considering how badly injured she already was, he held back some of the power of the attack to ensure that he didn't inflict anything other than bruises.

She can't take much more of this. She must be on the verge of collapsing.

As Bao extricated herself from the wreckage of the table, she wiped the blood off her lips with her sleeve.

"Chieftainess Bao, it's time to concede," Sunan said. "If I hit you with Rebuke of the Dragon, I could seriously injure you." After flexing his right hand experimentally, he confirmed that he had full range of motion back, and slowly curled his fingers into dragon claws as he walked closer to Bao.

Bao slowly looked up and into his eyes, and his heart trembled from the ferocity which seemed to stab into his soul.

"I don't know how you managed to unleash so much power with your strikes," she said, "but one thing I can tell clearly is that you Golden Dragon people don't know anything about dianxue! Phoenix Torment!"

Lurching forward with blinding speed, her left hand formed a vicious-looking hook that stabbed toward Sunan's temple. His right hand shot up to block her strike, and he realized that the move with her left hand was a feint and that the true attack was coming from her right hand. Before he could even consider defending with his left hand, her right index finger pushed down into the base of his neck by his collarbone.

Intense pain exploded from the point of impact. It felt like white-hot lava was coursing through his blood vessels and qi meridians, burning him from the inside out. In order to prevent himself from screaming, he clenched his jaw as he staggered back. Veins bulged on his neck and face, and he began to shake violently. Even his vision began to grow dim, as if he were teetering on the verge of lapsing into unconsciousness.

After a moment, the sensation passed, and he stood there, panting. He reached up to feel the spot where she had struck him with her finger, half expecting to find a gaping wound gushing with blood. Surprisingly, there was no wound at all.

What did she do? What is this dianxue?

Even more surprising was that, instead of following up with another attack, she simply stood across from him in a ready stance.

Taking a deep breath, he said, "That was impressive, Chieftainess Bao."

"You strike with great power yourself, Sect Leader."

The two of them stood there looking at each other, and both of them seemed to be thinking the same thing.

She was also holding back. If we push things any further, one of us is going to be seriously hurt.

"Chieftainess Bao, I think the two of us could learn a thing or two from each other. I'm curious to learn more about this dianxue of yours."

She nodded. "And I'd very much like to know how you released so much energy. I've never seen anything like that before."

"Why don't we continue our discussion with more food and drink?"

"Very well. There's a new type of alcohol in the north, something called sorghum wine. Do you happen to have any on hand?"

"Sorghum wine? That stuff burns like fire!"

Bao chuckled. "That's exactly why I like it!"

***

New tables were hauled in, and soon the dinner resumed. Bao explained dianxue, which her Pure Phoenix Sect had begun to explore recently. It was a discipline focused on attacking and manipulating pressure points throughout the body. By striking certain points and flooding them with qi, it was possible to immobilize and injure an opponent, but at the same time, it could be used for beneficial purposes. In turn, Sunan explained how to cathartically draw upon higher levels of power and how it came with the risk of injuring oneself in the process.

Sorghum wine flowed until certain disciples from both sects began to look around blearily and even lay their heads down on the table.

Sunan never noticed how Bao always seemed to have two cups of alcohol, one of which rested near her knee, beneath the table.

Eventually it got so late that Sun Mai had to remind Sunan that the local ward curfew time was approaching. If they didn't leave now, they would be forced to spend the night at the Heavenly Meat Palace.

"Chieftainess Bao, where is your Pure Phoenix Sect staying?"

"An inn near the Thunder Gate," she replied. "Across from the fabric emporium."

"I know the place," he said. "It's definitely not appropriate for heroes like you. Tie Gangwen, has anyone taken up residence in the former mansion of the Golden Immortal?"

"No, Sect Leader."

"Very well. First thing in the morning, take Chieftainess Bao and her people there. That will be her new home in Daolu."

CHAPTER 39
WIND

The Golden Immortal's old mansion wasn't very spacious, but it was better than an inn. Minor renovations were made, and soon the Pure Phoenix Sect had an official headquarters in Daolu. Some of the former followers of Lord Shu chose to part ways while others remained behind.

Despite Bao's protestations, her followers insisted that she take the main bedroom, which had previously been occupied by the Golden Immortal himself. She made some minor cosmetic changes to suit her style, and yet couldn't shake the feeling that something was odd about the place.

Immediate changes were made to the organization of the Pure Phoenix Sect. They had enough reserve funds to have uniforms tailored for everyone. They also instituted official ranks and duties. It only took a few days for word to spread through the city that a new force comparable to the Golden Dragons was rising up.

Bao even agreed to recruit new followers. However, the best idea came from Li Runfa, who suggested that they teach anyone to fight, as long as they were willing to pay. Bao disagreed initially, but when Li Runfa proceeded to explain how quickly they would run out of money if they didn't establish a source of income, she gave in. However, she emphasized that they had to keep the practice as secret as possible to prevent attracting the attention of either Sunan or the Demon Emperor.

But her main concern was Sunan and his Golden Dragons. After their initial meeting and exhibition match, she hadn't had any further dealings or communications, but she was sure that such a stable state of affairs wouldn't last.

Members of the Pure Phoenix Sect were instructed to not cause any conflicts with the Golden Dragon Sect and to always defer to them no matter the circumstances.

One of the first major missions she gave to Li Runfa was to get more information about Sunan. It took him a few days before he was ready to report his findings.

"It's already difficult to distinguish what is truth, what is fabrication, and what is exaggeration," he said. "One thing is for sure: Nobody knows where Sunan came from. Based on his accent, he's almost certainly from this general vicinity, the north. As for his specific origin, everyone had a different story, and from what I can tell, they are all speculation. Everyone does agree that he wandered into the city from the mountains and almost immediately befriended Sun Mai, who was nothing more than a down-and-out scholar at the time.

"Sunan made a name for himself fighting in the local platform fights. He defeated a man called the Killer of Daolu by cutting his head off, or perhaps by caving his chest in. Stories differ. Later, he killed the local crime lord, Iron Awl Hu, although I can't quite determine why. Some claim that he was avenging a loved one. Some say he was rescuing a maiden. Some are convinced that he simply wanted more power.

"There are even more stories that I can't verify. Rumor has it that he and Sun Mai killed a squad of Lions of Peace, or maybe just one, depending on who tells the story. That may be possible considering they made that very claim to us when we first met. Some people say that they are demon hunters, while others are convinced of the opposite—that they are building an army of demons to serve the Demon Emperor.

"I find the latter unlikely. On the very day that we arrived at the city, one of his key advisors was revealed to be a spy. And no ordinary spy at that. It was the Love General herself."

Bao gasped. "The Love General?"

Li Runfa nodded. "Indeed. Do you remember when we crossed the bridge, we saw a woman with red hair? That was her. Apparently Sunan was furious that she had lied to him. His men wanted to kill her, but instead he banished her and threatened to have her executed if she ever returned."

"So he's probably not interested in serving the Demon Emperor."

Li Runfa shrugged. "It's hard to say. But if he is, banishing the Love General and threatening to have her executed wouldn't be a good way to start."

"We need to find out for sure." Bao rested her chin on the palm of her hand. "The Bone General will return, and when he does, we need to be prepared."

"Prepared? For…?"

It was Bao's turn to shrug. "I don't know. I don't want to run again, but… we can't fight him. Can we?"

The two of them looked at each other for a long moment.

She shook her head. "We have time to think about it. Although probably not much. Before the time comes, we absolutely must ascertain Sunan's stance. If the Bone General demanded that we be handed over, perhaps Sunan would comply to curry favor."

"Should I arrange a meeting?" Li Runfa asked.

After a long moment of hesitation, Bao nodded again. "Yes. I need to present him with a gift, though. The Butterfly Festival is coming up, and that would provide the perfect excuse. Do we have anything from the forest stronghold that we could offer?"

"He runs the underworld of an entire city," Li Runfa replied. "What could we possibly give him that he doesn't already have access to? Maybe you should use the Phoenix Crown?"

"I don't want to use that on people who aren't truly my enemy. I already affected him with the power of the phoenix demon in the past. He won't take kindly to me trying to manipulate him with it again."

"Maybe you could give him something... personalized?" The two of them sat there silently for a moment, until Li Runfa tilted his head to the side. "How about some calligraphy? You've written a few lines of poetry in the past, haven't you?"

"When I was drunk!" Bao responded, laughing.

Li Runfa chuckled. "You would never be able to tell from the poetry itself. It really is quite beautiful. Why don't I buy some fine canvas and ink? Considering your background, your calligraphy really is above average."

That much was true. Having been raised in a noble family, she had trained in calligraphy from an early age.

"Very well, make it happen. Buy the finest materials, though."

Later that night, Bao lay in bed trying to sleep, her mind swirling with countless thoughts. She hated it when she wasn't in control of a situation, and right now she felt anything but in control.

Be confident, Bao, she told herself. *You've gotten this far, and you're not going to stop here... Where is that gust of wind coming from?*

All of a sudden, Bao realized that the room was somehow drafty, even though the windows were sealed tight. Frowning, she climbed out of bed, licked her finger, and tried to determine where the wind was coming from.

It took a few minutes of investigation, but she soon tracked the source to a wardrobe in the corner of the room. Given that it was constructed directly into the wall itself, she'd left it there while redecorating the room. Upon opening the wardrobe and looking inside, she found that it was completely empty. However, she could definitely detect a faint breeze coming from inside, and could even see the flame of her candle flickering.

She began to run her hands up and down the inside of the wardrobe, and after a moment she found a spot where a knot of wood wobbled slightly when her hand passed over it. She moved her hand back and pushed down, and a clicking sound rang out, and she felt the entire wardrobe move slightly.

Frowning, she grabbed the edge and pulled, and to her surprise, the entire wardrobe opened like a door, revealing a steep staircase which descended into the darkness.

Tie Gangwen mentioned that the Golden Immortal disappeared mysteriously. Perhaps this is how he did it.

Grabbing her knives from under her pillow, as well as an extra candle, she entered the doorway and began to climb down the stairs.

The passage descended steeply for quite some distance before she reached a tunnel carved through the bedrock beneath the city. As soon as she set foot on the tunnel floor, the flickering of her candle grew more pronounced as the wind picked up. Cupping her hand in front of the candle to protect it, she began to walk down the corridor.

Soon, the tunnel veered to the left, and she found herself at an iron door. At first she intended to pass it and find out where the tunnel led to, but as she did, the wind shifted, very nearly blowing out her candle. Apparently the wind was coming from behind that iron door.

She turned back toward the iron door, which surprisingly was not latched, bolted, or locked in any way. Keeping her hand cupped protectively in front of the candle, she pulled the door open.

Before she could make another move, a blast of wind enveloped her, blowing the candle out in the process.

Despite the lack of a candle, she could still see. Behind the iron door was a small room roughly six paces wide and six paces long. At the far end of the room was a stone altar, atop which was a chunk of orelike metal that emanated a soft blue light. The blue light filled the room and spilled out into the tunnel, providing just enough illumination to see clearly.

A stiff wind blew about in the room, also emerging out into the corridor.

What is this place?

After a moment of consideration, she thought back to the fallen star which had contained the phoenix demon.

Could this be another type of fallen star?

Another moment passed, and she gritted her teeth and stepped into the room.

The wind immediately slammed into her with such force that she nearly flew off her feet. Not only did it buffet her like a punching giant, it stabbed at her like thousands of needles. Immense pressure weighed down on her from above. Hunching her shoulders and bending her knees, she took another step.

The forces pummeling her increased dramatically, causing her hair to whip around her wildly and her clothing to flap back and forth.

She took another step, and she was halfway to the stone. The pressure grew, and she felt almost like her skin was being flayed.

With her fourth and fifth steps, the intensity increased even more. She felt like she was in the middle of a tornado at the bottom of the sea. Blood began to leak out of her left nostril, and her ears popped.

And yet she managed to take the final step, placing her directly in front of the altar, which she gripped with both hands.

Looking down at the stone in front of her, she could tell that it was very different from the fallen star. This rock looked almost like liquid, with blue streaks running through it that emanated soft light.

Remembering her experience with the fallen star, she quickly produced a handkerchief from within her sleeve that she placed over the rock. The wind died down.

Breathing a sigh of relief, she gingerly wrapped the rock up in the handkerchief and then did her best to straighten her hair. Wiping the blood off of her nose and lips, she began to fumble her way through the darkness back toward her room.

I wonder if a magic wind rock will be enough to impress Sunan.

CHAPTER 40
POETRY AND DREAMS

Wind stone?" Sunan asked, looking skeptically down at the box he held in his hands.

"I know it sounds unbelievable," Bao replied. "But it's true. I think wind stone is a fitting name, but you can call it anything you want. Whatever you do, don't open that box without proper preparations."

"And where did you find it?"

"The rock? I discovered a secret passage in the mansion you provided for us. Halfway through the passage is a chamber where I found the rock. The passage itself ended in a locked iron door. I can't be certain, but based on the direction the passageway follows, I think it leads… here…"

Sunan and Sun Mai exchanged a glance.

"I can show you the passage, of course," Bao said.

Sunan looked back at the box. "That would probably be good. Later. It wouldn't surprise me at all that the residences of the Golden Immortal and Iron Awl Hu were connected. But why would they have a magic rock like this?" With that, he handed the box over to Sun Mai.

Sun Mai took the box and began to examine it closely. "Those two were wrapped up in all sorts of things. Maybe they were planning to sell it? Or make it into a weapon?"

"Sect Leader Sunan," Bao said, "I know of a man who can forge things like this into weapons or objects of great power. Perhaps it would be worth visiting him."

Sun Mai knocked on the lid of the box with his knuckle. "You know, I've seen a lot of things in my life, but I've never seen anything as overtly magical as you describe. It really creates a tempest around it?"

Bao nodded. "It can be quite destructive."

Sun Mai fingered the latch that held the lid shut. "But how could someone forge a weapon out of it if creates a tempest? And how could this tiny little box contain a storm?"

"I'm not sure, Chief Minister Sun. When I first acquired the rock, I covered it with a piece of cloth, and that was enough. Furthermore, the tempest seems to be limited to a range of about six paces."

"I don't know, it all sounds a bit unbelievable to me."

Time seemed to slow down for Sunan as Sun Mai unlatched the lid of the box. Although Sunan didn't particularly like Bao, nor did he trust her implicitly, he saw no reason why she would be lying about the gift of the magic rock. She seemed to be trying to get on his good side with it, and she had repeatedly warned them not to open the box without making advance preparations.

When Sunan saw Sun Mai unlatch the lid, his scalp began to tingle with foreboding. "Sun Mai, don't—"

Before he could finish his statement, Sun Mai lifted the box up to eye level and cracked open the lid by just a hair.

Bao's eyes went wide. "No! Don't—"

As soon as the lid opened, the entire room filled with a raging tempest. Sun Mai let out a shriek as he was sent spinning off to the side and was slammed into the wall. Sunan and Bao were both thrown violently to the edge of the room, smashing through tables and other room decorations. The members of the Golden Dragon Sect and Pure Phoenix Sect were likewise flung head over heels in all directions.

As for the box, as soon as Sun Mai was thrown off of his feet, he loosened his grip on it, allowing it to fall to the ground. Being at the very middle of the tempest, it seemed to be completely unaffected by the wind. As screams and bellows filled the room, along with the howling of wind, the box landed on the ground, and the lid snapped shut.

Just as quickly as it started, the tempest in the room vanished. A protracted silence followed, which was broken when one of the scroll paintings in the room fell off the wall and landed on the ground with a crash.

Sunan struggled free from the wreckage and looked over at Sun Mai, who was slumped almost upside down against the wall.

"Still seem unbelievable?" Sunan asked.

***

No one was seriously injured by the tempest blast, although one of the Golden Dragons ended up with a broken arm. By the time everyone was out of the room and checked on, it was getting near the dinner hour, and Sunan suggested they continue their conversation at the Heavenly Meat Palace.

Bao agreed, and before long they were chatting over mounds of meat and jugs of alcohol.

When Bao suggested they drink sorghum wine, Sunan agreed.

Sunan was well aware that Bao's visit and gift came with an underlying purpose. She was clearly trying to earn his favor, or perhaps make a request. However, as the evening wore on, she made no mention of any such thing.

This dinner went much more smoothly than the last, and no fighting challenges were issued.

Sunan was surprised to learn that Bao enjoyed reading and had even read some of the same adventure stories he had enjoyed when he was younger. He soon noticed that Bao avoided talking about her childhood or family background, something he was more than happy to accommodate, as he himself did the same.

The evening wore on, and the sorghum wine began to take effect on some of the other disciples. Even Sun Mai eventually slumped over on the table and started snoring.

Because it was the eve of the Butterfly Festival, there was no ward curfew, and thus no need to leave the restaurant early.

Eventually, it was late, and the only customers left awake in the Heavenly Meat Palace were Sunan and Bao, and both of them were quite drunk.

"Did I ever tell you I can write poetry?" Bao said, her speech only slightly slurred.

"No, you didn't. That's incredible. I couldn't write poetry to save my life! Can you write some now?"

Bao's eyes widened. "Of course! Do you have a brush and paper?"

Sunan called a waiter over, who rushed to fetch some paper, a brush, and ink.

After dipping the brush into the ink, Bao closed her eyes. "Okay, let me think for a moment."

She took a deep breath, and then began to write in her flowing calligraphy.

The fiends, a tempest dark and foul,
A shining—

As she wrote the second line, Sunan jumped in and said the words, even before she could finish writing them.

"'A shining pillar paints the sky!'" he said. "I've seen that before. I even know the next line! 'Golden droplets spin and howl!'"

Bao looked over at him, her jaw dropping and her eyes going wide. "How did you do that?"

Sunan shrugged. "I've seen that poem before…"

Bao looked down at the poem. "But where? I composed this poem just now. The words were on my tongue, just waiting to be put onto paper."

A chill ran up Sunan's spine. "An intruder was spotted outside my window recently, a girl in a gray robe. My lieutenant Yuwen Huo chased her to the temple of Supreme Judge Yu, but when Sun Mai and I went to investigate, she had just left, and all that was left were some burning papers. That poem was written on one of the pieces of paper. There were some lines before it too. 'The graceful Bird due south takes wing, from north to east the clouds surge forth, from south to west fair feathers sing.' There was another line before the first, but it was too badly burned to understand, and the same with the lines past the passage I read."

Bao's hand began to tremble. "They all go together…" she said, her voice quavering.

"What do you mean?"

"I wrote all the lines separately, but they go together. And they even rhyme. 'The shining Wyrm strides ever north, the graceful Bird due south takes wing, from north to east the clouds surge forth, from south to west fair feathers sing. The fiends, a tempest dark and foul, a shining pillar paints the sky, golden droplets spin and howl…' Except, I never wrote that last line…"

She quickly wrote the last line onto the piece of paper, then looked back up at Sunan. "You said it was a woman in a gray robe?"

"Yes. And apparently she's adept at using qi."

"This… this… I don't understand. When I wrote the first two lines of the poem, a woman in a gray robe caused a huge scene. She even supposedly caused a man's head to explode as she fled.

This woman already has the entire poem written down? I've never seen it before, I'm certain. So how did the poem come to be in my thoughts?"

Sunan felt the hairs on his arms and neck standing on end. "It's not the first time this woman in gray has been seen around me, either. Sun Mai claimed to have seen her before. In fact… it was the same night I had those strange dreams."

"Dreams?" Bao said.

"I often have strange dreams, almost visions. Golden light shining… and a black wind. Golden clouds. A strange symbol…"

Their eyes locked, and it was almost as if both could feel the other's heart pounding.

"Sect Leader Sunan, may I ask, when was the first time you had a dream like that?"

Sunan took a deep breath. He had never talked to anyone about his dreams before, and he had most certainly never talked about the first time he experienced them. Perhaps it was because of the alcohol, or perhaps it was because of the bizarre connection between his dreams and Bao's poetry, but he felt the overwhelming urge to speak.

"I was raised in a village near the Bay of Yu. Life was happy there. I had a dad and a mom, and three sisters. But the Demon Emperor destroyed all of that. The village was burned, and my family… they all died. I fled into the Huang Mountains, where I lived alone for a long time. It seemed like years, but I guess it was only a few months.

"That was where I learned about qi, and in fact, it was shortly after the qi entered me that I started dreaming. I've always thought that the dreams had to do with the qi, but now I'm not so sure.

"Chieftainess Bao, I'm not sure where you come from or what your background is, so I don't know if you've ever seen things like what I've seen. *Horrible* things.

"I think about my family a lot. My parents. My sisters. I miss them. And that's why I don't think I can ever work for that bastard, the Demon Emperor.

"He sent his people to try to recruit me, you know. Trying to decide what to do is torture. Objectively, it would make sense to give in to him. That would be best for the city here, for the Golden Dragons. I've even heard stories implying the Demon Emperor is actually a good person, and that he's being manipulated into doing evil. But I'm not sure if I believe those stories.

"I don't know what to do, Chieftainess Bao. I hate the Demon Emperor, but I can't fight him! He has armies and magic and demons on his side. I mean, he himself is demon! He's so powerful that even if I ran from him, he would probably be able to chase me down and kill me." He shook his head.

"I really don't know what to do."

He looked over to see Bao staring him in the eyes.

.

CHAPTER 41
URGENT NEWS

Bao held Sunan's gaze for a moment that, on the one hand, seemed like an eternity and yet also passed as quickly as a raindrop splashing into a puddle.

Then she looked down into her empty drinking vessel.

"I've never told anyone my surname," she said quietly. "I always worried that if my people knew what it was, they would reject me. I think that in the beginning they actually would have, but by now they probably don't care. My surname is Shangguan. Have you heard of it?"

Sunan's eyes widened. "You mean the Shangguan Clan from Yu Zhing?"

"Yes," she said with a nod.

Sunan thought for a moment. "When I was young, I read a book about the noble clans of Yu Zhing. Shangguan. Nangong. Gongsun. Sima… There were some more, I think."

"Yes," Bao continued. "I was born Shangguan Bao of the Shangguan clan. Originally there were ten noble clans. Shanguan.

Nangong. Gongsun. Sima. Gongye. Dongmen. Zhongli. Xuanyuan. Yangzi. Situ. There was a rebellion when I was young, and some of those clans were completely wiped out. Nangong. Dongmen. Zhongli. Those clans were executed en masse, even the elderly and the babies. Although the other clans survived as a whole, none of them escaped completely unscathed.

"I was very young, but I'll never forget watching my mother be tortured and burned alive. It was at one of the mass executions that the Demon Emperor himself presided over. I remember one of my cousins... I really loved her, like a sister. The Bone Slicers cut her hands and feet off, then extracted the bones and stabbed her to death with them.

"I still have nightmares about those days." Bao shuddered slightly, then shook her head to clear it. "Later I was kidnapped by some criminals. When the Bone General invaded their headquarters, I fled with some of them, which was how I escaped Yu Zhing. But the Bone General doesn't give up so easily. He sent people after us, including an ogre.

"I managed to kill it, and we wiped out the entire force that had been sent against us. Unfortunately, the Bone General still managed to find out what happened, and he's been chasing me ever since.

"Sect Leader Sunan, the reason why I gave you the wind stone is because... I know that the Bone General will come for me. It might be tomorrow. It might be next month. It might be a year from now. But he will come. And just like you... I don't know what to do. At least, not at this moment. As far as the future, I know exactly what I'm going to do.

"The Demon Emperor is a vile bastard who is turning Qi Xien into a living hell. He deserves to die. He must die. And I will kill him. I might not have an army, but I have people who will follow me into battle. I might not be a warrior, but I become a better fighter every single day.

"I have complete and utter confidence in being able to do this,

Sect Leader Sunan. The only question is when. Maybe I'll lead an army into battle to crush him. Maybe I'll sneak into his chamber at night and slit his throat. I don't know exactly how I will do it. But I know that in the end, the Demon Emperor will die, and I'll be the one to make it happen."

The truth was that the sorghum wine was fueling Bao's speech just as much as her self-confidence. She had never given voice to any such sentiments in the past, nor had she ever really pondered the matter in any detail. In the heat of the moment, though, the words spilled out of her mouth with burning passion.

As she spoke, a fire seemed to flicker to life in Sunan's eyes, and by the time she finished speaking, his hands were clenched into fists and a smile just barely turned up the corner of his mouth. Without a word, he reached out and grabbed the nearest flagon of alcohol, which he used to fill both of their drinking vessels.

"Chieftainess Bao, your words have pierced my heart and soul. I felt lost before, but now I realize why that was. I was ignoring the truths that existed in my own heart. The Demon Emperor killed your family, he killed my family, and he has killed countless other families across Qi Xien. If we do not put an end to his reign of horrors, then who will?

"Regardless of how qi came into the world, it is a gift, and its greatest recipients are the two of us. I don't know if I believe in the Upper Realms, and the immortals, and Xian Nu Shen. Even if they do exist, it seems that they have no regard for the world of man. We must be responsible for our own fates and destinies. If you wish to slay the Demon Emperor, I will stand by your side, and so will my people. What do you say we swear an oath?"

With that, he raised his drinking vessel into the air.

"I, Fan Sunan, hereby swear that I will devote my life to the downfall of the Demon Emperor. Be it by sword or flame, be it by fair means or foul, he shall die. As sect leader of the Golden Dragon Sect, I hereby swear loyalty to Chieftainess Shangguan Bao and the

Pure Phoenix Sect. Henceforth, we shall strive relentlessly toward our mutual goal of bringing peace and justice to all of Qi Xien!"

Bao's eyes shone with a cold, piercing light as she raised her own glass and said, "I, Shangguan Bao, hereby swear to devote my life to the death of the Demon Emperor. Be it by sword or flame, be it by fair means or foul, he will be exterminated. As chieftainess of the Pure Phoenix Sect, I hereby swear loyalty to Sect Leader Fan Sunan and the Golden Dragon Sect. Henceforth, we shall live with one goal in mind: bringing peace and justice to Qi Xien, and bringing destruction to the Demon Emperor!"

And then, they drank.

***

Two years went by.

The Pure Phoenix Sect and the Golden Dragon Sect entered a formal alliance. Both sects increased their recruitment and training efforts, although they did their best to do it in the most discreet method possible.

Because of their various duties, as well as their focus on personal training, Bao and Sunan had little time for personal matters. Although they saw each other fairly often at formal banquets and other occasions, there was little time to develop their friendship.

There always seemed to be some matter that needed to be handled in Daolu that required the attention of one or the other. A few of the incidents that occurred would become tales told for years to come.

For instance, Sun Mai had a famous debate with An Jian, the mysterious owner of the Delightful Wind Shop, a debate which lasted for three days and three nights. Another time, Sunan dueled the leader of the beggars in Daolu in front of a packed house in the Green Elephant Emporium. After gaining victory, Sunan also won the respect of the beggars in the city. One of the most famous stories was how Bao outdrank the ten most famous drinkers in the city, all in one night.

Every month or two, a letter would arrive for Sunan from the Love General, but he refused to read even one of them and demanded that they be burned.

They made a few attempts to do further research and investigation into the so-called wind stone, but all such attempts were useless. Even just cracking open the box unleashed a huge tempest.

One of the most shocking revelations was that Sun Mai's apprentice Little Mao was actually not a young man, but rather, a young woman. Even more astonishing was that she was actually Mao Yun's sister, Mao Mei.

After months of attempting to hide her face from Mao Yun, he managed to catch sight of her at a banquet, and the truth was revealed. Mao Yun wasn't very happy about his sister being the apprentice of Sun Mai, but he had little say in the matter. Sun Mai seemed a bit confused when his apprentice stopped wearing the robes of a scholar and instead dressed like a fashionable young woman, but after consulting the moon about it, he declared that it was destiny.

By the end of the two-year period, both sects had grown large. The Golden Dragon Sect had roughly two hundred members. They were organized into four primary divisions, each one led by a Dragon Lord, two of whom were Yuwen Huo and Tie Gangwen.

As for the Pure Phoenix Sect, they numbered roughly one hundred fifty members, organized into three divisions, each one led by one of the Claws of the Phoenix.

After all of the intense training, the key figures in both sects made significant advancement in terms of martial arts.

Sunan, Sun Mai, Bao, and Mao Yun had all reached the point where a seventh breakthrough was in sight.

The Dragon Lords Yuwen Huo and Tie Gangwen, as well as the Claws of the Phoenix, Liu Jiahui, Lin Qingxia, and Yang Ziqiong, had all reached five breakthroughs.

As for the rest of the members of the various sects, they were a mix of levels, with more than half having reached one breakthrough, more than thirty percent two, and the rest having experienced three or four.

They formed a powerful fighting force, but Sunan and Bao both agreed to try to keep the true level of that power hidden. The longer they could last before the Demon Emperor came for them, the better.

It was well into the second year before reports began to filter in that the situation in the empire was changing. After decades of unrest, the south had finally been stabilized, and troops were beginning to move north again. At Sun Mai's urgings, they began to send spies across the Chezou River to infiltrate Tung-On and Fan.

Soon reports came in. Troop levels in Tung-On were rising dramatically. Over the course of only three months, the number of soldiers in the city increased from only a few thousand to over ten thousand. Perhaps even more. Reports differed. There were also large numbers of chariots.

Only a fool would be unable to see what was happening. When the reports from most spies indicated that twenty thousand troops were now stationed in and around Tung-On, and that the Fire General had been spotted in Fan, Bao and Sunan called a meeting. Everyone was present, including the Dragon Lords and the Claws of the Phoenix.

"The Fire General is the spear that slashes across the battlefield," Bao said. "If he leaves Fan for Tung-On, then it means war will be coming to the land north of the Chezou River."

"He'll obviously strike Nansun first," Sun Mai said. "Perhaps we should flee while we have the chance."

"For once, I agree with the little scholar," Mao Yun said. It had been some time since the two resolved their conflicts from the past, and they had even developed a bit of a friendship. "We could escape into the Huang Mountains, maybe head for Lun Shan."

"Or the Yangu Plains," Liu Jiahui said.

Bao looked over at Sunan. "Sect Leader Sunan, what do you think?"

Sunan took a moment to respond. "We can't fight an army of thousands with only a few hundred people. Even if you count the soldiers and constables of Daolu, we're still completely outnumbered. Besides, the Demon Emperor's soldiers can use qi also. Perhaps a preemptive retreat would be the best. But... I don't feel comfortable simply abandoning the populace."

"Sunan," Sun Mai said, "don't forget what Kong Zhi said. 'Sometimes true courage is knowing when not to fight.'"

Sunan looked down at the map laid out on the table in front of him. Before he could respond, the lieutenant of the first division of the Golden Dragons entered and clasped his hands respectfully. "Sect Leader, urgent news. Magistrate Pei Bai was just assassinated. And so was Sheriff Song. Daolu is now completely leaderless."

CHAPTER 42
QINGGONG

Located not too far away from Tung-On was a stretch of rolling terrain that created a valley, lined on either side by trees. A long line of troops originating from Tung-On was marching into that very valley.

On one of the hills above the valley sat three figures on horseback. Although none of the soldiers in the army looked at them twice, any ordinary citizen of Qi Xien who saw them would be left trembling from fear, except for perhaps the first, who was a woman.

She had long red hair and was stunningly beautiful. If Sunan were here, he would instantly recognize her as the Love General. Next to the Love General was a monstrous figure with tusklike teeth and dangerous eyes, wearing armor that seemed to be crafted from bone. If Bao could lay eyes on him, she would immediately identify him as the Bone General.

As for the third figure, he was someone that neither Sunan nor Bao had ever seen, and he was even more intimidating than the Bone General. Although he had similarly monstrous features, his shoulders were much broader, and he was taller. His face was crisscrossed with scars, and he was missing an ear. Whereas the Bone General was like a wicked-looking blade, this third figure was like a weathered battle-axe.

He wore a spectacular suit of yellow and orange armor, crafted expertly from interlocking plates of steel. While the Bone General's armor seemed to be crafted with the intention of striking terror into the hearts of those who beheld it, this yellow and orange armor seemed designed to intimidate. It radiated power, almost as if it were magical, as if even the strongest sword or fastest arrow could simply bounce off it like a pebble thrown at a boulder.

The third figure was the Fire General. He was responsible for training the Demon Emperor's soldiers and leading them into battle. He was as skilled a strategist as he was a fighter, and he was feared by anyone in Qi Xien who dared to lead troops against him.

The three generals looked down into the valley, where three glowing doorways could be seen. They were just large enough for men on horseback to ride through, three abreast, and they were clearly devices of powerful magic. Most shocking of all was that the troops who entered the doorways emerged in another location, far away from Tung-On.

The Bone General snorted coldly. "You must have paid a heavy price to persuade Gar-El to use three Krahang doors to teleport the army to Daolu."

"Quite the contrary," the Fire General replied. "He insisted on it. He originally wanted me to use four, but I convinced him that three would be sufficient."

The Bone General looked over at the Fire General with narrowed eyes. "Why does he think Daolu is so important?"

"The chief shaman performed a divination. Supposedly this Sunan is the key to everything. If he builds a power base in Daolu, Gar-El will fall. If we take the city and defeat Sunan, Gar-El will reign for more than a thousand years in peace."

The Love General shook her head. "The chief shaman said all that? I'm still convinced that half of his supposed prophecies are nothing more than drunken ramblings."

The Fire General looked over at the Love General. "You've certainly taken a liking to that human form you're wearing. You haven't gone soft, have you?"

The Love General's lips curled into a sneer. "I think not. However, I still can't believe we're wasting three Krahang doors just to try to take this city."

"The chief shaman might be a bit of an eccentric, but his divinations are no joke. He has correctly predicted far too many things throughout the years. Even the revolt in the south would have been much more successful were it not for his assistance. If he says that Sunan is our doom, only a fool would ignore him."

After a long moment of silence, the Love General said, "I still think it's a mistake. Sunan could be turned to our side."

The Bone General's expression was as cold as ever. "Our goal is to take the city. A single human is of no importance, no matter how good of a fighter he is. If I didn't know you better, I might also think you've gone soft."

The Love General declined to respond. A gust of wind blew, lifting her hair as she looked down at the troops entering the portals. Although no one could see, a flicker of hesitation passed through her eyes as she tucked her hair behind her ear.

***

Daolu was already in complete and utter chaos. Although the government and the constables had never been well respected, they were the official force of law in the city. With the sudden deaths of Magistrate Pei Bai and Sheriff Song, the city was now without any leadership whatsoever.

Sunan was the de facto leader, although that was mostly due to his control of underworld elements. There were many commoners in the city who had only heard whispers of his name, or at most, stories of some of his deeds. Although the Golden Dragons were well-known, to many people they were simply another iteration of Iron Awl Hu's organization.

And of course, Bao and the Pure Phoenix Sect were even less understood.

Under normal circumstances, the sudden death of either the sheriff or the chief magistrate would have been followed by one of their minions succeeding them. The Hen-Shi Empire still ruled in the north, with Emperor Tian residing in Nansun, to the west of Daolu. However, Emperor Tian had more pressing concerns, such as the buildup of troops in Tung-On, and he didn't provide a single response to inquiries sent via messenger bird.

Had it been a single death, Sunan might have been able to "suggest" a temporary replacement for either of them until Emperor Tian officially intervened. But when both men were killed in the same night, it struck fear deep into the hearts of the constables, the government agencies, and the populace in general.

The next day, Sunan contacted Sorghum God, the leader of the beggars in the city, whom he had defeated recently in a duel. With his cooperation, the beggars mobilized to help the Golden Dragon Sect and the Pure Phoenix Sect keep the peace.

It took about three days, but soon the city calmed down and returned to a semblance of its former order.

And that was when the armies appeared.

Only a few days before, all reports had indicated that the Fire General was massing troops in Tung-On, leading Sunan, Bao, and everyone else to the assumption that they were many days away. Even if they marched at full speed and bypassed Nansun, they couldn't reach Daolu for ten to fourteen days.

Besides, it seemed much more likely that the Fire General would first take Nansun, which was where Emperor Tian remained holed up. Even if Emperor Tian fled, leaving the city wide open, it would still take days for the Fire Emperor to occupy it effectively before marching on to Daolu.

Because of all of that, Bao and Sunan were both completely shocked when reports began to pour in of armies sighted to the west, north, and east.

"Impossible!" Sunan said. "We have confirmation that the Fire General was in Tung-On only a few days ago. Could this be another army?"

"But from where?" Mao Yun asked. "There are no major cities to the north or the west. Where did they come from?"

Something clicked in Bao's mind. "I remember hearing a story once. Supposedly, when the Demon Emperor conquered Huisheng, his army mysteriously attacked from both east and west simultaneously. At the time, no one could explain how soldiers came to be on the east side of the city. Some people even said the Demon Emperor flew the army over the city during the night."

"A flying army?" Sun Mai said. He rubbed his chin. "Seems improbable… but at the same time, completely fantastic!"

From the city walls of Daolu, it was possible to see three encampments being set up in the three cardinal directions. Furthermore, it was to the great shock of the entire city that the bridge crossing over the Chezou River to the south caught fire and burned down overnight.

All paths had been cut off.

Surprisingly, the city did not descend further into chaos. Most people were so scared that they didn't even want to leave their houses, and the city went depressingly quiet.

Eventually, a command pavilion sprang up in the eastern army's camp. It was a white tent with three banners flapping in the wind in front of it. Each banner was a different color: yellow, white, and black respectively.

No one paid much attention to the banners. That is, until an emissary from the Fire General arrived with an ultimatum.

> *To whom it may concern:*
> *This city is property of the King of the Pure Ones. Send out the ones named Sunan and Bao, as well as any of their subordinates. They will not be killed or harmed. You have three days to comply.*
> *If you comply on the first day, when the yellow banner flies, everyone in the city will be spared. If you wait until the second day, when only the white and black banners fly, then the soldiers in the city will be killed, and the populace spared. If you wait until the black banner flies alone, then everyone in the city will be killed or enslaved without the slightest bit of mercy shown.*
> *We have 20,000 troops, more fighters than the entire population of your city. You have no hope and no other options. Consider well.*
> *With full sincerity,*
> *The Fire General*

Word of the letter was not spread among the populace. Despite hours of debate, no consensus could be reached about what to do. Sun Mai suggested that the key figures from the Golden Dragon Sect and Pure Phoenix Sect try to cross the Chezou River by boat, during the darkness of night. The suggestion was met with grumbling. According to Mao Yun, there were enough supplies in the city to sustain them for several days. On the other hand, an army of 20,000 would be very difficult to feed for very long, especially so far away from any supply chain.

"But," Sun Mai said, "what if they *do* have flying troops or magical means of transportation?"

"A flying army?" Mao Yun said. "Are you serious?"

"Anything's possible," Sun Mai replied.

Late into the night, they adjourned their meeting to sleep. Back in the former residence of the Golden Immortal, Bao and Mao Yun sat in a courtyard, drinking yellow wine.

After a protracted silence, Bao said, "I know what we have to do."

Mao Yun's eyebrows rose.

Bao grinned. "Kill the Fire General."

"And how do you plan to do that?" Mao Yun asked.

"A small group of us can sneak into his command pavilion. They would never expect us to do such a thing. Think about it. We killed an ogre once already, and that was before we became truly powerful fighters. If we put an end to the Fire General, his army will dissolve. Even if the Bone General gets sent to fill his spot, we should have plenty of time to make our escape, either to the south or the west."

Mao Yun thought for a moment. "I'm not sure, Bao. Assassination? We've never done anything like that before."

"Come on, Mao Yun, you have to have some confidence in yourself! We've made significant progress in our martial arts recently, especially the lightness arts. What did Sun Mai call them again?"

"Qinggong," Mao Yun replied.

"Right," Bao said. "Classical Fei again. With our qinggong abilities, we could get into that command pavilion in the blink of an eye. We slice the Fire General's throat and return to the city before anyone knows what's happened."

Mao Yun seemed to be wavering, but Bao simply grinned. "Come on, man up! Go get the Claws of the Phoenix. We leave within the hour."

CHAPTER 43
SURPRISE!

As luck would have it, it was a cloudy night. Dappled moonlight bathed the city in both shadow and light, making it very easy for Bao and her group to slip over the rooftops toward the eastern wall of Daolu.

There were five of them. She and Mao Yun took the lead, with the Claws of the Phoenix following close behind. All of them wore black clothing that revealed little more than their eyes.

Flying Death, or Liu Jiahui, was one of the Pure Phoenix Sect's most preeminent masters of qinggong. He had developed a technique which came to be called Drift of the Butterfly Fish that even some of the lowest-ranked members of the sect could use to float through the air for long distances. In the hands of masters like the Claws of the Phoenix, the effects were even more spectacular.

Lin Qingxia, the Throat-Slitting Phoenix Ghost, was similar to Bao in that she fought with knives. She had a reputation for ruthlessness, and before joining the Pure Phoenix Sect, was rumored to have been a fugitive murderer, although Bao was convinced otherwise.

Lastly was Yang Ziqiong, who was called the Blood Drinker. She had developed a dianxue attack that, as of yet, no other disciple had managed to master. By striking a series of acupoints on the chest and shoulder, she could cause the victim's throat to explode.

This late at night, all of the city wards were closed according to curfew, but that posed little obstruction for such top experts from the Pure Phoenix Sect.

It only took a few minutes before they were in the shadows of the Dragon Gate, the main barbican gate on the twelve-meter-tall eastern wall. From this vantage point, they could see the Fire General's army encamped some distance from the city, beyond the fields of wheat and corn. The command tent with its three flapping banners seemed especially prominent among the other tents.

The entire group seemed to radiate a murderous aura, and their eyes were filled with both coldness and determination. They didn't seem to notice the chill breeze which ruffled their black clothing as they stood there gazing at their target.

Even from this distance, it was possible to make out the soldiers patrolling the perimeter of the camp. According to plan, the would-be assassins spent a few minutes analyzing the patrol patterns and identifying the temporary watchtowers that had been erected.

A moment later, a fluttering sound reached their ears, and the entire group went on guard.

A shadow descended from higher up on the Dragon Gate, and before any of them had a chance to react, someone was standing only a meter or two away from them. He wore the robes of the Golden Dragon Sect, and the skin on his face and neck was a bright blue color, giving him a dramatically terrifying appearance.

"Blue Devil Yuwen Huo," Mao Yun said softly.

Yuwen Huo nodded respectfully. "Is that you, Mao Yun? Out for a stroll, are we?"

Mao Yun looked at Bao.

In the years that she had been in the city, Bao had encountered Yuwen Huo on numerous occasions and had come to like the man. He was fiercely loyal to Sunan and a good fighter, one of the best in the Golden Dragon Sect. Pulling the black cloth away to reveal her face, Bao said, "We're going to kill the Fire General. Care to join us? How is your qinggong?"

Yuwen Huo's eyes narrowed, and he turned his head to look out at the distant command tent. After a moment, he looked back at Bao. "Does Sect Leader Sunan know about this?"

She shook her head. "We don't have time for meetings and debate. The plan is to strike quickly. Be in and out in only a few minutes. The slightest sign of trouble, we flee. There's really nothing to lose. I'm completely confident we can do it. If you wish to join us, here."

She had a sack slung over her shoulder, which she loosened. Inside was a long black cloak which she'd brought along for emergency purposes, as well as a few strips of black cloth. Everyone in the group had similar emergency items in case they need extra levels of disguise while on the mission.

Yuwen Huo looked at the black cloak in Bao's hand, and after a moment, a slight smile appeared on his face. "Nowadays Sect Leader Sunan has too many things to worry about. He's too weighed down with responsibility. In the old days, this is exactly the kind of thing he would have done. It's been a long time since I've been in a real fight."

He reached out and took the cloak, throwing it over his shoulders. After tying the strip of cloth around his nose and mouth, he looked just as capable as them of melting into the shadows.

"What about your qinggong?" Liu Jiahui asked.

"I haven't mastered that butterfly move of yours, but I have my own abilities. Let's just see if you can keep up."

Without another word, he stepped off the city wall and dropped toward the ground. A moment later, he vanished, moving so quickly than none of them could even see him. In the blink of an eye, he was almost a hundred meters away from them, waiting in the shadow of a tree.

"Showoff," Liu Jiahui said.

Bao chuckled. "Let's go."

The entire group leapt off the city wall, using the Drift of the Butterfly Fish to float through the air like leaves. They couldn't quite match the speed that Yuwen Huo had just attained, but they didn't touch the ground the entire time, alighting softly in almost the exact location Yuwen Huo was waiting.

From that point on, Bao and her people relied on another fundamental qinggong technique, Leap of the Swan, while Yuwen Huo dashed forward at incredible speed with his own technique. In that manner, they made their way through the farmland and across the open land to the Fire General's army.

Eventually they stopped in a copse of trees a short distance from the perimeter of the tents. Just when they were about to dash toward the camp, the clouds parted, casting brilliant moonlight down on the entire camp.

Bao raised her hand to stop the group. They waited patiently for a while until the clouds once again swallowed up the moon. When everything was in shadow, and the patrolling guards had passed, they dashed forward.

Considering the high level of their martial arts, it was a relatively simple task for them to slip through the camp unnoticed. A few soldiers were out and about, but most were huddled around fires chatting and drinking, or even asleep in their tents.

Bao was a bit surprised. *Somewhat lacking in discipline for everything I've heard about the Fire General.*

After weaving through the camp for a short time, they were in the shadows of a tent just across from the command tent, which was guarded by two soldiers who were obviously veteran fighters. The moment of truth had arrived.

Drive away your fear, Bao, she thought to herself. *Be confident!*

Bao looked over at Lin Qingxia and Yang Ziqiong and gave them a slight nod. The two women blurred into motion, leaping out of the shadows as quickly as vipers. Before the two guards could react, the two Claws of the Phoenix unleashed their most powerful moves in cathartic fashion.

Yang Ziqiong's Blood-Drinking Stab was executed to perfection. Her hand stabbed into the guard's acupoints, and an instant later, his throat exploded, sending blood shooting out like a fountain. Yang Ziqiong expertly dodged to the side to avoid the blood, then reached out to slow the guard's fall so he didn't make any noise.

As for Lin Qingxia, as she dashed forward, she began to spin like a top, her long knives flashing through the night with such incredible speed that the guard had no hope of defending himself. The knives bit into his neck, tearing through flesh and bone with no mercy. A second later, his head tumbled to the ground a few meters away. Lin Qingxia quickly grabbed the shoulder of his torso and lowered his corpse to the ground.

Surprisingly, the guards only seemed have experienced two or three breakthroughs in their qi cultivation and were killed almost instantly.

Bao pointed to the entrance of the tent, and the group leapt into motion.

Yang Ziqiong and Lin Qingxia ran into the tent only a few seconds before the rest of the group. Yuwen Huo and Mao Yun made it in next, with Liu Jiahui and Bao coming up last.

As soon as Bao was in the tent, time seemed to slow.

As expected, the Fire General was not alone. Based on reports from the walls of Daolu, soldiers came in and out of the tent on a regular basis, and estimates had placed the number of people inside between four to six at any given time. Sure enough, there were six people present at the moment.

Shockingly, only three of them were human soldiers. One was an old man, clearly a veteran of many battles, with an eye patch and a perpetual snarl. The second was a handsome young man wearing gold jewelry over his armor. The third was a middle-aged woman with angry eyes that opened wide with shock.

Next was the Fire General, wearing his resplendent armor. He was leaning over a wide table that filled most of the tent, atop which was stretched a map of Daolu.

Standing only a few meters away from the Fire General was a woman in a red dress, with long red hair. As soon as Bao laid eyes on her, the hair on the back of her neck stood up.

I passed her on the bridge the day we came to Daolu. That's the Love General!

However, the sight of the Love General made almost no impression on Bao at all compared to the final figure in the tent. Sitting in a chair off to the side, hands steepled in front of him, was a sinister-looking figure in a suit of bone armor.

The Bone General. How did they get here? None of the reports mentioned other ogre generals.

Although everyone in the tent seemed shocked, Bao and her people had been expecting the unexpected, and they didn't hesitate.

Being the first into the tent, Yang Ziqiong and Lin Qingxia attacked first. Yang Ziqiong headed to the left side of the table, her target being the Love General. Lin Qingxia went in the opposite direction, attacking the young man with the gold jewelry.

Lin Qingxia used the same move she had on the outside, spinning like a top, blades whizzing toward the young man. However, the young man was an expert fighter. A sword appeared in his hand and flashed through the air to block the knives. His left foot flew through the air, kicking Lin Qingxia in the side and sending her smashing into the table.

As for Yang Ziqiong, she once again used the Blood-Drinking Stab, and cathartically at that. Her hand blurred through the air toward the Love General's sternum, and then her shoulder. The move was executed perfectly, and the Love General's eyes went wide.

However, all she did was cough. Her throat did not explode, and not a drop of blood could be seen. In fact, her mouth twisted into a snarl, and her own hand shot out, a palm striking Yang Ziqiong's shoulder.

Yang Ziqiong screamed with intense pain, staggering backward and then dropping to her knees.

As Bao was preparing to unleash her own secret move on the Love General, the Bone General rose to his feet and waved his hand in front of him in one fluid motion.

Three wickedly serrated bone knives flew through the air, one toward Yang Ziqiong, one toward Bao, and one toward Yuwen Huo.

The first knife landed true, stabbing directly into Yang Ziqiong's eye.

CHAPTER 44
CITY WALLS

In the heat of combat, there was no time for an emotional reaction. Bao called upon a move that Sunan had taught her during one of their sparring matches: Dragon Cleaves the Clouds. She flipped backward and kicked the Bone General's knife, sending it spinning off to the side, where it stabbed into the table.

As she flew through the air, she heard a muffled shout from Yuwen Huo, and out of the corner of her eye, could just barely see him staggering backward as a knife hit him in the shoulder.

Then she landed. As she did, Yang Ziqiong toppled backward to land face up on the ground, blood pooling out beneath her head.

On the other side of the room, Lin Qingxia lurched to her feet and flung herself toward the young man in gold jewelry, joined by Mao Yun.

Bao looked over at Yuwen Huo and saw him pulling the knife out of his shoulder and tossing it to the ground. Without the slightest pause, completely ignoring the pain from the knife wound, he launched toward the Love General with Slash of the Dragon's Tail.

Bao had been hit with Slash of the Dragon's Tail before and knew the incredible power it could unleash. However, it was to her shock that the Love General simply blocked the kick with her forearm as if blocking a blow from a child.

The momentum of Yuwen Huo's leap was completely thrown off, and he fell awkwardly to the ground.

Bao gritted her teeth. *Now is not the time for shock. I have to be confident.*

Without any further hesitation, she leapt forward and shoved her hand out toward the Love General.

"Phoenix Palm!" she shouted, striking with such speed that the startled Love General was incapable of blocking her. Bao had been working on the Phoenix Palm for quite some time, and although it was not yet completed, it was already devastatingly powerful. It was a vicious technique, so dangerous that she had never even tested it out on a person. It was designed to permanently alter the flow of qi through the target's meridian points, doing almost irreversible harm to their vital energies. Hitting the Love General with this technique would most likely leave her so stunned and hurt that the flow of battle would instantly change.

Bao's mouth turned up into a grin as her fingers jabbed into a series of acupoints, and then she slapped her hand down onto the Love General's shoulder.

Nothing happened.

Bao felt qi flowing out of her in what should have been a devastating blow to the Love General's meridians. Instead, she felt like she was pouring a bucket of water over a cliff.

The Love General snarled and leveled a kick at Bao's waist. Bao was too shocked to react, and she took the kick without defending herself. The next thing she knew, she was tumbling backward head over heels. It took only a few seconds for her to lurch to a halt and then struggle to her feet next to Liu Jiahui, who was so stunned that he hadn't even moved yet.

The sight that met Bao's eyes when she looked up sent coldness stabbing into her heart.

The Bone General crouched next to Yuwen Huo, holding a knife at his neck.

"How many more of you are there?" the Bone General growled.

On the other side of the table, Lin Qingxia and Mao Yun were barely holding their own against the young man in gold, who had been joined by the old man with the eye patch.

Meanwhile, the Fire General was staring right at Bao, his face completely expressionless.

"How many?" shouted the Bone General.

Yuwen Huo spit in his face, and the Bone General slashed his knife across his throat.

"NOOO!" Bao screamed. But she could do nothing to prevent the blood from spurting out of Yuwen Huo's throat and across the Bone General's face.

The Bone General licked the blood off of his lips and slowly rose to his feet.

The old man with the eye patch growled "Smash of the Ogre God!" and thrust out with both of his hands. A blast of green energy surged out from his palms, smashing into Mao Yun and knocking him backward several paces.

The fight had only just begun, and two people out of their group of six were already dead. Not a single enemy had even been wounded. Three of their opponents were ogres, who somehow seemed impervious to all of their attacks.

How is this possible? I killed an ogre before. They're not invincible!

Now was not the time for contemplation. Bao was no fool, and she had the sickening realization that if they kept fighting, they would be slaughtered. The only option now was to flee.

But how? They won't hesitate to cut us down from behind.

Her eyes flickered back and forth, and she realized that their only hope was to rely on a trick that had already saved her once in the past.

As the Bone General took a step forward, Bao's hand snaked out and grabbed the oil lamp that hung from the tent wall.

"Retreat!" she yelled as she hurled the lamp toward the table with all the power she could muster.

The lamp shattered, sending oil splashing in all directions, which instantly ignited. Bao's frustration burned just as hot as she turned around, pushed Liu Jiahui out of the tent, and followed.

Mao Yun came close behind, followed by Lin Qingxia, and the four of them began to run at top speed through the camp.

Dammit! DAMMIT! It wasn't supposed to happen like this!

They were only a few seconds away from the command tent when Bao sensed footsteps behind them. Looking over her shoulder, she saw that they were being pursued by the Bone General and the young man from the tent. Farther back, the flicker of flames ate away at the inside of the command tent, and smoke was already rising up into the night.

Hoarse shouts were ringing up, and the camp was beginning to stir.

Bao gritted her teeth and tried to pick up some speed. Now that they weren't skulking in the shadows, they could move even faster than before.

And yet the walls of Daolu seemed very, very far away.

***

The Dragon Gate on the east wall of Daolu had a towering pagoda above the gate itself, which served as the watchtower.

For many centuries, the north had been a relatively peaceful place, and the guard towers of Daolu had been mostly for show. But when the Demon Emperor arrived, all cities in Qi Xien changed.

Walls were repaired. Guard towers reinforced.

But decades had passed in Daolu without the Demon Emperor so much as crossing the Chezou River. Things grew lax.

Then came the assassination of the magistrate and the sheriff, which sent the local soldiers and constables into chaos.

Thanks to the efforts of Sunan and Bao, all of the guard towers on the city walls were manned, which had been no simple task considering there were nearly fifty of them altogether. As for the Dragon Gate, it held mostly members of the Golden Dragon Sect, as well as a few scattered city soldiers.

In the past, it had been commonplace for the soldiers to sleep during their night watch, but not now. The fact that encamped armies had surrounded the cities ensured that all of the guards were on the highest level of alert.

One of the guards happened to be looking out at the camp to the east when he noticed something flickering in the middle of the camp. Squinting, he leaned out to try to see things a bit more clearly. After a moment, his eyes widened.

"Sir!" he called out.

The officer in charge of the Dragon Gate was a lieutenant of the Golden Dragon Sect, a man named Sima Zikang. Although he was a capable fighter, he had risen through the ranks more because of his quick wit and excellent command of strategy and tactics.

"What is it?" he asked, hurrying over.

"Sir, look. The command tent. It's on fire!"

Sima Zikang peered out into the night. Sure enough, the command tent in the middle of the army camp appeared to be aflame. At first Sima Zikang was inclined to ignore the matter. A fire in a tent among the enemy forces was not unheard of. But then something toward the edge of the army camp caught his attention.

Four figures ran out from the camp, moving at incredible speed as they headed directly toward Daolu.

"Sir, do you see that?" cried one of the other Golden Dragons.

Sima Zikang nodded.

"Are they attacking us?" another soldier blurted.

Sima Zikang chuckled. "Calm down. They're not going to attack us with only four people. However, those people are clearly using qinggong to speed up their movements. I wonder if they—"

Before he could finish his sentence, two more figures sped out from the tents. Apparently two people were giving chase, and all of them were heading in the direction of Daolu.

Who could it be? Sima Zikang thought to himself. *Escaped prisoners? But they haven't taken any prisoners yet. Defectors?*

As the figures drew closer, Sima Zikang took a deep breath. "Disciple Chen, Disciple Wang, Disciple Zhang. Ready your bows. We might need to loose arrows. Also, send word to Dragon Lord Yuwen about what's happening."

As his orders were carried out, Sima Zikang watched the group racing across the landscape. As they got closer, it remained impossible to determine who the group of four was, considering they were wearing all black. However, of the two pursuing figures, it soon became obvious that one of them was a hulking figure wearing a suit of armor made from bones.

Sima Zikang gasped. "The Bone General! Send word to Sect Leader Sunan! Men, ready your arrows. Wait for my word to fire!"

The group of four was now about a hundred meters away from the wall, which was about the limit of the range of the composite bows wielded by the three Golden Dragon Sect disciples that Sima Zikang had just called out.

It was at this point that the Bone General waved his arm. Sima Zikang couldn't see what exactly he threw. Whether it was a knife, a needle, or something else, it didn't matter. It hit its target, and one of the four fleeing figures tumbled to the ground.

Even as the black-garbed figure struggled to stand, the Bone General closed in. Reaching out, he ripped the black hood off of the figure, and long, wavy black hair spilled down.

"A woman?" exclaimed Sima Zikang. To his horror, the Bone General drew a long dagger from behind his back and stabbed it into the neck of the black-garbed woman. He viciously ripped the blade through her neck, circling it around until the body dropped to the ground. Then he then held the head up high for a moment, blood splattering down all over his arm, before tossing it off to the side.

"Loose arrows!" Sima Zikang said. "And where is Dragon Lord Yuwen? He was here in the Dragon Gate earlier. Get him over here. And get Lord Sunan!"

CHAPTER 45
A GOLDEN SPEAR

Although Sunan's hands were clenched into fists of rage, tears welled up in his eyes. "Dead? Yuwen Huo is *dead*?"

Bao looked down at the ground and nodded slowly.

"What were you thinking?" Sunan barked so loudly that he was almost yelling.

Bao's voice was barely audible as she replied, "We didn't know that the Bone General would be there as well. And... the Love General too."

Sunan shook his head slowly. "The six of you just sauntered into the Fire General's command tent? Even if he was alone, what makes you think you could kill him?"

A flicker of anger passed through Bao's eyes. "I've killed ogres before."

"Sure, sure you have." Sunan snorted coldly. "You need to stop telling that story like you beat the creature in a duel. After all these years, everybody knows what really happened. You crushed that ogre under a pile of boulders. Boulders, Bao! Did you have a pile of boulders in your bag when you went to the Fire General's tent?"

Bao's jaw twitched. "It could have worked. If we'd killed the Fire General, the army would have been thrown into chaos!"

"Yuwen Huo wasn't just a Dragon Lord, Bao. He was my friend. You got my friend killed!"

Bao looked up, eyes filled with both flames of anger and tears of sorrow. "Well, my friends are dead too, did you ever think of that? I didn't want this to happen! Lin Qingxia and Yang Ziqiong were like my sisters!" She couldn't hold back the tears anymore, and they began to stream down her cheeks. "It was a good plan, and we all agreed to it! I didn't force Yuwen Huo to go along. He wanted to! He knew you wouldn't agree, but he went anyway!"

Sunan slapped his palm down onto the table next to him with a resounding thud. "You're damn right I wouldn't have agreed. You know what I would have said? 'It's too dangerous. You won't be able to tell who is in the tent until you get inside. What if you're outnumbered? What if they have better fighters? You could get yourselves killed!' And guess what? That's exactly what happened! Dammit, Bao, you always talk about confidence this and confidence that. But have you ever heard of a thing called *overconfidence*? Just because you *believe* you can do something doesn't mean you're guaranteed to succeed. You wanted to throw their army into chaos? Well, you did the exact opposite! Yuwen Huo was my friend, and Lin Qingxia and Yang Ziqiong were your friends. But they were also top leaders in our sects! Now everyone is more scared than they were before! Dammit, Bao. DAMMIT!"

Sunan resisted the urge to smash the table into splinters with his fists. He thought back to when he'd first gotten to know Yuwen Huo, when he was just a new recruit. He thought about how they had trained and sparred together, and how they had fought the river demon. Two tears leaked out onto his cheeks, but he quickly brushed them away and closed his eyes. Breathing deeply, he tried to force his feelings away.

A long moment passed, a moment that seemed like an uncomfortable eternity of silence.

Finally, Sunan opened his eyes and looked at Bao. She was staring down at her hands, which were trembling and wet from the tears that were dripping down her cheeks and off her chin.

He had the urge to comfort her but suppressed it. "Leave," he said.

Bao took a deep breath. "Sunan, I—"

"Leave! Just leave, Bao. I don't want to talk to you right now." He averted his gaze.

Bao took a shaky breath and rose to her feet and left.

Sunan sat alone for a few minutes, wrestling his thoughts and feelings back under control. Finally, he called Sun Mai in.

"Any new developments?" he asked.

"No," Sun Mai replied. "The command tent fire was quickly put out. The Fire General's troops are definitely well-trained."

Sunan chuckled bitterly. "So she didn't even manage to burn down a single tent."

Sun Mai didn't respond.

Another moment of silence passed before Sunan said, "Promote Sima Zikang to Dragon Lord. We don't have time for all the proper ceremonies now, but make it formal. Let him pick who to replace him as lieutenant."

Sun Mai voiced his assent, then cautiously asked, "What about… rites for Yuwen Huo and the others?"

Sunan shook his head. "There's no time for anything fancy. Do what's necessary to make sure he rests in peace. I've heard the stories about corpses coming back to life, and that's the last thing we need right now."

He tapped his finger in thought, then continued. "I don't know much about this Fire General, but from the stories I've heard, I can't imagine that he'll let an act like this go unanswered. Especially with the Bone General there to advise him. Double the guards on the walls, but don't use anyone else from the Golden Dragon Sect or the soldiers or constables. Keep them rested and ready for combat. Use militia for the guard duty. I have a bad feeling…"

"Bad feeling?"

"Yes. There will be fighting tomorrow. And dying. We need to be ready."

***

Sure enough, the following day at dawn, the fighting began. The Fire General sent a force of roughly two thousand men from the north to attack the Thunder Gate, and two thousand from the east to attack the Dragon Gate. The vanguard of each attacking force was made up of heavy shieldmen, followed by a large contingent of spearmen and a smaller group of crossbowmen.

At the Dragon Gate, newly appointed Dragon Lord Sima took the initiative to send out a cavalry charge against the incoming force, followed by light infantry. The cavalry troops were mostly Golden Dragon Sect fighters who had trained in firing bows from horseback, and they quickly flanked the Fire General's soldiers, peppering them with arrows that pinned down the crossbowmen and threw the formation of heavy shieldmen into chaos.

That, in turn, gave Daolu's light infantry time to close in. Although the light infantry was composed mostly of ordinary soldiers and militiamen, they were led by qi fighters from the Pure Phoenix Sect. Almost immediately, they began to wreak havoc on the heavy shieldmen, and they even managed to start killing some of the spearmen.

Most of the Fire General's men were qi fighters, but they seemed completely surprised by the onslaught and were quickly pinned down by the fighters from the Pure Phoenix Sect.

Soon, the two thousand men who had attacked the Dragon Gate were forced into retreat. The light cavalrymen pursued them for a short time but then turned and headed back to the Dragon Gate, along with the light infantry. Overall, Sima Zikang's defensive strategy couldn't have gone any better.

Things didn't go as smoothly at the Thunder Gate in the north of the city, which was under the command of another one of the Dragon Lords, Guan Yunchang. He was a tall, well-built man known for his unusual strength and hand-to-hand combat skills. However, when it came to tactics and strategy, he was sadly lacking.

Unlike Sima Zikang, his plan to repel the two-thousand-man force was to simply shower them with arrows. Unfortunately, the heavy shieldmen provided good cover, and a hail of arrows from the crossbowmen soon forced Guan Yunchang's men to withdraw from the turrets and battlements.

The two thousand men suffered almost no casualties, and soon they occupied the gate structure. Once inside, a few muffled booms rang out, and the gate itself was blasted open. Guan Yunchang led his men to fight back, but they were too disorganized. They were quickly pushed back, and fighting erupted on the streets of Daolu itself.

Thankfully, chaotic melee combat was when Guan Yunchang was in his element. He and other key figures from the Golden Dragon and Pure Phoenix Sects rallied the Daolu troops in a valiant fight in which nearly two hundred enemy soldiers were killed before they were finally pushed back out through the gate. Of course, the Fire General's soldiers were well-trained, and they were also no strangers to close-quarter fighting. In the end, close to a hundred from the Daolu side lost their lives.

The first day of combat ended rather early. Apparently, the Fire General had only been probing the city, as he didn't send any more forces out to attack.

When the Thunder Gate was inspected, they found signs of fire and smoke, leading to rumors that there were fire demons in the army, monsters that could destroy the city gates with a single breath of fire from their nostrils. That did little to help morale.

Engineers went to work repairing the Thunder Gate as best possible, but it wouldn't be back to its full strength for quite some time.

Sunan was not happy with Guan Yunchang. Although he had led the fight to slay two hundred of the enemy, the dozens of Daolu fighters who had died included many from the Golden Dragon Sect and the Pure Phoenix Sect. Considering the enemy army numbered 20,000, and the two sects didn't even have a thousand total members, such casualties were severe.

Because of Sima Zikang's success at the Dragon Gate, Sunan appointed him as acting general and gave him command of the entire city. Sima Zikang immediately set about devising an overall defense strategy, preparing various plans and backup plans for the following day.

***

The next morning, the Fire General attacked the White Rat Gate on the western wall of the city. However, that seemed to be little more than an exploratory skirmish, as in the afternoon, he again attacked the Thunder Gate in full force. This time he used enormous crossbows to fire burning bolts at the walls. Some areas of the wall were seriously damaged, and a few of the burning bolts made it into the city itself, setting some buildings ablaze. The gate was once again breached, and fighting broke out in the city.

However, Dragon Lord Sima Zikang had anticipated this development and had made advance preparations. The Fire General's troops were quickly routed and pushed back out the gate. Unfortunately, the damage to the gate was even more significant than last time.

***

During the first two days of fighting, no one saw Chieftainess Bao. Rumor had it that the Claws of the Phoenix had demanded she relinquish any military authority during the siege. The truth was that she felt as if she had no face left to appear in public.

Mao Yun cajoled and threatened her, but she refused to leave her room. As the fighting raged, she lay in bed staring up at the ceiling.

She thought about the dagger piercing into Yang Ziqiong's eye. She thought about Yuwen Huo and the grin on the Bone General's face when he'd slit his throat. And she thought about how she had looked back to see the Bone General holding Lin Qingxia's severed head in the air.

A few times, she beat her pillow in rage.

Three emotions fought back and forth inside of her heart. One emotion was sorrow. Sorrow for the death of her friends, and even sorrow at disappointing Sunan. Another was shame. Shame for trying to be a hero but turning out a fool. The third was rage. Rage toward the Bone General for killing Yang Ziqiong, Lin Qingxia, and Yuwen Huo. Rage toward the Demon Emperor for causing everything. And even rage toward Sunan for how he'd berated her and sent her away so dismissively.

I'm hurting too, Sunan.

Late in the night of the second day, the rage and sorrow wiped out the shame. Then, in that time before sunrise, when the night was darkest, her rage battered the sorrow down and down and down until it was so deep in her heart that she managed to lock it up and forget about it.

Finally, she sat up in bed, fists clenched on her knees.

What happened is my fault, but that doesn't mean I need to run around like a criminal. If she was going to avenge Yang Ziqiong, Lin Qingxia, and Yuwen Huo, then she needed to bring the fight to the

Bone General. Maybe the ogres had some magic that made them invincible to their martial arts, but they were not immortal. They could be killed. *And I'm going to kill the Bone General!*

She jumped off the bed and was just preparing to go give Sunan a piece of her mind when she realized that a slight breeze had just touched her neck. She frowned slightly and turned to look behind her.

To her shock, the wardrobe in the corner of the room was wide open, and a man was standing in the doorway, holding a torch. He was tall and handsome but also tough-looking. He wore golden robes, and he was holding a short golden spear in his left hand.

Bao's hands flicked, and her knives dropped out of her sleeves into her hands.

"Who are you?" she growled. "And what are you doing in my room?"

The man took a step forward and leveled his spear at her. Smiling, he said, "That's the same question I wanted to ask you."

CHAPTER 46
A MESSAGE

Two men stepped out of the door to flank the man in the golden robes. As soon as Bao laid eyes on them, she knew who they were.

Lions of Peace. Could I take the two of them out, and this guy in the golden robes too? He doesn't look like a fighter.

"Not only did you take my room," the man in the gold robes said, "you took my tempest stone. Where is it?"

Bao narrowed her eyes. "Tempest stone? You mean the wind stone?"

A cold light flashed through the man's eyes. "So you did take it. Tell me where it is."

He took another step forward, and two more Lions of Peace entered the room. Bao knew there was no possible way for her to fight them. Besides, there were surely more soldiers further back in the corridor.

That was when the man's golden robes, coupled with the words he had just spoken, caused everything to click in Bao's mind.

"You're the Golden Immortal!" she said, raising her right hand and pointing a knife at him.

"I am," he replied, flashing her a smile. Despite his smile, his eyes still radiated coldness. "Now let me take a wild guess. A young woman with knives. In my room. With my tempest stone. I would bet money that you're Chieftainess Bao of the Pure Phoenix Sect."

Bao didn't respond. *I need to get out of here. He couldn't possibly have come from Sunan's mansion, could he? If not, then where did he come from? Does the tunnel somehow go past the city walls? That would mean... that the Fire General can get inside! No. He already* is *inside!*

"I can see what you're thinking," the Golden Immortal said. "You're trying to decide whether to fight or run. Before you choose either, wait a moment and hear me out. This silly war doesn't have to happen. The fighting can end right now."

Bao almost chuckled in response, but she wasn't in the mood. "How? By us surrendering? That's not going to happen."

The Golden Immortal's smile widened a bit. "No, that would be foolish. I am not here as a representative of the Fire General. As you know, the Fire General is the spear that slashes across the battlefield. The King of the Pure Ones has other servants, people who are not interested in killing and destruction. For example, the Love General."

"You work for the Love General?"

"I don't work for her. I represent her. Surely you know the level of authority she commands in the empire."

"Of course. The dove of peace who woos allies."

The Golden Immortal took another step forward, placing himself within five paces of Bao. His slight movement allowed more men to enter the room. This time, they weren't Lions of Peace; they were ordinary soldiers. Furthermore, Bao could tell from the shadows behind them that there were even more of them in the corridor.

"Chieftainess Bao, believe me, this is a fight you can't win. It doesn't matter how cleverly your men defend the wall. It doesn't matter what fancy fighting moves you've developed. The Pure Phoenix Sect and the Golden Dragon Sect number in the hundreds. You can't fight an army of thousands. You must be able to see that. Even a bear can be crushed by an avalanche."

Bao clenched her jaw. "The Bone General is here. He hates me. Been trying to kill me for years now. There's no way he would pardon me for my supposed crimes."

The Golden Immortal shook his head slowly. "That is a thorny problem. But believe me, the ogre generals all have equal standing and sway before the King of the Pure Ones. Right now, the empire needs allies, not martyrs. Think of how many lives you could save!"

Bao wanted to believe his words. She truly did. But they were too good to be true. She remembered things that Sunan had told her about the Love General, who was clearly an adept schemer, someone who wouldn't think twice before lying to get what she wanted. Besides, what kind of diplomatic envoy was made of up a bunch of soldiers who snuck into a besieged city via a secret tunnel?

Bao lowered her knife. "Very well," she said. "I think—"

Before she finished her sentence, her left hand shot out with lightning speed, sending her knife flying toward the Golden Immortal's face. She spun in place and crashed through the door.

The Golden Immortal's golden spear arced through the air, knocking the knife to the side. "Li, Xu, you're with me. Everyone else, carry out the mission!"

While the words were still leaving his mouth, he burst into motion, followed closely behind by two of the Lions of Peace.

As the Golden Immortal emerged from the door, another knife flew toward him, which he batted away just as easily as the first one. Bao was already halfway across the courtyard and had leapt up onto a decorative rock. From there she called upon her qinggong to fly into the air toward the western wall of the residence, over which the glow of dawn was just beginning to spread.

As the Golden Immortal sped forward in pursuit, he pointed his golden spear out in front of him with his right hand, then found a button inlaid in the base of the spear and pushed it with a click.

A twanging sound rang out as the spearhead broke apart into four hooked pieces, which blurred through the air toward Bao. Each of the four pieces was connected to a thin golden thread which, in turn, were part of a fine golden rope connected to the base of the spear.

The four hooks and the golden rope moved faster than the eye could track, and before Bao could reach the wall, they wrapped around her left ankle.

Before she knew what was happening, the Golden Immortal swung the spear to the side, sending her tumbling out of the air and onto the ground of the courtyard. The hooks detached from her ankle in the process, and she flipped head over heels until she splashed into the small pond in the corner.

She rose up, soaked and dripping, the Golden Immortal closing in with the two Lions of Peace. He pushed the button on the bottom of the spear again, and the hooks and rope swished back into place, returning the spear to its original shape.

The brief time it took for him to reassemble his spear gave the Lions of Peace a bit of a lead on him, and they reached the pond first. They lashed out with sabers, and water droplets flew about as Bao dodged both attacks.

Then she unleashed the same move that had failed so spectacularly on the Love General.

"Phoenix Palm!" Bao grinned as her fingers jabbed into a series of acupoints, then slapped her hand down onto the shoulder of the Lion of Peace.

The man screamed and staggered back, twitching visibly. As he did, the red outline of a palm was just visible on his shoulder.

The Golden Immortal was shocked, but that didn't prevent him from extending his spear once again.

It clicked, and as before, the spearhead broke apart into four hooks as it shot toward Bao.

This time, though, she was prepared.

"Dragon Cleaves the Clouds." She flipped backward, sending the hooks flying off to the side, and she landed a few paces back.

The other Lion of Peace slashed out again with his saber, but she dodged it easily, and before the Golden Immortal could reassemble his spear, she leapt up onto the wall and disappeared.

"Dammit," growled the Golden Immortal. In his years away from Daolu, he had focused hard on training, and he had already achieved a sixth breakthrough in his qi cultivation and was proceeding toward his seventh. Were it not for the fact that he had been so intent on capturing Bao alive, he would likely have beaten her soundly.

Behind him, soldiers were pouring into the courtyard. There were already dozens of them, and the flow didn't seem to be slowing in the slightest. After taking a moment to issue a few more orders, he leapt onto a decorative rock formation and then flew up onto the wall. It immediately became obvious where Bao had disappeared to.

"Iron Awl Hu's mansion," he murmured.

***

The former residence of Iron Awl Hu was now the headquarters of Sunan and the Golden Dragon Sect. Although it was well guarded, Bao was one of the highest-level martial artists in Daolu. She had spent much of her younger days hopping over walls and running through the back alleys in Yu Zhing, and besides, she was familiar with how the mansion was guarded.

With her qinggong, it was a simple task to scale the wall, and before any of the guards even realized it, she was outside of Sunan's room.

The guards outside the door stared at her in shock for a moment before drawing their weapons.

"Intruder!" one of them shouted.

"That's Chieftainess Bao, you idiot!" the other growled.

"Is Sect Leader Sunan awake?" she said. "If not, wake him." *I don't have time for this.* "SECT LEADER SUNAN!"

A muffled grunt could be heard from inside the room, then a crash. A moment later, the door swung open to reveal Sunan, bleary eyed but dressed in armor, a saber gripped in his right hand. Because of the siege, he had taken to sleeping in his armor. When he saw Bao standing there, his eyes widened.

"Bao? What are you doing here?"

"The Golden Immortal is in the city. He tried to kill me. Well, capture me."

"The Golden Immortal?" Sunan said incredulously.

"He's here with the Lions of Peace. And soldiers. Hurry!"

Not waiting to give any further explanation, she dashed out and leapt up onto the wall of the residence, to be joined almost immediately by Sunan as well as two other Golden Dragons.

At almost the exact moment that they alighted on the wall, three figures appeared on the wall of the Golden Immortal's residence to the east. A second later, five more figures appeared, then even more, until the entire wall was filled.

In the middle was the Golden Immortal himself, flanked by a Lion of Peace and dozens of soldiers.

"Sect Leader Sunan," the Golden Immortal called out, "did Chieftainess Bao pass along my message?"

Sunan turned his head slightly to look at Bao. "Message?"

She snorted coldly. "The Love General wants to recruit you. And me."

"I take it you said no?"

"I didn't say anything. I just threw a knife at his face."

Sunan chuckled.

The Golden Immortal pointed his spear at Sunan and Bao. "You have two choices: submit or die. Choose quickly."

Bao's hands clenched into fists. "He's strong. And that spear he has is dangerous. We can't fight him and all of those other people at the same time."

Addressing one of the Golden Dragons, Sunan quietly said, "Get word to the chief minister and Dragon Lord Sima. We'll try to buy some time here."

The man nodded and dropped off the wall.

When the Golden Immortal saw that, his eyes flickered with cold light. "That's answer enough for me. Kill them!"

CHAPTER 47
EXPLOSIVE FLIGHT

Sunan squinted his eyes shut as he smashed through the wooden windowpane and into the Drunk Ox Wine Shop. He caromed off a wooden shelf inside the room, sending several jugs of wine and alcohol smashing to the ground before landing in a heap in the corner of the room.

As he struggled to his feet, a blur crashed through the fragments of the window, and the Golden Immortal was standing over him.

"You should have submitted," the Golden Immortal said, pulling his spear back to deliver a blow.

As Sunan had come to find over the course of the past few minutes, there was something special about the Golden Immortal's spear. Not only could it shoot out hooks to bind an opponent, it was incredibly tough. Sunan had made the mistake of trying to block a blow from the spear with his forearm and had nearly received a broken arm as a result.

Earlier, the Golden Immortal led the Lions of Peace and the other ordinary soldiers in a rapid charge on the Golden Dragon headquarters. Fierce fighting had broken out, with Sunan and Bao teaming up against the Golden Immortal.

With so many people involved in the fighting, chaos quickly ensued, and the sheer number of people the Golden Immortal had at his command put the Golden Dragons on the defensive. For each of his soldiers who fell, there was always another to take his place, with more lurking off in the background and jumping up onto the estate walls.

Before long, Sunan and Bao found themselves fighting on the north wall of the estate, which overlooked the Drunk Ox Wine Shop.

By that point, Sunan, Bao, and the Golden Immortal had all received minor injuries, but nothing more. Then the Golden Immortal landed a lucky kick on Sunan's chest, sending him flying off the wall of the estate and into the shop itself.

Sunan's saber had been ripped out of his hand during the fall. His shoulder and knee ached, and blood was oozing out of his mouth. Just when the Golden Immortal was about to strike with his spear, a hoarse shout rang out, and any remnants of the poor window were completely obliterated as Bao flew into the room.

"Phoenix Palm!"

Sunan had seen Bao unleash Phoenix Palm on two different soldiers who had been foolish enough to interfere with their fight with the Golden Immortal. The results had been devastating, and although the soldiers hadn't been killed, they had been immediately rendered incapable of fighting.

This was the first time he'd seen her try the move out on the Golden Immortal.

Lips pursing into a frown, the Golden Immortal twisted to the side. "Golden Dodge!"

Spinning away from her attack, he twirled through the air, landing a kick on Bao's side that sent her smashing into another nearby shelf. More bottles of wine and alcohol crashed to the ground, a few of them landing on Bao herself.

By this point, the floor was slick with wine.

As soon as the Golden Immortal landed, he pushed the button on the bottom of his spear, and the claws blurred into motion, latching on to Bao. Then the Golden Immortal jerked the spear to the side, sending her smashing into another cabinet of wine jugs and into Sunan, knocking him down again.

Pushing the button again caused the hooks to release and the rope to snap back into the spear.

"I'm done playing games," the Golden Immortal said. "The Love General ordered me to try to get you to submit. But this a war zone, so the Fire General's orders take precedence. He said that if you refused to surrender, I was to kill you. I guess it's time to put away the toys"—he tossed the golden spear off to the side—"and use the real weapons!"

With that, he pulled a pair of crimson gloves out of his robe, which he put on each of his hands. Then he clenched them into fists, and they burst into flame.

"A little gift from the Fire General," he said, grinning.

Bao and Sunan struggled to their feet and got into ready stances. Both of them were bloodied and panting, sore from the protracted fighting. They were tired, tired in a way that they could never have imagined before, so tired that everything seemed to blur. This was different from sparring; this was real combat. Unlike the mismatched duels that both of them had fought in the past, it hadn't ended after only a round or two.

"It's better this way, anyway, Sunan," said the Golden Immortal. "I've been wanting to beat your ass into a pulp ever since you showed up at the Green Elephant Emporium all those years ago. Finally, the time has come. Strike of the Golden Fists!" He leapt high up into the air and smashed downward with his fists.

Sunan tried to counter the move, but it was too powerful. The fists slammed into his neck and left shoulder, shooting crushing pain through his body and sending him lurching backward, vision swimming.

Bao lashed out with a fist strike of her own, but the Golden Immortal easily countered it, then kicked straight out, knocking her back.

"You two are out of your league. I've trained with the top fighters in the King of the Pure One's forces. The two of you are just groping around in the dark. Strike of the—"

Before the Golden Immortal could finish speaking, someone interrupted him.

"Sword of the Scholar!"

"Slashing Axe!"

Wine jugs exploded as Sun Mai and Mao Yun burst into the wine shop, unleashing both of their signature moves. An illusory blade shot out from Sun Mai's fingers, and as Mao Yun waved his axe through the air, a ripple spread out, destroying numerous cabinets and wine jugs as it closed in on the Golden Immortal.

The Golden Immortal was caught totally unawares. The ripple hit him first, slashing his golden robes and causing blood to spurt out from his chest. Then Sun Mai's illusory sword hit him, destroying more of his clothing and gashing his thigh. However, things weren't over yet.

Over the years, Sun Mai had refined and perfected his Sword of the Scholar into something spectacular. Furthermore, he was unleashing it with cathartic power. As soon as the initial blade hit, eight more illusory blades appeared and spun toward the Golden Immortal in a tempest of destructive power. He staggered backward, blood spurting out of one wound after another. One of the blades nearly severed his left arm at the elbow, and he let out a miserable scream.

Clutching his left arm, he growled, "You're *dead*. All of you!"

Before anyone else could make another move, he blurred into motion, flying out of the same window he had entered.

"You're not getting away this time!" Sun Mai shouted, leaping into the air after him. "Come on, Mao Yun!"

Mao Yun looked over at Sunan and Bao. "Chieftainess, Sect Leader. The situation is bad. Full-scale assaults have begun on the north and east walls. Dragon Lord Sima has requested your presence at the Dragon Gate."

Sunan nodded. "You back up Sun Mai, we'll go to Zikang. Capture the Golden Immortal alive if you can. Kill him otherwise."

Mao Yun nodded, then leapt after Sun Mai.

All of a sudden, Sunan and Bao were alone in relative silence. They looked at each other.

"Bao, about what I said before…"

She shook her head. "It doesn't matter. Come on, we have to get to the Dragon Gate."

As soon as they stumbled out of the shambles of the Drunk Ox Wine Shop, they could see smoke rising up from locations all around the city.

"This isn't good…" Bao said.

The sounds of fighting could be heard from the north, presumably from the Thunder Gate. Although they were closer to the Thunder Gate, Sima Zikang had set up his command post at the Dragon Gate, so that was where they headed. They ran as fast as they could in their bruised and battered condition. A few minutes later, the Dragon Gate loomed up ahead. To Bao and Sunan's relief, it had not been breached. However, the sounds of fighting could be heard from the other side, and crossbow bolts were flying over the wall.

They hurried into the gate and past the guards to Dragon Lord Sima Zikang's command room. As soon as they entered, he looked up at them, face ashen.

"Sect Leader, Chieftainess…"

"How bad is it?" Sunan asked.

"Bad, sir. The Thunder Gate has been breached yet again, as

expected. Defenses here are holding, but I'm not sure for how long. They're pushing harder than they have so far. I think they'll breach the Dragon Gate within two hours. Worst of all is I'm getting reports that there are enemy troops in other parts of the city. I'm not sure if that's true, but fires have sprung up in numerous locations."

"It's true," Sunan said. "The Golden Immortal led his men through a secret passage. Can you send men to the Pure Phoenix headquarters to try to contain them?"

Sima Zikang looked down at the map of Daolu on the table, upon which were figures representing the main squadrons he had positioned throughout the city. "I don't think so," he said. "Not quickly enough. Sect Leader... I think we may need to resort to the Explosive Flight of the Dragon and Phoenix."

Bao cocked an eyebrow. "Explosive Flight of the Dragon and Phoenix?"

Sima Zikang nodded. "Chieftainess Bao, while you were... resting, we came up with some contingency plans. I think now is the time to enact just such a plan."

Sunan frowned. "Are you sure we can't salvage this? There are other contingency plans. Why not the Subtle Flight or the Dashing Flight? Why the Explosive Flight? They haven't even so much as shot an arrow at the White Rat Gate, after all."

"Sect Leader, even the greatest general or fighter must know when to back down. People are dying. We are vastly outnumbered, and we are facing elite warriors who have magic and demons on their side. We might not be able to retake the Thunder Gate today. Plus, we don't have enough men to spare to comb through the city and track down the infiltrators. That's not to mention that we have no idea how many troops came through the secret tunnel, or if more are coming through. We need to get out of Daolu now. If we don't, we won't have a chance to slip away during the night or break through their lines in an early-morning blitz. We will die here. Of that I'm certain."

A long moment passed in which no one spoke.

"Fine," Sunan said. "Begin the Explosive Flight of the Dragon and Phoenix."

Sima Zikang nodded decisively and turned away to begin the work.

Sunan looked over at Bao. "The Explosive Flight of the Dragon and Phoenix is a retreat tactic relying on a few precisely planned and targeted explosions. The resulting fire and smoke will give us the screen we need to get most of our people through the Zhen Gate and across the Chezou River. A few of the Golden Dragons and Pure Phoenixes will cast aside their robes and weapons and remain behind in civilian clothing to act as agents."

"Explosions? How?"

"You know how sorghum wine is flammable? Sorghum God has built stockpiles in a few key locations, and we've packed the surroundings with pine needles and other flammable materials. It will create plenty of smoke. Come on, we need to get moving."

Bao's mind was racing, and even as Sunan turned to leave, she reached out and grabbed his sleeve. "Wait."

He looked back. "What is it?"

"I've made a terrible mistake."

CHAPTER 48
A ZHEN BIRD

Smoke choked Daolu. As the Fire General's troops poured into the city, fires raged, and the citizens who couldn't cower in their houses ran screaming into the streets. In certain key locations, Golden Dragon and Pure Phoenix fighters held firm against the enemy soldiers. However, most members of the sect were already fleeing via the prearranged routes established by Dragon Lord Sima.

A gentle breeze had sprung up, ensuring that the smoke didn't rise high up into the air. Instead it spread out through the city.

Everything was descending into chaos.

Sunan and Bao stood on a rooftop adjacent to the Pure Phoenix Sect headquarters, strips of cloth tied around their noses and mouths to protect against the smoke.

From that vantage point, they could just barely see into the courtyard, which was occupied by a handful of the Fire General's troops. No more soldiers had appeared over the course of the past few minutes, leading them to believe that whatever force had been led into the city by the Golden Immortal had already dispersed. This relatively small group must have been left behind to stand guard.

"You're sure your Phoenix Crown is down there?" Sunan asked.

"It has to be. When the Golden Immortal arrived, we started fighting almost immediately, and then I ran to find you. There was no time for him to search the room."

"What if one of his men found it?"

Bao shrugged. "Anything's possible. But I locked it in an iron chest in a hidden compartment under the bed. They seem more interested in burning the city than searching for loot." Bao looked over at Sunan, her eyes flashing. "Sunan, that crown is dangerous. If it ends up in the wrong hands…"

Sunan tightened his grip on the saber he held in his right hand. "You don't have to try to convince me it's dangerous. Sun Mai and I are both very familiar with what it can do."

Bao wanted to tell Sunan that the power of the Phoenix Crown was different than the raw power of the spirit of the phoenix demon in the fallen star's unrefined form, but now didn't seem the proper time. "None of those soldiers down there look very intimidating," she said. "I'd wager they're all in the first level or so."

"Agreed. I still haven't recovered from the fight with the Golden Immortal, but those soldiers shouldn't prove to be much of a problem."

Bao hefted the spear she'd picked up along the way. "We don't have much time. Let's go."

Without another word, she leapt through the air toward the courtyard. Sunan flew along right behind her.

They descended on the soldiers like a force of nature, showing not even the slightest scrap of mercy. Bao stabbed a soldier through the heart with her spear, then slammed the haft into the nose of another, sending him flipping backward. Sunan severed a head, then unleashed a swinging kick that sent two soldiers tumbling backward.

Bao's initial assessment had been correct—these soldiers were not powerful qi fighters, and as such, it wasn't even necessary for Sunan and Bao to use any of their high-level techniques to defeat them.

There were more soldiers than they initially realized, but virtually every move they made resulted in soldiers dying or being rendered unconscious. A few soldiers inside the buildings rushed out to join the fight, and yet, barely a minute later, not a single one of them was left standing.

Bodies littered the courtyard left and right, and blood flowed everywhere.

Bao and Sunan were panting slightly, but neither one had received even a cut or bruise.

Sunan wiped the blood off of his saber with a rag and then sheathed it at his side. Bao tossed the spear aside and picked up a pair of butterfly swords laying off to the side. "Come on."

They were soon inside Bao's bedchamber, where she quickly opened the hidden compartment and pulled out an iron box. After unlocking it with a key she kept strung around her neck, she confirmed that the Phoenix Crown was safe.

Sunan looked over at the wardrobe leading to the tunnel. "That's where he came from?"

Bao nodded. "The wardrobe was locked, which means he must have a key or some other method to open the door from the inside."

"I just wonder how he got into the passage to begin with. We searched it thoroughly after you discovered it. Maybe we should investigate further…"

"No," Bao said. "Too dangerous, and not enough time."

Sunan frowned but nodded his head. "You're right. Let's go."

***

As the flames raged higher in the city, the soldiers and constables of Daolu, along with the members of the Golden Dragon and Pure

Phoenix Sects, fled the city. A select few shed their uniforms and stayed behind.

As for Bao and Sunan, they raced through the slums of Daolu toward the Zhen Gate, which was the arranged evacuation point. Upon arrival, they climbed up into the barbican to look out over the city. Much of it was obscured by smoke, but even still, the devastation was already apparent. Sunan gritted his teeth and shook his head.

"Damn you, Fire General," he murmured. "And damn you too, Demon Emperor."

"This almost seems too easy," Bao said.

"What do you mean?"

"Like we're being allowed to flee. The roads leading from the Dragon, Thunder, and White Rat Gates were all locked down, but the Zhen Gate was completely unguarded. It doesn't make sense."

"Maybe it does, Chieftainess," a new voice said. It was none other than Dragon Lord Sima Zikang, flanked by Sun Mai and Mao Yun. Sima Zikang looked haggard and exhausted, and both Sun Mai and Mao Yun had clearly seen better days.

"What do you mean?" Bao asked.

"The Fire General would prefer for us to flee. A protracted siege wouldn't benefit him, nor would the destruction of the city."

"But he set fire to the damn place!"

"To *some* of it," Sima Zikang corrected. "Not all. We probably set more fire than he did."

Sunan looked over at Sun Mai. "What of the Golden Immortal?"

"We wounded him but didn't manage to finish the bastard off," Sun Mai said.

Mao Yun made a sound almost like a growl. "I have a feeling this won't be the last time we run into him."

A short moment of silence followed, which was then broken by Sima Zikang. "Sect Leader. Chieftainess…"

Sunan turned away from the city. "I know. It's time to leave."

***

Not too far north of Daolu's Thunder Gate, three figures on horseback looked at the blanket of smoke covering the city and the formations of troops pouring into the shattered gates.

They were the Fire General, Love General, and Bone General. They were not alone. However, the soldiers and guards who accompanied them were arranged in formation out of earshot.

Different expressions could be detected on the faces of the three ogre generals. The Fire General's lips curved up into the slightest of smiles. The Love General seemed conflicted. The Bone General appeared to be struggling to contain his rage.

"I can't believe you're just letting them escape!" the Bone General snarled.

The Fire General didn't bother to look over at the Bone General. "My concern is taking this city, not routing the enemy. You never were a big strategist, Gu."

The Bone General turned his head and spat on the ground. "You know I hate that name. The language of this place sounds like a monkey vomiting up its intestines."

The Fire General chuckled softly. "This is our home now. After all the decades that have passed, you surely realize that, don't you?"

Without another word, the Bone General turned his horse and left. A few minutes passed in which the Fire General and the Love General simply watched the troops entering the city.

A wind blew, carrying with it the acrid odor of smoke. The Love General sighed inwardly. "Thank you, Huo."

The Fire General looked at her out of the corner of his eye. "You shouldn't thank me. This was a strategic decision. I care not for your politicking and scheming."

"I know that. But after you've conquered everything there is to conquer, there will still be much work to do to keep this empire in one piece. We're going to need people like that Sunan on our side."

The Fire General snorted. "You've grown soft, Ai. You might be the diplomat among us, but don't think you can hide that look in your eye from me. You've let that human boy work his way into your heart, haven't you?"

This time it was the Love General's turn to snort. "How much of a fool do you think I am?"

"I never said you were a fool. But you and Gu both seem to get obsessed with the wrong things. Do you know how much time he's wasted chasing that girl here and there? And why? Because she got lucky and killed one of his agents?"

"You know it's not as simple as that. Gar-El is very protective of us. He was the one who gave the order sentencing her to death."

"That was years ago, Ai. Much time has been wasted while Gu chased her all over the map, time that could have been spent on much more important affairs." Not giving the Love General a chance to pursue the topic, the Fire General said, "Daolu is ours, and it will be safe to enter by the time the sun sets. Will you be joining me? There will be plenty of work trying to ferret out the spies and the traitors."

"Isn't that Gu's job?"

"Indeed it is. But I suspect he might have other things on his mind. A young girl, perhaps…"

A long moment passed, and the smell of smoke grew stronger.

"I hate conquered cities," the Love General said. "Too much smoke and too much blood. I'll head back to Yao Gong Palace."

***

The escape from Daolu was relatively orderly, but some chaos couldn't be avoided. Soldiers and constables mixed in with the Golden Dragon Sect and the Pure Phoenix Sect, and they were joined by a large number of ordinary citizens of the city who didn't wish to stay behind.

Crossing the Chezou River was difficult considering the bridge had been burned at the beginning of the siege, but by making use of boats and other methods, they managed to get to the other side of the bank. A few people made their way directly south or even to the east. However, the vast majority followed Bao and Sunan to the west, toward the mountains which surrounded Zhifu Shan, one of the five legendary peaks of Qi Xien.

The first night outside of Daolu, they made camp on the border of the Little Demon Forest, which led to the foothills of the mountain. Although sentries were posted, everyone was exhausted and out of sorts, and the camp was haphazardly set. Furthermore, there were hundreds of people in it.

Because of that, nobody noticed a shadowy figure fly into the camp late at night and land on the branch of a tree not too far from Sunan's tent.

It was a zhen bird, an avian creature with a long neck, a copper-toned beak, golden claws, and purplish feathers. Zhen birds were not unheard of in the north of Qi Xien, and at first glance, this one seemed just like any other zhen bird, albeit somehow more beautiful. And yet, if anyone were there to look at its eyes, they would see them staring fixedly at Sunan's tent, gleaming with something that seemed to far surpass the intelligence of ordinary animals.

As the night wore on, the zhen bird remained on the branch, almost as if it were standing guard over Sunan.

CHAPTER 49
TWO BOXES

An Jian was an ordinary man. At least, he seemed that way. Although he was no martial artist, his eyes flickered with an intelligence that was outright frightening. That was one reason why he rarely looked anyone in the eye.

Currently, he was looking over the smoldering ruins of the Delightful Wind Shop, which had once stood right next to the headquarters of the Pure Phoenix Sect, the former residence of the Golden Immortal. An Jian had run the shop for a few years, selling beautiful fans decorated with poetry of his own creation. In the short time that he had operated the shop in Daolu, he had built up quite the clientele in the city, especially among the rich and powerful.

The shop was now nothing more than cinder and ash.

In the final hectic moments of the battle, An Jian had fled the burning shop with a handful of his fans, one of which he held in his hands right now. Looking down at the fan, he smiled.

"I must admit I failed to foresee that Daolu would be destroyed ahead of schedule. How very interesting." A curl of acrid smoke floated toward An Jian, which he waved away using the fan. The truth was that An Jian had once been one of the most powerful martial artists alive. But that was in a different life. A different time.

"Despite living directly in the shadow of Sunan and Bao, they slipped away before I could make my move. The closest I could get was that debate with Sun Mai. What a waste of time." An Jian looked around at the smoldering city. "Thankfully, it's not too late. All my years of preparation ensured that. The seeds that have been cast out will eventually grow to fruition, and then I will make my move.

"I still have decades of time to work with if necessary. The arrows hidden in the darkness will fly straight into the hearts of Sunan and Bao, and then the matter will be concluded." He chuckled. "It seems the time has come to do a bit of traveling."

With that, he began to stroll in the direction of the Zhen Gate.

***

After a short, fitful night of rest came another long day of travel, then a bit more rest. They skirted the edges of the forest during the day, then camped among the trees at night. The process repeated a few times until the group was about a week west of Daolu, beneath the towering mountain peak that was Zhiu Shan.

Bao was in a rotten mood. Flames of anger licked at her heart, and with each passing day, the anger grew hotter, and her temper shorter. The more she thought about the events that had occurred, the more frustrated she became with herself, and the more she hated the Demon Emperor. And especially the Bone General.

The faces of Lin Qingxia, Yang Ziqiong, and Yuwen Huo passed through her mind constantly. She relived the fight with the Golden Immortal and was continuously pricked by the stinging humiliation of having been defeated.

By the time they camped in a ravine at the foot of Zhifu Shan, Bao felt like she was about to explode. Not bothering to eat an evening meal, she left the camp and began to climb the mountain alone. An hour later, she settled down cross-legged on a stone outcropping that jutted out from the side of the mountain and formed something like a platform.

From this height, she could see forest stretching out to the east and the Chezou River far to the north, but little else. Daolu wasn't visible, nor was any smoke from its burning. The camp, farther down the mountain, was relatively well hidden in the ravine.

As she sat there looking at the sun preparing to drop down over the horizon, she forced herself to breathe in and out. Assuming the same posture she had invented years ago, she began to meditate. Instead of forcing the qi through a prescribed path, she allowed it to flow freely through her body.

Because of the rage inside of her, the qi seemed to flow more quickly than usual, but it also distorted slightly and fell into a different path than it normally did. To Bao's surprise, the flow of qi inside of her was taking a unique shape, and she surmised it was because of the anger that burned in her heart.

Over the course of the following hour, she continued to meditate, analyzing the flow of the qi and trying to memorize the pattern of its flow through her meridians. Strangely, her rage had subsided, but the qi had grown more powerful, rushing through her body like a screaming river. Her eyes shot open, and they glowed with a faint red light.

She still felt like she was about to explode, but this time it was not from anger. Leaping to her feet, she let out a growling shout and released the energy through the tips of her fingers. Five streams of crimson light snaked out, slashing into the rough rock at her feet, hewing out five fingertip-deep furrows that emanated faint maroon smoke.

Panting, Bao looked down at her fingers. Of all the techniques she had seen and used, this seemed the most terrifying. If it could slash holes into rocks, what could it do to human flesh? Most terrifying of all was that she could sense that the technique wasn't complete. There was potential to fuel it with even more power than she had. What would happen then?

What made it so powerful? My rage?

Closing her eyes, she turned her attention inward again and found that, to her surprise, she was completely calm. Earlier, the fury inside of her had burned seemingly beyond her control, but now there was nothing.

After a moment of contemplation, she sat down cross-legged and slipped into a meditative state once again. The qi began to flow, and this time she tried to send it along the same path as before. However, as minutes passed, and then hours, she failed over and over again. She could vaguely remember the outline of the path, but she couldn't reproduce it.

Before she knew it, an entire night had passed. As the light of dawn began to rise up from the mountain behind her, she opened her eyes.

"Dammit," she murmured. Shaking her head slowly, she rose to her feet.

It was in that exact moment that she heard her name being called behind her.

"Bao!"

She turned to find Sunan hurrying over.

"Were you out here the whole night?" he asked, looking alarmed.

She looked around in surprise at the murky dawn sky. "I guess so. I was hit with some enlightenment."

She subconsciously looked down at the five furrows she had slashed into the boulder.

Sunan reached her and followed her gaze down to the furrows. "Is that…?"

She nodded. "A new technique. But I'm having trouble

reproducing it." After a moment of silence, she continued. "You came all the way up here looking for me?"

"Yes, something happened. Follow me."

They hurried back down the mountain and into the camp. Bao immediately noticed a buzz of activity. At one point they passed a large pavilion, within which she saw Mao Yun, Sun Mai, Sima Zikang, Liu Jiahui, and other high-ranking members of the two sects.

"Is there some sort of meeting going on?" Bao asked.

"Yes," Sunan replied. "Up to now we've been running like crazy. Disorganized. We need to fix that, so the men are talking about how to divide up the new recruits."

"New recruits? I was gone for a night. Why does it feel like it's been a week?"

Sunan chuckled. "We have soldiers, constables, and plenty of ordinary citizens to take care of now. Those who are willing to join our sects will be divided up in the best way possible. Any who don't wish to join will be sent on their way once it's safe."

As they talked, Sunan led Bao through the camp to what she recognized as her own tent.

Sunan stopped outside and gestured at the tent flap. "After you."

She pushed the flap aside and entered the tent. It was small inside, cramped for two people, especially considering that there was a wooden table set up inside.

"During the unpacking last night," Sunan went on to explain, "I personally took care of your items, especially... that." He gestured at the iron box on the table.

"My Phoenix Crown."

"Yes. While taking care of your Phoenix Crown, I happened to notice something very interesting. Watch this." With that, Sunan unstrapped the burlap sack which had been tied to his back. Reaching into the sack, he pulled out a small wooden box, a box that Bao recognized.

"Is that the wind stone?"

"Indeed. Observe." Holding the wind stone's box in his right hand, he stepped toward the table and extended it toward Bao's box.

As the wooden box and the iron box neared, a faint droning sound reached Bao's ears. At first it was almost undetectable, but as the boxes got closer to each other, it became clearer and clearer. Then Bao noticed the air between the two boxes distorting, in the same way waves of heat would rise up from the horizon on a hot day.

Sunan brought the two boxes so close that they were almost touching. The distortions turned into ripples, which spread out for less than a meter in each direction, and the droning sound became even louder.

"What is this?" Bao whispered.

"I don't know. Throughout all the years, we never brought the Phoenix Crown and the wind stone into the same room with each other, let alone put them next to each other." A moment passed, then Sunan pulled the wooden box away and put it back into the burlap sack. "I shudder to think what might happen if I opened the wooden box. Or the iron box. Or both of them at the same time."

Bao reached forward and put her hand on the cool surface of the iron box. "The Phoenix Crown and the wind stone almost seem like they belong together."

"Exactly. Bao, I remember you mentioning someone adept at forging objects of power. The same one who forged your Phoenix Crown."

She looked over at him and smiled. "It's time for a trip to Mount Fohe."

CHAPTER 50
METEOR HAMMERS

The Pure Phoenix Sect had always been a bit smaller than the Golden Dragon Sect. Before the siege of Daolu, the Golden Dragon Sect numbered a bit over 200 members, whereas the Pure Phoenix Sect only had about 150 or so.

Casualties during the fighting had been significant but not heavy. After camping at the foot of Zhifu Shan, a census revealed that the refugees included 156 Golden Dragons, 126 Pure Phoenixes, 23 constables, roughly 300 soldiers, and hundreds of commoners. The majority of the constables and soldiers expressed interest in joining one of the sects or the other. Only about half of the commoners were interested.

There was some disagreement among the leadership of the two sects regarding how to split up the new recruits. The Golden Dragons, of course, wanted to retain the edge they'd had in Daolu, whereas the Pure Phoenixes were pushing for a leveling of the numbers.

Even after squabbling for the better part of the morning, Mao

Yun and Sun Mai couldn't come to an agreement.

Mao Yun slapped his thigh. "Our sects should be on equal footing, Brother Sun Mai! Even Kong Zhi said, 'Have no friends who are not your equals!'"

Sun Mai chuckled coldly. "Please, Brother Mao Yun. Are you really trying to match wits with me? Quoting Kong Zhi? Even children know that quote. However many quotes of Kong Zhi you know, I know ten times as many. No. A hundred times. Maybe a thousand! For example, Kong Zhi also said, 'Never impose upon others what you would not choose for your own self.'

"Would you choose to intentionally make yourself weak? I think not! Besides, Kong Zhi also said, 'The beginning... er, um... the beginning state is the perfect state!' In the beginning, the Golden Dragon Sect was roughly thirty percent larger than the Pure Phoenix Sect. That ratio should be maintained, don't you think?"

Mao Yun narrowed his eyes. "'The beginning state is the perfect state?' I've never heard that before. Did you just make that up? You did, didn't you? That's not a saying of Kong Zhi."

Sun Mai snorted coldly. "A little test, Brother Mao. Thankfully, you passed it." His eyes suddenly turned up in thought. "That is a great statement, though. Perfect for my scripture." Looking at one of the nearby Golden Dragons, he said, "Quick, go write that down! I need to remember it!"

As the man hurried off to find writing utensils, Bao and Sunan entered the tent.

Both sides laid out their arguments, and in the end, Sunan insisted that the sects' numbers be equal.

"Now is not the time to vie for superiority," he said. "Our two sects need to work together, not compete with each other."

Sun Mai and some of the other Golden Dragons grumbled a bit, but they abided by his wishes.

Those among the new recruits who wished to join one sect or the other were allowed to do so. Those who had no preference were divided up to ensure that both sects had roughly three hundred members.

The Golden Dragon Sect now had six major divisions, each one led by a Dragon Lord. One of those Dragon Lords was Mao Yun's sister, Mao Mei. Sun Mai retained his title as chief minister, and of course, Sunan was still the sect leader.

The Pure Phoenix Sect was organized into four divisions, with each division led by one of the Claws of the Phoenix. The only surviving member of the original Claws was Flying Death, Liu Jiahui. One of the newly promoted Claws was Wang Tian, who had distinguished himself during Bao's hunt for the fei beast. Mao Yun was given the title Phoenix General, with powers and responsibilities similar to Sun Mai's. Bao, of course, remained chieftainess.

Of the commoners, only some showed talent in terms of qi cultivation, and they were allowed to officially join one of the two sects. Most others had skills that were not martial in nature, but they were valuable nonetheless and were organized into a large outer sect that was officially separate from either of the two main sects. Among that group were cooks, blacksmiths, tailors, and even a fan-maker named An Jian.

The necessary formalities, ceremonies, and rites took an entire day. The following morning, the newly reorganized Golden Dragon and Pure Phoenix Sects broke camp and headed south. Their destination was a cave somewhere at the foot of Mount Fohe.

The ordinary sect members weren't privy to the details, but the Dragon Lords, the Claws of the Phoenix, and other higher-ranking leaders were told that they sought a skilled blacksmith named Ruan the Flamingo.

The journey south was relatively uneventful. Master Wang Tian, newly promoted Claw of the Phoenix, had originally been a hunter, and he had also been to Ruan's cave before. He led the way as they left the shadow of Zhifu Shan and headed toward the towering peak that was Mount Fohe.

A few days later, they made camp on a plateau that jutted out from the foot of Mount Fohe, which was only about an hour's ride from the location of Ruan's cave. They had decided that showing up at his doorstep with a small army wouldn't offer the best impression.

After camp was set and lunch eaten, a small group headed toward the cave, including Sunan, Bao, Mao Yun, Sun Mai, Mao Mei, and Wang Tian, as well as about ten ordinary members of each sect.

As the sun shone down, they threaded their way through the mountain foothills, keeping a moderate pace.

When they arrived at the cave, Bao immediately sensed that something was off. Things looked different from before.

"Chieftainess Bao," Wang Tian said. "Look. The door."

When Bao turned to look at the door leading into the cave itself, she realized it was open. In fact, a moment later, a gust of wind caused the door to swing wide open, then it slammed shut momentarily before opening again.

The group immediately tensed up, and the sound of swords pierced the air, as well as spears being unstrapped and arrows nocked, as they prepared to defend.

"Bao?" Sunan said.

Bao slid out of her saddle and pulled two long daggers out from her belt. "Something's off. Mao Yun, you stay here. Wang Tian, you're with me." Making quick eye contact with three of the other sect members, she continued. "You three as well."

Sunan picked three Golden Dragons. Leaving Mao Mei with her brother, he and Sun Mai joined Bao as she padded cautiously up to the door.

Once inside, they found that the corridor was well-lit, just the way it had been last time Bao came. Keeping her daggers in a ready position, Bao led them slowly down the corridor toward the main room, where she had met with Ruan previously.

Nothing seemed out of the ordinary about the corridor or the room, and yet somehow the strange feeling that prickled at the base of Bao's neck wouldn't go away.

"This all looks the same," she said quietly to Sunan, "but my feelings tell me that something's wrong. Where is Ruan?"

Sunan gripped his saber with two hands as he looked around. "No signs of a fight…"

Before they could confer any further, a voice echoed out from one of the doors at the other end of the room. "Well, what have we here?"

A man emerged, tall and well-built. He was dressed in red robes, and his head was shaved clean. A chain was wrapped around his right forearm, at either end of which was a metal ball carved with a monstrous face. As the man entered the room, others followed— men and women of varying ages and builds—all of whom wore red robes and had shaved heads. The entire group seemed to be armed with the chainlike weapons.

Before Bao or Sunan could react, eight red-robed men and women were facing them.

"Are you friends of Ruan?" Bao asked, gripping her daggers.

"Friends?" the man said. He chuckled. "I think not. Ruan has committed crimes worthy of death. However, he managed to scuttle away before he could be punished. What of you people? Are you friends of this Ruan?"

Bao immediately cursed the fact that she had left her Phoenix Crown in her saddlebag.

"We've never even met Ruan," Sunan said. "We've only heard of him by reputation. If he's not here, then we'll just take our leave." He took a step back, as did everyone else, including Bao.

"You'll not take another step," the man said. He suddenly sniffed the air. "Is that… the stench of blood? And of demons? Who are you people, exactly?" He slowly began to swing the chain back and forth with his right hand.

Sun Mai took a step forward and clasped his hands formally. "I am Chief Minister Sun of the Golden Dragon Sect. Friend, I like your hairdo, but considering I don't know your name, I am unable to compliment you properly. Would you please grace us with your honored surnames and explain from whence you come?"

A cold glint flashed through the man's eyes. "I am Blackleaf of the Hen-Shi Sect. We come from the Demon Maelstrom. Golden Dragon Sect, you say? I've heard of you people."

"We're quite famous," Sun Mai said immediately. "Brother Blackleaf, although I've never heard of your Hen-Shi Sect, I'm sure it's a powerful organization. I am the highest-ranking Golden Dragon here. Since Ruan the Flamingo isn't present, our group will now take our leave. Farewell!" With that, he clasped his hands in formal fashion and then turned to leave.

"Do you take me for a fool?" Blackleaf said. "It's true, the Golden Dragon Sect is very famous, as is the Pure Phoenix Sect. There are even pictures of the famous leaders of those sects, Young Dragon Sunan and Heroine Bao. Do you really think I wouldn't recognize its two most famous leaders, who are standing directly in front of me?

"And do you really think that the Hen-Shi Sect, we, the most devoted followers of Hen-Shi, sworn to rid the world of all those who would kill or harm others, would possibly allow the bloodstained hands of people like you to remain within Qi Xien?"

He extended his right hand, allowing the two monstrous iron balls to drop down until they almost touched the ground. "Our meteor hammers smite the wicked and cleanse the world of violence. And now, they will cleanse the world of you scum!"

Without another word, he swung the meteor hammer through the air, launching it directly at Sun Mai.

***

Several days to the north, a horse entered a ravine. A camp had recently been set up in the ravine, and little had been done to erase evidence of its presence.

Seated on the horse was a hulking figure clad in bonelike armor. Flanking him were a few other men in similar attire.

After entering the ravine, he looked around, sniffed the air, and said, "There's no need to lurk about. I know you're here."

A flash of gold could be seen from a nearby tree, and a moment later, a man dropped to the ground a few meters away.

"Greetings, Bone General," the man said, adjusting his golden robes.

"Greetings, Golden Immortal," the Bone General replied. "So, you're chasing them too?"

"Indeed." The Golden Immortal's eyes flashed. "I have unfinished business with that boy and that girl."

"What of your arrangement with the Love General?"

"We've parted ways."

"Interesting. Well, I happen to have unfinished business with those two as well. The King of the Pure Ones expressed a disturbing lack of concern but has indicated that I may hunt them down to my heart's content. I intend to destroy their ragtag army and then watch them die in torment. Do you care to join me?"

The Golden Immortal grinned. "As long as I get to be there to watch them suffer."

CHAPTER 51
SULFUR. SALTPETER. CHARCOAL.

Blackleaf and his fellow comrades from the Hen-Shi Sect looked impressive and spoke in a very domineering fashion, but the truth was, they couldn't match up to the Golden Dragon and Pure Phoenix Sects in terms of experience or skill.

Sunan and Bao had led their forces to fight ogres, hunt monsters, and kill demons. They had fought in tournaments, on city walls and on rooftops, in back alleys, forests, and rivers. In terms of martial arts, they had forged their own paths, and built their skills by means of both trial-and-error, and hard work.

The Hen-Shi Sect, on the other hand, was a reclusive group that had just begun to flex their muscles in the outside world. Although Bao and Sunan would have no way of knowing it, Blackleaf and the other seven from the Hen-Shi Sect had never actually fought anyone of a similar skill or power level as themselves. Although they possessed unusual strength, and despite the fact that their meteor hammers were capable of inflicting shocking levels of damage, in the end, experience trumped strength.

Sun Mai easily evaded Blackleaf's initial surprise attack. In the moments that followed, the other Hen-Shi Sect fighters hurled their meteor hammers out with astonishing force. However, only one of the meteor hammers hit its intended target, slamming into one of Sunan's Golden Dragons. The man was sent flying backward until he slammed into the wall with a sickening crunch.

All the other meteor hammer attacks were countered with ease. Then the Golden Dragons and Pure Phoenixes fought back.

Two of the Hen-Shi Sect fighters were killed in the first volley.

The rest of the fight lasted for only a few breaths of time.

In the end, five of the original eight red-robed fighters were dead. The Golden Dragon who had been hit in the first attack was the only casualty on their side.

The three enemies who survived, including Blackleaf, were quickly bound and gagged.

After a more thorough search, they confirmed that Ruan was nowhere to be found. From the look of things, he'd left in a hurry.

The cave was much larger than they'd anticipated. In fact, it wasn't so much a cave as a cave network, which Ruan had only used parts of. As for the deeper recesses, they had clearly been occupied in times past, perhaps by a local warlord or bandit.

It didn't take long for Bao and Sunan to agree that it was a good place to make a temporary base. They immediately sent word back to the camp, then turned their attention to Blackleaf.

After his gag was removed, the man merely glared at them icily but didn't say anything. Bao and Sunan exchanged a glance.

"Why did you come for Ruan?" Bao asked.

Blackleaf simply stared at her.

"Why did you attack us?" Sunan growled, his hands tightening into fists.

Blackleaf snorted. A moment passed, then he said, "I already told you, Young Dragon. We are sworn to rid the world of all those who would kill or harm others. I don't know how many lives you've taken, but I can tell that your hands reek of blood. It is our duty to cleanse the world."

Bao reached over and picked up one of the meteor hammers. Hefting it, she said, "You want to cleanse the world of killers… by killing them? Isn't that a bit of a contradiction?"

"It's called fighting poison with poison," Blackleaf replied. "When the world is clean, the instruments of cleansing will also be cleansed. This is not the Perfect Realm, and thus we must use imperfect methods to achieve that which is pure."

Bao and Sunan looked at each other again and could see the odd expressions in each other's faces.

"It's a good thing our friend Sun Mai isn't here at the moment," Bao said, "otherwise I think he might be interested in debating you. But I'm not. I couldn't care less about philosophy. Tell us why you came looking for Ruan and where he is now. If you do, we'll let you go."

Blackleaf's eyes narrowed. "You expect me to trust the word of wicked murderers like you? You killed five of us!"

"After you attacked us with no warning and killed one of my men!" Sunan barked. "Truth be told, I don't care what you call us or what you accuse us of. If we wanted to kill you, you would be dead." He picked up the gag and took a step forward. "Tell us what we want to know."

"Or what?" Blackleaf said

"Just tell us what we want to know. You have my word you'll be on your way before the moon rises tonight."

Blackleaf looked at Sunan, then Bao. Then he took a deep breath. "An object of great power was stolen from us. The branch of a tree that once grew in Emo-Cheng."

"The underworld?" Bao asked. In the past, she wouldn't have believed his words for even a moment. However, her view of the world had changed after her encounter with the phoenix demon.

"Yes, the underworld. Our sect acquired a branch of the Epoch

Tree, which we intended to use in our fight against evil. However, that branch was stolen from us."

"By Ruan?"

"By another. I only know that his surname is Du, and that he is a man of vast intelligence and cunning. As we followed him across the lands, we soon realized that his destination was Mount Fohe, and considering that was the case, it was obvious that he sought Ruan the Flamingo. Ruan is known to us; his skills border on inhuman.

"The truth is that we only arrived here shortly before you did, and we found that both Ruan and Du were gone, presumably having fled to parts unknown.

"So now you know the whole story. The time has come to live up to your end of the bargain."

Bao swung the meteor hammer back and forth slowly. "How do we know you're telling us the truth?"

Blackleaf frowned. "Search the area. I would wager my life that you'll evidence of the passage of Ruan and Du. Du came here on horseback. Presumably Ruan had a horse or mule as well. My guess is that they headed west. The passage to the Demon Maelstrom is southeast, in the Southern Desert, so Du will obviously not return to the east or the south. The way north is mountainous and inhospitable to travelers. The Kushen Basin, however, is the perfect place for a fugitive like Du. From there, he could easily head to Naqan or somewhere else in the east."

Bao slowly lowered the meteor hammer to the ground and looked over at Sunan. "I'll go find Wang Tian."

After being promoted to Claw of the Phoenix, one of Wang Tian's first acts had been to gather some of the best hunters, scouts, and trackers in the sect to form a special team that, with Bao's permission, he called the Eyes of the Phoenix.

It only took minutes from the moment they were mustered until they found Du and Ruan's tracks. Just as Blackleaf had surmised, they had fled to the west, Du on horseback, Ruan riding a mule.

Wang Tian immediately assigned two of the Eyes of the Phoenix to begin following the trail. Meanwhile, Bao returned to Sunan and Blackleaf.

"He was right," Bao announced.

A sneer flickered on Blackleaf's face, but it vanished just as quickly as it appeared. "Now you owe me my freedom," he said.

Sunan nodded. "You'll have it. You'll be escorted south and then set free with no weapons. If we see you near our camp again, we won't be so merciful."

With that, Sunan and Bao left to confer with their advisors and the other leaders of the two sects.

In the end, it was agreed that Sun Mai and Mao Yun would lead a group of ten to try to catch up to Du and Ruan. They would leave the following morning at the crack of dawn, with the fastest horses available. Bao and Sunan would remain behind to continue to consolidate the newly reorganized sects and focus on training.

***

Things were a bit chaotic as the Golden Dragon Sect and the Pure Phoenix Sect made a temporary home in the caves at the foot of Mount Fohe. After the cave assignments were doled out and everyone settled in, fan-maker An Jian set out to explore.

Shouldn't this mountain be called Fone, not Fohe? he thought. It was true that in later times, this mountain would come to be called Fone, instead of its current name of Fohe. However, despite all the knowledge that rested in An Jian's head, he couldn't come up with any theories why that might be. *If I had even the slightest martial arts ability, I might have been able to get close enough to them to use poison.* Sadly, he'd lost all of that on the journey here.

The caves were lit by lamp or candle, and most of them were very cold. However, not every place could be described as chilly. For example, one side cave had been set up as a kitchen. Fires were stoked and cauldrons hung to stew meat and vegetables. In another location was a room that the previous owner of the cave had used as a forge. Already, the sects were expanding the forge and using the existing setup to repair equipment and craft new weapons, especially sabers, as well as spears and arrowheads.

It was toward the forges that An Jian headed. Upon arrival, he found that luck was with him. Dragon Lord Zhou, one of the newly promoted leaders of the Golden Dragon Sect, was currently presiding over the activities. The cave was already very hot, and Dragon Lord Zhou, a stout, middle-aged man with a scraggly beard, was sweating profusely.

An Jian hurried over and offered formal greetings.

"You're An Jian, right?" Dragon Lord Zhou said.

"I am!" An Jian replied. "I'm honored you would remember my name."

"I remember you ran a fan shop back in Daolu, right? Delightful Breeze or something like that?"

"The Delightful Wind Shop."

"Right, right. You don't happen to have any fans for sale right now, do you?"

"For sale? Dragon Lord, do you really think I would deign to sell things to fellow members of my sect? I'm a member of the outer sect now! Here..." He pulled a fan out. "Dragon Lord, the poem on this fan is special. I came across it in a scroll that merchants brought from the distant lands of Naqan. By luck, a friend of mine back in Daolu was able to translate the original poem. Well, in any case, it might provide you a bit of respite from this hellish heat!"

He handed the fan over to Dragon Lord Zhou, who took it in hand and examined the poem.

"'The wind, snapping trees, dissolving mountains, serenity.' What does it mean?"

An Jian chuckled. "I'm just a simple fan-maker, not a poet. All I know is that it sounds lovely to the ear and looks beautiful when put to the pen. Good luck, Dragon Lord Zhou!"

As An Jian left, Dragon Lord Zhou began to fan himself.

An Jian smiled. "Thus it begins," he murmured to himself. "Next, I need to find some sulfur. Sulfur. Saltpeter. Charcoal. Although Divine Fire has not yet been invented in this era, all the ingredients exist. Bao and Sunan won't have any idea what hit them."

CHAPTER 52
DOORS AND PADLOCKS

Days passed, and slowly life in the cave fell into a rhythm. The newly organized sects focused on training the new disciples and helping the long-time disciples push toward breakthroughs. Temporary fighting platforms were built out of wood and hide, set up outside of the cave for training purposes. Dragon Lord Sima Zikang ran drills with various battlefield formations.

A guard station was erected higher up on the slopes of Mount Fohe, a location from which much of the lands to the west were visible. In addition to that, mounted patrols were sent out regularly to patrol the area within a two-day ride of the cave. Bao and Sunan wanted as much advance notice as possible if the Demon Emperor decided to send a force against them, be it large or small.

Roughly two weeks later, a discovery was made.

Bao and Sunan were having a casual sparring match on one of the fighting platforms when Li Runfa hurried up. During the reorganization of the Pure Phoenix Sect, Li Runfa had refused to publicly accept any title or position. However, as a member of one of the original groups led by Bao from the south, he was well respected, and his words carried almost the same weight as the Dragon Lords, if not more.

Li Runfa leaned up against the side of the platform and watched Bao and Sunan exchange blows for a minute or two. When they stopped to rest, he said, "Chieftainess, Sect Leader, I found something interesting."

Taking a drink of water from a skin bottle, Bao hopped down to the ground and looked over at him expectantly. Sunan jumped down to stand next to her.

"It's..." Li Runfa hesitated for a moment. "Well, I think it would be better if you saw it yourself."

Bao handed the skin bottle to Sunan. "Very well, lead the way."

With a nod, Li Runfa headed back into the cave entrance. It took a few minutes for them to wind their way through the main parts of the cave toward one of the deeper caverns. There were quite a few shafts leading farther into the depths of the earth, and at Li Runfa's suggestion, they had been slowly exploring those shafts and the smaller caverns they led to.

At a certain point, Li Runfa reached an area where two young men in the garb of the Pure Phoenix Sect waited, holding oil lamps. One of the young men handed a lamp to Li Runfa, who then continued down into the darkness.

As they proceeded, the tunnel grew narrower and shorter, until they were forced to duck their heads down. The tunnel twisted and turned and even branched off a few times. At one point, they had to squeeze through a crevice so narrow that it almost required them to hold their breath, lest they get stuck.

The entire time, both Bao and Sunan could tell that they were climbing ever downward into the bowels of the earth. It was an unnerving feeling.

Eventually the tunnel opened into a cavern so large that the lamplight didn't reach the ends.

The sound of dripping water echoed about, and a shallow lake spread out in front of them.

"I sure hope you know the way back, Master Li," Sunan said.

Li Runfa chuckled. "Don't worry, I have a very good sense of direction. Come on, we're almost there."

He strode out into the lake, which started out ankle deep but soon reached their calves.

At the far end of the cavern, the rock floor rose up again, and they stepped out of the water. That was when they saw the door.

There in the wall of the cave was a door made of stone. The door appeared to have been crafted from stone hewn from the wall itself. No hinges were visible, which indicated that the door would likely open inward. Securing the door was a sturdy-looking padlock, roughly the size of a melon.

The surface of the door was ordinary, with no decorations whatsoever. In fact, were it not for the large padlock, it would have been difficult to spot the door to begin with.

Bao peered at the door. "How did you manage to find this, Li Runfa?"

"Luck, I suppose. I really can't say how far down the tunnels and caverns go, but I can say that we've only scratched the surface of what's down here. My lamplight just happened to touch this door earlier this morning. If my head hadn't been turned in the right direction in that moment, I would have passed it by."

Sunan stepped forward. Grasping the padlock, he tugged it back and forth a bit. "Seems sturdy."

"It is," Li Runfa said. "I toyed with it earlier for a minute or two. Although it looks plain on the outside, the inner workings are complex. I didn't have the tools at the time, though, so I couldn't perform a true assessment."

"Presumably you have the tools now?" Bao asked.

He grinned. "Of course. Shall I?"

Sunan stepped back and took the lamp while Li Runfa pulled out a set of tools.

Sure enough, the padlock was no simple piece of machinery. Time ticked by, although it was difficult to say how much, considering they were surrounded by nothing but darkness and the sound of dripping water.

After what was surely an hour or so, Li Runfa shook his head. "This lock is… almost godlike. I can tell that it's going to take me time. How about I take you back to the surface and then come back to work on it alone?"

The others nodded.

***

It wasn't until the next day that it occurred to Bao that they hadn't heard from Li Runfa since he'd escorted them to the surface. After inquiring, she was told that he had been working on the lock for the entire time since.

The next day, the news was the same.

An entire week went by.

News was starting to spread through the camp, until eventually everyone was talking about it.

On the ninth day, a disciple came to find Bao and Sunan and gave them the news.

"Master Li opened the lock!"

After climbing back down into the darkness, through the tunnels, and across the lake, they found themselves standing once again in front of the door. Li Runfa looked exhausted, his hair disheveled, his clothing rumpled. But he was smiling.

"Just as I said before, godlike." He hefted the huge padlock in his right hand a few times. "I'm going to have to take this back up and study it well."

"Excellent work, Master Li," Sunan said.

Li Runfa clasped his hands respectfully. "Many thanks, Sect Leader Sunan." Then he placed his palm on the surface of the door and asked, "May I have the honor?"

"Go ahead," Bao said.

With that, he pushed the door open. It slid open quietly, without the slightest creak or moan. Behind it was a corridor, clearly hewn by human hands, which sloped down and to the left.

Since Sunan currently had the lamp, he led the way, and they followed the corridor down. It seemed to have been carved in a spiral, which led down several meters to another door and another padlock.

"Interesting," Li Runfa said, stepping forward to examine the lock. "The other lock was made from lead, this one seems to be iron." Without another word, he produced a long metal hook and slowly inserted it into the lock. After moving it around a few times, he looked back at Bao and Sunan. "This is going to take some time."

The days marched by. One day. Three days. Seven days. The camp was abuzz with rumors about what lay behind the door.

"I bet it's a treasure. Our sects are going to be rich!"

"What if it's actually a passage to the underworld?"

"Maybe it's a prison! What if there's some kind of ancient monster inside?"

On the ninth day, word came.

"Master Li opened the lock!"

Behind the door with the iron lock was another tunnel that spiraled down, just like the first one had. This second tunnel led to another door and another padlock. This padlock was made from copper.

Despite the increase in the quality of metal, this new lock took Li Runfa exactly nine days to open, just like the other locks. After that was another lock, this time one of steel. It also took nine days to pick.

Time blurred and rumors swirled.

Eighty-one days later, Li Runfa opened the ninth lock. Each lock was a progression of increasingly precious metals. The first was lead, then iron. After that, copper, bronze, and steel. The final four locks were made from metals that no one could identify, and yet all of them took nine days to pick.

On the eighty-first day, Bao and Sunan took Tie Gangwen and Sima Zikang along with them to meet Li Runfa in the depths of the earth beneath Mount Fohe.

Li Runfa stood in front of the door, holding a padlock made of strange greenish metal that actually glowed with soft light. He seemed mesmerized as he stared at the lock, running his finger slowly in a circle around the keyhole.

As Bao and Sunan approached, he looked up.

"I'm quite certain that this is the last lock and the last door," he said. "I can't say why. It just… feels that way." He reached out and placed his hand on the surface of the door. "May I have the honor?"

Bao nodded.

He pushed the door, and something like a sigh could be heard, a sigh originating in ancient times.

Behind the door was a cavern, and as they stepped in, they could sense that it was even bigger than the lake cavern up above.

They had come prepared with the most powerful lamps they had, which they now lit. Everyone present, including Bao, Sunan, Sima Zikang, Tie Gangwen, and Li Runfa, held up shining lamps, sending flickering light out in all directions.

The cavern floor was mostly smooth, and unlike the other caverns, there were few stalactites or stalagmites visible, and those that were there seemed relatively newly formed.

They proceeded into the cavern, and moments later, Tie Gangwen said, "Look, up ahead."

A pit became visible, and as they neared its edge and looked down, they gasped.

Bones could be seen at the bottom of the pit. At first they

assumed the bones were simply jumbled at the bottom, but as the lamp light spread out, they realized that they were looking at a skeleton. No, not a skeleton. Skeletons.

Two enormous skeletons filled the bottom of the pit, intertwined almost in an embrace. They formed a circle, with the torso of one of the skeletons resting within the tail of the other, and vice versa.

"Is that the skeleton of… a dragon?" Sima Zikang asked.

"I think it is," breathed Tie Gangwen. "And that other creature. It's…"

"A phoenix," Li Runfa said.

CHAPTER 53
THE TIMELESS MASTER

Sunan and Bao both had the same reaction. Their eyes glazed over, and without a word, they placed their lamps on the ground and then sat down cross-legged. In unison, they closed their eyes and began to meditate.

Nine days passed.

At the beginning of the nine days, everything in the cavern remained as dark and silent as before. But then fluctuations began to roll out from Sunan and Bao, something like vibrations that stirred the blood and qi of anyone present.

Bao and Sunan's closest friends and advisors took shifts to stand guard over them.

After nine days, the fluctuations became so intense that the air around Bao and Sunan began to distort. By the eighteenth day, they were surrounded by something that looked like an enormous shimmering circle.

After the eighteenth day, the circle began to glow, casting light out into the cavern and more fully illuminating the skeletons.

"Where did they come from?" Tie Gangwen asked.

He and Liu Jiahui were currently sitting cross-legged at the mouth of the cavern.

"You know the legend of the five peaks, right?"

"How the five tallest mountains in the realm were created by a specific dragon and phoenix?"

"Exactly."

"But Mount Fohe isn't one of those five peaks…"

Lie Jiahui shrugged. "Maybe there are more than five mountains that were created by dragons and phoenixes."

Tie Gangwen grunted in response.

After twenty-seven days, the distortions surrounding Bao and Sunan seemed to divide into two sections, like two interlocked teardrops.

After thirty-six days, the two divided sections began to slowly rotate in an endless cycle. The light shining out from the distortions grew more intense.

On the forty-fifth day, smaller individual distortions appeared within each side of the symbol, as if the two sides were beginning to change shape.

After fifty-four days, blurry figures became visible within the sections that made up the symbol.

Deep in the night on the sixty-third day, Liu Jiahui and Tie Gangwen were once again standing guard. Far above them, outside of the caves, clouds covered the moon and stars, cloaking everything in complete darkness. Inside the cave, however, the light shining from the symbol was so bright that it was difficult to look at it for any length of time. However, the figures within each side of the image were now relatively clear.

"I see it now," Liu Jiahui said.

"See what?"

"The dragon. And the phoenix. Inside that image."

Tie Gangwen looked over at him. "Don't tell me it took you

this long to figure out that the symbol would be a dragon and a phoenix?"

Liu Jiahui snorted. "Of course I realized it! But you couldn't see it clearly until just now. How many days has it been?"

"Sixty-three. Do you want to bet how many more days this is going to last?"

"I'm not stupid."

After seventy-two days, the dragon and the phoenix in the symbol became crystal clear, and the entire cavern began to vibrate.

"You know what this means, right?" Liu Jiahui said.

"What?" Tie Gangwen replied.

"It's not going to be long before we have one big sect instead of two smaller ones."

Tie Gangwen looked over at Liu Jiahui, a thoughtful expression on his face.

On the eve of the eighty-first day, virtually all of the leaders of the sect gathered at the mouth of the cavern. The symbol was now glowing so brightly that it was impossible to look at for more than a second or two. The cavern pulsed with vibrations, and a faint roaring sound could be heard.

When a certain time on the eighty-first day arrived, the dragon and phoenix that made up the symbol separated. The dragon seemed to come alive, swirling through the air down toward Sunan. Although it moved with incredible speed, it seemed to slow to a crawl. When the dragon slammed into Sunan's forehead, intense rumbling sounds filled the cave, and a shock wave blasted out in all directions. An explosion of bright light filled the area as the dragon merged into Sunan's forehead and then disappeared.

The exact same process occurred with Bao and the phoenix. With the graceful flutter of its wings, it shot down into Bao's forehead, fusing into her within the blink of an eye.

As quickly as that, it was over. Darkness once again filled the cave.

Bao and Sunan opened their eyes and turned to look at each other. On Sunan's forehead, the shining symbol of a dragon was slowly fading away, and Bao, of course, had a phoenix symbol.

"Do you understand?" Sunan asked.

"Yes." Bao reached her right palm out toward Sunan, who extended his left palm to meet hers.

When their hands touched, it was just barely possible to hear a rumbling roar and a piercing howl.

***

Nearly six months had passed since the discovery of the door deep below Mount Fohe, but nothing eventful had occurred during that time. Sun Mai, Mao Yun, and Wang Tian had not returned, nor had they sent word.

After Sunan and Bao emerged from their extended session of meditation, they didn't offer any explanation for what had occurred, and when asked directly, they gave cryptic responses.

That only fueled the rumors that filled the camp.

Sunan and Bao didn't seem to care.

More time passed. Training went on as usual. Every few days, people would show up at the cave, either looking for Ruan or asking about the two sects that now occupied his former abode. Slowly but surely, the sects were growing.

One day, Li Runfa once again interrupted one of Sunan and Bao's sparring sessions.

"Someone is asking for you, Chieftainess," he said. Then he lowered his voice. "Thankfully I was the first person he talked to. He said he wanted to speak with Shangguan Bao…"

Bao and Sunan exchanged a glance.

"Did he give his name?" Bao asked.

"Yes, Chieftainess. He said he's an old friend of yours. Gongye Zheng."

Bao's eyes brightened. "Gongye Zheng? Take me to him!"

A few minutes later, Sunan and Bao were seated in a small audience chamber across from a somewhat elderly man wearing the nondescript clothing of a farmer or craftsman. Leaned up against him on the wall was a very large object wrapped in a cloth bundle. Despite the clothing, it was impossible for him to change the way he held himself. He sat straight in his chair, with his chin tilted slightly upward, not arrogantly, but in a way that seemed to command power.

"Uncle Gongye," Bao said, "I almost didn't recognize you! What are you doing here?" Few people in Yu Zhing had ever noticed Bao or been kind to her, but Gongye Zheng was one of those few. One of the pillars of the Gongye Clan, he had somehow managed to survive the purges of years past, yet had avoided being sucked into the sycophantic cliques that catered to the Demon Emperor and his court.

Gongye Zheng smiled. "Yu Zhing has become far too dangerous, Bao'er. I faked my own death and then slipped out of the city under the cover of night."

Bao sighed. "From what I've heard, Yu Zhing only continues to get more and more dangerous as the years pass. Uncle Gongye… how did you know to find me here?"

"Even in Yu Zhing, people are talking about the events of Daolu a few months ago, about the two sects led by Young Dragon Sunan and Fierce Phoenix Bao. There are wanted posters being put up in the major cities of the empire. It didn't take long for me to put the pieces of the puzzle together."

"Wanted posters?" Bao exclaimed.

"Yes!" Gongye Zheng reached into his robe and pulled out a many-folded piece of paper. After opening it up, he handed it over to Bao.

It was a wanted poster with a picture of herself and Sunan.

"This doesn't even look like me!" she protested.

"Let me see that," Sunan said, reaching over to grab the poster. He snorted. "My jaw is definitely not that large!"

Gongye Zheng chuckled. "To be honest, I doubt anyone else knows your true identity, Bao'er. I apologize for speaking your true name to your man earlier. I should have been more careful."

"Don't worry, Li Runfa is quite circumspect. Uncle Gongye, what exactly are you doing here? Do you... want to join us?"

Gongye Zheng shook his head. "I'm just passing through. I plan to leave this part of the world far behind me. I'm going to Naqan, where the Demon Emperor is nothing more than a story told to children to scare them into behaving. I've always wanted to lay eyes on the Huo Sea. I heard a story once that when you watch the sun set over the ocean, you can see a blue flash of light that brings you luck for the rest of your life.

"Bao'er, word of your camp here is spreading. If I heard about it, you can be sure that the Demon Emperor knows you're here. I worry that you are not safe here."

Bao nodded. "I know, Uncle Gongye. We don't plan to stay here for long."

Gongye Zheng sighed. "I can sense in my bones that great change is coming. First there was the Battle of Daolu, and then the Uprising of Xuanlu. I have a feeling that more such incidents will occur. Perhaps the Demon Emperor's days truly are numbered."

"Uprising of Xuanlu?" Sunan asked. "What happened in Xuanlu?"

"You haven't heard yet? A great revolt occurred, led by the Timeless Master, a man named Li Buwei. It all centered around an execution planned by the city magistrate. A young woman was accused of cursing the Demon Emperor publicly and was sentenced to death. That young woman was Qixia the Butterfly, a very popular singer and dancer in the city. The incident caused widespread anger, and just as the sentence was about to be carried out, a band of masked men broke onto the scene, killing the Demon Emperor's soldiers and saving the young girl.

"It's hard to say what the truth is, but according the stories I heard, more than half the city rose up to support the revolt. Maybe the event was planned in advance, or maybe it was spontaneous. Half of the Demon Emperor's soldiers were killed, and the others were expelled from the city. Armies were sent from both Huisheng and Yu Zhing to restore order. In the end, Li Buwei and Qixia the Butterfly fled, although nobody knows to where."

Gongye Zheng shook his head. "I'm not sure how Li Buwei managed to fight so effectively against the Demon Emperor. If the tales are to be believed, he seemed to have foreknowledge of everything the soldiers were about to do. There are even whispers that he can see into the future. I suppose that's why people took to calling him the Timeless Master.

"According to the rumors, powerful martial artists are rising up all over the empire, people who can fight with superhuman strength and speed. Perhaps Li Buwei is one of them. Perhaps you are too, Bao'er?" Gongye Zheng looked at Bao with a strange gleam flickering in his eyes.

Bao smiled. "Times are changing, Uncle Gongye, that is a fact." He nodded.

"Lord Gongye," Sunan said, "it's getting late. Would you care to dine with us? I would love to hear more stories about these martial heroes."

"Of course, Sect Leader Sunan. I have many stories to tell!"

***

"Did you say Li Buwei?" the Bone General growled.

The soldier nodded.

The Bone General's hand clenched into a fist. "You're dismissed," he said.

The soldier hurried out.

"Who is Li Buwei?" the Golden Immortal asked.

"In your language, 'buwei' means nothing, but in the language of the King of the Pure Ones, it is very significant. I can't be sure, but…" The Bone General trailed off. Brows furrowed, he looked off into the distance, clearly lost in thought.

A long moment passed.

Finally, the Bone General rose to his feet. "I must speak in person to the King of the Pure Ones."

"But our plan…"

"Will continue as we have discussed. The reinforcements will be here soon, led by one of my top agents, a man named Geng Long. After he arrives, begin making the preparations. I will return after I speak to the King of the Pure Ones. Fear not, Golden Immortal, we will crush Sunan and Bao. A little uprising led by this 'Li Buwei' will do nothing to stop that."

CHAPTER 54
COUNCIL MEETING

Sunan and Bao entertained Gongye Zheng for three full days. He told many stories about events that had occurred in Yu Zhing during the years in which Bao had been gone and recounted rumors and tales of the martial heroes who were rising up in different parts of the empire.

Most such heroes were declared outlaws by the Demon Emperor and had huge bounties placed on their heads. There was the Purple Cavern Killer, who lurked in the shadow of Mount Rong, and the Twin Giants of Zhaoze Swamp. Rumors swirled about a vicious brute from Hui Sheng who was known as the Executioner of the South. And far, far to the southwest was Hua Pi the Skin Dancer. Those were the most famous of the martial heroes, but there were others.

Sunan was shocked to learn that copies of his Wu-Sunan fighting manual were proliferating throughout the empire. Supposedly, many of the martial heroes were using it as the basis of their newfound fighting skills. Because of the rigorous training involved in this new way of fighting, many had taken to calling it "kung fu," based on a Classical Fei word that meant "hard work."

On the morning of the fourth day, they saw Gongye Zheng off as he made his way west toward the Kushen Basin, and beyond it, Naqan.

"There's something he's not telling us," Bao said as they watched him leave.

Sunan looked over. "What do you mean?"

"I'm not sure," she said. "Don't worry. I trust Uncle Gongye with my life. But there is more to his journey to Naqan than simply fleeing the empire. Likely something to do with that big bundle he carried around with him." She shrugged. "It's probably not important. Everyone has their secrets."

The dinner that evening was much simpler now that they weren't entertaining important guests.

At one point, Li Runfa said, "Sect Leader, Chieftainess, I wonder if we should start reaching out to these martial heroes. In times like these, we could use as many allies as we can get."

"I was thinking the same thing," Liu Jiahui added.

"It's worth considering," Sunan said. "Perhaps after we move camp?"

"And when will that be, Sect Leader?"

"As soon as Sun Mai and Mao Yun return."

After dinner, Sunan and Bao decided to personally check in on the guard tower, which had been erected high up on the mountain. They set out alone into the crisp night air, taking their time as they hiked up the mountain.

At one point as they scrambled to the top of a tilted boulder, Sunan asked, "What do you think of this Li Buwei character?"

"The so-called Timeless Master?" Bao asked. "Hard to say. You know just as well as I how quickly tales can become distorted over time. Who knows what really happened in Xuanlu... However, I'd be interested in meeting him."

"Li Runfa is right. We could use allies."

"Perhaps more than even we realize." They stopped to rest for a moment at the top of a boulder. From this vantage point, they could see down to the entrance of the cave, where some of the disciples of the two sects were taking advantage of the coolness of evening to do some sparring. "Sunan, remember our fight with the Golden Immortal?"

"The one in which we almost got killed? Of course."

"It was a desperate fight, but…"

"But…?"

Bao crossed her arms and sighed. "But… that was nothing. When I faced the ogre generals, I felt like I was a fly attacking a tiger. My most powerful move, the Phoenix Palm, did absolutely nothing to the Love General. All of that power disappeared like a rock thrown into the ocean."

Sunan looked at her, disbelief flickering in his eyes. "Perhaps you just missed?"

"I didn't miss. The strike landed true." Bao closed her eyes. "I used to mention a lot how I killed an ogre, and I did, but… it really was just a stroke of luck. Short of crushing them with rocks, or maybe filling them full of arrows from a distance, I don't know how we could kill them."

Sunan didn't say anything at first. A long moment passed. "Bao, I'm sorry for going so hard on you that night…"

"You don't need to apologize. I made a mistake. A huge mistake. I understand that." She opened her eyes and looked over at him. "But I won't ever make a mistake like that again. I learned my lesson. In fact, I should be the one apologizing. Both of our friends died because of me."

Sunan took a deep breath. "What's done is done, and we can't change it. But I agree, we can make sure things like that don't happen again. I'm really starting to think we should contact this Timeless Master, and maybe some of the other martial heroes. I don't think the Demon Emperor and the Bone General are going to give up until the both of us are dead. They'll keep sending people after us. Whether it's assassins or armies, we need to be ready."

Suddenly a shadow flashed by on the ground. Sunan and Bao looked up to see a bird flying overhead.

"That must be the zhen bird I've heard people talking about," Bao said. "People say it's a good omen."

The zhen bird circled around and then landed on a nearby rock outcropping.

"I'm not much of a believer in that kind of thing," Sunan said. "Come on, let's keep going. The guard tower is just up ahead."

***

As was his custom, An Jian was taking a nightly stroll out of the cave. At one point, he stopped and sat down on a tree stump. Looking up the mountain, he could barely make out Sunan and Bao standing on a boulder farther up the mountain. A cold flicker passed through his eyes.

"So close and yet so far," he murmured.

With that, he pulled out a fan and placed his palm down on its surface. Then he closed his eyes. Moments later, images and sounds appeared in his mind.

He saw Dragon Lord Zhou, seated at a table with some of the other Dragon Lords and soldiers. In the middle of the table, a tiny arena had been set up with pieces of wood, in the middle of which were two crickets. The table was littered with peanut shells and cups of sorghum wine.

"Place bets!" one of the Dragon Lords said, instigating a flurry of activity as everyone present put down money on which cricket they thought would win the next fight.

This particular match was different than the others. Dragon Lord Zhou was the only one to place his money on the smaller cricket, provoking jeers among his companions.

"Come on, Big Bro Zhou, there's no way that baby cricket of yours can take out my Elephant Smiter!"

"Oh, yes he can!" Dragon Lord Zhou shot back. "My Young Dragon is destined for greatness."

"You named your cricket after Sect Leader Sunan?"

Laughter filled the room.

"Listen," Dragon Lord Zhou said, brandishing his fan, "ever since I got this magic fan, my luck has changed."

"That's a magic fan?"

"Absolutely! See this poem? 'The wind, snapping trees, dissolving mountains, serenity.' Do any of you know what that means?" His question was met by quizzical looks. "I didn't think so. But I know! It was written by a prophet king in Naqan! After I started meditating about the true meaning behind the words, I've been able to see the world much more clearly!"

Another Dragon Lord laughed, then reached out and grabbed his drinking vessel.

"Very well, then," he said. "Come on, everyone, let's drink to Big Bro Zhou and his Young Dragon cricket!" The soldiers lifted their cups high into the air.

"Ai, I can't drink too much," Dragon Lord Zhou grumbled. "There's a council meeting in the morning!"

An Jian was just about to sever the connection to the fan when he heard: "Oh, come on! Sect Leader Sunan and Chieftainess Bao never ask us Dragon Lords to say anything. Drink. Drink! To your health!"

An Jian's ears perked up. Bao and Sunan had been in secluded meditation deep in the heart of the mountain for months. Although that had given An Jian plenty of time to build up a sizeable stockpile of Divine Fire, it had left Bao and Sunan completely beyond his reach.

Everyone around the table drank, then began to cheer as the

handlers provoked the crickets into fighting.

Severing the connection to the fan, An Jian murmured, "Time to make a move."

***

Dragon Lord Zhou stumbled, bleary eyed, out of his cot the next morning and promptly rushed outside to empty the contents of his stomach. After trudging back into his room, he put on his Dragon Lord robes, tucked his fan into his belt, and prepared to head to the council meeting. Just before leaving the room, he looked down and noticed an ornate box sitting at the foot of his cot. It was about the length of his forearm, relatively plain, and had a complex design carved on the lid.

"Hmm, what is this?" he muttered, rubbing his eyes.

Take the box to the council meeting.

"I guess I should take it to the council meeting," he said. Picking up the box, he headed through the cave tunnels toward one of the central chambers that was being used as the command room. It was currently being guarded by two members of the Golden Dragon Sect.

"Greetings, Dragon Lord!" they said in unison.

"What's that box?" asked one.

Dragon Lord looked at them in confusion. "Box?" Then he glanced down and realized that he was carrying a box.

It's a gift for Sunan.

"Oh, it's a gift for Sect Leader Sunan."

Dragon Lord Zhou passed the guards and entered the command room. To his surprise, there were only three other people present—two Dragon Lords and one of the Pure Phoenix Sect's Claws of the Phoenix.

"I'm early?" he blurted.

One of the other Dragon Lords chuckled. "You're early, Big Bro

Zhou. I thought you said you didn't want to drink too much last night."

Put the box on the table.

Groaning, Dragon Lord Zhou put the box down onto a table at the side of the room and slumped down to the ground against the wall.

***

An Jian watched as Dragon Lord Zhou sat down on the ground and closed his eyes.

"Drunken fool."

Time passed. Based on how Dragon Lord Zhou was seated, An Jian could only see about half of the room. More people arrived, all of whom An Jian recognized. A Dragon Lord. One of the Claws of the Phoenix. Tie Gangwen. A few other lower-ranking members of both sects.

Suddenly, one of the Dragon Lords whispered, "Big Bro Zhou, wake up! The sect leader and the chieftainess are coming!"

An Jian watched as Dragon Lord Zhou scrambled to his feet and looked in the direction of the door. Then he clasped his hands and said, "Greetings, Sect Leader! Greetings, Chieftainess!"

Dragon Lord Zhou felt something tugging at his heart and mind.

Press the circular knob on the left corner of the lid.

Without even thinking about it, he reached over and pushed a circular knob of wood that had been carved into the bottom left corner of the lid.

CHAPTER 55
TWO KNIVES

Dragon Lord Guan Yunchang was standing next to one of the Claws of the Phoenix, Zhang Jing. It was with some derision that he watched Dragon Lord Zhou stumble into the meeting room, place a box on a nearby table, then slump down against the wall.

Leaning over to Zhang Jing, he said, "This is the fourth council meeting in a row he came in drunk."

"Drunk or hung over?"

"Same thing." Dragon Lord Guan had to hold back from spitting onto the ground. A minute or so later, faint snoring could be heard in the room. Guan's lips curled up into a sneer. Leaning back over to Zhang Jing, he said, "Watch this."

With that, he cupped his hand over his mouth and said in a loud voice, "Big Bro Zhou, wake up! The sect leader and the chieftainess are coming!"

Dragon Lord Zhou scrambled to his feet, clasped his hands, and said, "Greetings, Sect Leader! Greetings, Chieftainess!"

Of course, Sunan and Bao were nowhere to be seen. Dragon

Lord Guan immediately let out a loud guffaw. Others in the room began to chuckle.

Then, for some strange reason, Dragon Lord Zhou reached over toward the box he'd placed on the table. He pushed his finger down on the surface of the box, and a soft clicking sound could be heard.

The room exploded.

***

The atmosphere in the room was heavy. A new council chamber had been set up, and it was occupied by about ten people, including Bao and Sunan, Li Runfa, Sima Zikang. Some faces one would expect to be present were nowhere to be seen.

For a very long time, no one spoke.

Bao broke the silence.

"How many dead?"

"Five," Li Runfa replied softly. "Dragon Lords Guan and Zhou, Phoenix Claw Zhang. Two others, lower-ranking members of the council."

"And you said Tie Gangwen was injured?"

"Yes, Chieftainess. He… well, his arm was completely ripped off. The doctors aren't sure if he'll make it through. There were other injuries as well. Dragon Lord Wang lost an eye. Phoenix Claw Li suffered some serious burns."

Another very long moment passed in which no one spoke.

"What was it?" Sunan asked. "What could burn so hot and fast?"

"The people in the room said it happened in the blink of an eye," Li Runfa said. "An explosion. Intense heat, obviously. Dragon Lord Zhou got the worst of it. He was… completely shredded to pieces."

Dragon Lord Sima Zikang had been just a few meters down the hall from the entrance to the council chamber and had thus been spared even the slightest injury. "People are saying it was magic," he said.

Li Runfa frowned. "Considering everything we've seen in recent years, I can't deny the existence of magic. But I don't get the feeling that something magical caused this. The room smelled strange."

"It just smelled like fire to me," Dragon Lord Sima said.

"Yes, that's true. But there was something else. Maybe sulfur."

Bao clenched her fist. "If there's even the possibility it might involve magic, we need to investigate further. Get Smiling Luo involved."

"I wish Sun Mai were here," Sunan murmured. Then he looked over at Li Runfa. "Do we have any idea who might be responsible?"

Li Runfa shook his head. "Dragon Lord Zhou was at the center of the blast, so it must have originated with him. But he seems an unlikely to be the one truly responsible. Before joining the Golden Dragon Sect, he was nothing more than a server at the Heavenly Meat Palace. He was skilled in martial arts, but was no practitioner of magic, nor a man of alchemy. There must be someone else behind it."

"Hold on a moment," Dragon Lord Sima said. "Brother Li, did you just say that you smelled sulfur?"

"Yes, why?"

"Just yesterday I asked Alchemist Yang to make some galenite elixir for me. He said that he couldn't because he had no sulfur on hand. Someone had recently bought his entire supply."

Bao's eyes narrowed. "I'm no alchemist, but I'm pretty sure that not even a huge pile of sulfur could burn that hot. Or fast. And it definitely wouldn't explode."

"It's still worth investigating," Li Runfa said. "I'll look into it."

The meeting went on for several more hours. Discussions were made regarding who to promote as replacements for the officers who had been killed. They talked about heightening security and even decided to look further into the backgrounds of all members of the two sects, starting with the newest ones.

The longer the meeting stretched on, the more Bao's mood turned sour. Worst of all, there didn't seem to be any target upon whom to focus her anger. Whoever it was that had attacked the council meeting, he or she was hidden completely in the shadows. Even that person's motives were unknown. Had Bao and Sunan truly been targeted? Had it been one of the other officers? No amount of speculation could provide a clear answer.

At a certain point, Bao felt like she couldn't sit there anymore. "I need some fresh air," she announced, then rose to her feet and left the room.

As she paced through the corridor, she happened to hear one of the Pure Phoenix Sect members mention that the guard tower farther up the mountain had reported some suspicious movement to the southwest.

"When was that?" Bao asked.

"Greetings, Chieftainess! It was only a few minutes ago. Chang Peng of the Eyes of the Phoenix is putting together a team to go investigate."

"I see. Many thanks."

She headed toward the stables. Although Chang Peng was surprised to see her, and even more surprised that she wanted to join what was little more than a patrol, he didn't say anything. Minutes later, she was outside of the caves, breathing the fresh mountain air.

Their group consisted of six men and two women, plus Chang Peng and herself.

After riding a few minutes, the trees started to grow thicker as they entered a forested area. "Chieftainess," Chang Peng said, "why don't I go ahead and scout a bit? I can move a lot more stealthily on my own."

Bao nodded in agreement, and Chang Peng rode out ahead of the group.

Bao continued along at a steady pace. *This is exactly what I needed. I can feel myself calming down already.*

Ten minutes later, Chang Peng returned. "Chieftainess, I found them, up ahead in a clearing. Two men, lightly armed. One has a saber, and the other has a whole bunch of knives sheathed at his waist. They have horses but aren't mounted at the moment. Chieftainess, based on their clothing, I'd say they're definitely not from the north. Looks more like the fashion of Yu Zhing or Xuanlu to me, although I'm no expert."

After a moment of thought, Bao said, "Let's approach on foot." Picking one of the men at random, she said, "You stay with the horses."

With that, the group dismounted and proceeded through the forest with Chang Peng in the lead.

Thirty meters away from the clearing, Bao sent three people to the left and three to the right to flank the clearing, taking Chang Peng and one other with her to approach the clearing directly.

They're probably just passing travelers. I'll tell them to be on their way, and that will be the end of things.

Soon the clearing was visible through the trees up ahead. The group moved along quietly, using qinggong to keep their footfalls light and nearly inaudible.

When Bao stepped out into the open, she saw two men sitting with their backs to her, their horses tethered to trees a few meters away.

Not very perceptive, are they? she thought, smirking.

"Greetings, travelers," she said. Although her voice was calm, she flexed her fingers in preparation to unleash Torment of the Phoenix if necessary.

Both men looked over their shoulder at her, but the one on the left was a bit faster than the other. As soon as Bao saw him, her eyes went wide. He wore an eye patch and had three pale scars running down the opposing cheek. She recognized him! Back on the docks of Yu Zhing, she had clawed his eye out in a late-night scuffle.

He clearly recognized her, and as he rose to his feet, his hand clasped the hilt of the saber strapped to his waist.

Bao's eyes flickered to look at the man on the right, and when she saw his face, she felt as if her mind had been struck by a thousand bolts of lightning. She recognized him, too. His was a face she would never be able to forget, even if she wanted to.

"You?" she blurted.

He was none other than Geng Long, who had led her on midnight adventures through the alleyways and along the rooftops of Yu Zhing. He had kissed her on a moonlit night and held her hand as they gazed at the stars together. She would never forget the terror she had felt when she went to meet him, only to end up in a cold iron cage, or the hope which had surged in her heart upon hearing his voice outside, thinking that he had come to rescue her. Never could she forget how her heart had plummeted when she realized that it was Geng Long who had landed her in that cage.

The calm she had felt moments ago shattered, and rage began to boil in her heart.

For some reason, Geng Long didn't seem surprised to see her. "Bao…" he said.

The man in the eye patch took a step forward. "She doesn't look much different from before. Not very impressive."

Bao's mind was spinning so hard she almost couldn't think, and her eyes were beginning to go hot with anger.

"We're just passing through, Bao," Geng Long said, taking a step backward. "We'll be on our way now."

The man in the eye patch snorted. "There are only three of them," he said. "We could take them. Let's just kill her now and be done with it."

"Shut up, Xie Song," Geng Long said.

Bao's anger was already beginning to burn out of control, swirling through her along the same meridian pathways that she had forged in the mountains to the north. Geng Long's attention had shifted to his companion Xie Song, so at the moment, he didn't notice how Bao's eyes had begun to glow red.

Xie Song's expression was one of complete derision. "Don't you know who Geng Long is, *Chieftainess* Bao? He's a Bone Slicer now!"

"Shut the *fuck* up, Xie Song!" Geng Long barked, eyes flashing daggers at Xie Song before turning back to look at Bao.

Xie Song looked over his shoulder at Geng Long. "What, don't tell me you're afraid of this bitch. Are you?"

Bao screamed and slashed her hand out in front of her, sending five crimson streams of light snaking through the air.

Geng Long's eyes went wide, and he immediately kicked off with his left foot, sending himself shooting backward in a blur.

Xie Song looked back at Bao just in time to see five shining streams of light rushing in his direction. Before he could even react, the light hit him, cutting through his body as easily as a sharp knife cuts through bamboo. Blood and gore exploded in all directions as Xie Song's body was sliced apart. He didn't even have a chance to scream.

"*Fuck!*" Geng Long shouted. "Bao, what are you doing?" Two knives appeared in his hands as he landed on the ground some distance away.

Bao strode forward, leaving behind the shocked Chang Peng and the other members of the Pure Phoenix Sect.

Not deigning to even respond to Geng Long, she reached back with her hand to unleash another deadly strike, drawing cathartically on her own qi, ignoring the resulting pain and the wave of weakness which seemed to be building up inside of her.

Five crimson streams of light whipped toward Geng Long, but fortunately for him, he was ready. He leapt up into the air with astounding agility and speed, completely avoiding the five streams of energy, throwing both of his knives toward her.

As soon as she unleashed the cathartic blow, Bao felt a weakness sweeping through her, causing her knees to tremble. With what little energy she had left inside, she lurched to the left to avoid the flying knives. Even so, one of them slashed her forearm, sending pain tingling up toward her shoulder.

As she toppled to the ground, Geng Long utilized a bizarre qinggong technique to blur into motion and disappear into the nearby tree line.

Chang Peng rushed over to find Bao lying on the ground, unconscious. Her face was ashen, her forearm bleeding, and most disturbing of all, the skin around the wound on her forearm was a sickly black color.

Cursing to himself, Chang Peng picked Bao up in his arms and hurried back toward the horses.

CHAPTER 56
A VIAL

Bao regained consciousness the next day, but she was so weak that she could barely say more than a word or two before closing her eyes again.

Alchemist Yang, Smiling Luo, and the other doctors tended her wound and attempted to treat the poison, but nothing they had done so far seemed to do any good. On the second day, the veins leading up her arm toward her neck were starting to turn dark. Sunan was already getting a very bad feeling.

The mood in the cave complex had turned very grim. The Eyes of the Phoenix returned to the clearing where the fight took place and found that although the body of the man Bao had killed remained in place, the two horses were gone. They tracked the horses some distance to the northwest before the trail vanished.

Meanwhile, upon being questioned, Alchemist Yang revealed that he'd sold a large amount of sulfur to a maker of fans named An Jian. However, when Sunan sent men to bring An Jian to him for questioning, the man was nowhere to be found.

Sunan ground his teeth in frustration.

By the third day, the darkness of Bao's veins had spread closer toward the base of her neck.

Supposedly, the most famous doctor in the land lived far to the south in the Zun Valley, but a journey like that could take a month, and Bao already seemed to be hovering on the brink of death.

Regardless of what challenges Sunan had faced up to this point, he'd always felt as if he had options to pick from or opportunities to seek. But in this situation, he felt completely helpless. He could do little more than sit at Bao's bedside and watch over her.

When everyone else left the room and no one was around to see, he would reach out and hold her hand in his.

"Come on, Bao," he said quietly. "You tamed a phoenix demon, you can beat a little poison, right?"

***

An Jian was heading east, cursing under his breath in words that didn't even exist in this time.

"I got too eager," he muttered under his breath. "Lost my patience. Well, it won't happen again. Enough of these games. I'll just go to the King of the Pure Ores and reveal the truth. Consequences be damned."

His first goal was to get out of the Mount Fohe region. Aware that people from the two sects would be looking for him, and might even be trying to track him down, he stayed away from anything that even resembled a path.

The day after he left the caves, he reached the foothills of Mount Fohe and was starting to breathe easier. Until he rounded a mountain boulder and saw a woman standing about six meters ahead of him.

She was middle-aged, her long black hair bound at the top of her head, her gray robes functional and nondescript. She held a sheathed sword in her left hand.

Inwardly, An Jian's heart sank, but outwardly, he maintained a calm expression. "Greetings, fellow traveler."

The woman looked back at him with a cool expression. "I have to admit that your choice of names was clever. Arrogant, but clever."

There's no point in trying to keep up the facade, he thought. Reaching down slowly, he pulled a fan out of his belt and began to slowly cool himself. "So, you brushed up on your Classical Fei, I see."

"Yes. I should have thought earlier about how 'An Jian' is Classical Fei for 'Hidden Arrow.' Your face is different, but your voice is the same. I can only imagine what lengths the Demon Emperor of the future went to in order to send you back here."

"And I can only imagine what it's been like to hide in the shadows like you have for the past… how long has it been for you? Twenty years. Thirty?"

"I'm happy to pay the price. The Demon Emperor will not be allowed to succeed. I will guide Bao and Sunan to fulfilling their destiny."

An Jian stopped fanning himself. "You're trying to change the stream of time, girl. Bao and Sunan's fates have already been set. You're actually *interfering* with their destiny. Back when we first met, things were… rushed. May I ask for your honored surname?"

"Just call me Hui."

Fanning himself again, An Jian took a step forward. "I have a question for you, Miss Hui. Are you a murderer?"

"Excuse me?"

"It's a simple question. Here we are in the middle of nowhere, two enemies whose differences couldn't ever possibly be reconciled. Are you going to simply cut me down in cold blood? That's called murder. Is that what the Dragon-Phoenix Sect has become? A bunch of murderers?"

Hui chuckled coldly, slowly reaching her right hand over to grip the hilt of her sword. "You are a profound master, Hidden Arrow, not a helpless baby."

An Jian shook his head slowly. "Come now, Hui. I know that you can sense the truth. I have no martial arts abilities. My martial arts are gone, and I'll never get them back. That was the price to be paid for my journey back in time. I am like any other frail mortal. After all the years that have passed, you have surely become a profound master yourself, so you should be able to sense it with ease. I couldn't fight you even if I wanted to, and you could kill me as easily as turning over your hand."

He took another step forward.

Hui's eyes flashed with a dark light. "Stop right there."

"Or what?" An Jian said, smiling coldly. "You'll murder me? I'm no martial artist any more, just a maker of fans."

"You're one of the greatest villains in the world. Probably second only to the Demon Emperor himself. Killing you wouldn't be murder. It would be carrying out a death sentence that was issued upon you by all righteous sects of the martial world."

An Jian stepped forward again. "We aren't in that world, Hui. We're in a different world, and a different time. I'm not the profound master, you are. Think about it. You might well be the most powerful martial artist alive. Why don't we work together? You know the truth! The Demon Emperor isn't what the stories make him out to be. With our knowledge, we could steer him in a new direction. Maybe Sunan and Bao don't need to be his enemy. Maybe—"

Without warning, An Jian swept his fan through the air, pushing his thumb down onto a tiny button at the base of the fan. A faint whirring sound could be heard, and then a blast of needles shot out of the top of the fan.

The three steps he had just taken had halved the distance between himself and Hui, putting him only about three meters away from her, the perfect range for such an attack. The needles screamed through the air, spiraling out to form a deadly net.

However, An Jian's suppositions had been correct. Hui was now a profound master, and she had spent decades focused on almost nothing but training.

"Deflecting Canopy!" she barked, spinning her sword out in front of her.

One after another, the needles were deflected, with the majority of them flying back toward An Jian.

He grunted with pain as he felt himself being stabbed in the shoulder, the thigh, the forearm, and other places.

In the blink of an eye, the fight was over.

An Jian lay prone, staring up into the sky. The needles in his fan had been coated with hellebore, one of the most lethal poisons to ever be devised by men. He could already feel his throat swelling up and his heart twitching with pain.

Hand trembling, he reached into his robe to where a small vial rested, which was the antidote. He managed to pull the antidote out, but before he could unstop the cork, Hui loomed over him, the blade of her sword pushing against his wrist, preventing him from opening the vial.

This can't be it. I can't die here. Not like this.

"A liar and a manipulator down to your last breath," Hui said. "I guess that's what I should expect from the infamous Hidden Arrow."

An Jian's mind raced. "I know how to get back to the future," he said.

"I don't believe you."

"Let me take the antidote. Then tie me up. I promise, there is a path home."

Hui smiled sadly. "Even if there is, I don't want to walk it. I've made peace with myself. I will live out my days in this time. I will make sure Bao and Sunan fulfill their destiny." Oh so slowly, she reached down and took the vial out of An Jian's hand. "And I will also see the world rid of one of the vilest evildoers to ever walk its lands."

Hui dropped the vial on the ground and stepped on it with her heel, crushing it.

An Jian looked up at the clouds.

So this is how it ends.

***

Sunan paced back and forth in front of the cave entrance as he waited for the approaching group to arrive. Scouts had brought word that, at long last, Sun Mai and Mao Yun had returned. Sunan almost couldn't suppress the urge to run out and meet them.

Sun Mai was in the lead, riding next to Wang Tian. Behind him were Mao Yun and a grim-looking fellow wearing scholarly robes similar to the type Sun Mai favored. Further back was a man with one leg and a crutch slung over his shoulder.

Sun Mai was smiling broadly, but as he got closer and saw the worry on Sunan's face, his smile began to fade.

The group stopped a few paces away from Sunan, where Sun Mai said, "Greetings, Brother Sunan. Allow me to introduce Du Qian, scholar and former court official."

Sunan's jaw was clenched a bit tighter than normal as he clasped his hands formally. "Greetings, Master Du."

"Greetings, Sect Leader."

Sun Mai, never one to beat around the bush, said, "What happened?"

"It's Bao," Sunan replied. "She was poisoned."

"*What?*" Mao Yun exclaimed, leaping off his horse. "Has she been treated?"

Sunan shook his head. "No treatments seem to have any effect."

Sun Mai dismounted, as did the rest of the group. "What type of poison?"

Sunan shook his head. "We don't know. According to the men who were with her, she was cut by the knife of a Bone Slicer. The wound turned black, and her veins are going dark."

"Vosh sap," Du Qian said.

Sunan looked over at him. "What's that?"

Du Qian stepped forward. He had hard eyes, and his eyebrows tilted up in a menacing fashion. His thin lips seemed to be constantly pursed, and he walked with his back as straight as a board. "The poison that Bone Slicers use for assassinations. It's vosh sap." With that, he reached into his robe and pulled out a vial. "This is the antidote."

Sunan's eyes narrowed. "You just so happened to have the antidote to the Bone Slicers' poison, tucked away in your robe, in the exact moment in which one of our people was poisoned?"

"Sunan," Sun Mai said, "Du Qian used to be an official in the Demon Emperor's court. He has access to many secrets and many resources."

Sunan's heart began to thump in his chest. "You trust him?" he asked of Sun Mai. Sun Mai nodded.

Du Qian looked Sunan in the eye. "Truth be told, Sect Leader, the wise choice would be to distrust me. But if Heroine Bao has been poisoned by vosh sap, then she is in mortal danger. How long ago did it happen?"

"Three days."

"There's still time. Vosh sap comes from… a different realm, and it works more slowly here than in the land of its origin."

"A different realm?" Sunan frowned slightly. "You mean the Perfect Realm?"

Sun Mai guffawed. "Come on, Sunan, you know that the Perfect Realm isn't real."

Du Qian looked over at Sun Mai. "This again?"

Sun Mai's eyes flashed. "Didn't we agree not to get into this argument again, Du Qian?"

After a moment, Du Qian nodded. Looking back at Sunan, he said, "I'm not referring to the Perfect Realm. Nor the Imperfect Realm, nor the Lower Realms. The Demon Emperor and his ogre generals come from another place entirely, and that is also where the vosh sap poison comes from.

"As part of my plan to escape from the court, I procured a few vials of this antidote, just in case the Bone Slicers came after me. Which they did. Luckily for me, I fled to a place where even they didn't dare to enter.

"However, that's a story for another time. If Heroine Bao was poisoned three days ago, then we need to administer the antidote immediately."

He held the vial out toward Sunan.

CHAPTER 57
THE SHAN

Bao woke to find a strange man staring deep into her eyes. It was a bizarre moment. Although she didn't know him, she didn't feel threatened or fearful. A moment later, she realized that he was feeling for her pulse at her wrist. Then he blinked and retracted his gaze, pulling his hand away before stepping back from her.

"She'll be fine," he said to someone behind him.

Bao turned her head slightly and caught sight of Sunan, Sun Mai, and Mao Yun.

Sunan stepped around the man to stand bedside. "How do you feel?"

Bao took a moment to decide how to answer the question. "Weak."

Sunan nodded. "Allow me to introduce Master Du Qian. It was his antidote that saved you. That poison was very nasty."

Du Qian clasped his hands formally. "Greetings, Heroine Bao."

"Greetings, Master Du Qian."

"You drew cathartically on your qi, Heroine. It almost damaged your soul."

Bao tried to sit up in the bed but failed. "My soul? How can you tell that?"

"I've been studying the way that qi flows through the body, and I've come to realize that every person has five souls inside of them. From what Sun Mai has told me of this cathartic method of drawing on qi, it has the potential to damage or even destroy those souls. Please be careful in the future. I'll take my leave now. Please let me know if there's any other way I can be of help." He looked Bao in the eyes once more as he turned to leave.

Something about the way he looked at her pierced all the way into her heart, although she wasn't sure exactly why or how that could be. Then he was gone.

"How long have I been asleep this time?"

"This time?" Sunan asked.

She smiled weakly. "I once went unconscious for a few months straight."

"You were only out for three days."

Bao's thoughts drifted back to the events which had led to her recent state. "What happened to Chang Peng and the others?"

"They're all fine. It was Chang Peng who brought you back."

She thought for another moment. "Tie Gangwen?"

"He's alive and recovering."

"Did I miss anything else important?"

"We've decided to move the camp. Sun Mai and Mao Yun are back, as you can see. Plus, your encounter with the Bone General's men confirms our suspicion that the Demon Emperor is watching us. Once you've recovered, we'll make preparations to leave."

"I'm recovered," she said, struggling again to rise to a sitting position. Unfortunately, she only got up onto her elbows before falling back down.

"Rest, Bao. There are no armies marching on us. We can afford to wait a bit longer."

***

Bao recovered much more slowly than she would have liked. It took four days before she was able to even sit up for any length of time. For her, those four days were like an eternity. For everyone else, they sped by.

In accord with decrees passed down by the leaders of both sects, training intensified. More rigorous forms of sparring were introduced, and while there were more injuries, the fighters in both sects made even greater progress. Alchemist Yang and the other doctors were busier than ever, and even Smiling Luo provided help with some newly invented techniques that drew upon magic to be a bit more effective.

Thanks to the intensive investigations into the backgrounds of all members of the sects, two spies were identified. Upon the advice of Li Runfa, though, nothing was done about them.

"As soon as you know who the spies are," he said, "they start working for you."

Tie Gangwen had awoken from his coma. He would live, but the loss of his arm was a heavy blow to his psyche.

One of the most important events to occur during Bao's short convalescence was that Sunan had a meeting with Ruan the Flamingo.

The rooms which had been Ruan's quarters had been left untouched after the caves were occupied by the two sects, and that was the location of the meeting.

Sunan and Ruan were the only ones present. Currently, they sat together at a table, atop which sat a solitary box.

Ruan eyed the box. "A wind stone, you say?"

"That's what we've been calling it. Bao said that you have

experience working with things like this."

"That's true. I've never seen a rock that makes wind, but I've seen other powerful objects like it. Most of them fell from the heavens above."

"From the Upper Realms?"

"If that's what you call them, then yes." Ruan reached out and pulled the box closer to examine it in detail.

"*Don't* open it," Sunan warned again.

Ruan nodded. After examining the box physically, he produced various tools of his trade, which he used to perform measurements and other readings. The entire process lasted for ten minutes.

When it was over, Ruan sat there quietly for a moment. "I need to perform a ritual," he said. "It will take some time to prepare. Stay if you wish."

With that, he began to prepare paper talismans, which he used to seal all of the entrances to his chambers. Then he set to work inscribing a large circular sheet of paper with numerous complex designs and magical symbols. In the very middle of the piece of paper was a blank area the size of the box. Having accomplished these tasks, Ruan lit several sticks of incense.

Then he slowly placed the box down on the blank spot on the large piece of paper.

"You're going to open it?" Sunan asked.

"Yes. Don't worry, the ritual will keep us safe."

Sunan swallowed and looked around for something to hold on to. Unfortunately, nothing sturdy was nearby.

Before he could say anything, Ruan slowly opened the lid of the box. Visible streams of wind exploded out from the rock, and yet they were contained in a sphere roughly the same diameter as the piece of paper under the box. The wind streams lashed back and forth violently, but they were powerless to escape the barrier which had been erected.

Ruan went on to make further investigations into the rock and the wind.

Upon finishing, he used his crutch to reach in and close the lid of the box. The wind died down immediately.

"Very interesting," he said. He rubbed his chin with his thumb for a while, then looked over at Sunan. "I have an idea of how to work the wind stone into an object of power."

"An idea?"

"I won't get into the boring magical aspects. Suffice to say that the power in this stone is something that requires special tools to work with. Tools that I don't have."

"And who has such tools?"

"Wait here a moment." Ruan hopped over to a nearby shelf, which contained a sizeable collection of books and scrolls. After picking through them, he pulled out a large leather-bound book, which he carried back and plopped down on the table next to the box. "Have you heard of this?"

Sunan looked at the book. Inscribed on the cover in bold calligraphy were the words "Classic of Mountains and Rivers."

"Yes," he said. "There was a copy in the village where I grew up. I read most of it as a child."

Ruan raised his eyebrow. "You actually read the *Classic of Mountains and Rivers*?"

Sunan smiled wryly. "Well, I was mostly interested in the pictures."

Ruan chuckled. "That makes sense. Although the title implies that it's a geography, it's even more well known as being a bestiary, and the illustrations are definitely eye-catching." He opened the book and began to leaf through the pages. "As you probably know, according to the legends, it was more than ten thousand years ago that Xian Nu Shen created Qi Xien on top of Mount Zhizhu. In the early days, the lands did not look as they do now. They were filled with five thousand mountains and five thousand rivers, which were arranged into eastern, southern, western, northern, and central regions.

"The part of the world we live in now was once the Eastern Mountain and River Region. One of the ancient tribes that lived in that region was called the Shan."

"The Shan?" Sunan thought for a moment. "In Classical Fei, Shan means—"

"No. It's not Classical Fei. Their name comes from a language much older than that."

"I thought Classical Fei was the oldest language in the world."

Ruan looked up from the book. "That's what people who don't know much about the world think." He looked back down and continued leafing through the book. "The Shan were a people who were supposedly born of the wind and worshipped it as their god.

"Gushan?"

"Gushan is the wind god, yes, so perhaps the Shan are connected to him. I'm not sure." At this point, he found the page he was looking for. "Here."

After reaching a certain page in the book, he flipped it around for Sunan to look at. The *Classic of Mountains and Rivers* was essentially a bestiary of the ancient world and somewhat of an almanac. This entry was devoted to a tribe of creatures called the Shan. Sunan recognized the picture, which he had seen when looking through the book as a child. It depicted a strange creature with no head. Its facial features were part of its torso, and it wielded an axe and a shield.

"As you can read there, the Shan believed that the wind of the world was created by the breath of Xian Nu Shen, and that by worshipping it, they could hear her words. The most interesting part is right here. Look." He pointed at a passage toward the end of the entry for the Shan people.

Sunan began to read aloud. "The Shan beasts were learned of the craft of winds. The smite of their... what's this character?"

Ruan looked over. "Empyreal. It basically means 'heavenly.'"

Sunan continued. "The smite of their empyreal hammer did shatter the Tempest Crag, and thus formed the tempest stones of the Era of Creation." He looked up. "Hmm… according to Bao, the people who originally possessed this stone called it a tempest stone."

Ruan reached out and tapped the *Classic of Mountains and Rivers*. "Our best bet is to try to find that empyreal hammer."

Sunan sighed. "But where would we even begin? Is the *Classic of Mountains and Rivers* even to be trusted? I mean, if a race of headless people existed in the world, wouldn't everyone know about them?"

Ruan pulled the book back over and looked down at the information about the Shan. "You might be surprised what exists in the Banyan Region. It's right in the Demon Emperor's own backyard, and yet he hesitates to send troops into those forests and jungles. Many of the beasts and peoples described in this book still lurk in the shadowy valleys of the Banyan." He closed the book. "I've heard rumors that you plan to leave these caves. Is that true?"

"It is."

"If you plan to stay within the borders of the empire, I can think of few better, or safer, places than the Banyan. If you go there to find the empyreal hammer, perhaps I could tag along."

***

The Golden Immortal was in a foul mood. "I thought you were supposed to be a top Bone Slicer, Geng Long? You let Bao walk right into you and even kill Xie Song? *Dammit.*"

Geng Long spat on the ground and started twirling a knife through his fingers. "Shut the fuck up, Geng Jin."

"That's Golden Immortal to you, cousin. Nobody knows my real name, and I'd prefer to keep it that way."

Geng Long snorted coldly. "Whatever. They lost my trail. They'll never find us. What's our next move?"

The Golden Immortal closed his eyes to think for a moment. "We don't have enough men for an all-out assault, so we wait."

"More waiting."

"Yes, more waiting. Until the Bone General gets back, we don't do anything unless we're absolutely sure nothing like this will happen. And that includes scouting their perimeter. If I'm not mistaken, they'll be moving camp soon. Even they can't be so stupid as to stay in one place for very long."

Geng Long grinned and threw his knife into a nearby tree. "We can strike them on the road. An ambush."

The Golden Immortal nodded. "The only question is where they'll head. Probably Naqan, through the Kushen Basin. Either way, we wait. How much more poison do you have?"

Geng Long pulled out another knife and started playing with it. "Plenty. I definitely hit Bao, so that bitch is probably dead already. Half of our job is done." He chuckled coldly.

CHAPTER 58
AN ANCIENT CHARACTER

As the days passed, Bao quickly regained her strength. A week later, orders were issued to both sects to begin packing for travel. The caves were to be abandoned.

The preparations took two full days, and emotions among the members of the two sects were mixed. Some people were glad to be out of the cold, dark caves. But for many, those caves had been their home for many months, the only stable place of dwelling they had possessed since abandoning Daolu.

On the eve of departure, a grand feast was held for the leadership of the sects. Bao and Sunan were present, as were the Dragon Generals, the Dragon Lords, the Phoenix Generals, the Claws of the Phoenix, and other high-ranking officers. It was Bao's first time appearing in public after being poisoned, and it was a happy occasion.

After the feast, Sunan returned to his quarters and fell into a deep sleep. When he woke up, it was raining.

"Raining?" he murmured, looking up into the sky. Sure enough, drops of water were plopping down onto his face. "That's strange. The rain is hot."

At this point, he realized that the clouds up above were the color of gold. Sticking his hand out, he let some of the rain water collect in his palm.

"The rain is golden too?" A sudden realization hit him. "I'm dreaming again, aren't I?"

He watched as the hot golden rain began to fall harder and harder. Wind began to batter at his hair and clothing, sending the rain whipping about in the air.

He remembered something. A line of poetry. "Golden droplets spin and howl."

Sunan looked down and saw that he was floating in the air. Down on the ground, a strange symbol was visible. As soon as his eyes took in the full shape of the symbol, they went wide.

"*That* symbol…"

It was spinning in unison with the vortex, and it was the source of the golden light.

"A shining pillar paints the sky."

Rumbling sounds filled heaven and earth, and Sunan felt his innards vibrating in response.

He closed his eyes, and when he opened them again, everything was dark. He was back in his sleeping chamber. He reached up and wiped his face with his hand, half expecting it to come away wet with rainwater.

The only thing he felt was a few beads of sweat on his forehead.

His first impulse was to hurry over to Bao's quarters and tell her about the dream, but showing up outside her door in the middle of the night probably wouldn't be appropriate, so he settled back down and calmed his breathing.

Closing his eyes, he mentally reviewed the images he had just seen and began to ponder what they meant.

It wasn't until the late hours of night that he finally fell asleep again. This time, it was a dreamless sleep.

***

The following morning was a busy occasion as the sects formed ranks outside of the cave, and then began to make their way south, heading for the Banyan Region. Ruan traveled with the group, as he had discussed with Sunan, and Du Qian chose to accompany them as well, saying that there was safety in numbers.

Of course, the truth to Du Qian's decision was a bit more complicated than that, and as the group headed out, he continuously fiddled with a withered tree branch that he usually kept secure in the wide sleeve of his scholar's robes.

The current plan was to follow the mountain range south to where the mountains jutted out to the east. From there, they would make their way down into the Banyan Region itself. Although this route would bring them uncomfortably close to the rumored location of the Demon Emperor's palace, there would be many intervening kilometers of rough and uninhabited mountain terrain. The likelihood that they would encounter any Demon Emperor forces would be very low. According to Du Qian, the inhospitable mountains in that part of the empire were viewed as little more than rock and scrub, and they weren't even patrolled.

Although Sunan burned to talk to Bao about his dreams, he waited until the sects took time to rest and eat a short noon meal.

Bringing Sun Mai with him, he found Bao underneath the shade of one of the towering redwood trees that peppered the foothills of the mountains. She sat there with Mao Yun, eating a simple meal of steamed buns.

When Sunan sat down across from Bao, she looked at him quizzically. "Something happen?"

"I had another dream," he said. With that, he went on to explain everything he could remember, leaving out the details about what the symbol looked like for the moment. When he was finished with the description, he said, "Something struck me during the dream. When that golden-colored rain started falling, I remembered a line of poetry..."

Bao tilted her head to the side. "Golden droplets spin and howl..."

He nodded. "And that symbol sending golden light shining up into the sky."

Bao's face turned a bit paler. "A shining pillar paints the sky."

"It could all be coincidence, except for the symbol itself. It looked like this." Using his index finger, he traced an outline into the ground at his feet.

Sun Mai leaned over to look at it. "A circle with a curved line in the middle?"

"There's more," Sunan said. Picking up a twig, he traced a few more details onto each side.

"That looks like a dragon..." Sun Mai said. "And the other side is..."

"A phoenix," Bao concluded. "That was the symbol you saw in your dream?"

"Yes," Sunan replied. "I'm sure of it. And before you suggest that it appeared because of what we saw in the cave beneath Mount Fohe, let me point out that I saw the symbol in a previous dream. Back in Daolu. It wasn't until last night that I connected the two."

"So that's the symbol that appeared in the cave?" Sun Mai asked. He looked over and studied it more closely.

"A crude version," Sunan said with a wry grin.

Bao chuckled. "Li Runfa is somewhat of an artist. He told me that he made a more detailed sketch. I'm sure he'd be happy to show you, Chief Minister Sun."

Sun Mai stroked his chin. "Interesting. Very interesting. So, one of you dreams of dragons and phoenixes, and the other writes poems about them. Very, very interesting."

"What do you mean?" Bao asked.

Sun Mai looked over at her. "What do you mean, what do I mean?"

"What do you mean that I 'write poems about dragons and phoenixes'?"

"You know. The wyrm and the bird in your poem. They're obviously a dragon and a phoenix."

Bao's eyes narrowed. "How did you come to that conclusion?"

"Oh, I figured that out a long time ago. Didn't I tell the two of you?"

Bao and Sunan stared at him, and even Mao Yun cocked an eyebrow.

"I didn't, huh? Hmm. Well, I'm pretty sure I already put the information in my notes for my scripture. I guess it slipped my mind to say anything. That happens sometimes, you know. I tend to think of things and then after——"

"Sun Mai," Sunan said, "get on with the explanation!"

"Right. Well, in your poem, Heroine Bao, you have this character: 龑." He traced it into the ground. "You pronounce it 'wyrm.' Back in Daolu, I was doing some research into the ancient practice of talking to the moon, and I came across that very character in a dictionary from the Era of the Great Emperor."

"The Era of the Great Emperor?" Bao said, sounding surprised. "The Hao Dynasty? That was nine hundred years ago, wasn't it?"

"The dynasty was founded about nine hundred years ago, yes, but this dictionary was more recent. Probably about four hundred years old. Even in that dictionary, the character 龑 was listed as archaic. However, it seemed to be used synonymously with the character we use today for 'dragon.' They even look alike." He traced the character 龍 into the ground. "See? The top half of 龑 is 龍."

Bao and Sunan looked down at the characters and then looked back up into each other's eyes.

"What does it mean?" Mao Yun asked.

Sun Mai shook his head. "You seem to be having dreams and writing poems about the same thing. Perhaps you two knew each other in a past life and are recalling ancient memories?"

"Or what if they're messages from Xian Nu Shen?" Mao Yun asked.

Sun Mai's expression darkened. "Mao Yun, you know how I feel about that. The Perfect Realm—"

"I know," Mao Yun said. He tapped his temple. "The Perfect Realm is up here."

Sun Mai smiled. "Exactly."

Mao Yun rolled his eyes.

They continued to discuss the poem and the dreams, but they didn't reach any concrete conclusions. Before long, it was time to begin marching again.

Slowly but surely, the two sects were putting Mount Fohe behind them.

***

A zhen bird soared gracefully through the air high above the two sects, flying to and fro, almost like an escort. After the noontime break, the sects continued south until evening began to fall, whereupon they set up camp.

The zhen bird took that opportunity to alight onto the branch of a redwood sapling some distance away from the camp.

Mere moments after landing, a voice spoke out into the air. "It took me a while to deduce your identity, Love General."

The zhen bird turned to see a woman in a gray robe standing a few meters away. Her long black hair was bound at the top of her head, and she held a sheathed sword in her left hand.

The zhen bird cocked its head and adjusted its wings.

"There's no need for any further deception," the woman in gray said. "I should kill you on the spot, but instead I'll give you a chance to explain yourself. You've been following Bao and Sunan for some time now. Why? What tricks are you up to?"

A moment passed, and then the zhen bird hopped off the branch. As it did, its body flowed into a different form, and by the time it landed on the ground, it looked like a beautiful woman with fiery red hair bound above her head with an ebony hairpin.

"Why should I tell you anything about what I'm doing?" the Love General asked. "Who are you, anyway?"

"You don't know me," the woman said. "But I'm here to protect and guide Bao and Sunan. I'm a bit concerned by the fact that one of the Demon Emperor's ogre generals is trailing them." She took a step forward and extended her sword. "You have three breaths of time to give me an answer."

The Love General's eyes narrowed as she studied the woman further. "You're powerful. More powerful than any human I've encountered."

"That's right. And I'm not afraid of you, ogre. Where I come from, there are no ogre generals. They were all killed by people like me."

The Love General's eyes widened for a moment, but then just as quickly, they narrowed again. "You might be the most powerful human fighter in this world, but I've faced people even more powerful than you. If you're a friend of Sunan's, then I mean you no harm. I'm here to watch over him."

"Not likely," the woman said. "I know all about you, Love General. Never a greater liar existed in Qi Xien. I think I'll be doing the world a favor by getting rid of you this day."

The Love General's eyes flickered with a gleam of anger. "Try your best, swordswoman. I haven't killed anyone in quite a while. They might call me the Love General, but I'm no stranger to a fight." She waved her hand, and the long ebony hairpin flew out, allowing her hair to tumble down around her shoulders. As for the hairpin, it arced through the air around her, rapidly growing in size until it was a long spear, which she grabbed midair and pointed in front of her. "I don't know who you are, but if you push things too far this day, you'll die."

"I'm Hui from the Dragon-Phoenix Sect. Allow me to show you a technique that hasn't even been invented yet. One of the most powerful sword strikes ever created. The Perfect Strike of the Phoenix."

The Love General grinned and brandished her spear. "I've seen a lot more techniques than you might think."

CHAPTER 59
SCROLL PAINTING

"Dammit!" growled Geng Long, throwing another knife into a nearby tree trunk, which was already somewhat of a pincushion. "The Bone General is certainly taking his damn time getting back here. And how the hell did Bao survive that vosh sap? Fuck!"

"Enough with the language," the Golden Immortal growled in irritation.

Geng Long snorted. "Fuck you. I'll talk however I damn well please." He threw another knife.

"The Bone General will return when he feels like returning. In the meantime, we have a decision to make. Now that Bao and Sunan are out in the open and moving, should we strike?"

"Why wouldn't we? If we don't get them now, it will only get harder. They might be marching south for now, but it's not like their destination is Yao Gong Palace."

The Golden Immortal looked down at the map he'd spread out on the ground. "But where are they going? It would have made more sense to just head directly west into the Kushen Basin, or to Nangu."

Geng Long squatted down next to the map and pointed to a certain spot in the mountains farther to the south. "My guess is here. There's a story I heard about how Supreme Judge Yu once fought some mountain god. Supposedly Supreme Judge Yu threw his spear, but the mountain god dodged it, and the spear stabbed into the mountains. It was such a powerful blow that it hewed out a valley from here"—he pointed at a spot near the Banyan Mountains—"all the way to the Earthly Sea in the far south, which your map doesn't even show."

"A valley that goes from the Banyan Mountains all the way to that sea of sand? That's over one thousand kilometers! Maybe even two thousand!"

Geng Long shrugged. "It's just a story, but I've talked to people who've entered the valley before. If it really leads all the way to the Earthly Sea, then Sunan and that bitch could have a straight path to freedom." With that, he rose to his feet and walked over to the tree trunk, where he started plucking his knives out of the wood.

The Golden Immortal continued to study the map. "You said you have some tricks up your sleeve?"

Geng Long chuckled. "Finally got the balls to attack them, huh? Yeah, I have some tricks. The Dark Cloud bandits' headquarters isn't too far away from here, I can get in touch with them if I have to. They have about five hundred men ready to fight, more if I ask them to call in their reserves."

"How could such a huge force of bandits exist right under the shadow of Yao Gong Palace?"

"The Demon Emperor has a lot of trump cards hidden here and there. This is one of them, and luckily for us, they're under the command of the Bone General. In addition to the Dark Cloud bandits, I have this…" He produced an ornate-looking scroll case, crafted from wood and carved with terrifying-looking creatures and beasts.

"What's that?"

"Magic. Dark magic. If you're serious about attacking them, this will ensure our victory. There's no way that Sunan and Bao can deal with an army of slink demons from the underworld."

***

Hui leaned back against the tree and pushed her hand down over the wound on her thigh, hoping to staunch some of the blood flow. She had other more superficial cuts and wounds, ensuring that her gray robe was now more than half soaked with blood. But the thigh wound was the worst of all. Hui could tell that the stab of the Love General's spear had missed the major blood vessel, otherwise she would already have passed out and would most likely be dead.

I was careless, she thought. *Careless and unlucky. I can't believe ogres are this strong. Maybe I should have just spoken to Sunan and Bao directly.*

The Love General stood over her, spear leveled at in the direction of her throat.

Hui looked up at her with a grimace. "Well, go ahead and do it."

The Love General looked down at her for a moment, then waved her hand, causing the spear to shrink back down into the form of an ebony hairpin, which she placed into her sleeve. "I have no desire to kill you. What I said was the truth. I'm here to watch over Sunan."

Hui wasn't sure what to think of this. "But why? You're one of the ogre generals! It's your scheming that led to the Massacre of the Yangu Plains!"

The Love General frowned. "Massacre of the Yangu Plains? Are you mad? The King of the Pure Ones hasn't even sent a single soldier to the Yangu Plains."

Hui shook her head to try to clear it. "You *will* be responsible. In the future."

"In the future? What are you? A prophet? An immortal?"

"It doesn't matter. Even if you don't kill me, I'm still dead. I'll bleed to death unless someone treats this wound."

The Love General looked down at Hui for another long moment, then reached into her robe and produced a medicinal pill bottle. "Crush these pills into a paste and apply it to the wound. You'll recover within a few days."

She tossed the pill bottle down to Hui.

"Why are you doing this?" Hui asked.

"I don't know who you are or where you come from, but I can see you mean Sunan no harm. For the moment, that's enough for me to trust you. Unfortunately, you lack fighting experience, and eventually Sunan himself will surpass you. How will you help him then?"

Hui looked at the medicinal pill bottle for a moment, then back up at the Love General. "Knowledge."

The Love General's eyes narrowed for a moment, and then she nodded. "Don't get in my way again."

With that, she lowered herself into a crouch, then leapt into the air, transforming back into a beautiful zhen bird, which slowly flew higher and higher into the evening sky.

***

The two sects continued to march south through the unnamed mountains. Considering how far away they were from the most populated and "civilized" parts of the empire, these mountains were considered relatively wild lands. No maps existed that Sunan and Bao could procure, so they were forced to send out scouts and rely on the information brought back before making decisions about the exact path of travel.

One morning, as the sun was just rising, Sunan sneezed and woke up. After opening his eyes, he found an envelope lying next to him on the ground, his name written on the front in flowing calligraphy. Upon opening the envelope, he found a piece of thin paper folded inside with the following message.

Sunan: The Golden Immortal leads bandits and soldiers to attack you from the east and south. Lead your people into the ravine to the west. Hurry.

Not bothering to wake Bao, he went directly to Wang Tian and showed him the message. Wang Tian didn't need any orders. He immediately woke four of the Eyes of the Phoenix and sent them out to scout.

Sunan inquired with the guards on duty, but none of them had seen anyone enter or exit his tent. After the Eyes of the Phoenix left, Sunan finally went to wake Bao.

When she saw the message, she frowned. "This calligraphy looks like it was written by a woman."

Sunan frowned. "Perhaps. Sun Mai's calligraphy is fairly flowery, and he's not a woman."

"True," Bao replied. "Whether it's a man or woman doesn't matter too much. Whoever it was, how did they get a message into your tent? And how do they know that the Golden Immortal is leading troops our way?"

No amount of supposition or theorization on their part led anywhere. Preferring to play things safe, they roused the camp and issued orders to prepare to march in battle formation. Dragon Lord Sima Zikang's decision to train in military formations during their time at Mount Fohe had not been a waste.

As the camp was being cleared and the ranks were forming, the scouts returned from the east and south within minutes of each other.

"Chieftainess. Sect Leader. It's true. There seem to be about four hundred men marching on us from the south."

"There are men coming from the east, too. Perhaps three hundred."

The two sects immediately began to march to the west. Not too much time passed before the scout returned from that direction.

"Chieftainess. Sect Leader. There is indeed a ravine to the west. It seems like an ideal location to hole up for a fight. I rode the length of the ravine, and I even scouted the northern ridge. I didn't see anything untoward."

At this point, Bao and Sunan handed control of both sects over to Dragon Lord Sima. As they closed in on the ravine, he personally deployed the troop formations, including sending a contingent of archers to the north ridge, which was slightly higher than the south ridge.

By the time the enemy troops arrived, the two sects were completely arrayed for battle.

The enemies seemed to be mostly bandits, wearing a mishmash of armor and carrying a variety of weapons. A few Demon Emperor soldiers could be seen among them, and in the lead of the entire force was a very familiar face: the Golden Immortal.

"Where's Geng Long?" Bao muttered through gritted teeth.

"Who's that?"

"The one who poisoned me," she replied, her eyes flashing with flames of rage. "I knew him back in Yu Zhing. I expected him to be here too."

When Sunan looked over and saw the look in Bao's eye, he decided not to ask any more questions.

The Golden Immortal didn't waste any time. With a simple gesture and a barked command, he sent his men charging toward the mouth of the ravine, pinning down the archers on the north ridge with crossbow fire.

The bandits had numbers on their side, but the two sects were superior fighters, and their front line didn't budge. In fact, it began to creep forward.

Dragon Lord Sima remained on horseback, barking out orders as necessary.

After the fighting had been going on for roughly half an hour, Dragon Lord Sima approached Bao and Sunan.

"Sect Leader. Chieftainess. Something seems odd here. These bandits aren't fighting to break our lines. They seem hesitant. Like they're waiting for something."

"A trap?" Bao asked.

"Perhaps." Dragon Lord Sima looked back in the direction of the fighting. "Plus, they have hundreds of men in reserve. We may want to consider breaking through their lines and bringing the fight to the Golden Immortal."

After observing the fighting for another minute or two, Bao looked over at Sunan. "Sect Leader, I have an idea."

Before she had a chance to speak any further, Sunan squinted his eyes and pointed at the south ridge. "What's that?"

Bao and Dragon Lord Sima turned their heads.

"Is that the Bone General?" Dragon Lord Sima exclaimed.

"No," Bao replied. "But it's a Bone Slicer all right. Same type of armor. That's Geng Long!"

"What is he doing up there?"

Bao began to walk toward the south ridge. "I don't know, but it can't be good."

Before she even took two steps, Geng Long cupped his hands around his mouth and yelled, "Hey Bao, I have a little gift for you. Hope you enjoy it. Bitch!"

With that, he pulled an ornate scroll case out and opened it. A scroll painting unfurled, although from such a distance, it was impossible to make out any details on the painting. However, the details didn't matter. As soon as the scroll opened, the ink on its surface began to swirl and bubble. Rumbling sounds could be heard, like distant thunder, and then a shadowy figure emerged from the scroll.

It stood about knee high and resembled a skinned cat, with blood dripping down its exposed muscles and a vicious-looking face complete with glowing green eyes.

Then another appeared, and another. After jumping out of the scroll painting, they began to leap off the edge of the south ridge and scramble down the slope.

More and more of them poured out of the painting. Soon there were ten, then twenty, then fifty. They emerged in seemingly endless waves, emitting yowling screeches that grated at the ears and tugged at the soul.

Geng Long began to laugh uproariously.

CHAPTER 60
AN OFFER

If Dragon Lord Sima Zikang was shocked by the sight of dozens of catlike demons racing down the slope, he didn't show it. Before the first of the creatures could even get halfway down to the bottom of the slope, he shouted, "Golden Dragon squads four and six, Pure Phoenix squads five and seven, reform to the south!"

Four squads of fighters ran to meet the cat demons.

Within moments, bizarre, otherworldly screeches filled the air, and blood began to splash. The Golden Dragons and Pure Phoenixes soon found that although the bizarre cats were ferociously strong and terrifyingly vicious, they could die just as any living animal could die.

However, the cat demons had not stopped pouring out of Geng Long's painting.

"Dammit," Sunan said. "How many of those things does he have?"

Dragon Lord Sima began to shake his head slowly. "There are already enough to threaten to overwhelm us. Any more and…"

The demons continued to pour out of the painting, accompanied by Geng Long's maniacal laughter.

Sunan gritted his teeth. "Who is this psycho…?"

"The biggest bastard in the world," Bao snarled.

However many cats the fighters killed, more popped up to replace them.

The lines were holding but clearly wouldn't continue to do so for much longer.

"Sunan," Bao said, her voice low. "I think we need to use that technique."

He looked over at her. "Are you sure?"

"I'm sure."

Sima Zikang turned his attention from the cat demons to look at Bao and Sunan. "Which technique are you talking about?"

Bao clenched her fists. "The technique we learned in the cave beneath Mount Fohe."

"You learned a technique there?"

Sunan took a deep breath. "Yes. We saw an ancient battle. Or rather, participated in it. There was a war in which a dragon warrior and a phoenix warrior fought against an army from Emo-Cheng. An army of demons. In the end, the dragon and the phoenix combined their power into a single strike…"

"And wiped out the entire army of demons," Bao concluded. She took a step forward. "Sunan, are you ready?"

He gritted his teeth. "I… I don't know. We've never even practiced this."

"We practiced it on that ancient battlefield."

"That wasn't us! What if we can't control it?"

A demon cat pounced on one of the Pure Phoenixes and ripped his throat out. Two nearby Golden Dragons hacked the cat with their sabers, killing it. Then they lunged to fill the spot vacated by the now-dead Pure Phoenix fighter.

"Dammit!" Sunan muttered. "Bao…"

"Look, Sunan, you have to trust yourself. Be confident in your abilities and your skill. We did this before in that ancient illusory world. We can do it again."

Sunan took a step forward. "Fine. Let's do it. Let's unleash the Dragon Phoenix Strike."

Bao looked over at him and grinned. "You mean the Phoenix Dragon Strike? This was my idea."

He chuckled. "Fine. The Phoenix Dragon Strike. Dragon Lord Sima, once we start moving, have the men make room."

Dragon Lord Sima nodded.

Without any further discussion, Bao and Sunan accelerated into a run.

Behind them, Dragon Lord Sima called out, "Squads four through seven, Rippling Willow Formation!"

The Golden Dragons and Pure Phoenixes fighting the cat demons quickly began to execute one of the many maneuvers they had practiced. As Bao and Sunan neared, they formed a wedge shape, then surged forward, pushing the cat demons back in a sudden vicious charge. Then, just as quickly, they fell back, inverting the wedge shape to leave a wide opening in the middle.

The cat demons were taken by surprise. As their front lines scrambled to recover from the sudden charge, Bao and Sunan leapt into the gap that had been opened. They touched hands left to right and extended their other hands forward.

Neither of them spoke a word, nor did they shout the name of the technique, as had become the convention among qi fighters.

As their hands shoved forward, a flood of qi erupted, two blazing streams of energy, one of which vaguely resembled a dragon, the other, a phoenix. The streams of energy combined, causing intense rumbling sounds to echo in all directions. The ground trembled, and a powerful wind kicked up.

When the blast of energy slammed into the first of the demon cats, they trembled, and their eyes began to bulge. Then, after only a breath of time passed, they exploded into clouds of blood, gore, and bone.

Then the cat demons behind them exploded, one after another.

The massive wave of energy surged up the steep slope, completely destroying every cat demon it touched and also destroying any plants and vegetation in the area. Blood began to fall like rain, accompanied by the miserable screams of the cats.

Geng Long's eyes went wide as he stood there, the scroll painting still held in his hand, still belching out more cat demons.

As the flood of qi energy bore down on him, his jaw dropped, and his hand began to tremble.

It was only when the energy was about six meters away from him that he finally reacted, dropping the painting, planting his foot down, and pushing backward in an attempt to evade the blast.

However, he was too slow. The scroll painting was caught up by the flood of energy and shredded into pieces, and then the blast slammed into him.

Geng Long let out a miserable scream as he was sent tumbling backward like a kite with its string cut.

He flipped head over heels, blood spraying out of his mouth. By that point, he was out of Bao and Sunan's line of sight, but they could hear his cry, and then it was cut short with a thudding sound.

It was in that moment that the blast of energy faded away, and the fighters relaxed the ready stances they had assumed before looking around. The few cat demons that hadn't been caught up in the blast were being dispatched by the Golden Dragons and Pure Phoenixes that were near the outskirts of the blast radius.

At the entrance to the ravine, the fighting had stopped. Bandits and Demon Emperor soldiers alike were looking over toward Bao and Sunan and the blood-soaked ravine wall, their expressions that of shock and horror. Even the Golden Dragons and Pure Phoenixes fighting on the front lines were clearly shaken.

As for the Golden Immortal, his eyes were wide, and although no one could see it, his hands were trembling.

A short moment of silence followed.

Bao and Sunan were breathing heavily. They had just unleashed a powerful cathartic attack that had killed nearly a hundred or more cat demons, draining them significantly. However, they still had a bit of energy left to fight.

The silence was broken by Dragon Lord Sima. "Push the attack! Elephant Crushing Formation!"

A cheer rose up from the Golden Dragons and Pure Phoenixes, and battle cries began to ring out as they executed the offensive formation, pushing hard against the bandits and soldiers.

Bao's eyes flashed with flames of fury. "If Geng Long didn't die, then I'm going to finish the job."

Without another word to Sunan, she sped up the slope.

Sunan looked at the fighting, then turned his head to Dragon Lord Sima.

Sima Zikang quickly assessed the battlefield, then said, "The Golden Immortal is fleeing. The battle is ours. Go."

Sunan nodded, then sped after Bao.

***

Geng Long was no fool. He had grown up on the streets of Yu Zhing, stealing, scheming, plotting, conniving, and even murdering his way into positions of power. Eventually he'd wormed his way into the Bone Slicers, where he felt right at home.

When Bao and Sunan unleashed power that seemed to surpass the level of mortal beings, Geng Long was temporarily stunned into immobility. By the time he regained his senses and attempted to evade the blast, it was too late, and he was thrown back violently from the edge of the ravine.

Thankfully, he had chosen to wear his Bone Slicer armor for the battle, something he rarely did. He preferred to skulk in the shadows and slice throats, not fight on a battlefield. It was his decision to wear that armor that saved his life. Not only did it provide a level of protection from the tail end of the blast of energy, it absorbed some of the force of the blow he sustained when he slammed into a tree a few meters away from the edge of the slope.

By that time, the pain wracking his body forced him into a position of clarity. And because of the intense sensation of deadly crisis that rose up from the pit of his stomach, his reactions were even quicker than normal.

As he fell toward the ground, he twisted to the left. Landing in a crouching position, he didn't hesitate to burst into motion. Drawing upon the energy in his body, he moved with speed that surpassed even the best qinggong techniques of the Pure Phoenix Sect.

In the blink of an eye, he was gone.

***

Bao leapt onto the south ridge only to find it completely empty, other than the blood and gore left behind by the slain cat demons, plus the shredded remains of the scroll painting.

However, in the distant trees, she noticed a blur of motion and began to race in that very direction.

A moment later, she heard breathing and footfalls behind her and identified them as Sunan's. However, she didn't take the time to look back, instead keeping her gaze focused on the spot where she'd detected motion moments before.

Drawing upon the qinggong techniques of the Pure Phoenix Sect, she raced through the scattered trees, heading in a general southeasterly direction.

It took only a few moments to reach the spot where she'd seen the motion. However, nothing was in sight.

"Damn you, Geng Long," she muttered.

Sunan stopped next to her. After looking around vigilantly, he said, "No clue which way he went?"

"None. That bastard. One of these days I'm going to skin him alive. Then he can join those cats of his in hell!"

***

The Bone General had just finished a noon meal of roast chicken and was looking out over the Fei River. That was when he noticed a zhen bird flying toward him from off in the distance. His eyes narrowed, but as the bird neared, his expression turned into something more like a sneer.

Just as the zhen bird was about to land in front of him, it blurred, transforming into the Love General. This time, she did not wear the form of a human. She assumed her true form, that of a powerful ogre.

"You look much better that way," the Bone General said. "In this form, you're truly beautiful."

She ignored his comment. Smiling slightly, she said, "I came to inform you that your pet humans just led an all-out assault on Sunan and the girl."

The Bone General's brows furrowed. "And...?"

"Oh, it was a failure. I can't believe you lent your Slink Demon Scroll to that two-bit thief you let join your Bone Slicers."

"Geng Long used the Slink Demon Scroll? Then how could the battle have been lost?"

The Love General looked out at the waters of the Fei River. "Oh, Sunan and the girl destroyed the demons and the scroll. It was quite spectacular. Plenty of blood. You probably would have enjoyed the scene."

Rage flickered in the Bone General's eyes. "And Geng Long?"

"Escaped. Barely. Along with that cousin of his."

"Why didn't you help them?" the Bone General growled.

"And do your job for you? No." She looked back at the Bone General. "I'm here today to make an offer."

CHAPTER 61
CHRYSANTHEMUM LAKE

The two sects fared well in what later came to be called the Battle of the Cat Demons. Only a few unlucky members of the sects lost their lives in the fighting, whereas casualties among the enemy were relatively high.

After the flood of cat demons was destroyed, the tide of battle turned. Before Bao and Sunan even returned from their pursuit of Geng Long, the bandits and Demon Emperor soldiers had turned to flee. The Golden Immortal had long since fled.

After regrouping and tending to the wounded, the two sects emerged from the ravine and resumed their march south.

The Eyes of the Phoenix confirmed that the enemy forces were not regrouping, and that they were not being pursued. As night began to fall, they made camp on a stone shelf outcropping.

After the evening meal, Sunan lay in his tent trying to find sleep. However, his mind was filled with the events of the day, and slumber eluded him. While he lay there pondering whether or not to practice some Wu-Sunan forms under the moonlight, a voice spoke from outside the tent.

"Sect Leader Sunan, are you awake?"

It was Mao Yun.

Sunan grabbed his saber from the ground next to him and then emerged from the tent.

Mao Yun nodded in greeting. "Sect Leader, it's Bao. She went off on her own. To think, she said. I'm worried about her being out by herself. Remember when she stayed out all night on Mount Fohe?"

"She refused to let you accompany her?"

Mao Yun nodded. "She headed up there," he said, pointing up to the mountain ridge that loomed above them.

"I understand," Sunan said. "I'll go check on her."

With that, he left the camp and began to climb the mountain. Thankfully, the moon was bright, and although there was no path, the vegetation was sparse, making the way up relatively easy. After about twenty minutes, Sunan had reached the summit, where he saw Bao sitting cross-legged on a boulder.

Taking a deep breath, he approached the boulder. When he was a few paces away, Bao looked over her shoulder, and when she saw Sunan, nodded slightly. Taking that as an invitation, or at least a lack of dismissal, he hopped up onto the boulder and sat down next to her.

She said nothing, so neither did he. He placed his saber down next to him and then put his hands on his knees. Closing his eyes, he took a deep breath of the crisp night air, then performed some breathing exercises. After some time passed, he opened his eyes again. Stretching out as far as the eye could see was a wilderness of scattered trees and rugged rocks. Far off in the distance, a river was visible, which Sunan assumed was the Fei.

More time passed, and the silence grew weighty.

What should I say? he thought. *Or should I say anything at all? Should I just sit here?*

Before he could make his decision, Bao spoke.

"Have you ever wanted to kill someone?" she asked.

He was a bit taken aback. "Well, I've killed people before in battle."

She shook her head. "That's not what I mean. I mean, have you ever wanted to hurt someone? To make them scream as they die."

He shivered inwardly. "I... I guess not." She didn't say anything in response, so after a long moment passed, he continued, "I suppose you're thinking about the man from earlier today. What was his name?"

"Geng Long," she replied in a voice that sounded like metal grating on rock.

"Gong Long," he echoed. "From Yu Zhing? What... what happened with him? Was he... a friend?" He looked at her out of the corner of his eye and could see that her hands were clenched into fists as they rested on her thighs. Her jaw was tight, and she was breathing heavily. Her hair was somewhat in disarray, as if she hadn't even looked in a mirror since the fighting earlier. For some reason, it made her seem particularly attractive.

"He was more than a friend. I loved him. Or at least, I thought I did."

Sunan had absolutely no idea what to say in response, so he simply looked out at the moonlit landscape.

After a long moment passed, Bao continued. "Back when life seemed like nothing but a monotonous chore, I met him, and he made everything wonderful. We explored the city at night and had adventures. At least, they seemed like adventures back then. After everything that's happened since then, I think they were more just child's play. One night, we got into a fight, and then... he kissed me." Her voice quavered. "After that night, he kissed me more. I used to dream about leaving the city with him."

Sunan saw her clenching her fists even tighter.

"I dreamed of running away with him to the south. Of having a family. It was stupid. So stupid. Agh!" Despite her bellow of anger, Sunan could see something glistening on her cheek.

She's crying? At some point, his heart had begun to pound with emotion, except, he wasn't sure exactly which emotion it was. Was it anger? Jealousy? Or perhaps something else entirely?

"It was all a lie, Sunan. He was toying with me. Getting me to trust him so that he could sell me. That fucking bastard!"

Her tone was that of fury, but Sunan could see more tears streaming down her face. "Sell you?" he asked.

She laughed bitterly. "Yeah. To a gang in Yu Zhing. 'A project.' That's what he called me. I'll never forget what he said. 'I set her up for a whole year.' He sold me to a gang so that they could ransom me for money. I was only there for a few days before the Bone General came. Mao Yun was there. He was the one who set me free. And then I ran." She took a deep, shaky breath. "I've been running ever since. I never thought much about it afterwards; there was never time. But then he showed up here and..." Her voice broke, and she began to weep. It started out softly but grew louder and more choked, until finally she leaned over, placing her hands flat on the boulder to support herself as her tears poured down her face.

Without even thinking about it, Sunan reached and put his hand on top of hers.

Time passed, and slowly her crying faded. Sunan pulled his hand away, and she straightened up. After wiping her face dry, she breathed in and out a few times.

"Am I wrong to want him dead?" she asked.

"No," he said immediately. "I would do it for you if I could."

She sniffled and chuckled. "You'd do that for me?"

"Sure."

The two of them sat there for some time looking out at the wilderness.

"Bao, let's join forces."

She looked over at him. "What do you mean? Aren't we already allies?"

Her eyes were swollen and bloodshot from the weeping, but for some reason, it only made her look more charming.

"I mean more than just allies," he said. "Let's combine our two sects. It will only make us stronger. This won't be the last time we face a powerful opponent. Whether it's the Bone General or the Demon Emperor or that bastard Geng Long, we'll be stronger if we're united. What do you say?"

She looked away from him, turning her gaze to the stars above as she thought. "Okay."

"We can call it the Phoenix Dragon Sect," he said.

She smiled. "I took the Phoenix Dragon Strike. Let's make it the Dragon-Phoenix Sect."

***

The following morning, they informed the top leaders of both sects regarding the decision. However, no official announcement was made. Everyone agreed that it would be best to wait until reaching the Banyan Region before discussing the particulars of how to restructure, and then they would hold the necessary rites and ceremonies.

The sects proceeded south. Generally speaking, the traveling was uneventful. A minor stir occurred when people noticed that the zhen bird, which had been following them since the early days fleeing from Daolu, had disappeared. Many took that to be an ill omen. However, a few days later, the zhen bird was spotted again, and hearts calmed.

Crossing the Banyan Mountains proved more difficult a task than they had imagined, especially considering that most of the peaks of the mountains in this area were snow-capped year-round.

They ended up winding their way deeper into the mountains to the west before finally finding a passage through.

When they finally began their descent into the Banyan Region itself, the temperature began to rise sharply, and the air grew more humid. After weeks of trudging about in icy winds, it was a bit of a relief.

As they approached the foothills of the mountains, a lake became visible off in the distance. It was enormous, almost a sea.

"Chrysanthemum Lake," Sun Mai said. "The most tranquil body of water in the empire. They say that even during thunderstorms, not a wave can be seen on its surface."

As they proceeded down into the foothills, the trees grew denser. It took a full day of travel to reach the shores of the Chrysanthemum Lake. Just as Sun Mai had said, the lake was so still it almost looked like glass. The waters were clear, making it possible to see ancient fallen tree trunks at the bottom of the lake, a multicolored spectacle that seemed almost like another world. The lake stretched so far that the opposite shore wasn't visible.

After reaching the shore of the lake, the sects rested while the Eyes of the Phoenix scouted for a suitable location for a permanent camp. By evening, they were setting up tents in a forest clearing near a waterfall that fed into the lake.

As the camp began to take shape, a zhen bird landed onto a nearby tree.

***

Later that evening, Ruan the Flamingo was standing at the lake shore, looking out at the water, when he heard footsteps behind him.

It was none other than Du Qian, who came to a stop next to him.

"I've given you your chance to think," Du Qian said.

Ruan nodded. "Can I see it again?"

Du Qian looked at Ruan with narrowed eyes for a moment, then reached into his robe and pulled out the withered tree limb, only about as long as his own forearm. It was so dark that it was almost black, except for the thin silver veins running up and down its surface. He handed the tree branch to Ruan.

Ruan carefully took the branch and began to examine it closely. "You're absolutely sure of its origins?"

Du Qian nodded. "It's a branch of the Epoch Tree, of that I'm certain. As for how the Hen-Shi Sect got their hands on it, I can't say for certain. It wouldn't surprise me at all if they simply stole it. In any case, can you work with it?"

Ruan sniffed the branch. "I can. Based on the power flowing through it, I can tell you that it will be a long process. And the final result... will probably be something large."

"Neither of those matter, as long as I get results."

"You'll get results. Shall I begin work?"

Du Qian thought for a moment, then nodded in the affirmative.

Ruan tucked the tree branch into his sleeve.

CHAPTER 62
ZUN SHAN

Although Sunan and Bao weren't aware of it, rumors were beginning to spread through the camp.

"Did you hear about how Sect Leader Sunan and Chieftainess Bao spent the whole night together on top of a mountain a few weeks ago?"

"People are saying that they're a couple now!"

"If they get married, what will happen to the two sects?"

"Supposedly they're already secretly engaged."

"You don't even know the half of it. I heard that she's pregnant!"

"That wouldn't surprise me at all. I was walking by Bao's tent the other night, and you wouldn't believe the sounds I heard!"

It didn't take long before some of the leadership of the sects caught wind of the rumors. It was Mao Yun who took it upon himself to try to stem the tide of gossip. He well knew that if Bao or Sunan ended up hearing about such rumors, especially some of the more salacious ones, it would be a huge loss of face.

However, the rumors wouldn't stop, and were compounded

by the fact that Sunan and Bao had taken to spending more time with each other. The truth was that because of the well-established routines led by the other sect leaders, Bao and Sunan had few responsibilities. Usually, martial arts forms were practiced first thing in the morning, followed by sparring sessions. The time after the noon meal and accompanying rest was set aside for meditation and self-reflection. Then came battle formation practice with Dragon Lord Sima. The final hours before dinner were for various other sect-related activities, and the evenings were free time.

Other than when official duties required their time, Bao and Sunan were often seen sparring together, creating new martial arts techniques, or sitting by the lake chatting.

It was Sun Mai who came up with the solution to the problem.

"It's time to announce that we're forming a new sect!" he announced.

Bao and Sunan looked at each other.

"Are you sure it's time?" Sunan asked.

Sun Mai smiled broadly. "Of course! There's no need to beat around the bush. Plus, the Bixie Moon is approaching, the perfect time for new beginnings!"

"I agree on this point," Mao Yun chimed in. "The main question we have is what to call the sect."

"Well," Bao said, "that's already been decided. It will be the Dragon-Phoenix Sect. But the Bixie Moon is only a week away. Is that enough time for all the preparations?"

"More than enough," Sun Mai said. "Li Runfa and I have already worked out the emblem to use. Look!" He produced a sheet of paper with an ink drawing on it, depicting an intertwined phoenix and dragon.

Sunan's eyes widened. "Is that...?"

"Yes," Sun Mai said. "This is the very same image which appeared above the two of you in the cave beneath Mount Fohe. Fitting, don't you think?"

"We won't really need to change the uniforms very much," added Li Runfa. "Assuming the sect still has separate divisions for the Dragons and Phoenixes."

Things proceeded in a whirlwind. The announcement was made, and the date was set for the following week. Thankfully, the buzz of excitement that swept through the camp quelled some of the rumors about Sunan and Bao.

When the day came, a grand ceremony was held officially uniting the two sects into one larger sect. Many of the titles held by the officers remained the same. However, Sun Mai stepped down as the chief minister to focus on his work with his scripture, which he said was nearing completion. He was replaced by Tie Gangwen, who assumed the title Dragon General.

In the time that had passed since Tie Gangwen's grievous injury, he had developed new ways to manipulate qi, and he was now just as formidable a fighter as he had been in the past. In fact, because his surname meant 'iron,' people had taken to calling him the One-Armed Iron Titan.

After some debate, new titles were also created for Sunan and Bao. From the day of the ceremony onward, they came to be known as Dragon Sovereign Sunan and Phoenix Sovereign Bao. Neither Sunan nor Bao were very pleased with such ostentatious titles, but no amount of protestation on their part could convince the other leaders to accept anything else.

With the addition of the new recruits that had filtered into the sect over the months, the new Dragon-Phoenix Sect had roughly seven hundred members, divided equally into the Golden Dragon Division and the Pure Phoenix Division. Each division was further separated into seven legions, led by Dragon Lords and Claws of the Phoenix respectively. Because a new legion had been formed in each division, new leaders needed to be chosen, and at the suggestion of Dragon Lord Sima, those leaders would be decided by holding a tournament.

The day after the opening rites and rituals, and the night of feasting which followed, the tournament began. It was a grand occasion that began first thing in the morning with thirty-two competitors, sixteen from each division. The rules for the competition were similar to the platform fights back in Daolu, although any blows that would inflict serious injury were strictly forbidden. The losers of any given match would be removed from the competition.

The thirty-two competitors were all well-known members of the sect, people who were skilled fighters and had distinguished themselves in various ways, either in the fighting in Daolu or during the following months.

The first round of the competition took an entire day, with sixteen spectacular fights. Some of them ended quickly, others were protracted struggles that lasted for multiple rounds. Another night of feasting was held, and the following day, the sixteen winners from the first round fought fierce battles until only eight remained. Of those eight fighters, five were men and three were women. One of the men who stood out from the others was from the Golden Dragon Division. His name was Lin Cuirou, a name that was almost too beautiful for a man.

Lin Cuirou was known for two things. First was his love of emeralds. He bedecked himself with all sorts of emerald jewelry, everything from rings to necklaces to a headband with a gaudy emerald festooned in the middle of it. Second, he was known for his good looks, of which he was very proud. He was handsome to the point of being pretty, with unusual green eyes that would make most women swoon to look into. Because of his good looks and his love of emeralds, other members of the sect had given him the humorous nickname Emerald Hunk.

At the beginning of each match, Lin Cuirou would instruct his opponents not to strike him in the face, and none of them did. That is, until the final round, during which he was up against a burly

Golden Dragon who landed a fist strike right on his cheek.

In response, Lin Cuirou went berserk, unleashing Slash of the Dragon's Tail with cathartic speed and power.

Despite countering with a move called Golden Willow Shield, his opponent was thrown violently out of the fighting arena.

It was a spectacular scene that left everyone in the audience cheering. As for Lin Cuirou, he hurried in search of a mirror to check his face for any permanent damage.

The final two battles of the tournament couldn't have been more opposite. The match which determined the new leader for the Pure Phoenix Division lasted for ten brutal rounds and ended with a complete knockout. In contrast, the match for the Golden Dragon Division ended within moments with a beautifully executed strike by Lin Cuirou.

In the end, Lin Cuirou was promoted to Dragon Lord, and a stocky woman named Ma Ge became the new Claw of the Phoenix. Long ago, Ma Ge had been a close follower of Sunan, but in the years since, she had taken a liking to Bao.

A few weeks passed, and because of how exposed their camp left them, the decision was made to continue traveling south. The sect traveled slowly along the bank of the Chrysanthemum Lake for about three days until they reached the southern shore, where the scouts had found a wide valley that made the perfect location for a more permanent camp. The valley was closer to the lake, and it would be much more easily defended, leaving everyone feeling a bit more secure.

The area north of Chrysanthemum Lake, which bordered the Banyan Mountains, was uninhabited. However, that was not the case south of the lake. Several tribes of indigenous people called that area their home, and although they were suspicious of outsiders, once they were convinced that the Dragon-Phoenix Sect was not part of the empire, they accepted their presence.

In fact, some of the nearby tribes seemed very interested in the fighting abilities of the sect, prompting Sunan and Bao to make arrangements to teach them.

The Eyes of the Phoenix were tasked with scouting the area and making maps. As the weeks went by, the scouts traveled farther and farther away from Chrysanthemum Lake, even into the Jian Shu Forest, which filled most of the Banyan Region, and was more of a jungle than a forest, despite its name.

Sunan had long since explained to Bao about the Shan people and the empyreal hammer. It took no convincing on his part for her to agree to have the Eyes of the Phoenix begin to look for clues.

Time passed. The first interesting word that came back from the Eyes of the Phoenix had nothing to do with the Shan.

Wang Tian himself brought the news to Bao and Sunan as they drank tea near the shore of the lake.

"See those mountains to the southeast?" He pointed. "That's where Zun Shan is located."

"*The* Zun Shan?" Sunan asked.

"Yes," Bao said. "Another of the five great mountain peaks. What of it, Wang Tian?"

"One of the Eyes of the Phoenix was exploring the area and found a staircase cut into the very rock of Zun Shan."

Bao frowned. "A staircase on Zun Shan? I learned about all of the five peaks and never heard anything about a staircase."

"I know," Wang Tian said. "I studied a thing or two about them myself, and I have never heard any such tale. However, it didn't seem to be a surprise to any of the locals when we made some inquiries. The staircase is located on the western face of the mountain, and it isn't visible from the foot of the mountain. Even the entrance to the staircase is difficult to find. My man only stumbled across it by chance.

"What's the most intriguing, though, isn't the staircase itself. It's what's at the end of the staircase: a temple."

Bao put down her teacup. "A temple on Zun Shan? How is that possible?"

"Your guess is as good as mine. I'd like to go see it for myself. Would you two like to come along?"

And thus, three days later, Sunan and Bao found themselves climbing a staircase up the side of Zun Shan. In addition to Wang Tian and two other Eyes of the Phoenix, they were joined by Sun Mai, Mao Yun, and about ten other members of the sect.

The air got colder and thinner the higher they got. Eventually the staircase ended at the mouth of a cave. Columns had been carved into the sides of the cave opening, although they were worn and crumbling with age.

Just as Wang Tian had said, the mouth of the cave led to a temple complex that was shockingly large. It took the small group an entire day just to explore the main areas. It contained a huge grand hall, seven smaller halls, and numerous passages and rooms.

"Who could have built a place like this?" Sunan asked at one point.

"Perhaps the Suk," Sun Mai replied. "Or perhaps other forces more ancient than we can imagine. The architecture is like nothing I've seen before."

Bao ran her finger along the wall, which had obviously once been carved with a fresco, but it was now so worn down that it was almost impossible to make out any details. "You know, this place is more than large enough to hold the Dragon-Phoenix Sect..."

CHAPTER 63
A DEBATE

The cave temple on Zun Shan had water springs in it, and it was the type of location that only an insane general would lead an army against. Everyone agreed that it would make the perfect headquarters for the sect. Work began immediately to renovate and adapt it into a suitable location to hold a large group of people like the Dragon-Phoenix Sect.

It was not a project that could be accomplished overnight. At the absolute minimum, it would be many months before the work was complete.

After everyone returned to the camp near the south bank of Chrysanthemum Lake, Sun Mai said that the trip up the mountain had led him to new enlightenment and that he needed to go into secluded meditation to work on his scripture.

"When I come out," he said, "my scripture will be complete."

Over the course of the years, Sun Mai had stopped referring to his scripture as a "classic scripture." Although few people noticed that, Sunan did.

While Sun Mai went into seclusion, life went on as usual in the Dragon-Phoenix Sect. The Eyes of the Phoenix continued to scout and explore the Banyan Region, focusing mostly on the areas to the east of Zun Shan and the camp. Work continued on the cave temple.

One month after Sun Mai went into seclusion, Wang Tian brought a report back to Sunan that clues had turned up regarding the Shan people. Sunan was of a mind to go investigate himself, but at the urging of Bao, he held back. Instead, Wang Tian took on that responsibility.

Another month passed.

One night, when the moon had just turned full, Sunan and Bao were taking an evening stroll by the lake when they caught sight of a robed figure standing knee deep in the waters of the lake, staring up at the moon. As they neared, it became obvious that it was a man, though neither of them recognized him from behind, mostly because his head had been completely shaved.

When they were about ten meters away, the man looked over his shoulder at them.

"Sun Mai?" Sunan blurted. "Your hair!"

Sun Mai looked back out at the lake. "Yes, I've parted ways with it."

Bao and Sunan stopped at the edge of the water.

"Sun Mai, why are you out in the water?" Bao asked.

"I felt hot," he replied. "And I haven't spoken with the moon for some time now." He turned and walked back to the shore. "I finished my scripture. Would you like to take a look?" He held out a bamboo scroll.

Sunan took it and began to unroll it.

As he did, Sun Mai said, "Mao Mei and I will start making copies in the morning."

Sunan began to read the text by the moonlight. First his eyes narrowed, and then they widened as he realized that he could hardly understand any of it. However, the reason for that was not because it didn't make sense, but because it seemed incomprehensibly profound.

There were some passages that he remembered coming up in conversations with Sun Mai in the past.

Beliefs are just systems.

The beginning state is the perfect state.

Seek the truth and pursue the actual.

However, the elucidating texts that went along with the statements seemed stunningly deep.

For example, the section on "seek the truth and pursue the actual."

Seek the truth and pursue the actual. Truth is the experience; the actual is the corporeal. Without the truth, does the actual exist? Without the actual, what is truth? The experience is perceived, the corporeal is experienced. Without being perceived, does the cosmos exist? Without the experience, does the perception exist?

It went on like that for several more lines of text. Each aspect of the scripture made Sunan's mind spin. Based on what he knew about Sun Mai, he had expected the scripture to be a random collection of sayings and thoughts, but even just glancing at a few parts of it, he could tell that the entire body of text was actually unified.

Bao was looking over his shoulder, and her eyes were just as wide as Sunan's.

"You wrote this, Sun Mai?" she asked.

A slight smile appeared on Sun Mai's face. "I did."

Sunan took a deep breath. "Sun Mai, this is incredible. I... I don't even understand it."

Sun Mai looked out over the lake, his eyes glittering as if with starlight. "There are some parts which I know to be true but have yet to fully grasp the meaning of. Please, take your time examining it, and give it to Mao Mei when you're finished. I haven't slept for two months. I need to rest." With that, he turned and left.

Sunan and Bao sat down by the lake to read the scripture, bathed by cascading moonlight.

The moon slowly crawled across the sky.

At one point, Bao shivered. "I never thought Sun Mai was serious when he said that the Perfect Realm doesn't exist. But after reading this... it makes me wonder."

***

Bao wasn't the only one who began to wonder. In the following days, copies of the scripture were made, and slowly they began to circulate through the camp. Most members of the Dragon-Phoenix Sect were generally familiar with Sun Mai's ideas and arguments, but this scripture was different. It was as if all of the rambling, disjointed things Sun Mai had said through the years had been run through a sieve, refined, reshaped, tempered, and forged into sword that stabbed directly into the heart of the Dehuan beliefs that most people in the empire held dear.

Of course, most members of the Dragon-Phoenix Sect had come from lowly backgrounds. They were soldiers, ruffians, bandits, as well as many who had started out as commoners with a knack for using qi. However, there was one person in the camp who was anything but ordinary when it came to the scholarly arts, and that was Du Qian.

Sun Mai had started out as nothing more than a poor street scholar who barely made a living with his skills. In sharp contrast, Du Qian had risen up through the imperial exams until he occupied a position in the Demon Emperor's court. He was a scholar among scholars, a man of learning and tradition who both firmly believed in the ancient Dehuan teachings and could also explain and expound upon them. The Demon Emperor was responsible for many repugnant acts, but one thing he had left untouched were the traditions set forth by the famous philosopher Kong Zhi, which were the basis of the Dehua belief system.

At first, Du Qian refused to even look at the scripture, but as the discussions raged through the camp, he eventually gave in. When he finally sat down and began to read, his hands gripped the bamboo scroll tighter and tighter. His jaw clenched, and flames began to burn in his eyes.

"This is ridiculous!" he muttered angrily. "Heretical ravings!"

He had to suppress the urge to physically throw the scroll away.

Meanwhile, Sun Mai had slept for a week straight. Upon emerging, he shaved his head again, and then had a light breakfast of rice congee in the middle of the camp. Something about him seemed different. He seemed calmer, more tranquil, even introspective.

As he was finishing his meal, Du Qian stalked up, holding a bamboo scroll in his hand.

"Scholar Sun!" he barked, looming to a stop over Sun Mai and holding the scroll out in front of him. "I demand that you renounce this trash immediately! If you don't collect the copies and destroy them, *I will*!"

Sun Mai rose to his feet, a tranquil smile on his face. "Brother Du Qian, I'm sorry you don't like my scripture. But I most certainly will not destroy it. In fact, there are more scriptures to come. This is only the first volume of thirteen."

Du Qian snorted coldly. "Scholar Sun, there are so many erroneous aspects to this 'scripture' of yours that I could write an entire treatise about them. Look at this!" He jerked open the scroll, found a passage, and read it out loud. "'If a text is not read, does it exist? The truth of a text is the experience, not the ink and the paper.'" Du Qian threw his head back and laughed. "This is how children think! Literally! Cover your face with your hands, and a baby will think you've left the room. Reveal your face, and the baby rejoices upon your return. Laughable!"

Sun Mai's smile never left his face. "Perhaps we could learn a thing or two from the simple minds of children, Brother Du Qian.

My analogy of the written text explores the meaning of the deeper things in life. For example, the *Sayings of Kong Zhi*. Without a person like you to read and understand the sage's sayings, of what use are they? The world depends on us experiencing it. If none of us were here, would the cosmos exist? If it did exist without us, would it continue to run the same as it does now? What is the cosmos? What is reality?"

Du Qian shook his head. "Your words run in circles and go nowhere. Reality is reality. It exists beyond the shadow of a doubt. Look around you! Your presence doesn't affect whether or not the sky is above us or the ground is beneath our feet!"

Sun Mai didn't seem affected at all by Du Qian's words. "Brother Du Qian, what I am questioning is the very nature of existence. As I'm sure even you would acknowledge, your existence is contingent upon your being conscious to experience it. If you went permanently unconscious, you would eventually cease to exist. Therefore, our conscious perception of the world around us is crucially important. Even more important is the fact that we can *change* reality! We can learn new things and invent new things.

"The Dragon-Phoenix Sect is a perfect example. The Dragon and Phoenix Sovereigns Sunan and Bao imagined a new future, and then they made it happen by founding a new sect. Another example is martial arts. New techniques are being created every day, things which never before existed! We lowly humans can change reality and the future! Is that not an amazing thing?"

Du Qian hesitated for a moment. "Fine. I'll concede that humans can change the future. But that doesn't mean a mere thought on our part can change reality. In your scripture, you essentially argue that the Perfect Realm is not real. That's impossible! The world around us is a *reflection* of the Perfect Realm, and only by making that reflection as close as possible to the true Perfect Realm can we achieve peace and happiness. Even you reflect this thought in your statement that 'the beginning state is the perfect state.' The divisions between the realms are absolute and must be maintained. By implying that there are no such divisions, or that there aren't even any realms to divide, you create the potential for catastrophe of a cosmic level!"

Sun Mai's eyes glittered. "Brother Du Qian, I know that you believe in a non-metaphorical Perfect Realm that exists high above our heads in the sky. But how can you prove its existence? Have you been there?"

"I haven't been *there*," Du Qian replied, "but I've been to the Lower Realms! I've seen the demons and monsters that lurk beneath our feet. Powerful forces exist in the underworld, Sun Mai, and pretending they don't exist won't keep you safe."

Sun Mai chuckled. "Brother Du Qian, I know full well what terrors exist beneath our feet. And that only goes to prove my point. Does it really make sense that concrete evidence exists of the Lower Realms, and yet not a single shred of evidence can be found that the Perfect Realm exists above our heads?

"Darkness and evil spread in the world, and powerful immortals and gods look down and ignore us? If such all-powerful beings exist in the heavens but ignore us mortals down here, how could you view them as being perfect? Even you, a lowly mortal, would stoop to help an injured bird if you came across it, wouldn't you? How then could those supposed perfect immortals in the heavens ignore our suffering down here? If, as you say, our world is a reflection of the Perfect Realm, then explain the Demon Emperor."

"He… he…" Du Qian spluttered. It took him a moment to collect his thoughts. "He's not from this world! He's from—"

"Another realm?" Sun Mai asked. "Within the same cosmos or a different cosmos?" He shook his head. "Brother Du Qian, I don't claim to have all the answers to all the questions that exist. But I do believe that asking questions is the only way to determine the true nature of reality. I'm willing to hear more of your arguments regarding my scripture. Why don't we go for a walk by the lake, and we can further this discussion?"

Du Qian suddenly seemed a bit calmer than before. Placing the scripture scroll into his sleeve, he nodded. "Very well. Let's begin with your statement that beliefs are just systems. How do you reconcile that with what Kong Zhi said in the *Rites of Wan Mei?*"

CHAPTER 64
FLYING CROCODILES?

When Sun Mai and Du Qian returned from the lake, Du Qian was by no means convinced of anything that Sun Mai had been trying to persuade him of. However, he no longer wanted to kill Sun Mai. Furthermore, they reached an agreement whereby every day for the following month, they would have a public debate about one of the topics raised by Sun Mai in his scripture.

During that month, the debates were attended by virtually all members of the Dragon-Phoenix Sect. In some of the debates, Du Qian came out the clear winner, in others. he was completely flummoxed by Sun Mai's confounding logic, or lack thereof. As a result of the debates, many members of the Dragon-Phoenix Sect grew more firm in their belief of the traditional Dehuan teachings. However, many people were swayed by Sun Mai.

Something else happened during the month of debates. News and stories reached the sect about the exploits of other famous martial artists throughout the empire.

For example, a feud had developed between the Purple Cavern

Killer and the Twin Giants of the Zhaoze Swamp. According to stories brought back to the camp by the Eyes of the Phoenix, the Purple Cavern Killer and his apprentice eventually challenged the Twin Giants to a duel. The four of them met in the salt mines south of Zun Valley, where they fought for three days and three nights. No one was present to witness the duel, but it ended in a shocking turn of events: The Twin Giants and the Purple Cavern Killer became sworn siblings.

In an even more astonishing development, the Executioner of the South had sold his services to the Demon Emperor, earning him widespread hatred among the martial artists.

Traders from the Dai Bien Forest brought tales of Hua Pi the Skin Dancer, tales so fantastic that many people refused to believe them. Furthermore, not all the stories were consistent. In some versions, Hua Pi was a midget who had stolen shapeshifting powers from a demon. In other versions, Hua Pi was no midget at all, but rather a beautiful woman with a demented soul who relished the screams of the victims she skinned alive. The only common theme was that Hua Pi was a terrifying figure no one dared to offend.

One of the most popular figures in the stories was the hero Qian Chengsi, who was also called the Stone-Footed King. He had supposedly traveled south from the Yangu Plains on a mission to bring justice to those who trembled under the iron fist of the Demon Emperor. Stories about his exploits reached the sect via information gathered by the Eyes of the Phoenix, as well as from groups of passing refugees. There were multiple stories about Qian Chengsi, but the most sensational was how he had robbed the treasury of Tung-On, then fled to Mount Dao, where he was tracked down by three Lions of Peace, whom he then killed in a fight on top of a cliff.

However, the most sensational tales to reach the camp were about the Timeless Master, who was becoming a figure so well-known that many people considered him to be even more famous than Sunan and Bao. The Timeless Master already had a group of heroes following him that was almost as large as the Dragon-Phoenix Sect. He had a sworn brother now, a great hero named Pei Fu. Rumor had it that the two of them had begun work on a palace somewhere in the southern Banyan Region.

Recently, they had led a force of disciples to execute the corrupt magistrate of Zun City. Not only did they succeed in their mission, on their way out of the city, they ran into a squadron of Demon Emperor soldiers led by none other than the Hate General. A bloody battle was fought in which the Hate General's squadron was completely routed. As for the Hate General, he fled into the swamp north of Zun City, barely escaping with his life.

When Bao heard about the Timeless Master defeating an ogre general, she felt both jealous and irritated, but she also couldn't help but feel a bit of admiration. Of course, little did Bao know that stories of her own exploits, as well as Sunan's, had a similar impact on the many people who heard them.

As the month of debates between Du Qian and Sun Mai drew to a close, the Eyes of the Phoenix finally brought back word about the Shan people.

The Shan was actually a blanket term for a large group of smaller tribes scattered through the north, though mostly the northwest, Banyan Region. From what the Eyes of the Phoenix had seen, most of them looked like normal people, nothing like the bizarre depiction in the *Classic of Mountains and Rivers*. One of the Eyes of the Phoenix insisted that she had glimpsed a headless man among a group of tribesmen she'd spotted, although many of her fellow scouts made fun of her story.

Considering that there was not much to do in the temporary camp other than train and spar, it took little convincing for Sunan to persuade Bao to join him on a trip down the Southern Fei River to look for the mythical Shan people.

Preparations took more than a week, mostly because they needed to prepare a large raft upon which to travel down the river.

Traveling on foot through the thick jungle would have added an element of danger that they preferred to avoid. After word came through that the raft had been acquired, a group set off, including Bao, Sunan, Mao Yun, Wang Tian, Ruan the Flamingo, and five lower-ranking members of each division of the sect. The goal of the journey was to move quickly and without fanfare down the river to Shan territory and determine once and for all whether the mythical version of the Shan people could be found, and whether or not the empyreal hammer truly existed.

They set out from the temporary sect headquarters on a bright, sunlit morning, traveling in a roughly southeasterly direction toward the Southern Fei River. After a full day of travel, they were completely out of the foothills of the mountains and well into the jungle that was the Jian Shu Forest.

From there, the pace slowed. It took about two days to reach the bend in the river where the raft was waiting. Once aboard, their pace quickened as they floated down the Southern Fei.

Occasionally they caught sight of local tribes on the banks of the river, fishing, hunting, or washing. Sometimes there were children playing.

As evening was falling on the first day of travel, Sunan sat by himself at the edge of the raft, fingering a bracelet made of cloth and beads. He had put the bracelet together himself recently; it was a traditional craft that most children in his home village had been adept at.

Should I give it to her? he thought. He looked down at the bracelet for a long moment. It reminded him of his mother and sisters, for whom he had made such bracelets every summer growing up. *It's silly, isn't it? Why would she want a stupid bracelet like this?*

A moment later Wang Tian approached and sat down next to him. Sunan quickly put the bracelet away.

"We'll need to set up camp soon," Wang Tian said. "Thankfully this part of the forest is relatively safe."

"What do you mean *relatively?*"

Wang Tian chuckled. "Well, for one thing, there are no flying crocodiles."

Sunan laughed out loud for a moment. Then, noticing Wang Tian's expression, he said, "Wait, you're serious, aren't you?"

"Of course. You haven't heard the stories of the flying crocodiles down south?"

"Sure I have, but I thought you could only find them in places like Nangu, not the Banyan…"

"Well, that's mostly true. From what I've heard, flying crocodiles can only be found south of the Zun River, so we shouldn't see any up here."

They camped upon the riverbank, and woke early to proceed on their way. An overland trip through the forest would have taken at least ten days in perfect travel conditions, but using the raft cut the travel time down significantly. It was roughly noontime on the third day when they concealed the raft and proceeded inland on foot. Travel progressed rather slowly because of Ruan the Flamingo, but with the assistance of other members of the sect, they managed to set a decent pace.

"My scout spotted that headless man about half a day's travel from here," Wang Tian said.

He led them up a tributary of the Southern Fei, more of a stream than a river. After they had walked along for about two hours, they reached a small pond, where they stopped for a short rest.

Bao knelt down next to the pond and had reached her hands into the water when a strange gruntlike clicking sound echoed out.

Sunan looked up into the trees on the opposite side of the pond, and the blood drained from his face. Sitting there in the branch of a tall tree was an enormous crocodile staring directly at Bao.

As Bao looked up from the water, the crocodile dropped out of the tree and began to fly directly toward her. Before anyone could react, the beast was only about two meters away from her, its jaws opening to reveal a mouthful of sharp teeth.

There was no time to ponder the situation. Sunan quickly leapt into the air toward the flying crocodile, unleashing Rebuke of the Dragon.

Just when the crocodile's jaws were about to snap down on the shocked Bao, two illusory dragons slammed into it, knocking it out of the air and sending it splashing down into the pond.

Sunan landed right next to Bao, drawing his saber as he did. Bao rose to her feet, stepping back and pulling out two daggers. The rest of the party also drew their weapons.

That was when more grunting and clicking sounds filled the air. Upon looking up into the surrounding trees, they saw three more flying crocodiles looking at them from within the canopy above.

"Dammit, Wang Tian," Sunan said. "I thought you said the flying crocodiles lived south of the Zun River!"

"They do!" Wang Tian cried. "These things shouldn't be here."

A raspy voice spoke out from farther within the trees. "They're mine."

As the words were spoken, an old man stepped out into the open. He wore hide garments, and his long white hair hung loosely over his shoulders. His clothing was embroidered with deep-blue cloth, and his right arm was covered with a complicated tattoo. At first, Sunan assumed he was one of the local tribesmen, but Wang Tian's words quickly proved him wrong.

"You're from Zhaoze Swamp, aren't you?" he said.

The old man smiled, reaching up to stroke his scraggly white beard. "You're a sharp one, aren't you? That's right, I'm originally from the swamp. Enough with the chitchat. Hand over your valuables, and then I'll be on my way."

Mao Yun's eyes went wide. "You're trying to rob us?"

The old man let out a low whistle, and the flying crocodiles made more grunting sounds. As for the crocodile that had landed in the pond, it remained under the surface of the water, staring up at Bao.

"I'd prefer to think of it as you people donating to my traveling expenses," he said with a crooked grin.

Bao took a step forward. "Look, old man, we don't have the time for this. Take your lizards and scram."

Within the wooden travel pack strapped to Bao's pack was her Phoenix Crown, but before she could even consider taking it out and putting it on, a cold gleam flickered in the old man's eyes, and he said, "Wrong answer."

Then he made a clicking sound, and the crocodiles all flew into the air.

CHAPTER 65
THE SPEAKER

Flying crocodiles descended from the trees, and the crocodile in the pond burst out with snapping jaws as it attacked Bao. Whizzing sounds could be heard as the old man launched a handful of darts.

He's a qi fighter, thought Bao. As she dodged to the side to avoid the crocodile, Sunan's saber spun through the air to deflect the darts.

Fierce fighting broke out, with two or three members of the Dragon-Phoenix Sect each taking on one of the crocodiles.

As Sunan flew off to fight the old man on the other side of the pond, Bao fostered the spark of rage which had just leapt up in her heart, using it to alter her qi flow.

She had no attention to spare for Sunan or anyone else. She alone fought the flying crocodile which had initially ambushed her. After evading its initial lunging bite, she threw a knife toward its eye, but the blade merely glanced off the top of its head. Then it swung its tail, catching her off guard and sending her flying backward through the trees.

As she was struggling to her feet, it flew toward her again. She focused solely on manipulating the qi within her body, building it up to unleash in the powerful attack she had first invented at the foot of Mount Fohe. In a critical moment like this, there was no time to worry about what Du Qian had said about the danger of cathartic moves like this.

She waited until the last possible moment before dodging to the side, and then she roared in a rage as she swung her hand through the air. Five bands of red energy shot out, slicing through the flying crocodile's armored hide as if it were nothing more than wet paper.

The crocodile didn't even have a chance to react before it was falling to the ground amidst a shower of blood and gore.

The old man fighting Sunan let out a bellow of grief and anger, but he wasn't able to break free from his fight with Sunan.

Bao looked around and saw that the other members of the Dragon-Phoenix Sect were holding their own against the three surviving flying crocodiles. Without hesitation, she leapt to join Sunan in fighting the old man.

Before she could get close enough to land a blow, though, the old man suddenly inhaled deeply and then expelled the breath out of his mouth in a violent blast toward Sunan. Sunan was flung backward, landing hard on his back on the other side of the pond.

Bao slashed her remaining knife toward the old man's throat. The old man dodged, throwing a dart toward her face, which she kicked aside with Dragon Cleaves the Clouds.

As Bao and the old man fought back and forth, Wang Tian and another Dragon-Phoenix fighter faltered in their fight against another of the flying crocodiles, forcing Sunan to leap to their aid.

Moments later, the old man unleashed the same move he had used on Sunan, expelling a powerful breath backed with internal energy. Bao attempted to avoid the move but was hit dead on and flew backward until she slammed into a tree, which knocked the wind out of her.

As she flopped to the ground, gasping for breath, the old man leapt high into the air and threw two darts at her. Her hands were planted on the ground as she struggled to push herself to her feet, and her knife lay a few meters away from her. There was no time for Dragon Cleaves the Clouds or any other move that she could think of.

That was when a blur passed in front of her eyes, resolving itself into the form of Sunan. His sword screamed through the air, knocking down one of the darts. However, the second dart slammed into his shoulder, and the force of the blow sent him spinning off to the side.

Another spark of rage burned to life in Bao's heart as she rose to her feet and struggled to suck in a breath of air.

In that same moment, a growling cry rose up as Mao Yun delivered a killing blow to one of the other flying crocodiles.

As Bao began to circulate her qi to deliver another slash of rage, the old man made a clicking sound, then leapt backward at incredible speed. In the blink of an eye, he vanished into the trees. The flying crocodiles shot into the air, disappearing moments later. Almost as quick as the fight began, it ended.

Bao intentionally kept her rage simmering in case the retreat was a feint, but she turned toward Sunan, who was just now struggling up. She stepped forward to offer a helping hand, then she saw the dart embedded in his shoulder.

"That looks like it hurts," she said.

He grimaced and reached up to touch the dart. "I've had worse," he said.

"Really? When?"

Gripping the exposed end of the dart, he pulled it out and sucked in a deep breath. "Good question."

He tossed the dart to the ground next to him.

Luckily, none of the other Dragon-Phoenix Sect members had received any significant injuries in the short skirmish.

"That's not poisoned, is it?" Mao Yun asked.

Bao squatted down and picked up the dart. The only thing that she could see on the surface was blood. She sniffed it. "Doesn't appear to be. Do you feel anything strange inside of you, Sunan?"

Sunan closed his eyes for a long moment. "No. Just pain."

After taking time to clean Sunan's wound and bind it as best they could, they proceeded on up the stream.

Eventually, Wang Tian pointed out into the forest. "The clearing is just up ahead. That's where the headless man was spotted."

They immediately struck out toward the clearing. Soon, the trees began to clear, and they could see an open space ahead of them. It was also possible to see that the clearing was occupied.

Sitting in the very center, out in the open, was a young woman wearing hide clothing similar to that worn by the old man they had just fought, except that hers was patched with yellow cloth. She sat cross-legged on a low, wide boulder, her eyes closed and her hands resting on her knees.

As Wang Tian cautiously led the way into the open, the young woman's eyes opened.

"I've been waiting for you," she said. "Greetings, Young Dragon. Greetings, Fierce Phoenix." Before anyone could respond, she rose to her feet and hopped nimbly off the boulder. "Please come with me. The True Shan are waiting for you."

The group exchanged glances, but there was little time for discussion, as the young woman was just about to disappear into the trees.

Sunan was the first to step forward and follow.

The young woman led them farther into the forest, where the terrain began to slope upward.

"There's a mountain up ahead," Wang Tian said. "Unnamed, as far as I know."

The young woman stopped walking and looked over her

shoulder. "It has a name. Shenshi Shan." With that, she continued on.

Bao frowned slightly as she walked along next to Sunan. "She has a very strange accent, but I think the name of that mountain is Classical Fei. If I'm right, it means 'holy rock' or something like that."

"Interesting."

The ground sloped upward with increasing steepness. Eventually, they reached a valley filled with small huts and bustling with people dressed like the young woman.

When she led the group into the village, many eyes turned in their direction. However, no one seemed particularly surprised by their arrival, and everyone went about doing whatever they had been doing moments before.

"Welcome to Zhenshan Village," the young woman said. "The True Shan are waiting in the holy cave at the end of the village. Come."

Bao leaned toward Sunan. "It's definitely Classical Fei," she whispered. "The name of their village means 'true shan.' It's hard to say what that 'shan' means, though. Originally I thought it meant mountain, but now I think it might means 'virtue' or maybe 'benevolence.'"

At the end of the valley was a cave that seemed very ordinary in nature. The young woman came to a stop just outside. "I am not worthy to enter," she said, "and neither are the rest of you, save for the Young Dragon and Fierce Phoenix. Please, go in."

Mao Yun lowered his voice and said, "Are you sure this is…"

"Safe?" the young woman completed. "Of course. The True Shan are the epitome of benevolence. They have been waiting for you."

Sunan patted the box with the wind stone in it and then walked into the cave. Bao followed.

The initial tunnel was dark, but faint light gleamed up ahead.

They walked forward cautiously until the tunnel bent to the left, then the right. Then it opened up into a small cavern.

A bizarre sight met their eyes, causing both of their jaws to drop. A fire burned in the middle of the cavern, its flames violet and tinged with green. Seated cross-legged around the fire in a semicircle were five creatures that were obviously the 'headless men' that Wang Tian's scout had spotted. They were clearly not human. Each one had two large eyes on its chest and a wide mouth on its stomach. Their limbs were slender, their fingers and toes longer than a human's. They wore nothing except for loincloths crafted from vegetation.

When Sunan and Bao entered the room, the creatures' eyes were closed, but only a moment later, they opened, and they seemed to shine with profound light.

Sunan swallowed hard to still his beating heart, then clasped his hands and bowed. "I am Fan Sunan. Greetings, Seniors."

Bao followed suit. "I am Shangguan Bao. Greetings, Seniors."

The creatures blinked, and then the one in the center smiled. "We are the Shan," he said. His voice was deep and sonorous, and his accent lilting, something the likes of which neither Sunan nor Bao had ever heard before. "I am the Speaker of this generation. Please, sit and hear my words."

After only the slightest hesitation, Sunan and Bao both sat down cross-legged. Including the five Shan, they now formed a complete circle around the fire.

"We Shan are an ancient people," the Speaker said. "Back when the world was filled with rivers and mountains, we were numerous. Now, our numbers have dwindled, but we have not forgotten the words whispered to us by the ancient winds. For countless generations, our people have waited for a phoenix and a dragon to appear among you humans. According to the ancient winds, that phoenix and dragon would either lead the world into a new era of progress or drag it into darkness.

"The ancient winds told our ancestors that it was only by helping the human phoenix and the human dragon to succeed in walking their path to completion would the world progress as intended. Therefore, there is no need for you to request our assistance. We offer it willingly.

"We know that you possess one of the holy tempest stones." His eyes turned to face Bao. "The instant you touched it, Fierce Phoenix, we sensed you.

"Presumably, you wish to use the empyreal hammer to forge the tempest stone into an object of power." He smiled. "You need not request permission; we give it freely."

Bao and Sunan were at a loss for words.

"Senior Speaker," Sunan said, "we… we…"

The Speaker smiled. "Words are not necessary. We understand. The matter of the tempest stone and empyreal hammer is settled. However, there is another matter we wish to speak of with you, and an offer we wish to make.

"Since ancient times, we Shan have sought truth in the winds, by means of the wind dream. Considering that you are the Young Dragon and the Fierce Phoenix, would you like to join us in a wind dream to seek guidance about the coming days?

"Perhaps we could even catch a glimpse of the future…"

CHAPTER 66
PING

The Speaker produced a conch shell so weathered by time that it looked like a stone teardrop. Its surface was as smooth as jade, and it was just barely possible to see arcane magical symbols and designs carved into the surface. The Speaker raised the conch shell to the mouth on his stomach and then blew into the end.

A blast of wind emerged from the other end of the shell, which, when it touched the violet flames, sent sparks showering out in all directions. The sparks swirled through the cave, spinning around and around until they formed a vortex. With each moment that ticked by, each spark began to shine, until the violet light filling the cave was so bright that Sunan and Bao both closed their eyes.

Everything went still, and then a rushing sound filled their ears.

They opened their eyes to find themselves flying through the air. When they looked down and around, they didn't see their bodies. It felt as if they were simply the wind, streaming through the air. Next to them were five other streams of wind, which were the other True Shan.

One might think that being the wind would impart a feeling of freedom, but it was actually the opposite. They were like drops of water in a river, tiny streams of wind in a raging torrent that swept through the sky. Whispering, murmuring voices echoed in their ears, although it was impossible to make out any distinct words.

A moment later, the voice of the Speaker could be heard, faint, as if it were coming from the other side of the world.

Don't struggle. We will follow the winds wherever they take us.

They were flying along a mountain range filled with towering peaks and stunning valleys. They raced along until the mountains began to drop toward the ground. Then a body of water became visible up ahead.

That's the Mei Lian Sea! Bao said. Or thought. She wasn't sure which. They flew along the edge of the sea until a city rose up on the horizon. *Yu Zhing!*

The winds swept them past Yu Zhing and then north, swirling around the mountain Gor Shan before speeding up the Fei River. They passed Fan, following the river west. Bao was almost sure she caught a glimpse of the inn where she and Mao Yun had first gotten drunk together all those years ago.

Are we going to Mount Fohe? Sunan wondered.

Whether or not that was the initial destination would never be known. Halfway up the Fei River, something changed. Before, they had been speeding along completely unobstructed. But suddenly the winds around them trembled. Then they were tugged off course, pulled south, away from the river.

In addition to the rushing sound of winds, rumbling sounds filled the air.

What's this? the Speaker asked. *The winds are being pulled south against their will...*

As they shot south, mountains rose up ahead of them. Just barely visible in one location in those mountains was a towering palace.

Is that…? Bao said.

Yao Gong Palace? Sunan continued.

The Speaker suddenly spoke in an urgent voice. *The lair of the Demon Emperor. This wind dream has been interfered with. We must leave!*

As they sped toward the palace, they saw a black tempest spring into being, surrounding the entire palace. Then, golden light began to shine up into the heavens. When Bao and Sunan looked up, they were shocked that the sun, the moon, and two dazzlingly bright stars had formed a square up above. Moments later, golden clouds began to fill the sky.

The winds around them were screaming, not because of the speed with which they flowed, but because of fear. Terror.

Sunan and Bao felt themselves shaking violently as a golden-colored rain began to fall around them.

Then their eyes opened.

***

In the middle of the Banyan Region was a mountain that would, in later generations, come to be called Mount Heiping. As a young girl, Hui had once traveled with her master to a secret temple on Mount Heiping. The sect there had been their ally in resisting the Demon Emperor, and she had learned much from them.

After her encounter with the Love General, she decided that she needed to rethink her mission and seek enlightenment on how to proceed. She had traveled south, passing the slow-moving Dragon-Phoenix Sect and entering the Banyan ahead of them. Just as Bao and Sunan had recently done, she rafted down the Southern Fei, then hiked through the jungle to Mount Heiping.

Along the way, she encountered a few dangerous situations, but they were nothing a profound master like herself couldn't handle.

To her surprise, she found that in the location of that future secret temple, there was already a structure in existence. It was also a temple, clearly an ancient one at that, little more than an outline of walls, and almost completely overrun by vegetation.

Something about the place seemed to resonate with her, leading her to wonder who might have built such a structure and why it had been erected in this specific location. She also wondered whether it was connected to the temple she remembered from her youth.

After clearing out a space for herself and erecting a temporary shelter, she sat down cross-legged to meditate and pray.

Time flew by, and she was so engrossed in meditation that she lost track of the time. One day, only moments after the Speaker took out his conch shell far to the north, a tremor ran through Hui. Then her hand twitched, and she opened her eyes and shot to her feet.

"Someone has interfered with my Trance Touch incantation."

***

Countless violet sparks fell down to the ground of the cave, where they danced spasmodically until fading into nothing.

The Speaker slumped in place. Sweat covered his body, and it was the same with the other True Shan, as well as Bao and Sunan.

"What was that?" Bao asked.

"My dream," Sunan said, reaching up to massage his temples.

Surprise flashed in her eyes. "You mean *the* dream?"

"Yes."

"You've had that dream before?" the Speaker asked.

Sunan nodded. "Something like it. Black winds. Golden light. Rain."

Bao thought for a moment, then said, "And then there's my poetry…"

They proceeded to explain a bit about their dreams and poetry.

The Speaker listened thoughtfully, and when they were finished, he sat quietly for a long moment.

"Wind dreams cannot be interfered with externally." His eyes turned up in thought. "Well, perhaps that isn't necessarily true. Or could it be that…" He lapsed into silence.

After another long moment, he sighed. "I must confer with my brothers and sisters about this. For now, please retire to the quarters which have been prepared for you. You may use the empyreal hammer, but you may not take it with you. It must be used in the forges here in the valley. Take this." A command medallion appeared in his hand that appeared to be crafted from shells. He tossed it to Sunan. "If we achieve any enlightenment regarding the wind dream, we will call for you."

***

Ruan went to work immediately, and the days began to pass. As for the rest of the group, they spent time training and sparring. A few of the members of the Shan tribe were already proficient in the cultivation of qi and had begun to fuse it with their traditional fighting style. Although none of them were as powerful as Bao or Sunan, the diversity of their combat arts provided new insights to the members of the Dragon-Phoenix Sect.

An entire month went by. On a few occasions during that time, Sunan almost brought himself to give the cloth bracelet to Bao, but he never did.

One day, Ruan returned from the forges with a long wooden box. It was simply crafted, decorated with a carving of a dragon that had powerful gusts of wind surrounding it.

"It's done," Ruan announced, handing the box to Sunan.

"Is it safe to open?"

Ruan nodded. "It was very difficult to contain the power of the wind, but the job is done."

Sunan opened the box to reveal what appeared to be an ordinary saber.

"It took shape on its own," Ruan explained. "Just like the Phoenix Crown. To be honest, I'm not sure what its powers are."

Sunan reached into the box and grabbed the saber by the hilt. When he did, he felt a tingling sensation in his arm, like wind flowing through him. The effect faded away quickly.

He performed a few forms with the saber.

"Good weight and balance," he commented.

After a few moves, in which nothing out of the ordinary happened, he shrugged. "Perhaps it needs to be used in real combat to reveal its powers."

"Likely so," Ruan said. "The power of the wind from that stone is definitely inside of it."

"What should I call it?" Sunan mused.

"The Blade of Tempests?" Mao Yun said.

"Too wordy," Bao said.

"The Broadsword of Winds?" Wang Tian offered.

Sunan and Bao looked at each other, then shook their heads.

"The Wind Saber," Sunan said.

Bao smiled. "I like it."

***

Over the course of the past month, the True Shan had sent no word regarding the dream. Now that the Wind Saber was complete, Sunan and Bao inquired of the tribe elders and were informed that they could leave.

The same young woman who had led them to the tribe brought the news. "If the True Shan wish it, they will contact you," she said. "Now, if you're ready to go, I'll lead you back to the river."

And thus began their return to the western Banyan Region.

Pushing the raft upstream with poles was still faster than

traveling on foot. Days flowed by, and eventually they disembarked and began to head on foot back toward Chrysanthemum Lake. As time continued to pass, the little cloth bracelet Sunan had tucked away in his robe started to seem heavier and heavier.

They were noticed by a Dragon-Phoenix Sect patrol when they were about a day from the camp.

"Dragon Sovereign Sunan! Phoenix Sovereign Bao! Greetings!" The disciples who met them excitedly went on to explain that the new sect headquarters was complete and that the sect had merely been waiting for their return before moving into Zun Shan.

They hurried back to the temporary camp as quickly as possible.

Upon arriving, they were received by Sun Mai and leaders of the sect. Everyone was in high spirits and itching to move into the new sect headquarters.

"I've been there myself," Sun Mai said. "It's a grand sight to be sure. However, considering you've been gone for so long, a feast is in order. Tonight we dine and drink, and we shall worry about Zun Shan tomorrow."

Just when the festivities were beginning, a guard hurried over to Bao and Sunan. "Dragon Sovereign Sunan, Phoenix Sovereign Bao, a visitor has arrived and seeks an audience."

"Who is it?" Bao asked.

"A young lady surnamed Ping. She says she brings a message from the Timeless Master!"

CHAPTER 67
A LETTER

Ping was pretty but not beautiful, with a charming smile that radiated sincerity. She wore ordinary garments and was unarmed. Strapped at her waist was a corked gourd bottle with the character "alcohol" painted on it.

Clasping her hands formally, she said, "Greetings, Dragon Sovereign Sunan. Greetings, Phoenix Sovereign Bao. I am Ping Fangrou, loyal disciple of the Timeless Master. Because of the unique style of martial arts I've developed, my friends call me the Drunken Crane. I am here to offer formal greetings on the behalf of the Timeless Master and to deliver a message.

"Dragon Sovereign, Phoenix Sovereign, it was not my intention to interrupt your feast. I'll take my leave now and return in the morning." With that, she bowed and prepared to leave.

"Hold on," Bao said. "There's no need to leave. Please, join us!"

"Yes, please do," Sunan added. "I'm curious about this unique martial art of yours."

Ping Fangrou hesitated. "I really couldn't prevail upon you in such a fashion…"

"Nonsense," Bao said. "We insist."

Ping Fangrou's smile lit up the room as she once again clasped her hands. "If you insist!"

The tables were rearranged so that Ping Fangrou could sit near Bao and Sunan. Food and drink were served, and a few pleasantries were exchanged.

Then, Ping Fangrou filled her drinking vessel. Almost immediately, the fragrant aroma of sorghum wine rose up.

"Sorghum wine!" she said, her eyes lighting up. "It seems the rumors are true!"

Sunan filled his own glass and looked over at her. "Rumors?"

Ping Fangrou chuckled. "Forgive me, Dragon Sovereign. Most stories about the Young Dragon and the Fierce Phoenix have to do with your adventures and martial arts. But other stories exist that I find more interesting. I'd heard that the two of you are fond of sorghum wine, although I'd always wondered if it was true or not." She looked at Bao. "I've also heard that you are especially skilled in the art of drinking, Phoenix Sovereign."

Bao smiled. "I won't deny it, Heroine Ping." She raised her cup. "Welcome to the Dragon-Phoenix Sect. I wish you good health and long life!"

"Many thanks! I will drain my cup, but please do not feel obliged to follow suit!" With that, Ping drained the entire cup of sorghum wine.

"Don't drink too quickly, Heroine Ping!" Sunan said, chuckling.

Ping smiled and refilled her drinking vessel. "Fear not, Dragon Sovereign. The truth is that I'm somewhat of an expert when it comes to drinking. Actually, my style of martial arts benefits from the boost provided by a healthy bit of alcohol!"

"Really?" Bao said, clearly intrigued.

"Really!" Ping Fangrou replied. "With enough alcohol inside of me, I'm almost impossible to hit! And my blows become difficult to predict and counter."

Bao laughed in response.

Ping Fangrou raised an eyebrow. "Phoenix Sovereign, I'm not joking! I can demonstrate if you'd like, but I need to drink a bit more."

Bao was slightly taken aback but could see the sincerity in Ping Fangrou's expression. They continued to eat, drink, and chat, until roughly two hours had passed. Every time Ping Fangrou drank, she drained her cup but encouraged those she was drinking with to drink more slowly.

Gradually, her eyes became slightly cloudy, and her speech just barely slurred.

Eventually, the conversation returned to martial arts. By that point, despite the fact that Ping Fangrou had drank more than anyone else, she actually seemed to be less inebriated than before.

Bao's head was spinning slightly. "Heroine Ping, I really am intrigued by this martial arts style of yours. What do you say to an exhibition match? You and me. Right here, right now!"

Ping Fangrou's eyes widened. "Oh no, Phoenix Sovereign. I'm definitely not worthy of your martial arts. Besides, you're clearly much more skilled and powerful than me!"

"Nonsense," Bao said, rising to her feet. "I can tell that you're not much behind me. And I promise not to use any of my more powerful techniques. Please, humor me!" She extended her hand toward the open space in the middle of the room.

Ping Fangrou hesitated for a moment, but then her smile widened and she stood up. "Very well, Phoenix Sovereign, if you insist!"

As she walked over toward the open area, she stumbled, lurching to the left and almost falling to the ground before jerking her torso back in the opposite direction and then shuffling to a stop. Chuckles sounded from the crowd of gathered members of the Dragon-Phoenix Sect.

"Be careful, Heroine Ping!" someone called out.

"Yeah, don't get yourself knocked out before the fighting begins."

Ping Fangrou turned to face Bao, swaying back and forth in place.

Bao took a ready stance. "Are you sure you're up to a fight, Heroine Ping?"

"Of course," she replied, striking a stance. It was an odd stance, in which she leaned back slightly and held her hands loosely out in front of her, her fingers curled as if holding a drinking vessel.

"Is there a name for this stance of yours?" Bao asked.

Ping Fangrou chuckled. "Stance of the Drunken Cat! Phoenix Sovereign, please, you make the first move."

"Very well." With that, Bao dashed forward and lashed out with a palm strike. She didn't draw upon any powerful technique, sticking to an ordinary blow. She even held back a bit of strength.

However, just when she was sure her palm strike was about to land on her opponent's shoulder, Ping Fangrou twisted and stumbled to the side, and Bao's palm struck nothing but air.

The slightest of frowns could be seen on Bao's face as she spun, sending a kick flying toward Ping Fangrou's waist.

However, Ping Fangrou swiveled in a circle, and Bao's foot caught nothing but fabric. Bao's frown deepened.

"You'll have to do better than that, Phoenix Sovereign!" Ping Fangrou said with a respectful nod of her head.

Bao threw a few more palm strikes and kicks, and yet Ping Fangrou evaded every single one. Bao was soon fighting at full strength, but whenever her blows were about to land, Ping Fangrou twisted or lurched or stumbled in an unpredictable way.

Bao's frown had turned into a smile. "Very impressive! All right, no more holding back. See if you can dodge my Fury of the Phoenix."

She swept her arms through the air, unleashing a wide beam of blinding white light that sped directly toward Ping Fangrou.

"Woah!" Ping Fangrou blurted. "Drunken Dodge!" With that, she bent, dipped, and weaved in an elegant flow of drunkenness, narrowly evading Bao's Fury of the Phoenix.

"I think I need to learn a few of your moves, Heroine Ping!" Bao said. "However, I have a question…" Bao unleashed a few more kicks and palm strikes, all of which Ping Fangrou evaded.

"Ask away, Phoenix Sovereign. I could do this all day."

"Can you do anything but dodge? Fury of the Phoenix!" She swept her arms out again, sending another wide beam of light shooting toward Ping Fangrou.

Ping Fangrou yet again evaded the blast. "I wouldn't dare to strike at you, Phoenix Sovereign!"

Bao grinned. "If you don't, then I'm going to knock you flat on your face! Phoenix Torment!" Bao's finger shot with lightning-like speed toward Ping Fangrou's neck.

Just when she was sure that her blow would land, Ping Fangrou said, "Dip of the Drunken Cobra!" Her torso then bent back at a seemingly impossible angle, causing Bao's blow to swing wide. Ping Fangrou's head nearly touched the ground before she sprang back and thrust her palm toward Bao's shoulder.

Bao's eyes went wide, but there was no time for her to adjust her momentum.

Ping Fangrou's blow landed with a smack.

It was a mundane attack, not a powerful martial arts technique, but it was a blow nonetheless, and Bao, already drunk and off balance, stumbled backward.

Gasps rang out in the room, and everything went quiet.

The blood drained from Ping Fangrou's face, and she suddenly didn't seem drunk at all.

A moment of silence passed, which actually lasted for only the briefest of moments, but to Ping Fangrou it seemed like an eternity.

Then she clasped her hands and bowed deeply.

"Phoenix Sovereign, please forgive my impertinence!"

Bao brushed her shoulder off and laughed. "Are you kidding me? That was amazing! Incredible!"

As Bao hurried forward to lift Ping Fangrou up from her bow, Sunan began to clap, then Mao Yun, then Li Runfa, until soon the entire room was cheering. Ping Fangrou smiled, and her cheeks turned a bit more flushed than they had been before.

"Come, come," Bao said. "Let's sit and talk more about this drunken martial art of yours! How did you come up with it?"

***

The following morning, many in the sect woke with pounding heads and dry throats. After a morning of recovery, preparations began to move the sect. As the members of the sect bustled about packing belongings and readying pack animals, Bao and Sunan met again with Ping Fangrou, who requested that only the three of them be present.

"It is with great pleasure and solemnity that I offer you this message from the Timeless Master," she said, holding out a sealed envelope with both hands.

Sunan took it respectfully, and then he broke the seal.

"Dragon Sovereign," Ping Fangrou said, "the Timeless Master insisted that only the two of you read the letter, although not out loud. He also requested that you burn the letter after reading it."

Sunan's eyes widened, but after a moment he nodded. "I understand."

"I'll take my leave, then," Ping Fangrou said, hurrying out of the tent.

With that, Sunan pulled the letter out of the envelope and unfolded it. After glancing it over, he handed it to Bao. "You read it first. You read faster anyway."

Bao began to read the letter silently.

Dragon Sovereign. Phoenix Sovereign.

I regret that I cannot personally come to visit you. Matters here are at a critical juncture, and I cannot leave.

I have sent this message to you with one of my most trusted disciples, Ping Fangrou. Do not hesitate to make use of her skills while she is with you.

I need to share information with you about the Demon Emperor, information that few people in the world are privy to. Unfortunately, I cannot reveal why I have such intimate knowledge of him, and I can only hope that you will trust my words. If we can ever meet in person one day, I will offer a more detailed explanation.

The Demon Emperor is not from this world, and he is a force more powerful or dangerous than you can imagine. He was a twisted and evil person even before coming to these lands, and in fact, the only way he opened a portal to come here was by killing thousands of innocent people in his home world.

The events that led to his arrival in Qi Xien left him injured and damaged, but with each year that passes, he recovers more of his previous power. Before long, there will be no one in this world who can challenge him, not even the Gods and Immortals in the so-called Perfect Realm.

We must bring an end to the Demon Emperor!

Although I cannot be sure, I think it is fate that allowed some of us to rise up as powerful martial artists. Those of us who wield these powers must work together. We must grow stronger and work as a team. We must fight!

I've heard tales of people fleeing to distant lands such as Naqan or the lands of the Hechi. Believe me, that is just a delaying of the inevitable.

I propose an alliance within the martial world, a sect of

sects, whose power will rival the empire's. When we are strong enough, we can emerge from the shadows and launch an assault on Yao Gong Palace, close the breach between worlds, and destroy the Demon Emperor.

Please think long and hard about my words, and when you are ready to respond, send word back with Ping Fangrou.

It is with the greatest respect that I conclude this long letter. I hope that next time, we can meet face to face!

Li Buwei

CHAPTER 68
BRONZE DRUM

I, Fan Sunan, hereby swear that I will devote my life to the downfall of the Demon Emperor. Be it by sword or flame, be it by fair means or foul, he shall die. As sect leader of the Golden Dragon Sect, I hereby swear loyalty to Chieftainess Shangguan Bao and the Pure Phoenix Sect. Henceforth, we shall strive relentlessly toward our mutual goal of bringing peace and justice to all of Qi Xien!

I, Shangguan Bao, hereby swear to devote my life to the death of the Demon Emperor. Be it by sword or flame, be it by fair means or foul, he will be exterminated. As chieftainess of the Pure Phoenix Sect, I hereby swear loyalty to Sect Leader Fan Sunan and the Golden Dragon Sect. Henceforth, we shall live with one goal in mind: bringing peace and justice to Qi Xien and bringing destruction to the Demon Emperor!

Those were the words that had been spoken by Sunan and Bao years ago in Daolu. Neither of them had forgotten the oaths they had given voice to that night, but never had they been presented with a chance to actively pursue the goals they had both sworn to pursue.

Now, the Timeless Master was essentially expressing the same sentiments that already existed in their hearts: The Demon Emperor must be brought to an end!

After reading the letter, Sunan put it down on the table and looked at Bao. "Do we even need to discuss our answer?"

She shook her head. "This fight against the Demon Emperor needs a leader, and I have the feeling this Timeless Master is that leader."

"At some point we need to meet him in person."

"Agreed."

Bao wrote the response to the Timeless Master, which they handed over to Ping Fangrou to deliver back to him.

Then, Bao set about burning the letter from the Timeless Master, with Ping Fangrou present to witness it.

"Dragon Sovereign, Phoenix Sovereign, may I presume so much as to ask the nature of your response? Although I didn't read Master Li's letter to you, I'm aware of the request he made. As for your letter, it will remain sealed, of course, but my heart already itches to know how you have responded."

Bao smiled. "Of course we agree."

A grin broke out on Ping Fangrou's face. "Wonderful!"

"Heroine Ping," Bao continued, "I truly hope that we can meet again soon. I'm going to ponder the drunken martial arts you use, and next time, let's see if you manage to get another blow past my defenses!"

"I can hardly wait, Phoenix Sovereign." Ping Fangrou clasped her hands and bowed deeply, then turned and left.

Bao rose to her feet to leave, and Sunan followed suit. However, before she could walk out, Sunan said, "Bao, um…"

She turned. "Yes?"

"I, well… I made something for you. Kind of silly, I know, but back where I grew up, we used to make things like this a lot." He pulled out the bracelet he'd made and handed it her.

Bao blinked and took the bracelet. "You made this?" she asked, looking down at it.

Sunan cleared his throat. "Yeah, I know it's silly, you don't have to wear it or anything."

"I don't think anyone has ever made me anything before. I mean, not as a gift." She looked up into his eyes. "Thank you."

"It's nothing," he said. "All right, I have some packing to do. I'll see you again in a bit." With that, he hurried past her and left the tent.

Bao looked back down at the bracelet, and a faint smile appeared on her face.

***

Sunan hurried through the bustling camp toward his own tent. The entire way, he could feel his face burning and was convinced that it was as red as an apple.

That was so stupid. She's definitely laughing at me now.

Before he could put any more thought into it, he arrived at his tent and found Sun Mai standing there waiting for him.

Sun Mai smiled, and as soon as Sunan saw that smile, his heart flip-flopped. It wasn't Sun Mai's usual smile. There was something profound about it, something both sad and happy at the same time.

"What's wrong?" Sunan asked.

Sun Mai took a deep breath. "I think the time has come for me to leave."

Although Sunan was surprised, he wasn't quite shocked. He had suspected for some time that something like this would happen eventually, especially after Sun Mai had stepped down as chief minister to work on his scripture. "Where will you go?"

Sun Mai's gaze shifted toward the southeast. "I want to go to Rong Shan."

"Mount Rong?" Sunan understood. "One of the five peaks?"

"Yes. I've been to Zhifu Shan and Zun Shan. The remaining of the five peaks are Gor Shan, Lu Shan, and Rong Shan. I feel that to truly understand the world, I should climb all five of them."

"And after that?"

"I don't know. I need to spread word about my teachings, and I can't do that unless I move around. By the way, what message did the Timeless Master send?"

"He wants us to join forces to fight the Demon Emperor."

Sun Mai nodded. "I guessed as much. When the time comes to strike the final blow, I hope to be there as well."

"Me too. Are you going out alone?"

"I would like to take a few of my pupils with me, as long as you and Bao agree. Mao Mei is one of the brightest, but she's a Dragon Lord, so she will stay behind. A few of my other students such as Shisan and Guo Fu have already expressed interest in joining me."

"Of course. Take anything you need from the supplies."

Sun Mai reached into his robe and pulled out a bamboo scroll. "Take this, Sunan. It's a copy of my scripture, one that I personally transcribed."

Sunan accepted it. "You know, Sun Mai, even though we never swore any oaths, I feel like we are brothers."

"Me too." He reached out and clasped Sunan's arm. "Forever."

"Forever," Sunan said.

***

The Dragon-Phoenix Sect settled into their new headquarters. The official name was the Dragon Phoenix Temple, but most disciples in the sect took to calling it the Palace of Sunan and Bao.

Days went by, and the sect began to fall into routines. Days turned into weeks, weeks into months.

Seasons came and went.

Eventually the seasons turned into years. At first, Sunan and Bao had assumed the True Shan would eventually send them a message, but no word ever came.

The sect continued to grow slowly, and it didn't take long before Sunan and Bao did exactly as the Timeless Master had suggested and began to actively resist the Demon Emperor. Teams of disciples numbering three to five were sent to most of the major cities, including Huisheng, Zun City, Xuanlu, Yu Zhing, Fan, and Nansun. They even sent teams to the more distant locations like Qi Fao and Ti Fan. Of course, far to the north in Daolu, spies had been left behind after the city fell, and contact had long since been established with them.

The tasks assigned to such teams were to destabilize the Demon Emperor's organization. Weapon supplies were stolen, treasuries raided, key buildings burned to the ground. There were even certain cases of important officials suddenly dying in the middle of the night…

Sunan and Bao went out on some of the most difficult tasks and missions of all. Although they itched to meet with the Timeless Master in person, the timing was never right, and their paths never crossed.

Stories of martial heroes swept through the lands. More powerful fighters were rising up everywhere, and the Dragon-Phoenix Sect wasn't the only one causing problems for the empire. The Timeless Master had made contact with many in the martial arts world, and thanks to his leadership, the resistance was relatively organized. Rumors were also spreading that the nomadic tribes in the Yangu Plains were uniting under the influence of a powerful leader, and that raiding parties were beginning to harass the north.

Something else happened that caught everyone off guard. The teachings of Sun Mai caused a huge upheaval among the common people, the martial arts circles, and the scholars. For generations, the teachings of Kong Zhi had been the guiding spiritual force in Qi Xien, as embodied in the religion known as Dehua. According to

Dehua, the world of man was imperfect, but humans could aspire to perfection by emulating the principles of the Perfect Realm and by following the will of the Enlightened Goddess Xian Nu Shen.

However, Sun Mai's scripture provided a very strong argument that the Perfect Realm was a mental construct. The mere concept was viewed as heretical by many, especially the traditionalist Dehua priests and the scholars. As for the Demon Emperor, he cared little for the religious beliefs of the populace, as long as it didn't interfere with his rule. Therefore, nothing was done to suppress the new teachings and beliefs, which were spreading like wildfire.

Sun Mai even produced a second scripture devoted to the subject of dialogue, detailing why having open conversations with people of all sorts was important. That was another huge deviation from Dehua, which emphasized etiquette, strictly defined social roles, and following traditions.

In some ways, this religious revolution was more momentous than the struggles between the martial artists and the Demon Emperor.

In addition to advancing in their martial arts, Sunan and Bao spent more and more time with each other. Hardly a day went by that they didn't dine together, and their sparring sessions often lasted entire mornings. This did not go unnoticed by the members of the sect, and soon the once-forgotten rumors began to spread again.

"I heard a rumor that Dragon Sovereign Sunan and Phoenix Sovereign Bao are going to get engaged soon!"

"Back in Daolu, they weren't enemies, but they definitely weren't friends. Who would have thought this would happen one day?"

"You people are thinking too much into it. They're just carrying out their duties as leaders of the sect…"

"They didn't look like they were carrying out any duties when they went on that moonlit stroll the other night…"

Although few people took note, Bao often wore a cloth bracelet.

***

The Bone General was sipping tea when the Golden Immortal rushed into the room.

"The opportunity has finally come!" the Golden Immortal said.

The Bone General looked up. "It's about damned time!"

"This just came from my contact in the Dragon-Phoenix Sect." The Golden Immortal put an opened envelope on the table, which the Bone General picked up.

After reading the letter in the envelope, the Bone General chuckled. "They're going to Zhaoze Lake to see the pearl tigers? Are they children?"

The Golden Immortal snorted coldly. "More like fools."

"It doesn't matter. This the perfect opportunity. Zhaoze Lake is only about three days from here. Prepare the bronze drum. We leave immediately."

***

As Hui descended a mountain she now knew to be Shenshi Shan, she held a weathered seashell in her hand. She had spent months in Zhenshan Village with the True Shan and had experienced mind-opening enlightenment the likes of which she had never before experienced in life.

But now she faced a crossroads.

"Do I go back and finish my work with Bao and Sunan?" she murmured. "Or follow the advice of the True Shan? What would Master have done?"

She hiked through the jungle for some distance until she was back at the Southern Fei River, standing in front of the small boat she had procured from some local tribesmen.

Climbing into the boat, she looked to the west. "Zun Shan and the Palace of Sunan and Bao?" Then she looked east. "Or the Eastern

Archipelagos? The Defeat at Heart's Ridge will come eventually, and if the True Shan are right, those islands are very likely the key to success. The Kun-Peng Pipes. I could be gone for years…"

After a long moment of contemplation, she shoved her boat off the riverbank and turned it east.

CHAPTER 69
FOOTPRINTS

A biting wind swept the upper reaches of Zun Shan as a small group emerged from the Dragon Phoenix Temple and began to make their way down the mountain.

Proceeding carefully down the mountain path was a group that included some of the top figures in the Dragon-Phoenix Sect. In addition to Sunan and Bao were Mao Yun, Wang Tian, Lin Cuirou, and Li Runfa. Including the other lower-ranking members of the sect, they had a group of twenty. After the formation of the Dragon-Phoenix Sect, Li Runfa had again declined to take any formal position or title. However, in a secret meeting with Sunan and Bao, they agreed to his proposal to act as the sect's spymaster.

"Was it really necessary to spread rumors that we're going to look at the pearl tigers?" Bao asked.

Li Runfa chuckled. "I know of at least three members of the sect who are sending regular reports out to other groups. I've confirmed that one of them is working for the Timeless Master, and one of them is probably an imperial informant. But I'm not sure about the other. In any case, if I know of three, I wouldn't be surprised if there are more."

"I get it," Bao said, "you want to control the information. But pearl tigers? Really? Who would be stupid enough to believe that we would climb down the mountain and go all the way to Zhaoze Lake just to see some fluffy white tigers?"

"Good question," Li Runfa said with a wry smile. "In any case, this meeting with the Scorpion Swordsman of Zhe Valley is too important to leave to chance."

"I still can't get over these names. Scorpion Swordsman?" Bao laughed.

"Don't forget you control a group called the Claws of the Phoenix, one of whom is known as Flying Death. And don't get me started about Dragon Lord Lin Cuirou's nickname…"

"The Emerald Hunk?" Bao rolled her eyes. "Well, in any case, I'm very curious to see this Scorpion Swordsman's technique. How many men does he lead?"

"Fifty. They're already part of the loose coalition created by the Timeless Master, the same as us, but they have no formal alliances with any other groups. Having formal allies like them to the south would definitely be a benefit to us."

Upon reaching the lower parts of the mountain, they didn't go north toward Chrysanthemum Lake, but rather south toward the Heiping Valley. It was a journey of several days, two of which were spent traveling along the southern bank of Lake Liyu, which occupied the center of the valley. After leaving the lake, they circled the foothills as they headed southwest toward Zhaoze Lake.

Zhaoze Lake was nestled in the foothills of the very same mountains that eventually rose up into Zun Shan and also the same mountains that formed Heiping Valley. It was considered one of the major lakes in the southern regions, along with other large lakes like Chrysanthemum Lake, Lake Liyu, Bixie Lake, and Nai'an Lake.

However, it was the smallest of that group and was unique

in that it had a large island right in its center, which was where the pearl tigers called their home. The pearl tigers also roamed the surrounding hills, but they were heavily concentrated on the island itself. In many parts of the Banyan Region, the white hides of pearl tigers were used in ceremonial attire, and occasionally, live tigers would become the pets of powerful tribe leaders.

At one point when Sunan and Bao were walking along in relative privacy, Sunan said, "I heard that the growl of a pearl tiger can put you to sleep if you're not careful!"

"Oh?" Bao said.

"Yeah, I'm kind of excited to see them. I read about them in a book once when I was young."

"Oh," Bao replied.

He looked over at her. "What, you're not excited about seeing the tigers?"

"Um, sure. But our mission is to meet the Scorpion Swordsman, not see some tigers. Besides, what's the big deal about some tigers, even if they are white?"

Sunan gave a light snort. "Well, I've never seen a tiger."

Bao's eyes widened. In Yu Zhing, tigers were not exactly common, but they were no rarity among the extremely rich noble houses. "Really? Oh, well in that case, maybe we *should* visit the island after all."

One night, about half a day's journey from the lake itself, they struck camp. The area was relatively remote, with nothing even resembling human habitation. The closest thing to it was a trading post a few hours south, on the bank of the Zun River, which was usually the final stop for trading caravans before braving the mountain passes that led to the Kushen Basin.

Although the temperature toward the summit of Zun Shan was frigid, this far south, things were much warmer and more humid, so some of the group slept under the stars while others pitched tents among the scattered trees.

The mood in the group was one of anticipation, both to see the lake and the tigers and to see the Scorpion Swordsman.

In a nearby tree was a zhen bird, preening its feathers. As the moon rose and the night grew deep, the zhen bird fell asleep.

***

Meanwhile, back in the Dragon-Phoenix Sect, Du Qian and Ruan the Flamingo were walking down a passage toward one of the many storerooms in the depths of the palace.

Walking as quickly as he could with his crutch, Ruan said, "I have to tell you, Master Du, I've never created anything like this before."

Du Qian sniffed. "I would imagine not, considering it took you over two years."

"To be honest, the branch you provided, despite having become the heart of the object and the source of its power, only makes up a tiny portion of the final version. As for that case full of magic bronze you provided from Naqan, I used every last bit of it, just like you requested."

"And the iron nails from Dhamma?"

"Yes, I used all of them."

They reached a door, which Ruan unlocked with a heavy iron key. He pushed the door open and then led the way in, holding his lantern high to illuminate the room.

The sight which met their eyes caused Du Qian to gasp. "This…"

Ruan grinned. "Impressive, isn't it? Shall we go for a ride to test it out?"

***

At first, everyone assumed that Sunan was sleeping late. It was only after the morning meal was finished and they began to break camp that they realized he wasn't in his tent at all.

Then the assumption was that he had left to meditate or practice his Wu-Sunan forms in solitude.

Bao packed his tent for him.

However, as the morning wore on, he never returned to the camp, and anxiety began to mount, especially in Bao.

"The lookouts didn't see anything?" Bao wondered, her voice tight with anxiety. "They didn't fall asleep, did they?"

"Xu Zhang was on guard during the third watch," Mao Yun said. "He remembers Sunan walking out of the camp in the night, presumably to relieve himself. He didn't think much of it, and when the end of his watch came only a few minutes later, he forgot to mention the situation to Yin Zheng, who replaced him. Yin Zheng didn't see any movement for the entirety of his watch."

"Could he have fallen victim to some beast? A pearl tiger?"

Mao Yun shook his head. "I refuse to believe that the Dragon Sovereign would be bested by a giant fluffy cat. Impossible."

"Maybe the Scorpion Swordsman kidnapped him?"

"Without a fight? Unlikely."

Wang Tian had already begun to scour the area for clues, and before long, turned up just that.

"Look here," he said, pointing to the ground. He and Bao were currently about a hundred meters away from the campsite. "These are Sunan's footprints. And right about here, they just disappear. But look at this. This is the remnant of another footprint, leading away from the camp. Look how big it is."

The footprint looked to be half again as big as any ordinary human footprint.

Bao's face drained of blood.

"This way," Wang Tian said. He led the way a bit farther south. "Here's another. Whoever this person is, he's not only huge, he's light on his feet and knows how to walk without leaving many tracks. However, the farther away from the camp he gets, the less he cares about being followed." More and more footprints appeared, until even Bao was able to follow them with little trouble.

Roughly five hundred meters south of the camp, they found hoofprints.

Bao took a deep breath. "That horse must have been huge."

Wang Tian nodded. "It's a warhorse to be sure, a big one. The only time I've ever seen someone riding a horse that big…"

"Was back in Daolu." Bao's hands clenched into fists. "There's only one person this could be…"

The person to speak the name was neither Wang Tian nor Bao. A female voice echoed through the trees, a voice that could only belong to someone spectacularly beautiful.

"The Bone General."

Bao swiveled in the direction of the voice, daggers dropping down into her hands out of her sleeves. Wang Tian pulled the short bow off of his back and nocked an arrow.

A woman stepped out from behind a tree some distance away. She had long crimson hair and wore pink robes. Her face was beautiful in an almost otherworldly way, her figure both lithe and curvaceous.

Bao's jaw tightened. "You… You're the Love General. What are you doing here? What did you do with Sunan?"

"I did nothing. It was the Bone General."

"Why should I believe that? I know all about what happened between you and Sunan. He told me. You've been obsessed with him for years." Bao had her wooden travel pack strapped to her back, within which was her Phoenix Crown. However, considering how bizarre ogres were, she didn't dare to try to use it so overtly.

"I didn't reveal myself to get in an argument with you, girl. Listen to me, and listen well. I mean you no harm, and I mean Sunan no harm. It's the opposite, in fact. In a moment of laxness, I failed to prevent the Bone General from taking Sunan in the night.

"You wish to speak of obsession, child? The Bone General

mastered that art long before you were even born, and right now the object of that obsession is you. He will not rest until he has you, and when he does, you cannot even imagine the torment you would experience before you die. To reach that goal, he's taken Sunan.

"He will use Sunan as bait to get to you, and once he has you, he'll probably make you watch Sunan's torturous death as part of the twisted punishment he wants to inflict on you.

"We need to act quickly. Go back and get your top fighters. Mao Yun. Lin Cuirou. Ouyang Jian. Chang Peng. Yin Zheng. If we hurry, we might be able to catch the Bone General off guard. I don't think he realizes I'm here, and that will give us a slight advantage."

Inwardly, Bao's heart was pounding with both fear and hesitation, but outwardly, she kept her face cold and stony. "There's no way I could possibly trust—"

"I don't need your trust, girl. I need your strength. I would do this alone, but as I'm sure you can imagine, I'm no match for the Bone General in a fight, and he'll definitely have men with him. Probably that Golden Immortal. Time is of the essence here. The Bone General tends to be impatient, and I fear that if we don't act quickly, he will harm Sunan."

She stepped forward. "There is no time for hesitation. Are you with me, or not?"

***

Some distance to the south, in a small town that functioned as a trading post, was a large inn. Inside, a single candle illuminated the cramped extents of one of the rooms. Lying on the bed, bound with thick leather straps, was Sunan. His eyes flashed with anger and also a bit of fear, but he didn't move.

The Bone General loomed above him, toying with a serrated knife.

"Are they on the way yet?" he asked.

Leaning up against the door was the Golden Immortal. "Not yet."

The Bone General placed the tip of the knife on Sunan's cheek and gently ran it down his face toward his throat, exerting just enough pressure to push down onto his skin without cutting it or drawing blood.

"They'd better hurry," the Bone General said. "I'm in a mood to slice bones."

CHAPTER 70
FIERCE FIGHTING

Bao stood about two meters to the left of the Love General, in a copse of trees on a hill slightly northeast of the trading post.

A thousand thoughts were running through her head.

Is Sunan safe?

What is the Love General's true goal?

Will she betray us?

Should we betray her?

The trading post was not quite large enough to be called a town, but it was big enough to have a main road running through the middle, as well as a public square. As Bao looked down at the place, she saw someone hurrying out of the trading post's eastern gate. It was Wang Tian.

"I understand that you hate and distrust me," the Love General said suddenly.

Bao glanced at her out of the corner of her eye but didn't respond.

The Love General sighed lightly. "Although, I do have to remind you that you're the one who tried to kill me first."

"What?" Bao said. "When did I try to kill you?"

"Back outside of Daolu. I was simply sitting there at the table, you and your people burst in and tried to kill me."

Bao's jaw tightened as an image flashed through her mind of a knife stabbing into Yang Ziqiong's eye. Then she remembered how her Phoenix Palm had disappeared into the Love General like a pebble tossed into a lake. It was true that the Love General hadn't struck the first blow; she had to admit that. And neither had the Love General been directly responsible for any of the casualties that night among Bao and Sunan's friends.

"If you're really trying to help save Sunan," Bao said, "then tell me why I couldn't hurt you back in that tent. Hitting you felt like... it felt like hitting a soft pillow."

"We ogres, our home..."

"You're from another realm, I know."

The Love General's eyes flickered with the briefest moment of surprise. "Yes, we are not from this world. Suffice to say, the divine energy that you call qi doesn't affect us in the same way. We are connected to it intimately, but we cannot use it and are mostly immune to its effects. It's a function of the natural and magical laws that govern the universe and is a complicated matter that even I don't fully understand. However, although ogres are mostly immune to qi... each and every one of us has a weakness."

Bao looked over in surprise. "Weakness?"

"Yes. A different weakness for each ogre, again, a function of the natural and magical laws around us. I hope you'll forgive me if I decline to tell you my own. Ogres are very protective of that secret. Of course, considering my vast network of agents throughout the empire, and my skills, I've managed to uncover the weaknesses of three of the other four ogre generals. The Bone General's weakness is..." She took a deep breath. "Paper."

A laugh escaped Bao's lips before she could even think to stop it.

"Paper? What are you going to do, throw a book at him?"

"Very funny. No, no books. But I did take the time to make these." The Love General reached into her robe and pulled out a small cloth bundle wrapped with twine. She quickly unbound the bundle and pulled back the cloth to reveal four white spikes, each slightly longer than the length of an average hand, as thick as a thumb at the base, narrowing into a razor-sharp point.

Bao's eyes widened slightly. "Those are…?"

"They're made from paper," the Love General said. "Back where I come from, this technique is used to create art. You boil the paper into a pulp, then add a sticky substance. After that, you can mold and shape it to your liking."

She took two of the spikes and offered them to Bao. "Here."

Bao took them. They were very light, but they were solid and well balanced.

"Like I said," the Love General continued, "the technique is designed to make art, not weapons. You'll only be able to use each one once, and you will have to strike his eye, or perhaps his neck."

Bao hefted the spikes in her palm for a moment. "I could project it with qi from a distance."

The Love General nodded. "That would work. We are immune to qi itself, not to physical objects propelled by it. The only other option would be to get close enough to personally stab him with it. I don't know about you, but I wouldn't want to be in a fight with the Bone General where I had to get that close to him."

"Me either."

"Don't use one of the spikes unless you're absolutely sure you can strike true. Once he realizes we know his weakness, he will be on guard, and our advantage will be lost. If you propel it from a distance, do it when he's distracted, otherwise he will surely deflect the attack."

Bao nodded. Looking at the spikes one last time, she tucked them into her sleeves.

The Love General did likewise.

As had been planned, Wang Tian went far to the east before circling back around and heading back to Bao.

The first thing he said upon returning was, "I found him. They're holed up in that large building in the middle," Wang Tian said. "It's an inn. Phoenix Sovereign, there's a trading caravan approaching from the east. About thirty merchants and traders. If we intercepted them…"

***

"Are they *blind*?" the Bone General growled. "An infant could have followed the tracks I left."

"I'm not sure," the Golden Immortal said. "A trader came in from the west about an hour ago and then continued on to the east. Other than him, nobody has come or gone. Should I go out and scout around a bit?"

"No. If they recognize you, we would lose the element of surprise. We wait." He slowly pushed the tip of his knife against the skin on Sunan's neck, until a small bead of blood pooled. "Once I have the girl, you can carve this one to pieces however you wish."

There was a soft knock on the door, which the Golden Immortal opened. One of the Bone Slicers slipped in.

"Bone General, Golden Immortal, a merchant caravan just arrived, about forty men strong. Stopping here on their way to Naqan. Doesn't seem to be anything out of the ordinary with them. There is still no sign of the girl and her people."

The Bone General gritted his teeth. "That little bitch is really starting to piss me off. I thought she was smarter than this. Fine, let's bring the fight to her. We move out immediately."

Sheathing his dagger, he expertly reached out with his finger and jabbed a spot on Sunan's neck, rendering him unconscious. Then he threw him over his shoulder and reached out to grab a small bronze drum sitting on the table next to the door. The Golden Immortal quickly opened the door and hurried out ahead of him. Then the two of them followed the Bone Slicer down the short hall toward the stairs that led to the common room.

The arrival of the merchant caravan had the inn buzzing already, as the new arrivals began to pour into the common room.

"Filthy commoners," the Bone General muttered under his breath, making sure that Sunan's head bumped hard into the wooden wall of the inn as he turned the corner to descend the stairs. "I pray one of them gets in my way so that I can lop a head off."

Once on the floor of the inn, the Golden Immortal headed toward the door, followed by the Bone General. Meanwhile, the Bone Slicer went to get the other Bone Slicers, who were betting on cricket fights in a small private room in the back.

It was when the Bone General and the Golden Immortal were about halfway to the door that the Golden Immortal happened to turn his head to look at some of the merchants who were sitting at one of the tables. His gaze passed over one of them, a tall, broad-shouldered young man with a well-trimmed goatee. After his gaze left the young man, he looked back, and then his eyes narrowed. He stopped walking.

"Bone Gen—"

Before he could finish speaking, the young merchant threw his cloak off and pulled an axe out from under the table.

The Golden Immortal's eyes widened, and before he could say another word or raise his golden spear to defend himself, the young merchant swung his axe.

"Slashing Axe!" Mao Yun shouted. The wave of his axe sent a ripple through the air that slammed into the Golden Immortal's chest. Blood spurted from the wide gash that opened up, and the Golden Immortal staggered backward, crashing into a table behind him.

More merchants threw their cloaks off and drew weapons. Two

of them stepped forward to block the path of the Bone General.

The Bone General viciously kicked the nearest one in the chest, sending him tumbling head over heels.

Shouts rang out from the back of the room as the Bone Slicers leapt into the fray.

The Dragon-Phoenix Sect fighters held nothing back as fierce fighting broke out. The handful of actual merchants in the room were screaming and fleeing in terror. Tables were overturned and chairs smashed.

Lin Cuirou single-handedly took on the highest-ranking Bone Slicer, and the two were soon exchanging a flurry of palm strikes and kicks.

After being caught flat-footed, the Golden Immortal jumped to his feet and leapt toward Mao Yun, sparks flying as his golden spear clashed with Mao Yun's battle-axe.

Then the Bone General leaned to the side as a knife whistled through the air past his ear. As he turned to look in the direction the knife had flown from, his lips twisted into a vicious, bloodthirsty grin.

There, only a few meters away from him, was Bao, holding another knife in her left hand.

"So," the Bone General said, "you did come after all."

"Give me Sunan," she said, drawing a third knife from her belt.

The Bone General hesitated for a moment, then took a step forward and said, "Take him!"

With that, he hurled Sunan directly at Bao.

Despite being taken aback, Bao quickly dropped her knives, planted her feet, and stretched her arms wide to catch Sunan. As Sunan flew through the air, the Bone General held the bronze drum out in front of him and raised his other hand as if to strike it.

Bao caught Sunan, staggering backward under his weight and the force of impact but managed to stay on her feet.

It was in this moment of chaotic fighting that the Love General, who was still sitting off to the side, cloaked and hidden, shouted, "Watch out, Bao, that's the Drum of Midbar!"

CHAPTER 71
SENDING A MESSAGE

The Bone General's hand descended to the surface of the drum, and a sound louder than the loudest thunder exploded into the room. Everything began to vibrate, from the tables to the doors to the teeth of the Dragon-Phoenix fighters and the Bone Slicers. Hands trembled visibly, and some people even dropped their weapons. Everyone stopped fighting.

A bronze beam of light spiraled out from the drum, heading toward Bao with lightning speed, and at the same time, in slow motion.

Bao had no time to think, so she immediately sent qi rushing to the meridians in her legs as she used one of the Dragon-Phoenix Sect's qinggong techniques to try to evade the light. The edge of the brightness slashed through the leg of her trousers as she leapt to the side with Sunan in her arms. Because of his added weight, she wasn't able to successfully complete the move, and she landed hard on her back roughly a meter to the left of her original position. The bronze light hit the table that she had been standing in front of, wrapping around it and dragging it toward the drum. Apparently the table couldn't withstand the force crushing down on it, and it shattered into splinters.

As the light began to fade away and the crushing pressure in the room vanished, the Bone General looked over at the Love General and growled, "What do you think you're doing, Ai?"

"What are *you* doing, Gu? You don't know what the Drum of Midbar will do to humans!"

"I've tested it!" he replied, his voice grim. "It will hold them!"

As they exchanged words, Bao rolled over and climbed to her feet. Sunan was still unconscious, and considering his size and weight, picking him up and trying to move around didn't seem wise at the moment. The pressure from moments ago had stopped the fighting in the room, and everyone was currently focused on the two ogre generals.

As Bao got to her feet, the Love General threw the cloak off her shoulders and took a few steps forward, drawing an iron dagger with a pearl hilt, the blade of which was so polished it was almost white. She also reverted from human form to ogre form, leaving her taller, with broader shoulders and a sturdier frame.

The Bone General snorted. "The Dagger of Sarilla? You're going to try to fight me with that?"

Bao took a step forward, first feeling her sleeve to confirm the location of the paper spike hidden therein, and then she drew a knife with her other hand.

"I'm not interested in fighting you, Gu," the Love General said. "You know that. But we made a deal, remember? Why aren't you living up to it?"

"We did have a deal," he replied. "Fine. Live up to your part, and I'll live up to mine."

When the Love General didn't respond, a very bad feeling rose up in Bao's heart. She suddenly felt as if she were in a cage with two angry, hungry tigers. Just when she was about to take a step back, the Love General spun in place and lunged toward her.

Considering how close they were to each other, Bao had no time to react. Before she could even blink, the Love General's enormous ogre hand latched on to her throat.

A faint choking sound escaped Bao's lips as she swung her knife toward the side of the Love General's head. However, the Love General easily blocked the blow with her white dagger. "Sorry, girl," she said. "But Sunan wasn't meant for you anyway." With that, she lifted Bao up and hurled her through the air in the direction of the Bone General.

Bao tumbled head over heels, flopping onto the ground two meters away, placing her almost exactly halfway between the Love General and the Bone General. As she once again crawled to her feet, the Bone General lifted his hand and swung it down toward the drum.

However, as his hand began to descend, Lin Cuirou, who moments ago had been fighting one of the Bone Slicers, threw an iron ball out in front of him, projecting it with a blast of qi that caused it to accelerate with unbelievable speed.

In the moment before the Bone General's hand reached the drum, the iron ball struck, twisting the drum and pushing it to the side. The Bone General's hand still managed to hit the surface of the drum, albeit at an awkward angle. The entire room shook as a thunderous roar again filled the ears of everyone present. The bronze beam of light spiraled out, but the beam shot right past Bao and instead headed toward the Love General.

The Love General's eyes went wide, and she leapt to the side, but she wasn't fast enough to avoid the bronze light. The beam latched on to her ankle, yanking her off her feet and dragging her toward the drum.

She let out a shriek of dismay, and she even tried to grab at a nearby table, but it did no good. "Dammit, Gu, you'd better free me as soon—"

Before she could finish her sentence, her foot made contact with the drum, and her body began to ripple and distort as she was sucked inside. In the blink of an eye, she and the bronze light were gone.

The pressure in the room vanished, and the Bone General looked down at the bronze drum. "Well, that's one way to end your meddling, Ai," he said. "Maybe I should have done this a long time ago."

As he looked away from the drum toward Bao, she gritted her teeth and took a step forward. Lin Cuirou let out a shout and used a qinggong move called Pounce of the Lion, leaping high into the air and then shooting down toward the Bone General.

Ordinarily, Pounce of the Lion was used to pin an opponent, immobilizing them and even inflicting damage via momentum and qi. However, the Bone General was no ordinary opponent, and before Lin Cuirou could complete the move, the Bone General reached out, grabbed him by the hair, and slammed him into the ground.

Lin Cuirou let out a muffled grunt and grabbed the Bone General's wrist with both hands.

By that point, Bao was within striking distance and didn't hesitate to swing her knife toward the Bone General's neck. The Bone General immediately dropped the bronze drum and used his freed hand to grab her forearm. The knife came to a stop a hand's breadth from his neck.

"You never learn, do you?" he said with a cruel grin. "I'm going to enjoy your screams when I slice the flesh off of—"

Bao sent her left hand shooting out. Within it was the paper spike, which she stabbed right into the Bone General's right eye. Screaming with rage, Bao used the heel of her palm to shove the spike as deeply as she could into his head.

He did not cry out in pain or shock. In fact, it was difficult to determine if he had even seen the blow coming. His grip on

Lin Cuirou's hair loosened, and he dropped Bao's other hand. Faint wisps of smoke joined the blood which spurted out of his eye as he swayed in place for a moment and then fell down flat on his back.

Bao stood there breathing heavily, the Bone General's hot, red blood flowing from the middle of her palm down to her fingers, where it began to drip to the ground below. Lin Cuirou looked down at the Bone General with a grim expression.

The Dragon-Phoenix Sect fighters were looking over with wide eyes, and the Bone Slicers' faces were covered with expressions of complete and utter astonishment.

Bao wasn't sure how she felt. For years now, the Bone General had been stalking her, always lurking in the shadows of her mind. Even in the security of the palace on Zun Shan, she had always feared that he would step out from a corner to try to take her head.

And here he was, lying dead in front of her, an enemy who had haunted her dreams from Fan to Tung-On to Daolu.

"Finally," she murmured.

The blow to the psyches of the Bone Slicers caused by the sight of their leader being cut down ensured that the rest of the fight didn't last for long. The Dragon-Phoenix Sect outnumbered them, and they showed absolutely no mercy. All of the Bone Slicers were killed. The few who weren't cut down in the heat of battle fell on their own weapons rather than be captured. The Dragon-Phoenix Sect suffered only one casualty, with the rest of the fighters coming out with only a few minor wounds. In the final moments of the fight, the Golden Immortal tried to make an escape, but Mao Yun's axe took his head off in one vicious blow.

It took Sunan about an hour to regain consciousness, and when he saw the pile of bodies heaped in the corner, with the Bone General on top, his eyes went wide.

The bronze drum, which had sucked the Love General into its depths, now seemed like nothing more than a simple bronze drum. They wrapped it up tight with cloth and resolved to study it further after they got back to Zun Shan. What they would find was that it was sealed with powerful magic that surpassed their comprehension. Eventually it would be buried deep in the caverns of Zun Shan, never again to see the light of day. At least, not for many, many generations.

That night, they burned the bodies of the Bone Slicers and the Bone General, keeping the Bone General's identity medallion as proof of their victory over him. Before lighting the blaze, they removed the Bone General's head and put it in a box.

Lin Cuirou accepted the task of delivering it to the Demon Emperor. He and two of the other members of the sect would make the long journey up the Zun River to the city of Jin Yu. From there, they would skirt Mount Hai'an and head north to Yu Zhing, where they would surreptitiously deliver the head to the city magistrate. By the time it reached the Demon Emperor, Lin Cuirou and his companions would be long gone from the city.

The round trip would take at least two or three months, but the message that would be sent to the Demon Emperor would be well worth it. Even though he had magical methods of keeping track of his ogres, it would be a different thing to personally see the rotten, withered head of one of his generals tumble out of a box in front of him.

The following day, they provided compensation to the owner of the inn for the damages caused by the fight. The man seemed to be in shock. After all, everyone in the empire knew how the Demon Emperor treasured his ogres. One could only imagine his rage when he found out that one of them had been killed, and an ogre general at that.

With that, the Dragon-Phoenix Sect proceeded to their meeting with the Scorpion Swordsman. When he saw the identity medallion of the Bone General and heard their tale, he immediately agreed to join a formal alliance with the Dragon-Phoenix Sect.

CHAPTER 72
ZHIZHU CORAL

Two weeks after returning to Zun Shan, Sunan realized something that made his heart sink: Bao had stopped wearing the cloth bracelet.

At first he thought it was a fluke. But soon there was no mistaking it. She never wore the cloth bracelet anymore.

The first day, his reaction was to rationalize why she had stopped wearing it. Perhaps she felt it didn't match her clothing or thought that it was too childish. The second day, he tried to convince himself that he didn't care. The third day, he canceled his usual sparring session with Bao and spent the day in secluded meditation.

During his meditation session, he focused almost completely on pushing thoughts of Bao and the bracelet outside of his head. However, such efforts were useless.

Worst of all was that with Sun Mai gone, he had nobody to talk to. It was only after Sun Mai's departure that Sunan realized he had no other close friends. Even the long-time members of the

Golden Dragon Division all viewed him with a certain reverence that precluded closeness.

In the past, Sunan had never thought much about how often he and Sun Mai talked to each other, but now it was painfully obvious. Of course, having a conversation with Sun Mai had often been as frustrating and useless as trying to juggle a handful of oiled ferrets. But if nothing else, Sun Mai was trustworthy, and to Sunan, having someone to confide in was an asset that he only realized the value of after losing it.

A day of meditation did little good to clear his mind. On the morning of the fourth day, he rose early, tossed a thick cloak over his shoulders, and stalked toward the main gate of the palace.

The guards there were surprised to see him, and before they could inquire why he was leaving the palace, he muttered something about going for a walk to get some fresh air.

It was cold outside, with a stiff morning wind that bit to the bone. Sunan began to climb farther up the mountain, scrambling up the boulders and steep inclines that would eventually lead to the highest peaks of Zun Shan. Based on the extensive scouting the Dragon-Phoenix Sect had done of the mountain, it was completely safe.

Sunan did not plan to climb very high. After hiking for about an hour, he sat down cross-legged on a rock outcropping and looked at the landscape stretching out below. It was a cloudless day, and the scenery was breathtaking. He could even see the mirrorlike Chrysanthemum Lake off to the north.

Taking a deep breath, he closed his eyes and focused on the qi in his body. To his surprise, he found that his qi flow had been altered and was streaming through different meridians than it usually did. For some reason, it felt soothing, and even pleasant. Drawing on his qi reserves, he poured more power into the flow, strengthening it, reinforcing it, speeding it up.

Sunan had no way of knowing it, but the reason his qi flow

had been altered was that the spot he had chosen to sit on was itself a meridian, a place where the natural energies of heaven and earth flowed through the mountain toward its summit. Another thing that Sunan was completely unaware of was that the top of the mountain was a very unique place in all of Qi Xien, a place where the natural meridians were especially powerful. By sitting down to meditate and perform breathing exercises on that natural meridian, he allowed his own qi flow to be altered, much the same way that a compass might be affected upon nearing a powerful lodestone.

The longer the qi flowed through his body on this new pathway, the calmer Sunan got, until his heart felt as tranquil as the surface of Lake Chrysanthemum.

Before he realized it, three hours had passed. That was when he detected the sound of someone climbing up the mountain from down below.

He opened his eyes, and let his qi flow return to normal. However, the calm remained.

A few minutes later, Mao Yun appeared on the rock outcropping.

"May I join you, Dragon Sovereign?" he said.

Sunan looked over his shoulder and nodded. Mao Yun sat down next to him cross-legged, wrapped his cloak around himself, and looked out at the scenery.

"A bit better view up here than down by the palace entrance," he commented.

"Indeed," Sunan replied.

A moment passed.

"Dragon Sovereign, you've seemed... distracted over the past few days."

It suddenly dawned on Sunan why Mao Yun had come, and the calm from moments before was interrupted by a spark of emotion in his heart that seemed to contain anger, embarrassment, and melancholy all at the same time.

"I'm fine," Sunan said.

Mao Yun nodded. "Dragon Sovereign, may I speak plainly?"

"Of course, Mao Yun. You know I don't care about formalities, especially among friends."

"Very well. I think I know why you were so… distracted. It was the cloth bracelet, wasn't it?"

Sunan's heart suddenly leapt up into his throat before dropping down into his stomach. "W-w-what?" he stammered. "What bracelet?"

Mao Yun chuckled. "Sunan, you have many talents, but lying isn't one of them. Most people didn't notice that bracelet, but I noticed. Bao and I have been close for years now, and we're even sworn siblings. That's a secret, by the way. We swore our oaths way back in Daolu.

"Anyway, as her sworn brother, do you think I wouldn't notice how she took to wearing that cloth bracelet all of a sudden? I didn't even need to ask her to know who gave it to her.

"I'm guessing that when she suddenly stopped wearing the bracelet a few days ago, it got you… distracted. Am I right?"

For some reason, Sunan felt very, very foolish. Sighing, he shook his head. "Was it that obvious?"

"No, no, no. Sunan, even Bao didn't notice! But she's my sworn sister, so part of my responsibility is to be looking out for certain things. Things like this. So I noticed."

"It's stupid, I know," Sunan said. "Those bracelets, back where I come from, they…"

"I know. Sunan, I was born in Yu Zhing, as was my father, but my mother was originally from Qi Fao, so I know all about those bracelets. They're relatively common among the villages and towns that surround the Bay of Yu. And I also know what it means when a young man gives a bracelet like that to a young woman who isn't a family member."

Red heat began to seep up Sunan's neck onto his face, and he suddenly felt as if he were being strangled. He tried to think of some way to respond to Mao Yun's words, but the only sound that came out of his mouth was a slight gurgling noise.

"Sunan, the reason Bao took that bracelet off is that she cherishes it."

At first, Sunan wasn't quite sure he'd heard correctly. Then his eyes went wide and, without even thinking about it, he turned to look at Mao Yun. "What?"

Mao Yun sighed. "She's been wearing it for a while now, and it was beginning to fray. It was even soaked with the sweat of far too many sparring sessions. During the battle with the Bone General, it was also splashed with some of his blood. So she took it off, carefully cleaned it, and then put it in a jade box, which she keeps in her room. Sunan…" He chuckled softly. "Maybe it's because I'm watching all this happen from an outside perspective, but sometimes I wonder just what the two of you are thinking! You run one of the most powerful sects in all of Qi Xien, you've fought and killed ogres, you've experienced visions of ancient times, you've defended against armies, you've slaughtered hordes of demons, but when it comes to each other, you might as well be fumbling around in the dark with your ears plugged!

"I told Bao that you would be upset if she stopped wearing the bracelet, and she responded that I was being silly and that you wouldn't even notice. Sunan, I'm not much older than you, but at the moment, I feel like someone from the elder generation talking to a little boy. You must know what's happening between you and Bao. You do, right?"

Mao Yun's words struck Sunan's gut like physical blows, although he tried not to let that show on his face. Clearing his throat, he said, "We're… we're just friends and the leaders of the—"

Mao Yun burst out laughing, cutting Sunan off. "Sunan, you said for me to speak plainly, and so I shall. The two of you are falling in love! You don't have to admit it, but you know it's true. This situation with the bracelet makes it clearer than ever."

Sunan was at a complete loss of words. "I... I..."

"Sunan, we in the martial world live different lives than those in the mundane society of Qi Xien. That much has become clear over the past years. In ordinary society, things like these would be arranged by your families and the matchmakers. But neither of you have families to make such arrangements. You two need to do things differently. We're not part of society anymore, and you don't need to conform to all those ancient customs."

After Mao Yun finished speaking, the only sound that could be heard was the cold mountain wind. A long moment passed, a moment that seemed to stretch for an eternity. However, Mao Yun could sense that it was a moment in which he shouldn't speak, so he held his tongue and waited for Sunan to break the silence.

When he did, he only spoke six words.

"All right, what should I do?"

***

In the Zun Peaks, in the southwest of the Banyan Region, was a fortress built into the face of a cliff, which had come to be called the Grotto of the Timeless Master. In a stone chamber deep in the fortress, a meeting was currently underway, led by the Timeless Master himself, Li Buwei.

Those who had never seen the Timeless Master generally expected him to be tall, dashing, and heroic looking. The reality was quite the opposite. He was rather short, even stocky, with blunt features that made him look different from the average inhabitant of Qi Xien. However, his eyes glittered with a profound light that made him seem extraordinary to the extreme.

Also present in the stone chamber were other heroes associated with the Timeless Master, including his wife the famous swordswoman Lady Qixia, his sworn brother Pei Fu, Drunken Crane

Ping Fangrou, a new arrival to the fortress, Hero Qian Chengsi, as well as many others.

The Timeless Master was staring down at a table covered in maps, one of which showed the Banyan Region, and the other, the Dai Bien Forest.

The other heroes at the table were also studying the maps, frowns on their faces.

"Is the matter at Bixie Lake that important?" Lady Qixia asked.

The Timeless Master nodded. "Yes, and we can't afford to go down there without a sizeable force. We still don't know the truth about this Hua Pi character or where his loyalties lie. If he forms a coalition opposed to us, we would be in a very dangerous position. And ignoring his invitation would be tantamount to a direct insult. So the question is, what do we do about Huisheng?" He looked over at Qian Chengsi. "Are you sure your information is correct?"

Qian Chengsi nodded. "Absolutely. I saw it with my own eyes. The Zhizhu Coral is in Huisheng."

The Timeless Master looked back at the map. "The Demon Emperor never leaves the Zhizhu Coral in any city for longer than four months. That means time is limited. We have to strike quickly."

"We don't have enough people to split them between Huisheng and Bixie Lake," Lady Qixia said.

"I know. It seems the matter of the Zhizhu Coral must be handed over to someone else. Perhaps the Dragon-Phoenix Sect? If they hurry, they could get to Huisheng in time."

Ping Fangrou smiled. "Should I prepare for a trip to Zun Shan?"

The Timeless Master nodded. "Leave within the hour."

CHAPTER 73
MAGISTRATE ZHOU

I didn't tell you about the cloth bracelet?" Bao asked. Then she leaned her head to the side to dodge the stab of the spear. Pushing the haft to the side, she used Phoenix Torment on her opponent, one of the city guards of Huisheng. The man let out a muffled shriek, then tumbled down the rooftop amidst a clatter of roof tiles, before falling over the edge and disappearing into the darkness of night.

"Cloth bracelet? No, you didn't." Only a few meters behind Bao, Ping Fangrou was also fighting one of the city guards. As the man's spear slashed through the air, she swayed backward at an odd angle to avoid it, then snapped herself toward him and punched him in the chest, sending him flipping head over heels across the rooftop.

On a few nearby rooftops, and within some of the dark alleys below, other Dragon-Phoenix fighters were also tangling with various city guards.

Having dispatched the last of the group set specifically after them, Bao and Ping Fangrou began to speed across the rooftop, heading south toward the docks. "Yeah, he made a cloth bracelet and gave it to me as a gift."

"Made it himself? Wow!"

"I guess it's a tradition from up by the Bay of Yu."

"That's so sweet!"

They leapt over the gable end of the rooftop and flew to the air, landing on the roof ridge of the adjacent building.

"I wore it for more than two years straight," Bao said, "until it was about to fall apart."

"Then what? He made you a new one?"

Bao chuckled. "No, you wouldn't believe what happened. That dolt Sunan."

Before she could continue, the whistle of arrows flying through the air could be heard.

"More guards," Ping Fangrou said. After leaping forward into a tumble to avoid two arrows, she continued running across the roof ridge. "So, what happened? What did Sunan do?"

***

"Dragon Sovereign," Lin Cuirou whispered, "I heard some news about you and the Phoenix Sovereign. Is it true?"

"There's no need for formalities," Sunan replied in just as low a voice. "Just call me Sunan."

Lin Cuirou and Sunan were crouched in the eaves of a pagoda in a temple overlooking the city magistrate's palace complex, well concealed in the shadows cast by the crescent moon, which hung low over Huisheng. Lurking nearby were numerous other Dragon-Phoenix fighters, all of them armed to the teeth and dressed in dark clothing, complete with masks to cover their noses and mouths.

By chance, Lin Cuirou had been returning from Yu Zhing and his mission to deliver the head of the Bone General when others from the sect arrived in Huisheng for the mission they had accepted from the Timeless Master. The addition of another Dragon Lord made Sunan and Bao even more confident in the success of the mission.

"Anyway," Sunan continued, "I'm not sure exactly what you heard, but it's probably accurate."

Lin Cuirou grinned. "Congratulations! How did you win her over?"

Sunan shook his head. "I wonder that myself just about every day. A handsome fellow like you probably understands women a lot more than someone like me. I'm really just a villager, you know."

"The founding emperor of the Lin dynasty also started out as a villager, so there's no shame in that. Although I do have to say, with my good looks, women tend to throw themselves at me left and right. So, you're correct about that part."

Sunan chuckled. "Well, in any case, the news you heard is true. Bao and I are enga—"

Before he could finish his sentence, a commotion broke out in the magistrate's palace below. Servants and guards alike poured into the main square in the middle of the complex, many of them bearing lanterns affixed to long poles.

There was much shouting and yelling, and it seemed as though the entire complex was being mobilized. A moment later, the magistrate himself appeared, clearly having been awoken from his sleep. Despite that, he held a sword in his right hand as he called out orders to the scrambling guards and servants.

"That's him?" Lin Cuirou asked.

"Yes, that's him." Sunan's grip on the hilt of his Wind Saber tightened. "Magistrate Zhou, the most hated city administrator in all the south. Last month, he had twenty children executed as punishment for accusations of treason leveled against their clans. Take out Magistrate Zhou, and Huisheng will be completely leaderless."

"So that's why the Timeless Master sent you here?"

"No, this part of the plan was devised by Bao." Sunan closed his eyes for a brief moment to begin circulating his qi. "All right, let's go."

***

"I truly envy you, Bao," Ping Fangrou said, stepping onto the gable end of the roof and then leaping out into the air. "In our society, it's usually the matchmakers who—"

Before she could finish her statement, a pebble shot through the air toward her torso, moving at such incredible speed that it was virtually impossible to dodge. Ping Fangrou managed to twist to the side, preventing the pebble from striking her head on, and instead it clipped her shoulder. Even still, she felt like she'd been kicked by a horse.

The blow sent her spinning through the air, and she just managed to pull her momentum under control before she hit the wall of the building. By a sheer stroke of luck, her feet landed on the wall, and she pushed out, somersaulting to the ground below.

Bao had been just behind her, so instead of leaping to the next building, she leapt down to join Ping Fangrou below. They were in a small rear courtyard of what appeared to be a grain warehouse. It was mostly empty with the exception of a few bags of grain piled up against one wall, as well as a few push carts.

"Are you all right?" Bao asked.

Ping Fangrou had landed in a crouch and was now rising to her feet, rubbing her shoulder. "I'm fine. But whoever threw that pebble is very, very strong."

A cold chuckle drifted out into the cool, night air. "Strong is one word you could use," a deep voice said.

Moments later, someone blurred through the air and dropped down at the opposite end of the courtyard.

The mere sight of him would cause most people to grow weak

in the knees. He was more than two meters tall, with shoulders as broad as an ox and fists the size of melons. He had a guandao cradled in his arm and was bare chested, revealing rippling muscles covered by countless tattoos. The scenes depicted by the tattoos were horrific—every imaginable form of torment was inked in grisly detail, almost as if the most terrifying torture chambers of Emo-Cheng were embodied in this hulking man.

There were trees of knives, vats of boiling oil, burning flames, and worse.

Bao rarely needed to fight with weapons anymore, but she still kept knives in her sleeves, and she quickly checked to make sure they were ready.

"Who are you?" she said.

"I'm Kang Zhenya, also called the Executioner of the South. I have to admit that your plan to steal the Zhizhu Coral was a clever one. But when a clever mind meets an iron fist, it doesn't take a genius to figure out which one will come out on top."

With that, he swung the guandao out and pointed it straight out at Bao. That in itself was an impressive display, considering most guandaos weighed upwards of ten kilograms. And this one looked much larger and heavier than the ordinary type.

However, based on Bao's experience, she could tell that in terms of qi level, this man was not her match. She had her Phoenix Crown in a cloth pack strapped to her back, but in this situation, she didn't feel the need to resort to such means to deal with someone like this.

"Ordinarily," she said, "I would be much more inclined to bandy words with you. But I'm in a bit of a hurry. Why don't you step aside and let us be on our way? If you do, you might live to see the light of day."

Kang Zhenya immediately threw his head back and laughed uproariously. "I might live to see the light of day?" He laughed again. "You think two little girls like you can win in a fight against the Executioner of the South?"

Bao took a step forward. "Since you hurt my friend Ping's shoulder, I think it would be best if she rested for this fight. I'll kill you myself if I have to."

Kang Zhenya laughed yet again. "Very impressive. Do threats like this usually work for you?"

"I don't usually threaten. I just kill." She took another step forward.

Kang Zhenya's eyes flickered, and this time, instead of laughing loudly, he merely chuckled. "You kill people? And who did you kill last, a sick beggar on the street?"

"The Bone General."

Kang Zhenya subconsciously took a step back. "W-what? What did you just say?"

"I'm Phoenix Sovereign Bao of the Dragon-Phoenix Sect. The last person I killed was the Bone General. I stabbed him in the eye, cut his head off, and burned his body like trash."

Kang Zhenya swallowed hard before gripping his guandao in both hands and assuming a ready position. "Girl, there is no way that you—"

"I rescind my offer," Bao said. Two knives dropped down into her hands as she began to run forward at full speed...

***

The instant Magistrate Zhou saw black-garbed figures dropping out of the shadows, he knew that he was facing a deadly crisis. The guards in his palace were trained qi fighters, but considering the type of martial artists that had been rising up throughout the empire recently, he had no faith in their ability to defend against a major assault, especially when outnumbered.

Sure enough, as soon as the black-garbed figures clashed with the guards, the guards were on the defensive. Within moments, one of the guards fell, pierced through by a spear. Half a moment later, one of them lost a head.

Gritting his teeth, Magistrate Zhou spun, preparing to run toward the library, where a secret passage led outside of the complex. However, before he could take more than three steps, a black-garbed figure blocked his path, a young man with a saber.

Magistrate Zhou was actually one of the top martial artists in the city, so it was without hesitation that he lashed out with his sword.

The young man reacted with lightning speed, his saber flashing through the air to deflect the sword.

The instant the two weapons touched, a wave of coldness swept up Magistrate Zhou's arm, leaving it tingling on the verge of going numb. He quickly took a step back.

His lips turned up in a sneer. "What kind of a coward are you, attacking from the shadows, hiding your face? Some kind of thieves or bandits, I assume?"

The young man slowly reached up and loosened the black cloth stretched out across his nose and mouth. As the cloth fell, his face was revealed, handsome, with sharp eyes and lips that seemed to form a faint, perpetual smile.

"I'm Dragon Sovereign Sunan of the Dragon-Phoenix Sect. I've come here to execute the judgment laid forth upon you by the martial world of Qi Xien. For your treasonous collusion with the Demon Emperor, and crimes against morality, you have been sentenced to death."

The blood drained from Magistrate Zhou's face. A moment later, he lashed out with the sword again, but it was only a feint. As Sunan raised his saber to defend, Magistrate Zhou spun on the balls of his feet and prepared to make a dash for the front gate.

That was when another black-garbed figure blocked his path.

"Before you accuse me of being a coward..." Lin Cuirou removed the black strip of cloth, flashing a smile as he said, "I'm

Lin Cuirou, the most handsome hero to ever walk the face of Qi Xien. And you, Magistrate Zhou, will pay for your crimes tonight!"

Taking a deep breath, Magistrate Zhou leapt forward and swung his sword at Lin Cuirou.

CHAPTER 74
A SECRET

The Dragon-Phoenix Sect's assault on Huisheng could not have been executed more perfectly. The body of Magistrate Zhou was strung up from the main gate on the south side of the city, and the city guard was routed. The guards who survived the fighting either fled the city or shed their armor and uniforms and tried to blend back into the populace.

Of course, it wouldn't take long for troops from Xuanlu to come and restore order, but at least the Dragon-Phoenix Sect had bought the city a few days of freedom. The attack also sent another clear message to the Demon Emperor: *Your days are numbered!*

The only people to whom Bao and Sunan had revealed their true identities were now dead. The so-called Executioner of the South had been inhumanly strong, but he was skilled in little more than executing prisoners. Bao had made short work of him.

As such, the populace at large had no idea who had struck in the night.

With the Zhizhu Coral safely in hand, they headed south for

about a day before veering west through the northern foothills of Rong Shan. As they skirted the enormous mountain, Sunan couldn't help but wonder if Sun Mai had found his way there and whether he had gained more enlightenment for his scripture.

At Bao's suggestion, one of the Eyes of the Phoenix was sent to see if Sun Mai was in the area, with orders to spend no more than a week looking for him. Meanwhile, the rest of the sect pressed onward.

Eventually they reached a place where the Zun River bent south a bit, which was where Tie Gangwen was waiting with a small squad, guarding the boats they had prepared before the assault on Huisheng.

Before long, they were heading west upriver, leaving Huisheng far behind. On their initial journey to Huisheng, they had boated down the Southern Fei River to Xuanlu, then made the rest of the trip over land. Therefore, for most members of the Dragon-Phoenix Sect, this was their first time on the Zun River, and there were many sights to see. From fishing villages and endless swamps to riverside shrines and majestic temples, there was something alive about the Zun River that the rivers to the north seemed to lack.

Eventually they passed Zun City and headed into Zun Valley, whereupon the banks of the river soon became thick with jungle vegetation. A few days west of Zun City, they disembarked and began to head north, led by Ping Fangrou in the direction of the Grotto of the Timeless Master. As had been suggested in the Timeless Master's handwritten message, Sunan and Bao would deliver the Zhizhu Coral to him in person, which would be the perfect occasion to meet face to face and discuss the future of Qi Xien and the martial world.

They hiked through the jungle for about two days before breaking through the vegetation to find themselves standing at the base of a mountain that stretched off to the north and whose west face was made up of sheer cliffs, almost as if the side of the mountain had been hewn off by some towering giant.

"We're here," Ping Fangrou said. "Come on."

She led the way forward until they were at the base of a smaller cliff that jutted out of the base of the larger cliffs. It appeared to be over a hundred meters tall and was almost completely vertical.

Lin Cuirou leaned his head back to look up toward the top of the cliff. "Please don't tell me we have to climb to the top of this thing…"

Ping Fangrou chuckled. "Of course not." She stepped forward to a section of the cliff where a wrist-width crevice could be seen, then produced a long iron key, which she inserted into the crevice. Upon twisting the key, muffled clanking sounds could be heard, whereupon an ingeniously camouflaged door swung up.

Ping Fangrou put the key away. "I'll lead the way."

After entering the door, they realized that the hundred-meter-tall cliff they had just passed through was mostly a facade. Now they were in front of a lavishly decorated main gate, which barred a path that led deeper into the mountains. Two guards stood on either side of the entrance, and they greeted Ping Fangrou with respectful formality as she led the Dragon-Phoenix Sect members inside.

Beyond the gate, the path became a wide stone staircase that led to a spectacular palace. There, Ping Fangrou summoned servants to bring tea and snacks.

Ten minutes later, a booming voice filled the entire palace.

"Dragon Sovereign! Phoenix Sovereign! Welcome to my humble home!"

The Timeless Master was not as Bao and Sunan had imagined him. In their minds, he was tall and slender, with long flowing hair and eyes that sparkled like starlight.

Instead, he was short and rather stocky, with a wide nose and round eyes that didn't seem characteristic of the people of Qi Xien. And although there was something strange about his eyes, it wasn't the sparkle of starlight. A profound glow within them flickered like the embers of a burning campfire.

Bao and Sunan immediately shot to their feet, clasped their hands, and bowed deeply.

"Greetings, Timeless Master!" they said in unison.

The other members of the Dragon-Phoenix Sect scrambled to kowtow as their voices continued to echo out.

"Greetings, Timeless Master!"

The Timeless Master threw his head back and laughed. "It's my honor to be in the presence of such heroes! Your timing couldn't have been better; I only arrived back yesterday myself. Please rise and follow me. I have plenty of food and drink prepared. Dragon Sovereign, Phoenix Sovereign, do me the honor of walking by my side!"

The Timeless Master's fortress was massive, rivalling Sunan and Bao's palace on Zun Shan. After strolling through numerous passageways, they found themselves in a banquet hall, where an impressive spread of delicacies awaited them.

For the following three hours, they feasted and chatted. Sunan and Bao sat with the Timeless Master in the position of honor, with other heroes of both sects spread out in the rest of the hall. Soon, the room buzzed with conversations about the kung fu of the martial heroes.

At one point, Tie Gangwen, the One-Armed Iron Titan, challenged Hero Qian Chengsi to an exhibition match, leading to widespread cheering among everyone present. The din made conversation almost impossible, and so the Timeless Master looked over at Sunan and Bao and said, "Come with me. There are more things I wish to discuss... in private."

Just as Tie Gangwen and Qian Chengsi were removing their outer robes in preparation for their friendly duel, the Timeless Master, Sunan, and Bao slipped out and began to head through the cool, dark corridors of the stronghold. As they walked along, the

Timeless Master called a passing young man to join them, who he then left at the entrance to a side corridor they entered, telling him to prevent anyone from entering.

The corridor led up to a lamp-lit chamber, where a wide stone platform overlooked a still pool of water. Stone steps led from the platform down into the water.

"These springs are mainly used for bathing and washing," the Timeless Master said, "although Ping Fangrou trains in the water sometimes. She says the way it slows her movements is the perfect way to mimic the effect of alcohol on the body, and it helps her to understand martial arts in a different way. As for me, I like to come here to think. It's very peaceful."

The faint sound of dripping water echoed about occasionally within the chamber, a perfect complement to the flickering shadows cast by the lamplight.

The first thing the Timeless Master asked about was something that hadn't been discussed during the dinner.

"So," he said, "are the rumors true? The two of you…?"

Sunan grinned, as did Bao, although she covered her mouth with her hand.

"Yes," Sunan said. Then he cleared his throat. "We're… we're engaged to be married."

The Timeless Master clapped his hands loudly. "Wonderful! Simply wonderful! Have you set a date for the wedding?"

"The first lunar month is coming…" Sunan said.

"Ah, an auspicious time for weddings," the Timeless Master said. "Well, if I can't come to the wedding, I'll certainly send a gift."

Both Sunan and Bao clasped their hands formally. "Many thanks, Timeless Master."

The Timeless Master smiled. "In private, we can dispense with the formal titles. My name is Li Buwei, please just call me that. Actually, my name is the perfect segue into the subject I wish to discuss.

"One of the main reasons I wished to meet with you in person is to tell you a secret. It is a secret with profound ramifications that, if revealed to the wrong person at the wrong time, could be a major disaster to our cause. At the moment, few people are privy to the truth of the matter. My wife is one, as well as Ping Fangrou and Qian Chengsi. Outside of my organization, though, the only ones who know the secret are my enemies, and I fear that some of them might use it as a weapon to undermine the resistance to the Demon Emperor.

"Sunan, Bao, you will be the first outsiders I reveal this secret to. Will it be safe in your keeping?"

Sunan nodded immediately. "Of course, Li Buwei. I swear it."

"As do I," Bao echoed.

"Very well," Li Buwei said. "My name, Li Buwei, is not my birth name, and in fact, the surname Li is not the surname I inherited from my father. It was my mother's surname, and she is the one who gave me this name. My birth name is Hanno alu-Bukhra." He looked first into Sunan's eyes, then Bao's. "It sounds strange, does it not? Not a name you might expect to hear in Qi Xien. And that is because it is a name that comes from another world.

"I was born here on Qi Xien, but my father was not. He comes from a different world, a different realm. Whatever words you use to describe it, he is an alien to these lands, in every sense of the word."

There was a pause as he looked at them for a few moments.

"My father is the Demon Emperor."

To say that Sunan and Bao were surprised would be an understatement. Sunan's eyes went as wide as saucers, and Bao's jaw dropped. Both of them subconsciously took a step back, and their hearts began to pound.

Before they could say anything, Li Buwei continued. "Yes, I can imagine how shocking this news must be, and you can see how damaging it could be to our cause if it became public. First, let me reassure you, I am nothing like my father. When I was born, he was too busy scheming to take over this world to spend any time with me. Short of holding me in his arms occasionally, I might as well not have existed. Although, I was there in Yao Gong Palace to watch firsthand as he carried out his vile plans.

I was raised by my mother until I was eight years old, which was when she displeased my father and was executed. I was there for the execution."

The muscles in his jaw tightened, and he stopped talking for a moment. "After that, my father did his best to twist my mind and make me become like him. I put on a show of conforming, but eventually I reached a breaking point and parted ways with him.

"As you can imagine, he was not happy about that, and he has never given up in trying to track me down and... well, I don't know. Perhaps drag me back to Yao Gong Palace to be *reeducated*. Or maybe he'll just try to have me killed. I'm not sure.

"Back in my initial letter to you, I alluded to this secret of mine, and now you know the truth. You also know why I am so convinced of how evil my father is. I know the story of his youth, and although I won't go into the details of the tale right now, suffice to say that he has always been driven by a lust for power, a lust that he will satiate at any cost."

Li Buwei sighed and looked down into the water of the pool. As for Sunan and Bao, they stood there, still too stunned to speak.

A long moment passed.

Finally, Li Buwei said, "I suppose you'll need some time to think about what I've told you, and I'm sure you'll have questions later. However, there is one more thing I wish to discuss in private, and that is the Zhizhu Coral."

CHAPTER 75
SHOCKED TO THE CORE!

Y ou've heard tales of Mount Zhizhu, correct?" Li Buwei asked. Sunan and Bao nodded.

"Of course you have," Li Buwei continued. "Everyone has at least heard tales about the enormous mountain upon which Qi Xien and all the other lands rest. However, imagine for a moment the distance involved if you traveled from Yu Zhing, which overlooks the Mei Lien Sea, all the way to Fal Tasu in Naqan, which looks out over the Huo Sea. Do you know how far that is?"

Bao's eyes turned up in thought for a moment. "An immense distance… Perhaps three thousand kilometers?"

"Closer to five thousand," Li Buwei said. "Now take that distance and double it. That is how far down Mount Zhizhu stretches into the ocean."

"The oceans are ten thousand kilometers deep?" Sunan asked, shocked.

"On average, yes. The Zhizhu Coral comes from such depths, from the very base of Mount Zhizhu itself. As such, you can imagine how valuable it would be even if it were nothing more than an ordinary piece of coral. As for how my father managed to acquire it, even I don't know.

"Of course, it is much more than a simple piece of coral. It was once a part of Mount Zhizhu, the very mountain upon which our entire world rests and survives, and as such, it is connected to the fabric of reality of which we are part. It is a connection that will remain in place for all eternity, at least, as long as the coral and the mountain both exist.

"The resonance between the coral and the mountain manifests as powerful, magical fluctuations that pour out from the coral. Only the most powerful of magic users would be able to sense the fluctuations, and even then, only after performing certain rituals and spells. Which is exactly what my father did. In any case, the fluctuations affect all living beings within a certain radius of the coral, stirring their hearts and minds, slowly fostering a sense of euphoria.

"The effect takes time, and it would be virtually impossible to identify as something out of the ordinary, at least up to a point. Essentially, the Zhizhu Coral makes everyone around it feel happy. However, once it reaches a certain level, the euphoria will begin to turn into a mania that rapidly devolves into insanity.

"The Zhizhu Coral is one of ways that my father has managed to subdue and control Qi Xien. By moving the coral from city to city within his domain, he keeps the populace inexplicably happy. The effect created will last for many months after the coral is gone, allowing my father to essentially suppress any negative emotions in the places he controls, quickly winning over the populace of newly conquered cities."

Li Buwei shook his head. "In my opinion, it is an insidious and vile method of control. Removing the Zhizhu Coral from his arsenal of tools is merely one step in the long-term plan to remove him from power."

Bao and Sunan had not even been given time to recover from their shock regarding Li Buwei's identity, only to be slammed with this new bit of shocking information. Apparently, Li Buwei was finished with his explanation, as he maintained his silence and simply looked over at them.

After a long moment passed, Bao said, "What will you do with the coral? Destroy it?"

"No. I fear that damaging the resonance between the coral and Mount Zhizhu could have catastrophic ramifications. I plan to seal it with magic and then bury it in a place no one will ever find it. I'm not sure if you're aware, but many of the mountains in these lands contain caverns and tunnels which naturally inhibit magical fluctuations. They are like voids in the world around us. There is one particular mountain in Suk territory to the west that has such void pockets. Perhaps that is where I will bury the Zhizhu Coral. Right under my father's nose, so to speak…"

The conversation went on for a few more minutes, after which they returned to the dining hall. The match between Tie Gangwen and Qian Chengsi had ended, and another match had begun, pitting Lin Cuirou against the Timeless Master's sworn brother, Pei Fu.

Everyone was in very high spirits.

***

The Dragon-Phoenix Sect stayed in the Grotto of the Timeless Master for a full week. Martial arts tips were exchanged and bonds formed.

For the first time, the members of the Dragon-Phoenix Sect felt as if they were truly a part of the newly forming world of martial arts that existed in Qi Xien. They had brothers- and sisters-in-arms, fellow heroes who were willing to fight and risk their lives for the good of the people. For their home.

Of course, Sunan and Bao spent many hours in private

discussing Li Buwei's shocking revelations. In the end, they could find no reason to distrust him, and they even went to the extent of reassuring him of their intentions to support his cause.

At dawn on the eighth day, it was with much ceremony that the Timeless Master saw them off. He even personally escorted them to their boats on the Zun River. That was where the true farewells were said, and the Dragon-Phoenix Sect began to make their way west up the Zun River, toward Zun Shan.

The trip was relatively uneventful. On a few occasions, they made contact with local tribes, engaging in trade at one point and even picking up a new recruit or two. Eventually they reached Zhaoze Swamp, a misty, dank place that abounded with mosquitos, snakes, and a variety of other unsavory beasts.

On one occasion they even saw a flying crocodile, whereupon Bao said, "Remember that old man we fought?"

"Up north?" Sunan replied. "Yes. I wonder what happened to him. He was no weakling."

"That old man?" Wang Tian said. "He goes by the name Kind Devil Fuling. After his run-in with you, he's only ever been seen in the Dai Bien Forest. Rumor has it he's taken up with Hua Pi the Skin Dancer."

Zhaoze Swamp was so large that it would possibly take days to travel from one end to the other. However, instead of following the river west, which would have led them to the very same trading post where they had defeated the Bone General, they headed north along a tributary that led to Heiping Valley and Lake Liyu. Roughly a day after the swamp gave way to jungle, they reached one of the most impressive sights south of the Banyan Mountains.

The Falls of Sura.

One of the tallest waterfalls in all the lands, it sent water crashing down fully a thousand meters.

Cut into the mountain rock next to the waterfall was a steep staircase leading up to the area beyond.

It was a hair-raising climb, but everyone made it safely, after which they retraced the same path back to Zun Shan that they had taken after the final encounter with the Bone General.

After returning to the palace, preparations began for the wedding.

An auspicious date was set during the first lunar month, and invitations were sent out to key figures in the martial arts world, such as the Scorpion Swordsman and the Timeless Master.

As the date approached, the activity in the sect reached a fever pitch. The entire palace was thoroughly cleaned and decorated, and much work went into the crafting of spectacular wedding garments for both Sunan and Bao.

Important martial artists from across the empire arrived one after another, even the Timeless Master. Much to the delight of both Sunan and Bao, Sun Mai returned, along with his most trusted apprentices, who had once been members of the Dragon-Phoenix Sect themselves. Most members of the Dragon-Phoenix Sect were recalled from their various missions and assignments throughout the empire.

Because of all the hustle and bustle, there was no time to sit down and reminisce with Sun Mai. However, both Sunan and Bao could tell at a single glance that he had changed since they last seen him. At one point, he and Sunan clasped forearms, whereupon Sunan's eyes went wide.

Leaning forward, he lowered his voice and said, "Sun Mai, your martial arts… how far have you progressed?"

A faint, enigmatic smile appeared on Sun Mai's face. "Far. Very far."

"You've surpassed me, haven't you?"

Sun Mai nodded slightly. "I've reached a level of mastery that is profound to say the least. After the wedding, we can sit down and discuss it a bit more."

Although the occasion was a wedding, this was also one of the first times in which the top figures of the martial arts world were gathered together in one place. There were some whispers of fear regarding what would happen if someone chose attack them in this moment, but everyone was confident that with so many top-level fighters together, not even the Demon Emperor would be so reckless.

When the actual day of the wedding came, Sunan donned his wedding garment, which was crafted from crimson brocade silk, embroidered with nine golden dragons that were so lifelike they seemed to be on the verge of leaping off of the garment and flying about the room.

Sheathed at Sunan's waist was his Wind Saber, for which Ruan the Flamingo had crafted a beautiful scabbard of red lacquered leather, inlaid with a design of blue pearls that flowed like the wind. Although no one would be able to tell just by looking at it, the scabbard contained a spell formation which focused the energies of the Wind Saber in on itself, allowing it to build up shocking levels of power the longer it remained sheathed.

As for Bao, she decided to buck the long-standing traditions of Qi Xien and wear a blue wedding gown. None of the wedding guests had ever seen a blue wedding gown before, but it matched perfectly with her Phoenix Crown and was embroidered with a single silver phoenix that seemed even more lifelike than the nine dragons on Sunan's garment. The phoenix's eyes were made from rubies that glittered brilliantly, even during the dark of night. Of course, when wearing her Phoenix Crown, she was careful with her wording so as not to unwittingly unleash its power upon the guests.

Bao and Sunan also forwent many of the customary traditions for Qi Xien weddings, which would eventually become a precedent among members of the martial world.

The ceremony itself was simple. They kowtowed to heaven, to earth, and to the Timeless Master. Then they shared a cup of tea.

As simple as that, and they were married. Bao put away the

Phoenix Crown as soon as possible, still fearing that it might accidentally wreak havoc.

Then the banquet began.

There was much toasting, followed by performances and acts of all sorts and kinds. Ten of the most beautiful female disciples from the Pure Phoenix Division performed a graceful dance, and several of the Golden Dragons played a ballad. One of Sun Mai's apprentices, Shisan, recited a 1,500-year-old poem written by Emperor Lin from the Era of the Thundering March. Three of the Timeless Master's disciples performed a comedic interpretation of the Goddess Xian Nu Shen creating the world.

Later, there were martial arts performances. Ping Fangrou had a new drunken martial arts routine, which solicited a challenge to a duel from Bao. However, no amount of persuading could convince Ping Fangrou to fight Bao on her wedding day, so they agreed to postpone the match until a later date.

Liu Jiahui had recently invented a qinggong technique that left everyone in the audience gasping in awe, and the Scorpion Swordsman performed the marvelous feat of slicing ten needles down the middle in a single blow. Tie Gangwen and Hero Qian Chengsi had an exhibition match that turned out to be more a comedy routine than a fight. Tie Gangwen repeatedly used the fact that he was missing an arm to flummox Qian Chengsi, but he was eventually defeated after Qian Chengsi bound his left leg up. The "One-Armed, One-Legged Duel of Legend" quickly became the talk of the martial world.

Eventually, the time came to give gifts. There were almost too many to count, everything from weapons to clothing to books.

The Timeless Master provided them with an ornamental rock that he mentioned, in passing, came from another world. Sun Mai handed them a bamboo scroll, personally written by him, which he said was the second volume of his scripture.

However, the most impressive of all the gifts came from an unlikely individual: Du Qian.

He preceded his gift with much fanfare and even a flowery speech, after which he left for a few minutes. When he returned with the gift, everyone was left shocked to their core.

CHAPTER 76
A ROPE AND A SACK

An enormous bronze chariot burst into the room, manned by none other than Du Qian. It wasn't just the chariot that was bronze—the horses pulling it were of the same material, except for their eyes, which glowed bright blue. It was obviously a war chariot made for battle, with spikes on the wheels and thick protective armor, although the design seemed ancient and even somewhat simplistic.

The horses pulled the chariot into the middle of the hall in dramatic fashion, whereupon they stood stock-still, almost as if they were nothing more than statues. Du Qian hopped off the chariot and with a flourish of his arms said, "Phoenix Sovereign. Dragon Sovereign. Allow me to present to you an artifact of incredible power. Crafted by Ruan the Flamingo using a branch from the Epoch Tree as its axle, this is the Chariot of Qi Xien!

"It was created by magic both ancient and mysterious and will give you an edge in the fight against the Demon Emperor that no one else in the land possesses."

He ran his hand down the side of the chariot. "As you can see, it is large enough to fit four or five people. The magical horses which pull it never get tired, and most shocking of all, they can drive the chariot with no one at the reins! You heard me correctly. Once in the chariot, simply say the words 'chariot, take me to…' and say any place in the world, and the chariot will take you there.

"Furthermore, the speed the chariot can attain on an open road vastly exceeds that of any ordinary chariot or horse. Best of all, the horses need no rest or food. The chariot can ride without stop through a cloudy, moonless night, or even dark caves and caverns beneath the surface of the earth. Not even the fastest steeds from Kushen would be able to overtake it. With the Chariot of Qi Xien, you will be able to move across the lands with incredible speed, and in complete safety. For example, the trip from here to Daolu, which would normally take weeks, can be made in only five to seven days.

"Dragon Sovereign. Phoenix Sovereign. Ruan and I have been preparing this gift for many, many months. Years, even. Please accept it with our most humble congratulations!" With that, he clasped his hands and bowed deeply.

Bao and Sunan were, of course, completely stunned, as was everyone else in the room. In fact, at first, nothing met Du Qian's speech other than astonished silence.

A long moment passed, after which Sunan said, "Master Du, this… this is incredible!"

Du Qian smiled and opened his mouth to say something in response, but before he could, Sun Mai rose to his feet.

"Brother Du Qian," he said, "this is indeed most impressive." Looking over at Sunan, he said, "Dragon Sovereign, may I have the honor of inspecting this marvelous gift?"

"Of course, Sun Mai."

Sun Mai stepped forward to look more closely at the chariot, starting with the horses. "Brother Du Qian, I presume that you tested the powers of the chariot, correct? It really can go anywhere in the world?"

"Of course, Brother Sun Mai. Over the past months, Ruan and I have taken the chariot to locations such as Zun City and the outskirts of Xuanlu. And of course, Daolu."

"How did you get it down the steep steps leading to the bottom of the mountain?"

Du Qian smiled. "This chariot is driven by ancient, powerful magic. Do you really think a few steps would pose a problem for it? We even told the chariot to take us to Naqan. It began to speed to the west, but we interrupted the journey. In any case, rest assured, it can take its riders anywhere."

"Anywhere?" Sun Mai said, looking up, an expression of slight surprise on his face.

"Anywhere," Du Qian said confidently.

Sun Mai walked around and hopped up into the chariot itself. "According to the legends I have read, the roots of the Epoch Tree burrow down so deep into the earth that they provide an anchor for Qi Xien within the flow of time. I wonder how that affects the powers of the chariot?"

Du Qian frowned slightly. "What do you mean?"

"Brother Du Qian, you crafted the chariot using an item of power that comes from a different realm. Doesn't that mean that the chariot can transcend the world we see around us? Might it not reveal secrets regarding the very nature of the world itself?"

Du Qian seemed slightly taken aback. "Perhaps it could—"

Before he could finish his sentence, Sun Mai smiled, picked up the chariot reins, and said, "Chariot, take me to the Perfect Realm."

Gasps echoed out from the audience, and yet… nothing else happened.

Du Qian's face drained of blood, and he took a step back.

Sun Mai cleared his throat. "Chariot, take me to the Upper Realms."

Nothing happened.

"Chariot, take me to see Xian Nu Shen. Chariot, take me to see Hen-Shi and Gushan. Chariot, take me to see Supreme Judge Yu."

Nothing happened.

At this point, Du Qian's face darkened. Hurrying forward, he hopped up into the chariot next to Sun Mai. "Now listen here, Sun Mai—"

"Chariot, take me to the moment when Xian Nu Shen created the world."

Muffled rumbling like distant thunder filled the ears of all present. Time seemed to slow... and then stop. Brilliant colors burst out from the chariot, surrounding the entire thing, filling the eyes of all onlookers until all they could see was painful whiteness. Then... the chariot vanished.

After the light faded away, cries of shock filled the room, and numerous individuals shot to their feet, including Sunan and Bao.

Only a moment later, though, more rumbling sounds and blinding light filled the room, and the chariot was back.

It looked different. Its previously smooth and lustrous surface was now riddled with damage, as though it had been hacked at with blades and beaten with clubs. There were even arrows protruding from a few areas and what appeared to be teeth marks.

Du Qian and Sun Mai were in the chariot, although they looked very different as well. Sun Mai's head was no longer cleanly shaven. His hair hung past his shoulders, and he was completely disheveled. He also had a scraggly beard, and his robes were stained with both dirt and blood, seemingly on the verge of falling off his body. Du Qian was similarly bedraggled.

However, what was most shocking about the scene was neither the chariot nor its two riders.

Instead, it was what hung on the outside of the chariot, on its wheels, and even clinging to the horses. Corpses. Dozens of them, complete with rotting flesh and protruding bones. Some of them even dripped with viscous blackish fluid that was apparently partially congealed blood.

As soon as the chariot appeared in the room, it became clear exactly what type of corpses these were, as their heads moved, and they looked around with snarling grimaces. Almost instantly, they began to hop off of the chariot and look around at the stunned wedding guests.

One of the corpses seemed older and somehow more limber than the other corpses.

"Well, well," she said, opening her mouth to reveal long, razor-sharp teeth. "You've brought us to some lovely food!"

If the sight of a talking, reanimated corpse wasn't shocking enough as it was, when people looked over at her, cries of astonishment and shock filled the room.

"*Mao Mei?*" Mao Yun blurted.

This reanimated corpse looked almost exactly like his own sister, Mao Mei!

Mao Yun's head swiveled, and moments later locked on to another young woman sitting some distance away from him, who was looking at the reanimated corpse, her jaw dropped and her eyes as wide as saucers. That young woman was also Mao Mei.

There were two Mao Meis in the room, one of them young and very much alive, the other a withered corpse with sharp teeth bared in a vicious grin.

"Feed, my children," said the corpse version of Mao Mei. "Feed to your hearts' content!" Cackling, she leapt off of the chariot toward the nearest wedding guest, and before the man could react, she buried her fangs into the base of his neck.

The other reanimated corpses began to hop in different directions toward other wedding guests.

Thankfully, virtually everyone present was a martial hero of some sort or another, and most of them reacted quickly. Within moments, fierce fighting had broken out between the wedding guests and the reanimated corpses.

Meanwhile, the corpse version of Mao Mei remained latched to the neck of the initial victim, who was struggling to push her off.

At this point, Du Qian vaulted out of the chariot. "Sun Mai," he shouted, "prepare the Encompassing Emerald! Everyone else, listen carefully. These jiangshi are immune to normal attacks. Hit them with fire or energy!"

With that, he leapt toward the corpse Mao Mei, pulling what appeared to be nothing more than a crude hemp rope out of his robe, the end of which had been tied into a noose. However, when he hurled it through the air toward Corpse Mao Mei, it began to glow with a faint violet light.

As for Sun Mai, he jumped out of the chariot and settled down cross-legged right in the middle of all the fighting. Closing his eyes, he clasped his hands together in front of him and began to meditate.

Corpse Mao Mei apparently sensed the noose flying toward her head. She dropped her victim, shoving him away from her and flying backward in an attempt to dodge the noose. However, she was just a moment too slow, and although the noose didn't manage to settle around her neck, it snagged her right wrist.

Not hesitating for even a moment, Du Qian jerked on the violet rope, causing Corpse Mao Mei to spin through the air and slam into the ground only a meter in front of Sun Mai.

"This trick again?" Corpse Mao Mei said. "It didn't work last time, and it won't work this time either!"

Sun Mai's eyes snapped open, sending bright green light spilling out into the room. "I've improved it a bit since our last encounter," he said.

The green light began to spin around Corpse Mao Mei, who could only look on in shock as it formed something that looked like an enormous, illusory emerald, with her in the very middle. Letting out a screech, she violently kicked the emerald, but other than a thudding sound, it did nothing.

"This won't work, you fools!" Corpse Mao Mei shrieked. "I wasn't reanimated by some bungled ritual. I'm a servant of the Five Ghosts! I command power beyond your imagination! You can't kill me!"

As she continued to rave, the illusory emerald began to shrink down. Sun Mai remained in place, his eyes glowing with brilliant green light as they remained fixed on Corpse Mao Mei. Seconds ticked by, and the emerald slowly shrank. Corpse Mao Mei began to scream. Incredible invisible forces were causing immense pressure, engulfing her from all directions, applying pressure that even her powerful undead body could not resist.

The pressure mounted, and her screams increased. She attempted to batter her way free from the emerald, but no amount of thrashing on her part produced a successful result. Her body began to twist and distort, and eventually one of her legs snapped. Then an arm was crushed, and her neck twisted at an unnatural angle. Soon her screams were reduced to muffled grunts. And then, after only about a minute had passed, she was crumpled into nothing more than a ball of flesh, crushed bone, and oozing black liquid.

Moments later, the emerald faded away, and the lump of flesh plopped to the ground. Sun Mai's eyes returned to their normal color.

Du Qian didn't hesitate, pulling out a burlap sack that seemed equally as ordinary as the hemp rope had. Dashing forward, he threw the sack over the lump of flesh and tied it closed with the hemp rope. As the knot was secured, a flash of violet light swept across the surface of the sack, after which it continued to look as ordinary and unimpressive as before.

It didn't take long for the wedding guests to use a variety of fire and energy attacks to blast the other animated corpses to pieces.

From the moment the chariot had disappeared to the moment

it had returned and fierce fighting had broken out to the moment that the fight ended, only a few short minutes had passed.

Now, eerie silence filled the entire wedding hall.

CHAPTER 77
A MOMENTOUS EVENT

It was only by a great miracle that no one in the wedding feast was seriously hurt. The reanimated corpses, or "jiangshi" as Du Qian had named them, fed on qi, not flesh. The handful of unfortunate guests who had been bitten were already beginning to recover, and other than some flesh wounds, everyone came out of the ordeal unscathed.

The wedding guests were sent away with the promise of further explanations after Bao and Sunan conferred with Sun Mai and Du Qian to get more details about what had occurred. After the bodies of the jiangshi were disposed of, the key leaders of the Dragon-Phoenix Sect remained behind in the hall with the chariot. Also present were Du Qian, Ruan the Flamingo, the Timeless Master, Sun Mai, and a few other top figures in the martial world such as the Scorpion Swordsman and the Purple Cavern Killer.

At first, everyone was entranced with the chariot, but a moment later, the Timeless Master asked the question that was on everyone's mind.

"What happened?"

Du Qian shook his head and maintained silence.

Seeing that Du Qian didn't feel like talking, Sun Mai began to explain. "When I told the chariot to go back to the moment when Xian Nu Shen created the world, I was trying to prove a point, or perhaps, be funny or dramatic. Little did I know that the chariot can truly travel through the streams of time.

"We did indeed go back to the moment when Xian Nu Shen created the world, and it was…" He trailed off, seemingly at a loss for words.

"Spectacular," Du Qian said. "Terrifying. And…"

He and Sun Mai exchanged a glance.

"Incomprehensible," Sun Mai said. "Du Qian and I still do not see eye to eye on everything, but I think that both of us now look at the world in a different way. Perhaps I will record some of what we saw in the thirteenth volume of my scripture." He hesitated. "Or perhaps not. The knowledge we now possess could be very, very dangerous."

The Timeless Master turned to look at the chariot. "If what you say is true, and this chariot can travel through the stream of time, then perhaps we could use it as a weapon in our war against—"

"No!" Du Qian and Sun Mai said.

"It's too dangerous," Du Qian said. "First of all, there is no such thing as *a* stream of time. There are many. Countless streams, intersecting, crossing, flowing together and apart constantly. The fact that Sun Mai and I made it back here is almost a miracle. Changes made in one stream of time can affect other streams and can even destroy them or the original stream. We have seen it with our own eyes. In the wrong hands, that chariot could be the undoing of the fabric of the universe, and in the right hands… well, even the hands of those with good intentions can slip and make mistakes. The chariot… it must be destroyed!"

"Du Qian, my brother," Sun Mai said, "don't forget what *that* person told us."

Du Qian's eyes flashed with intense light. "About the chariot being… infected?"

"Yes. Destroying it would be too dangerous. The best thing would be to cripple it somehow, then seal it away in a place that no one would ever find it."

Du Qian nodded, then turned to Sunan and Bao. Clasping his hands formally, he said, "Dragon Sovereign. Phoenix Sovereign. Ruan and I created this chariot with the intention of providing you with another tool to fight the Demon Emperor. Instead, what we created is a deadly abomination. Please, I beg your forgiveness, and at the same time, implore you to allow me to be the one to fix the problem. I will find a way to disable the powers of the chariot, then seal it beyond the reach of mortal hands."

However, not everyone in the room could be so easily convinced to abandon such a powerful weapon. The debate which followed lasted for many hours, during which time Sun Mai and Du Qian revealed some of the things they had seen on their journey and some of the terrors they had faced. Apparently a close bond had grown between the two scholars during their days traversing the streams of time, and although they still did not agree on all matters of philosophy, they were now close enough to consider each other friends.

In the end, everyone was convinced of the danger of keeping and using the chariot, even the Timeless Master. In fact, Li Buwei even claimed to know of the perfect place in which to seal the chariot, and he offered to help Du Qian and Ruan to go about burying it.

The following day, Du Qian, Ruan, and Li Buwei left. Afterward, more wedding festivities and formalities went on. Then the guests began to depart.

Within a few days, routines in the Dragon-Phoenix Sect were starting to return to normal.

Before leaving, Sun Mai sat down with Sunan as promised, to discuss martial arts.

"I didn't spend as much time recently on my scriptures as I'd hoped," Sun Mai explained, running his hand over his freshly shaven head. "However, I gained much enlightenment when it comes to kung fu. To some extent, we've long since identified the four major branches of martial arts, some of which we've already begun to describe using Classical Fei. I believe that we should officially codify those four branches into four disciplines: qinggong, the arts of lightness; dianxue, the skill of manipulating pressure points; neigong, the internal martial arts; and waijia, the external martial arts."

Sunan looked up in thought. "Yes, it makes sense. My Dragon Cleaves the Clouds would be waijia, an external use of martial arts. Your Sword of the Scholar draws upon internal energy and would be considered neigong. Bao's Phoenix Torment is obviously dianxue, and the Flight of the Phoenix developed by Liu Jiahui is qinggong."

Sun Mai nodded. Pulling out a bamboo scroll, he handed it to Sunan. "Remember this?"

Sunan took it and looked at the title. "*Wu-Sunan, the Ultimate Fighting System.*" He chuckled, unrolling the scroll to examine the contents. "It already seems so simplistic."

"In some ways, yes," Sun Mai replied with a faint smile. "But there are still profound truths in there that even later generations of martial artists may benefit from. Sunan, in the coming months and years, I plan to focus solely on my scripture. However, it occurred to me that it might be worthwhile to begin recording the various martial arts techniques that are being invented. In the past, we codified your original martial arts routine into Wu-Sunan. It would probably benefit posterity to do the same with all of the Golden Dragon and Pure Phoenix moves that have become common. And even some of the rarer techniques."

Sunan nodded, rolling the Wu-Sunan scroll back up. "It's a

good idea. I'll talk with Bao about it. Unfortunately, with both you and Du Qian gone, we will now be short a scholar."

Sun Mai chuckled. "I'll tell you what. One of my apprentices is particularly bright when it comes to martial arts. I'll leave Shisan behind for the time being, and he can help with the effort. There's something else important that I need to mention to you, something that I realized during an extended session of deep meditation. We already know that each breakthrough leads to a higher level of martial arts. Including your first breakthrough in the Huang Mountains, how many have you experienced throughout the years?"

Sunan didn't even need to think to provide the answer. "Six."

"So, you're in the sixth level. As for me, I've experienced eight breakthroughs."

Sunan's eyes widened. "Eight?"

"Yes. And I'm on the verge of a ninth. What I can tell you is that the seventh breakthrough is a watershed, and when it happens, new doors are opened up in your mind and heart, doors that you are currently unaware even exist. The inner workings of qi become clearer, and you also come to understand how your actions affect the world around you. The concept of karma is an old one, but with the profound mastery of martial arts that comes with the seventh breakthrough, it becomes something far more tangible.

"I believe that the term profound master is an appropriate title for one who has made that seventh breakthrough. Although I personally don't feel the need to be addressed in such a way, I imagine that soon more disciples of the Dragon-Phoenix Sect will reach that level of power, and I suggest you consider using it."

Sunan was a bit taken aback. "Of course. But… I can't help but wonder how many breakthroughs are possible."

"I don't know. I suspect many. And considering the levels of power I've already achieved with eight breakthroughs, it wouldn't surprise me if I could eventually use my understanding of qi cultivation to live forever."

Sunan's jaw dropped. "Like an immortal?"

"If such beings exist, then yes. Another thing, Sunan, a piece of advice, or perhaps a warning. Fortresses in cliffs and palaces in mountains might seem to be places of safety, but we live in a world of magic and superhuman martial arts. Such places are not invincibly secure. Please be careful, and don't get complacent up here on the top of Zun Shan."

With that, Sun Mai rose to leave.

Sunan also stood up. "Oh, by the way, I got some news."

Sun Mai raised an eyebrow expectantly.

"Back when we made our escape from Daolu, much of the city burned to the ground. Including the Heavenly Meat Palace. But it's been rebuilt. Perhaps one day we can go back and have some spicy prawns together."

Sun Mai looked at him for a long moment, then threw his head back and laughed. "Absolutely, my brother. Absolutely."

***

Eventually, life in the Dragon-Phoenix Sect returned to normal. The squads that had been assigned to duty outside of the sect returned to their posts, and those that remained behind focused on training.

Unrest was building within the empire. After the theft of the Zhizhu Coral, the Demon Emperor was forced to resort to even more harsh and brutal crackdowns to keep the populace under control. Things might have been worse were it not for the increasingly large-scale conflicts with the nomadic tribes from the Yangu Plains and the Chai Yun. They were now united in unprecedented fashion and were raiding with a ferocity the likes of which was unheard of in the history of Qi Xien.

The resistance against the Demon Emperor being coordinated by the Timeless Master continued, but with the increased vigilance of the Lions of Peace and other military and government forces, it was more difficult to do anything safely.

There were even some casualties when missions went wrong.

However, passions were running high, making it easy to find new recruits, and overall, the Dragon-Phoenix Sect was growing in number.

The most momentous event, however, was one that no one in the Dragon-Phoenix Sect knew about. One evening, in the middle of the thirteenth lunar month, Bao brought wonderful news to Sunan.

"I'm pregnant."

CHAPTER 78
MORE NAMES

Sunan laughed with more joy than he ever had in his life. He stepped forward and embraced Bao, who also started laughing, although it only took a moment for her laughter to turn into tears.

"I don't even know how to be a parent…" she murmured.

"It's easy," he said. "You feed them. Change their swaddling. And let them sleep. No challenge at all! Let's go make an announcement. Everyone in the sect is going to be thrilled."

"No, let's wait," she said. "For safety's sake…" She could only imagine what might happen if the Demon Emperor and his forces learned that she was with child, and thus more vulnerable than ever.

As it turned out, it only took a week for an event to occur which completely reinforced Bao's fears. It was with a grim face that Wang Tian brought news from the heart of the empire, in the form of a single sheet of crumpled paper.

"Look at this," he said, carefully flattening the piece of paper. "It's a letter from the Demon Emperor himself, to the magistrate of

Yu Zhing. It's a miracle that the Eyes of the Phoenix were able to get this."

Magistrate Li,

The time has come to deploy the three assassin squads you have been training. Send them to kill the leaders of the Dragon-Phoenix Sect, Sunan and Bao. They are holed up in a fortress on Zun Shan, a place not easily reached by armies or infiltrators. I am sending this letter with my newly appointed Bone General, Geng Long, who will give further instructions on how to carry out the mission. The assassin squads from Xuanlu will also join the mission. Furthermore, I have come to suspect that this Sunan and Bao have kidnapped my Love General. If you find any clue regarding her whereabouts, you will be rewarded handsomely.

The King of the Pure Ones

A meeting was held shortly after. Present were Sunan and Bao, as well as Wang Tian, Mao Yun, and Li Runfa.

Although everyone was indeed thrilled to hear of Bao's pregnancy, they were equally perturbed that assassins were being deployed specifically to target Sunan and Bao.

"I don't feel safe here," Bao said.

Li Runfa drummed his fingers on the table but didn't say anything.

"This is surely the safest place to be," Mao Yun said. "Surrounded by friends and guards."

"And spies," Li Runfa said. "I'm currently aware of five infiltrators, but there could be more. And considering that most recruiting goes on outside of the headquarters, it's becoming more and more difficult to screen the newcomers."

"If you know who the infiltrators are, why not just expel them?"

"It's not the ones I know about that worry me."

Wang Tian reached into the folds of his garment and pulled out a map of Qi Xien, something that all Eyes of the Phoenix carried with them. Unfolding it and laying it out onto the table, he said, "If you left Zun Shan, where would you go? Perhaps Zhe Valley? The Scorpion Swordsman would probably be willing to take you in."

Li Runfa shook his head. "We would be even less sure of who may or may not be an agent of the Demon Emperor. If you leave, it must be in secret, and so must your destination."

Wang Tian looked down at the map and frowned. "The Dai Bien Forest? Apparently the Timeless Master worked out a deal with Hua Pi the Skin Dancer."

Li Runfa shook his head again. "Hua Pi doesn't control the entire Dai Bien Forest, only parts of it. The entire area is far too unstable. Besides, the man's a maniac."

"What about the lands of the Hechi?" Sunan said.

"The goat people are peaceful," Li Runfa said, "that much is true."

"It's the journey I would worry most about," Wang Tian said. "To get there, you would have to take a ship from either Yu Zhing or Qi Fao. Qi Fao is too far to the north, and Yu Zhing is essentially the seat of the empire."

Another long silence filled the chamber.

Finally, Bao said, "What about Naqan? My Uncle Gongye is there, and it's about as far from the Demon Emperor as you can get."

Naqan was definitely the farthest point from the empire in terms of civilized lands. It was so far away that it wasn't even mentioned on Wang Tian's map.

As the moments ticked by, everyone turned to look at Li Runfa. Finally, he shrugged. "Naqan would be a good choice. But the journey would be an arduous one. It would be hard to calculate directly, but I would guess at least three months. Maybe four."

"That's a long trip," Sunan said, frowning.

"What about Nangu?" Li Runfa suggested. "It's well beyond the borders of the empire but closer than Naqan. The journey would be much shorter. Perhaps a month?"

Bao thought about it for a moment, and then nodded.

Of course, a decision like that couldn't be made so quickly. The discussion went on late into the night and continued the following day. Eventually, a plan was finalized. Preparations were made, and a week later, the plan was carried out.

An official announcement was made in the sect that Sunan and Bao had both received enlightenment in a dream and were traveling to the lands of the Hechi to search for an ancient scripture. They set out accompanied by Wang Tian and a select group of the Eyes of the Phoenix, as well as Mao Yun and a few of the most loyal and old-time members of the sect.

However, once they reached the bottom of Zun Shan, the group split up. Wang Tian and his Eyes of the Phoenix headed west into the Jian Shu Forest and the Southern Fei River. But Sunan, Bao, Mao Yun, and their handful of companions headed south, their true destination, of course, being Nangu. They also changed out of their Dragon-Phoenix Sect garb, donning nondescript travel clothing.

They went through Heiping Valley, giving the inn where they had fought the Bone General a wide berth. They wanted to make sure their passage south was witnessed by as few eyes as possible, or perhaps none. Before long, they were in Zhe Valley.

The journey was relatively uneventful. On a few occasions, they ran into bandits or wild animals, but considering the level of their martial arts, such encounters posed little threat. Crossing the mountains into Zhe Valley took longer than expected, but after that, travel went smoothly as they followed the Zhe River directly south.

Upon reaching the southernmost reaches of Zhe Valley, the other members of the sect headed north, with Bao and Sunan continuing south via boat down the Zhe River, with only Mao Yun as their escort.

The first thing they noticed upon entering the Nangu Region was the humidity. All three of them had traveled through the jungles and swamps of the Banyan Region, but Nangu was even more lush with vegetation, and hotter. Oftentimes it was difficult to see from one bank of the river to the other because of the mists that floated about.

They quickly found that the Nangu Region was a dangerous place. All sorts of strange creatures and animals were lurking about.

At one point when passing a lagoon, Sunan pointed at a flock of pink birds. "Are those flamingos?" he asked in awe.

Bao looked over. "Indeed. Now you see where Ruan got his name."

They all chuckled.

Eventually they abandoned any attempts to make camp on the riverbank at night. They headed down the river as quickly as possible to a city located at the mouth of the river, where it flowed out into the Yao Yun Sea. From there, they booked passage on a ship that was heading west to a smaller city that they hoped to make their final destination.

The Nangu Region was inhabited by a race of people who called themselves the Kithiri, and they worshipped the wind god, Gushan. For the most part, they looked just like the people to the north, except that they had skin the color of bronze and spoke many strange languages and dialects, most of which were grouped under the general classification of the Singh language.

"I studied a bit of Classical Singh as a child," Bao said, "but have forgotten most of it."

Although Bao, Sunan, and Mao Yun stuck out a bit, the Kithiri were used to travelers and didn't pay them much heed.

After many days of travel along the southern coast of the continent, they reached their final destination, the city of Sunharee Machalee, which in the Classical Singh language that the locals spoke meant "golden fish." It was built on the shores of a bay of the same name, and though it was a small city by the standards of the empire, it was large for Nangu.

They spent a bit of time in the city, where they found a guide named Vihaan, who spoke the Daoyun language they were used to using. With Vihaan's help, they learned a bit more about the local culture, and then, considering how cheap things were here compared to the empire, they spent a bit of money to purchase some land south of the city. They had brought an entire case of gold taels with them, ensuring that money would not be a problem during their time away from the empire, at least not for many years to come.

Over the course of the following week, Mao Yun and Sunan built a small cabin there overlooking the bay. Behind the cabin, they tilled a bit of land, where they planted some grains and vegetables. They also bought a few pigs and chickens, some fishing equipment, including a small boat, as well as various household items like a stove, quilts and blankets, and other things.

When the work was done, Bao and Sunan looked at their new home, and they were happy.

For Bao, there was something fresh and romantic to it all. She had been raised in the finery of a noble clan, in one of the most advanced and richest cities in the world. To her, a little cabin overlooking a bay, with a vegetable garden in the back and a rooster to wake them up in the morning, was like something from a story.

For Sunan, it reminded him of home. As he stood there, his arm wrapped around Bao's shoulder, he thought of his own childhood and the countless times he'd collected eggs from the chickens in the mornings or wrestled with the pigs on cool spring evenings. Bao couldn't tell because she wasn't looking at his face, but tears had actually welled up in his eyes.

Mao Yun left the next day.

"I'll be back in six months," he said. "You'll need help when the baby comes."

Bao blushed. "I'm sure the Kithiri midwives will be fine, Mao Yun. You don't need to come all the way back to—"

"You can't stop me!" he interrupted with a grin. "Take care, you two."

With that, he headed back north to the Banyan.

For years, Bao and Sunan had been up to their necks in either danger, intrigue, mystery, or martial arts.

But now, things were different. The pace of life slowed down, and everything was simple. They would wake with the sun to tend to the garden and the animals, and then go fishing in the afternoon. In the evenings, they would sit in front of the cabin and drink the local spiced tea as they watched the sun set over the waters of the Bay of Sunharee Machalee.

They made a few friends in the city, including a local fisherman named Lawat, who it turned out had a bit of a talent for qi cultivation, which was a rarity this far south. Lawat agreed to teach them Classical Singh in exchange for some lessons about qi manipulation.

Soon, Bao's belly began to swell, but that didn't stop her from helping with the daily tasks of life.

Time began to speed by.

In their third month in Nangu, they asked Lawat to take them to the best midwife in the city. She was a kindly woman, typical of the Kithiri, albeit somewhat plumper than the average citizen. She felt Bao's pulse at her wrist, rubbed her belly, and finally did a few other tests. For the most part, the methods used by Kithiri midwives seemed similar to those used in the north.

When she was finished, the midwife said something in Classical Singh that neither Bao nor Sunan could understand. "Aap *judava* bachon ko janam denge."

Bao responded in her own heavily accented Classical Singh. "No understand?"

The midwife smiled. Pointing at Bao's belly, she replied with a few words of Daoyun. "Baby is two." She held up two fingers on her right hand. "Two baby."

"*Twins?*" Bao exclaimed in Daoyun. She quickly switched back to Classical Sing. "Me, two baby?"

The midwife nodded. "Judava. Two baby. Boy, boy? Boy, girl? Girl, girl?" She shrugged. "Judava."

"Twins…" Bao said, taking a deep breath. She looked over at Sunan. "We need to think of more names!"

CHAPTER 79
GROWING UP

True to his word, Mao Yun returned six months later. Since the cabin had no extra room for him, he pitched a tent behind the garden.

By this time, Bao's belly was so large she had trouble walking normally.

It turned out that Mao Yun was the most nervous of the three of them about what was to come. Bao was more excited than anything, and Sunan was simply jumpy with anticipation.

Mao Yun brought the latest news of what was happening in the empire. The raids from the Yangu Plains had turned into a full-fledged invasion, forcing the Demon Emperor to send most of his armies north to protect the recently completed Grand Canal that connected the Chezou and Fei Rivers.

The majority of the fighting was focused around the Bay of Yu. Qi Fao had been sacked, and last Mao Yun had heard, the Yangu tribesmen and Chai Yun barbarians were pressing south toward Nansun.

Because of the unrest in the north, the resistance led by the Timeless Master was gaining traction. Martial artists in all the major cities had created secret societies devoted to the overthrowing of the local governments, and more broadly, the empire itself. Of course, that included numerous members of the Dragon-Phoenix Sect.

On the eighth day of the ninth lunar month, they called for the midwife to come from the city. After all of the months of practice with the language, both Sunan and Bao could speak Singh conversationally and had no trouble communicating with her.

The following day, on the ninth, Bao gave birth to twins, a boy and a girl. In the traditional culture of Qi Xien, it was the custom to call upon astrologers to help with the naming of newly born children, but being so far from home, there were no astrologers who spoke Daoyun, and when it came to profound matters like astrology, neither Bao nor Sunan were qualified to discuss them in a foreign language.

But, as Mao Yun had mentioned to Sunan years before, they were no longer normal members of society.

So Sunan and Bao came up with their own names. Their son was Fan Jinlong, and their daughter, Fan Chunfeng. Their given names came from Classical Fei and literally meant "golden dragon" and "pure phoenix."

Everything went smoothly, and according to the midwife, the two babies were exceptionally strong.

Bao recovered quickly, and she and Sunan soon fell into the same type of routine that most new parents did—catering to the children and dealing with lack of sleep.

Thankfully, Mao Yun was there to help. For the most part, he took over the responsibility of caring for the livestock and crops, as well as the fishing.

Six months went by in a blur. Eventually the babies fell into a pattern of sleep, and Sunan resumed his previous duties. Mao Yun said his farewells and promised to come back in another six months.

Even at six months of age, the two babies were already showing their personalities. Fan Jinlong seemed like his mother, somewhat feisty and always looking for something new to amuse himself. They took to calling him Little Dragon. As for Fan Chunfeng, she took after her father. She seemed fascinated by everything around her and would always take the time to thoroughly study anything she got her hands on, mostly by chewing on it Her parents began calling her Little Phoenix.

Time marched on. For Sunan and Bao, the things that had been so important in the past, the matters which had once been their passions in life, slowly began to slip into the backs of their minds. The seething hatred they had for the Demon Emperor became distant. Sunan still thought about his childhood, but it was more with reminiscence than with the bitter grief and rage that had gripped his heart for so long since that fateful summer night. Bao never forgot Geng Long or the nightmares she had endured in Yu Zhing, but now her focus in life was her children.

Although neither of them forgot the oaths they had sworn years before to bring an end to the Demon Emperor, the joy of watching Little Dragon and Little Phoenix grow was the most important thing in life now. In their little corner of the world, separated from all the chaos of the empire, their life was a simple one.

As promised, Mao Yun returned just in time for the babies' first birthday. He brought gifts and news.

Everything north of the Chezou River had been taken by the Yangu and Chai Yun, and their new allies, a race of barbaric giants from far to the north called the juren. According to the reports Mao Yun had read, the juren had four arms, gray skin, and white hair and were savage in ways that surpassed anything that existed in Qi Xien. As for how the Yangu and Chai Yun hordes had convinced them to join the fight against the Demon Emperor, it was hard to say.

In fact, most people had no idea why the hordes were invading to begin with. The Timeless Master had reached out to their leaders with an offer of alliance but was completely ignored.

In addition to the invasion, the Timeless Master's resistance was growing in momentum, ensuring that the Demon Emperor was feeling pressure on all fronts. Things were not going well for his empire.

Around the time that Bao and Sunan had first fled south, there had been a flurry of activity as agents of the Demon Emperor searched for them. However, with more pressing matters of concern for the empire, the death sentence that had been issued against them was gradually pushed aside to become a thing of the past.

Mao Yun stayed for a month and then left. This time, he didn't return for another year, for the children's second birthday. The news was not as exciting this time. The war was at a deadlock, with the forces of the Demon Emperor holding the Chezou River against the invaders.

In one interesting bit of news, Daolu had been occupied but mostly left untouched, including the Heavenly Meat Palace. In fact, the invaders apparently enjoyed the fare there, and as a result, the restaurant had doubled in size.

By now, Little Dragon and Little Phoenix could walk, and they were already beginning to say a few words. To Mao Yun's delight, Sunan and Bao had also begun to train them in the fundamentals of martial arts, and the children loved wrestling with their Uncle Mao.

As the children grew older, life grew easier. The relatively remote location in which they lived was a perfect place for meditation, so after the initial two years of raising twins on their own, Sunan and Bao finally got back to their routines of training. And of course, since Little Dragon and Little Phoenix had been building a foundation almost from the moment they were born, they also joined in.

Most martial artists back in the empire would have been shocked to learn that by their third birthday, both children had already made their first breakthrough in qi cultivation. As for Sunan and Bao, they also began to progress again, edging closer to the profound master level.

Mao Yun returned for their third birthday, of course, to bring news and gifts. The Demon Emperor's forces had undertaken a major offensive, recapturing Daolu and Nansun and pushing the invaders back north toward Qi Fao and the Bay of Yu.

Three-year-old Little Dragon and Little Phoenix were turning into skilled fighters for their age, and by teaming up, managed to force their Uncle Mao to use a real countering technique during one of their "wrestling matches." Mao Yun was completely taken aback for a moment, but then he roared with laughter.

"Excellent kung fu!" he declared.

Shortly after Mao Yun left, both Bao and Sunan made breakthroughs, reaching the profound master level. The qi flows within their bodies became clearer, and they came to an understanding of how karma connected to them with the world at large.

It was during the same year that Lawat made his sixth breakthrough. Both Bao and Sunan were very excited to have a skilled combatant with whom to spar. Of course, they made fairly frequent trips into the city for the sake of the children, who soon made friends with the local children. Because of the environment, both Little Dragon and Little Phoenix were completely fluent in the local Singh dialect as well as Daoyun, which they used at home.

The years whizzed by.

Because of the large amount of gold they had brought with them from the north, and the fact that they could live almost completely off the land, there was no need for anyone in the family to work at any specific trade or occupation.

Other than family chores, they spent their time devoted to the martial arts.

Every year, Mao Yun would return for the children's birthday and to bring news. By the children's fifth birthday, they had made two breakthroughs, which was around the time that they demanded their parents stop calling them by their nicknames in public. Furthermore, because both Sunan and Bao had long since taken to using only their given names, the children did the same. From then on, they were Jinlong and Chunfeng. By the children's tenth birthday, they had each made four breakthroughs and were just as skilled as Sunan had been back in his days of platform fighting in Daolu.

After ten years of living in Nansun, both Bao and Sunan had progressed quite a bit. Sunan had reached his tenth breakthrough, and Bao was right behind with nine.

Over the years, they developed powerful new techniques. Sunan created a mystifying counter called Blink of the Dragon, and Bao conceptualized a way to use the rage attack she had developed years before into something terrifyingly powerful that she called Rage Holocaust.

In addition, they experimented a bit with the powers of the Wind Saber and the Phoenix Crown.

Among the gifts Mao Yun took to bringing were various books and texts from the north, items which Bao and Sunan felt were important for the education of Jinlong and Chunfeng. Before long, they had quite a collection including *The Book of Fortunes, The Classic of Mountains and Rivers, The Rites of Wan Mei, The Sayings of Kong Zhi*, as well as various histories of Qi Xien. Mao Yun also brought two new volumes of Sun Mai's scripture, along with a personal note from Sun Mai himself, providing a bit of news as well as some personal insights into his latest scriptures.

Both children were voracious readers and quickly memorized all the classics.

There were a few adventures here and there. On one occasion, the family pigs were stolen by a band of marauding monkeys. Sunan and Lawat tracked the monkeys far into the jungle to the east, and a spectacular battle ensued before the pigs were rescued. On another occasion, Bao and Chunfeng inadvertently exposed a gang that had been selling fake Wuxing sorghum wine.

Something more momentous occurred once when Sunan and Jinlong were out fishing. A sudden storm struck, dragging them far out to sea, where they were stranded on an island, unable to leave because of a sea monster that circled the island for two weeks straight. As it turned out, it was actually a stroke of good fortune, as Sunan and Jinlong discovered that the island was a natural meridian. Meditating for a single day there was like meditating for ten in most other places in the world. The island soon became a frequent destination for the entire family and provided an incredible boost to their martial arts.

During Mao Yun's return trip for the children's twelfth birthday, a sudden disaster struck Lawat's family. His wife and two children were all stricken by a pernicious illness that, according to the local healer, could only be cured by means of a special type of ginseng that grew to the west. Sunan, Bao, Jinlong, Chunfeng, and Mao Yun joined Lawat on his journey to search for the root.

It turned out to be a much more difficult task than they had imagined, taking them on a journey of many weeks, into a land of endless swamps. They faced numerous dangers, including bandits, monsters, and the like. However, it would have been hard to find a group as well equipped for such challenges in all the lands.

It was on their adventures to the west that Bao used Rage Holocaust for the first time, and it left everyone dumbstruck with its sheer power. In the end, they returned with the ginseng just in time to save Lawat's family.

The most dangerous situation arose when the children were twelve. Tribes of seemingly intelligent monkeys from the deep jungle went onto the offensive, pouring out from the trees to attack the humans in the area. What started out as raids quickly turned into a full-scale invasion by an entire army of primates. Sunan and

Bao's log cabin was completely destroyed, and the entire family fled to Sunharee Machalee city.

In addition to Lawat, there were a few other qi fighters in Sunharee Machalee, and Sunan rallied them to help defend the city from the army of vicious monkeys. That was the first time Sunan used Blink of the Dragon in a real combat situation, and it was just as shocking as Bao's Rage Holocaust.

The "siege" lasted for only a few days before the monkeys were routed and driven back into the jungle.

The destruction of the log cabin turned out to be somewhat of a blessing. After all, it had grown quite cramped and worn out over the past decade. Sunan, Bao, Jinlong, and Chunfeng built a new log cabin, making it bigger, with separate rooms for Jinlong and Chunfeng, and even a spare bedroom for when Mao Yun came to visit.

Ironically, shortly after the new cabin was built, Mao Yun returned for the children's thirteenth birthday, and this time he brought a guest with him.

When Bao saw who it was, her eyes lit up.

CHAPTER 80
GATES

"Uncle Gongye!"

Rushing forward, she threw her arms around Gongye Zheng.

"I couldn't stay away from Qi Xien," he explained, "so I came back for a visit. I ran into Mao Yun in Zun City and managed to pry the good news out of him after a few cups of sorghum wine."

"A few cups! That's all?" Bao looked over disapprovingly at Mao Yun. "Are you losing your skills as you get older?"

"He drugged the wine," Mao Yun exclaimed.

Gongye Zheng laughed heartily. "I did no such thing!"

As usual, news came in from the north. After more than a decade of fighting, a major development had occurred. The leader of the invading tribesmen had been assassinated by Bone General Geng Long, after which the alliance began to fall apart. After retaking all of the major northern cities, the Fire General then led the Demon Emperor's army north into the Yangu Plains to wreak vengeance upon the tribes there.

Some were even calling it a massacre.

Unfortunately, drought and famine had struck the lands south of the Chezou River. As such, the secret societies that had been so involved in fighting the Demon Emperor over the past decade shifted their goals to helping the populace. According to the Timeless Master, in times of tragedy, the people shouldn't be forced to suffer.

During dinner on the first night, Gongye Zheng gingerly brought up a topic that many members of the martial world in the north were thinking about. "You've been away for a long time," he said. "Do you plan to go back?"

"Originally we planned to go back as soon as the children could walk," Sunan said. "But then the northern invasion started, and we feared chaos could break out if the Yangu and Chai Yun tribesmen and the juren crossed the Chezou River. Plus, with the Timeless Master there to coordinate the resistance against the Demon Emperor, it didn't seem that we were needed. For the children's sake, we decided that staying outside of the empire was still the best thing."

Mao Yun cleared his throat. "Truth be told, talk has been spreading in the sect."

Sunan frowned. "What sort of talk?"

"Both divisions are growing… discontent. People are wondering why you've been away for so long. For the first decade, Li Runfa and I spun enough stories to forestall any questions. By the way, after your quest in the lands of the Hechi, you sailed to the Sea of Bing in search of an immortal elixir. And then you went to the lands north of Naqan to confer with a guru regarding a martial arts technique. But people have begun to suspect that we aren't being honest. I've even heard a few rumors that the two of you are dead."

Bao chuckled. "Rumors of our death…"

"Bao, Sunan," Gongye Zheng said, "I suspect that your days of peace will have to end eventually. Perhaps the martial world as a whole can do without you, but not the Dragon-Phoenix Sect. Stories have spread as far as Naqan about your exploits, you know.

Despite your long absence, you are the heart and soul of the sect you founded. Unless the two of you retire outright and appoint a new Dragon Sovereign and new Phoenix Sovereign, you'll have to go back sooner or later."

"Father," Chunfeng said, "why don't we just go back? Sitting around farming and fishing down here is a big waste of time!"

"It's not safe, Chunfeng," Bao said, her eyes flashing. "You know that."

"Come on, Mother," Jinlong jumped in. "Could it really be more dangerous than fighting an army of monkeys? Or bandits and monsters in the Earthly Sea?"

"That's right, Mother," Chunfeng said. "We're not children anymore. We're almost as old as you were when you left Yu Zhing."

In a rare moment, Bao was so taken aback that she couldn't respond.

A brief, awkward silence followed, after which Sunan laughed loudly. "We'll go back eventually. For now, let's just enjoy the dinner and worry about less important things. Mao Yun, have you heard anything about Sun Mai recently?"

"As a matter of fact, I have. He's completed more volumes of his scripture. He now has a total of…"

Strangely, the very night in which Gongye Zheng and Mao Yun arrived, Sunan had a dream, the first one in more than a decade. For the time being, he and Bao kept that information to themselves.

Mao Yun only stayed for two weeks as opposed to the month he usually stayed. When he went back north, he carried a formal decree handwritten by Sunan and Bao, with various instructions for the sect that they hoped would strengthen the conviction of its members. The message also implied that they would be coming back to the north soon.

Gongye Zheng stayed behind. At first, he slept in the extra room in the log cabin, but after a few weeks went by, he declared that he was going to find lodging in the city and that he planned to stay nearby for a long period of time.

Both Bao and Sunan were delighted, and Jinlong and Chunfeng were also excited, having taken immediately to their elderly "Granduncle Gongye."

A few months after Sunan's dream, Bao slipped into a meditative trance that lasted for two whole days. Upon emerging from the trance, she did not need to ask for ink and paper, for Sunan had it prepared and waiting for her. She immediately penned the following words:

The shining Wyrm strides ever north,
The graceful Bird due south takes wing,
From north to east, the clouds surge forth,
From south to west, fair feathers sing.
The fiends, a tempest dark and foul,
A shining pillar paints the sky,
Golden droplets spin and howl,
The sun, the moon, two stars align.
Heaven and earth turned inside out,
The crash and clash of night and day,
All compass points unite and shout,
The Lions seal the fiends away.

When she finished, she put down the brush, took a deep breath, and said, "That's it."

Sunan looked at her, his eyebrows raised.

"It's finished," Bao explained. "There are no more lines to come."

"How do you know?"

She shrugged. "I just know."

They analyzed the poem as best they could but couldn't come to any conclusions about what it meant.

After talking about it for nearly an hour, Sunan finally said, "I wish Sun Mai were here."

Bao smiled faintly. "Me too."

Gongye Zheng breathed new life into the family and quickly took primary responsibility for educating Jinlong and Chunfeng, especially when it came to matters such as calligraphy, painting, music, and the like.

The children spent more time in the city than ever, giving Sunan and Bao more time to meditate and cultivate their martial arts. Although they sparred frequently and often invited Lawat and other local qi fighters to join them, both of them secretly yearned for a real fight.

Mao Yun didn't return for the children's fourteenth birthday. At first Jinlong and Chunfeng were hurt, but when they realized that their parents seemed very worried, their attitude changed. The whole family felt as if a weight had suddenly begun to tug at their hearts.

Although they had always depended on Mao Yun to bring the latest news regarding the martial world, Sunharee Machalee was not so out of the way that news didn't reach it.

Everyone was talking about how the Demon Emperor had invaded the Yangu Plains and massacred almost all of the tribes there. The gory, horrific stories trickling into the city were enough to make one's heart crawl with fear, and the local Kithiri were starting to worry about what would happen if the Demon Emperor looked south.

As the children's fifteenth birthday neared, and Mao Yun didn't come at the usual time, the mood in the family turned very grim. Even Gongye Zheng seemed worried.

The birthday came and went, and although they celebrated, the joy of the occasion was greatly dampened.

A week after the birthday, Mao Yun finally arrived, and as soon as the family saw the look in his eyes, they knew that he did not bear good tidings. Although he smiled when he saw Jinlong and

Chunfeng, nothing could hide the weariness in his expression or the sorrow in his eyes.

Bao and Sunan prepared a curried fish dinner, and it was only after putting some food in his belly that Mao Yun began to relate the news from the north.

"After the drought ended and food became plentiful, the Timeless Master said it was time to prepare for the final assault. While the Demon Emperor carried out his massacre of the Yangu tribes, the secret societies in the major cities intensified recruiting efforts and made major strikes against several important targets. Everyone in the martial world was excited. Within a few short weeks, many important officials were assassinated, leaving the heart of the empire in chaos.

"But as the major sects prepared to mobilize and march on Yao Gong Palace, something completely unexpected happened. The Bone General led a massive assault on the Grotto of the Timeless Master."

Bao frowned. "But that grotto is an impregnable fortress. Unless they opened the front gates wide from the inside, no army could ever breach their defenses. At least, not by any means I can think of."

"You're right," Mao Yun said. "And in fact, in the years since you visited, those defenses were even shored up and strengthened. However, no number of defenses could have protected the grotto from the magical gates."

"Magical gates?" Sunan asked.

"The Demon Emperor can use magical gates to move whole armies vast distances in the blink of an eye. We only learned of this fact after the assault on the grotto. Each gate can only be used once, and there are a limited number of them at the Demon Emperor's disposal. Apparently, the Timeless Master was aware that such gates had been used in the past, but he believed there were no more in existence. Either the Demon Emperor had gates held in reserve, or he created new ones."

Bao's eyes flickered. "Daolu. That's how he did it."

Mao Yun nodded. "Yes, we realized this after learning of the gates. It was always a mystery how he surrounded us so quickly back then. I even remember arguing with Sun Mai about whether or not the Demon Emperor's armies could fly."

"So, what happened, Uncle Mao?" Chunfeng asked. "I bet the Timeless Master fought a duel with the Bone General, didn't he?"

"We don't know for sure," Mao Yun said.

Sunan frowned in confusion. "What do you mean?"

"All we know is that the Timeless Master was defeated."

Chunfeng and Bao both gasped. Sunan's eyes went wide, and Jinfeng's hands clenched into fists. As for Gongye Zheng, a grim look filled his eyes.

"The Timeless Master's family and disciples put up a spectacular fight. According to the survivors, for every disciple who died, three Demon Emperor soldiers were killed. It was a bloodbath."

"Survivors?" Bao asked. "Who? How many? What about Ping Fangrou? And Lady Qixia?"

Mao Yun shook his head. "Ping Fangrou didn't make it out alive. Neither did Qian Chengsi or Lady Qixia. And the Timeless Master himself... well, no one witnessed his fall, but he was never seen after the initial assault, whereas the Bone General was. I think the result of their battle is obvious.

"A small group of survivors managed to flee with their lives, led by the Timeless Master's sons. They fled through the jungle and made their way to Zun Shan, where we took them in. However, after learning of the gates, we didn't feel safe, and we abandoned the palace. Upon the advice of Li Runfa, all of the outsiders who had in infiltrated the Dragon-Phoenix Sect over the years were either expelled or executed. Most of the lower-ranking members of the sect were dispersed, sent into hiding in various cities and locations in the Banyan, where they await a call to action. The leadership fled south to Zhe Valley, where they were taken in by the Scorpion Swordsman.

"Even now, they wait there. Dragon Sovereign. Phoenix Sovereign. You must return. The martial world as a whole is now completely leaderless. The sects have been thrown into chaos, and the Demon Emperor is rapidly consolidating his power. We fear that he might even have regained control of the Zhizhu Coral."

He looked at them gravely. "If you don't come back now, the fight may be lost for all time."

CHAPTER 81
JOURNEYS

Sunan and Bao didn't need any persuading. They decided to leave the following week.

It took a bit of time to take care of their affairs and belongings. After all, they had lived near Sunharee Machalee for a decade and a half, and no matter how much they had always viewed themselves as outsiders, they had definitely put down roots.

Over the years, Lawat had turned into not only a close friend but a skilled qi fighter. As the only local who had reached the profound master level, he was somewhat of a legend. After much discussion with his own family, he decided to join the party heading north as a way of repaying Bao and Sunan for their help years ago when his family fell ill.

However, when it came to Jinlong and Chunfeng, even after much discussion, the family couldn't come to an agreement. The children wanted to join their parents on the journey back to their ancestral homeland, but Bao was staunchly opposed, convinced that the danger was too great.

"The entire purpose of our coming south was to protect the two of you!" she said. "I won't allow you to be sent right into the tiger's mouth."

"Stop treating us like babies, Mother," Jinlong said forcefully. "We're far more skilled fighters than you and Father were when you fought in the Siege of Daolu!"

"That's right, Mom," Chunfeng said. "We can take care of ourselves. It's not fair for you to keep us away from our homeland!"

Sunan didn't seem willing to side with either his wife against his children or vice versa, and he only offered a few words of input here and there.

After nearly an hour of arguing, Gongye Zheng finally joined the conversation.

"I have an idea," he said.

Everyone looked over expectantly.

"Jinlong, Chunfeng," he said, "would you be willing to help out your Granduncle Gongye? I have an important mission to go on and a long journey. Having the two of you along to protect me would leave me feeling much more at ease. You could give your parents some time to handle the important matters back home before you join them."

Bao frowned. "What mission are you talking about, Uncle Gongye?"

Gongye Zheng stroked his beard as he continued, "Back when I met you at Mount Fohe, I said that I wanted to flee the empire to somewhere safe, that destination being Naqan. The truth is that there was a lot more to the story than I revealed. I was on a mission for the Timeless Master and Lady Qixia, a mission which, to this day, nearly two decades later, I have yet to fully accomplish. Now that Li Buwei and Qixia are dead, I can delay no longer. The mission must be seen to its end."

Chunfeng's eyes glittered. "A mission for the Timeless Master and Lady Qixia?"

Gongye Zheng smiled. "That's right. You know the story of how Li Buwei rescued Lady Qixia, right?"

"Of course!" Jinlong said. "It was during the Uprising of Xuanlu. Qixia the Butterfly was accused of cursing the Demon Emperor publicly and was sentenced to death. Just as the sentence was about to be carried out, a band of masked men broke onto the scene, killing the Demon Emperor's soldiers and saving the young girl. Of course, those masked men were led by Li Buwei. He fled with Qixia into the Banyan, where they got married and eventually became the leaders of the martial world."

"Yes," Gongye Zheng said. "You know the story well. However, there are some details that were never made public. The executioner actually swung his blade down toward Qixia, but her struggling caused him to miss on the first strike. Moments later, Li Buwei and his men burst onto the scene, and fierce fighting broke out. During the melee, Qixia grabbed the executioner's blade, turning it upon the executioner himself and taking his head. However, because the blade was so large, Qixia couldn't control it, and it spun off to the side, where it struck a golden tripod that was actually a powerful magical item.

"When the blade struck the cauldron, something like a crack of thunder was heard, and a wave of energy blasted out through the entire room, knocking everyone off their feet.

"Apparently the blade was imbued with powerful magic during that incident. Lady Qixia took it with her when they fled into the Banyan, hoping to unlock its secrets. However, she and Li Buwei soon realized that the powers of the blade were beyond their ability to control. Therefore, they entrusted the blade to me, instructing me to take it as far away from the empire as possible and place it in safekeeping until someone appeared who could use it against the Demon Emperor."

Jinlong frowned. "But Granduncle Gongye, you were never with Lady Qixia and the Timeless Master. You're from Yu Zhing.

Why would they entrust the blade to you?"

"Clever kid!" Gongye Zheng said. "You see, Lady Qixia's surname is Guo, and her father, Guo Minghan, was the chief constable in Xuanlu. However, before holding that position, he was a mid-ranking constable in Yu Zhing, and for years he had been a drinking companion of mine. After his transfer to Xuanlu, we kept in contact, and he was aware that I detested the Demon Emperor and planned to leave the empire for Naqan. Therefore, when the matter of the magical blade came up, he was the one who arranged for me to take it to the far corners of the earth."

"But Granduncle Gongye," Chunfeng said, "I don't understand what you mean when you say that the mission is not accomplished. Didn't you live in Naqan for years?"

"I did, and I spent almost a decade of my time there preparing a special place to store the blade, an underwater vault of sorts. However, in the hopes that I would eventually find someone worthy of wielding it, I never fully sealed the vault entrance. For some reason, I feel that now is the right time to finally complete my mission.

"Jinlong, Chunfeng, will you two be my escorts back to Naqan? Being the born martial artists that you are, perhaps one of you could unlock the secrets of the blade and wield it in the fight against the Demon Emperor. And if not, you can help me to seal the vault once and for all. Afterward, we can return to the empire. By that point, your parents would surely have been able to keep you safe."

As Gongye Zheng spoke those final words, Sunan and Bao exchanged a glance, and Bao nodded ever so slightly. As for Jinlong and Chunfeng, this tale of a magical blade buried beneath the sea, once wielded by the now-dead heroine Lady Qixia, had already begun to tug at their hearts and minds.

"Children," Sunan said, "what do you think?"

"Father," Jinlong said, "Granduncle Gongye shouldn't make such a difficult journey on his own. He needs escorts!"

"That's right," Chunfeng said. "Besides, what if that magical blade has powers that can help in the fight against the Demon Emperor? Jinlong and I are probably stronger than Li Buwei and Lady Qixia were when they sent it to Granduncle Gongye to take to Naqan."

She looked over at Bao, who looked over at Sunan with a knowing look. "Well, I don't know," said Bao. "It sounds dangerous."

"Think about it, Mother, it makes sense. Jinlong and I can go to Naqan to help with the blade. By the time we finish and come back to meet you, you'll have had plenty of time to make sure things are safe."

Bao was somewhat torn. At this point in her life, her children were more important to her than anything, especially her desire for revenge. She truly did feel that it was too dangerous to bring them right into the middle of the chaos that was the empire and the martial world. On the other hand, the idea of sending them away to the other side of the world was equally heart-wrenching. However, the latter decision seemed the safer of the two.

"Very well," she said. "It makes sense."

Jinlong let out a whoop of excitement, and Chunfeng grinned and clenched her hands into fists.

The week of preparations seemed to fly by. When the day came to depart, the entire family stood on the docks of Sunharee Machalee. Sunan, Bao, Lawat, and Mao Yun would boat up the Zhe River to Scorpion Villa, the home of the Scorpion Swordsman.

As for Gongye Zheng, Jinlong, and Chunfeng, they would make the journey to Naqan over land. There hadn't even been a discussion of them going by ship. The waters to the west were infested with pirates, making any such journey far too dangerous. They would travel the mountain passes north to the Kushen Basin, and then go straight west all the way to Naqan.

Sunan embraced his children and gave them a few parting pieces of advice. Bao tried hard to keep her tears from flowing but failed. Even Mao Yun's eyes were a bit damp. Being Kithiri, Lawat was a very complicated individual, but even he seemed to be moved.

With that, they parted ways. As the ship slid out of the harbor, Sunan and Bao kept their eyes glued to the docks and the sight of their children waving goodbye.

The first days of the journey were made mostly in silence. However, as they settled into the rhythm of travel, they soon resumed their normal routines of meditation, martial arts forms, and sparring.

The trip north was mostly uneventful. Having made the journey on multiple occasions, Mao Yun knew exactly where to stop along the way to find the best and safest accommodations. He knew which stretches of the river were prowled by bandits, and how to avoid them. He even knew a bit about the river currents.

Overall, things went very smoothly.

"I can't believe you made this journey every year for so many years," Sunan said to Mao Yun.

Mao Yun smiled. "Bao is my sister, and you're my brother-in-law. And I love those children like my own."

"Speaking of which," Sunan said, "after all the years, why haven't you married yet?"

Mao Yun chuckled. "Don't tell Bao, but it won't be long before I am," he said.

Sunan's eyes widened in shock.

Eventually they reached the northernmost stretches of the Zhe River, where they abandoned the boat and began to hike north toward Mount Peng.

It took three days to reach Scorpion Villa, where the Claws of the Phoenix and the Dragon Lords were waiting. To some extent, it was an emotional reunion, and yet the leadership of the two divisions viewed Sunan and Bao with such awe and reverence that they didn't dare treat them with excessive familiarity.

There were many familiar faces, including Liu Jiahui, Tie

Gangwen, Li Runfa, Mao Mei, Lin Cuirou, Sima Zikang, Ma Ge, Wang Tian, and others. Of the original group of fourteen leaders, a few had perished in combat throughout the years, but the majority had maintained their position. All of them had advanced significantly in their martial arts, with Liu Jiahui, Tie Gangwen, Mao Mei, and Lin Cuirou all being in the profound master level, although not quite as advanced as Bao and Sunan.

After the initial formalities and pleasantries, the Dragon-Phoenix Sect held its first official meeting in more than fifteen years.

CHAPTER 82
WOMEN AND CHILDREN

The meeting began with each Claw of the Phoenix and each Dragon Lord providing a detailed report of their division, including the martial arts skills of all their key disciples, where those disciples were hiding in the Banyan, and any developments in those areas.

Secret codes and methods of communication had been established, whereby the entire sect could be mobilized within days and meet in any number of predetermined meeting points, including Zun Shan, Chrysanthemum Lake, the Falls of Sura, or even more distant locations such as Zun City, Huisheng, or Xuanlu.

Li Runfa was the last to present his report. Being the spymaster of the sect, he naturally had access to deeper resources than the other leaders.

"After the death of the Timeless Master, the Demon Emperor turned his attention to other powerful martial artists in the empire and issued warrants calling for their arrests or deaths. In fact, he's already captured the Twin Giants of the Zhaoze Swamp. All of the top martial artists have gone into hiding, and unfortunately, since the Timeless Master was the one taking the lead, we don't have any way of contacting them all. In fact, we don't even know the full extent of how many martial artists were part of the alliance.

"What I find even more worrisome is that almost immediately after the Grotto of the Timeless Master fell, the Bone Slicers began to recruit heavily. Although I don't have precise figures, their numbers seem to have quadrupled in the recent months.

I fear that they are planning something…"

"That monster Geng Long is still the Bone General?" Bao asked.

"Yes, Phoenix Sovereign. No attempts to take his life have been successful. According to my reports, I suspect he's long since reached the profound master level."

Bao frowned. "Kill one Bone General and another one pops up in his place."

"Indeed."

After a moment of silence, Sunan said, "What about Sun Mai?"

"His teachings grow more popular with every new scripture that he puts into circulation. However, the fact that Sun Mai himself is such a powerful martial artist makes him just as much a target of the Demon Emperor as any of us. He tends to stick to the more remote parts of the empire, preaching and gathering followers for his religion."

"Gathering followers?" Sunan said, sounding a bit surprised. "Religion?"

Li Runfa chuckled. "Yes, only a few years ago, he began to call his teachings by the name Qi Zhao. In Classical Fei, that means—"

"Rising light?" Bao said. "Something like that?"

"That's right," Li Runfa said. "According to my latest reports, Sun Mai was last seen in the western parts of the Dai Bien Forest, not too far from here, actually."

Sunan looked over at Wang Tian. "Is there any way we could reach out to him? I have some important matters I wish to discuss."

***

Somewhere beneath the streets of Yu Zhing was a wide corridor, in the middle of which was a channel filled with flowing water. At the end of the corridor was a wooden door, heavily guarded by burly men in bone armor. Beyond the door, which was bolted and barred from the inside, was a chamber that had been decorated with countless bone sculptures.

In the middle of the chamber was an enormous bone table, seated around which were several men all wearing bone armor far more ornate than that worn by the guards outside. Only one person at the table wasn't clad in armor. He was the rather handsome man who lounged in the seat of honor, wearing black silk robes and a crown that appeared to be made from interlocking finger bones.

One of the other men at the table was middle-aged, with a long scar running down the side of his neck. "Bone General Geng," he said, "the recruitment quotas have all been met, and the training is going well."

"How much longer until the plan can be carried out?" Geng Long asked.

"In terms of training, immediately," the man with the scar said. "Each squad will be led by one of the Bone Slicer Elites, with the new recruits mostly serving as muscle and extra hands."

Another man at the table was young, with cold eyes and thin lips. Leafing through a pile of paper in front of him, he said, "The Bone Slicer Elites are all here in Yu Zhing. From the time you issue the order to execute the operation until they all reach their target destinations and strike, I would say less than a month. Presumably the best thing would be to set a specific date upon which to act. Give them plenty of time to arrive and scout things out."

Geng Long nodded. "Any developments with the Dragon-Phoenix Sect?"

The cold-eyed young man shook his head. "They remain in

hiding, and we only have tabs on about a quarter of their disciples. As for the leaders, we are fairly certain they fled south, either to join the Scorpion Swordsman in Zhe Valley or Hua Pi the Skin Dancer in the Dai Bien Forest."

"No word of Bao or Sunan?"

The only response was another shake of the head.

"Dammit," Geng Long said. "I was sure that the death of that scum Li Buwei would draw them out of hiding. They must have had children. That's the only explanation for why they would leave for so long." A sinister gleam appeared in his eyes. "If we could include those children in this plan, then everything would be perfect."

"Bone General," said the man with the scar, "after the first stage of the plan is carried out and we move on to the second, I wouldn't be surprised if the Dragon Sovereign and the Phoenix Sovereign show their faces."

"If they don't," said the cold-eyed young man, "then by the time they do, it will be too late."

***

Fifteen years of absence couldn't be made up for in a single afternoon meeting. Days began to speed by in which Bao and Sunan were brought up to speed on all the details of things happening in the empire.

Plans were hatched and strategies outlined as the Dragon-Phoenix Sect prepared to pick up where the Timeless Master had so tragically left off.

Wang Tian left to track down Sun Mai, and in a very strange turn of events, returned only a week later.

Sun Mai was with him, as well as a few of Sun Mai's disciples.

He and Sunan embraced, and then Sunan clasped his shoulder. "What are you doing here?"

Sun Mai smiled. "Last month I had a dream in which I learned of your imminent return. How could I not come to see my brother?"

"You couldn't have come at a better time. Bao and I have some dreams to discuss with you, and some poetry."

"Ah." Sun Mai's eyes glittered. "The poem is done?"

Sunan nodded.

"Excellent," Sun Mai said. "Over the years, I've meditated on the subject quite a bit, and I have some insights you'll find particularly interesting."

"We can talk more later. First let's catch up on years past. Are you almost finished with your scripture?"

"I'm reaching the end. Look." He pulled a bamboo scroll out of his sleeve. "The latest volume. I've yet to share it publicly."

***

When Liu Shasha sold her last steamed bun of the day, she packed up her vendor's cart and began to push it through the cramped streets toward her little house at the edge of Zun City. Tucked into the palm of her left hand was a tiny roll of paper that a random customer had handed her along with a few spades for a bag of buns.

After pushing her cart some distance away from her usual selling spot, she ducked into an alley, looked around to make sure she was alone, and then unrolled the little slip of paper.

A tiny line of characters appeared, which she couldn't even read without putting the piece of paper right in front of her nose.

Shasha, I hope you are well. Good news! Momentous events are coming, and we may be reunited soon. Please kiss the children for me.
—Tian

Liu Shasha sighed as she ripped the paper into tiny bits and scattered them in the alley. "Stay safe, husband," she murmured. "Come back to us soon."

With that, she continued pushing her cart down the street until she arrived at home.

Liu Shasha sold steamed buns, but she was not just a simple street vendor. Her husband was Wang Tian, who led the Eyes of the Phoenix for the Dragon-Phoenix Sect. Although Liu Shasha was only a member of the outer sect, her husband had taught her a bit of martial arts. She had even made a breakthrough with qi cultivation, which made her far tougher and able to take care of herself than the average woman.

Furthermore, she was cautious by nature and was not the type to blithely stroll through life unaware. As such, she immediately noticed that the main gate of the residence was open. Considering that her parents were responsible for watching over her two-year-old toddler and five-year-old child, that gate was normally kept shut and barred from the inside.

But here it was cracked open, as though someone had just entered or left.

Eyes narrowing, Liu Shasha reached into the fold of her robe and pulled out a curved knife from Dhamma that her husband had given her as a gift years ago.

Abandoning her vendor's cart, she stepped forward carefully, knife held in a ready position.

After pushing the gate open carefully, she looked into the courtyard beyond it but didn't see anyone or anything.

"Sheng'er?" she said. "Ling'er? Mother? Father?"

There was no response.

Keeping her knife ready, she stepped into the courtyard. As she did, she detected a blur of motion within her peripheral vision, coming from the left. However, despite her modest abilities in martial arts, she was completely incapable of reacting. In the blink of an eye, the figure to her left stabbed his finger into her wrist and then her neck. Her hand loosened, and even as the knife fell to the ground, she began to collapse.

Before she fell to the ground, the figure reached out and caught her.

Suddenly, she found herself staring into the face of a man wearing a set of bone armor.

"A feisty one, huh?" the man said. Chuckling, he threw her over his shoulder, which was when she caught sight of her children and her parents, bound, gagged, and leaning up against the far wall of the courtyard, flanked by two tough-looking men in grayish garments.

The man holding Liu Shasha crouched down and then leapt into the air, flying up until he was on the courtyard wall. "Grab the rest of them and let's get going," he said. "We have two more sets of targets in Zun City before we leave for the north."

***

In the dense forest north of Huisheng was a lake whose shores were covered with black and white stones. Close to the lake was a small encampment occupied by a few of the wives of some lower-ranking members of the Dragon-Phoenix Sect, as well as their children and a few old-timers. They had only been camped here for a few months. The location had been selected mostly because it was a few days outside of the city, a place that few people would ever visit for casual purposes.

The lake teemed with fish, and there were plenty of berries, roots, vegetables, and even fruits available for foraging in the forest. Combined with a few pigs and chickens brought from the city, it was the perfect location to get away from the world for a short time.

However, when three men in bone armor showed up, flanked by a group of ten muscular fellows in gray clothing, the little camp devolved into terror.

Within minutes, the entire group of nearly two dozen women, children, and old-timers were bound and thrown over the shoulders of the men, who disappeared into the forest.

***

In locations all over the empire, from Yu Zhing and Xuanlu to the Zhaoze Swamp and the depths of the Banyan Region, similar scenes played out. In a single day, hundreds if not thousands of women, children, and elderly folks were snatched up and taken away.

CHAPTER 83
PULSES

When the first report of a kidnapping came in, Wang Tian didn't pay it much heed. Over the years, the Dragon-Phoenix Sect had become one of the largest and most powerful organizations in the martial world, with nearly six thousand disciples split among the two divisions. As such, there were always bound to be minor incidents among members.

But almost within the hour of the first report, a second report came in. It was only the previous year that the Dragon-Phoenix Sect had taken to using birds to send messages, something that was not common in Qi Xien.

When the third report came in, Wang Tian brought the matter to Sunan and Bao's attention. Things only got worse as the day wore on.

One of the reports caused Wang Tian's face to drain of blood. "Shasha," he murmured, his eyes widening.

"Wang Tian?" Bao said.

He slowly rolled the small strip of paper up. "They took her. And my children."

There was little need to wonder who *they* were.

By the end of the day, fourteen reports had come in regarding kidnappings of family members of the Dragon-Phoenix Sect.

"We have to do something!" Bao exclaimed. When she thought about how she would feel if Jinlong and Chunfeng had been taken by the Bone Slicers, it caused her to shudder in terror.

"We don't even know where they've been taken, Bao," Sunan said.

"But we will eventually, and being stuck down here in Zhe Valley will only delay how long it will be before we can act."

Sunan looked over at Li Runfa. After fifteen years, Li Runfa's hair was mostly gray, but his eyes were as sharp as ever. "You're probably right, Phoenix Sovereign." He looked down at the maps that were spread out on the table. "It might not be a bad idea to relocate to somewhere closer to the heart of the empire."

After a moment passed, Sun Mai reached out and put his finger down on one of the maps. "What about here?" he said.

Li Runfa's eyes narrowed. "That's where the Purple Cavern Killer and his apprentice challenged the Twin Giants to a duel, isn't it?"

"You have a good memory," Sun Mai said. "The salt mines there were once owned by a rather rich tribe that controlled most of the northern tributary of the Ghezhong River. However, they resisted Hua Pi the Skin Dancer as he attempted to unify the Dai Bien Forest, and they were eventually wiped out. The mines were abandoned about ten years ago, and have been ever since."

Li Runfa leaned closer to the map. "That would put us within about two days of the Zun River. Definitely an ideal location." He looked up at Bao. "However, once we leave this villa, it will be much more difficult to get any news. At the moment, all reports are sent to this location, and that will continue until we issue orders for the sect to regroup."

Bao ground her teeth in frustration, and a long moment passed.

"We wait a few more days," Sunan said. "If we don't get any news by then, we can head to those salt mines."

Wang Tian's hands were clenched into fists. "Phoenix Sovereign, I hereby request leave to—"

"Denied," Bao interrupted, trying to keep a stern look on her face despite how her heart ached. She thought back to when Sunan had been kidnapped by the Bone General and how she had barely been able to stand still because of the anxiety. And that had only lasted for a few short hours. "Running off on your own won't do any good. There's obviously a purpose behind all of this. We need to figure out what it is so that we can get your family back safely, and the families of all the other members of the Dragon-Phoenix Sect. Then we can go in prepared."

Lips pursed tightly, Wang Tian nodded. Of course, everyone in the room knew that if Wang Tian had expressed such a desire, other lower-ranking members of the sect scattered about in the world would likely have the same urge to take action.

The news they were waiting for came in two days later.

"Heart's Ridge," Li Runfa said. "That's where they're going, I'm almost certain of it. I got three separate reports all indicating the same thing."

"Heart's Ridge?" Sunan looked down at the map. "I haven't heard of it before."

"About five years ago, the Demon Emperor began construction of a fortress here." He pointed to a location on the map where the Banyan Mountains dropped down toward the Mei Lien Sea. "It's about two days south of Yu Zhing and never really had a name before. But when they started building the fortress, they uncovered a large, heart-shaped rock, and thus the name."

"It's a huge structure," he continued, "one of the largest fortresses ever built by the Demon Emperor, perhaps the only larger one being Yao Gong Palace itself."

"Fortress?" Dragon Lord Lin Cuirou said. "Or prison?"

Li Runfa looked up. "If I recall, it was your man who infiltrated the construction team, wasn't it?"

"That's right. He said that the depths of the fortress are filled with countless tunnels and corridors with cages and barred chambers. Dungeons the likes of which don't exist anywhere in Qi Xien."

Li Runfa looked back down at the map. "Yes, I always wondered what use the Demon Emperor would have for so many cells. He doesn't tend to keep prisoners alive for very long. Now it all makes sense."

Bao reached up to massage the bridge of her nose. "Are you telling me they've been planning this for five years?"

"It's hard to say," Li Runfa replied. "Dragon Lord Lin, how much do you know about the fortress itself?"

"The reason my man infiltrated the construction team," Lin Cuirou replied, "is because my division of the sect was in charge of the roads connecting Yu Zhing, Xuanlu, and Huisheng. Heart's Ridge overlooks the path between Xuanlu and Yu Zhing, so it was only natural for me to try to keep tabs on what was being built there. Furthermore, I had my man create a rough map of the entire structure. I figured it wouldn't hurt to have some detailed information about the Demon Emperor's second-largest fortification, one that essentially controls the land path between south and north."

All eyes in the room were focused on Lin Cuirou. A moment later, Bao broke the silence. "Go get that map."

***

They set out the following day. Other than Sunan and Bao, the forces of the Dragon-Phoenix Sect included seven Dragon Lords, seven Claws of the Phoenix, Phoenix General Mao Yun, Dragon General Tie Gangwen, and the spymaster, Li Runfa, a total of seventeen.

A report had come in indicating that at least one of the Scorpion Swordsman's disciples' family had been kidnapped, so the Scorpion Swordsman himself joined them, bringing thirty of his top fighters.

Sun Mai also joined them, and he had five disciples with him.

As such, it was a group of over fifty of the top martial artists in the lands who set out from Scorpion Villa toward Heart's Ridge.

Scorpion Villa itself was located in the mountains north of Zhe Valley and also overlooked the westernmost stretches of the Ghezhong River, which ran through the north of Dai Bien Forest. Since the Scorpion Swordsman often had dealings with Hua Pi the Skin Dancer, he maintained a small travel hub on the river, only two days' march from the villa. Normally manned by two of his disciples, it was stocked with travel supplies and also had a cache of ten large bamboo rafts, each one large enough to hold ten people.

Soon, they were speeding down the Ghezhong River into Dai Bien Forest.

On the second morning of what was likely going to be a seven-day journey to the salt mines, Sunan, Bao, and Sun Mai finally discussed the matter of the dreams and poems.

"For more than ten years, I had almost no dreams," Sunan explained to Sun Mai, "at least not the dreams of gold. The dreams I did have seemed more like memories of previous dreams. When they returned, they were stronger and clearer than before. Like true visions of another time and place.

"For a period of months, I had the same dream over and over again, until the details were burned into my mind as if by a branding iron. By now, I can recall each part in complete detail.

"I am looking down at the ground, where numerous colored dots swirl into a shape that looks very much like the dragon-phoenix symbol that makes up the insignia of our sect. A black hurricane sweeps across the symbol, which begins to emanate golden light. The light causes golden clouds to form, and then golden rain begins to fall. A wind screams, and a vortex springs up to cover the symbol and the hurricane. Meanwhile, the sun, the moon, and two stars in the heavens form a perfect square overhead. Golden light connects the four heavenly bodies, which descend to the earth in that square form. Black and white lightning crash, and in the end, two golden lions are all that are left behind."

Sun Mai nodded. "And the poem?"

Bao immediately recited the poem:

The shining Wyrm strides ever north,
The graceful Bird due south takes wing,
From north to east, the clouds surge forth,
From south to west, fair feathers sing.
The fiends, a tempest dark and foul,
A shining pillar paints the sky,
Golden droplets spin and howl,
The sun, the moon, two stars align.
Heaven and Earth turned inside out,
The crash and clash of night and day,
All compass points unite and shout,
The Lions seal the fiends away.

Sun Mai nodded, then closed his eyes for six hours straight. When he opened them, he sighed.

"There are many similar elements between the poem and the dream, and some elements which are not possible to reconcile at the moment. For example, what are the 'colored dots' in the dream, and what are the 'compass points' mentioned in the poem?

"In any case, there is something I've come to suspect over the years. It only hit me after Du Qian and I took that journey on the chariot. Afterward, my meditations on the subject of time led me to certain speculations. Sunan, do you mind if I check your pulse?"

The way Sun Mai seemed to suddenly change conversation topics in the middle of his sentence reminded Sunan of the old Sun

Mai, and he smiled. Pulling back his sleeve, he extended his wrist, which Sun Mai reached out and grabbed lightly with his thumb and forefinger.

A moment later, Sunan felt a soft energy enter through his wrist, slowly spreading out through his meridians until it filled his entire body. An hour later, the energy dissipated, and Sun Mai opened his eyes and looked at Bao.

"Bao?"

She nodded, pulled back her sleeve, and extended her wrist.

Another hour passed.

Finally, Sun Mai released Bao's wrist and opened his eyes again.

"As I suspected," he said. "The evidence is almost impossible to detect. Only a profound master who has made multiple breakthroughs would notice that…"

CHAPTER 84
A POTION IN A VIAL

Sun Mai's eyes flashed. "Both of your meridians have been… touched."

"Touched?" Sunan said.

"Perhaps manipulated is a better word, although I don't think there was any ill intent involved."

Rubbing her wrist, Bao said, "So you're saying that my poem and Sunan's dreams are the result of someone manipulating the qi in our bodies?"

"Something like that," Sun Mai replied, "although I can't be sure of the details. I suspect that someone has been reaching out from the shadows to send you a message, likely a message to do with a confrontation with the Demon Emperor. After all, you both saw images similar to Sunan's dream when you went on that wind dream with the True Shan and got close to Yao Gong Palace. Whoever this person is, he likely views himself as your friend and ally."

"But why wouldn't he just speak to us directly, or even send a written message?"

Sun Mai sighed again. "Likely for the same reason that we chose to seal away that chariot all those years ago. Interfering with the streams of time is a very dangerous thing."

"*Time?*" Sunan exclaimed. "You think this person, whoever he is, traveled through time?"

"Perhaps. The fluctuations in your meridians, they remind me of certain other fluctuations I've felt before."

"The chariot?" Bao asked.

Sun Mai nodded. "Perhaps you have had a hidden ally on your side this entire time, slowly prodding you in the direction of victory, telling you secrets from the future."

"I had the first dream in the Huang Mountains, decades ago..." Sunan said. Both he and Bao were clearly shaken.

After a moment, Sun Mai continued, "Sunan, the colored dots that made up that symbol, you said they were golden and silver, correct?"

"That's right."

"Just like the uniforms of the two divisions of the Dragon-Phoenix Sect..."

***

On one particular mountain peak in the Banyan Mountains was a cave that overlooked Heart's Ridge and the Mei Lien Sea. That cave was where Hui had set up camp a few days before. For fear of attracting the attention of the Demon Emperor's forces in Heart's Ridge Prison, she chose not to light a fire, despite the fact that snow blanketed the mountain at this elevation. To stay warm, she relied on thick garments and clever manipulation of the qi in her meridians.

She was sitting at the mouth of the cave, looking down at the prison, thinking about stories she remembered from her childhood.

"The Defeat at Heart's Ridge," she murmured. "So much tragedy. The betrayal of Lin Cuirou. The death of far too many heroes. Mao Yun. Tie Gangwen. Wang Tian. Ma Ge." She sighed. As a young girl, she had heard the whispered names of those heroes who had died in the Defeat of Heart's Ridge a thousand years in the past. At that time, they had been little more than names.

Over the years, she had seen all of those heroes with her own eyes and had even spoken with a few of them in passing. They were real people to her now, and the thought of them falling in battle in a treacherous trap was heartrending.

In the history she knew, the Defeat at Heart's Ridge had been a crushing blow to the Dragon-Phoenix Sect. Bao and Sunan survived, but most of their closest friends and their most powerful fighters lost their lives. The resulting anguish and fury prompted Bao and Sunan to marshal the heroes of the land in a reckless assault on Yao Gong Palace that was an even worse defeat than Heart's Ridge. Neither Bao, Sunan, nor any of the other martial heroes had returned from that assault, which had been the turning point that solidified the Demon Emperor's power for the following millennium.

Hui looked down at the musical instrument she held in her hands, a set of pipes crafted from long, tubular shells, inlaid with pearl, jade, and gold and inscribed with tiny magical symbols.

Hui had spent a decade in the Eastern Archipelagos acquiring the pipes and had paid a heavy price to do so. She had lost a finger on her left hand, had been stabbed in the abdomen, and had even sacrificed half of the blood in her body in a ritual that nearly cost her her life. In the end, she returned to the mainland feeling battered but victorious.

"The Kun-Peng Pipes," she murmured. "Were the True Shan right? Can these pipes really turn Heart's Ridge into a victory instead of defeat?"

She had to believe that the pipes did possess that power. If they didn't, then her torturous adventure in the Eastern Archipelagos would turn out to be a cruel joke on the part of fate.

"I spent so many decades holding back, refusing to interfere, terrified of causing damage to the streams of time. And now I intend to smash at them with a hammer. Is this the right thing to do? Is this what Master would have done?"

As the cold mountain air blew against her face, Hui looked down at Heart's Ridge Prison and fingered the images of fish and birds carved into the Kun-Peng Pipes.

"It won't be very long now. Not very long at all…"

***

It was from the salt mines that the leaders of the Dragon-Phoenix Sect went about organizing one of the most complicated tasks they had ever undertaken: regathering the sect.

The empire was huge, but the Dragon-Phoenix Sect was no small organization, with over six thousand disciples between the two divisions. Even if the lower-ranking disciples—the ones who had only made one or two breakthroughs in qi cultivation—were left out, there were still thousands of members.

To move such a large number of people through the empire unnoticed would be no simple task.

Therefore, a three-pronged approach was finally decided upon. The disciples who had dispersed to locations north of the Banyan Mountains would gather in Yu Zhing. Those who had scattered into the Banyan Region and Jian Shu Forest would gather in Xuanlu. A smaller group, mostly the elite disciples and top fighters, would go to Zun City, which was very close to the salt mines.

After the orders were sent out, the leaders in the salt mines had little to do other than wait. A few of them left on important tasks, such as meeting with key disciples in their division or retrieving powerful weapons or artifacts that would likely be useful in the coming days.

Thankfully they did receive updates via the information

networks operated by Li Runfa, as well as the Eyes of the Phoenix, who reported in to Wang Tian.

Li Runfa's speculations were proved correct: All of the captured women, children, and elderly folks were being taken to Heart's Ridge. There were a few reports of martial heroes attempting to raid the prison fortress there, presumably in an attempt to free certain captives.

No such attempts were successful.

There were a handful of other martial artists who joined them. Blackleaf from the Hen-Shi Sect seemed very irritated to be forced to work with them, but he clearly recognized that there was strength in numbers. Kind Devil Fuling also appeared, the same old man who had tried to rob them years ago on a tributary of the Southern Fei River.

Disturbingly, there were reports of ships being built in a makeshift shipyard just below the fortress. They were supposedly huge, with multiple masts and decks, apparently designed to hold large numbers of people.

They could only speculate why such ships were being built. On the one hand, it seemed to indicate that the captives in Heart's Ridge Prison were meant to be kept alive. On the other hand, it also indicated that there was a plan to move the prisoners to another location. But where?

To the north, the Yangu Plains were now mostly a desolate wasteland. To the south was Dhamma, and beyond that, Nangu. Farther in the deep ocean was the Eastern Archipelagos and the Desert Island of the Hechi. None of those places seemed likely destinations for a large group of captives, not unless slave camps were constructed to hold them, but then what had been the point of building a huge prison?

It was a source of much debate among the leaders of the sect, but in the end, no one could come up with any good theories, not even Li Runfa.

However, it did impress upon them the fact that time was running out.

***

Lin Cuirou was one of the leaders who had left the salt mines on important business. Currently, he was sitting at a table in a teahouse in Zun City, examining himself in a copper mirror, when a man in tan robes sat down at the table next to him.

"Have you tried the white monkey tea?" the man asked.

Lin Cuirou's eyes flickered away from the mirror for a moment to look at the man. He seemed ordinary in every way, neither tall nor short, neither handsome nor ugly. He was the type of person who was instantly forgettable.

"I prefer the yellow leaf tea," Lin Cuirou said.

"But that's only suitable when the west wind blows."

"All winds blow from the central plains."

The man in tan chuckled. "You picked a nice table. Very private."

Lin Cuirou smoothed his eyebrows out and then put the mirror away. "Do you have it?"

"Of course." The man in tan reached into his robe and pulled out a small jade vial, which he placed on the table.

Lin Cuirou reached out to grab it, but before he could, the other man's hand shot out and clamped down on his wrist.

"Do not take the potion until at least one of them is dead," the man said. "I cannot emphasize this enough. The King of the Pure Ones is taking a big risk by providing the payment for your services in advance. He won't take kindly to duplicity."

Lin Cuirou jerked his wrist out of the man's grasp and then took the vial. "I'm not a fool," he said. "In addition to the main effects of the potion, it will also give me superhuman strength, correct?"

"That's right," the man said, pulling his hand back. "You will live forever, your beauty will be like that of a statue, and you will be so strong that no hand will be able to harm you."

"What if I need that strength to do the killing?" Lin Cuirou asked. "Seems kind of silly to wait until after the deed to gain extra strength."

The man in tan rose to his feet. "Kill at least one of them, then take the potion. Afterward, you will have a status higher than you can possibly imagine."

CHAPTER 85
NORTH TOWER

W hen the time was right, they left the salt mines and headed northeast to the Zun River. After rafting east, they turned into one of the main tributaries that headed almost directly north.

At one point on the journey upstream, they could see a mountain off to the west that was now the tomb of Li Buwei, the Timeless Master. The mountain loomed on the horizon for an entire day, casting a somber mood upon the leaders of the sect.

Eventually the waters grew too shallow, and they disembarked, hiking through the trees and low-lying foothills of Mount Hai'an until they were no more than a day's walk from the Southern Fei River.

That was where they holed up in some caves high on the cliffs of the north side of Mount Hai'an. Mao Yun and Tie Gangwen were the only ones to proceed onward. Tie Gangwen went north to Yu Zhing to lead the forces from there, while Mao Yun went east to Xuanlu. The appointed time had already been set for the departures from Yu Zhing, Xuanlu, and Mount Hai'an. If the timing was right, the entire sect would reunite just below Heart's Ridge.

Anxiety mounted with each day that went by. It was as if everyone could sense the friends and family being held captive only a few short days away on Heart's Ridge.

Time went by both at a crawl and in a flash. On the appointed day, they left the cliff caves and marched north, crossing over the Southern Fei River and heading northeast. Their timing was perfect, and in the exact moment that they crossed the river, a large group of people appeared on the road from the southeast, led by Mao Yun.

For most of them, it was their first time seeing Bao and Sunan in almost two decades, making it a joyous and exciting reunion. For others, it was their first time to ever lay eyes on Bao and Sunan. To them, the legendary Dragon Sovereign and Phoenix Sovereign were almost like gods whose stories they had heard recounted, sung, and even acted out. Despite the solemnity of the occasion and the dire circumstances, it was still an amazing and almost surreal experience for everyone.

The formalities were kept to a minimum, and then they headed north.

Soon, Heart's Ridge rose up ahead, as well as the fortress prison built atop it.

As Sunan and Bao led the group north, Tie Gangwen appeared, leading the rest of the sect south.

It was on the shore of the Mei Lien Sea, right at the base of the Banyan Mountains, that the Dragon-Phoenix Sect assembled in full for the first time in many years.

Dragon Sovereign Sunan and Phoenix Sovereign Bao stood at the head of the sect, flanked by Dragon General Tie Gangwen and Phoenix General Mao Yun. Behind them were arrayed the seven Dragon Lords and the seven Claws of the Phoenix leading the fourteen halls.

When in hiding in Xuanlu and Yu Zhing, the various members of the sect had worn random and nondescript clothing. But here, they donned their official robes. The Dragon Division was clad in gold and the Phoenix Division in silver. It was a splendid and grand sight as they stood in formation, the sun shining down on them, the sea wind at their back.

Off to the side was Sun Mai with his people, and next to them were Blackleaf and his red-robed Hen-Shi Sect disciples, as well as other famous martial artists such as Kind Devil Fuling with his flying crocodiles.

After everyone was assembled and they were prepared to march, Bao put her Phoenix Crown on her head, and Sunan pulled out his Wind Saber, although he kept it sheathed. No one else could sense it, but as soon as the two objects were out in the open near each other, a resonance formed between them. To Bao and Sunan, it felt like tiny vibrations tugging between the two objects. During their many years in Nangu, they had experimented with the crown and the saber, and they knew how powerful they could be when used in unison. Now was the perfect time to draw upon that power.

Bao hoped that by using her Phoenix Crown, they would be able to simply walk into Heart's Ridge Prison. But that wasn't the only plan. Despite the sect having been separated for quite some time, over the years, Dragon Lord Sima Zikang had relentlessly trained the sect in their formations, and at the moment, they were ready for virtually any outcome.

If troops came out to meet them with spears and swords, they would use the Foxes in the Thicket formation. If arrows were loosed upon them, it would be Tiger Exploits the Boulder. If they needed to scale the outer walls, the sect's top qinggong experts would be utilized in Cloud of Bats. And those were only a few of the tricks Sima Zikang had up his sleeve.

The Dragon-Phoenix Sect was ready. They had come to take back their friends and family. And nothing could stop them.

***

Heart's Ridge Prison was a hulking structure whose architecture was not the type normally seen in Qi Xien. It had four towers, one in each corner of the prison, all of which were facing in the cardinal directions.

The north tower was the tallest of the group, and the room at the very top of that tower was set aside for use by the prison warden.

At the moment, the warden was in that tower, but he wasn't seated behind his table like he normally would be. That spot was occupied by none other than Bone General Geng Long, who was fiddling with four jade pendants laid out in front of him.

"Bone General, sir," the warden said, "the Dragon-Phoenix Sect is assembling down below."

Geng Long looked up. "Hm? Oh. Yes, as expected."

"Er, Bone General, it's quite a large group. Close to ten thousand from the look of it."

"Yes. The largest sect in the land now that I slaughtered that bitch Li Buwei."

The warden cleared his throat. "Sir, even with the Bone Slicers you brought, we don't even have two thousand men in the prison. This structure was designed to keep people inside, not the other way aroun—"

"Yes, yes. Have the men put up a good fight." He waved his hand dismissively. "Be off with you. Bring me updates as necessary."

As the warden hurried off, a slightly confused expression on his face, Geng Long picked up one of the jade pendants and held it closer to his face. It seemed ancient, and one could imagine how the faded whitish-green had once been as vibrant as a field of fresh grass in spring. But now it was faded and dull, and there were even dark spots on the surface that looked like rot.

A creature was carved on the surface of the pendant, something that looked like a half snake, half dragon, with two claws and a long tail.

"Flood dragon…" Geng Long murmured. "I really can't wait to see what you look like." A twisted smile slowly spread out across his face.

***

Just as the warden had said, the Heart's Ridge Prison had not been designed with a siege in mind. There was no narrow path leading up to its main gate, nor any impressive barbicans or ramparts.

The Dragon-Phoenix Sect marched up the slope leading to the fortress, stopping just out of bowshot.

Then Bao, Sunan, Tie Gangwen, and Mao Yun approached the gate on foot.

As they walked out in front the sect, the gate opened, and a young man in a suit of armor walked out, flanked by five soldiers. All of them looked very nervous but were trying to put on a front of confidence.

The two groups stopped a few meters apart, whereupon the young man in armor frowned and said, "I am Lieutenant Xue Lihu of the Heart's—"

Bao was in no mood for chatter.

"We are the Dragon-Phoenix Sect," she interrupted. "Open the gates and let us in immediately."

Lieutenant Xue's eyes widened for a brief moment, and then he nodded. "We'll open the gates right away." Turning on his heel, he added, "Should we notify Bone General Geng that you're here?"

Suddenly all the veins in Bao's body ignited with fury. "What did you just say?"

Lieutenant Xue stopped in his tracks. "Ma'am?"

"Bone General Geng Long is here?"

"Why, yes, ma'am. He arrived only a few days ago for an inspection."

Bao's eyes flickered with a cold light. After exchanging a glance with Sunan, she said, "Take me to him."

***

Geng Long was carefully applying some poison to a wickedly serrated knife when the door burst open and the warden hurried into the room.

"Bone General, they're inside already!"

Geng Long looked up. "What?"

"I don't know what happened. The guards just opened the gate. None of them even put up a fight!"

"Spineless cowards!"

The warden shook his head. "Bone General, there must be some magic at work. Not even your Bone Slicers at the gate did anything. They simply dropped their weapons and sat down on the ground."

Geng Long sheathed his dagger and rose to his feet. "Dammit, what other tricks do they have that we're not aware of? Well, it doesn't matter. This just means things will move a bit faster than planned."

"Sir, should we activate the Krahang door?"

"*Fool!*" Geng Long bellowed. "That door is worth a thousand times more than the lives of everyone here combined! It's to be used only *after* the Dragon-Phoenix Sect has been wiped out! You think the Five Ghosts would be happy if we reneged on our agreement?"

***

Bao couldn't be everywhere at once, so there was some fighting as the Dragon-Phoenix Sect spread out through Heart's Ridge Prison. But they had numbers on their side, as well as passion, and no amount of resistance could stop them for long.

No one interfered with Bao and Sunan at all as Lieutenant Xue led them through the corridors toward the north tower of the prison. They were joined by Sun Mai, Lin Cuirou, and Ma Ge.

However, after making the long climb up the tower and cautiously entering the room at its top, they found no trace of Geng Long or the prison warden.

"I-I-I don't know where they are," Lieutenant Xue stammered. "They should be here!"

"That bastard probably ran as soon as he knew we were coming," Bao spat. "No matter. Whether he turns up now or later, I'll kill him. Let's get back down to the main courtyard."

At the bottom of the tower, just as they were about to head toward the main courtyard, Lin Cuirou said, "Dragon Sovereign, according to my man on the construction crew here, there's a secret storage chamber not too far from here. It might contain some items we could use in our fight."

"Sounds interesting," Sunan said, looking over at Bao.

She nodded. "You go with Lin Cuirou. I'll take charge of the evacuation."

Lin Cuirou turned and headed down the corridor in the opposite direction, a slight smile on his face. Sunan hurried after him.

CHAPTER 86
LOOK!

Lin Cuirou led the way through a few winding corridors and down some staircases until they were beneath the main level of the prison. Soon they reached one long corridor with a door at the end.

"I doubt it's unlocked," Lin Cuirou said. "You wait here, Dragon Sovereign." With that, he hurried to the end of the corridor to confirm that the door was locked.

"Locked," he called out. Taking several steps away from the door, he lifted his left foot up and said, "Glamorous Stomp!"

He slammed his foot down, which caused a burst of green energy to surge out around him. Without pausing, he took another step forward, and the green energy grew stronger. A third step, and the energy transformed into a finger-thick streak of blinding light that snaked forward across the ground, slamming into the door, which subsequently exploded into a shower of splinters.

The Glamorous Stomp was a move invented by Lin Cuirou

himself, and it had become quite popular, especially among the Dragon Division.

"The way's clear, Dragon Sovereign," he said, entering the room and then stepping aside to allow Sunan to pass.

Sunan hurried forward and found himself within what appeared to be a storeroom. However, a single glance revealed that the room was completely empty.

"Lin Cuirou, are you sure—"

Before he could finish speaking, he sensed a powerful force bearing down on his neck, and instinctively leaned forward in a dodge, after which, a sword sliced through the air above him. Spinning and leaping back, he swept his sheathed Wind Saber out to find Lin Cuirou lunging at him with a stabbing attack.

"What are you doing?" he cried, swiping the sword to the side with his Wind Saber. When the blade of the sword made contact with the sheath of the Wind Saber, a blast of energy erupted, and Lin Cuirou was shoved backward three paces.

"Sorry about this, Sunan," Lin Cuirou said, wiping a tiny drop of blood off the corner of his mouth. "But some things in life are more important than ideals. If I don't kill you this day, the Bone General will."

Anger flashed in Sunan's eyes. Although Lin Cuirou's actions were befuddling, there was obviously no time to ponder the situation. "So that's how it is," Sunan said. "Very well. Wind Devastation!"

He snapped his sheathed Wind Saber out in front of him, sending a stream of bluish wind energy spiraling toward Lin Cuirou at incredible speed.

However, Lin Cuirou was a profound master, just the same as Sunan, and he had been planning this ambush for a very long time. He had even visualized how the fight between him and Sunan would play out. Although Sunan had been gone for many years, and no one in the empire was aware of what techniques he might have invented during that time, Lin Cuirou had extensive combat experience, and he was confident in being able to handle anything Sunan threw at him.

There was no time to dodge or leap to the side, so instead, Lin Cuirou reached out with the four fingers of his right hand curved like hooks.

"Four Emptinesses of Death!" Lin Cuirou growled. Shockingly, his four fingers pierced into the blue wind energy, stopping its motion. Lin Cuirou's entire arm began to tremble violently, sweat popped out on his forehead, and his eyes turned completely bloodshot.

However, to the shock of Sunan, the wind energy simply faded away into nothing. Shaking his hand out as if to loosen it, Lin Cuirou chuckled. "And now something special I've been working on just for you. The next version of my Glamorous Stomp. I still haven't named it yet. Maybe I'll go with Dragon Decapitation Steps!"

Before Sunan could do anything else, Lin Cuirou stomped his foot down, causing energy to surge up around him that was ten times more intense than the energy from his third step before. Then he took two more steps forward, and the energy continued to build, filling the entire chamber with blinding light, causing everything in the area to vibrate on the point of collapse.

When his foot stomped onto the floor after having taken his third step, an arm-thick streak of light shot toward Sunan across the floor.

"Blink of the Dragon," Sunan murmured, closing his eyes. In the instant that his eyelids closed, he completely vanished. The arm-thick streak of light shot past the point where he had just been standing, slamming into the rear wall of the chamber, causing an enormous blast that sent shattered stone and clumps of soil showering out in all directions. Even many of the stones that formed the roof of the chamber fell to the ground.

A moment later, Sunan opened his eyes, reappearing in the same spot as before.

Lin Cuirou gritted his teeth. "Damrnit, you're really making things hard, aren't you? Fine. No more holding back."

Hands blurring, Lin Cuirou produced two objects, one being a small jade vial, the other being a metal sphere. In one smooth motion, he popped open the jade vial, then launched the sphere into the air, sending it speeding toward Sunan.

Sunan, couldn't see anything particularly incredible about the attack with the metal sphere, so he simply swept his Wind Saber out to deflect the sphere. However, when the surface of the scabbard made contact with the sphere, a clicking sound rang out, and the sphere popped open, releasing a cloud of powder into Sunan's face.

As Sunan leapt backward, coughing, Lin Cuirou chuckled and said, "And now my reward!"

Laughing loudly, he said, "You're dead for sure now, Sunan. That poison will kill you within a day no matter what you do! Therefore, according to my agreement with the King of the Pure Ones, I am free to drink this potion!"

Lifting the jade vial up to his lips, he drank the contents and then tossed the vial off to the side. A moment later, a tremor passed through him, and a faint green light began to shine out of his eyes. "But waiting that long would be a real shame. I think I'll rip your head off your shoulders first!"

Shaking visibly, Lin Cuirou began to laugh, softy at first, but then louder and louder until it turned into maniacal raving. "I can feel the power erupting inside of me! You're dead, Sunan. Dead!"

Sunan gripped his sheathed Wind Saber in a ready position as he watched Lin Cuirou twitching. Shockingly, the green light began to shine from Lin Cuirou's veins, many of which were bulging out of his skin. His hands were clenched into fists, and his muscles were taut. Next, to Sunan's shock, Lin Cuirou began to grow larger and taller, until he ripped through his upper garments. Then he threw his head back and roared, whereupon green flames erupted from his eyes, ears, nose, and mouth. As the flames swirled about, his hair caught fire, melting it into nothing but ash.

Lin Cuirou's laughter had ceased.

"This power," he said through grated teeth. "It's too much. I can't… It's killing… me… Damn you, Demon Emperor."

Closing his eyes, he pressed his palms together in front of his chest and took a deep breath, apparently attempting to slip into a meditative trance.

Meanwhile, the green light had spread beyond his veins. His skin was now glowing, so brightly that Sunan had to avert his eyes. A sound filled the air like the roar of countless beasts and demons, increasing to such volume that Sunan clamped his hands over his ears.

A long moment passed, although Sunan wasn't sure how long it was exactly. On the one hand, it seemed like the blink of an eye, but on the other, it seemed like an eternity. Eventually the light and the sound faded, and Sunan opened his eyes.

The sight which met his eyes caused his jaw to drop. Right there in the spot where Lin Cuirou had been standing was what appeared to be a slab of semi-translucent jade, with Lin Cuirou seemingly trapped in the middle of it. He had been transformed into something not human anymore, as if he were part of the jade itself. He looked almost like a statue, except that his eyes were open and appeared to be staring directly at Sunan.

His hands were held in front of his chest, palm to palm, just like they had been moments before.

In the eerie quiet that filled the area, Sunan took a tentative step forward, then another, until he was in front of the jade slab. As he did, Lin Cuirou's eyes seemed to follow him, even though they didn't move. Finally, Sunan reached out and touched the jade, to find that it was as cold as ice. After a moment, he shook his head and sighed.

"What have you done to yourself, Lin Cuirou?" he thought. "Are you still alive in there?"

Considering the size of the slab of emeraldlike jade, there was no way Sunan could move it on his own. Resolving to come back later for it if possible, Sunan quickly sat down cross-legged and cast his senses inward to check his blood vessels for traces of poison. At the moment, he couldn't find a single trace of anything out of the ordinary.

"Was it a bluff?" he thought. After a few minutes passed, he rose to his feet. Shaking his head, he began to make his way back to the main courtyard.

***

With Bao's Phoenix Crown, and the fact that Dragon-Phoenix Sect vastly outnumbered the soldiers in the prison fortress, they met no serious resistance.

By the time Sunan made it back up to the ground level, the evacuation had already begun. Families were being reunited, but there was no time for extended reunions. Everyone began to file down to the beaches below, where they formed back up into ranks according to the divisions of the sect. It was a large group, nearly twenty thousand in total, so the entire process took quite some time.

No one saw even the shadow of Bone General Geng or any other high-level Bone Slicers. As for the news regarding Lin Cuirou, Sunan told Bao, Mao Yun, and Li Runfa, who all agreed that now was not the time to reveal the information to the sect as a whole. They simply said that he had fallen in a cowardly attack by a Bone Slicer.

It was late in the afternoon before all of the imprisoned friends and family members were freed and the prison was emptied. The Dragon-Phoenix Sect and the other miscellaneous martial artists made a huge conglomeration of people that stretched from the area where the land sloped up steeply toward the prison, all the way to the sand of the beach.

When the task was accomplished, Sunan and Bao, as well as the other leaders of the sect, prepared to march south according to the plans they had made back in the salt mines.

The two divisions would split, one going up the Southern Fei River with the intention of reoccupying the palace on Zun Shan, and the other would go to infiltrate Xuanlu. Only two of the boats in the nearby shipyard were complete, so a smaller group would use them to sail down to the Zun River, then up it toward Zhe Valley and the Scorpion Villa.

As the sect leaders were conferring about the final details, Wang Tian suddenly interrupted, "Dragon Sovereign. Phoenix Sovereign. Look!"

Everyone turned to find that two people were walking up the beach toward them, some distance away.

***

High atop the mountain above Heart's Ridge, Hui stood on a ledge, looking down at the sprawling group of people that was the Dragon-Phoenix Sect.

"The time has come," she murmured. Raising the Kun-Peng Pipes to her lips, she took a breath.

CHAPTER 87
KUN-PENG

The two figures approached from the south, too small to make out clearly at first. However, as they drew closer, their features became clear.

The first one was none other than Geng Long.

He wore his Bone General armor and had something slung over his back in a sack.

Roughly a hundred meters to the west of him, and a bit farther back, was a tall, burly man with a long scar running down the side of his neck, also clad in bone armor, with a similar sack hanging over his shoulder.

As soon as Bao saw Geng Long, her heart began to thump, and she felt her rage beginning to burn. However, instead of the hot, uncontrollable rage from years ago that burned like wildfire, this rage was like a sea of lava, slow moving but destructive.

Bao immediately pulled out her Phoenix Crown and put it on her head.

"Geng Long," she growled, then she took two steps forward.

Next to her, Sunan also stepped forward, his Wind Saber at the ready. Although nobody noticed it—not even Sunan himself—he was sweating more than usual, and he had begun to cough occasionally.

The other leaders of the Dragon-Phoenix Sect, as well as Sun Mai and Blackleaf, all stirred, some of them drawing weapons. Others simply got into ready stances.

When Geng Long was about fifty meters away, Bao raised her voice, imbuing it with some qi to make it boom like thunder.

"Do we really have to do this right now, Geng Long?"

Responding with his own qi-imbued voice, Geng Long said, "That's Bone General Geng to you, bitch."

His profanity and disrespect caused cries of anger to rise up from the Dragon-Phoenix Sect, and the air soon filled with the sounds of weapons being drawn.

"How dare you!"

"This bastard needs to die!"

"The Phoenix Sovereign killed two of the Demon Emperor's generals already. It seems today is the day to kill a third!"

Geng Long subsequently flung the sack off his shoulder, sending it thumping into the sand in front of him. Whatever was inside the sack was relatively large, reaching all the way up to Geng Long's waist. Reaching out, he untied the sack, allowing it to slip down to reveal a four-sided cauldron, greenish-colored and covered with carvings of demonic creatures.

The Bone Slicer a bit farther west followed suit.

"I was hoping to kill you myself, Bao," Geng Long said. "But I suppose watching you get killed will have to do."

"Come fight me one on one," Bao replied. "We'll see who kills who. The last two times we met, you ran away like the coward rat you are."

Geng Long's jaw twitched for a moment, but he didn't respond directly. Instead, he reached into a pouch at his waist and pulled out a jade pendant, which he held out directly over the cauldron.

"It's time to end this nonsense," Geng Long said. "And ironically, the Dragon-Phoenix Sect will be brought to death... by dragons." Chuckling, he crushed the jade pendant and dropped the pieces into the cauldron.

Immediately, rumbling sounds that seemed to come from another time and place filled the air. The ground began to vibrate beneath their feet. A moment later, black flames erupted from the cauldron, shooting dozens of meters up into the air as they radiated not heat, but intense cold.

Then a howl echoed out, hoarse and grating, seemingly filled with rage and sorrow and hatred.

A moment later, another howl echoed from the west, where the Bone Slicer had crushed a similar jade pendant and tossed it into the cauldron he had been carrying.

Before anyone could do anything, two more pillars of freezing black flame shot up far to the north, on the other side of the amassed Dragon-Phoenix Sect.

The howls erupting from within the cauldrons joined together in a vicious, angry harmony that caused the skin to crawl and the heart to tremble.

The ground continued to tremble harder and harder, until it was quaking with such intensity that it was difficult for some of the lower-level Dragon-Phoenix Sect fighters, as well as the ordinary family members, to keep on their feet.

Meanwhile, the four cauldrons were expanding, growing twice, three times, ten times larger than before.

Finally, a burst of cold air far more frigid than the previous coldness spread out in all directions as an enormous figure burst out of Geng Long's cauldron.

It was like a huge snake, with long horns and cold eyes, as well as two viciously clawed talons. It was huge, fully one hundred meters long, with scales so black they glinted with violet light. Shockingly, much of the creature was in a state of decay, as if it had been dragged up from the grave. There were even bones visible on many parts of its body, and in some areas it was possible to look right through it to the other side.

As the creature shot out of the cauldron, it howled with rage, then flew through the air in a spiral before coming to a stop just above Geng Long.

Even as gasps of shock and cries of alarm could be heard from the Dragon-Phoenix Sect, another of the creatures shot up from the cauldron to the west, and then two more off in the distance, behind the sect.

"What are those things?" Sunan said faintly.

"If I'm not mistaken, they're flood dragons," Sun Mai replied. "Although, they have other names, depending on which texts you read. These ones appear to be reanimated corpses."

"How do we fight them?" Bao said.

Sun Mai shook his head. "I don't know."

With that, Geng Long raised his arm above his head. "And now, let the slaughter beg—"

Before Geng Long could finish speaking, a piercing sound entered the ears of all present, boring into their ears and down into their minds. It was a long, resonant, vibrating call that resembled that of some winged creature of the heavens.

It was so loud, that many people clamped their hands over their ears and closed their eyes. Even Sunan and Bao winced, and Geng Long's eyes flickered.

A moment later, the pitch of the sound rose, and then fell, then began to twist and spiral into what was clearly a song of some sort.

It was an ancient, melancholy song that was somehow tinged with righteousness and vigor.

Next, an enormous crashing sound rose up from the water out in the bay, causing everyone to turn their heads and see a huge plume of water surging up into the air, as if an enormous object had just dropped down into the water.

As eyes widened and jaws dropped, a shape bulged out of the water some distance from where the water was still spraying out in all directions.

Something emerged silently from the depths of the bay, a creature the size of a whale, or even larger. However, it was no whale, but a fish with bright blue scales and long fins.

The fish sailed through the air for a moment before splashing back down into the water, unleashing another eruption of water and sending huge waves rolling out across the bay.

Everyone stared in shock, and the fish again leapt up into the air. This time, its fins rippled and distorted as they spread out, growing larger and longer. Iridescent blue and yellow feathers began to sprout out from its scales. Its tail flapped back and forth, also growing larger and longer, transforming into what looked more like long feathers.

The fish's mouth changed shape, becoming a hooked beak, above which were black shining eyes.

As these transformations took place, the four flood dragons seemed to recoil, edging away from the direction of the water.

This time, the fish didn't land back into the water. Its fins transformed into wings, its tail into tailfeathers, its dorsal fin into a feathered crest that ran from the top of its head all the way down its back.

Legs sprouted out, long, with viciously taloned claws that glinted in the evening light.

Just when the bird reached the apex of its leap from within the waters of the bay, it flapped its enormous wings, propelling it toward the beach at incredible speed.

"Kun-Peng, it's you," Sun Mai breathed.

As Kun-Peng flew across the bay, each flap of its wings caused waves to spread out on the surface of the water below. At one point, it let out a piercing cry that seemed to resonate with the deafening song that filled the air.

The flood dragons howled in fear and terror.

Although it wasn't clear to anyone what exactly was happening, the Dragon-Phoenix Sect, and especially its leaders, could somehow sense that this huge bird bore them no ill intentions. Perhaps it was the way the flood dragons were edging backward, or just the aura of the enormous bird itself, but somehow they felt like bullied children, backed into the corner of an alley, only to have an adult suddenly appear to save them.

As Kun-Peng neared, its size became clearer—it was enormous. Its wingspan was fully twice the length of any of the flood dragons.

With each beat of its wings, it moved forward at incredible speed, and it was only moments away from the shore.

"Dammit," Geng Long growled, "what the *fuck* is that thing?" Reaching into another belt pouch, he pulled out what appeared to be a hardened clump of clay, which he crushed in his fist. Green smoke began to rise up from the shattered remnants of the clay, which he then tossed into the cauldron in front of him.

In response, the cauldron shook visibly and began to emit intense humming sounds.

"Kill that bird!" Geng Long shouted.

The flood dragon nearest him shivered for a moment, then coiled up into a tight ball before shooting toward the incoming Kun-Peng.

Moments later, the other three flood dragons similarly began to charge toward the Kun-Peng, apparently having been given compelling orders just like the first one.

Under the stunned gazes of the Dragon-Phoenix Sect, four one-hundred-meter-long flood dragons charged toward the gargantuan Kun-Peng with its two-hundred-meter wingspan.

Wind from Kun-Peng's wings swept across the beach like gale-force gusts as it bore down on the reanimated flood dragon corpses.

The first to reach the giant bird was the flood dragon that Geng Long had summoned. Right before they were about to slam into each other, the flood dragon opened its mouth and screamed, letting out a blast of black liquid colder than ice. It shot out like water from a fountain, causing cracking sounds to fill the air.

Kun-Peng was huge, but that didn't mean it wasn't agile. It pulled its wings in and spun to the side, completely dodging the blast of freezing black liquid, then lashing out with its talons to grab the flood dragon.

As for the black liquid, it sailed past the spot the Kun-Peng had just occupied, slamming into the water of the bay, much of which was frozen upon impact.

Meanwhile, Kun-Peng dropped down toward the ground, crushing the flood dragon into the earth below on a spot only about a hundred meters away from the Dragon-Phoenix Sect itself. The ground quaked as the flood dragon was shoved into the soil. Kun-Peng lashed its sharp beak down toward the creature's throat. However, before its beak could make contact, the second flood dragon arrived, sending a blast of freezing liquid toward Kun-Peng's torso. Kun-Peng lurched to the side just in time, managing to escape the blast, but losing its grip on the first flood dragon, whose head snaked around as it snapped at Kun-Peng's leg with viciously sharp teeth. The second flood dragon closed in, similarly lashing its jaws at Kun-Peng's right wing.

The developments that were taking place were almost too shocking for the Dragon-Phoenix Sect to process.

Kun-Peng and the two flood dragons were beginning to fight back and forth, causing the ground to shake violently. However, there were still two more flood dragons closing in.

Although Kun-Peng was vastly larger than the flood dragons, it was already having trouble tangling with two of them. If two more joined the fight, it was easy to imagine how quickly the battle could turn in the favor of the flood dragons.

The first person to recover his senses was Sun Mai. Of everyone present, he had the most experience with mystical phenomena like this. After all, he had traveled the streams of time, had glimpsed things that no other mortal had ever glimpsed, other than Du Qian. In fact, although no one present would have any way to know it, and perhaps no one ever would, Sun Mai had witnessed Kun-Peng's birth, countless years in the past.

Sun Mai's hands clenched into fists as he raised his voice. "Profound Masters, this mighty bird is Kun-Peng, a righteous servant of the Enlightened Goddess. Who will join me in taking the fight to one of these wicked flood dragons to buy Kun-Peng a bit of breathing room?"

CHAPTER 88
EXCHANGING BLOWS

Mao Yun was the first to step forward. Brandishing his axe, he said, "Let's take the head off of one of these worms!"

The One-Armed Iron Titan Tie Gangwen flicked his sleeve and growled, "It's been a long time since we fought side by side, Grandmaster Sun."

"I will fight," Lawat said. As usual, he was dressed in traditional Kithiri garb and wielded the long, sickle-shaped blade that was common in Nangu, a look which had earned him the nickname Golden Djinn.

One by one, the profound masters voiced their intent to join Sun Mai in fighting one of the flood dragons.

"That one!" Sun Mai said, pointing to the farthest of the dragons, which was speeding in an arcing path that would bring it past them within seconds. "Keep the fight away from the rest of the sect!"

With that, Sun Mai leapt into motion, calling up his qinggong to speed away from the sect, his robes flapping in the wind. The other profound masters followed, preparing weapons and martial arts techniques. Despite being expert fighters, each of them having combat experience far beyond most other people in the world, none of them had ever fought an enemy as enormous as this.

As for the flood dragon, it was completely focused on Kun-Peng, and it didn't notice the lowly humans converging upon it from the side.

As Sun Mai neared it, he waved his fingers through the air. "Sword Rain of the Scholar God!"

More than two dozen illusory swords sprang into being around him, which then slashed through the air toward the flood dragon.

The flood dragon was taken completely by surprise as the volley of swords slashed into the base of its neck with such force that it twisted to the side, lost altitude, and slammed into the ground, sending dirt and sand flying out in all directions.

As it did, the nearest of the profound masters unleashed further attacks, including a blast of energy that resembled a spear, a flying dagger that blazed with white fire, and a violet lightning bolt.

Before the flood dragon knew what was happening, it was hit again and again with numerous attacks, causing it to howl in anger.

However, after the initial surprise, the creature snapped its head around to glare in the direction of the approaching heroes, its eyes shining with blue light. Although a few rotting scales had been knocked off or melted, it didn't seem seriously hurt.

The flood dragon seemed to inhale, whereupon Sun Mai shouted, "Don't let the liquid touch you, and definitely don't let it get past us to touch the sect!"

A moment later, a blast of frigid black liquid erupted from the flood dragon's mouth, heading not only toward the profound masters, but the rest of the sect behind them.

Sun Mai spun to the side with barely a moment to spare. Some of the liquid even hit the corner of this robe, freezing it into a solid mass that shattered a moment later.

"Sleeve Cyclone!" Tie Gangwen growled, spinning his long sleeve in a circular motion, which sent wind screaming out in front of him to meet the black liquid.

The cyclone began to suck up the black liquid, and yet it was clearly not on the same level as the flood dragon's attack. A moment later, the wind began to collapse, having neutralized only about half of the black stream of liquid, which continued to stream through the air.

"Lava Arrow!" Wang Tian let loose an arrow, which transformed into a stream of burning, molten rock.

When the freezing black liquid and the burning lava touched each other, a high-pitched screech rang out, along with a shock wave that sent clouds of dust and sand up into the air.

Sun Mai landed off to the side, drew a sword from his side, and called out, "Press the attack. Kill it before it releases another blast!"

Moments before, when Sun Mai had been calling for the profound masters to intercept the flood dragon, not all of them had joined him. Sunan and Bao had remained behind as well.

"You two," Sunan said, pointing to two of the remaining profound masters. "Go handle that Bone Slicer to the west." Next, he looked at Blackleaf from the Hen-Shi Sect. "Can you take care of the Bone Slicers to the north?"

Blackleaf nodded and led his men away immediately.

"Ma Ge," Sunan continued, "you stay with me and Bao."

"I can handle him myself," Bao said through gritted teeth. She took a step forward.

"Maybe you can," Sunan said, stepping to follow her, "but the safest thing—" Before he could finish his sentence, his legs buckled, and he dropped forward onto his knees. Then he reached up and placed his right palm on his chest.

Bao turned to look at him, a slight frown of concern on her face. "Sunan?"

Ma Ge kneeled down and felt the pulse at his left wrist. "Poison," she said a moment later.

Bao's eyes widened. "Lin Cuirou poisoned you?"

Sunan settled backward into a cross-legged position, placing his still-sheathed Wind Saber across his knees. Closing his eyes, he said, "Yes. I thought perhaps it was a trick, but apparently not."

"You—"

"Go," Sunan interrupted. "Take care of that bastard once and for all. I can handle a bit of poison. Lawat, you back her up." Resting his hands on top of each other in his lap, palms up, he began to meditate.

Bao looked over at some of the lower-ranking members of the sect a few meters away. "You six, come stand guard over the Dragon Sovereign!"

With that, she turned toward Geng Long. "I've been waiting for this moment for a long time."

Moments before, Geng Long had been transfixed by the shocking fight erupting between the flood dragons and Kun-Peng. However, his attention was quickly drawn back to Bao as she began to walk toward him across the sandy soil, with Ma Ge following close behind. Although he was surprised to see Sunan sitting cross-legged in meditation, he ignored him.

"Just you two against me?" he said loudly. "Feeling suicidal?"

"This will be one on one," Bao replied. "The only question will be how long it takes for me to kill you. You stay back, Ma Ge. Don't interfere unless absolutely necessary."

Geng Long chuckled coldly, reaching over his shoulder to unstrap what appeared to be the femur bone of some enormous animal, the end of which had been sharpened into a point. The surface of the bone itself had been carved with countless strange symbols. It was pitch black, although it was impossible to tell whether that was by natural occurrence or because it had been dyed.

Geng Long gripped the unsharpened end with one hand, then

slowly ran the index and middle finger of his other hand down the length of the bone, muttering words in an incomprehensible language.

Countless bone spurs erupted from the strange symbols on the pitch-black bone, and the bone itself began to grow longer. Originally, it had only been about half a meter long, but in the blink of an eye, it was a full meter in length, and then two. In the end, it was a full three meters long!

Geng Long slowly lowered the enormous weapon to rest on his shoulder. "Even if ten of you came at me at once, I'd still cut you all in half."

Bao wasn't in the mood for banter, nor did she care for a protracted fight.

"Drop that weapon," she said, glaring into his eyes.

As soon as the words left her mouth, she could sense the power of the Phoenix Crown flowing out and boring into Geng Long's mind.

Geng Long's eyes widened, and the hand which gripped the bone sword twitched. However, a moment later, his eyes narrowed.

"So that's how you got into the fortress," he said. "Nice trick. Thankfully, the King of the Pure Ones trained me well. Mind tricks like that won't work on me."

Bao was now only twenty meters away from Geng Long. Considering that her Phoenix Crown didn't affect Geng Long, she decided to draw upon her next most powerful move. Some qi fighters preferred to start with their weakest moves and save the powerful ones for later in the fight when, presumably, the opponent was more tired and had used enough of their own techniques to reveal a weakness. But not Bao.

Using her rage to channel her qi along the same pathways as she had discovered years ago on Zhifu Shan, she slashed her right hand through the air and growled, "Rage Holocaust."

Five beams of red energy shot out from her fingers, which rapidly expanded in width until they merged with each other, forming a one-meter-wide column of destruction that hewed a massive furrow into the quaking ground as it bore down on a shocked Geng Long.

There was no time for Geng Long to ponder the situation or how to defend himself. Reacting on pure instinct, he swung his bone sword off his shoulder and, in the final moment before the column hit him, assumed a defensive stance with the sword held out horizontally in front of him.

The instant the column of energy made contact with the bone sword, red sparks erupted in a fountain, and Geng Long was shoved backward. He tried to dig his feet into the soil to hold his ground, but it did no good. Intense rumbling sounds filled the air as he was pushed backward one meter, two meters, five meters, ten meters…

The entire time, red sparks sprayed out in all directions, including onto Geng Long himself. When they hit his bone armor, they sizzled, leaving behind nicks and scratches, and when they touched his flesh, they smoked and burned. Geng Long howled at the top of his lungs, drawing on all of his energy to push back against the column of energy.

At the thirty-meter mark, he finally stopped moving. He shoved his bone sword forward with all the strength he could muster. As he did, the bone sword's serrated edge tore into the column of energy, ripping it apart right in the middle, sending a tempest of red sparks out in all directions as the column was completely destroyed.

As the energy faded away, Geng Long stood there panting at the end of a seventy-meter-long trench that separated him from Bao. His bone armor was in bad condition, and his face was covered with countless burns and patches of melted, seared flesh. And yet, a wild gleam could be seen in his eyes as he once again hefted his bone sword up onto his shoulder.

"Impressive, Bao. Much better than last time. Too bad you won't be able to use that move again anytime soon. Also, now I'm at the perfect distance to use one of my favorite techniques. Bone Meteor!"

As he spoke, he stamped his right foot down onto the ground, releasing a burst of energy that sent a minor shock wave rolling out as he shot up into the air.

To Bao, it looked like a qinggong technique, although she couldn't be certain. Geng Long became a blur as he shot up in an arcing path, reaching a height of about twenty-five meters before he began to plummet back down toward her. As he sailed through the air, he spun his enormous bone sword like a wheel, creating a black blur that virtually crackled with qi energy.

Bao's first instinct was to run to the side, but even as she did, the black blur changed course, as if it were locked on to her person. As it closed in, she realized that she had no choice but to meet the blow, and yet she had no weapons to do so other than the daggers in her sleeve.

And two ordinary daggers were definitely not enough to stop that wheel.

CHAPTER 89
SOULS

Sunan closed his eyes and tuned out the sounds around him.

Back in the fortress, he hadn't felt any effects from the poison. He hadn't even been able to detect its presence in his blood. Only after the complete evacuation, when the sect leadership began to confer, did he break out into a cold sweat. Then before he knew it, his heart was racing, and he had begun to cough.

It had been imperceptible at first, and the appearance of the flood dragons and Kun-Peng had been so shocking that he had been swept up in the events.

Now, as he cast his awareness inward, he became more aware than ever of the racing of his heart. With every passing moment, it beat faster and faster.

So that's why I didn't notice it before. It's only in my heart. Although Sunan was no physician, he knew that the human body had limits.

If my heart doesn't slow down, he thought, *what will happen? Will it stop? Or collapse?* Whatever happened, it would fatal, of that he was sure.

He attempted to breathe more slowly to calm himself, and he also tried to slow his qi flow. However, none of those things did any good. Bit by bit, his heart raced and raced toward what was certain death.

I need to calm my heart, Sunan thought. *Calm.*

He thought back to years before when he'd climbed almost to the very top of Zun Shan to meditate. His qi flow had been altered during that state of meditation, leading him into a state of profound calmness. In the years that had followed, he had contemplated how his qi had flowed and had replicated it on a few occasions. However, other than the state of deep calm, it had never proven particularly useful.

He altered the flow of his qi to match that same qi flow he had discovered on Zun Shan.

Within moments, his heart rate stabilized. Then, as he continued to send his qi flowing through those particular meridians, the beating began to slow.

However, as his heart began to calm, he noticed countless minute objects flowing out from it into his blood vessels.

That's the poison.

His heart was beating as calmly as if he were floating on the top of a lake. But the poison was still present inside of him. To Sunan, it seemed as if hours had passed, but from the moment he had fell to his knees until his heart calmed, only a few breaths of time had passed.

Is Bao safe?

He opened his left eye just a crack, and the sight that met his eyes almost caused his heart to begin racing again.

Bao was standing about twenty meters away or so, looking up at what appeared to be an enormous black wheel falling out of the sky directly toward her. She almost seemed rooted in place, as if she couldn't move.

When Sunan focused more closely on the black wheel, he realized that it was Geng Long, wielding a sword that was so exaggeratedly long it was almost comical. However, there was nothing comical about the energy fluctuations rolling off of him. Even with this one brief glance, Sunan could tell with certainty that if Bao were to be struck by this technique, she should be grievously injured, perhaps even killed.

Sunan took his right hand off his knee and grabbed the hilt of his Wind Saber.

"Bao!" he shouted, drawing the Wind Saber from its scabbard and throwing it in her direction.

He had kept his Wind Saber sheathed for a very long time, not even drawing it during his fight with Lin Cuirou. The scabbard within which it was sheathed was the same one Ruan the Flamingo had created for him to wear on his wedding day. The spell formation in that scabbard could focus and build up the power of the Wind Saber over time, allowing it to reach shocking levels.

When Bao heard Sunan calling her name, she glanced back and saw his Wind Saber speeding toward her in a blur.

During their years in Nangu, they had done a bit of experimentation, and they were sure that if the Wind Saber and the Phoenix Crown were used together, the resonance between them would unleash devastating force. However, because of the volatile way the two objects reacted to each other's presence, they had never actually gone so far as to use them together in a fight.

But it was a critical moment, and there was no time to ponder the situation.

As the black blur that was Geng Long descended, Bao reached out and grabbed the Wind Saber. Ripples of power coursed through her meridians, causing her to gasp. The Phoenix Crown began to shake, creating vibrations that perfectly matched the ripples of power. Within the blink of an eye, the Phoenix Crown and the Wind Saber connected to each other, using her body as a channel of communication.

Although the connection itself was beyond Bao's control, she could sense that somehow the Wind Saber was tugging at the phoenix demon sealed inside of the crown, causing it to let out a miserable, enraged shriek.

"Shut up, you oversized chicken," Bao growled through gritted teeth.

There was power stored inside of the Wind Saber, but with the addition of the essence of the phoenix demon, that power began to expand exponentially. Bao's hand began to tremble, and then her entire arm.

The energy seemed to be growing at an exponential rate and was rapidly reaching a point where it couldn't be contained. Bao quickly realized that if she didn't release that energy, it would almost certainly harm her, and it could potentially kill her.

***

Meanwhile, Kun-Peng was locked in a vicious struggle with three flood dragons. The flood dragons were no match for the enormous bird in terms of raw strength, but they clearly had the advantage in terms of mobility and speed. Kun-Peng was like a sovereign of the sky and was not the type of creature built for close-quarters combat.

The bird had its beak latched on to the neck of one of the flood dragons and was just about to rip its head off when another of the flood dragons bit onto the base of its wing.

Releasing the first flood dragon, Kun-Peng jerked the second flood dragon away, then lashed at it with enormous curved talons.

That was when the third flood dragon head-butted Kun-Peng on the back, sending it staggering forward.

Of course, considering the enormous size of the beasts, their battle caused the ground to shake and sent intense rumbling sounds out in all directions.

Thankfully, the flood dragons' black liquid attack didn't seem to be something that could be used again in a short period of time, for none of the flood dragons had unleashed that attack a second time.

As Kun-Peng and the three flood dragons fought back and forth, Sun Mai and the profound masters continued to hold their own against the lone flood dragon. In their battle, they were the ones who lacked strength but had the advantage in mobility and speed.

With one powerful martial arts technique after another, they slashed and battered the flood dragon, simultaneously using their qinggong to avoid the deadly attacks being leveled against them. So far, not a single one of the profound masters had been seriously injured.

***

Geng Long was only two meters away from Bao this point. There was no time for lengthy planning or strategizing, and she knew she couldn't simply attempt to block Geng Long's technique. She had to unleash an attack of her own.

She did her best to focus the terrifying energy buildup and then swung the Wind Saber out in front of her. White and blue light erupted out to meet the pitch black of Geng Long's attack, and when the two forces met, a deafening droning sound filled the air, a sound like a thousand boulders being shattered by lightning.

Geng Long's eyes went wide, and his mouth twisted into a snarl. And yet that snarl quickly vanished as he realized that he was being pushed backward.

The white and blue light erupting from the Wind Saber shone brighter and brighter as it shoved Geng Long and his bone sword away from Bao, slowly at first, but then faster and faster.

Moments before, the bone sword had defended against and eventually destroyed the Rage Holocaust. However, against the combined might of the Phoenix Crown and the Wind Saber, it was like a dried branch trying to stop a rolling boulder.

The droning sound continued to increase in pitch, and the white and blue light grew brighter, until it was like a sun shining on a battlefield.

Within moments, the beam of light erupting from the Wind Saber was so large it was about to envelop Geng Long. It was to his shock that cracks began to spread out on the surface of his bone sword.

A moment later, the sword began to shatter, starting at the tip, working down the blade to the spot where his two hands held the base of the weapon. Next, his suit of bone armor began to split apart and fall off. Then, when there was nothing left to stave off the deadly white and blue energy, Geng Long found his skin melting.

An enraged, terrified scream of pain and disbelief escaped his lips as his muscles were reduced to ash, and then his bones were incinerated.

And the energy of the Wind Saber was still not fully unleashed.

Geng Long was reduced to nothing more than a shadow, which then disappeared into the sunlike light of Bao's attack. She turned her head to the left.

There, Kun-Peng was in the middle of fighting two flood dragons. Moments before, the gargantuan bird had finally managed to rip the head off of one of the flood dragons, which it tossed into the waters of the bay. There, the decapitated corpse transformed into countless motes of black light that faded away into nothing.

The other two flood dragons had both received injuries of some sort. One of them had a gash on its back that almost cut through its entire body. The other had one of its legs ripped off.

However, Kun-Peng was also in bad condition, with numerous wounds that bled scintillating green blood. One of the flood dragons had latched its jaws onto the bird's right wing, while the other circled around through the air, apparently intent on attacking Kun-Peng from behind.

As the second flood dragon prepared to do just that, a beam

of white and blue light slashed through the air like a whip toward it. Before it could react, the light slammed into the flood dragon, incinerating half of its body in the blink of an eye.

Only then did the light finally fade away.

Bao sagged in place, lowering the Wind Saber until the tip rested on the ground in front of her. Sweat was dripping down her face, and her entire body was trembling.

Although Geng Long's attack hadn't even come close to touching her, she still felt as though she had been injured. Closing her eyes, she cast her senses inside of her, but she couldn't find any internal injuries. And yet she somehow felt incomplete.

Suddenly, she recalled something Du Qian had mentioned decades ago. *Every person has five souls inside of them. The cathartic method of drawing on qi has the potential to damage or even destroy those souls.*

Bao took a deep breath. *Now's not the time to worry about souls.*

CHAPTER 90
REVELATIONS

Hui stood high up on the mountain, freezing wind buffeting her face and sending her robes and hair whipping about as she watched events playing out down below. The sight of enormous Kun-Peng rising up from the water was awe-inspiring. Although she had met Kun-Peng face to face in the Eastern Archipelagos, the creature had been in fish form, which she had only glimpsed in the depths of a murky subterranean lake.

To see the creature out in the open was breathtaking.

It was little surprise to Hui that the profound masters of the Dragon-Phoenix Sect leapt into the fray with the flood dragons. She could well remember the tales she had heard as a girl regarding the Defeat at Heart's Ridge. During that battle, it hadn't just been the profound masters who joined the fight. Even the weakest members of the sect put their lives on the line to defeat the monsters thrown at them by the Bone General. Although they had destroyed the flood dragons in the end, most of the heroes lost their lives in the process.

But this time, things were playing out very differently. Less than a minute after the initial fighting broke out, Kun-Peng had destroyed one of the flood dragons.

Moments later, a brilliant white and blue light filled the battlefield, and Hui's eyes widened, then narrowed as the light grew uncomfortably bright, even from the great distance at which she observed it.

"What is that?" she murmured. To her shock, the light curved through the air and slashed one of the flood dragons in two before winking out. That light was something that had not been mentioned in any of the stories Hui had heard.

"Something new? It seemed to contain the fluctuations of both the Wind Saber and the Phoenix Crown. Don't tell me... someone is wielding the saber and the crown at the same time?"

In the history Hui knew, it wasn't until the final confrontation with the Demon Emperor that the secret powers of the saber and crown had been revealed. According to the stories, after Sunan fell in battle, Bao picked up his Wind Saber and unleashed a devastating attack with it. However, by that point of the fight, even such a powerful attack did little good. The Demon Emperor was wounded, but he struck back with a vicious blow that killed Bao. Afterward, the Demon Emperor took control of the Wind Saber and the Phoenix Crown, which only strengthened his iron grip over Qi Xien and gave him another tool to expand his conquest throughout the continent.

In any case, Sunan and Bao definitely did not combine the power of the two objects in the Defeat of Heart's Ridge.

"Things are already changing..."

With a second flood dragon already dead, the fight didn't continue for much longer. Kun-Peng ripped the third dragon to shreds, and moments later, the profound masters finally battered the fourth one into oblivion.

What had once been a crushing, demoralizing, and bloody defeat had become a momentous victory.

Hui worked hard to suppress the smile from breaking out on her face. She failed, and it blossomed across her face.

"Time to send you away, Kun-Peng," she murmured, raising the pipes to her lips.

***

After the final motes of black light that were the remains of the fourth flood dragon faded away, the profound masters looked around in both shock and triumph.

A moment later, Kun-Peng let out a piercing cry, then leapt into the air, wings sending a blast of air out in all directions. Perhaps it was because of the frenzy of events, or perhaps because of the sea breeze, but almost no one seemed to notice that, in accompaniment with Kun-Peng launching into the air, the faint sound of music was floating through the air. It was nothing like the triumphant, symphonic blast of noise that had summoned the creature, and in fact, it was only Sun Mai who noticed it.

As Kun-Peng flew high into the sky and then disappeared to the west, Sun Mai looked up toward the top of the mountain, his eyes glittering.

***

Although the Dragon-Phoenix Sect was far away at the bottom of the mountain, Hui was a profound master with keen eyesight, and she could just barely make out some of the figures down below.

After defeating the flood dragons and watching Kun-Peng fly away, the profound masters converged at the front of the sect, presumably to confer about what action to take next. Feeling more pleased than ever about how everything was playing out, Hui closed her eyes to meditate and restore some of the energy she had expended to power the Kun-Peng Pipes.

Time passed.

The wind blew.

After a while, just when Hui was about to rise to her feet and gather the few belongings in the cave to leave the mountain, she realized that she wasn't alone anymore. Her eyes slowly opened, and she turned her head to find a man standing several paces to the side.

He wore long robes and had a clean-shaven head, and she knew who he was the instant she laid eyes on him.

"Sun Mai," she said. "Excellent qinggong. I didn't sense your approach at all."

Sun Mai nodded politely. "May I ask your honored surname?"

Hui slowly rose to her feet, then clasped hands and bowed deeply. "Fan Hui of the Dragon-Phoenix Sect."

Sun Mai's eyes widened. "Fan...?"

Hui nodded. "Golden Dragon Division."

Sun Mai looked a bit closer at her. "There's something about your aura. Those fluctuations..."

"They are similar to the fluctuations from that chariot you rode into the past."

"How?"

Hui took a deep breath. "Master Sun, considering that we are now talking to each other face to face, I think that attempting to hide the truth would be pointless. However, I must request that you keep the information I'm about to tell you strictly in confidence. Considering that you have traveled through the streams of time yourself, I'm sure you can understand why I'm... hesitant to disturb their flow."

"The streams of time? So my speculations were not too far from the truth. You come from a different stream of time?"

Hui looked down at the Dragon-Phoenix Sect at the bottom of the mountain. "To be honest, I'm not completely sure. I believe that I come from this same stream, further down the flow."

Sun Mai's eyes flickered. "From the future."

"Yes."

"And you came… to change the past?"

"To change the past, and thus, change the future. In the future that I come from, the final assault on Yao Gong Palace was a complete failure. The Demon Emperor slaughtered… all of you. The Dragon-Phoenix Sect barely survived, and the Demon Emperor ruled the lands with an iron fist for a thousand years."

Sun Mai looked at her quizzically, as if sensing there was more.

"The religion you created, Qi Zhao, died with you."

"The Dragon-Phoenix Sect operated in secret in the centuries that followed the defeat, resisting the Demon Emperor where possible and attempting to help the common people. Eventually, an ancient artifact was recovered, a ruined chariot, the axle of which contained shocking power."

Sun Mai wasn't sure whether to chuckle or shake his head. "Du Qian's chariot?"

"Exactly. The chariot was in complete disrepair, but the main source of its power, the wooden axle, contained the power of time, and it was reforged by an expert swordsmith into what came to be known as the Sword of Time. Of course, there are many other factors that led to the axle of the chariot becoming the Sword of Time, but they aren't important.

"I was born around the time that the chariot was discovered, and I became the apprentice of the hero who had been chosen to use that sword to go back and fix the mistakes of the past. Sadly, in the very moment before the ritual was complete, my master was killed, and I took his place."

"You've been guiding us all along, haven't you?" Sun Mai said, his expression unreadable. "That was you back in Daolu, wasn't it? In the temple of Supreme Judge Yu?"

"Yes, that was me. I was careless that night."

"I even saw you years before that, didn't I?"

Hui smiled. "I was especially careless in the early years. You see, most experts from my era believed that streams of time should only be altered indirectly. They were convinced if someone interfered too directly, it could lead to catastrophic results."

Sun Mai nodded. "That much is true. I've seen it with my own eyes."

"That is why I always used the most indirect means at my disposal to try to influence the outcome of the fight with the Demon Emperor. Today was the first time in which I ever interceded with such a heavy hand."

"Without Kun-Peng," Sun Mai said, "the battle would have been a devastating loss. A massacre."

"Close to that," Hui replied. "It became a legend called the Defeat at Heart's Ridge, and it prompted Sunan and Bao to lead a foolhardy assault on Yao Gong Palace. Interfering with the events at Heart's Ridge was never part of the plan. However…" She looked off toward the distant horizon, the wind playing with her hair. "Perhaps it was a weakness on my part, but I just couldn't bear to see so many heroes die."

A thousand questions burned in Sun Mai's head, but his heart was pounding in anxiety. Having traveled the streams of time, he knew that Hui was right to worry about how her interference could lead to disaster. In fact, the more he thought about the implications of what she was telling him, the more he wished to be out of her presence.

"I should leave," he said. "But before I do, I have two final questions. First, could it be that another reason you are so hesitant to personally interfere is because of the blood which runs through your veins? That and your surname, Fan?"

Hui continued to look out at the sky for a long moment. "Yes."

Sun Mai nodded. "Second question. Sunan's dreams and Bao's poetry. They came from you, correct?"

"Yes. The culmination of generations of rituals performed and enlightenment sought by the profound masters of the Dragon-Phoenix Sect in my era."

"Over the years, we have discussed and analyzed the dreams and poetry at great length, but we are still not completely sure of the implications of every detail," said Sun Mai. "Now that we have already met and talked with each other, perhaps you could spare a moment to clarify a few points."

"Of course."

Sun Mai and Hui were accompanied only by the cold winds as they quickly discussed a few aspects of the dreams and poetry. Finally, Sun Mai clasped his hands respectfully.

"Heroine Fan, it was truly a pleasure to meet you. I fear I can hardly comprehend the sacrifices you have made in your quest, and I will forever hold you in the highest esteem. Unless you object, I would like to record some of your story in my thirteenth scripture, a scripture that I will only allow the most qualified of profound masters to study."

Hui thought for a short moment. "Very well, Master Sun. And now, you really should take your leave. Farewell."

Sun Mai turned to head back down the mountain. In the last moment before he disappeared, Hui's voice reached his ears.

"One more thing. Hidden in Vault #456 in the Heart's Ridge Prison is a magical door. Someone like you should have no problem understanding how it operates…"

Sun Mai's eyes widened in shock, and there was a whistling sound as an iron key flew toward him. Without looking back, he reached up and grabbed the key, then began to speed down the mountainside toward the beach, his robes rippling in the wind.

CHAPTER 91
IT HAS THREE

From the moment the flood dragons had emerged from the cauldrons to when Kun-Peng flew away over the horizon, only a few short minutes had passed.

After the fighting was over, the Dragon-Phoenix Sect and the other groups on the beach stood there in shock, almost uncertain if what they had witnessed was real or not.

However, the evidence left behind of the fighting was anything but illusory. And yet, that evidence was mostly superficial damage to the soft ground at the base of the mountain. The next heavy rain that came along would likely wash away all traces of the momentous battle.

After unleashing the power of the Phoenix Crown and the Wind Saber, Bao felt drained. There was also a pain deep inside of her that left her quite unsettled. Placing the Phoenix Crown back in its box, she sheathed the Wind Saber and handed it to Ma Ge. Then she sat down cross-legged in front of Sunan to meditate.

Sunan was also in the middle of meditating as he attempted to expel the poison from his body.

As more disciples hurried over to stand guard over them, Mao Yun and Tie Gangwen took charge, sending profound masters out to confirm that the other Bone Slicers had been defeated, as well as to calm the ordinary members of the sect and confirm that no one had been injured.

Soon the profound masters began to regroup near Sunan and Bao, where an atmosphere of tense anxiety began to mount. Murmured whispers could be heard occasionally as the profound masters discussed the events that had just played out.

"Do you think there are more Bone Slicers nearby?"

"Doubtful. That group was likely stationed in the prison itself and slipped out to prepare their little trap. They were trying to crush us with those dragons, not get involved in a real fight."

"What are the Dragon Sovereign and Phoenix Sovereign doing?"

"I heard that the Dragon Sovereign was poisoned. I'm not sure about the Phoenix Sovereign. Maybe she's helping him with the poison?"

"Perhaps she's just recovering from that incredible technique from earlier."

"What was that white and blue light?"

"She was using the Phoenix Crown and the Wind Saber together. Can you believe that power? I wonder if anybody who uses those two items together could wield power like that?"

Sometime later, Bao opened her eyes and rose to her feet. Upon looking around at the small crowd surrounding her and Sunan, she said, "Are we prepared to leave?"

"Yes, Phoenix Sovereign," Tie Gangwen replied.

It was then that Sun Mai spoke up. "Phoenix Sovereign, may I have a word?"

***

Sunan recovered roughly an hour after he had first slipped into deep meditation. Almost immediately, Bao and Sunan pulled him to the side for a private discussion.

It wasn't long after that when Sunan called out, "Dragon Lords and Claws of the Phoenix, we will begin the evacuation as previously planned, within the hour. Prepare to move out. Mao Yun, Tie Gangwen, Wang Tian, Li Runfa, come with us."

Without any further explanation, Bao, Sunan, and Sun Mai drew upon their qinggong to speed back in the direction of the fortress.

The group of four whom Sunan had called out didn't hesitate to follow. As for Li Runfa, he was not skilled in qinggong, so Wang Tian grabbed his forearm and pulled him along. Seemingly within the blink of an eye, the group of six was gone.

The leaders of the sect immediately began to break into the various groups that would head in different directions away from Heart's Ridge.

***

"How did you find out about the magic door?" Sunan asked as they hurried through the dim corridors of the prison. The lamps they carried cast strange shadows in all directions, making the place seem quite eerie.

Sun Mai didn't respond for a very long moment. "I can't tell you."

Sunan glanced over at him in surprise. "Can't tell me?"

Sun Mai ran his hand across his pate, which was already starting to show a bit of a shadow from his hair growing back. "You'll have to trust me on this, Sunan. Besides, I have more things to tell you that will make this magical door seem like nothing."

Unsure of what to make of Sun Mai's claim, Sunan simply lapsed into silence.

Eventually, they reached an iron door with the numbers 456 carved into the rock above it. It was a sturdy door secured with a heavy padlock that members of the Dragon-Phoenix Sect had attempted unsuccessfully to break open during the evacuation of the prison. There were many such areas within the prison. After all, the sect's mission had been to rescue their friends and family, not loot the fortress.

Sun Mai pulled an iron key out of the sleeve of his robe, which he used to unlock the padlock. Then he pushed the door open and entered, holding out the lamp in front of him.

The room was empty except for a single item: a long, sturdy wooden chest.

Mao Yun was the one to step forward and open it, revealing a collection of six long metal bars, some of which were straight and some of which were curved. From the grooves and tongues at the ends of each of the bars, it was obvious that they were designed to interlock.

Mao Yun looked over his shoulder at Sun Mai, then Sunan and Bao.

Sun Mai stepped forward and glanced at the bars. "Let's set it up. It should only take a moment."

Sure enough, assembling the bars was a simple task, and within moments, a large door frame stood tall in the middle of the stone chamber. It was wide enough for three men to enter on horseback and stood on its own with no need of support.

"It looks a lot less impressive than I imagined," Li Runfa said. "How do we use it?"

Sun Mai reached out and put his hand on the surface of the door, then closed his eyes. A moment passed, whereupon a smile appeared on his lips.

"She was right," he murmured in a voice so soft no one could make out clearly what he had said.

"Sun Mai?" Sunan asked.

Sun Mai looked up. "It's simple. Any profound master can activate the door with little more than a thought. In terms of where it can lead, the possibilities are many. As far as I can tell, I can open the other end of the door in any location that I have visited in the past, and any location where the door has been."

A few people gasped.

"Why don't we use it to get the sect back to the palace?" Tie Gangwen asked.

"Based on everything we know," Wang Tian replied, "the magical doors can only be used once. Wouldn't it be better to use it... offensively?"

Sun Mai lowered his hand. "My thoughts exactly. Our plan to get the sect to safety is still a good one. With this door in our hands, I think the time has come to discuss something of utmost importance." He looked at Sunan. "Your dream." Then at Bao. "And your poem."

***

The two divisions of the Dragon-Phoenix Sect mostly went separate ways, taking their friends and loved ones with them. A small group consisting mostly of other martial artists such as Blackleaf and Kind Devil Fuling commandeered the boats in the harbor. The Pure Phoenix Division headed south to infiltrate Xuanlu and perhaps Huisheng. The Golden Dragon Division would head up the Southern Fei River toward Zun Shan.

Other scattered groups from both divisions headed in other directions. The current plan was for the sect to temporarily vanish from the world.

Everyone, from the ranking officers to the ordinary non-martial artists from the outer sect, was anxious to get away from Heart's Ridge. As such, no one needed any persuading to hurry off in whichever directions they had been assigned.

Because of that, few people noticed something strange happening. After emerging again from the prison, Mao Yun and Tie Gangwen began to circulate among the leadership figures of the sect, both the profound masters and others among the most skilled and powerful fighters.

By the time the sun set, the sandy land between the mountains and the bay were empty. The two divisions of the sect were gone, leaving only a lonely wind behind to caress the battered and broken evidence of the spectacular battle.

**

Roughly an hour north of the city of Yu Zhing was a cave network that, many years ago, had been an oft-used way station and supply depot for one of the criminal gangs that operated in the city.

It was the very same cave network where Bao and Mao Yun had spent the night when they fled Yu Zhing all those years ago.

For years, the caves had been completely abandoned, but after the Dragon-Phoenix Sect began to carry out operations in the major cities of the empire, they had been refitted and expanded for use in the operations of the local secret societies.

About two years prior, when the entire martial world was burning with passion under the leadership of the Timeless Master, one particularly ambitious local leader had expanded the caves, hoping to build a small army to use to overthrow the government in Yu Zhing. Later, after the death of the Timeless Master, when many martial artists had scattered and gone into hiding, the caves had been abandoned again.

Now it became the gathering place of the most powerful martial artists in the world.

It started with a small group of seven, including Bao, Sunan, Mao Yun, Wang Tian, Tie Gangwen, Sun Mai, and Li Runfa. Although, strictly speaking, Li Runfa couldn't be considered a powerful martial artist; his skills lay in other areas.

More of the leaders and top fighters in the sect began to show up a few days later. One by one, they were assigned housing within the caves, with a few, mostly Eyes of the Phoenix, being sent into the city disguised as beggars or merchants to gather intelligence.

Over the course of the following two weeks, roughly a thousand of the Dragon-Phoenix Sect's most famous and powerful figures arrived.

None among the group knew exactly why they were gathering in Yu Zhing, at least, not yet. One night, after all the other members of the sect who had been ordered to come to Yu Zhing had arrived, the small group who had originally discovered the magical door had a meeting in the most secure area of the cave network.

"Now that the elites are gathered," Sun Mai said, "we can finally begin training."

"We also need more information about Yao Gong Palace," Bao said. "We have the magical door, which can get us inside, but we don't even know the layout of the place, let alone who or what we'll be facing once we're on the inside."

"My Eyes of the Phoenix can be of some help," Wang Tian said. "Why don't we send a pair up into the mountains to survey and scout the area?"

"That won't be necessary," Li Runfa said quietly. "After all these years, the time has come to reveal a secret that only the Dragon Sovereign and Phoenix Sovereign ever knew."

As all eyes in the room came to rest on him, he continued. "The Dragon-Phoenix Sect doesn't have two divisions. It has three."

CHAPTER 92
A BEAR IN A CAVE

What?" Wang Tian blurted.

Tie Gangwen's eyes went wide, and even Mao Yun seemed completely taken aback.

"In some ways," Li Runfa said, "it's a complicated story, and in other ways, very simple. Haven't you ever wondered why I never devoted myself to studying martial arts? It is because I was focused on other matters. To explain, I have to go all the way back to when we were fleeing north and stopped in Tung-On. When browsing through the back-alley shops there, I found an ancient text, which described a ritual of incredible..." After trailing off for a short moment, he continued. "Perhaps power is not the right word, but usefulness.

"One of the key ingredients to complete the ritual was the blood of a raksha demon. Raksha demons are terrifyingly ferocious things, and as you can imagine, getting the blood of one was no easy task. Mao Yun, do you remember the three Zhou brothers?"

Mao Yun nodded.

"The four of us teamed up, and after many years of plotting and planning, we managed to track down a young raksha demon and kill it. Sadly, First Zhou and Second Zhou were killed in the battle. Later, Third Zhou and I used the blood of the raksha demon to complete the ritual, and we made these." Reaching into his sleeve, he pulled out what appeared to a mask made of leather or skin.

Without further explanation, he placed the mask on his face, whereupon his facial features blurred. Moments later, they became clear again. As of that moment, Li Runfa didn't look at all like Li Runfa, but rather the spitting image of Sunan. He even looked physically larger than he had before. Even more shocking was that everyone present, despite being profound masters with incredible senses, and also the ability to detect and analyze auras, couldn't tell any difference between Li Runfa's qi fluctuations and Sunan's.

"Surprisingly," he continued, his voice now that of Sunan's, "the changes go down into the muscles, bones, and even blood."

Then he peeled the mask off his face, whereupon his features returned to normal. "The masks come with other… benefits as well. I realized immediately that with tools like this at my disposal, I could build the ultimate intelligence agency, which is exactly what I did. With the blessing of the Dragon Sovereign and Phoenix Sovereign, the Raksha Division was born. Third Zhou and I began to recruit, picking the best of the best from our sect and also bringing in fresh blood." He looked over at Wang Tian with an enigmatic smile. "We even have a few former Eyes of the Phoenix. Remember Chang Peng?"

Wang Tian frowned slightly, apparently neither amused nor pleased. "I thought he died trying to infiltrate the chief shaman's dungeon…"

Li Runfa shook his head. "He didn't. Unfortunately, we only have a few masks, and we have been unable to track down any more raksha demons in the years since. Therefore, we are few in number. However, over the years we have infiltrated many of the most powerful organizations in the empire and have gained access to some of the most secret locations. That includes Yao Gong Palace."

At this point, Bao couldn't help but ask, "You have an agent inside of Yao Gong Palace?"

Even she had not been made aware of this point.

"Yes," Li Runfa said. "It was a very difficult task, but Third Zhou himself managed to take the place of one of the palace servants, which was how he managed to make this." Li Runfa pulled a leather tube out of his robe, which he opened. Within it was a patch of animal skin rolled around a weathered piece of paper. As he unrolled the animal skin out in front of the gathered group, it quickly became obvious what it was.

"Is that a *map*?" Mao Yun asked. "Of Yao Gong Palace?"

"Indeed," Li Runfa replied. "And this"—he unrolled the paper—"is detailed information about everything from the guard patrols to the meal schedule to the times and places when the Demon Emperor appears in the open for ceremonies and the like."

Tie Gangwen shook his head. "Master Li, if your Raksha Division can get a map of the Demon Emperor's palace, and even a schedule of his daily affairs, what other things might you have been able to do throughout the years to help us? How many times did we sent men to infiltrate the enemy, only for them to be discovered and executed? Those masks could have been of incredible use!"

Li Runfa looked back at him with a sharp glint in his eyes. "Do you really think our division didn't help on missions throughout the years? During the most important operations, there was always a Raksha agent helping from the shadows. How do you think we were able to steal the Zhizhu Coral so easily? Or what about the assassination of the chief shaman? Or the Uprising of Nansun? None of them would have been possible without the Raksha Division.

"Think of all the intelligence I have brought to the table over the years, maps and schedules just like the ones in front of you. Do you really think our ordinary intelligence wing could have access to so much dangerous, secret information? You never asked how I got such information, and I never offered to reveal my sources, an arrangement I don't think anyone in the sect found fault with.

"The Raksha Division was the most powerful tool at the disposal of the Dragon-Phoenix Sect, a trump card that I was not willing to reveal until the time came to strike the final blow."

"And that time is now," Sunan said. "Master Li, I presume you've studied the map and the schedule already and have identified some ideal places and times to consider?"

"Yes. However, now that the secret of the Raksha Division has been revealed, I have another bit of information that I must share. Before I do, please allow me to preface my words by saying that I fully believe in this plan to eliminate the Demon Emperor once and for all. The profound masters of the Dragon-Phoenix Sect are the most powerful warriors in the world, and if steps are not taken to end the Demon Emperor now, I fear the world will be lost for all time.

"However, perhaps better than anyone else here, I understand how powerful the Demon Emperor is. And that is because a Raksha agent was in the Grotto of the Timeless Master when it fell."

All eyes had already been on Li Runfa before, but now they were even more sharply focused on him.

"According to the stories that have begun to spread since the fall of the Timeless Master, he was killed during a decisive duel with Bone General Geng. However, the truth is much more chilling. The Bone General and the Timeless Master didn't fight until the very end of the battle, when almost everyone else in the grotto had been slaughtered. The Timeless Master defeated the Bone General easily, but he didn't manage to kill him. And yet, the Timeless Master was not fated to survive. The Demon Emperor himself came to finish the job.

"My Raksha agent was there, hidden, to witness the entire tragic spectacle. After the dust settled, she escaped and recorded this." He pulled out a many-folded piece of paper, which he put down in front of him. "Names and descriptions of some of the techniques the Demon Emperor used, as well as a brief account of the final moments of the Timeless Master."

As Sunan reached out to pick up the piece of paper, Li Runfa shook his head. "The Demon Emperor is terrifyingly powerful, that much is certain. Were it not for some immensely powerful magical weapons the Timeless Master had at his disposal, objects none of us were aware that he possessed, he would never have lasted for even a single round of combat. He also had a powerful protector, someone the Demon Emperor called a Sertori, although I'm not sure what that means."

Sunan unfolded the piece of paper and began to read it. "Some of these techniques seem familiar," he said, "things I've seen used by Demon Emperor soldiers, such as Dancing Steel. But Vortegan's Whirling Catastrophe? How bizarre. What does 'vortegan' mean anyway?"

"Likely a transliteration," Bao said. "Not surprising considering the Demon Emperor is from another realm."

Sun Mai's eyes sparkled. "Another realm?"

"Another realm. Another world. Call it whatever you wish to call it." She sighed. "I almost can't believe that in the end, the Demon Emperor really did kill his own son."

Li Runfa's eyes widened. "You knew that the Timeless Master was the son of the Demon Emperor? My Raksha agent reported that the Demon Emperor said as much in the final moments of their fight, but even I wasn't sure if that information was accurate."

"We've known for many years. He told us himself and swore us to secrecy," Bao said. "What a tragic end to the story of Li Buwei."

Before Sun Mai or any of the others could ask any of the questions burning in their minds, Sunan said, "Listen to this." Then he began to read from the slip of paper. "'The Timeless Master struck blow after blow. However, neither the edge of his blade nor the power of his qi could harm the Demon Emperor. Any wounds inflicted would heal before a second blow could be struck. He was essentially impervious to attack.'"

When Sunan finished speaking, silence filled the room. A long moment passed, then Sunan looked up at Sun Mai. "Is this why I've heard you mention sealing him and not killing him?"

Sun Mai didn't respond at first. After rubbing his chin in thought for a moment, he nodded. "Truth be told, I was not aware of this particular detail, but it makes sense, given what I do know. If an ordinary man had a bear to deal with, it would be much wiser to seal the mouth of its cave with a boulder than to try to slit the beast's throat with a knife."

Bao gritted her teeth. "The oath I swore was to see him dead!"

Sunan reached out and placed his hand on Bao's knee. "Seal the bear in its cave, and it will starve to death. Or at least, there it will be trapped until you can collapse the cave itself."

Another long moment passed, and Bao nodded. "I agree. Li Runfa, you said that you've worked on a way to take some of the long-standing troop formations and power them with magic? A massive spell formation?"

"That's right. All we need is an area large enough to fit roughly a thousand people."

"Presumably you've identified the times and places you think are the best options to unleash the spell formation?"

"You presume correctly, Phoenix Sovereign."

"The floor is yours."

CHAPTER 93
ALTERING THE FORMATION

Hui was very careful as she followed Bao and Sunan north toward Yu Zhing. The last thing she wanted to do was alert them to her presence now. When she thought back to all the mistakes she had made through the years, she couldn't help but shake her head.

It's almost like the only thing I do is make mistakes, she thought. *I can't believe I let Sun Mai just walk right up to me.*

Over the years, she had become very adept at using her Trance Touch, and she had come to realize that it had other applications than what it had originally been designed for. It had been developed with the intention of putting certain thoughts into the heads of Bao and Sunan, thoughts which would lead them down the course to sealing the Demon Emperor.

Later, Hui realized that it could also be used like a weapon. However, the thought of entering a person's mind to cause harm, even an enemy, was repugnant to her. Throughout all the years, she had only ever done so once, in the direst of circumstances—at the bottom of the sea in the Eastern Archipelagos.

Another application was much more practical. As she made more breakthroughs, and as she became more adept at manipulating the Trance Touch, she realized that by carefully focusing its power, it was possible to use it like a second set of eyes, eyes that could move about at great distances. In other words, if utilized properly, she could "observe" people without ever getting close enough for them to see or even hear her.

It was this ability that helped her to keep track of the movements of the Dragon-Phoenix Sect. After confirming that they were holing up in a cave network north of Yu Zhing, she found a hiding place for herself a safe distance away where she could watch over them. As one profound master and top expert after another joined them in the caves, Hui's heart began to beat with anxiety.

They're really going to do it, aren't they? They're preparing to assault Yao Gong Palace.

Soon, they began to train, and for the first time, Hui was able to see in person the formation that she had only ever observed in visions. To her surprise, the profound masters seemingly mastered the formation within only a few days. Although they weren't fully powering it with qi flows, their movements were fluid and in perfect coordination.

Yet again, as she had been through the years, Hui was struck by how different things were in this era. Qi cultivation breakthroughs came quickly and more easily, and the martial artists all seemed more naturally talented. Some of that surely had to do with how fresh and new qi was to the world. After all, Hui had also advanced much more quickly through her breakthroughs than was common where she came from. As for how everyone seemed to be innately skilled in martial arts, she couldn't think of any explanation for it.

After a few days of training, an even more shocking development occurred with the Dragon-Phoenix Sect: They began to alter the formation.

What are they doing? she thought, her spine tingling in anxiety.

However, it didn't take long for that anxiety to become admiration as she realized that they were experimenting with alternate ways to run and power the formation. *Of course. There will surely be fierce fighting. What if the formation is interrupted in the middle and needs to re-form? Or what if some of the heroes fall in combat?*

Yet again, Hui was struck with a sense of frustration at her own incompetence. Why hadn't the profound masters of her own time thought to do the same thing?

Hui was convinced that the Dragon-Phoenix Sect was fully capable of taking care of itself.

They don't need me anymore. Not to give advice. Not to protect them. Definitely not to guide them. The end is coming.

With that, she began to head east. Whether she hiked through the mountains, made her way through the Southern Desert, or took the easy northern route, the journey to Yao Gong Palace would take at least ten days.

From what I've seen of how Bao and Sunan do things, they'll continue to train for at least another month.

***

As the days went by, the profound masters grew more and more comfortable with the formation, as well as the variations. Their movements were quick, fluid, and flexible. They could maintain the formation with as many as half of the original required number of participants, and they could also keep the structure intact when moving back and forth across the landscape at triple the speed they could when they had first begun training.

Eventually it reached the point where all of the leaders were fully satisfied. They were convinced that the sect was as prepared as it could be.

"The day after tomorrow is the spring equinox," Sunan announced. "It is the day we will make our move. Sun Mai will activate the magical door, and the Dragon-Phoenix Sect will rid these lands of the Demon Emperor for all time.

"It was decades ago in the Huang Mountains that I first experienced a vision of the events that will unfold the day after tomorrow. I have seen them play out over and over in my head, and I know beyond the shadow of a doubt that we will succeed."

"The Dragon Sovereign is right," Bao said. "The mnemonics of the spell formation were imparted to me by the Enlightened Goddess herself, Xian Nu Shen. It is our destiny to put an end to the injustice and horror of the Demon Emperor, and we will do it the day after tomorrow!"

The bit about Xian Nu Shen was pure speculation on Bao's part, but based on the cryptic information Sun Mai had given them, she knew that the matter of her poetry was something far beyond ordinary in nature.

"Rest well this afternoon," Mao Yun said. "The Phoenix Sovereign and I will go into Yu Zhing to procure food and alcohol. Tonight, we feast. Tomorrow we meditate. And then... we fight!"

After a bit of cheering, the profound masters dispersed to rest. As for Bao and Mao Yun, they disguised themselves as grain merchants and headed into Yu Zhing with Li Runfa and Ma Ge.

***

Sun Mai and Sunan climbed to the top of the hill above the cave entrance and sat down on a boulder to watch Bao and the others heading toward Yu Zhing.

After the carts disappeared around a curve in the path, Sunan lay back on the boulder and closed his eyes. The warmth of the sun caressed him from above while heat radiated up from the stone beneath his back. It was a very pleasant sensation.

As for Sun Mai, he sat there cross-legged, his back straight, the wind slipping gently over his clean-shaven scalp.

For a long moment, the two of them sat there in silence.

Finally, Sunan opened his eyes and looked at the clouds above. "My children memorized your other scriptures. Did I tell you that already?"

Sun Mai's eyebrows shot up in surprise, and a smile spread out across his face. "You didn't."

"Jinlong's favorite is the fourth volume, while Chunfeng prefers the fifth. They once got in a heated debate over the merits of each."

Sun Mai chuckled. "I wish I could have been present for that."

"After all of this is over, you can meet them. Maybe you can even deliver the final volumes of your scripture to them personally."

"Yes, I will. There's another thing we need to do afterward. Something very important."

Sunan rose back up into a sitting position. "What's that?"

Sun Mai turned to look at him. "Celebrate at the Heavenly Meat Palace! We'll eat mountains of spicy prawns and drink rivers of sorghum wine!"

Sunan immediately burst out laughing.

***

After entering Yu Zhing, Li Runfa and Ma Ge went to procure food, leaving Bao and Mao Yun to get the alcohol.

Ironically, despite having been drinking partners for years, neither Mao Yun nor Bao had ever had a single drink together in Yu Zhing.

For Bao, it was a very strange thing to be back in the place where she had grown up. Generally speaking, everything looked the same. Some of the shops here and there were different, but almost everything was as she remembered it.

When they passed by the Shangguan Clan compound, strange emotions tugged at her heart. Mao Yun saw her glance over at the main gate and softly said, "Want to go take a look?"

She shook her head. "My heart never belonged to that place."

Suddenly feeling melancholy, she looked away from her ancestral home.

They found an alcohol shop in the city, where they purchased jugs of sorghum wine, yellow wine, pear blossom wine, and virtually everything else the shop had available. After filling up the cart, they turned and headed back toward the city gate.

"Last time we left this place," Mao Yun said, "it was definitely not through the city gate."

Bao chuckled. "Who would ever have thought that our next visit would be under these circumstances? Buying alcohol before storming the Demon Emperor's castle."

Mao Yun laughed. They lapsed into silence for a bit.

"I wonder where Jinlong and Chunfeng are," Bao said.

"In Naqan by now, surely," Mao Yun replied.

"I miss them."

"Me too, Bao." Mao Yun sighed. "After this is all over, and we're all reunited, where will you settle down? Have you and Sunan talked about it?"

"Talked about it, yes, but we haven't made any decisions. He doesn't want to go back to the Bay of Yu, and he certainly doesn't want to live in Yu Zhing. Nangu is too far away, and the palace on Zun Shan… well, it doesn't seem like a good place for a family. It's too cold."

"Perhaps a place like Chrysanthemum Lake," Mao Yun murmured.

"Yes, we talked about that, actually. Maybe we can build a manor there for all of us to live in, right there on the edge of the water. You would be welcome to join us. We could build a whole wing just for you."

Mao Yun smiled. "Perhaps. There's another person who I would have to ask before agreeing to something like that."

Bao looked over in surprise. "Mao Yun?"

He blushed and cleared his throat but didn't elaborate.

Smiling, Bao chose not to pursue the matter, but she couldn't help but wonder which young woman had managed to work her way into Mao Yun's heart.

Eventually they passed out of the city gate and headed north toward the caves. Some distance away, Bao looked over her shoulder and wondered if she would ever see Yu Zhing again.

CHAPTER 94
THE ATTACK BEGINS

There had been much discussion regarding how exactly to carry out the assault on Yao Gong Palace, but in the end, it was Dragon Lord Sima Zikang's plan that won the approval of the leaders.

The time was easily established: the Demon Emperor's yearly ritual, performed at dawn during the spring equinox. From the information in Third Zhou's report, it was called the Heavenly Submission Ritual and was one of the key ways the Demon Emperor maintained power in Qi Xien. Although he would be surrounded by guards, he would be directly in the open and relatively isolated from the rest of this palace.

The main question was how to charge into the square where the ritual would be held. Some of the leaders argued that they should open a portal directly into the square itself, perhaps right in front of the altar that the Demon Emperor would be standing in front of.

But in the end, Sima Zikang's arguments won out.

The final plans having been made, the Dragon-Phoenix Sect

assembled just outside of the cave network, during the time before sunrise that was often the darkest part of night. Like most organizations, the Dragon-Phoenix Sect had all sorts of ceremonial robes befitting the status and rank of each member. But on this day, they did not dress for ceremony—they dressed for a fight.

The members of the Golden Dragon Division wore golden garments, and the Pure Phoenix Division wore silver. Some people imitated Sunan and wore armor. Others, such as Flying Death Liu Jiahui, who relied heavily on qinggong techniques, wore none.

Everyone was armed to the teeth.

After the group was assembled, Sun Mai and Mao Yun erected the magical door, and then Sun Mai placed his hand on its surface.

Looking over his shoulder, he made eye contact with Sunan, who gave a slight nod.

No words were spoken.

Sun Mai closed his eyes, and the door began to vibrate.

***

To the west of the Southern Desert, high in the Banyan Mountains, was a fortress that loomed like a glimmering blue specter over the lands of Qi Xien.

It was a palace fortress, designed both to awe and to defend, with numerous towers rising into the sky and countless tunnels dug into the rock of the mountains beneath it. Similar to Heart's Ridge Prison, its architecture did not seem native to Qi Xien.

Currently, it was dawn, and the full moon was just visible in the west as the sun peeked up over the lands to the east.

As the sunlight spread out, one of the first things it touched was a huge open square constructed to the west of the palace, which had been built in a way to perfectly capture the dawn sun during the spring equinox.

As it happened, today was the equinox, and a grand ceremony was being held in that square.

Visible on the west side of the square was an altar crafted from pearl and gold, and standing in front of it was the most feared person in the entire world: Yao Feng, the Demon Emperor.

At first glance, he almost looked like an ordinary person, except that he was shorter than average, and quite stocky. His facial features did not seem like someone from Qi Xien, but they were not so foreign as to be alien. He wore a violet robe embroidered with golden creatures of myth, as well as a crown of pearls and numerous types of jewelry, from golden rings to diamond necklaces.

Arrayed in military formation a few paces behind him were a group of figures who would strike fear into the hearts of anyone who looked at them: ogres. There were fifteen of them, all with slightly different facial features and builds, but each and every one of them was tall, powerfully built, and clad in ceremonial armor. These were none other than the Demon Emperor's personal guard, who all held the rank of general in his army but never left his side.

Lined up behind the ogres was a group of about fifty people, most of whom appeared to be ordinary people from Qi Xien, intermixed with shorter, stockier individuals who seemed more akin to the Demon Emperor in their facial features. Most of the group was made up of men, but there were also women. All of them wore identical robes and were armed with long, pitch-black spears. This mixed group of fighters were all elite martial artists assigned to guard the Demon Emperor, experts who were fanatically devoted to him but did not rank quite as high as the ogre guards.

Behind the ogre guards and elite fighters was a sizeable force of ordinary soldiers, armored and well armed, and then a large group made up of what appeared to be court officials, servants, and the like.

At the head of this congregated group of devotees, the Demon

Emperor stood in front of his grand altar, hands held aloft as he prayed for his empire.

At one point in the ceremony, one of the ogres stepped forward and offered a ceremonial jade pitcher to the Demon Emperor.

The Demon Emperor took the pitcher, which was filled with the fresh blood of children, and stepped forward to pour it over the altar.

However, before he could even take a second step, his eyes narrowed.

***

The Dragon-Phoenix Sect entered Yao Gong Palace via a subterranean chamber almost directly beneath the large square. From there, they proceeded through the tunnels as quickly as possible, cutting down the handful of guards they ran into before they could even make a cry of warning or sound an alarm. At a certain corridor, the force split up. The Golden Dragon Division headed south and the Pure Phoenix Division went north.

The shining Wyrm strides ever north,
The graceful Bird due south takes wing.

The profound masters and expert fighters of the Golden Dragon Division poured out of the southern entrance of the square, using qinggong to move as quickly and silently as possible. Then they began to unleash deadly attacks upon the gathered forces in the square.

They did not discriminate between soldiers and servants. Except for Third Zhou, who had long since fled the fortress, every person in the place was a devoted follower of the Demon Emperor and was not deserving of mercy.

Within moments of the Golden Dragon Division's appearance in the square, the Pure Phoenix Division's fighters burst onto the scene from the north, similarly unleashing savage violence on the Demon Emperor's forces.

The sudden surprise attack caught the people in the square completely off guard, and dozens were killed in the opening salvo.

However, even the lowest-ranking soldiers in Yao Gong Palace could be considered top-rated fighters in the empire as a whole. Most of them were veterans of many battles, killers whose hands were so stained with blood they could never be washed clean. Within moments of the initial attack, the ordinary soldiers had shields raised to defend themselves, and were also unleashing attacks of their own.

As for the officials, servants, and other non-fighters, they scattered in terror.

The goal of the Dragon-Phoenix Sect was simple—they needed to clear enough space within the square to get into formation. Once the formation was in place and its power focused on the Demon Emperor, they would be mostly safe.

But there was no way the Demon Emperor's forces would simply let them get into formation right then and there.

From the moment the first of the profound masters leapt out into the square, to when the non-fighters began fleeing in terror and the soldiers turned to fight, only a few moments passed.

As the ordinary soldiers began to form up in ranks, the elite fighters and ogre guards also turned.

And of course, the Demon Emperor himself noticed what was happening, and his eyes began to flicker with rage. Never before in his entire time ruling the lands of Qi Xien had any enemy ever dared to assault him openly, much less in the middle of Yao Gong Palace, the seat of his power and the most well-defended fortress in existence.

Snarling, he tossed the jade pitcher down, splashing blood all over the ground, and then he began to perform an incantation, gesturing with both hands, chanting words in a strange language.

Meanwhile, more fighters were rushing into the square, releasing countless deadly attacks of incredible power.

Illusory beasts and weapons slammed into the soldiers left and right. Fire and lightning fell from the sky. Booms filled the air. Blood spattered everywhere, and the aroma of charred flesh began to fill the square.

Before the Demon Emperor's elite fighters could spring into action, dozens upon dozens of soldiers were killed. Some were decapitated, some crushed to death, some burned alive. Their shields did little good. Despite all of them being skilled qi fighters, when facing the wrath of such a large group of top-level fighters, they were cut down like dried weeds.

Sunan and Bao were in the lead, their expressions grim as they unleashed one attack after another in their attempt to blast the ordinary soldiers out of the way and begin to establish the formations.

But that was when the elite fighters waded into the mix, fighting back with powerful techniques that finally forced the Dragon-Phoenix Sect to begin to defend themselves.

And then the ogres joined in, and the battle grew more intense.

However, it was in that moment that the Demon Emperor shouted something in a strange language and threw his hands above his head.

Suddenly, the air above the square began to swirl faster and faster, picking up random objects from the battlefield such as dust, drops of blood, and even things like broken arrows and darts. The wind began to rotate faster and faster until it formed a screaming black whirlwind.

Down in the square, fighters from both sides looked up, expressions of uncertainty and fear playing out on their faces as the whirlwind descended.

The Demon Emperor looked on with a cruel grin on his face as the tornadolike vortex touched down on the north side of the battlefield, right between the two opposing sides.

"Vortegan's Whirling Catastrophe," he murmured. "It's been a long time since I've been able to see its destruction in action."

The whirlwind began to zig and zag across the square, mostly mowing through the Phoenix Division forces but occasionally swerving into the Demon Emperor's men, some of whom were able to avoid the winds, but many of whom were picked up and hurled violently left and right. Before long, the vortex had reached the Dragon Division forces.

The Dragon-Phoenix Sect ranks were instantly thrown into chaos, with numerous fighters being thrown pell-mell across the square. Even some of the leaders were caught up in the destruction, including Mao Yun and Liu Jiahui. As for the Demon Emperor's men, the front line of the fighting was currently made up of ordinary soldiers, so many of the unlucky ones who ended up caught in the maelstrom were severely injured or even killed.

After several long seconds that seemed like minutes, the whirlwind faded away, and the chaos was over.

The Dragon-Phoenix Sect forces were completely disorganized. Mao Yun, Liu Jiahui, and several other members of the sect had been thrown over the heads of the enemy soldiers and were now lying on the ground right in front of the elite fighters and ogres. Even Sunan had been affected and was sent staggering backward several paces before he lost control and tumbled into a sitting position.

The Demon Emperor took a step forward, shoving his sleeves back to reveal powerfully muscled arms.

"You think insects like you qualify to fight with the King of the Pure Ones?" he growled. When he spoke, it was in a strange, clipped accent the likes of which no one in the Dragon-Phoenix Sect had ever heard before. Taking another step forward, he raised his voice. "I slaughtered warriors twice as powerful as you before your grandparents were born. I've drunk the blood of more enemies than you have ever seen. I've lived through traps and ambushes ten times more devious and a hundred times deadlier than this little child's game. So unless you have something other than parlor tricks up your sleeve, the time has come for me to rip you to pieces!"

With every sentence he spoke, the volume of his voice increased until he was speaking in a roar. He continued to walk forward, and as he did, magical forces surged within him, causing him to grow physically larger. Something like a majestic divine light began to shine around him, something which struck fear into the hearts of the Dragon-Phoenix Sect and caused passion and faith to rise up in his own followers.

Within moments, he was double his original size, whereupon he clenched his hands into fists and leapt into the air.

CHAPTER 95
ARROWS

Slaughter them all!" the Demon Emperor roared. He began to float high up into the air, until he was at least ten meters above the square.

The soldiers, elite fighters, and ogre guards surged into action, attacking the Dragon-Phoenix Sect fighters with renewed vigor.

At the northern side of the square, Bao was fighting shoulder to shoulder with Ma Ge and Lawat. As she watched the Demon Emperor fly up into the air, she gritted her teeth and unleashed an attack that sent five soldiers flying backward, killing two of them. Then she blocked an incoming volley of arrows before sending out an attack at another group of soldiers.

Dammit, what is that bastard doing up there? And how is he flying? That's not qinggong! I can't sense any qi fluctuations at all.

She could see his hands flashing rapidly in front of his chest, his lips moving as he muttered what was surely the mnemonic to some type of magic. Then he closed his eyes, and Bao was struck with an idea.

What if we can *kill him?* she thought.

It wasn't a time for contemplation or thought. In one fluid motion, she placed the Phoenix Crown on her head and closed her hand around the hilt of Sunan's Wind Saber, which he had entrusted to her with the express purpose of giving her a chance to use their combined power if the opportunity presented itself.

This was just such a moment.

The Wind Saber had been sheathed ever since the battle of Heart's Ridge, allowing the powers within to simmer to a figurative boil. As soon as her hand wrapped around its hilt, the power thrummed between it and the Phoenix Crown.

She drew the blade and once again felt incredible energy building up.

After cutting down Geng Long and the flood dragon with the power of the crown and the saber, Bao had thought long and hard about what to call that blinding release of energy but had come up short. It didn't really matter.

The Demon Emperor appeared to be completing the casting of his spell, and as his eyes were opening, Bao slashed the saber through the air, and an enormous column of white and blue energy snaked out.

The Demon Emperor's eyes went wide.

***

After landing hard on the ground in what was essentially enemy territory, Mao Yun struggled to his feet along with Liu Jiahui and a handful of others from the Pure Phoenix Division.

Then the entire group of them watched in shock as the Demon Emperor doubled in size and flew up into the air.

Before any of them could react, the elite enemy fighters rushed toward them, followed closely behind by the ogre guards.

In a situation like that, many people would curse their luck and tremble in terror. But not Mao Yun. As far as he was concerned, his new positioning on the battlefield was an opportunity.

"Stand firm, all of you!" he cried to the Pure Phoenix fighters. "Buy some time for the rest of the sect!" Hefting his pitch-black battle-axe, he prepared to meet the charge of the enemy forces.

"You heard the Phoenix General," Liu Jiahui said. "Give them hell!"

Mao Yun swung his axe through the air, unleashing a blast of energy directly into the ranks of the elite fighters. Liu Jiahui turned into a blur as he used a rare offensive qinggong move to blast directly into the enemy lines. The other Pure Phoenix fighters fanned out and unleashed their most powerful techniques.

***

As soon as Sunan saw Bao reaching for her Phoenix Crown, he knew what was coming. Although he had been in the middle of meditation when she slaughtered Geng Long and the flood dragon, he had still been able to sense the energy she had unleashed at that time, and of course had heard her firsthand account of what had occurred.

As such, he knew exactly what type of attack was coming. He also knew what he needed to do.

Perhaps Bao would be able to take out the Demon Emperor by unleashing the combined power of the Phoenix Crown and the Wind Saber. But if she didn't, then it would be more important than ever that the two divisions of the sect get in formation as quickly as possible.

"Dragon General Tie," he shouted above the din of fighting. "Use your Titan Squad Array!"

Tie Gangwen and four members of the Golden Dragon Division grouped together in a smaller formation designed to maximize damage over a short period of time.

"Dragon Lords," Sunan continued, "use cathartic Dragon Pearl Formations immediately!"

Before the words had even finished leaving Sunan's mouth, the Dragon Lords did exactly as Sunan said, grouping into squads of three to blast at the enemy with Dragon Pearl Formations.

Whether it was the Titan Squad Array or the Dragon Pearl Formations, all of them were powerful trump cards that could only be used once or twice in a single battle. While Sima Zikang had cautioned to hold them in reserve until the battle situation was clearer, Sunan hoped that using them in this chaotic moment would open up the space they needed to fall into the larger Dragon-Phoenix formation that was their ultimate weapon.

The Dragon Division forces began to push the Demon Emperor's forces back across the square.

The Claws of the Phoenix on the north side of the square began to unleash similar trump cards to shift their position.

As both divisions of the sect moved into action, brilliant white and blue light began to spread out across the square, with Bao in the very middle of it.

***

When the Demon Emperor saw the massive beam of light closing in on him, he grabbed a jade pendant that was hanging around his neck. As his hand closed around it, it shattered, releasing a cloud of mist that formed the shape of a circular buckler.

In the moment before the beam hit him, he thrust his hand out, and the buckler slammed into it.

A high-pitched droning sound filled the entire square, accompanied by rippling pulses of energy that caused blood to seep out of the eyes, ears, noses, and mouths of the less powerful fighters on the battlefield.

***

Bao felt as if she had just slammed an iron rod into the trunk of an oak tree. Pain flowed up her arm, which spasmed and trembled physically.

Cracks spread out in the paving stones beneath her feet, and she had a feeling that the energy in the Wind Saber had only been partially released. Being the conduit for the release of the energy, she was like a hole in a dam through which water was gushing rapidly until it was unexpectedly plugged up. If that water wasn't allowed to drain properly, the dam would be destroyed, starting with the hole!

***

Ironically, the Demon Emperor felt something quite similar to Bao. Pain spread out through his arm, which began to shake as he was pushed ever so slightly backward through the air.

It had been a long time since the Demon Emperor felt pain. In fact, it had been a long time since he engaged in a fight with anyone remotely close to this level.

As such, a cold grin spread out on his face, and he pushed out against the beam of light.

***

The standoff between Bao and the Demon Emperor caused almost all of the other fighting in the square to cease, as everyone watched with bated breath.

Both sides knew that the result would decide the battle. For the Dragon-Phoenix Sect, this was their beloved Phoenix Sovereign, the person who was to lead the northern half of the spell formation. Were she to be injured, or worse yet, killed, it would be a devastating blow.

As for the forces of the Demon Emperor, their situation was even more grave. If the inconceivable happened, and he fell in battle, then the fate of his minions needed no strong imagination to conceive of.

As the buckler and the beam of light caused intense rumbling sounds to fill the square, one of the Demon Emperor's most devoted ogre guards reached into a belt pouch and pulled out what appeared to be a short arrow crafted from green bronze. He slowly loaded the bolt into the crossbow he held in his right hand and began to mutter some words in a strange language.

***

As Mao Yun watched Bao and the Demon Emperor engaging in what almost seemed like a battle of strength, a strange sensation began to creep up his neck. Turning his head, he saw one of the ogre guards slowly extending his right hand, within which was a crossbow.

It didn't take any calculation on Mao Yun's part to realize that the crossbow was aimed at Bao.

There was no time for pausing or hesitation.

As the ogre's hand squeezed the trigger, Mao Yun lunged forward.

The bolt left the crossbow, becoming a streak of light that, to Mao Yun's shock, split into two, then four, then eight, and then continued to split over and over again, rapidly transforming into a massive maelstrom of bronze bolts.

Eyes widening, he thrust his axe out to meet the bolts, shouting, "Jiahui, help!"

***

Although Bao could sense a commotion breaking out, and even

vaguely heard Mao Yun's shout, she had no attention to spare for the matter. Gritting her teeth, she pushed forward with the Wind Saber, ignoring the screaming of the muscles, bones, and tendons in her right arm as she did so. Even her blood felt like it was on the verge of boiling.

I'm not gonna back down, you bastard.

***

It was to the Demon Emperor's shock that he realized more power was building up in the beam of light, shoving him backward through the air and sending such intense pain up his arm that it wiped the grin off his face and caused sweat to break out on his forehead.

How are you doing this, human?

CHAPTER 96
TRICKERY?

Hui stood on the bough of a tree far away from Yao Gong Palace. She hadn't dared to get too close, but she simply could not resist the intense desire to watch the final battle take place. In all the years she had traveled throughout the empire, she had never come close enough to lay eyes on the palace.

"Yao Gong Palace," she murmured. "The gate through which the ogres entered our world. And the Demon Emperor."

Her heart was in her throat, her hands gripping her robes tightly.

She had no trick move up her sleeve this time. The Kun-Peng Pipes could only be used once per century, and none of the other relics and powerful items she had accumulated over the years would do any good.

All she could to was wait and watch.

From her vantage point, she could just barely make out what was happening in the square. The Demon Emperor flew up into the air, and then Bao yet again unleashed that blinding blue and white light.

Even after much thought, Hui couldn't figure out how Bao was using such a powerful attack. In the era that Hui hailed from, the heroes of the world had managed, on two occasions, to acquire both the Phoenix Crown and the Wind Saber, and although they had been a powerful combination, they had most certainly not led to a massively overpowered attack the likes of which Hui was now witnessing.

Is it strong enough to kill him? she thought. Although Hui would not bemoan the death of the Demon Emperor, wouldn't it mean that all of her decades of work would be rendered meaningless? She had traveled the streams of time to bring a message to Bao and Sunan, using both dreams and poetry as an attempt to teach them how to seal away the Demon Emperor for all time. Her mission was the culmination of decades of planning on the part of the most righteous profound masters of her era.

And yet it looked like the Demon Emperor might not live long enough to be sealed.

***

Everyone in the square watched in shock as the Demon Emperor lurched back through the air once, twice, and then a third time.

Then Bao let out a roar of rage as she pulled the Wind Saber back slightly and shoved it out in front of her.

The Demon Emperor howled at the top of his lungs, the sound of which merged with the piercing boom of the buckler exploding. The white beam of light slashed forward, completely incinerating his right arm and sending him tumbling out of the sky to slam almost directly into the middle of the square.

***

Mao Yun's black axe whirled rapidly, creating a black disc of light that slammed into the cloud of incoming bolts. Liu Jiahui waved his arm, sending a spiraling wind out that knocked at least half of the bolts out of the air.

Even so, a handful of bolts made it through, striking Mao Yun in the shoulder and thigh. A few others made it past him and struck other random members of the Pure Phoenix Sect. However, none of them reached Bao.

Mao Yun didn't even feel the pain of the bolts. Roaring, he slashed his axe out, sending a blast of energy toward the crossbow-wielding ogre. However, when his attack simply vanished into the ogre's jade-encrusted breastplate, he remembered a point that had been drilled into the sect during their training. It had slipped his mind in the heat of the moment.

Ogres are immune to qi!

Mao Yun's mind raced as he tried to decide what to do. The ogre in the jade breastplate put another bronze bolt onto his crossbow, pointed it straight at Mao Yun, and pulled the trigger.

More ogres were leaping into the fray, so this time, Liu Jiahui could not come to Mao Yun's assistance. As soon as the crossbow's retention spring clicked, the bolt shot into the air, buzzing as it transformed into a hailstorm.

Mao Yun gritted his teeth and once again began to spin his axe out in front of him.

***

Bao's blow had seriously injured the Demon Emperor, and it had apparently stunned him, as he currently lay motionless in the middle of the battlefield.

The surrounding enemy troops and fighters were clearly stunned, but that was one when one of the ogres shouted, "The King of the Pure Ones cannot be killed! Crush these worms!"

Chaotic fighting immediately broke out. Because of the use of the Titan Squad Array and the Dragon Pearl Formations moments before, and the push by the Phoenix Division, the battlefield was now quite lopsided, with the front line being more like a sinuous curve than a straight line.

As the Demon Emperor's forces roared and fought back with powerful techniques, the Demon Emperor twitched and lifted his remaining arm up, planting his hand on the ground next to him as if to push himself up.

***

Sunan sent a group of ten soldiers flying backward, killing half of them with the initial force of the blow. Turning his head, he saw the Demon Emperor struggling to his feet.

Bao was standing there, panting and struggling to lift the tip of the Wind Saber off the ground.

As for the battlefield as a whole, although it seemed chaotic, Sunan was very pleased to see that the main line between the Dragon-Phoenix Sect and the forces of the Demon Emperor had twisted into a wavelike shape.

The Demon Emperor was almost equidistant between himself and Bao.

This is the moment, he thought.

However, that was when his eyes flickered to the left to land on Mao Yun, who was facing a hulking ogre with a jade-inlaid breastplate and a handheld crossbow. The ogre pulled the trigger, and the bolt leapt from the crossbow, multiplying and dividing to become a hail of bronze that caused Sunan's eyes to widen.

Most terrifying of all was that the bolts were not only numerous—they thrummed with powerful energy. They were not ordinary bolts but were backed by powerful magic.

There was no time for Sunan, or anyone else in the square, to do anything to help Mao Yun. Everyone was involved in their own desperate fighting, especially those who had been tossed out of place by the whirlwind moments before.

Sunan could only watch as the hail of bolts raced toward Mao Yun, whose black axe twirled in front of him to create a black disclike shield of light.

As the brightly shining bolts slammed into the shield, the light began to flicker and tremble. And then, a moment later, it collapsed. A bolt slammed into Mao Yun's arm, and then his hand, and then his shoulder.

More bolts sliced into him, lifting him off his feet and sending him spinning backward through the air, splatters of blood flying out in curving arcs.

"*NOOOO!*"

The scream which echoed across the square came from Mao Mei, who had been fighting some distance away from her brother. At the sight of the hail of bolts slamming into him, she burst away from her opponents and leapt into the air, drawing on a qinggong technique to speed over the heads of the other nearby soldiers.

Spears and other blades lashed at her as she passed by, a few of them reaching their target and leaving her legs bleeding profusely.

Her brother landed hard on the ground and skidded across the stone floor of the square on his back. Mao Mei reached him and scooped him up into her arms.

Although he was a head and a half taller than her, and one of the mostly well-built and imposing men in the entire sect, she channeled her qi flow into her arms and picked him up with ease. She leapt into the air while the ogre with the jade breastplate put another bolt onto his crossbow and fired it at her back.

At that point, Sunan was forced to look away to counter an attack from one of the elite fighters.

***

When Bao saw Mao Yun flying backward through the air in a shower of blood, her heart lurched up into her throat.

Brother! she cried inwardly.

Unfortunately, there was nothing she could do.

In their planning and training, they had taken into consideration that some of the Dragon-Phoenix Sect would fall in the fighting. Even the possibility of Bao or Sunan being killed had been worked into the plan.

No matter who it was that perished, the plan *would* be carried out.

Gritting her teeth and burying her anxiety over what was happening to Mao Yun, she turned back to face the Demon Emperor, who by this point had pushed himself up onto one knee.

Looking up, he made eye contact with her and started to chuckle.

"I'm impressed," he said. "Very impressed. Unfortunately, if that's the best you have, then I'm afraid you've made a grave error in coming here today." Sneering, he turned to look at the stump of his arm.

To Bao's shock, the end of the stump, which moments ago had been cauterized and smoking, was now wriggling and pulsing. Then the darkened skin cracked and bulged and began to grow outward. The Demon Emperor's arm was regrowing itself right in the middle of the fight.

Just like the report from the Raksha agent had indicated, even the most serious of injuries were of little concern to the Demon Emperor.

Chuckling again, he began to rise to his feet.

Bao looked over the Demon Emperor's shoulder to make eye contact with Sunan, who was standing opposite her, right behind the Demon Emperor's back. Sunan nodded. Bao nodded back.

Bao's fingers interlocked, and she took a step forward, drawing deeply upon her qi flow.

Across from her, Sunan did the same thing, and a resonance built up between them, causing the air to vibrate.

The Demon Emperor's eyes narrowed as he regained his feet. He could sense the resonance, and in fact, it passed directly through him, like tiny waves that he could feel in the core of his being.

In a position very close to Sunan, Sun Mai was sending illusory swords flying across the battlefield toward one of the elite fighters when he looked over and saw what was happening. He tapped his foot on the ground, launching himself into the air at high speed to land and a bit to the left of Sunan. He had chosen to wear the robes of the Golden Dragon Division that day, and as he flew through the air, he almost looked like a golden cloud.

Locking his fingers together, he planted his feet and channeled his qi through his meridians in the prescribed fashion. Another resonance sprang into being between himself and Sunan, which bolstered Sunan's energy, causing the resonance between him and Bao to increase in intensity.

The Demon Emperor's eyes went wide, but before he could do anything, Ma Ge flew into position behind Bao, her silver Pure Phoenix robes fluttering like feathers.

Again, the resonance between Bao and Sunan grew stronger.

Next to abandon the fighting and leap into formation was Tie Gangwen, and then Wang Tian.

One by one, the most powerful fighters of the Dragon-Phoenix Sect sped like lightning to join the growing formation, like a stream of clouds and feathers swirling through the air.

From north to east, the clouds surge forth,
From south to west, fair feathers sing.

With each addition to the formation, the resonance grew more powerful, and the effects wider. Even with only six people in place, it began to pulse, sending out rolling ripples of energy that pushed against the soldiers, elite fighters, and ogre guards in the square.

As for the Demon Emperor, although his arm was growing out

rapidly, he found that his feet were locked in place.

"What trickery is this?" he growled. "Immolation!"

In response to his words, raging flames burst into being around him, flames so hot that the paving stones around him were immediately blackened and even began to pop and hiss. However, it did nothing to affect the resonance, which increased in intensity with every additional person who fell into place behind Sunan and Bao.

Within a few short moments, there were twelve people in the formation, and bright golden light intermixed with silver sparkles shone in the air between Sunan and Bao and around the people in formation.

***

From her position atop the tree, Hui could just barely see flickers of golden light in the ceremonial square in Yao Gong Palace.

"It's begun," she murmured.

CHAPTER 97
THE WORLD TREMBLED

The ogre guards and elite fighters howled in desperation as they struggled to unleash more attacks. The Demon Emperor snarled, "Vortegan's Whirling Catastrophe!"

Yet again, a black vortex swept through the square, but it was powerless against the defensive energies of the spell formation and did little more than toss debris here and there.

With each member of the sect that joined Bao and Sunan, more energy pulsed out in all directions.

With Sunan and Bao as the focal points, the resonance that had formed from the combined qi flow was locked tight on the Demon Emperor. Even after casting his immolation magic and Vortegan's Whirling Catastrophe, he was powerless to break free.

As the flames and winds faded away, he began to cast another spell in the hopes of freeing himself.

But then Sunan and Bao took a step forward, and the entire square shuddered as the power of the formation intensified.

The light on Bao's side was pure white, and the light on Sunan's side was golden. However, the white part of the light only served to brighten the golden side, and in the end it was pure golden light that began to rise up into the sky.

The fiends, a tempest dark and foul,
A shining pillar paints the sky.

High above, in what had once been a clear blue sky, clouds had begun to form, and when the light from below touched them, they also turned golden.

Twenty people were in formation, with more members of the sect leaping in with each second that ticked by.

As they did, the vibrations filling the air began to spread out, causing the fortress itself to shudder.

"Fools!" the Demon Emperor bellowed. "I can just create a portal and step away from this place!" However, no portal appeared.

A golden drop of water splashed down onto the paved surface of the square, only a few paces away from the Demon Emperor. Then another drop fell, and another, as rain began to fall. Strangely, when the rain touched the skin of the people in the square, it felt hot, not enough to burn, but enough to make the rain seem like something from a different world.

From the moment that Bao and Sunan had first taken their places at the front of the formation to the moment when the rain began to fall, barely a minute had passed.

It was obvious to the Demon Emperor's forces that something very dangerous was unfolding, and as such, the ogre guards began to shout orders to the elite fighters in an attempt to lead a charge against the formation itself. The first group, consisting of four ogres and ten elite fighters, tried to charge toward Bao, unleashing projectile weapons and qi attacks as they closed in.

However, the defensive energies of the formation itself crushed all the attacks before they could even get close to Bao. The ogres and elite fighters couldn't get within ten paces of her because of the powerful fluctuations rolling out.

As the golden rain began to fall in earnest, the formation grew, and the Demon Emperor struggled and howled. Soon the energy vibrations had spread out to shake the surrounding mountains, all the way down to their roots.

Some distance away, the tree Hui stood on had begun to sway back and forth, forcing her to reach back and grab ahold of the trunk to steady herself. A faint smile had appeared on her face.

The resonance between Bao and Sunan had become visible. It was like undulating bands of gold and silver waves, flowing back and forth between them, with the Demon Emperor trapped in the middle.

They both took another step forward, and then another, the formations moving with them. As the vibrations grew more intense, many of the Demon Emperor's soldiers began to flee in terror, and even some of the elite fighters had lost their nerve and were trying to escape.

Meanwhile, something else was happening that no one near Yao Gong Palace could see, not even Hui. High up in the heavens, far above the roiling golden clouds, two bright stars appeared on opposite ends of the sky. The dawn sun and setting full moon were also opposite of each other.

It was an astral phenomenon the likes of which had never been witnessed before.

The two stars, one red, one blue, linked together with the sun and the moon to create a perfect square.

Golden droplets spin and howl,
The sun, the moon, two stars align.

Astrologers from Naqan to Nangu to the Yangu Plains all looked up and marveled at what they were witnessing.

Within the empire, golden clouds were rapidly spreading out from the Banyan Mountains, and many of the astrologers there were oblivious to what was happening.

By now, more than two hundred members of the Dragon-

Phoenix Sect were in formation, and the energy fluctuations rolling out from Yao Gong Palace were causing the earth to quake as far north as the Chezou River and as far south as Zun Valley. The golden clouds were also churning in all directions.

Slowly but surely, Bao and Sunan advanced, getting closer and closer to the Demon Emperor, until they were so close they could almost touch him. His eyes were bloodshot, and his mouth twisted into a snarl, although only Bao could see that.

"How are you doing this?" he said, his voice grating. "Who are you? Where are you from? What Sertori is backing you?"

"I am Bao of the Dragon-Phoenix Sect. I don't know what a Sertori is, but I can tell you that the only person backing me is the Enlightened Goddess."

The Demon Emperor seemed inclined to spit on the ground but could barely move his mouth to speak. "Xian Nu Shen? She is nothing! A fractured mirror, a broken vase! Even that bitch Hen-Shi and the worm Gushan are nothing!"

Ignoring his words, Bao said, "Your days have come to an end, Demon Emperor. How does it feel?"

With that, she stepped past him, while Sunan took a step forward, placing him within the Demon Emperor's field of vision.

"How dare you call me the Demon Emperor! I am Gar-El! I am Yaum alu-Bukhra! I was the first Sertori ever to perform Thauma! I am the reincarnation of the god Senga! I shook the entire world of Gamandria! Ants like you don't even deserve to look at me!"

Sunan didn't understand even half of the terms the Demon Emperor had just used. "Babble however you wish," he said. "You can do nothing to stop us, Demon Emperor."

Then he took another step forward, this time moving away from Bao.

If the Demon Emperor had been able to move, he would have leapt forward and torn Sunan limb from limb, then used his shattered body to beat Bao into a bloody pulp. But he couldn't move.

"I killed Rashan of Shandee. I slaughtered a thousand Sertori, and they were powerless to stop me! I even fought the dragon Tanoor to a standstill! You call yourself a dragon? That was a real dragon, you puny bug! You don't stand a chance against me!"

Sunan ignored him and took another step forward.

"Immolation!" the Demon Emperor wheezed. Once again, flames appeared around him.

The resonance between Bao and Sunan grew stronger with each step they took, and this time the flames danced as weakly as a dying candle before winking out.

Meanwhile, more and more members of the sect were pouring in to join the formation. The formation was now powered by more than six hundred of them. Virtually all of the Demon Emperor's followers had fled, leaving behind only the ogre guards and a few of the most fanatical expert fighters, who were struggling uselessly to try to attack the spell formation.

Bao and Sunan took another step forward, pulling each half of the formation with them, and the Demon Emperor's left hand twitched. Although he couldn't move his arms or legs or even his head, he was still capable of very small movements. His hand trembled as he reached toward a ring on his left index finger. It was crafted from white jade and inlaid with a black pearl. It took supreme effort, but he managed to push his thumb against the ring. A black lightning bolt to shot up into the sky toward the golden clouds.

Moments later, another lightning bolt shot up, then another, causing intense crashing sounds to join the rumbling from the spell formation.

The Demon Emperor began to laugh. "You see? My resources are deep and powerful! This ring was a gift from the Five Ghosts!"

More black lightning erupted from the ring, crashing upward instead of downward as it bombarded the golden clouds.

Bao and Sunan's steps faltered momentarily as both of them felt bursts of pain stabbing into them from the resonance.

However, a bit of pain wasn't enough to stop them. Gritting their teeth, they both took another step forward. One of the black bolts of lightning faded away, and then another.

"Impossible," the Demon Emperor murmured, his bloodshot eyes widening.

Wind began to swirl in the square, causing the golden rain to become a blur that swirled round and round without cease.

With each step Bao and Sunan took forward, the black lightning grew weaker and weaker, until it faded away completely.

Bao and Sunan walked forward resolutely, taking the spell formation with them. By this point, they had both reached the spot previously occupied by the other. As for the formation, it was powered by over nine hundred members of the sect and stretched across the entire square from north to south and east to west. The only members who were not in the formation were the handful who had fallen in the fighting or were too injured to participate.

If anyone had been able to view the formation from high in the sky, it would look like a circle with a sinuous line running through it, one side bright white, the other side golden. It resembled the basic design of the symbol of the Dragon-Phoenix Sect!

Meanwhile, up the heavens, the sun, the moon, and the two stars on the horizon began to shine more brightly than ever, piercing through the layers of clouds until they were visible to everyone on the earth below.

Four bright spots of light up above created a perfect square that shone with such brilliance that soon no one could even look up, but they were forced to bow their heads and close their eyes.

All the lands were shaking, even Nangu and Naqan.

The entire world trembled under the power of the Dragon-Phoenix Sect.

Heaven and Earth turned inside out,
The crash and clash of night and day.

As for the Demon Emperor, he was screaming in his mind, trying to call upon ancient magics, desperately attempting to use other powerful items on his person. But he was rooted in place, and all such efforts failed.

The spell formation was complete.

But things weren't over yet.

The final blow was yet to be delivered.

CHAPTER 98
GOLDEN LIONS

All compass points unite and shout,
The Lions seal the fiends away.

Bao and Sunan sank down into cross-legged positions of meditation, as did everyone else powering the formation. As they closed their eyes and placed their hands in their laps, palms up, the energy fluctuations rolling off of the spell formation began to retract from the four corners of the continent, converging back on the Banyan Mountains.

Then they began to recite the very poem that Bao had taken years to complete. Although they spoke in a murmur, the energy of the spell formation caused their words to echo like thunder.

The mountains began to shake so violently that trees fell and boulders split open. Thankfully, Hui had picked one of the mightiest of the trees, and although it swayed back and forth like a reed in a storm wind, it didn't fall.

Cracks had long since spread out on the surface of Yao Gong Palace, and now it began to crumble. Towers fell and corridors collapsed, and many of the Demon Emperor's forces who hadn't been quick enough to flee earlier were crushed to death.

As for the surface of the ceremonial square, cracks had already begun to spread out across its surface, but it held its shape.

As Bao and Sunan sat there cross-legged, they became conduits for levels of energy that were literally shaking heaven and earth. The powers of the spell formation grew more and more intense as energy began to rush from all parts of the continent to converge on the two of them, then pour into the resonance, and finally, come to rest on the Demon Emperor.

Although the light shining in the square was so blinding that no one could even open their eyes to observe, if they had been able to, they would have seen strange magical symbols and designs on the Demon Emperor's skin as he continued to struggle in vain to free himself. A shining phoenix mark appeared on Bao's forehead and a serpentine dragon on Sunan's.

Bao and Sunan felt like rivers being flooded with oceans upon oceans of water. Their qi meridians had already been stretched to the limit, and many of them had burst. Now that the spell formation was drawing upon the full level of the power that it was capable of, the effect became more pronounced.

One by one, their meridians popped and shattered, and their blood vessels began to burst.

The forces ripping through them were too great for their physical bodies to process. Because of the resonance, there was no need for them to open their eyes to sense what was happening to each other, nor any need to use their voices to communicate.

What's happening, Sunan?

I don't know, Bao. But we can't let up. The sealing is almost complete, I can sense it.

The energy and the clouds that had filled the lands had retracted and were now focused within the Banyan Mountains. Brilliant golden light shone out to fill the entire empire as the mountains trembled and shook.

The intense levels of power were now causing problems for the other members of the Dragon-Phoenix Sect. Blood had begun to ooze out of the eyes, ears, noses, and mouths of many of them, especially those who had experienced only four or five breakthroughs.

Bao and Sunan could sense this.

Bao, open yourself to the power. It's too much for the rest of the sect to handle.

I know, Sunan. I know. Are we... are we going to die?

A long moment passed.

Perhaps.

Bao didn't say anything more, but Sunan could sense her determination as she opened herself up further to the flow of energy. He did the same.

By now, their meridians were completely destroyed, and their blood vessels were shattered. Even their bones were starting to crumble, and their muscles were being shredded to pieces. No one present could see it, but their skin looked as brittle as dried mud and was covered with countless cracks. However, the marks on their foreheads continued to shine as brightly as suns.

I don't want to die, Sunan. I want to see Jinlong and Chunfeng again. I want to build a house by a lake.

Jinlong and Chunfeng won't be safe as long as the Demon Emperor lives, Bao.

Although they were surrounded by a cataclysm of wind and thunderous roaring, to Bao and Sunan, everything seemed quiet and calm. Neither did they feel any pain as their bodies were destroyed.

It was at that point that both of them heard words being spoken into their minds, words that thrummed and echoed as if they were being spoken by more than one voice.

Young Dragon, Young Phoenix, you will not die. Your physical bodies are no more, but your immortal bodies await. You have done well. The time has come to leave the mortal realm. Open yourselves to us, and we will complete the seal.

Who are you? Bao asked.

We are Hen-Shi. We are Gushan. We are Xian Nu Shen.

Bao and Sunan were both stunned, but now was not the time to consider what was happening. Both of them could sense that the power coursing through them was on the verge of slipping past their control.

It was in that moment that Bao felt a new sensation, like a hand coming to rest on her shoulder. It was a soft, warm hand, but a hand that also seemed powerful beyond imagination.

She slowly relaxed.

Sunan also felt a hand come to rest on his shoulder, and calmness flowed through him.

The end had come.

***

Sun Mai was the first to feel the change.

The deafening roar which surrounded him suddenly whooshed into silence, and he could sense that the blinding light had vanished. He felt as if he were falling.

Opening his eyes, he found that the ceremonial square was crumbling around him. Of the nearly one thousand members of the Dragon-Phoenix Sect who had powered the spell formation, most still had their eyes closed as the slabs that made the floor of the square fell apart and tumbled downward.

Sun Mai saw others opening their eyes. Realizing that there was no time to ponder what was happening, he sprang into motion, sending his sleeves whipping out to wrap around several nearby Golden Dragons who he knew to be among the weakest present. Then he drew upon one of his most powerful qinggong techniques to fly through the air, tapping off of an occasional stone slab as he sped toward safety.

The other profound masters took similar action, and as other powerful qi fighters in the sect opened their eyes, they did the same.

Within moments, everyone in the sect was either flying away from the ceremonial square or was being carried away from it.

Rumbling sounds echoed out as a huge cloud of dust began to rise up. Most of Yao Gong Palace had already crumbled, and now the ceremonial square was collapsing.

By the time the members of the Dragon-Phoenix Sect found solid ground to stand on, the only thing left in the spot where the square had once stood was a crater.

Sun Mai looked around at the members of the sect, trying to find Bao and Sunan. They were nowhere to be seen.

Gradually, silence filled the air, and the dust settled.

That was when Sun Mai looked down into the crater itself, and his eyes widened.

Other members of the sect gasped and stared in shock at the bottom of the crater.

Amidst the rubble were three eye-catching objects. One was the Demon Emperor, still and unmoving, encased in what appeared to be a slab of translucent red stone, like jade or crystal. On either side of him towered two statues depicting golden lions, one male and one female.

When Sun Mai saw the golden lions, the hair on the back of his neck prickled up. Flicking his sleeve, he leapt and floated down to the bottom of the crater to stand in front of the male lion.

"Sunan?" he murmured.

There was no response. After turning to look at the female lion, he looked back at the male lion and then reached out to place his hand on the surface of the statue.

Sun Mai.

Sunan?

Tell the sect to stand guard there. Make sure the Demon Emperor is never freed. And then… come find us.

Where are you, Sunan?

The Immortal Realm.

***

The Demon Emperor had been sealed away, but his empire still existed. There was still much work to be done.

Some of the Dragon-Phoenix Sect remained behind to build a new fortress in the spot where Yao Gong Palace had once existed. They took it upon themselves to stand guard and ensure that the Demon Emperor never again walked the lands of Qi Xien. They would guard his sealed form, as well as the sealed forms of the ogres who had been caught up in the energy of the spell formation.

Other members of the sect went out into the world to fight the remaining ogres and other Demon Emperor loyalists.

Both the Phoenix Crown and the Wind Saber were damaged in the final battle, but they still became the most sought-after items in the martial world. They would be the source of schemes, intrigue, and outright battles for centuries to come.

Stories about Sunan and Bao spread through the lands. The tales of their exploits, including their final battle against the Demon Emperor, were varied and sometimes contradictory. But one common thread ran through them all: Sunan and Bao were heroic lovers who had led the fight against the Demon Emperor, and had saved the people of Qi Xien by sacrificing themselves.

A thousand years later

In a village near Qi Fao, a daughter had just been born to one of the local fishermen, and the local astrologer had come to help the parents choose a name.

As the astrologer set up the tools of his trade and began to consult his astrological charts, he said, "Congratulations, Mr. Fan. Your daughter's aura is already heroic and strong."

The fisherman laughed proudly. "Well, we are descendants of

Sunan and Bao, after all."

"Is that so?" the astrologer replied.

"Indeed. I have the genealogies to prove it."

"Interesting, I'll have to take that into consideration." With that, the astrologer went about his work. Eventually, he came up with an auspicious name that both parents were happy with.

After the astrologer left, the fisherman held his daughter in his arms and looked down into her eyes.

"You've been born into an era of peace, Fan Hui," he said. "The Era of the Glorious Emperor. But the blood of Sunan and Bao runs in your veins. If this world ever needs a hero, perhaps you can follow in their footsteps."

After a moment, he chuckled. "Oh, who am I kidding. I'm sure that won't happen."

Fan Hui reached out, grabbed her father's finger, and smiled.

The End

AFTERWORD

I hope you enjoyed *Legends of Ogre Gate*. If you are interested in knowing how things play out during the following 1,000 years in Qi Xien, check out *Wandering Heroes of Ogre Gate*, a tabletop roleplaying game published by Bedrock Games; this story is a novelization of the ancient, quasi-mythological history of that game universe. In the game sourcebook's Chapter 7: The World of Qi Xien – History, Religion, Customs, and Cosmology, you can find detailed information about the millennium that followed the showdown between Sunan and Bao and the Demon Emperor.

Scattered in other parts of the rulebook are all sorts of tidbits regarding things not addressed in the story. For example, there is a large section on the Timeless Master, which even has a detailed map of his grotto. You can also find out what happens to the religion Sun Mai created, and even more intriguing, what happens to the Dragon-Phoenix Sect.

Also available with some google-fu is *The Tournament of Daolu*, a game supplement based on the events of this novel, where you can find statistics for many of the characters, as well as maps, art, and plenty of other resources suitable for both gamers and non-gamers alike.

Thanks so much for reading! If you'd like information about my latest projects, please visit jeremybai.com.

Jeremy Bai a.k.a. Deathblade

ACKNOWLEDGMENTS

Legends of Ogre Gate was originally released in serialized form on WuxiaWorld.com. I would like to offer profound thanks to all of the beta readers who offered feedback and constructive criticism there, as well the team who helped me prepare the initial chapters for launch.

Many thanks to Brendan Davis from Bedrock Games, who worked closely with me to make sure the characters, events, techniques, history, and everything else conformed to the 'reality' of the Ogre Gate game universe.

And of course, I owe deep thanks to Ren Woxing, the owner of Wuxiaworld.com, who allowed me to post chapters on the website, despite the focus of the site being translated novels.